THE *American* HEIRESS BRIDES COLLECTION

Nine Wealthy Women Struggle to Find Love
in a Society That Values Money First

THE *American* HEIRESS BRIDES COLLECTION

Kimberley Woodhouse
Lisa Carter, Mary Davis, Susanne Dietze,
Anita Mae Draper, Patty Smith Hall, Cynthia Hickey,
Lisa Karon Richardson, Lynette Sowell

BARBOUR BOOKS
An Imprint of Barbour Publishing, Inc.

Print ISBN 978-1-63409-997-4

eBook Editions:
Adobe Digital Edition (.epub) 978-1-68322-146-3
Kindle and MobiPocket Edition (.prc) 978-1-68322-147-0

All scripture quotations, unless otherwise noted, are taken from the King James Version of the Bible.

Scriptures marked ASV are taken from the American Standard Version of the Bible.

This book is a work of fiction. Names, characters, places, and incidents are either products of the author's imagination or used fictitiously. Any similarity to actual people, organizations, and/or events is purely coincidental.

Published by Barbour Books, an imprint of Barbour Publishing, Inc., P.O. Box 719, Uhrichsville, Ohio 44683, www.barbourbooks.com

Our mission is to publish and distribute inspirational products offering exceptional value and biblical encouragement to the masses.

Printed in Canada.

Contents

The Heiress and the Homesteader

by Lisa Carter

Chapter 1

Montana Territory, 1880

How had this happened to her?

Eugenia Rutherford stared in dismay as the train chugged out of sight. When she told Daddy how they'd cast her off the train like a common criminal—he'd fix their wagon for good. Daddy didn't suffer fools gladly.

But then she remembered. She couldn't tell her father. She'd run away to prove a point.

The depot sign swung in a light July breeze. Surveying the hardscrabble mining town of Silver Strike, her nose wrinkled. Apropos, considering who she was—the daughter of one of the richest men in California. A silver king.

She just hadn't counted on being unceremoniously dumped in the middle of Nowhere, Montana. Maybe she'd gone too far this time.

No sign of a porter. Grimacing, she clutched her valise and picked her way over the railroad track toward the station. She couldn't wait to shake the dust off this one-horse town.

Visor shading his brow, a man pored over a train schedule at the ticket counter. She rapped her gloved knuckle on the pane of glass, and he jumped.

He scowled. "What?"

Not the usual deferential treatment to which she was accustomed. Her mouth tightened. Maybe Daddy needed to buy this whole stinking town and teach them a lesson.

"I'd like a ticket to Chicago, if you please."

He mumbled the price of a ticket.

"I'm Eugenia Rutherford, and I don't carry money."

"No money, no ticket."

She frowned. "Do you know who my father is, sir?"

"I don't care if you're the queen of Alibaba. No money, no ticket." And with that, he snapped the window closed.

"How dare you..."

But what now? She did a slow one-eighty and spotted the ornate Silver Strike Hotel at the end of what passed for Main Street.

Daddy would wire her some credit. Might as well get a decent meal and a room for the night. Although, what this last outpost of civilization considered a decent meal was anybody's guess.

◆ ◆ ◆

Next move, yours.

Cort crushed the telegram in his fist.

"Bad news, mister?"

Cort glanced at the telegraph operator. "The worst."

He'd found Mrs. Anderson's note when he returned to the house from the fields. She'd resigned and "borrowed" his buckboard, which she promised to leave outside the telegraph office. Hired right out from under him by the confounded sender of the telegram.

Women. They were all alike. Loyalty meant nothing. Good riddance to the lot of them.

Except. . . What was he going to do about Granny?

Since the stroke, she needed constant care. His energetic grandmother had shriveled into someone he no longer recognized. Her vivacious spirit reduced to a low ember. The doc told Cort not to expect her to live long.

Cort wouldn't wish to prolong her life. Not the way she was now. But he missed her. Really missed her.

He'd already left her too long alone at the homestead.

Ten-year-old Luke, from the foundling home, who ran errands for the telegraph office, plucked at Cort's shirtsleeve. "Who's gonna take care of ole Miz Dahlgren now?"

Cort exhaled. "A good question, young man. A very good question."

The boy stuffed his hands in his trousers, which needed patching. Something his grandma had done in her spare time—making new clothes for the children at the Home in Silver Strike near their old homestead.

"I'm purt near strong as a growed man." The boy flexed a nonexistent muscle. "I know the way to your farm. I happen to be in the market for extra work."

"Oh you are, huh?" Cort rolled his tongue in his cheek till a thought struck him. "How do you know where we live? I didn't realize you'd been to the homestead before."

"I delivered a telegram to Mrs. Anderson yesterday."

Another telegram?

"You didn't happen to read—I mean notice—what it said, did you? Or who sent it?"

Luke squared his thin shoulders. "I did not, sir. I am a professional."

Fair enough. Besides, Cort could well imagine who'd sent the first telegram to the farm. That blasted man was playing chess with people's lives. But to shanghai an elderly woman's nurse was diabolical even for him. And for what purpose?

Cort hadn't the foggiest idea. *Next move, yours.* What did that mean?

He scrubbed the back of his neck with his hand. The way Granny was fading, he didn't think he'd have long to worry about her situation. He'd truly be alone then.

Feeling a kinship with the orphan, he reached into his pocket. "I'll keep your offer in mind, young fella." He pulled out a penny. "Why don't you treat yourself and get something sweet at the mercantile?"

Luke drew himself up, all four foot eight inches. "I work for a living, sir. I don't take handouts."

An interesting attitude for a foundling, but he couldn't fault Luke's work ethic. Or his budding entrepreneurship.

"Call it an investment in the future. And remember me when you make your first million, okay?"

Luke grinned and took the coin. "All right then. I'll buy taffy. I can split it with the little guys at the Home."

Enterprising and generous. He ruffled Luke's windblown hair. No wonder his grandmother had been so involved with the orphanage before the stroke last winter stole her vigor.

Cort headed to the mercantile to leave an employment notice on the bulletin board. *Could use some divine help right about now, God.* He had to find someone to take care of Granny, at least through harvest.

◆ ◆ ◆

Hitching her skirt free of the mud clogging the street, Eugenia maneuvered past the wagons rolling down Main. She dodged the horses tied at the railing outside the mercantile and hurried to the boardwalk.

She stopped at the telegraph office to wire her father. "I'll be in the hotel restaurant waiting for his reply."

This wasn't turning out like she'd planned. In a snit last night, she'd thrown a few garments in her valise and stormed off to the train station near the Rutherford mansion in Sacramento. Her name—her father's name—had been enough to get her a seat in first class in lieu of an actual ticket.

Eugenia never bothered to carry money. She was a Rutherford. Rutherfords didn't need coinage.

She regretted the harsh words between her and her father. They'd always been close, but Daddy had to understand she was an independent woman. She didn't intend to be used as a marriage pawn to further his empire.

They'd argued over the copper king fellow, the latest in a long line of would-be suitors.

Eligible bachelors from the best families, as well as others who were self-made. But she'd turned up her nose at them all. Like the upstart copper king who'd had the nerve to call her spoiled.

Looking down her nose at him, she'd shown him the door last February. "I prefer a clean-shaven man to a rough-bearded yokel like you." Her father had been incensed at her behavior.

She was determined to marry—or not—at her own pleasure.

Most women married for love or money. She had no need for money—Daddy made sure of that. As for love?

She'd never been in love in her life. Nobody—including Daddy—could make her do anything she didn't want to do. And marriage topped the list.

Her widowed father had never denied her anything she wanted. Daddy needed to understand how determined she was to be in charge of her own destiny. It wouldn't take long for him to see things her way while she visited her dear friend, Muriel, in Chicago.

"I don't carry money." She smiled as the waitress presented the bill. "I'm Eugenia Rutherford, you see."

The waitress blinked at her. The people in this town didn't appear too bright.

"My father will compensate you for the meal and accommodations once he wires me the money."

The waitress opened her mouth then. And what followed wasn't pleasant. Outraged, Eugenia demanded to speak with the hotel manager.

"You're going to speak to the manager, dearie," snarled the waitress. "We know how to deal with moochers like you."

"Moocher? How dare—?"

The manager proved no more helpful than his staff. Instead, he wrapped his beefy hands around her upper arms and hauled her out of the chair.

"Unhand me," she yelled. "I demand you unhand me."

The manager towed her toward the lobby. "You'll pay your bill or we'll settle this with the sheriff."

Dragging her heels, she caught hold of the reception desk. "Sheriff?"

But he shoved her toward the front door. Making a spectacle. Of her, Eugenia Alice Rutherford.

"What 'bout her bag, Mr. Penrod?" the waitress called.

The manager grunted as Eugenia's shoe smacked his shin. "Toss it on the street."

And without further ado he tossed her onto the boardwalk.

Chapter 2

Cort emerged from the mercantile to find a crowd gawking outside the hotel.

The hotel manager dumped a squawking, screaming blond woman—petticoats and all—onto the boardwalk. The girl who waited tables screeched for the sheriff. For somebody—anybody—to help.

What on earth?

Cort crossed the street with long strides just as the caterwauling woman sprang at the manager. She swung back her fist. Cort inserted himself between the two as she threw a punch.

His chest deflected her well-aimed blow. He didn't even stagger. But caught off balance, she teetered. Arms flailing, she fell backward.

She landed with a plop and an oozing squish into what he preferred not to imagine. Laughter erupted from the crowd. Squeezing her eyes shut, the troublemaker moaned.

The telegram crinkled in his pocket. He got his first good look at the crazy woman. Suddenly, everything became clear.

And his stomach sank to the bottom of his boots.

Covered with muck, she was a sorry sight. Despite the expensive, now ruined dress, she was a bedraggled woebegone sort. He shouldn't laugh. But he couldn't help it.

He loomed over her. "Pride goeth before a fall, eh?"

"More like pearls before swine." She blew a strand of hair out of her eyes. "You are no gentleman."

He smirked as he offered his hand. "And you smell nothing like a lady."

At first, she refused to take his hand. But unable to stand up on her own, she gnashed her teeth and seized his hand. Ignoring the tingle of electricity of her skin against his fingertips, he pulled her free of the cloying mud. For his reward, she glared at him.

The sheriff pinned her arms behind her back. She cried out at his rough treatment. "We'll see how you like cooling your heels in a cell."

Her Royal Haughtiness probably deserved jail time, but Cort didn't like to see a woman manhandled. "Maybe we can work out something to everyone's satisfaction."

Cort angled toward the manager. "As long as the hotel is compensated, would you be willing to drop the charges, Mr. Penrod?"

Mr. Penrod straightened his string tie. "If she'd been able to pay her bill, we wouldn't be standing here now."

Sheriff Turnbull didn't loosen his grip on his prisoner. "Whatcha have in mind, Cort?"

"Granny's nurse quit this morning."

Murmurs of commiseration arose. His grandmother, one of Silver Strike's pioneering women, was a beloved figure.

"That's too bad."

"That's a raw deal."

"That's tough, son."

Cort nodded. "Fact is, I'm in a bind. I've got no one to watch out for Granny at the homestead while I'm in the fields."

He hooked his thumbs in his belt loops. "If I pay her bill, she can reimburse me by taking care of Granny till harvest is over."

Sheriff Turnbull curled his bushy, mustached lip. "She'll rob you blind the first chance she gets. And head for the hills." He shook the girl for added emphasis.

It took everything inside Cort to restrain himself from knocking the sheriff's hand off her arm. He kept his coiled fists at his side. "What about you, Mr. Penrod?"

The manager's forehead creased. "As long as I get what I'm owed—"

"You'll get what you're owed all right." The girl vibrated like a taut bowstring. "All of you. Soon as my daddy—"

"Stop talking. Right now." Cort's chest rose and fell. "I've never told a woman to shut up in my life, but so help me, if you don't close your mouth this instant—" She lunged at him.

Only the sheriff's grip prevented her from pounding him.

"You'll do what, farm boy?"

She was either the bravest woman he'd ever met—the whole town ready to lock her backside in jail and throw away the key—or the dumbest.

He couldn't decide which. Stubbornness, she possessed in spades.

"You take care of my grandma, or you can enjoy the cold comfort of the Silver Strike lockup." He relished having the upper hand with this slip of a miss for once. "Your choice."

◆ ◆ ◆

This was outrageous. This was extortion. Blackmail.

If Eugenia weren't so horrified, so totally without resources—so without Daddy—she'd tell this homesteader what he could do with his job offer.

She took a breath. "That won't be necessary. As I tried to tell Mr. Penrod before he assaulted me, my father will settle the bill. This has been a terrible misunderstanding."

Cort—wasn't that what the sheriff called him?—arched his eyebrow. "Only misunderstanding is you thinking you can go into a place of business, consume their product, and then refuse to pay."

"That's not what happened."

"It's exactly what happened."

The telegraph operator pushed to the front of the crowd. "Your father refused to send any money, Miss Rutherford."

Her mouth fell open. "What?"

"Says you made your own mess and now you can lie in it."

"H–He wouldn't do that. There's been a mistake." She lifted her chin. "He wouldn't abandon me here."

"Come on." The sheriff yanked her arm again. "It's jail for you till the circuit judge rides into town." He chuckled. "Next month."

"Wait." She tried pulling free. "This can't be happening."

"It's happening. So what's it going to be?" The Cort person tapped his dusty boot on the boardwalk. "I got things to do. Haven't got all day."

Switching tactics, she forced her eyes to water. "Please. . . Don't make me go with him." She made a show of blinking rapidly. "He's mean. I'm scared."

Cort What's-His-Name rolled his eyes. "Put a cork in it, Rutherford."

Eugenia glowered. "That would be Miss Eugenia Alice Rutherford to you."

"Save the theatrics for the stage. Jail or join the ranks of us nobodies who work for a living?"

And somehow she found herself in a buckboard wagon beside this homesteading philistine headed for the valley outside Silver Strike.

Clutching the edge of the seat, she cut her eyes at him and gave him a scathing appraisal. A tan Stetson topped his short, dark hair. He had reasonably symmetrical features. A strong, clean-cut jaw.

His thin lips were currently flattened to match his forehead in what appeared to be a perpetual scowl. Dark eyes framed lashes the envy of any girl. Although her heart fluttered, there was nothing remotely girlie about her new employer.

Employer. . . The notion sent a dagger through her heart. Silencing any would-be palpitations this dirt-farming homesteader evoked.

"If you're done sizing me up, Miss Rutherford. . . ?"

She stiffened. "Charming you are not."

His hands balled around the reins. But he kept his gaze fixed on the bend in the road. "I'm not required to be Prince Charming."

She sniffed. "No worries there."

A muscle ticked a furious beat in his cheek. "But I am your boss."

"You're not the boss of me. No one is the boss of me."

The homesteader looked at her. "That, I suspect, is the source of most of your problems."

His dark eyes glinted. "But you'll take care of my granny while I bring in the harvest or you'll find yourself in the lockup faster than you can say 'Eugenia Alice Rutherford.'"

She bristled. "You are a barbarian."

"Novel experience for you, isn't it, Miss Rutherford?" He didn't look the least repentant. "To find yourself without recourse or resources. Maybe you'll learn something from this experience of eating crow."

"Rutherfords do not eat crow." She sneered. "We serve it."

His eyes narrowed. "We'll see how you like dishing out hog slop and chicken feed. A comeuppance long overdue. And I, for one, intend to enjoy the show."

Chapter 3

As the horses cantered past the played-out Silver Strike mine, Cort stole a glance at the infuriated young woman beside him. Eugenia Rutherford was beautiful, make no mistake about that. A man could drown in those cornflower eyes of hers. He pushed up the brim of his hat with his index finger.

But he'd learned the hard way it didn't matter how exquisite the cup if the contents were pig swill. And this spoiled heiress was nothing but a vain, prideful minx. God help the man who ever took on the herculean task of taming this one.

The valley opened before them, and she gave a small gasp of pleasure. Despite his determination to remain unmoved in her presence, he felt a small sense of satisfaction.

"Pretty, isn't it?"

About as pretty as Eugenia Alice Rutherford, but he didn't say that out loud.

Eugenia scanned the pine-topped ridges running parallel to the valley. Sunlight gleamed on the golden tresses of her hair like the wheat awaiting harvest in his fields. Her hair had come loose from its elaborate updo and fell in shimmering, silky waves to her shoulders.

Silk. . . His hands flexed on the reins. But pretty is as pretty does.

Eugenia pointed at the prairie mansion looming beyond the trees. "What a glorious house."

Bucolic pastureland extended toward the mountain horizon. Bees droned above meadow flowers. Thoroughbreds grazed under the azure blue Montana sky.

He scowled. No surprise she'd be drawn there. Like called to like. "It's an eyesore on the landscape."

Not that anybody had asked him his opinion in building the eight-gabled monstrosity.

"Is that where we're going?"

He snorted. "No, we're not."

Come to think of it, he could hardly wait to show Miss High and Mighty the homestead.

"Perhaps I can appeal to their better nature. Perhaps they could extend me a loan."

"No better nature there." Cort clenched his jaw. "He's a cautious, exacting man. Owns most of the land in the valley."

He flicked the reins. "Started the mine, which gave Silver Strike its name. Later, he diversified from the silver lode to copper."

"Copper?" She whipped around, gazing over her shoulder as they bypassed the mansion. "Who lives there?"

"The McCallums."

Her mouth fell open. "The copper king?"

Cort gave her a sideways look. "You've heard of him?"

Her expression went from hopeful to downcast. "I've heard of him." She swallowed.

"Drives a hard bargain. Gets what he pays for and then some." Cort pressed his lips together. "It's also said he never forgets a slight."

She locked her fingers around the handle of the battered valise and dropped her gaze to the floorboard. "Oh."

"Want me to stop?" He pulled on the reins. "No skin off my nose. Long as I get what I'm owed." Maybe it'd be better to put an end to this right now.

His heart thudded. "Of course, that still puts me in a bind with what to do about Granny."

Despite what he told the sheriff, he wouldn't—couldn't bring himself to—hold her captive against her will.

"No." Her voice had gone small. "That won't be necessary. We have an agreement—I gave you my word."

"A woman of her word. Good to know." Some of the tension in his belly uncoiled a notch. "Haven't met one of those in a while. Wasn't sure they still existed."

Eugenia pursed her lips. "Then perhaps you ought to be more careful of the company you keep."

Something flared inside his chest. This was insane. What was he doing bringing someone like Eugenia Rutherford to the homestead? He ought to turn the wagon around and. . . His breath caught in the back of his throat.

Instead, he steered the horses off the main route and onto the less traveled, slightly overgrown path. In contrast to the enormous McCallum estate, he tensed, preparing for her reaction to the homestead.

He hunched his shoulders as they rode into the farmyard and passed the barn. "Needs a coat of paint. Maybe after harvest."

Perched on the edge of the seat, she said nothing. He pulled the reins short outside the rough-hewn house. The farmhouse needed a coat of paint, too.

Cort jumped from the wagon and tied off the horses. Good thing he wasn't trying to impress Eugenia Rutherford. There was an endeavor fraught with failure.

He ought to make her clamber down on her own. But the training of a lifetime—first his mother and then Granny—wouldn't allow him to treat a lady thus. Even an annoying, obnoxious lady like Eugenia Rutherford.

Cort offered his hand. Her mouth went mulish. He blew out a breath.

"Look, Miss Rutherford. It's not the queen's palace, but I've left Granny alone far too long, and the horses—not to mention me—are tired."

She allowed him to help her over the side of the wagon. Placing both hands around her waist, he swung her to the ground. Dried mud flew off her skirts.

He made a face. "You don't smell much better than the pigs you're going to slop behind the barn. You might want to wash up before you start supper."

She stiffened. "Pigs? I thought you were being facetious."

Taking the steps two at a time, he flung open the door. "You'll find I don't joke when it comes to the homestead or Granny."

Head held high, she strode past him into the house.

"And just so you're aware, Miss Rutherford. Any mess you tromp inside will be your responsibility to clean up. No maids here." He grinned and removed his hat. "You *are* the maid, Miss Rutherford."

◆ ◆ ◆

Eugenia wanted to take the hat out of his hands and grind it in his smirking face. But short of funds and facing jail time, her options were limited. Gritting her teeth, she stalked into the kitchen.

A big farm table—intended to accommodate a farmer's many children—occupied the center of the room. She assumed because of his desperation for a nurse, he had neither a wife nor children. She curled her lip, thinking on his cavalier treatment of her. Like anybody was stupid enough to marry the churlish homesteader.

Hands on her hips, she surveyed the small kitchen with the wood-burning stove. Neat and tidy, she'd give the homesteader that. Perhaps due to the handiwork of the disappearing nurse, if his outlandish story was to be believed.

The farmhouse was larger than it appeared from the outside. Rooms branched off from a hallway at the rear of the dwelling.

Cort cocked his head. "Granny?"

"Is that you, Cort, honey?" A quavery, thin voice called.

He shuffled over to a room, its door ajar. "I'm sorry I was gone so long."

Eugenia peered over his broad shoulder. The curtains were pulled shut. A slight figure lay huddled among the bedsheets.

Clothed in her nightclothes and bed cap, the elderly woman squinted in the dim light. "Who's with you, Cort?"

"I didn't catch Mrs. Anderson." His shoulders slumped. "I had to make other arrangements on the spur of the moment."

His grandmother's blue-veined hands fretted at the coverlet. "I'm sorry to be such a nuisance."

Cort took the old lady's frail hand in his. "You're not a nuisance."

Despite her hard feelings toward the homesteader, Eugenia found herself touched by his devotion to his ailing grandmother.

"I found you a new nurse." He stroked his grandmother's hand. "She'll take care of you until harvest is over. After that, I'll find you a more permanent nurse."

The old woman with her lined features held out her hand to Eugenia. "I'm Ingrid Dahlgren. But most folks call me Granny."

Her hair underneath the cap was silver white. "I've long outlived my usefulness, I fear. But I can't complain. Not after the full, rich life I've lived. And I don't mind. I've pined long enough for my dear husband and Cort's sweet mother, gone these many years."

Cort's mouth flattened. "You're no trouble, Granny." His voice roughened. "And you're not going to die. I won't let you."

Eugenia was struck by the vulnerability in his words. And she realized this wasn't some cruel joke Cort Dahlgren was inflicting on her. He—Granny—actually needed her. No one had ever needed her before.

Granny squeezed Eugenia's hand. "What's your name, dear?"

Her hand in Eugenia's was small, dry, and felt paper-thin. "I'm Eugenia Rutherford."

"The silver heiress?" Her dark eyes cut to her grandson and sharpened. "Cort, what have you done?"

"Eugenia accrued a debt in Silver Strike, which she's going to work off by taking care of you. Until harvest is over. No big deal."

Granny frowned. "Work at the homestead?"

He folded his arms across his chest. "What's wrong with the homestead?"

"Nothing. . ." Granny's chin wobbled. "But a young lady like herself. . . She can't know the first thing about. . .about. . ."

Eugenia flushed.

"She's not stupid." He threw Eugenia a shrewd look. "And I imagine what she doesn't know she'll figure out soon enough."

Not a ringing endorsement, but maybe his backhanded way of declaring her capable and intelligent.

"Cort, honey. . ." Granny's brow wrinkled. "A lady like her slopping the hogs and feeding the chickens?"

"Just because she's a silver heiress doesn't make her better than homesteaders *like us*." His eyes bored into Granny. "Trust me. I know what I'm doing."

He angled toward Eugenia. "You don't work, you don't eat."

"Cort!" Granny pinched her lips together.

Eugenia made a shooing motion with her hands. "Take care of the horses. Granny and I will be fine."

"I'm so sorry, dear," Granny whispered as soon as he departed. "I'm afraid I'll need your help with the bedpan."

Spots of color dotted her pale cheeks. "I'm so terribly, terribly sorry to be such a bother." Granny's brown eyes watered.

And for the first time in her life, Eugenia's heart stirred with compassion for someone other than herself. For the elderly woman, clearly embarrassed to be dependent. For what it must feel like to be helpless, sick, and old.

She folded back the quilt. "Don't you worry about anything, Granny. That's what I'm here for—to help."

Afterward, Granny surprised her. "If you don't mind, I think I'd like to try getting up. I'm rather tired of lying in the bed."

Eugenia smiled. "Of course." Somehow she managed to transfer Granny from the bed to the rocking chair next to the window. She drew back the curtain.

"There now." Granny eased her bony shoulder blades against the chair. "How wonderful to feel the sunshine on my face. To be able to see the sky and the mountains above my old home."

"Do you feel strong enough to sit here while I take care of those chores Cort mentioned?"

Granny's eyes twinkled. "I won't go far, I promise."

Eugenia paused at the threshold. "Just one thing, though. Um. . .exactly how does one go about slopping hogs, Granny?"

Chapter 4

Leaving Granny reading her Bible, Eugenia changed into the second-best dress she'd carelessly tossed into her valise before her hurried departure from her father's house.

Her cheeks heated in shame at the remembrance of her harsh words to her father. He must be so angry at her. Angry enough to wash his hands of her forever?

No more than she deserved for the selfish, childish way she'd behaved. Since her mother's death, they'd been each other's everything. And with her father suddenly excised from her life, she felt off-kilter.

Regret dogged Eugenia as she tucked the pale blue shirtwaist into the waistband of the blue-sprigged skirt. Not exactly farmhand material, but the best she could do under these trying and unforeseen circumstances.

She found a plain muslin apron hanging from a peg and ventured toward the barn. The horses whinnied from the nearby corral.

The barn was surprisingly tidy. Cort was a good steward of the land and his livestock. To all appearances, a hard worker. Pleasant smells of horseflesh, leather, and hay filled her nostrils.

As for the slop bucket...

She tried not to breathe as she squelched out behind the barn. Grimacing, she had a bad feeling her brand-new shoes were not going to survive this little misadventure into homesteading.

Would she? She sighed. The jury was still out on that one, too.

The sound of grunting pigs stopped Eugenia in her tracks. Her eyes widened, aghast at the huge, mud-daubed hogs wallowing in the pen. Her stomach turned over. She might never eat bacon again.

Holding her nose against the stench, she propped the bucket on the railing and tipped it into the trough. The contents sloshed. And—she groaned—splashed onto her apron.

Glancing from side to side to make sure no one—namely Cort Dahlgren—had witnessed her humiliation, she emptied the rest of the bucket and beat a hasty retreat.

Surrounded by fields of ripened ears of corn and stalks of wheat, the farm itself was picturesque. The house, cozier than her lavish home in Sacramento. And the red rose rambler twining above the porch eaves was deliciously fragrant and lovely.

Outside the chicken coop, she eyed the rooster with trepidation. Granny had said to distract the hens by scattering the feed and then to collect the eggs.

Retrieving the tin pail, she unlatched the gate and tiptoed inside. With a belligerent squawk at the invasion of his territory, the rooster advanced.

Her heart hammering, she reminded herself who she was—a silver heiress. And who this upstart bantam rooster was—a chicken.

Apparently though—like Cort Dahlgren—the rooster didn't care for silver heiresses. Wings extended, his sharp, pointy beak punctuated the air as he came after Eugenia. And somehow, the rooster got between her and the gate.

Her escape route blocked, she darted for the relative safety of the henhouse. But the rooster flew at her and counterattacked, nipping at her skirts.

Shrieking, she tossed the pail at the rooster's red-crested head. The rooster weaved. The pail rolled onto the ground.

Feathers ruffled, the hens launched themselves at the scattered feed. She covered her head with her arms and screamed again. The chickens ignored her, scratching at the ground.

With a swelling wave of laughter, Cort Dahlgren lolled against the fence post. She dropped her arms.

Glaring, she snatched up the pail. "So glad I could amuse you." With the chickens occupied, she marched over to the nests.

He laughed so hard, he clutched his belly. Tears rolled down his cheeks. "You show 'em who's boss."

Plunging her hand into the straw, she found an egg, which she gently laid inside the bucket. "I'd like to show you who's boss. . . ."

He howled again, slapping his hand on his knee. "If you could see your face. . ."

Lips tight, she collected the eggs. "It's all fun and games until someone gets a bucket upside their head," she hissed.

Which produced further hilarity from the homesteader.

Mustering as much dignity as she could manage, she sashayed out of the coop, her skirts swishing. And still he laughed.

Until. . .until a hen followed Eugenia out of the pen. The rooster and two more hens strutted into the barnyard.

"Shut the gate," Cort shouted. "Latch the hook."

He lunged, but too late as the henhouse emptied itself into the yard. "Of all the stupid—"

"Who're you calling—?"

"Don't just stand there." He dove for one of the scuttling hens. "Don't let them get away."

Squawking, clucking—and that wasn't only the chickens—they scurried after the escape artists.

"Go that way." He gestured. "I'll cut 'em off over there. And we'll herd them into the pen."

Arms spread wide and working together, they wrangled all the chickens inside the gate, except for the rooster. The bane of her entire existence. Other than Cort Dahlgren, of course.

She blew a strand of hair out of her face. Bested by a chicken brain? Eugenia Alice Rutherford thought not.

Hunching her shoulders, she cornered the rooster against the water trough. And pounced. Grasping on to its tail feathers, she and the rooster rolled in the dust.

"I'm losing him," she yelled. The rooster flapped its wings, weakening her grip.

"Cort," she screamed. "Help!"

His large, tanned hands closed around the rooster. "You can let go now, Genie. I got him." He smiled.

She liked the way he smiled at her—when he wasn't being overbearing. "Thank you."

He shut the rooster inside the coop. She brushed the dirt off her skirt.

Genie. No one had ever called her that before. And to her surprise, Eugenia found she rather liked it. Or at least the sound of her name on Cort Dahlgren's lips.

"You're going to run out of clean clothes." He slapped his dusty hat against his thigh. "But no worries, wash day is tomorrow." He gave her that cockeyed smile of his.

Her heart did a funny flutter-flop. "I'm sure I can handle it."

Cort stuck his hands in his pockets. "I've got to check on the horses, but I'll be in the house soon for supper."

Supper? She bit back a sigh. If it wasn't one thing, it was two dozen more. How did these farm women manage to draw an even breath?

"No need to hurry," she called to his back as he headed toward the barn. A broad, stalwart back, tapering to his strong, narrow waist. "Take your time."

Cort Dahlgren was definitely unsettling. More than she'd supposed from a mere homesteader. Much more in fact than she'd reckoned out here in the wilds of Silver Strike, Montana.

She wondered with an uncomfortable disquiet how long harvest lasted. And if it would last long enough. She mopped her suddenly perspiring brow.

Long enough for what?

◆ ◆ ◆

If Cort lived to be a hundred, he'd never forget the sight of the silver heiress doing battle with his rooster.

Grinning, he strode toward the house. The sun hovered in a final blaze of orange glory above the rim of the mountain range. And some of his resentment at her high-handed ways dissipated.

He bounded up the porch steps. The hinges creaked as he pushed open the door. His stomach rumbled. He stretched his arms over his head, loosening his tired, knotted muscles.

"Take off your boots, Cort." Speaking of a certain heiress. . . "I just swept."

Removing his hat, he ducked inside the kitchen. Eugenia hovered over a skillet on the stove. The table was set for three.

His gaze landed on the tiny figure of his grandmother ensconced in the chair beside the hearth. Toeing out of his boots, he hung his hat on a peg and padded across the wide-planked floor to her.

"Look at you," he whispered, pleased and surprised to find Granny out of bed.

She offered him a cheek to kiss. "I look good, don't I, darlin'? Thanks to Eugenia."

Granny did look good. The best he'd seen her in a long time. Her hair was coiled into the bun she'd worn throughout his childhood. She smelled of lavender. Out of her nightgown and in an actual housedress. The heavy, sorrowful weight he'd borne since her stroke lifted a smidgen.

His eyes flitted toward Eugenia. Thanks to Genie. No one was more surprised than he when the nickname slipped from his lips this afternoon. An endearment?

Cort shook off the notion. Disturbed more than he cared to admit. But Eugenia

Alice Rutherford had a funny way of growing on a person. Especially him.

"Thank you, Miss Rutherford."

"Don't thank me yet." She gave a small, somewhat thready sigh. "After wrestling chickens together, maybe we can afford to be a tad less formal."

His pulse quickened. Was the ice princess thawing? "Whatever you think."

She crouched in front of the oven. Using her apron, she opened the door and withdrew a pan. Her shoulders slumped. She clanged the pan onto the counter.

"I'm sorry, Cort." She sounded on the verge of tears. "I—I can't seem to do anything right."

Sorry about what?

Granny patted his arm. "Getting the oven temperature right takes practice. And with giving me a bath, she got distracted."

His grandmother pinned him with a look. "She tried her best. Please don't be too hard on her. She's crushed at the prospect of disappointing you. Again."

Eugenia Alice Rutherford, crushed? And since when did she care what a homesteader like him thought?

But she wrung her hands in the folds of her apron. As for the blackened lumps of dough on the tray? Biscuits, he supposed.

He gulped. "I—I like my bread toasted."

Eugenia's eyes glistened. "Toasted, not charcoaled."

Those beautiful eyes of hers...

He peeled away the top layer of the dough. "Charcoal is supposed to be good for the stomach. Aids digestion."

Eugenia's lips trembled. "The bottoms are burned, too."

"The insides are fine."

Not true, but he stuffed a portion of the undercooked middle in his mouth. He fought the urge to gag. Forced himself to chew and swallow.

"You cannot possibly like my biscuits." She planted her hands on her hips. "Cook wouldn't have fed this mess to the pigs." She sniffed. "Not that we owned pigs."

Cort noticed how the blue blouse accentuated the color of her eyes. His heart did an unexpected lurch.

He'd been too harsh. His expectations too lofty, perhaps he'd unfairly set her up for failure. She'd probably never ventured below stairs in the Sacramento mansion in her life, much less cooked or kept house.

"The pigs aren't picky." He wrapped a dish towel around the iron handle of the skillet. "They'll love it." He scraped the ruined contents into the scrap bucket.

She bit her lip. She had beautiful lips, he thought not for the first time.

"You must be hungry. . . ." Her eyes welled.

Something akin to lightning sizzled his brain. He could deal with her sarcasm and bossiness. Her tears? Not so much.

"Next time you'll do better."

Tiny lines feathered Granny's eyes. She smiled at him from across the room. "Exactly."

"Where are those eggs you gathered earlier?" He cleared his throat. "Scrambled eggs anyone?"

Chapter 5

She never realized how useless an existence she'd led as the pampered daughter of a silver baron.

Eugenia insisted on helping Cort scramble the eggs. Watching and learning as he poured the eggy contents of the bowl onto the heated skillet. At his elbow, her sleeve brushed his. The scent of hay and the enticing, musky aroma of Cort Dahlgren filled her senses.

Distracted by his nearness, she glimpsed a different side of him as they worked together to put dinner on the table. She'd been wrong about him being arrogant. She admired his gentle ways with his grandmother. And like his granny, he also possessed a gracious heart.

"You've helped Granny find her spark again." He smiled. "This is the happiest I've seen her in months."

Eugenia warmed at his words of praise. She slipped into the chair opposite Granny, and Cort eased into the chair at the head of the table.

When he steepled his hands to say grace, she bowed her head, too. Cort talked to God like a friend. Thanking God for the sunshine and the rain. The blessings of good work.

She'd never considered work as a blessing. She'd assumed everyone—those less fortunate than herself—tolerated work as a curse or, at best, a necessary evil.

"Thank You, God, for the blessing of our new friend, Eugenia. And for her loving care of Granny."

She blinked. Cort Dahlgren was thankful for her? She wasn't sure she deserved to be called a blessing. And her throat constricted when he called her his friend. It would be an honor to be Cort's friend.

Taking care of Granny hadn't proven to be the chore she'd imagined. What had changed since Silver Strike? She had the strange sensation maybe the only thing that had changed was her. Upon reflection, a change long overdue.

"I thank You, O God, for the good health You've given us to enjoy this food." Cort's voice grew husky. "And each other. Amen."

She felt his gaze travel over her face. Her hair. Her eyes. Her mouth. Eugenia quivered at the intensity in his eyes. They shared a long look.

"Amen," she whispered, breaking the spell between them.

Granny told Eugenia about her work at the orphanage in town while Cort dug into his supper.

"I miss the children." Granny fingered the lace edging her collar. "It has given my life meaning since my husband, Lars, died."

Eugenia glanced at Cort. He'd laid his head onto the table and fallen asleep. His forehead rested in the crook of his arm.

Remorse pricked her conscience. He'd put in a good day's work and then some. Especially after trailing the missing nurse to town and bailing Eugenia out of jail. She resolved to be more of a help to Cort and less of a hindrance tomorrow.

"Should we wake him?"

Granny gave her sleeping grandson a fond look. "Let him rest his eyes a few moments. Once he hired Mrs. Anderson, he set up a bedroll in the hay loft."

Eugenia wrapped her arms around the thin fabric of her dress. "It's kind of chilly once the sun sets, even if it is July. You think he'll be okay out there tonight?"

"Cort's tougher than he looks." Granny's face sagged. "He had to be, losing his parents so young like he did."

Something they had in common. Her fingers twitched with the desire to smooth the lock of dark hair out of his eyes. Instead, she moved the empty glass away from his elbow.

Granny rested her gnarled hands on the table. "Surrounded by old folks, he didn't have much of a childhood. He's always worked hard and felt a great responsibility to carry on the family legacy."

Eugenia could totally see that about him. "The homestead."

Granny dropped her gaze. "That and other family obligations."

Yet Cort had a refreshing self-confidence, unlike the preening conceit of most of the men she knew from higher society. And even more attractive was Cort Dahlgren's solid faith. Despite her father's example, not something until now she'd believed to be of much use.

She gazed around the kitchen. The parlor maid's room contained more articles of value than this poor farmhouse sported in its entirety. An abundance she'd taken for granted as her right.

But after today's unfortunate misunderstanding, she was learning she had no rights or entitlements. Nothing beyond her father's generosity. If her father had truly disinherited her, nothing stood between Eugenia and a hand-to-mouth existence.

She squared her shoulders. She wasn't Junius Rutherford's daughter for nothing. He and her mother had come from humble roots. And if Eugenia Alice Rutherford was forced to start over, she would.

At least, the Dahlgrens possessed their land. Cort's hard work to keep the homestead going in the face of incredible obstacles was nothing short of remarkable. And the more she came to know this enigmatic young man, her respect for him grew.

"Your grandson is a credit to you, Mrs. Dahlgren."

Granny wiped her mouth with a napkin. "Cort will make some woman a fine husband one day."

For inexplicable reasons, the thought of Cort taking a wife sent a pang through Eugenia.

Granny's eyes sparkled in the glow cast by the oil lamp. "Seeing the two of you makes me feel almost young again. I might yet be of use to those around me. That's what the good Lord put us here for, I reckon. To serve others."

Another notion Eugenia resolved to turn over in her mind.

She came to a sudden decision. "If you'd like to visit the children at the orphanage again, I see no reason why we can't work toward that goal each day."

Granny cocked her head. "It's a busy time on the farm. I didn't want to burden Cort with the half-baked wishes of an old woman."

"As long as you feel strong enough, I don't see any harm in trying." Eugenia tossed her hair over her shoulder. "And as for half-baked?" She shrugged. "I'm the queen of half-baked."

The next morning at the cry of that hateful rooster, she rose from her bed with aching muscles she'd never suspected she possessed. She found Cort already brewing a pot of coffee. Chagrined, she vowed to rouse herself earlier the next day and add no more duties to his workload.

She marched out to the chicken coop with a bucket and broom, armed for battle. Time to show that cockerel who was boss. It was with a great deal of personal triumph she emerged victorious—and unscathed—from the henhouse, a half-dozen brown eggs in her pail.

Cort was slicing a loaf of bread when she returned to the house.

Bread? Another task to learn. But no problem. Heady with the routing of the rooster, she felt ready to tackle anything farm life threw her way.

When she proudly—the good kind of pride this time—placed the plate of scrambled eggs on the table in front of Cort, his eyes lit with appreciation. "Quick study, aren't you?"

"I promise you something besides eggs for dinner."

He gave her that lopsided smile, which did funny things to her nerve endings.

After he headed to the barn, she turned her attention to helping Granny, who wanted to be out in the fresh air while Eugenia tackled wash day.

She dragged a chair out of the house and placed it under the shade of the giant oak. Her arm around Granny's waist, she helped Granny outside.

Granny's right foot dragged a little, but Eugenia noted a healthy color had replaced the old woman's previous pallor. And Granny had taken a few more steps than yesterday.

Eugenia spent the morning hauling water in a huge iron pot from the well to hang over the fire—per Granny's instructions. She gathered the sheets, the bedclothes, and soiled clothing. Using the homemade lye soap, she scrubbed at the stains and stirred the pot full of clothes. Her knuckles were soon bruised and raw from the scrub board.

Midmorning as the heat of the day increased, she transferred Granny into the house. She wiped her arm across her brow where perspiration beaded her forehead. The gingham work dress Granny found inside a trunk for Eugenia to wear was streaked with soot from the fire. Her hair hung in sweaty hanks to her waist.

Back and forth from the pot to the clothesline, she carried the wash. Her arms ached from stirring the pot, carrying the basket heavy with wet linens, and then pegging the clothes on the line.

When Cort emerged from the cornfield, she slumped. She'd forgotten about lunch. Heaving a sigh and leaving the wash, she lumbered toward the steps.

◆ ◆ ◆

Mounting the steps, Eugenia swayed, clearly exhausted.

Cort rushed forward and cupped her elbow in his hand.

"I should've had lunch ready. I'm sorry, Cort."

"No problem." He steadied her arm and ushered her inside. "I'll help you."

"It's not your job to do lunch. It's mine."

When he touched her hand, she sucked in a breath and wrenched free of his grasp.

His gut tightened. "What's wrong with your hand, Eugenia?"

She pressed her hand against her chest. "Nothing."

"Let me see," he grunted.

"Never mind." She avoided looking at him. "I need to get—"

"Ham sandwiches?" Granny leaned against the butcher block beside a tray of sliced ham.

Cort stepped around Eugenia. "You shouldn't be on your feet."

Granny shooed him away. "Stop fussing. I'm not an invalid." She threw Eugenia a smile. "I've still got a lot of life to live."

His grandmother arched her eyebrow into a question mark. "I'm assuming you've washed your hands?"

Cort frowned. "Speaking of hands... Eugenia, I insist you allow me to inspect yours." He hunched his shoulders. "Please, Genie?"

With reluctance, she withdrew her balled fist from the folds of her skirt. Stifling a sob, she uncurled her hand.

Cradling her hand in his palm, he winced at the bleeding, oozing sores. "Genie..."

She snatched her hand away. "I wasn't used to toting the water bucket."

He felt terrible. "It's too heavy for you. I should've realized you weren't used to that kind of labor." She had to be in tremendous pain.

"This is my fault." A rush of tenderness consumed him. "I'm so sorry, Genie. I'd rather be hurt myself than to see you hurt."

She lifted her chin. "It's my job to wash the clothes."

He took her hand again, careful not to rub the raw flesh. "But I'd never want to see your lovely skin marred...."

She shot him a quizzical look, and Cort flushed, realizing what he'd said.

Her face clouded. "My hands need to toughen up. Like me."

Cort stroked the back of her hand with his thumb. "I'll put ointment on it. We'll need to keep it bandaged to avoid infection." The back of his eyelids burned. "I can't tell you how sorry I am this happened."

He hated himself. He'd expected whining and laziness from the silver heiress, but instead she'd done her best to satisfy his demands and take care of Granny.

God, please forgive my misplaced pride....

After lunch, he helped her hang the last of the wash on the line to dry. He insisted that she and Granny rest during the heat of the afternoon. He was done with getting even. He wanted no part in putting Eugenia in her place. So he rode into town.

Where he sent a terse telegram of his own. Washing his hands in no uncertain terms of the entire scheme.

Chapter 6

Over the next week, Eugenia fell into a routine with her homestead responsibilities. Under Granny's tutelage, she mastered the intricacies of the stove and the fine art of pie making. Not just humble pie, either, as Eugenia's self-respect grew. She discovered there was a choreography to ensuring the food came off the stove at the same time.

Cort had taken to arriving for lunch with a handful of meadow daisies. The first time he produced the bouquet of wildflowers from behind his back she stared at him.

"For me?"

His gaze dropped to his boots. "I know they're not the lavish orchids you're used to, but—"

She grabbed for them as he started to backpedal. "They're beautiful."

Eugenia clasped the flowers to her pinafore, half afraid he'd take them back. "Thank you, Cort. I love them."

Something stirred between them.

His Adam's apple bobbed. "It's a hectic time of year on the farm. And most of all, thank you for your devotion to Granny."

She willed her heartbeat to settle. This was about showing his appreciation for her care of Granny. Nothing more.

But the next day, he brought Eugenia a handful of forget-me-nots from the woods. "Like your eyes. Except the flowers aren't as pretty."

And later that week, a cluster of wild, dark pink roses. She lifted the bouquet to her nose to inhale their fragrant, spicy scent.

His only explanation before taking his seat at the table? "I like the look of pink against your face."

It was a supremely proud day when she set a platter of fried chicken, a bowl of mashed potatoes, and a loaf of brown bread in front of Cort. Declaring herself not hungry, Granny excused herself to catch up on her reading.

His eyes crinkled, the lines fanning out from the corners as he smiled at her. "The chicken smells great, Genie."

Eugenia had never known this kind of satisfaction before. Too excited to eat, she watched while Cort tucked into the simple fare she'd cooked with her own two hands.

She'd pleased him. Her heart beat faster. And pleasing him, somewhere along the way, had become her highest goal.

After he ate his fill, he leaned back in his chair. "There's a dance coming in a few weeks."

Plate in hand, she paused in clearing the table.

"In the meadow beside the church on a Saturday evening to inaugurate the upcoming harvest."

Eugenia held her breath. Waiting. Hoping. Would Cort ask her to go to the dance? Sometime over the last few weeks their relationship had moved from outright hostility to friendship. As for something more?

When she didn't say anything, his forehead creased. He pushed away from the table. The chair scraped across the hardwood floor. He reached for the plate in her hands. His dark eyes searched hers.

Her heart stutter-stepped. He leaned closer, only the plate between them.

"Would you like to go to the dance, Genie?"

Her mouth went dry. What was he really asking?

"You like to dance, don't you?"

She nodded, her head bobbing like a fish caught on a hook.

"Good." He tugged at the plate in her hand. She wasn't ready to let go. Or allow him to move away.

She moistened her lips with her tongue. "Why do you want to go?"

He shuffled his feet. But he didn't let go of the plate they held between them. "I thought the dance might be fun."

"Fun?" Her breath came in short spurts.

His chest rose and fell. "Everybody deserves a little fun. Especially before the hard work of harvest begins."

Everybody. Not a personal invitation, then. She let go of the plate.

Her hand dropped to the folds of her gingham work dress. "I guess everyone in Silver Strike will be there."

Cort gripped the plate. "I—I meant. . ." Spots of color peppered his cheeks.

She wasn't sure she'd ever seen him flustered. He always seemed so in control of not only himself but his world.

Eugenia started to turn away, but he seized hold of her hand. Electricity sparked as his skin touched hers. Her lips parted in an involuntary O.

His eyebrows drew together. "I meant to ask if you'd allow me to escort you to the dance." His mouth twisted. "I realize it's not the kind of grand society function you're used to."

She lifted her chin. "I'm sure the dance will be lovely. Thank you for inviting me. For thinking of me."

"I'm always thinking of you," he growled. "I also realize I'm not your usual, well-heeled escort."

Taking the plate, she set it on the table with a dull thud. "Because you're a homesteader?"

A vein throbbed in his cheek. "Yes."

Silence stretched between them for a long moment. A throat-catching moment.

"I'm beginning to think Sacramento parties are vastly overrated." She tilted her head. "As are silver barons and copper kingdoms."

He took her hands in his. "So you'll go with me?"

She smiled. "I'd love to go. And I'll be proud to be on the arm of one of the hardest working, best men I've ever had the pleasure of knowing."

He gave her a winsome, boyish smile that set her heart soaring.

She realized he'd yet to let go of her hands, or she his. Instead, he raised her hand to his mouth and brushed his lips across her fingers. She gave a delicious shiver all the way down to her work boots.

"Thank you, Genie. I'm looking forward to it."

His hand over hers, he pressed her palm against the rock-hard muscle of his chest. Through the fabric, she felt the warmth of his skin. And the wild drumming of his heart in a beat to match her own.

There was a look in his eyes—she felt it, too. As if they both understood they were on the brink of a precipice. One dizzy step further toward either disaster or the cusp of something altogether wonderful.

Finally, he let go of her hands. With a promise—to be continued—in his eyes?

He forcibly swallowed. "Let me help you with the dishes. Together we'll get it done."

And she let him help this time. Because he was right. They did make a good team.

Chapter 7

The next few weeks were busy in preparation for harvest. Eugenia's hands took on calluses. And she helped Granny take back her strength. Each step earned with painstaking care.

Gradually, Granny regained her mobility. Still unable to walk long distances, she could move about the farmhouse and down the steps with assistance.

Today Eugenia had promised to take Granny to the orphanage to reunite with the children.

She arose in the darkness of predawn. She—who never in her life before coming to Silver Strike awakened before noon. She made Cort's breakfast and hastened to the small garden patch beside the house.

Early morning had become her favorite time, when the world shook off slumber and dew beaded the blades of grass. She lifted her face to the sky, streaked with the first brushstrokes of color. And she gave thanks for the beauty of another day.

She hoed to the rhythmic, croaking chorus of the frogs by the pond. And weeded to the melodic chirping of the meadowlarks. She'd also fallen into the habit of praying for Granny.

For Cort. For her father. For herself. And she found she carried the peace of the morning throughout the day.

After gathering the peas into her basket, she returned to the kitchen. She'd shell the peas later this afternoon. She untied her apron and hung it on its peg.

"Give me another minute, dear," Granny called from her bedroom.

"No rush." Eugenia drifted to her own bedroom and the pink-sprigged calico lying across the quilt on her bed.

With Granny's encouragement, Eugenia had taken an old dress from the brown leather trunk and altered the fabric to fit her figure.

On impulse, she held the dress against herself and peered at her reflection in the looking glass above the bureau. The dress had turned out nicely. Real question—would Cort Dahlgren think so?

In her widow's black bonnet and shawl, Granny joined her. "You did an excellent job."

Eugenia flushed, embarrassed to be caught admiring herself. "The ladies academy didn't teach me much of practical value. But my studies—such as they were—did include needlework."

Granny held the sleeve against Eugenia's face. "The color brings out the roses in your cheeks."

Eugenia turned this way and that in the mirror, admiring the calico. The color did wonderful things for her complexion. Still unmarred, thanks to Cort's insistence that she wear a bonnet outdoors.

Who would've believed someone of her station would ever need such fundamental skills? But if nothing else, she'd learned—the hard way—stations in life could change without warning. And it behooved one to be prepared.

Laying aside the gown, she helped the old woman navigate the steps. With Granny eager to see the children, Cort had already hitched the horse to the buckboard.

Spotting Cort across the open field, she lifted her arm. He waved. A warm feeling curled in her belly.

He'd been watching for them. For her. Her other favorite time involved evening, when she and Cort shared their day with each other.

No fanfare. No high drama. Just talking about favorite books and childhood memories. She—whose whirlwind social calendar had once been filled with one event after the other. Who knew she would find the simple life so fulfilling?

She slapped the reins, and the horse set off at a brisk trot.

Granny balanced the willow basket filled with eggs in her lap. "Won't be long till harvest."

Eugenia's heart skipped a beat. Harvest—her debt paid—and she'd be on her way. But to where? To her friend, Muriel, in Chicago? Or to Sacramento?

The farm felt like home now. Would there be a place for her at the homestead after harvest? A place in Cort's life? Is that what she wanted?

Granny's gaze roamed over the stalks of grain, golden in the late-July sunshine. "I haven't seen the fields this ripe and ready since my dear Lars was still alive."

The old woman let out a sigh. "I pray for Cort's sake the harvest is a good one this year. He's earned it."

"Have the harvests been poor?"

Granny fluttered her hand in the breeze. "Drought. The locusts came three years in a row. Many farmers hereabouts gave up their homesteads. Quit farming. Sold up to the McCallums."

Eugenia's mouth tightened. Sold out to the copper king. She knew his kind. Taking advantage of hard times. Gobbling up the surrounding acreage when the other farmers fell into trouble.

"Cort probably should've given up, too. But I loved the place, and he's held on for my sake."

She'd seen him walking among the rows of corn, early morning and late evening. His stride measured, his head bent. His face contented and proud as he surveyed the work of his hands.

Granny shook her head. "The homestead's not made a profit in years. This harvest, I expect, will be the last one. Time to let go of the past. Cort has his own life to live."

Cort give up the farm? He loved the homestead. What would become of him if he didn't have the farm? She could no more imagine Cort doing anything else than she could imagine herself—she gulped.

Than she could imagine herself content to return to the endless round of high society.

Her heart pounded. What would become of her? She'd never again be satisfied to wile away her days in useless pursuits. Mooching—the waitress at the hotel had been thoroughly correct—off the labors of others.

She squared her shoulders. And resolved to do everything in her power to ensure the harvest was a good one for Cort. So he didn't lose his beloved home. So vile Copper King McCallum didn't devour Cort's heritage.

The wagon jostled over a dip in the road.

"Whoa, there!" Granny clutched the basket. "Don't want to smash your profits."

Eugenia fastened her attention onto driving and off the uncertain future. "Sorry."

Another thing she'd learned about farm life? Apparently, whoever took care of the chickens had free and clear rights to sell the extra eggs at the mercantile.

Egg money, Cort called it. And declared it rightfully hers. She protested the first week. But he and Granny insisted.

The money became the first Eugenia had ever actually earned in her life. Every week since—when the mercantile owner dropped the coins into her palm—she experienced a tingle of satisfaction at the fruits of her labor.

Not a large amount of money. Pocket change really. But enough to mail a weekly letter to her father.

In the first letter, she apologized for her rude, selfish behavior. In subsequent letters, she told him of her chores, the joy of her days, and the surprising faith she rediscovered at the homestead. It grieved her that her father hadn't written her back, but despite his worrying silence, she continued to write.

The loss of their relationship gnawed at her insides. She'd taken so much for granted—most of all his constant support and enduring love. And like the self-centered child she'd been, she'd thrown everything away with her foolish petulance.

She wished he could see her now. Despite her humble lifestyle, she believed Junius Rutherford would've been proud of the person she prayed every day to become.

As for the rest of her egg money? She had to become practical, so she stashed the remaining coins in the toe of an old stocking. She'd need money once she left Silver Strike and the Dahlgren farm forever.

Without Cort and Granny, a forever she preferred not to contemplate. She aimed to enjoy her time with Granny and with Cort as long as she could.

Granny often quoted, "A forecast of rain on the morrow should never be allowed to mar the sunshine of today."

A lesson for life.

Next week the harvest commenced for area farmers. And this Saturday, the dance. Anticipation set her heart aflutter.

"After we visit the Home, I have my shopping list for the mercantile." Granny patted the bulge in her skirt pocket. "A few necessities. Food for the body. What about you?"

On the outskirts of Silver Strike, Eugenia allowed the horse to ease into a trot. "I have my eye on a strand of pink ribbon."

Granny smiled. "To match the dress."

Eugenia blushed. "Do you think I'm foolish to spend money on frivolity?"

"Not at all, my dear." Granny adjusted her bonnet. The sun was strong and bright. The sky, a panorama of blue. "I believe food for the soul is as much a necessity as feeding the body."

"Food for the soul..." Eugenia liked the play of the words on her tongue.

Granny's wise old eyes gleamed. "Gifts from the Father to His beloved children—if they have the heart to embrace such gifts. A feast for the senses."

She'd not thought of life that way before. A gift from a loving Papa. But it was true.

Like the dew on the squash blossoms. Or the trill of the bird. Food for the soul.

It amazed Eugenia sometimes how much she'd learned in the last month. And not just about farming. But about herself and most of all, God.

She'd received many gifts of love from her father. The least of which were of any monetary value. But she, foolish child, had been blind to their real worth.

Eugenia turned the wagon toward the sprawling, two-story house on the end of Main. Boys and girls spilled out of the foundling home. And seeing them, she missed her father even more. For without her father in her life, she felt as adrift as these orphans.

Setting the brake, she hopped down and tied the reins to the hitching post. Wiping her hands on her apron, the matron emerged, her weathered face wreathed in welcome. Eugenia helped Granny out of the wagon.

Instantly engulfed by the children, Granny rested the palm of her hand briefly on top of each child's head. Eugenia's eyes watered at the love between Granny and the children.

Talking a mile a minute, a boy by the name of Luke and an older girl, Vera, led Eugenia on a tour. The younger ones refused to let go of Granny's skirts and informed the old woman about what had transpired during her prolonged absence.

Eugenia was impressed by the family atmosphere and the meaningful instruction the Home provided. Each child learned early to care not only for themselves, but also for the concerns of others. All were required to keep the Home in proper working order.

The children received the usual reading, writing, and arithmetic at the Silver Strike schoolhouse. But each child was also trained for a marketable skill. Most importantly, seeds of faith were planted in the children's hearts and watered.

And Eugenia—as always her father's daughter—inquired about the Home's financial footing.

Matron Harris was candid. "We are dependent on donations. The good people of Silver Strike have been extremely generous in helping us to maintain the ministry."

The fiftyish woman threw a swift look at Granny. "In fact, the land upon which the Home sits was deeded to the Society by the McCallums."

Eugenia's eyebrows rose. As did her previous estimation of the rough-bearded suitor she barely recalled meeting once upon a time in Sacramento. Maybe the copper king wasn't as despicable as she'd believed.

Her heart was stirred by everything she'd seen at the Home. If only she had even a portion of her father's resources to invest in the lives of these children. If only she could do something to make a contribution to promote the good work done here.

After a time, she could see Granny visibly tiring, so she bade the children farewell. The matron and a circle of children followed them to the waiting wagon.

Moving the basket aside, Granny settled her skirts on the wooden seat. "We'll come again soon."

The eggs. Eugenia didn't have much, but she did have the eggs. A vision of a dark pink ribbon woven through her hair flashed across her mind. And the image of the coins in her drawer. Could she trust God to provide for her needs if she gave that away, too?

Shunting aside the doubt, she handed the basket to the matron. "It's not much, but maybe enough for tomorrow's breakfast."

Granny cocked her head. "What about your—?"

"Next time I come"—Eugenia hugged Vera—"I'll bring more eggs and flour, too."

Amid the matron's thanks and a flurry of waving from the children, she climbed onto the buckboard and steered the horse toward the store.

"That was an unselfish thing to do. I know how you've been eyeing that ribbon."

"It was little enough." She glanced at Granny. "I wanted to give the eggs to the children. And it felt good. To do something for someone else."

She patted the letter tucked into the pocket of her skirt. "I have enough from last week to send the letter to my father. The ribbon can wait."

"I'm so proud of you, Eugenia." Granny's eyes shone. "My dear girl, how far you've traveled from the self-possessed young woman who first arrived at the homestead."

Eugenia's mouth wobbled. "Self-obsessed, you mean."

She cringed, contemplating the spoiled creature she'd once been and never hoped to be again. What had made the difference?

Granny and Cort's selfless love for each other and for God. As well as her dawning realization of God's tremendous sacrificial love for her. As for Cort?

She wasn't sure how Cort felt about her. She liked to think she'd earned not just egg money, but also his respect. As for his love?

The one who held Cort Dahlgren's heart would be truly blessed. And for the love of a good man like him, she'd freely relinquish any claim of inheritance and society position ten times over.

But what would a hardworking homesteader like Cort Dahlgren possibly ever want with a useless silver heiress like her?

◆ ◆ ◆

Saturday evening, Cort's breath hitched at the sight of Eugenia. The dress was simple but lovely. And she'd done something different with her hair.

"Hey, you."

Eugenia's mouth curved. "Hey, yourself."

Cort smiled at the meadow flowers she'd woven into the strands of her hair like a crown of petals. The simple dress was far more beautiful to his way of thinking than any elegant ball gown.

His spirits dimmed at the thought of her real life in Sacramento. This homestead life—the world he, Granny, and Eugenia had created together—couldn't last forever.

Cort needed to tell her the truth. None of them could go on like this indefinitely. She—no matter how much he wished it—didn't belong here. Not on the homestead, most especially not with him.

She was used to finer things. This homestead adventure was a lark—at first maddening, ultimately inconvenient—but a lark nonetheless, a detour on the road of both their lives.

Eugenia would be angry, rightly so. He dreaded the scorn in her eyes like he'd fear a ravaging plague of locusts. After the dance, he promised himself. No more putting off what needed to be done.

He offered his hand as she stepped into the wagon. He untied the team of horses from the railing. The horses snuffled and pawed the ground.

Cort heaved himself onto the seat. "Hi-yup." He flicked the reins and steered the horses toward the road.

She waved to Granny. Standing—he swallowed against a lump in his throat—thanks to God's grace and Eugenia's stubborn refusal to accept defeat. They owed Eugenia so much. She'd given Granny back her life—a life of purpose.

But when Eugenia returned to her father, she'd forget about them soon enough. No doubt relieved to leave the hard work of the homestead behind. His heart quaked at the prospect of never seeing her again.

Perhaps, though, she'd remember him and their time together with fondness. Which, at this point, was all he dared hope for. To hope for more with someone like Eugenia Rutherford was an exercise in delusion.

And Cort—if nothing else—was a practical man. A prudent man. A cautious man.

The horses plodded down the country road toward town. After weeks of unhindered conversation, he found himself suddenly tongue-tied. Beside him, she sat with her gloved hands clutching the edge of the wagon seat. Equally at a loss for words?

Utterly unlike the Eugenia he'd come to know, appreciate, and. . . He caught himself up short. To love?

He clenched the reins. Yes. Because he did love her. So very much.

Cort stole a sideways look at her face. "The grain's ready to harvest."

Her shoulders relaxed a smidgen. "How do you know?" Was she as nervous as him?

"Checked the fields this afternoon." He cast a look at the darkened sky. "Monday morning, bright and early, we'll start. After a harsh winter and a wet spring, I'm hopeful we can get the crop in before a thunderstorm or, God forbid, a hailstorm flattens the crop."

"I'd like to help."

The wagon rocked side to side as the horses trotted along the road. He bit the inside of his cheek. This was a very different Eugenia Rutherford than the spoiled young woman he'd first met.

"I appreciate that, Genie."

She nestled closer to him on the seat. His heart sped up, liking her nearness. She tucked her hand in the crook of his elbow.

"I know how important bringing in the crop is to you and Granny." She squeezed his arm. "We're in this together. And we'll get it done together."

He had a hard time remembering to breathe with her this close. He couldn't think how he'd gotten himself ensnared in this scheme in the first place. But of course, he knew.

It was because of Eugenia. . . . For him, it always came back to Eugenia.

Somehow he suspected—the thought gave him no pleasure, only certain pain—it would always come back to Eugenia.

After next week she returned to her real life. He had just tonight. One night to fulfill the longings of his heart. To hold her in his arms. To dream of what could never be.

Futile, hopeless. He set his jaw. But if only for a brief time, he could pretend Eugenia Alice Rutherford was his.

Chapter 8

Under shimmering pinpoints of starlight, Cort held her in his arms, and they danced in the outdoor pavilion. When the musicians took a break, he pulled Genie into the small garden between the church and the schoolhouse.

The night air was heady with the scent of fragrant roses drooping along the length of the white picket fence. Beneath the pergola, she slipped into his embrace as natural as breathing. She turned her face to his. Her beautiful lips parted.

His pulse accelerated. If he didn't kiss her now, he feared his heart would break from longing. He bent his head. She closed her eyes.

Eugenia trembled in his arms. And his heart turned over in his chest. With love for this woman who was so much more than he'd ever believed.

He leaned closer. She gave a tiny involuntary inhalation. And Cort—who'd waited far longer for this moment than she'd ever suppose—could deny his heart no longer.

When his mouth found hers, she leaned into his kiss. And his senses drank in her essence.

Her breath fanned his cheek. "I never knew," she whispered. "I never knew it could be like this."

Cort never had, either. Hope surged. That he might woo her into staying. If she felt the same as he felt for her. . .

Lightning streaked across the sky. Thunder boomed.

He loosened his arms as couples hurried to waiting buggies, trying to outrun the rain.

They smiled at each other and shrugged. Laughing, they dashed for the wagon. The stars winked out, obscured by the blackness of the storm.

He'd had his dance with Genie. More than one. And his mouth curved at the remembrance of the feel of her lips on his.

All the way home, he wrestled in his mind about what to say to her. The time had come to reveal his true feelings. To ask Eugenia to stay by his side. And Granny's. To love them. As they—he most of all—loved her.

But as he helped her alight from the wagon, the threatening storm broke in a torrent of rain. Covering her head with her arms, she darted for the porch.

And the moment was lost.

He was half relieved, truth be told, to put off the inevitable. Tomorrow morning, he promised himself. Before breakfast.

Cort spent a sleepless night amid the violent strikes of lightning. And the morning dawned a vivid orange.

At the window—by the aqua-blue medicine bottles filled with wildflowers—Genie studied the sunrise over the fields.

No more stalling. He jammed his hands into his pockets. "Gonna be a hot one."

A pucker creased her forehead as she continued to stare out the window. "Does it appear that the sunrise has crept closer than normal?"

He followed the direction of her gaze. And the bottom dropped out of his stomach.

"Fire!" He whirled. "The fields are on fire."

◆ ◆ ◆

Eugenia ran outside to the farmyard. Probably a lightning strike that smoldered overnight. The entire harvest was in flames.

Beyond saving. And now the barn? She couldn't allow Cort's dreams to go up in smoke.

Inside the burning barn, the heavy wall of smoke and searing heat almost sucked the breath from her lungs. Coughing, she recoiled from the raging inferno.

Through the haze, she caught sight of Cort, struggling to free the horses from their stalls. The terrified horses reared. Their eyes blazed wild with fear.

Cort needed her help. He couldn't do this without her. He'd be trampled trying to save them.

Holding her apron against her nose and mouth, she plunged into the swirling darkness.

She grabbed several blankets and a bridle from the tack room. "Cort!"

He didn't hear her at first above the frightened screams of the horses. But when she nudged his arm, he whipped around. She pressed a blanket into his hands.

"No, Genie." He gestured. "Go back. I'll get the horses."

He disappeared into a stall without waiting to see if she obeyed. Which was just too unfortunate. Because she'd proven she wasn't any good at doing what she was told.

Cort was one man. And there were two horses.

Best-case scenario, he'd save one horse. Worst case? He'd die saving one or both. She didn't much care for either scenario.

The crackling roar of the flames licked at the hayloft above their heads, devouring everything in its path. The ceiling could collapse at any moment. There was no time.

She slipped past him into the other stall. The horse bucked. "Please, God," she breathed. "Help me."

Coaxing and cajoling, she managed to secure the bridle and drape the horsehair blanket over the bay's head. Holding her cheek against the coarse fabric, she whispered, pleaded, and tugged the horse out of the stall and into the open air.

In the barnyard, Cort swatted the other horse out of harm's way into the corral. Using his sleeve to cover his nose, only the white of his eyes were visible in his smoke-blackened face.

"Gen—" His eyes narrowed. "I told you—"

A barn beam crashed behind her. The bay bolted. She lost her footing. Her hand tangled in the reins.

"Let go!" Cort ran forward. "Let go, honey. He's dragging you."

In a stumbling run to keep pace with the charging horse, she experienced a sudden terror. If she went down, she wouldn't be getting up. "I can't. Cort!"

He threw himself in front of the horse, yanking the bridle. "Whoa, boy. Whoa."

She found her footing.

Fingers shaking, she pried her hand free of the reins. And Cort immediately released the horse into the corral.

Cort's strong arms encircled her waist. "Are you all right? You could've died. I told you—"

"Y–You know I—I was n–never one to listen too well." Her body quivered so hard only his strength kept her upright.

He buried his nose into her hair. "Genie. . . What were you thinking?"

She clung to him. "You needed my help to save the horses."

His grip tightened. "Horses I can live without. You?" His chest heaved. "Not so much. Don't ever scare me like that again."

She glanced over his shoulder to where Granny flapped a dish towel at the cinders peppering the porch. "The house."

Wetting the last of the grain sacks in the rain barrel, they prevented a shower of sparks from igniting the dwelling.

At the sound of splintering wood, Eugenia pivoted. With an immense creaking groan, the upper story of the barn collapsed. Fire engulfed the entire structure.

She gasped. "Oh, Cort. All your hard work."

He squeezed his eyes shut then opened them. "It doesn't matter."

"It does matter." Tears tracked across her cheeks. "What will you do now?"

Cort's mouth worked as he struggled to regain his composure. "I'll do what farmers always do. Somehow make do until next year."

Hours later, glowing embers still burned among the ruins of his hopes and dreams. He poked underneath the charred boards looking for anything to salvage. But it was no use.

Cort moved like an arthritic old man among the ashes. "I've lost the harvest."

"This wasn't your fault." She snagged hold of his shirttail. "And we saved the house."

His shoulders slumped. "The farm was my responsibility. Granny was counting on me, and I let her down."

It tore Eugenia's heart to see him so discouraged, so defeated. She understood how much the land meant to not only Granny, but to Cort also.

He scrubbed his hand over his sooty face. "Good thing most of my clothes are still in the house. I'll wash up."

Moving about the kitchen, she couldn't help staring at the paperwork he'd left on the kitchen table. The bank notices.

Her heart sank. McCallum would win again. She had no doubts the boorish copper king would turn the Dahlgrens out of their home.

Where would they go when the bank foreclosed? Granny had made such progress. Against the odds, battling the effects of the palsy. Would this obstacle prove too much? Would this break Granny's die-hard spirit entirely?

Eugenia sagged against the table. She couldn't let this happen. Not while she had the power to change things, to fix things for Granny and Cort.

Her new faith told her to trust God to provide. But what could she—?

She sucked in a breath. Perhaps God had already provided the answer—Eugenia Rutherford. There was one thing only she could do to make things right.

Eugenia shook her head. There had to be another way. Not when her heart had finally found a home. Here with Granny. With Cort.

She'd been so foolish. A stupid little girl. She'd had no idea how people struggled to survive. She'd taken so much for granted. Been so proud.

Proud of what? The fine houses and carriages? The silly plumed frippery that summed up her entire life? Her father's millions. Of which she'd earned not one penny.

But the notion—the solution to Cort's problems—wouldn't leave her. No matter how hard she pondered another remedy, this was the only one that offered the Dahlgrens a chance to hang on to the homestead.

And she wasn't the same bored, shallow child who arrived in Silver Strike. She'd grown up, thanks to Cort and Granny. For the first time in her frivolous life, someone needed her.

She'd found a purpose beyond herself in loving and caring for Granny. She bit back a sob. In loving Cort, too. Now, more than ever, Granny and Cort needed her. Needed her to do the hard thing.

The hardest thing of all. Like Granny talked about in the scripture. Wouldn't God want Eugenia to do the same? To sacrifice herself for those she loved.

Because there was no denying she loved them. Maybe—other than her parents—the only people she'd ever loved more than she loved herself.

Cort wouldn't understand. He'd try to stop her as long as he believed she cared for him. But she must find a way to convince him. To make him not only see the soundness of her plan, but steel herself against his contempt at her choice. She must ride away and never look back.

And do that which must be done.

◆ ◆ ◆

Cort realized something was wrong when he stepped into the kitchen. Beside the counter, Granny wrung her hands in her apron. Eugenia tended to the stove.

She'd changed out of the scorched work dress. Her hair piled into an elaborate chignon, she'd put on the grand, blue silk she wore that first day. His heart lurched.

As they fought the fire side by side, he'd glimpsed the young woman God meant for her to be. His Genie. His truest love.

She took Granny's gnarled hand in her now work-roughened one. "I'm so sorry."

"It's only wood, child."

He needed to tell Eugenia the truth. What he'd put off saying for weeks. And knowing Eugenia, she was liable to sock him in the gut when she learned what he'd done.

Which he would deserve, take like a man, and then beg her forgiveness. On his knees. He wanted nothing to stand between their future. He'd give his life to ensure her every happiness.

"Eugenia. . ."

She turned away. "Supper's waiting."

Granny's blue-veined hand cupped Eugenia's cheek. "I want you to know how proud I am of the fine woman you've become."

Eugenia stepped back. "I—I sliced some ham."

"I'm not hungry." Granny's brow wrinkled. "I think you two need to talk." She shuffled toward the rocker.

He moved toward the woodstove, but Eugenia shrank from him. "Genie..."

What was wrong? Had Granny told her? Did Eugenia despise him?

"The potatoes are nearly ready." She set to stirring the frying pan as if her life depended on it.

And he had the uneasy sensation his life might depend on what next she said to him. Or didn't say.

"I'm not hungry, either." He crossed the distance separating them and touched her elbow. "What's wrong, Genie?"

She shivered as his breath ruffled tendrils of hair dangling about her ear. "Nothing."

Eugenia scooted out of his reach. "Let me finish what I started, please."

There was a hard edge to her voice. A tone he hadn't heard since that first day in Silver Strike.

She plunked the platter of fried potatoes onto the table. She took an extraordinary amount of time—or so he thought—wiping clean her work space. Fiddling with the stove. Adjusting the plates and napkins. Stalling?

His stomach cramped. Two plates. Two napkins. Two sets of utensils. What was happening here? Why wouldn't she look at him?

She crouched beside his grandmother in the rocking chair. "Thank you for everything, Granny. For teaching me so much." Her voice quavered. "F–For seeing something in me I never imagined about myself."

"Genie—" He stopped at Granny's upraised palm.

His grandmother touched Eugenia's cheek with one gnarled finger. "God has great plans for you. Plans for a future and a hope. Never forget. Trust and believe."

With an abrupt motion, Eugenia rose, her skirt swaying. "Could we talk outside, Cort?"

And what he saw in her eyes made him want to run. To hide.

But he could do none of those things. His chest tightened as he followed her out to the corral. Leaning over the railing, the horses softly nickered.

She smoothed her hand over the bay's neck. "If you'd allow me to borrow a horse, I'll make sure he's returned to you."

He cleared his throat, thick with smoke inhalation and emotion. "Where're you going, Genie?"

She flinched. "I'm not Genie. I'm Eugenia Alice Rutherford, silver heiress. And it's time I started acting like who I really am."

Eugenia gulped. "Who I was always born to be."

He took hold of her arm. "You can be whoever you choose to be. Together we can—"

"That's just it, Cort." With great deliberation, she placed herself out of his reach. "There is no 'together.' There can never be an 'us.'"

Eugenia scanned the blackened fields and barn. In her expression he beheld a wistfulness, an aching sadness. And a steely resolution.

"Such a lovely, lovely dream. But only a dream." She shook herself. "From which, however, we must now awaken."

"I don't understand." He gritted his teeth so hard, his jaw ached. "I lov—"

"Don't." She fell against the corral gate. Panic streaked across her face. "Don't say anything else. Something you'll regret. Something which can't be undone."

"I don't regret a single moment I've spent with you over the last month. I realize you're scared."

He raked his hand over his head. His hat fell into the dust. "I'm scared, too. But don't stand there and deny what I've felt for you and what I know you've felt for me isn't real. Real love isn't safe. It's the biggest risk of all."

Eugenia's eyes flashed. "I'm more like my father than I supposed. A risk taker when it comes to big decisions. Willing to throw my lot and life where there'll be a better return on my investment."

He stared at her. "What are you talking about?"

"I've decided to accept McCallum's proposal."

"Why would you do that?" He seized her arm. "You can't—"

She flung off his hand. "I'm Junius Rutherford's daughter. I can do anything I want. And what I want is to marry the copper king."

"You don't mean that. You can't mean that. You love me. I know you love me."

She gave him a pitying look. "Don't be naive. Whether I love you or not is irrelevant in the larger scheme of things."

"Then enlighten me, Eugenia." His mouth thinned. "What is this about?"

"It's about my future." Her lips tightened. "And not to be cruel, but your lack thereof."

She looked at him down the length of her long, patrician nose. A feat, considering he topped her height by at least a foot. A gesture, which reminded him of the other Eugenia. And stirred an old anger that until now he believed he'd put behind him.

"It's about regaining Daddy's good graces. About not losing my inheritance. Taking my rightful place in society. And refurbishing my sadly neglected wardrobe."

He clenched his fists. "You're lying. I don't understand where this is coming from, but I know you. This isn't you."

"Don't be presumptuous, Cortland Dahlgren. You know nothing about the real me. What could a homesteader like you understand about the needs and desires of an heiress like—"

Her words shattered what little control he had left over his emotions. Wrapping both hands around her upper arms, he yanked her against his chest.

She pressed her hands against his shirt and shoved. "Get your hands off me."

He didn't budge so much as an inch.

"Allow me to demonstrate, Miss Rutherford. One last time, how well this homesteader understands an heiress." His mouth contorted. "Or at least, one particular heiress."

Crushing her lips with his own, he kissed her. For all he was worth. For all she meant to him. For all they'd meant to each other.

She made a sound in the back of her throat. Her knees buckled. She would've fallen to the ground, but he held her hard and fast.

"Cort. . ." she whispered, when he allowed her a breath.

She laced her hands behind his head and combed her fingers through the short hair at the nape of his neck. Closing her eyes, she kissed him back.

Thoroughly. Tortuously. Giving as good as she got.

He tottered. He would've fallen, except her hands propped either side of his shoulders and held him fiercely upright.

"Genie. . ."

Her eyes flew open. "No!" She thrust him from her.

Stumbling, he caught the fence.

Her eyes were wild, like a bird desperate to free itself from a snare. "This can't happen. I won't let this happen. I'm leaving."

Cort hardened his heart against the raw hurt swirling through his gut. "You're making a mistake. Don't do this. If you leave me standing here, I promise you nothing will turn out as you hope."

She brushed a lock of hair behind her ear. "You have no idea what I hoped. But hopes are for fools. And we can afford to be neither hopeful nor foolish."

Cort's heart pounded against his rib cage. "What makes you think McCallum will want you after you threw his proposal in his face in Sacramento?"

"How did—? Never mind." She rolled her eyes. "It was never me he was after. Therefore, no bruised pride on his part. He was after a shipping agreement via matrimony with one of Daddy's railroad enterprises. What I'm doing is for the best."

"Better for whom?"

She led the horse out of the corral. "Better for us both." She used the edge of the water trough to climb onto its bare back.

But as she headed toward the road, his hope disappeared in a cloud of dust. And he knew nothing could ever be right for him again.

Chapter 9

"She didn't mean it, Cort. That wasn't our girl talking."

He held himself taut, his anger barely leashed. "Maybe the plain and simple truth is we saw what we wanted to see. She never changed. She's still the same selfish snob she always was."

The rocking chair creaked. Gripping the armrests, Granny lumbered to her feet. He turned from his bitter contemplation of the blackened ruins of the barn—and his life—to lend his support.

"It's because of that girl you call self-centered that I'm able to walk and be about my business."

"But—"

"It'll take more than palsy to put this old lady under. And don't sell Eugenia short. Have faith in what you feel for her. Have faith in the strong, godly young woman she's shown herself to be."

"She's shown herself all right." His nostrils flared. "I ought to ride over there and give her the surprise of her life."

"Cort—"

He scowled. "Telling her what I should've said the moment she found herself mired in the mud on Main Street."

"Cort—"

He clapped his hat onto his head. "We'll see how high and mighty she is when the truth comes out."

Granny shook her head. "You should pray about this first. Before you do anything."

He grimaced. "If I cut through the woods, I'll reach the ranch ahead of her."

"Don't make things worse. Please. . ."

But he didn't see how things could get much worse.

The anger was the only thing keeping him on his feet. If he stood still even for a minute, the despair of shattered dreams would pierce his heart. Numbness would be a blessing. Anything to soothe the pain.

He skirted the road and rode the horse hard. Through the piney forest and over the ridge, he hunched over the horse's mane. Clamping his hat on his head, he let the horse run. He bit his lip so hard he tasted the metallic, copper taste of his own blood.

Barreling into the stable yard at the McCallum mansion, he swung to the ground.

He stalked past the startled stable boy and strode across the stone terrace like he owned the place. Which was just too funny. Considering why he was here.

Through the french doors, he charged into the parlor with its soaring, beamed ceiling and panoramic mountain view. He pushed past Mrs. Anderson, mouth agape.

"Where is he?" He jerked his head toward the hall. "The library?"

"Mr.—wait!" Her heels click-clacked behind Cort as she hurried to match his long strides along the corridor.

He flung open the door and barged inside, only to be confronted by the tall, leather back of the desk chair. The chair swiveled.

Cort glared at the man behind the desk. "I'm done with you."

The knocker banged on the front door, and the man's bushy eyebrows ascended. Apologetic, Mrs. Anderson bustled inside the library.

Cort jabbed his finger at her. "You were supposed to be working for me, not him." The pounding on the door continued.

The man's aristocratic mouth twitched. "I believe I have more than one surprise visitor today."

"I'm not playing your game anymore." Cort sneered. "You two deserve each other. I've had it up to here"—he brought the side of his hand level to his forehead—"with the both of you."

The man looked beyond him to Mrs. Anderson. "I think you better answer that now. Before our guest—Eugenia, I assume from our friend's apoplectic state—knocks down the door."

"Yes, sir. Of course, sir. Right away, sir." Taffeta skirts quivering, Mrs. Anderson dropped a curtsy.

The man raised his index finger. "Oh, and Mrs. Anderson?"

Midmotion, she halted.

"Give us about five minutes, if you please."

"As you wish, sir."

Mrs. Anderson bobbed another small curtsy before closing the library door behind her.

Cort rolled his eyes. "Anybody ever dare to tell you that you're not really a king?"

The man steepled his long-fingered hands on the mahogany desk. "Nor Eugenia a princess. But it'll take a stronger, braver man than me to break the news to her." His steely blue eyes twinkled. "Are you volunteering?"

Not trusting himself to speak, Cort wanted to smash something. Anything. He settled for crushing his hat between his hands.

The front door squeaked on its hinges. Mrs. Anderson's soft rejoinders turned into muffled exclamations of alarm.

"If you'd permit one more piece of advice?" Cocking his head, a self-satisfied smirk settled on the man's patrician features.

Cort ground the hat between his hands.

"Your choice, of course." The man's elegantly clad shoulders shrugged. "Perfectly within your rights to refuse."

His temper rose at the man's overweening arrogance.

"It might yet prove to be in your best interests not to show yourself to Eugenia right away." The man flicked a languid hand toward the brocade drapes. "Perhaps if you'd step behind—"

"You can't seriously be asking me to hide behind the curtain while you. . . You and she. . ." Cort slapped the hat against his thigh.

"Please, Cort. I'm praying you won't give in to a rash impulse."

He swallowed. Praying. . . Granny was right as usual—something he should've done before ever entering into this farce.

Watching this thing play out, he'd be further humiliated, trapped between them. But without another word, he slipped behind the curtain's concealing folds.

Through the fabric, he caught the creak of the chair as the man once more faced away. And in the foyer, he heard Eugenia's shrill demands to see Mr. McCallum.

Why had he come here? To have his nose rubbed into her rejection and her willingness to sell her soul to the copper king?

He leaned his forehead against the cool windowpane. Outside, a robin sang cheerily. Inside, his heart was heavy.

◆ ◆ ◆

"I've come to see Mr. McCallum, and I won't be denied, Mrs. . . ?" For the first time, Eugenia faltered.

The gray-haired woman in her early sixties curled her lip. "Why a nursemaid from the homestead next door need know my name, I'm sure I don't know."

Eugenia bristled, defense of the homestead on the tip of her tongue. But just in time, she remembered her purpose. No need to make an enemy yet. Not until this dragon lady gatekeeper allowed her access to the copper king.

Once she became McCallum's wife, she and this haughty housekeeper would have a conversation. About who was who and what was what. She wasn't Junius Rutherford's daughter for nothing.

She jutted her chin. Nobody did haughty better than Eugenia Alice Rutherford. She frowned. Or than the person she used to be. The person she wasn't so proud of now.

The woman glanced at the watch fob pinned to her embroidered shirtwaist. But as Eugenia contemplated ramming the door, the woman stepped aside. And ushered Eugenia into the massive foyer.

"Right this way, if you please, miss. And it's Mrs. Anderson to yourself."

Anderson. . . Where had she heard that name? She followed Mrs. Anderson past an ornate display of fresh flowers.

Mrs. Anderson's knuckles rapped briskly on a pine-paneled door. Hearing a muffled "Come," she turned the knob and swept Eugenia inside. "Eugenia Rutherford, sir."

She'd barely time to register the book-lined walls, expensive oil paintings, the mahogany desk and leather chair before. . .

. . .before Mrs. Anderson closed the door behind Eugenia with a soft click. Leaving her alone in the room—

The chair creaked.

Her heart palpitated. She wasn't alone. Her palms turned sweaty.

At the homestead, the way ahead seemed clear. But now. . .now her tongue cleaved to the roof of her mouth.

She had only vague recollections of the copper king coming to Sacramento last winter. She remembered a brown derby, the rough, scratchy beard, and dark eyes.

Eyes which became stormy when she had the butler throw him out onto the street.

She winced, recalling her high-handed behavior.

Would McCallum hear her out? Or do the same to her? No worse than she deserved.

Her knees quaked beneath her skirts. She smoothed her hands down her dress and frowned at the roughness of her palms against the silk. Mr. McCallum would laugh at her seen-better-days dress and callused hands.

She straightened. She had nothing to be ashamed of. Her hands were the result of clean, honest work. A badge of honor. And if McCallum—

Behind the chair, he cleared his throat.

Eugenia squared her shoulders. "Mr. McCallum, I'd like a word with you about an important matter of mutual benefit."

Silence, except for the steady ticking of the grandfather clock in the corner near the green drapes.

Eugenia pursed her mouth. "I'd like to apologize for our last meeting."

Tick. Tick. Tick. Or was that the beating of her heart?

"Our last meeting." She moistened her lips with her tongue. "At my father's house. In February. Mr. McCallum?"

Her breathing accelerated. He didn't bother to face her. Of all the rudeness. . .

But she caught herself. After the way she'd acted, she had no right to expect anything. And if she had to eat crow to save the homestead, she'd do that and more.

Tick, tock. Tick, tock. Time was running out.

"I've come to tell you that I've reconsidered the kind offer of your marriage proposal."

The man shifted in the seat, but otherwise, he said nothing.

She plowed ahead. "I realize how wrong I was to be so prideful. But I'm throwing myself on your mercy and asking you to reconsider marrying me."

Only the incessant ticking of the grandfather clock filled the study.

She took a deep breath. "Let's be honest, though. You don't love me, and I don't love you. You want access to my father's railroad."

Eugenia knotted her fingers in her dress. "I've greatly wronged my father. But he loves me—a love I took for granted until lately. I think I can make things right with him regarding the transportation of your copper. I'm willing to surrender my claim to his fortune."

Now for the hard part. "I need only one thing from you in return."

The chair tilted as the man sat forward.

"I—I need you to sign the homestead deed over to Cort Dahlgren, free and clear of any debts." There, she'd said it.

"Why?"

She jolted at his clipped voice. "B–Because. . ." Tears stung her eyes.

Eugenia dashed away the tears with the back of her hand. "Because I love Cort Dahlgren, and he loves that farm. I'd gladly spend the rest of my days working the homestead with him, but he needs the farm more than he needs me as his wife."

She trembled like an aspen leaf in a brisk autumn wind. Momentarily overcome at the prospect of the bleak, loveless future she faced with the man behind the desk. But she persevered.

"I'm not the same girl you proposed to in Sacramento, Mr. McCallum. I've changed. For the better, I think. And if you'll do this one thing for Cort, I promise you. . ." Her voice broke. "I promise you. . ."

This time she couldn't stop the flow of tears streaming down her cheeks. "I beg you, Mr. McCallum to hear my humble plea for Cort's farm." She clasped her hands under her chin.

In a rustle of skirts, she dropped to her knees amid the deep, plush carpet. "And then I promise I'll be the best wife you could ever imagine."

Chair squeaking, the copper king pivoted. But Junius Rutherford arose.

She gasped. "Father? I—I don't understand." She collapsed in a puddle of fabric. "I thought I was talking to—Why are you here?"

In a silk cravat and waistcoat, her father rounded the desk. Bending, he extended his hand to her.

"Daddy. . ." Her eyes awash, she inserted her hand into his. "I'm so sorry for the things I said. For running away. For everything."

He grasped her hand. "Oh, my darling child, how I've longed for this moment when we could be together again." He helped her stand. "With no distance between our hearts."

"But. . ." She couldn't look at her father. "After the way I treated you, I don't deserve your forgiveness."

"It's not a matter of deserving, my precious girl. I forgave you the moment the words left your mouth."

She lifted her gaze to meet his.

"We must forget about the past and embrace the future that lies before us." He raised her hand to his cheek. "With much joy, I anticipated this day. When your heart came home not only to me, but to the beloved heavenly Father your mother and I served with such devotion during our brief married life."

She tucked her head into his shoulder. And inhaled the comforting scents of her childhood—the trace of pipe tobacco, the clean aroma of the shaving lotion he wore.

Her father stroked her hair. "You've become the woman your mother and I dreamed you could be. Until after her death, in my grief I spoiled you and allowed you too much your own way."

"It's not your fault, Daddy. It's mine."

"Blame doesn't matter, not between you and me, dear child." Her father cupped her face between his hands. "We were separated briefly so one day, in the fullness of time, we could be together forever. United in spirit, heart, and true faith."

She hugged him close. "I'm ready to betroth myself to Mr. McCallum."

Junius Rutherford smiled. "You were wrong about Cort. He is a fine young man. The finest. He does indeed love that farm, but I think not more than he loves you."

"But the debts, Daddy. I must—"

"You must, of course, tell Mr. McCallum what you just told me. And I think you'll find him a fine man as well. Quite accommodating." Her father's mustache broadened. "To the most outlandish of schemes where love is concerned."

"What're you talking about?"

Her gaze followed the motion of his hand to the tall, hanging curtain. The fabric rustled. Her eyes widened.

"Eugenia, my darling girl, allow me to reintroduce you to the real copper king. Cortland McCallum, Esquire of Silver Strike, Montana."

The curtains parted. Her mouth dropped open. And Cort Dahlgren—McCallum?—came out from behind the drapes.

Chapter 10

Her eyes darted between him and Junius.

Cort felt ashamed of how he'd stormed over to the ranch. Ashamed for doubting Eugenia. Of his lack of faith in the woman he loved.

She'd been willing to bind herself to a man she didn't know, much less love, to save his farm. He could barely wrap his mind around that kind of sacrifice. That kind of love.

"Cort?" she whispered. "You're the copper king?"

Junius Rutherford fingered his snow-white goatee. "I'll leave you two to talk."

"Daddy—"

"No matter what Cort tells you, I take full responsibility for everything. It was my idea entirely."

"What idea?"

But the wily silver tycoon departed quickly. Leaving Cort alone to face the lion. . . uh. . .lioness.

"What's going on?"

Repositioning his hat on his head, Cort fixed his gaze on the carpet between them. She had every right to be angry. She'd hate him for deceiving her. His stomach turned to mush, dreading her condemnation.

But she deserved the truth. And he deserved her scorn.

Indignation wreathed her features. "Why did you pretend to be Cort Dahlgren, a homesteader?"

"I never said I was Cort Dahlgren. You assumed."

"An assumption you never bothered to correct." She quivered with fury. "Was the whole town in on the conspiracy to make a fool out of me?"

"There was no conspiracy. No one was out to deceive you—"

"Except you and my father."

"The townsfolk probably assumed Junius Rutherford's daughter would know Cort McCallum. And when you couldn't pay your bill after your father cut off your credit, the incident with Mr. Penrod and the sheriff was all too real."

"An incident you were quick to take advantage of." Her bottom lip trembled. "Was it revenge for Sacramento, Cort?"

"I can't say I wasn't still angry when you showed up practically on my doorstep in Silver Strike." He jutted his jaw. "And I'm not going to lie and tell you the irony of you slopping hogs and feeding chickens didn't occur to me. But then, you. . . We. . ." He bit his lip.

Hurt sharpened her beautiful blue eyes. "What about Granny? Was she part of this elaborate scheme to humiliate me, too?"

"No. . . She wanted me to tell you the truth immediately. And this was not about humiliating you."

"What then was this farce about?" Her eyes flashed. "Why pretend to care about me?"

"That was no pretense." He moved forward. "Granny loves you."

He swallowed. "As do I. Since the first moment I laid eyes on you at the wedding of a mutual friend last year in Chicago."

"At Muriel Treadwater's society wedding?" She blinked. "I don't remember meeting you."

Her mouth thinned. "Nor Cort McCallum, either. As for loving me? Does your idea of loving someone involve betrayal?"

"I never meant to. . ." Shame smote his heart. "After these past weeks together, I've come to realize what I felt that weekend wasn't real love. Only a shallow love at first sight."

She held herself aloof from him. And he didn't blame her.

He hung his head. "Real love must spring from proven character. From shared experiences. And now I've proven to you my utter lack of character."

"Cort. . . That's not—" She reached for him, only to let her hand fall. "Why did we not meet that weekend if you imagined yourself so in love with me?"

"I was too shy to speak with you."

She made a most unladylike snort. "You've not a shy bone in your body, Cort McCallum."

"I *was* shy. I am shy when it comes to expressing deep feelings. Feelings such as I'd never felt for anyone before. Feelings, which even now. . ." He gulped.

She stepped closer, and he took courage.

"You were knee-deep in potential suitors. And one by one, you cast them aside. Finding fault with each."

She had the grace to blush. "I acted horribly."

"Then I was called home." He gestured at the house. "Granny had suffered a stroke. The doctor believed her to be dying. I kept a bedside vigil beside Granny until the immediate danger passed."

He gave Eugenia a small smile. "Apparently, I blathered on about a certain silver heiress. When Granny recovered her powers of speech, she urged me to plead my troth to you post haste. So I hurried to Sacramento."

She sighed. "Where I took one look at your disheveled clothing, rough beard, and threw you out of the house." Her gaze dropped to her shoes. "Without the beard, I didn't recognize you."

He took Eugenia's hand in his. And she let him.

"I shaved the beard off when I returned to Silver Strike. I told myself I never wanted to see you again."

He squeezed her hand. "But I promise you, I truly, truly never meant for this. . .this deception to betray you."

◆ ◆ ◆

Eugenia let her shoulders rise and fall. "But how did I—we—end up in this scheme of my father's?"

He pushed back his hat with the tip of his finger. "Everyone believed Granny was withering away. She'd lost the fighting spirit that enabled her and my grandfather to pioneer this rugged land."

Cort cut his eyes to the window. "It was her husband—Lars Dahlgren—who made the first silver strike in the territory."

"Your grandfather Dahlgren? The town's named after his silver strike?"

Cort nodded. "My mother was their only child. Born on the homestead. Which they soon left for the lure of finer things."

He blew out a breath. "After the stroke, Granny's dying wish was to spend her last days where she'd been the happiest—on the homestead as a young wife and mother."

Eugenia laced her fingers in his. "And you, Cortland McCallum, out of love for her, wanted to make sure Granny's last dream came true. I remember now where I heard the name. Mrs. Anderson was Granny's nurse."

"Your father made her a job offer via telegram she couldn't refuse. I was in Silver Strike that day in a vain attempt to convince her to return to the homestead when I received a telegram, too."

She tilted her head. "Also from my father?"

"'Next move, yours,' it said." He scrubbed his hand over his face. "I had no idea what he was talking about until the commotion erupted outside the hotel. Later, he unveiled the plan he'd set in motion. He arranged a one-way ticket for you from Sacramento straight to Silver Strike."

She gaped. "He planned for me to live on the homestead as Granny's nurse?"

"A vision he left for me to implement."

She tapped her shoe on the carpet. "An arrangement into which I unwittingly and oh so conveniently fell."

Cort grimaced. "And he proceeded to set up residence in my house."

She shook her head. "So he could play puppet master with our lives and watch the drama unfold."

"Don't think too harshly of him, Genie. He loves you and wanted only happiness for you. He knew my parents quite well when he himself was a young man."

She deflated. "I won't stay angry at him. I know in my heart he desires only the kind of true love for me he once had with my mother."

"His motives, I swear to you, were pure and noble. Never to humiliate."

"Just to humble." She bit her lip. "And rightly so."

"You weren't the only one with a pride problem, Genie. You weren't the only one whose rough edges needed smoothing. After getting to know you, I realized I no longer desired your comeuppance."

He crimped the brim of his hat with his hand. "I rode over here Saturday morning to tell your father I couldn't go through with his scheme. I planned to tell you after the dance. But after we kissed. . ." He dropped his eyes to his boots.

Eugenia's pulse quickened. "What about after the kiss, Cort?"

"I thought once you knew the truth that I'd lose you for good. I told myself to wait till morning to tell you the truth. But the fire—"

"Everything went up in smoke."

His eyes bored into hers. "And you rejected not only Cort Dahlgren, but once again unknowingly rejected Cort McCallum, too."

"Rejecting you for your own good. I was trying to save the farm."

He took her into his arms. "There is no good for me without you. I don't understand why you believed marrying the copper king would save the farm."

Eugenia straightened the cuff of his sleeve. "You said McCallum held the title to the homestead." She couldn't resist the urge to touch him.

"So he does—I mean I do. It's all in the family."

Her brow puckered. "But the debts Granny spoke of. . ."

"What exactly did Granny say?"

Eugenia placed her palms on the broad length of his shoulders. "She said the farm hadn't made a profit in years."

"Which isn't the same thing as being in debt."

"No, you're right." It felt so right to be in his arms. "Once again, I assumed wrongly. Leaped to a false conclusion."

"The farm hasn't been worked in years. Not since Granddad built this house. I decided to bring in one last harvest for Granny's sake. Before she, too, passed."

Eugenia smiled at him. "I don't think Granny is going anywhere. Not anytime soon."

"Because of you, Granny found her will to live again." His voice turned gruff. "We're both so grateful for you."

Frowning, she removed herself from his arms. "Gratitude?"

He didn't allow her to drift far. "Gratitude, my dear Genie, I assure you is the very least of what I feel for you."

Something eased in her heart. "Why, Cort McCallum. . ." She fluttered her lashes. "Do tell."

His eyebrows rose. "And reinflate your vastly overrated opinion of yourself, which your father and I have gone to such great lengths to quell?" He smirked. "I think not."

She play punched his shoulder. "Fine then. Be that way. See if I—"

He swung her around. Her skirts swirled. "I love you because you never fail to surprise me. You make me laugh—"

"Usually at me."

"—I love your intelligence. Your joy of life. Determination—"

"Otherwise known as my obstinacy?"

He gave her that lovely, lopsided smile of his. "I'm not above admitting to a growing fondness for a beautiful, blue-eyed silver heiress."

"And I'm not above admitting to a growing fondness for Cort McCallum, or whatever he chooses to call himself henceforth."

Widening his stance, he peered at her upturned face. "Once upon a time, an heiress and a homesteader?"

She winced. "I'm the one who wasn't good enough for you."

"There's the thing, Genie." His dark eyes lit as if from within. "No one is good enough, not compared to God's indescribable goodness. Yet God loves us anyway."

"I love you, Cort. So much. And thanks to you and Granny, I discovered God's great love for me. A love I never comprehended before."

When Cort looked at her like that. . . Her heart ached with love for him.

"If you'll allow me." He nestled her closer. "I'll spend the rest of my life showing you how much I love you, Eugenia Alice Rutherford. Always and forever."

"Oh, Cort. God has been—is—so good to allow us this second chance to love Him and one another. I'll never take His love or yours for granted ever again, I promise you."

His eyes took on a teasing glint. "Shall we plan a grand honeymoon tour of Europe?"

She planted a light kiss on his lips. "Who needs Europe when you have Silver Strike, Montana, and a honeymoon homestead cottage? If Granny wouldn't mind vacating to the main house for a week or so."

"Definitely a week. Or so. . ." He brushed his mouth over her fingers. She shivered. Deliciously.

He stroked his jaw. "And I'll be sure to bring my razor. I have it on good authority, you prefer clean-shaven men to rough-bearded yokels."

Catching his chin between her thumb and index finger, she tugged his mouth till only inches separated his face from hers.

"What I will always prefer—Cort McCallum—is you. Any which way I can kiss you." She gave him a beguiling look. "Don't you ever forget it."

And he never did.

Lisa Carter and her family make their home in North Carolina. In addition to *Mule Dazed*, she is the author of seven romantic suspense novels and a contemporary Coast Guard romantic series. When she isn't writing, Lisa enjoys traveling to romantic locales, teaching writing workshops, and researching her next exotic adventure. She has strong opinions on barbecue and ACC basketball. She loves to hear from readers, and you can connect with Lisa at www.lisacarterauthor.com.

The Reluctant Heiress

by Mary Davis

Dedication

To the Displaced Modifiers—Donita, Jill, Carol, Faye, Heidi, Jim, Vikki, and Ross. Your input, encouragement, and support have been invaluable.

Chapter 1

Boston, 1905

Victoria Dewitt sprang to her feet in a swish of black silk despite her long corset. "I have to do what?" She directed her question to her late great-uncle's elderly attorney sitting behind his large cherrywood desk.

From the corner of her eye, she saw the young attorney off to the side bolt out of his chair a half a second after she did. Mr. Wellington was Mr. Frye's grandson and in attendance to observe.

The elderly man used his desk for support and shoved to his feet as etiquette dictated. "Miss Dewitt. . ."

"Did I hear correctly?"

"I am sure you did. Please return to your seat and allow me to finish."

She took several quick breaths and settled back into the padded chair, waiting for the elderly attorney to continue.

He sat, adjusted his spectacles on the bridge of his nose, and focused on her great-uncle's will before him. "'My grandniece and only living relation, Victoria Dewitt, has three months from the reading of my last will and testament to marry in order to inherit the totality of my estate, businesses, and holdings. I know this puts her in a predicament, but I don't want her to cloister herself away and mourn me out of some misplaced sense of duty. She should go live her life while she is still young.'"

Victoria harrumphed. Very unladylike. Mrs. Tishell from finishing school would have shot her a hot glare for such conduct. Ladies were not to "voice" their displeasure with words, *sounds*, or expressions.

Mr. Frye peered over his spectacles. "Your uncle wanted only to see you taken care of."

She doubted that.

"He loved you very much."

"He had a strange way of showing it." Since her arrival in his home fifteen years ago at the age of seven, her uncle had paid her very little attention. Attention she had desperately yearned for after her parents had died. Instead, he scowled at her from afar and hired people to look after her. "If he had, he would not have stipulated marriage as a condition in his will." *Predicament indeed.*

"Perhaps he wishes you to consider your future."

Mr. Wellington spoke up. "Are you against marriage?"

She swung her gaze to the onlooker. Did he really need to be here to witness her humiliation? Dust motes drifted in the shaft of sunlight between them. "Of course not. I just don't want to be forced into it. I wish to marry for love. And my uncle knew that. He didn't believe in love and wants to deprive me of it." As he always did. She doubted he even knew what love was.

"So the problem is not that you oppose marriage, but that you are not in love. Am I correct?"

"You are." She turned back to Mr. Frye, not wishing to acknowledge Mr. Wellington's scrutiny. He was probably just like her uncle, thinking a lady of twenty-two had no right to remain unmarried.

Mr. Frye cleared his throat. "Well, then, let us hope you fall in love in the next three months, shall we?"

Not likely. "One cannot put a time constraint on love." It happened when it happened.

The elderly man gave her a sympathetic look. "In the event you do not marry within the allotted time, you will receive a small monthly stipend." He rustled through the papers under the will.

"How small?" Would it be enough for her to live on? Running her uncle's household took a great deal of money.

He pulled out a piece of paper and handed it to her.

Across the top, in her uncle's meticulous script, was written *Budget*. How typically controlling of him. Her gaze skimmed to the total at the bottom. Not nearly enough to run the house. "What about wages for the household staff? The cost of the electric lights? Feed for the horses?" Then her gaze lit on a line of the budget. *Apartment Rental*. "I am not to remain in the house?"

"If you marry, you may live there comfortably the rest of your life. If not, your uncle made provisions to see to the dispersal of his assets."

Three months to find a suitable suitor after years of trite society parties, get said prospect to propose, plan a wedding, and marry. *Impossible!* And that excluded the element of falling in love, which would make the whole ordeal even more impossible.

She had always suspected her uncle resented her intruding on his orderly life. But to cast her out? "What about the household staff? Are they to be turned out as well?"

"No one will be going anywhere until the allotted three months are up. At that time, another portion of your uncle's wishes will be read, depending on what you have decided to do."

Her uncle had employed excellent staff. They should be able to find other positions easily enough. She would allow them to start looking right away. No sense making them wait.

"The rest of the details will be revealed in three months' time."

Mr. Wellington spoke again. "I am sure Mr. Helmsworthy didn't intend for anyone to suffer hardships."

She narrowed her eyes at the young attorney. He had no clue about the plight of women and servants. Both dependent on the generosity of men in a society constructed by men to benefit men.

She turned back to the older attorney and rose gracefully to her feet. "If that is all, I'll take my leave. I have much to think about and tend to."

Both men got to their feet. The elder barrister held out his hand. "There is more. If you'll take your seat again, I'll go over the particulars of the next three months."

Particulars? She eased back down, grateful for the chair to catch her.

"Your uncle has arranged a dinner party to be held in his home seven days from this reading."

A party? Honestly? "What kind of dinner am I to plan on such short notice? Who am I to invite?"

"Your uncle has already made all the plans. You need do nothing but be there. The parcel delivered to the housekeeper when the carriage came for you has all the instructions. I am sure Mrs. Fuller has things well in hand. She has likely already assigned tasks to the other staff and placed orders for food, flowers, and the like. You needn't worry about a thing."

"Can you at least tell me who is to attend and what the nature of the party is to be?"

Mr. Frye shifted his gaze from her. He removed his spectacles, pulled out a handkerchief, and proceeded to clean the lenses.

She glanced to the younger—annoying—attorney for an answer.

He shrugged and shook his head.

Did he truly not know? Or did he not want to tell her?

Mr. Frye fitted his glasses back into place, took a deep breath, and looked at her. "You are not going to like this."

She had attended dozens of her uncle's parties and knew how to conduct herself. "What is it? Am I to be paraded in front of every eligible bachelor in the state of Massachusetts?"

Mr. Frye neither confirmed nor denied her frivolous suggestion, but his eyes told her it was so. "Obviously, not *every* eligible bachelor."

Victoria slumped as much as her corset would allow. "So I am to be set on the auction block."

"It is not so dire as that. You have full choice in the matter. You do not have to accept any advances that you do not wish to." He continued to lay out other plans her uncle had for her over the next three months, including the number of gentlemen from the guest list she must allow to court her.

She calculated in her head. That would make the final blow on Christmas Eve. What a Christmas gift.

Mr. Frye motioned toward his grandson. "Mr. Wellington will be by your side *every* step of the way. During that time, he will see you have *every* opportunity to be successful in receiving your inheritance."

"What?" It was Mr. Wellington who sprang to his feet this time.

"Your only duty, starting now, is to be at Miss Dewitt's beck and call."

"Certainly there is someone else who would be better suited. Ford? Or Jefferies? I have my cases."

"Your top priority is seeing to Miss Dewitt. I would do it myself, but I am too old to be frolicking around. I trust only you with this delicate matter."

"Mr. Frye, I am capable of seeing to matters on my own." Though she rather liked the sound of having a man do her bidding for a change.

The older man glanced from her to Mr. Wellington and back. "This is not an issue either of you can argue and win. Now off with you both. I have work to complete."

This was going to be a long three months. She would rather her uncle had straight out disinherited her and be done with it, rather than dragging out her demise.

Victoria stood, and Mr. Wellington grudgingly escorted her to the door.

"Graham?" Mr. Frye said.

Mr. Wellington turned.

"I expect daily reports."

Mr. Wellington gave a nod and opened the door for her. After helping her on with her black velvet, floor-length cloak, he shrugged into his overcoat and put on his hat. Then he escorted her out of the building to the waiting carriage and opened that door as well.

She hesitated with a slippered foot on the step. "By your sour expression, one would think you were the one being forced into marriage." She climbed in.

He entered and settled on the seat opposite her. "When I attended law school, it was not to follow a privileged debutante around like a puppy dog."

The carriage heaved into motion.

Victoria fussed with her skirt folds. "I have no desire to keep your company either. Let's strike a deal. Neither of us wishes this arrangement. I release you from your duty." She held out her gloved hand to him to seal the agreement like gentlemen did.

He glanced at her hand. "I only wish you had the power to dispense such an indulgence. Do you forget I have to report back to my grandfather each day?"

She placed her hand back in her lap. "Tell him whatever you like."

"That would be dishonest. Besides, what do you suggest I do with my time? I can't very well return to the office and get any work accomplished."

He had her on the dishonesty. She didn't like that either. "You could do whatever you wanted."

"I want to progress in my field. To do that, I need to please my grandfather. To do that, I am stuck with you for the next three months. And you, with me."

Oh bother. Maybe she could find a way to excuse him from his mission while finding employment for the house staff and figuring out what to do herself. *Bother. Bother. Bother.*

The answer was simple.

Lord, send me my true love. Now, please. I don't have any time to waste.

Chapter 2

Graham Wellington swayed in the carriage as it pulled into a lane lined with maple trees in full fall colors but not yet releasing their vibrant foliage. The country mansion the conveyance stopped in front of was larger than he had anticipated. He smiled inwardly, because swarms of eligible gentlemen would be clamoring for Miss Dewitt's hand in marriage, and she would not be able to resist them all. He would be able to dispense with this business quickly. After all, women could be quite foolish when it came to romantic love.

He opened the carriage door, disembarked, and held his hand out to assist her.

She glared at it.

For a moment, he thought she might refuse.

But she placed her delicate gloved hand in his and alighted from the carriage as though she walked on air. "Thank you." She dipped her head toward him as she retrieved her hand.

The front door flew open. A plump middle-aged housekeeper and a tall butler descended the five steps. The housekeeper wrapped Miss Dewitt in her arms. "You're back! Come in out of the cold." The older woman ushered the younger inside.

The lanky butler had a droopy hound-dog face. He bowed to Graham. "Sir? Won't you come in?"

Graham drew in a deep breath and entered.

Miss Dewitt caught his gaze. "Mr. Wellington, this is our housekeeper, Mrs. Elaine Fuller, and Mr. Foster Dent, the butler."

Graham greeted them both.

The wide foyer had a round table on an oval, plush carpet atop a pale gray marble floor. A wide staircase curved up to the next floor, and a substantial crystal chandelier hung from a high ceiling.

Graham had not imagined anything as grand as this.

He studied Miss Dewitt as she tugged on each finger of her white kid gloves while she spoke to Mrs. Fuller.

The housekeeper took Miss Dewitt's gloves and cloak and handed them to Mr. Dent. "The preparations for the dinner party are well underway."

"I will not participate in this ridiculous ruse. I'm canceling it. Would you please notify everyone?"

Graham stepped forward. "You will not." What was she thinking? He turned to the housekeeper. "It is *not* canceled. Continue with everything. The party will go on as planned." He unbuttoned his coat and shucked it off his shoulders. "These are your uncle's last wishes."

Miss Dewitt turned to him. "Don't bother removing your coat. You may take your leave."

She was dismissing him? Not likely. He pulled his arms from his coat sleeves and handed the overcoat to the butler. "We have a party to prepare for."

"I think not. I won't be attending."

He held up his hands in exasperation. "You have no choice."

"Oh, but I do. Mr. Frye said I could choose to accept suitors' attentions or not. I choose not."

He glanced around the opulent foyer, evidence of how much wealth Mr. Helmsworthy had acquired. "You must attend if you hope to have any chance of keeping all this."

"I could pack a trunk right now and walk out."

He would like to see her trying to lug a trunk out of this mansion. Tugging it down the hall, bumping it down the stairs, and dragging it out the front door. She hadn't thought her escape through. "But you won't." She would be a fool. "Who would turn their back on all of this?" He held his hands out to indicate all that surrounded them.

"I would." She turned in a swish of black silk and ascended the wide curved staircase.

In awe, he watched her, trying to figure out how she could be appearing to. . .float?

Her threat was empty, of course. No one in their right mind would give all this up. For something as elusive as romantic love? And she wasn't fooling him with her bravado. Though she spoke cheerfully, he could hear the slight tremor in her voice at times. Had this just been too trying of a day? Or was she afraid?

He liked her spirit though. And their verbal sparring. But she wouldn't best him.

The housekeeper had left the foyer, but the butler stood silently waiting, still holding Graham's coat over one arm and his hat in his hand. At some point, the man had hung up Miss Dewitt's cloak and stashed her gloves.

Graham wasn't about to leave. "I'll wait in the library, if that will be acceptable."

"Very good, sir." The middle-aged servant slid back a pair of pocket doors to reveal the indicated room. "Can I have Cook prepare you a pot of tea?"

"No need to trouble her."

She had enough to do with the party preparations.

"If you intend to wait for Miss Victoria to return, you might be here awhile. I'll have a tray prepared in case you change your mind."

The butler obviously knew his mistress.

"Is there someone you could spare to deliver a message to my office? I don't want to take anyone away from their duties."

"Neil the stable boy could do it. He rides like the wind."

"Is he trustworthy?"

"Yes, sir."

Graham nodded his agreement and pointed to the desk on the far side of the room. "May I use some paper and a pen?" When the boy brought his papers and files, he could get some work done while he waited for the spoiled debutante to come to her senses.

"Mr. Helmsworthy preferred to use dipping nib pens and ink. He didn't like the newfangled fountain pens. The well and pens are in the top right drawer, stationery in the top left. I'll send for the boy."

"Thank you, Mr. Dent."

The servant bowed slightly as he pulled the doors together, disappearing behind them.

Lord, the next three months are going to be trying, aren't they? When I said I was going to work on patience, I didn't have this *in mind.*

If God was going to test his determination on this matter, he would rise to the challenge. And prevail.

Two hours later, he remained in the library seated behind the desk, his recently delivered legal case files and other papers organized on the surface.

The pocket doors slid back. Mr. Dent stood patiently in the opening.

"Come in."

The butler stepped only one pace inside. "Lunch is served in the dining room."

Graham had much work to do. "Would you bring a plate in here? I'll work while I eat."

"I think you will want to eat in the dining room."

Graham studied the older man and understood. Miss Dewitt was there. His chance to wear her down. He pushed back the chair and unfolded himself. "Yes, a break would be refreshing."

The butler's mouth pulled up at the corners ever so slightly.

The dining room held a large table, thirty feet long. Maybe forty. Graham had never seen such a table. How many could it seat? Thirty, or more, easily.

Victoria sat at the farthermost part adjacent to the end seat. Across from her, a place was set for him. She watched him approach and dipped her head toward the butler. "Foster informed me you were still here. I would have thought you long gone."

She had hoped, but he was not so easily put off. "My grandfather said I was to be at your beck and call. How would I complete my job if I left?" He bowed with a flourish of his hands. "I am yours to command." He straightened and studied her openly.

She returned his gaze without a hint of annoyance or being ill at ease with his regarding her.

After a moment, he touched the back of the chair. "May I?"

She nodded. "I wouldn't deny anyone food."

A young servant woman entered with two plates. She reached to set a plate in front of Miss Dewitt.

Miss Dewitt held up a hand. "Guests first."

The now flustered woman dipped in a slight curtsy. "Sorry, miss." She set the first plate in front of Graham.

"Thank you."

She set the second in front of Miss Dewitt.

"Thank you, Muriel."

"I'll get it right next time, miss."

The would-be heiress nodded at the young maid. "You did fine."

Muriel scurried out of the room with her head down.

Graham tilted his head toward Miss Dewitt. "That was kind of you not to scold her."

"Why would I do that? She did nothing worth scolding her for."

He had seen aristocracy give a servant a dressing-down for far less.

Without warning, she bowed her head and spoke a short blessing over the food.

Surprised, he barely lowered his head before she finished. He opened his eyes.

She poked at her chicken salad with her fork. "I expect you will leave after you eat."

Again, she was trying to get rid of him.

"I have very clear orders. I don't plan to fail." He took a bite of chicken.

"I have no intention of being the main attraction in a circus."

"Why not? For all you know, the man you are meant to fall in love with will be there. If you remain in your room, you could miss your chance at the love you so desire."

She took a sip of water. "I know what you are trying to do."

"What is that?"

"Appeal to my romantic nature."

"Is it working?"

She struggled to hide a smile and failed. She drew in a deep breath. "Imagine this..." She lifted her hands in the air. "All of this is yours. A party is held in your honor. The only guests are unmarried ladies, ranging in age from sixteen to sixty."

"Preposterous. A sixteen-year-old would be far too young for me."

"Age doesn't matter to a father when *he* can benefit from marrying his daughter off as a child bride."

He hated that practice. "And sixty?"

"Much older men often take wives twenty or thirty years their junior. Now, back to my story. Every single one of these women knows that you are looking for a wife, and they are vying intently, by whatever means they can, to marry you. Not because they care for you or even like you." She waved her hands in a graceful manner. "But for all this. You are just an unfortunate encumbrance to get what they want."

Distasteful indeed. "I'm sure this party will be nothing like that."

"I have been to many of these kinds of parties, and they are exactly like that."

"But these men don't know you're desperate to marry—"

"Desperate?"

"I didn't mean that. Let me rephrase." He drew in a deep breath. "They don't know your great-uncle is *requiring* you to marry. Is that better?"

"Not much."

"The only people who know about the will's stipulation are you, me, and my grandfather."

"Do you think these men stupid? They will assume I have inherited it all. So the will changes nothing for them. Only for me."

She had a point.

"The only thing this party will accomplish is to severely shorten the amount of mourning time they allow me. They will think it is all right to start calling on me and deluging me with invitations and making themselves nuisances."

Again she was right.

"I see your point. This is not an ideal situation. But these are your uncle's wishes, and the party *is* going to take place. And whether you attend or not, you will have gentlemen callers after that. Would it not look better for you to attend your own party than not?"

"First, this is not *my* party but my great-uncle's. I'll make a deal with you. I'll attend if..." She leaned forward. "If I get to invite an equal number of eligible ladies for you to entertain."

"Me?" He would think she would want them to distract some of the men. "Why me?"

"So you can see what it's like."

"What would ever possess me to agree to such nonsense?"

"So you can give your grandfather, your boss, a good report. Which sounds better? The dinner party went off without a hitch, and Miss Dewitt seemed to enjoy herself? Or Miss Dewitt locked herself in her room the entire evening? I dare say your grandfather wouldn't be pleased with the latter." With a self-satisfied smile, she settled back in her chair.

Cunning little minx, to say the least.

Spirited indeed. Maybe she would prove a worthy opponent after all.

Chapter 3

Victoria lay on the fainting couch in the parlor, resting prior to the guests' arrival. She needed to gather her wits before the evening's mental games commenced. Her black silk gown with a beaded lace overlay had already begun to stifle her. Or did the suffocating feeling come from the anticipation of an unpleasant, annoying evening?

She had managed to whittle the list of gentlemen down by five, leaving fifteen. One engaged, one married, one deceased, and two out of the country. Her attempts to get three more struck from the list—because they were so impossibly obnoxious—had been nixed by Mr. Wellington. He would soon see what it was like for her. She'd handpicked the ladies for tonight's party.

"Miss?" Foster's voice hovered next to her.

Victoria opened her eyes.

"The first carriage is driving up the lane."

Mr. Wellington stood from his chair. "Shouldn't you go upstairs?"

Swinging her feet around to the floor, she sat up. The beads of her dress tinkled against one another. "Whatever for?"

He stepped to her and proffered his hand. "So you can make a grand entrance after everyone has arrived."

How dramatic. She took his assistance and rose. "Some ladies might like all that attention on them at once. I prefer to welcome my guests as they enter, rather than rush around the room later to greet everyone in a hurry." She tugged at the top edge of her black gloves that covered her arms within an inch of the small puffed shoulder caps.

"That is quite thoughtful of you."

Did he truly think so? Or was he simply coddling her? She could tell he considered her a spoiled debutante with no feelings for others.

He obviously didn't see her need to marry for love and probably thought any man would suffice. For his duty, that was true, because he would have completed his obligation. But she would have the rest of her life with the chosen man. For better *or* for worse. Better to live as a pauper alone than *for worse*.

She strolled through the parlor doorway. "You'll join me in the foyer."

"That's not necessary. This is *your* party."

"Mr. Wellington, have you forgotten that you have guests to greet as well?"

At a throaty sound, she glanced back at him. Had he growled? Oh, this evening could be fun after all. After turning around, she indicated the spot next to her.

Mr. Wellington cut a stately and handsome figure in his evening suit. He pushed his mouth into a halfhearted smile and joined her.

She held up her index finger. "Remember to greet your guests with an authentic smile. One mustn't be rude."

Definitely a growl.

As the first carriage rolled to a stop, Foster opened the front door. A shock of cool air swirled around Victoria, but she had been trained not to shiver.

Four footmen stood at the ready outside, and one opened the carriage door.

She was pleased to see that the first to arrive were her good friends Stanley Browning and Millicent Amundsen, brother and sister.

Stanley bowed over her hand. "It is so good to see you again. My sister could hardly wait for your party."

Victoria gave Millicent a quick greeting hug, no more than a lean forward and back. "Thank you for coming on such short notice."

"I wouldn't have dared missed this."

"May I present Mr. Wellington, one of my uncle's solicitors." Victoria turned to him. "This is Stanley Browning and his sister Mrs. Amundsen, my dear friend. She is a year widowed and seeking a father for her two young sons."

Mr. Wellington shot Victoria a glance before bowing over Mrs. Amundsen's hand. "Pleased to meet you."

"As I am of you. Do you have any children? It can be so difficult to get children from two different marriages to get along. They become jealous of the new parent."

Mr. Wellington hesitated far too long. No doubt trying to devise an alternate answer to the obvious. When he finally spoke, his words came out choked. "No children."

"Very good. I look forward to speaking with you throughout the evening."

Victoria struggled not to laugh.

Three automobiles drove up next. Lord Hugh Claremont, whose overtures she had turned down several times. Reginald Parker, who fancied Edith Nicholas. And Gordon Montgomery, who fancied all women and had no plans to limit himself to just one, married or not.

What a guest list her great-uncle had put together.

Three women descended from the next carriage. She greeted them. "May I present Mr. Wellington. This is Patricia and Monique Linden. Sisters." She indicated the third lady. "This is their cousin Nancy Linden." Nancy batted her eyelashes nonstop.

Monique pushed Patricia forward and held out her hand. "How do you do?"

Mr. Wellington bowed over each of the three ladies' hands. "Very well."

As the trio glided away, Monique spoke louder than need be. "He is handsome, Patricia. Don't you think so?"

Patricia nodded.

Then came a wave of four more gentlemen, three in carriages and one in an automobile.

Rosemary Hudson arrived next, as tall as Mr. Wellington, graceful as a swan, and delightfully flirtatious.

She tapped his chest with her closed fan. "This could prove to be a delectable evening after all."

Then brothers Jonathan and Ellis Warner. Each lingered over Victoria's hand with a kiss.

Though she wanted to jerk her hand from their grasps, she refrained.

Eloise Madison scurried in, looking like little more than a child, as she didn't stand over five feet tall. She tilted her head back to look at Mr. Wellington. "My, you're a tall one."

Flora Young at eighteen, the youngest Victoria had invited, giggled and hid behind her fan.

Mr. Wellington bowed over her hand.

She giggled more and fluttered her fan. "I think I might faint."

Victoria straightened. "Mr. Wellington, please see Miss Young gets to a chair. I would hate for her to collapse."

Mr. Wellington shot her a stern look and took the young lady's arm. "Right this way, miss."

Flora giggled more.

Victoria allowed herself a small laugh. Oh, this *was* fun, even if she had to endure the gentlemen.

Another four gentlemen arrived, greeted her, and entered the parlor.

Foster bowed. "Everyone has arrived, Miss Victoria."

"Thank you." Putting on her "authentic" smile, Victoria joined everyone in the parlor.

The ladies had Mr. Wellington surrounded near the chair where he had seated Flora. He looked like a cornered animal. They were playing their parts perfectly.

After surveying the room's occupants, she headed around to the left to mingle among the guests.

She stopped at a cluster of men talking about baseball. She greeted them, exchanged pleasantries, and moved on.

Before she was even a quarter of the way around the room, Lord Claremont headed her off from the other direction. "I cannot tell you how pleased I was to receive your invitation."

She bit back the retort that jumped into her mouth and found something less derogatory to say. "The invitation came from my uncle."

"How can that be? He is gone."

"Before he passed, he saw to all the arrangements for this little soirée in the wake of his death."

"Wise of him."

More like controlling.

"He did not wish for you to linger in mourning."

"No chance of my doing that after this evening's festivities." At least she could wear black so gentlemen callers would be reminded of her recent loss. And she did so out of respect for her uncle.

He had seen to her every need. Even if he had no capacity to love, he hadn't been outwardly cruel. Though eager to have her marry, he had never forced her, no matter how many gentlemen he introduced her to.

Until now.

Foster entered the room and rang a handbell. "Dinner is ready."

Relief swept over Victoria. That took care of breaking away from Lord Claremont.

Without asking, he hooked her hand over his arm. "Shall we?"

Pulling free would be rude and, since it would be for only a moment, she allowed him to escort her into the dining room.

He pulled out her chair at the opposite end from where she and her uncle normally ate. Mr. Wellington would be at that end. She hadn't the desire to sit in her uncle's seat.

Lord Claremont glared at the place card to Victoria's right, the seat for the most important male guest.

Stanley Browning pulled out that chair. "I believe this is my seat."

Victoria knew it would be an affront to his lordship, but she had needed to make a point that he wasn't the most important to her. As a concession, she had allowed him the seat to her left. Any farther from her would have been tantamount to a public slap in the face and scandalous.

Mr. Wellington entered with his female entourage. He glanced her way.

"Your seat is at the other end with the ladies seated close by." Normally at such a dinner, the guests would be seated alternating between the ladies and gentlemen. But why bother? The men were here for her uncle's money, and the ladies. . . ? Well, because she had invited them to prove a point to Mr. Wellington. She knew how to survive a party such as this. But did he? He seemed to be handling himself so far. But the evening was far from over.

◆ ◆ ◆

Graham sat at the far end of the table with the widow Millicent Amundsen and her search for a father for her sons on his right. Patricia Linden settled in the chair on his left with her sister Monique beside her, listing all her sister's fine qualities.

"You see, I have a beau. But our parents won't allow Martin and me to be engaged or marry until Patty is, so both she and I are quite eager for her to find a husband. She is not getting any younger."

Patricia smiled sweetly. "I had a beau. We were very much in love, but he was thrown from his horse. Before he died, he told me he loved me and wanted me to be happy and find someone to love. I have no aspirations of finding love again, but I do hope I can."

He didn't need to know all that.

Widow Amundsen cleared her throat. "Love in marriage is overrated. If one has companionship, then the marriage is considered wildly successful. My two are good boys and young. They would think of anyone I marry as their father and not give you a moment of grief."

Not only was Graham not ready to be a father, he had no desire to take on a wife yet. This evening couldn't end soon enough.

Finally, Miss Dewitt signaled the meal had concluded by standing with the aid of the butler. "We'll have tea and coffee in the parlor." Everyone followed her like ducklings to the other room.

She floated to the red velvet sofa and sat. The men crowded around her, one situated on each side, some in the chairs adjacent to her, and the remainder standing around the sofa. She smiled at each one.

Servants brought out cups of coffee and tea.

Graham watched Miss Dewitt surrounded by admirers. How could such a beautiful creature be so frustrating? Even in mourning clothes of black, she exuded the epitome of elegance and grace. Only he, alone of the gentlemen callers, knew she cared for none of them.

After a bit, with a delicate twist of her alabaster wrist, Victoria flicked open her fan and fluttered it about, coyly glancing over it. Her eyes seemed pinched, with the creases at the corners more pronounced. Had she had enough for one evening? Should he call this party to an end? He was certainly ready for it to be over.

The way the men hovered around her, they reminded him of vultures. Opportunists, every one of them.

She lifted her hand a few inches to get the maid's attention. She had stationed the servant to remain within sight. Evidently just for this purpose.

The maid crossed silently and curtsied.

Miss Dewitt spoke, but he couldn't hear what she said. Probably some pretense to call her from the room. Permanently.

Should he stop it or allow her to cut the evening short?

The maid opened the french doors to the garden, exited the room, and returned in a trice with a delicate china teacup she handed her mistress.

A cool, fall breeze freshened the stagnant air. He hadn't realized how stuffy the room had become.

After Stanley Browning and Millicent Amundsen played several duets on the grand piano, the guests departed.

All but one.

Lord Hugh Claremont.

The vulture imprisoned her hand in both of his, delaying his departure.

She stood at arm's length, smiling courteously. "I must bid you good night, Lord Claremont. I truly am spent. It was good of you to come and to honor my uncle's request. Good evening."

Mr. Wellington smiled. Smart minx. She'd just made sure Lord Claremont knew she was not the one who had invited him.

But the man didn't release her.

Graham stepped toward them, took Miss Dewitt's hand from Lord Claremont's, and tucked it around his elbow. "Mr. Dent, will you see that his lordship gets to his automobile."

"I will see you again soon, Miss Victoria." Claremont's eyes narrowed, but he made no more foofaraw and left.

Graham didn't like *his lordship* being so familiar with Miss Dewitt by using her first name. Pushing the man from his mind, he turned to her. "Tonight wasn't so bad after all, was it?"

Her ever-present smile vanished.

He realized he still held her arm. "Admit it, you enjoyed yourself."

She heaved a heavy sigh. "I'm just glad it's over." The tension around her eyes faded.

"You can't fool me. I saw you smiling."

"What you *saw* was years of practice. Good night." She floated up the stairs. At the midpoint, she spoke but didn't turn around. "Don't bother coming before noon. I won't be up, and you'll be wasting your time."

Unexpected disappointment pricked. He wouldn't see her first thing? In that case, he would spend the morning at the office, report to his grandfather, and come here at noon. That would work out quite well for everyone.

Chapter 4

At noon the next day, Graham rode up to the Helmsworthy mansion on horseback. His report to his grandfather had been well received, and he had been able to accomplish a great deal of work while at the office.

He pictured the contents of his satchel. Besides the paperwork for his caseload, he was armed with lists and arguments to refute any excuse Miss Dewitt threw at him to worm her way out of the next stage of the requirements. Why did this feel as though he was heading to court?

The front door opened as he swung off his horse. Mr. Dent greeted him and motioned to the stable boy, who took charge of Graham's mount. The butler showed him inside, took his coat and hat, and stepped to the closed library doors. In only a week, Graham had fallen into a routine of working in the library until Miss Dewitt graced him with her presence. He was prepared for her.

The butler slid open the doors.

What he hadn't prepared himself for was a put-together beauty seated behind the library desk in a black velvet and lace gown with long sleeves and a high collar. Her hair perfectly coiffed and a healthy glow to her cheeks. Her appearance stole the breath from his lungs. He stood there mute, like an errant schoolboy brought before the headmaster.

She smiled like a cat who had cornered a mouse. "Have a seat."

He didn't like her being in the seat of authority and power, but he sat anyway. Best to give the impression of being amenable. "I thought you weren't going to rise before noon."

She had obviously been up for quite some time.

"The stress of last night's events kept me from sleep."

She *appeared* fully rested.

Unlike himself and his nightmares. Great vultures, in evening suits and black ties, swooped down and carried Miss Dewitt off. When he tried to rescue her, a swarm of ladies clawed at him, pulling him to pieces and scattering him in an abandoned field.

He mentally shook off the unpleasant thoughts. "Or was it that you didn't want me here first thing?"

She shrugged one slender shoulder. "Your later arrival did allow me some solitude to gather my thoughts."

More like excuses.

His attention remained on the shoulder she had so casually raised. He remembered it milky-white peeking from under the top of her sleeve last night.

Miss Dewitt folded her hands on the desk. "So, on to the next requirement of the will."

Graham stared. Compliancy? From Miss Dewitt?

"I see no point in this. None of the gentlemen in attendance last night are suitable candidates."

Not so compliant after all. But he had a counter prepared for what he had surmised would be her first and strongest argument. Did she truly believe she could outthink him? She didn't have the mental fortitude. "How can you be so sure after one evening?"

"Try six years of evenings, social events, and parties. This isn't the first time my uncle has tried to marry me off to one of these gentlemen, as well as others."

So, she knew the dinner party would be an exercise in futility. He found it a relief that she wasn't considering any of those vultures, but she needed to find someone. "If not one of them, then whom would you consider?"

Again, her indifferent shrug. "The eligible men have all been ferreted out."

"So, are you saying there isn't *one* worthy gentleman in all of Boston and the surrounding areas?" It would have been impossible for her to have met them all.

"Not at all." She waved a hand carelessly. "There were suitable Christian men. I either could not fall in love with them, or they found good wives."

"Lord Claremont seemed quite taken with you. And he comes with a title."

"I am not interested in a title. Lord Claremont's interest is aimed at my great-uncle's bank account and holdings. I'm merely standing in his way."

He couldn't argue with that. If not for his experience with the ladies, he might not have seen the disingenuousness of the men's overtures. "What, then, do you propose?" He knew she had likely put great thought into the matter.

"I declare my uncle the victor, put an end to this farce, and procure myself employment."

An unexpected guffaw shot out of him. "I'm sorry." He schooled his laughter. "I cannot picture you working. What would you do? Salesclerk at a millinery or flower shop?" He pictured her as a maid or cook. Disastrous. "You have no idea what it is like to work. People like you mistakenly think working is easy."

Her chin tipped up. "People like me?"

"The wealthy, who have never worked a day in their lives and have had everything handed to them."

"You have obviously never attended a finishing school for ladies. I have attended three."

"Three?" Had she failed out of the first two?

"My uncle was at a loss about what to do with me, so he sent me to finishing school, then found a *better* one, and then a *better* one. Very hard work indeed."

He raised an eyebrow. "Learning how to hold your little finger out when you drink tea?"

"Sitting up straight for hours without allowing your back to touch the piece of furniture you are seated upon. Not once."

He then noticed the space between her and the back of the chair she sat in. His posture was lax. He shifted forward. Within a few minutes, his back migrated toward the support of the chair again. How did she make it appear so natural?

She continued. "Keeping a conversation going when you have no interest in the subject nor the person prattling on."

She'd always seemed attentive when he'd spoken with her. Or had that been an act she had been taught to perfection?

"Knowing which gown is appropriate to wear to which function, sometimes changing four or five times a day. A considerable waste of time. Clothes you have to be cinched into that require another person to make it possible. Not to mention learning how to breathe in such garments so one doesn't faint. Slow, shallow breaths."

He never realized the difficulties. Or absurdities. Ladies made everything appear so effortless. "If you have put this much thought into your argument, then you must have ideas about the types of employment you would be qualified for." Then he could tell her why each one was unfeasible and ill thought out.

"I could teach at a finishing school for girls or be a governess. I could give private French or piano lessons."

He could conjure no arguments for those. In fact, he hadn't considered this line of thought. Why would someone of her high station ever contemplate working? But let her try. She would see it wasn't as simple as she thought when she had cracks in her hands and dirt under her fingernails. He doubted he would make any headway by opposing her. "Compromise?"

Her eyes twitched. "What are you proposing?"

"I won't discourage you from seeking employment *if* you continue with your uncle's course of action as it's laid out in his will."

She stood and held out her hand.

He rose slowly and hesitated a moment before unconventionally gripping her hand as though he were making an agreement with a man.

She pumped his hand once. "Agreed."

She'd agreed a little too readily, but he said anyway, "Agreed."

◆ ◆ ◆

Victoria mentally patted herself on the back. Getting her way had been easier than she had anticipated. She could endure a few outings with gentlemen—provided they behaved themselves—if it meant she didn't have to wait to pursue employment. She stepped out from behind the desk. "Cook has prepared a nice tomato bisque and finger sandwiches. I thought something light would be in order."

Mr. Wellington proffered his elbow to her. "Sounds delicious."

She rested her hand on his forearm and walked into the dining room. He seated her then sat. She said grace, and Foster served the soup and sandwiches.

He picked up his spoon. "We need to discuss the gentlemen who were in attendance last night."

She stopped, her finger sandwich midway to her mouth, then set it back onto her plate. "Must we tarnish a good meal with such talk?"

"I think it prudent to move forward. As you said, three months is not long to find a husband."

But plenty of time to secure employment. Then she could call this mockery to an end. "Very well. If you insist." She motioned to Foster.

He crossed to her. "Yes, miss?"

"Would you bring me the file on the corner of the desk? And a fountain pen, please."

He bowed, departed, and returned promptly. He set the file and pen on the table next to her.

Mr. Wellington stared at the retrieved items. "I thought your uncle had only dip pens."

"I am not my uncle. I tried to get him more up-to-date, but he refused. I'm surprised he didn't use a quill." She opened the file.

"You have a list of the men at the ready?"

"I thought it prudent to save time." She uncapped the pen. "Lord Hugh Claremont. Completely unsuitable." Overbearing, self-absorbed, tedious. She struck through his name with a flourish. "Gordon Montgomery. No." She crossed off his name with pleasure. "Reginald Parker. No." Crossed off. "Martin Mayfair. No." She read each name and struck through them with pleasure.

"What are you doing?"

"I am weeding out those who are ill suited."

"But you have eliminated every name."

She smiled. "So I have. I guess this task is done." She closed the folder and set the pen atop it. Now, she could enjoy her food.

He reached across the table and snagged her folder and pen.

That flew in the face of good etiquette, but she chose not to mention it and sipped her soup.

He flipped open the folder. "Jonathan Warner. He seemed like a nice enough chap and couldn't take his eyes off of you."

"Jonathan and Ellis Warner's business practices are suspect at best."

"Stanley Browning. He was nice, and you seemed to get on well with him."

"I do get on well with him. He's like a brother to me. To marry him would be like marrying my brother. Neither he nor I could tolerate that."

"Tobias Ring?"

She shook her head.

"You have to pick someone."

"I tried to get you to understand before the party that none of these men were suitable."

"Then other men."

Foster entered, saving her from further torture. He crossed to Victoria silently, holding out a silver tray.

She picked up the calling card, read the name, and placed it back on the tray. "Tell Lord Claremont I'm not receiving callers today, and put his card with the others."

"Lord Claremont is here?" Mr. Wellington smiled. "Invite him for lunch."

"Am I not allowed one day of peace?"

Foster looked to her for his order.

She heaved a heavy sigh to show her displeasure. "Invite him in."

Mr. Wellington pinned her with a stare. "You've had other gentlemen callers today? How many?"

She fluttered her hand as though lazily swatting at a fly. "I lost count after five. Hm. Maybe seven or eight. I didn't see any of them, but they all left their cards. I told you last night's affair would open things up for them to start calling."

Lord Claremont swept into the room as though it belonged to him. His afternoon suit and ornamental walking cane were a bit overstated for a casual visit. He hadn't been the oldest at the party, middle thirties, and had already burned through his inheritance. And now he wanted hers.

He scooped up Victoria's hand and kissed it. "So good of you to see me."

She motioned to her uncle's empty seat. "Won't you join us?"

He glared at the sandwiches. "I've eaten. I came by to invite you on an outing tomorrow."

Of course his lordship wouldn't eat anything with his fingers.

"I was just settling my calendar with my uncle's solicitor. I will inform you if there are any vacancies."

"Certainly every moment of your time cannot be taken up."

Oh, she would make sure it was. "There is so much to do in regards to my uncle's will."

When Lord Claremont glanced at Mr. Wellington, Victoria made a face to show how she felt about his lordship. Unladylike, but she didn't care. She wouldn't be a lady much longer but a working girl.

Failing to control a smile, Mr. Wellington glanced away.

"I will anxiously await to hear from you." Lord Claremont kissed her hand again and strolled out.

Her guest stared after Claremont longer than necessary. Possibly to make sure the man had left. He turned to Foster. "Mr. Dent, would you bring all the cards delivered today?"

Foster looked to her for permission.

She nodded.

He left and returned with a silver tray.

Mr. Wellington retrieved the cards and counted them. "Ten, including Lord Claremont's." He thumbed through the cards and sorted them into two piles.

She ignored him and sipped her soup one spoonful at a time.

He put his hand on one pile. "These you have already discounted." He picked up the others. "These are still open for discussion."

None of the gentlemen from last night were open for discussion. She continued spooning in soup.

He flipped through the cards. "Peter Strausberg. Winston Lockhart. Douglas Berg. Robert Lewiston. And Carlton Carver. Just an outing or two with each. What could it hurt?"

"Not Robert Lewiston. I won't even consider anyone who isn't a Christian." The others at least went to church and claimed to be Christians.

"Very well. Then how about—"

"Stanley Browning."

He gave her an indulgent look. "You said he was like a brother."

"Better to spend time with a brother. He can advise me."

"As you wish. We have the required five."

She dabbed the corners of her mouth with her linen napkin. "And I will choose five women for you."

"Me? You are the one—" He cut himself off, frowning. A few other emotions played across his expression.

Good. He was confused.

"Sir, do you expect me to go on outings with men without a chaperone?"

"Of course not. I will be with you every time any of these men call on you."

"Well, that will be awkward. It will be better if there are two women and two men." She pushed from the table and stood. "'Just an outing or two with each. What could it hurt?'"

She walked out before he could reply.

Chapter 5

On Monday morning, Victoria stood in her foyer, slipping her hands into a pair of fur-lined black leather gloves. Her dark gray wool coat had a black fox fur collar and cuffs and was fastened up to her neck. She secured her wide-brimmed hat on her head with tulle tied into a big bow under her chin. All ready to go.

Foster and Neil waited outside as Graham rode up the lane. The door opened, and Foster ushered her daily warden inside while Neil took care of his horse.

Graham eyed her. "Are you going somewhere?"

"*We* are going into Boston where I will be visiting Mrs. Marshall's School of Graces for Ladies, the Bancroft Finishing and Boarding School for Young Girls, and the Auckland Private School."

"We are going to all those places in one day?"

"That's just the morning. We'll lunch at the Majestic Hotel Dining Room before heading to the Catholic School for Girls and Madame Lafayette's Etiquette and Manners for Young Girls. I need to pick up a hat I ordered at Hampton's Millinery." His surprised expression was endearing, but she would not allow herself to giggle or even smile. "Finally, afternoon tea at the Lindens', where Mr. Peter Strausberg will be present, which should make you happy. Then, back here for a light supper."

He raised his eyebrows nearly to his hairline. "You have everything arranged, I see."

He didn't expect she would let him dictate her every move when Mr. Frye had said he was at *her* beck and call? "I have included both employment options as well as seen to the provisos of the will. If I am to take the time to go all the way into Boston, I must use the trip prudently."

"And you have leaned more heavily toward the employment side of things," Graham said.

"One doesn't want to seem too eager where gentlemen are concerned, lest one be considered wanton."

Foster stood ready at the door. "Are you sure you don't want Pierce to drive?"

"We'll be fine. You and the staff can rest and enjoy the day. I will need nothing from any of you until supper."

"Very good." Foster opened the door.

Graham rushed to her side to escort her out. He stopped short on the bottom step.

She turned to face him. "Is something wrong?"

"You have a horseless carriage?"

"We prefer 'automobile,' and we have two. This 1905 Cameron Runabout, as you can see, seats two. And a larger Buick model that seats four, two front and two back, with a canvas top for inclement weather. It isn't technically mine but my uncle's. Shall we?"

"I don't. . ." He stared at the yellow vehicle. "I've never. . ."

"You don't have to. I'm driving."

"You know how to drive?"

Though automobiles were still a new trend—one people said would pass—her uncle had bought the Buick last year after Victoria had cooed over the idea. She had bribed Pierce, the chauffeur, to teach her to drive it. This year her uncle had bought the smaller Runabout. "Yes. I am a thoroughly modern lady." She walked to the driver's side and waited for him to assist her.

He hurried to her side. "Not *thoroughly* modern."

She supposed not if she expected him to lend her a hand, as she had.

He helped her in and climbed in the other side. "Are you sure you don't want the chauffeur to drive?"

"If you're afraid, you don't have to come with me."

He settled his gaze forward.

Men could not bear to have their masculinity questioned.

Pierce stepped in front of the automobile and turned the crank. The engine started straight away. The chauffeur came to Graham's side. "No need to worry, sir. I taught her myself. She knows how to handle her. I wouldn't let her go if she couldn't."

The pallor of Graham's face told her he wasn't convinced.

Though tempted to drive fast and recklessly—but within control—to really shake him up, she would be considerate and drive with caution. She didn't want him to think poorly of her or find her unappealing. Easing the vehicle forward, she headed down the lane.

◆ ◆ ◆

Graham's skepticism had quickly faded, and he'd been impressed with Victoria's driving ability. She had command of the vehicle and didn't drive irresponsibly. He could see where one of these novelties could be fun for a time. But with their unreliability, they would likely never truly replace horses as some people had suggested. The wind created at motoring speeds made the cool fall air downright chilly. He had struggled not to visibly shiver.

Victoria had gone to the five schools on her list, leaving her notice of intent to teach. The matrons at each were surprised she wished to work, three of them assuming her offer was as unpaid charity help. Each, excited at the prospect of having such an influential lady in their school, said they would contact her soon. She would have employment in no time, at this rate.

He supposed it didn't matter if she gained employment or married. Either way, his duty would be done. He settled on that uneasy thought for a moment. No. Either way his duty wouldn't be completed until the final portion of the will was executed.

Having everything settled for Miss Dewitt sat better with him. That *did* mean spending more time with her, but he could tolerate that. It was only three months, after all. Well, now two and a half months. Had two weeks already flown by?

His stomach tightened when she stopped the automobile in front of a stately home half the size of hers. Patricia and Monique Linden would be after his attentions. He needed to focus on Victoria and her success in inheriting her uncle's estate, not be distracted by frivolous ladies and nonsense. He would need to see if he could strike a deal with Victoria to dispense with entertaining the ladies—an unnecessary stipulation. In exchange for his freedom, he could start helping her in her employment search.

Before the butler or footman could help Victoria, Graham jumped out and rounded the vehicle. He wanted to assist her. It was his duty, after all.

Servants led them through the front door.

The Linden sisters fluttered to him, taking his coat, hat, and gloves. Then they ushered him into the parlor where they sat him on the sofa and plunked themselves down on each side. Monique launched into her litany of all her sister's finer points. She really wanted to get her sister married so she could wed.

Peter Strausberg escorted Victoria in and seated her in a chair. He sat in one positioned far too close to her.

Taking care of Miss Dewitt was Graham's responsibility.

The butler entered the room. "Croquet is set up on the back lawn."

Monique fairly jumped to her feet. "Since it is such a nice day, we thought we would play croquet. You all go on out while I supervise afternoon tea preparations." She let her gaze flicker between Graham and her sister before she fluttered away.

Having only one sister assigned to him, Graham breathed easier. He rose and offered Patricia Linden his arm. He wished it were Victoria who accepted his assistance, but Mr. Strausberg already had possession of her.

When not in the open automobile with the chilly breeze buffeting one's face, the afternoon was pleasant indeed. Croquet would be a nice way to occupy the time where he didn't have to struggle to keep up his end of the conversation.

The trees had metamorphosed from their spring and summer greens to vibrant autumn plumage. But even in this colorful expanse with the green grass below the colorful trees and the blue sky above, Victoria, clad in black, stood out like a prized rose. After a moment, he drew in a breath, realizing he had forgotten to breathe.

Each participant chose a color, and the game was in play.

Victoria had no problem knocking Strausberg's ball far off course. But when Graham had the opportunity to do the same with Miss Patricia Linden's, he tapped it lightly. She smiled at him, blinking briskly as though she had specks of dirt in her eyes she was trying overly hard to extricate. Maybe he should rethink his strategy and play more ruthlessly.

The next time Victoria's ball hit Strausberg's, Graham said in a low voice, "Let the man win."

Victoria placed her booted foot on her ball. "You wish for me to lose on purpose? Whatever for?"

"Men don't like to lose. Especially to a lady. It will put him off."

"I see." She batted her eyelashes and let her mallet hover a couple of inches from her ball, lining up her shot.

Good. A nice gentle tap.

She drew in a deep breath, heaved the mallet far over her shoulder, and swung hard.

Graham winced in fear she would strike her own foot.

Clack!

Strausberg's ball sailed across the yard, almost stopped at the crest of a small rise, and rolled down the slope. His eyes narrowed and his lips thinned as he huffed and puffed after it.

Victoria smiled at Graham. "Silly me. I guess I hit it harder than I thought."

"You knew exactly what you were doing. Why would you do that to the poor man? He was one of the stronger candidates."

"Maybe to you. This lets me see what kind of a man he is and whether I could be married to him for the *rest* of my life."

He wanted to be mad at her and scold her, but her impish smile got the better of him and disallowed any negative feelings or thoughts.

Chapter 6

Victoria watched out the window. For today's luncheon, she had invited Mr. Lockhart, a nice enough fellow but not someone she could fall in love with, and for Graham, flirtatious Rosemary Hudson. An interesting combination all around.

Winston Lockhart stepped out of his automobile, a black Columbus Electric Buggy with a matching fold-down leather top and contrasting red interior. He had the top up today because of the frigid drizzle hanging in the air. So a walk in the garden would be out of the question. That meant being cooped up inside with awkward conversations.

Foster opened the door, and Mr. Lockhart entered with his head down against the rain. When he raised his head, his gray gaze fixed on Victoria, and he smiled. "Let me get out of this wet overcoat."

Foster helped him.

Graham leaned close to her ear. "He's easily twice your age."

"Not quite, but close. He'll turn forty in a couple of months after the first of the year."

"I didn't get a good look at him at the initial party. You aren't seriously interested in a man that much older than you, are you?"

"I'm not interested in *any* of the men on my uncle's list."

"Well then, this little social gathering is a waste of time."

She faced him. "What shall I do? Throw him out?"

"Not now that he's already here."

"But if he wasn't already in the house, I should have barred the door?"

He tossed her a don't-be-ridiculous glance.

"I told you none of the men were suitable. Do you believe me now?"

He grunted in response.

Soon after, Miss Hudson arrived and attached herself to Graham.

Victoria thought she would enjoy watching him squirm under Rosemary's attention, but she didn't like how the woman snuggled close, pawing at him and laughing like a ninny.

Graham wouldn't be saying anything that funny. He wouldn't wish to encourage Rosemary or any of the women.

Unless. . .he fancied Miss Hudson. Couldn't be.

Maybe Rosemary hadn't been such a good choice after all.

At luncheon, Mr. Lockhart sat next to her with Graham and Rosemary across from them.

Mr. Lockhart took a sip of water and set his goblet down. "I was surprised by your party so soon after your uncle's services. I would have thought you'd have taken advantage of a longer mourning period."

He had no way of knowing she didn't know her uncle well enough to mourn him. Though her uncle had kept his distance, she had longed to have an affectionate relationship and loved him. "My uncle wouldn't have wanted me to lock myself away." Obvious from the party and courting rituals he'd forced upon her.

She glanced across the table.

Rosemary had her long, slender fingers on Graham's forearm.

Victoria bristled.

His shoulders looked stiff and tense.

Rosemary needed to stop touching him. Her actions were far too bold.

Victoria tuned back in to Mr. Lockhart's monologue.

"When I first came to Boston in my early twenties, your uncle took me under his wing and treated me like a son."

In contrast to her being treated like a stranger who had invaded her uncle's well-ordered house.

"I think Joseph would be pleased if we courted."

If her uncle had chosen a husband for her and not left the decision up to her, would he have chosen Winston Lockhart, his makeshift son?

Rosemary giggled and leaned close to Graham.

Victoria pushed back her chair and spoke to Muriel. "We're finished with lunch. We'll have tea in the parlor." She would see to it that Rosemary and Graham didn't sit next to each other on the sofa.

◆ ◆ ◆

Several days later, Graham sat astride his horse on his daily morning trek out to the Helmsworthy mansion. A horseless carriage rumbled up the lane toward him. He guided his mount off the road and onto the grass.

His horse sidestepped as the automobile passed.

Victoria's chauffeur waved, but Graham couldn't see anyone in the back. After another twenty minutes in the saddle, he arrived at the stately edifice that never ceased to impress him.

Neil rushed out to see to Graham's horse.

Graham handed over the reins without a worry. "Thank you for taking such good care of my horse each day."

"Stable master says they aren't just a convenience and means to get around. They have personalities and feelings like people do." The adolescent servant stroked the stallion's neck. "They deserve kindness. If you treat them well, they will treat you well. They know when you like them."

Graham had not thought of his horse as much more than a means of transportation. Never thought about the potential of emotions. But he could see the horse responding to the young man by leaning closer and putting his chin on top of his head.

"Good boy," Neil cooed.

Graham patted his horse's withers. "Good boy."

The stallion turned his head and lipped the brim of Graham's hat as though to say, *Nice to finally meet the man on my back.* Graham smiled. "Give him an extra carrot or something."

"He likes apples."

"An apple then." Graham traipsed up the steps.

Mr. Dent stood waiting for him. "Good morning, sir."

"Good morning. Is Miss Dewitt up?"

The butler closed the door behind them and took Graham's hat and gloves. "She is and has gone into Boston. I thought you knew."

Graham stopped in the middle of unbuttoning his overcoat. So she had been in the backseat of the automobile after all. Even if he hurried, he doubted he could catch up to her before she disappeared into Boston traffic. "Where did she go?"

"Said she had some errands."

"Do you know what kind or where?" He removed his coat and handed it to Mr. Dent.

"She didn't say, but I think they had something to do with the telephone calls she received yesterday."

"Before I arrived?"

"Yes, sir."

"Did she say when she would return?"

"Not directly, but she left instructions for lunch."

So she could be back for lunch or just thought to feed him. "I'll be in the library working. Let me know when she returns."

"Very well."

Graham set to his tasks and completed everything he'd packed in his satchel in short order. He hadn't brought a lot with him, as his grandfather hadn't given him any new responsibilities and had assigned his current cases to others. Normally that would have irritated him, but he found he didn't mind. His present task of assisting Victoria was more important, if only temporary. And growing more appealing every day.

With nothing to do but wait for her to return, he perused the shelves. Mr. Helmsworthy had a wide variety of books, from shipping to gardening and from legal texts to building birdhouses. Graham wanted something recreational and found the shelves of novels. *Little Women. Pride and Prejudice. An Unwilling Guest* and *Because of Stephen* and a slew of others by a Grace Livingston Hill. This was definitely the romance shelf. No wonder Victoria was so fixated on love.

He pulled down a volume of *The Time Machine*. This was more to his liking. He got comfortable in a chair and opened the cover.

Midmorning, Mr. Dent slid the doors back no more than a foot and peered in.

Graham closed the book, happy for the distraction, and waved him in. "Is Victoria back?"

"Not yet. Mrs. Fuller has a tea tray for you. Shall I have her bring it in here or serve it in the parlor?"

"Here is fine."

The housekeeper brought in a tray with tea and cookies and set it on the serving table next to Graham's chair.

Mr. Dent stepped aside in the doorway for Mrs. Fuller to pass. "Is there anything else you require, Mr. Wellington?"

"This is fine, thank you." When the pair had just crossed the threshold, Graham spoke again. "Wait. There is something. Have a seat, both of you."

The housekeeper and the butler glanced at each other, but Mr. Dent spoke. "We would rather not, sir." He hesitated a moment before continuing. "Servants don't sit in the presence of others."

"You're not *my* servants." Graham motioned to the sofa. "Please. I insist."

Mr. Dent nodded to Mrs. Fuller. She sat awkwardly on the sofa. Mr. Dent sat in the matching chair to Graham's. "What can we do for you?"

"How long have you known Victoria?"

The housekeeper spoke before the butler could. "Ever since she arrived. Both of us."

"Tell me about her."

The pair gave each other uncomfortable sideways glances.

"I'm not snooping. I just want to know what she was like." After more reassurances, the pair of servants told of Victoria's arrival fifteen years ago and many stories of her growing up, as well as her kindness and generosity.

Mrs. Fuller sighed. "Those first years, she stuck close to me in the kitchen. Asking all sorts of questions and cooking beside me."

"Victoria can cook?"

"Nothing difficult. She mostly made cookies and cakes. She likes her sweets."

He never would have guessed she'd spent any time in a kitchen.

"One of my favorite episodes with her was the bunny incident." The butler's mouth turned up in a nostalgic smile. "She had managed to catch a young rabbit and snuck it up to her room. That night she was playing with it under her bedcovers."

"Oh dear." Mrs. Fuller put one hand to her chest. "That gave me quite a fright when I went to tuck her in. The bunny jumped out and scampered about the room."

Mr. Dent took the next turn with the story. "When I entered, it darted between my feet and out of the room. It took us two weeks to capture it and release it outside. The poor thing would have been dead if Cook and Victoria hadn't fed it."

They spoke of her more like parents than servants.

"You both care about her a great deal."

They nodded.

"What about her uncle?"

Mr. Dent answered. "He was a good man."

"Did he treat her well?"

"As well as he knew how." Mrs. Fuller replied this time. "The poor man didn't know the first thing about children. He was at a loss as to what to do when she was around. He would watch her out the window when she played in the yard. He gave me complete charge of raising her. Anything I told him she needed, he saw that she got it."

Muriel stepped into the room. "Miss is coming up the lane."

Mr. Dent and Mrs. Fuller shot to their feet. The butler tugged on the bottom of his jacket. "You won't speak to her of our conversation, will you?"

"Of course not. I appreciate your candor."

Graham met Victoria in the foyer as she came in the door. "You left before I arrived."

"I needed to go into Boston."

"And you didn't want me along."

"What need would there have been for you?"

Need? He was supposed to be with her. His duty. He *wanted* to be with her.

"I honestly didn't think you would want to go. It would have been a waste of your time."

Time with her was never wasted.

"I'm sure you were able to complete a lot of work in my absence."

What little he'd brought. "So what errands did you attend to?" Would she tell him about the telephone calls?

Her pretty pink lips pulled into a smile. "I had interviews at two of the schools I applied to. They said it was a matter of formality before presenting me to the schools' boards. And the other three schools are going directly to their boards."

"Congratulations."

She would have employment in no time.

And strangely, that made him happy. No more wily suitors.

◆ ◆ ◆

Victoria sat in the back of the Buick with Graham at her side. Today would be fun. Millicent had readily agreed to afternoon tea at her home. Millicent's brother, Stanley, would be pleasant company—a nice change from the others—and Victoria would get to see Graham with children.

The chauffeur parked in the circular driveway, got out, and opened the door. He held a black umbrella aloft.

Graham climbed out first and gave her his hand.

Millicent's butler came out holding up two more umbrellas.

Victoria stepped out and spoke to Pierce. "I could have driven."

"Indeed." Pierce dipped his head. "But that would have been unseemly for a lady of your station."

"I don't know that I'm concerned with that." She would soon enough be on her own, and people would think her most unseemly.

One side of the chauffeur's mouth curved up. "But others would."

"I suppose."

"If you drove yourself everywhere, I would be out of a job."

"Well, now, I couldn't have that."

His grin broke full. "Much appreciated, miss."

The butler led them inside where Millicent waited with three-year-old Richard clutching her hand and baby Ulysses on her hip. "I'm so pleased you made it. We have been looking forward to your visit all week."

After depositing the umbrellas in the stand, the butler took their coats, hats, and gloves.

Millicent pulled on Richard's hand, causing the boy to step forward. "This is my son Richard. Richard, say good afternoon to Mr. Wellington."

"Goo-noon." The boy turned into his mother's skirt.

"Say hello to Miss Victoria. You know her."

Richard smiled. "Huwoe."

Victoria squatted down. "Good afternoon, young man. You are getting to be such a big boy."

Millicent spoke again to Graham. "This is my little one, Ulysses. He's ten months old." She deposited the baby into Graham's unsuspecting arms.

Graham looked as though he wasn't sure what to do but shifted the child, getting a better hold on him.

"Right this way." Millicent led them into the parlor.

Stanley greeted them with a kiss to Victoria's hand and a handshake for Graham.

He was doing quite well with a baby in his arms. He looked like a natural.

The sight warmed Victoria's heart.

The servants set out tea, scones, strawberry preserves, and clotted cream.

Graham and Millicent sat on the sofa with Richard between them, and Millicent held Ulysses. Graham picked up Richard's small toy wooden horse from the floor and gave it to the boy.

Richard galloped the horse over to Graham's thigh and left it there.

Graham galloped it back to the boy.

And back and forth it went until Richard climbed onto Graham's lap. "Now you." The boy bounced. "Horsey ride."

"Richard, get down and don't bother Mr. Wellington." Millicent reached for her son's arm.

"That's all right. I don't mind." Graham took the boy's hands and bounced him on his knee. "'Trot, trot to Boston to buy a loaf of bread. Trot, trot home again. The old horse is dead.'" He let his knee drop, indicating the demise of the poor animal.

Stanley leaned toward Victoria. "He likes you, you know?"

"Nonsense. I'm nothing more than an obligation he would rather be rid of."

"If that were so, he wouldn't be entertaining your best friend's child."

She watched Graham. Could he truly have feelings for her that weren't associated with his duty?

The nanny entered the room. "I'll take the children now if you like."

"Yes, thank you." Millicent handed over Ulysses.

After a moment of fuss from Richard, the nanny had the three-year-old by the hand and left with her charges.

Graham repositioned himself on the sofa. "Mrs. Amundsen, your son is quite the cowboy."

"Thank you. You will wear out long before he does." Millicent pinned Victoria with her gaze. "Do tell him. He has been such a good sport about all this."

She didn't want to. Everything would be spoiled. But Millicent was right. Graham deserved to know. She gave her friend a nod of consent to tell him.

Millicent shook her head.

Graham narrowed his eyes. "What's going on?"

Victoria's insides tightened. "I. . .I have a confession to make."

He tilted his head. "I'm listening."

She didn't want to say but went on. "I told the ladies. . .that I invited to the party about my predicament." She took a deep breath. "I told them to be overly attentive to you." She regretted her actions and hurried on to explain before he could cut her off. "I needed you to understand what it was like for me."

Graham stared at her. "So the ladies hovering around me was all an act? The Linden sisters? Miss Hudson?" He shifted his gaze to Millicent. "And you aren't looking for a father for your sons?"

"I'm not opposed to marrying again, but he has to be the right man. You have been a darling, playing with my boys."

Graham's jaw muscles flexed.

Stanley chuckled. "I thought something was going on. My sister was quite out of character."

Victoria hoped Graham would see the humor in this.

Graham stood. "Mrs. Amundsen, thank you for a lovely time." He left the parlor, evidently angry with Victoria's deception, and headed out the front door into the rain.

"Oh dear." He was angry with her.

Millicent waved her hand in her brother's direction. "Stanley, go after him and explain."

"He'll get over it."

Victoria wasn't so sure. She rose. "I should go. Could you have Pierce bring round the car?"

A couple of minutes later, wrapped in her cloak, Victoria hastened through the rain to the open automobile door. "Hurry and see if we can catch up to Mr. Wellington."

Pierce drove faster than normal but still safely.

Not too far down the road, Graham strode along one side. When had she started thinking of him as Graham and not Mr. Wellington?

"Pierce, stop alongside him."

The chauffeur did.

She opened the door. "Please get in."

For a breath's length, she thought he might refuse, but he dipped the water off the brim of his hat in a stream and climbed in.

After Pierce had the automobile traveling at a more reasonable speed, Victoria chanced to speak. "I'm truly sorry for putting you through all that. You didn't seem to understand how things are for women. I needed you to have the smallest amount of understanding."

Graham removed his hat and burst out laughing.

She couldn't believe he was laughing. "I'm pleased you can find the humor in this."

"I thought about the way the ladies acted. At the time, I was shocked, but now I can see it was playacting."

"So, you're not angry with me?"

He shook his head. His shaggy brown hair sprinkled rain droplets inside the automobile. "I'm game for a good lark now and then."

"But you looked upset."

"I was trying not to laugh once I figured out the jig."

Pleased, she settled back in the seat, not bothering to wipe away the rain on her cheek from his hair, which was wavier than usual, being long and wet. She rather liked his untamed appearance. It gave him a roguish quality.

He gave her a rakish smile. "After this, I think I have earned the right to call you by your first name. If that is acceptable with you?"

"Quite acceptable."

"And you, Victoria, must call me Graham."

"I would like that, Graham." She liked that very much. It made them seem less like adversaries and more like friends.

No more than friends.

Chapter 7

Victoria stood before the full-length mirror in her room, inspecting her overall appearance. A slim, black velvet evening gown with black beads and black embroidery accompanied by long black gloves and a black lace fan. She *was* tired of all this black. But following convention was the least she could do out of respect for the man who had taken her in and seen to all her needs. The physical ones, at least.

A knock on her door.

"Come in."

Muriel stepped inside. "Mr. Wellington is downstairs."

"Thank you." Victoria scooped up the matching velvet shawl and followed the maid out of the room.

She stopped at the top of the stairs to take in Graham's appearance.

He looked dashing in his formal evening suit, with his wavy brown hair freshly cut. He turned and gazed up at her.

Her breath caught. *Handsome* popped into her head. *Yes, very handsome.*

She made her way down the staircase slowly to have reason to keep her gaze on him.

He didn't smile, only stared. "You. . .you're. . .stunning."

So he was pleased.

"You look quite debonair yourself."

"Who have you paired me with tonight?"

"Since the jig is up, I have invited Millicent." She wrapped her shawl around herself. "My friend will be pleasant company for you. We'll pick her up and meet Douglas Berg at the theater."

Graham helped her on with her hooded cloak and escorted her out to the waiting automobile.

An hour and a half later, Pierce pulled up in front of the Bijou Opera House.

Graham assisted both ladies out and ushered them inside. He took their wraps and deposited them in the coat-check room.

"Victoria," someone called from across the lobby.

She scanned the faces to locate Mr. Berg. Instead, her gaze lit on Lord Hugh Claremont, who strode in her direction.

Too late to pretend she hadn't seen him. But at least she had the excuse of finding Mr. Berg to pull away from him.

Lord Claremont loomed over her. Perfect white teeth gleamed through rosy lips. Something in his possessive smile spoke of victory. "You are a hard lady to gain an audience with."

For him, on purpose. How many times had she avoided this man's telephone calls in the past two months alone? And feigned headaches when he came calling? "Seeing to the contents of my uncle's will has consumed my time." She gave her closed fan a flourish. "We must be off to locate the rest of our party."

"Mr. Berg?"

Victoria's false smile wavered. How did he know? "Yes. Enjoy the show."

He gripped her arm. "I'm sorry to inform you that Mr. Berg won't be able to make it tonight. He asked me to attend you in his stead."

No. And she had thought she might actually enjoy this evening.

"Shall we go up to my balcony box?"

She glanced at Millicent and Graham, who both shrugged.

Victoria endured the first half of *Rigoletto* with Lord Claremont leaning toward her and whispering throughout the performance. She waved her fan toward him. "I can't hear." *With you hissing in my ear.* But he didn't stop.

At intermission, she fairly jumped from her seat and latched on to Millicent's arm. "Shall we go to the ladies' powder room?"

"Yes." Her friend hurried out with her, understanding Victoria's need to escape.

After the entr'acte, Victoria dreaded returning to Claremont's box. "Do you think the men would notice if we didn't return?"

"Only if they both have gone suddenly blind. Even then, I think they would be aware of your absence. You made it through one half, you can make it through the other." Millicent took her arm. "The second half will be better. I promise."

It couldn't be any worse, and she was that much closer to the end of the evening and returning home. She took a deep breath. She could manage. The opera was half over.

The men met her and Millicent in the lobby and escorted them up the stairs.

Behind her and Lord Claremont, she thought she could hear Graham grumbling. Then Millicent giggled.

Once in the box and preparing to sit, Millicent spoke in a slightly raised voice. "Mr. Wellington! That is a wholly inappropriate comment." She turned. "Victoria, do trade seats with me."

Her friend didn't give Victoria a chance to respond before slipping around her and sitting in Victoria's seat next to Lord Claremont's.

Victoria smiled and quickly sat next to Millicent. That left the seats on either side of the ladies for the gentlemen. Graham sat next to her.

Lord Claremont's scowl showed his displeasure, but he sat without complaint when the lights dimmed.

As the curtain rose, Graham whispered, "I didn't say anything improper to her."

"I know. She is giving me a reprieve from his lordship."

"Very kind of her." After a pause, he continued, "You were gone a long time. I thought you might have slipped out a side door."

"Millicent wouldn't let me."

He chuckled softly.

A soothing sound.

After the show, Graham retrieved their coats from the cloakroom. He helped Millicent on with hers first.

Pinning Victoria with his gaze, Lord Claremont shrugged into his overcoat. "I'll drive you home."

She didn't relish the idea. "I have my automobile and chauffeur."

"Mr. Wellington can use them to take Mrs. Amundsen home."

She didn't like the way he was making decisions for everyone. Nor did she know how to turn him down without ruffling his feathers too badly in public and causing a scene. She would definitely be thought of as unseemly then.

Graham draped her cloak around her shoulders. "As one of Miss Dewitt's solicitors, I am duty bound to be her escort until all the stipulations of the will have been met and dealt with."

Very smooth. She fastened her wrap at her neck as she spoke to his lordship. "Thank you for your offer. Good evening."

Lord Claremont scowled.

She smiled back as she turned to exit with Graham and Millicent. What she had wanted to say to Claremont was *Go away and stop bothering me*. He would not have taken that well and probably would have perceived it as a challenge.

Fortunately for her, she had her protector, Graham.

◆ ◆ ◆

Sitting behind the desk in the library, Victoria growled softly and wadded the letter.

"Something wrong?" Graham sat across from her.

"That is the fifth one."

"The fifth what?"

"Rejection. I don't understand. All the schools I applied to have turned me down. Stating that they don't have need of an additional teacher at this time or that their budget can't support another teacher. I even spoke to several parents who were interested in piano or French lessons for their daughters, and they have all declined my services as well. They were all so enthusiastic before." She had hoped to have a placement secured before Christmas and start after the first of the year.

"I'm sorry."

She pinned him with a stare. "Truly. Now you can say that you told me I wouldn't be able to work. What did you say? 'Your kind of people don't know what hard work is.' Or something like that." That he, of all people, thought poorly of her hurt most of all.

"That's not true. I was hoping you would gain employment."

"That is hard to believe. You've been pushing the marriage angle."

"But I agree that none of the gentlemen are suitable for you."

At least they could agree on that. She pulled out a sheaf of blank papers. "I will make a new list of potential pupils." She rummaged in the desk drawers for a fountain pen. *Bother.* She hadn't left one of hers in here. *No matter.* She thunked an inkwell onto the desktop then dug through her uncle's myriad of expensive nib pens. She held up her prize, an ebony-handled metal-tipped nib pen inlaid with mother of pearl. The one her uncle never allowed her to use. She opened the well and dipped the pen.

Graham leaned forward. "Is this really necessary? Go to the schools tomorrow and make inquiries. Shall I do it for you?"

She appreciated the indignation in his voice. "Not necessary. They each made it perfectly clear in their letters that they would not be hiring me." She thrust the letters, even the crumpled one, across the desk to him and went back to her list.

He would obviously never consider himself a candidate. Her uncle had fortunately not put any stipulations on what kind of man or his station she must marry. Graham could be considered right alongside Lord Claremont or a chimney sweep. But far more appealing than either.

She turned back to her task of finding employment. A couple of possible student names came to mind as well as an academy for boys. She touched the pen to paper. It scratched rather than flowed. Redipped. More scratching. She rotated it a little this way and that. A splotch of ink puddled on the paper. Holding the instrument up to the light, she noticed the tip was damaged.

She stared, turning it around and around, watching the light glint off the defect. Was this why her uncle never permitted her to use it? Why hadn't he said so? Rather than making her feel as though she wasn't good enough?

"These are an outrage." Graham slapped the letters back onto the desk. "You might have grounds to sue them."

She set the pen aside. "Why would I want to work at an establishment where I had to force them to hire me?"

"When you put it that—"

Foster opened the sliding library doors. "Mr. Frye is here to see you both."

Victoria glanced at Graham. Had he known his grandfather was coming today?

Graham shrugged.

She returned her gaze to the butler. "Show him in."

Graham stood.

The old man crossed the room with more agility than Victoria had expected and sat in the vacated chair. He flapped his hand about. "Pretend we have dispensed with all the greetings and pleasantries."

Graham shifted to sit on the corner of the desk. "We weren't expecting you."

"I come with disturbing news."

She couldn't imagine what would be more distressing than being forced to marry.

Mr. Frye opened his mouth to speak but said nothing for a long moment as though considering his words. "First, tell me your interest in Lord Hugh Claremont."

"Interest? I have no interest in him."

"Then you are not considering his lordship as a suitor?"

"Certainly not."

"Very well. Stanley Browning came to see me."

Victoria blinked, trying to catch up with the subject changes. Disturbing news. Then Claremont. And now Stanley. Why had Mr. Frye come? Did he even remember himself? "What did Stanley want?"

"He was paid a visit by Lord Claremont."

That connected two of the three. "Why would Lord Claremont do that?"

"He *asked* Mr. Browning to stay away from you. If he knew what was good for him. A veiled threat if I ever heard one."

And that connected the third. Disturbing news, indeed. "Why didn't Stanley come to me directly?"

"Well, he obviously felt it was enough of a threat he didn't feel safe to approach you."

Victoria eyed the pile of rejection letters and pulled them toward her. She shuffled through them then shook them in the air. "He did this as well."

Graham twisted toward her. "I doubt that."

"I don't."

"How can you be so sure?"

"This is exactly the kind of thing he would do to get his way. He knows all the prominent people who send their daughters to those schools and is either friends with board members or on the boards. So he would have known before I even left Boston. His title carries weight. And I'll bet he *asked* Mr. Berg to go away as well so he could take his place at the theater." She had tried to be nice but not anymore.

Graham grimaced. "I'll take care of Claremont."

How sweet of him to want to protect her, but he would only fuel Lord Claremont's determination, who would probably threaten Graham as well. "Don't bother. I know how to deal with him." Once and for all.

Chapter 8

Graham shook his head. "I can't believe you invited that man here, *to your home*." What was she thinking? Lord Hugh Claremont? The man who was trying to force her to marry him by threatening all other suitors and pressuring schools and parents not to hire her?

Victoria stood before Graham in a plain cotton black blouse and black wool skirt. Not her usual stylish attire. No trims, no ruffles, no bobbles. She almost looked like a peasant. But she carried herself with a grace and dignity that bespoke her station.

She gave her chin a slight tilt. "First, I did it to have the upper hand. My territory."

Smart.

"Second, this isn't my home but my uncle's. If I don't marry, it will be gone. Still not mine. If I do marry, it will become my husband's property and *still* won't be mine. So this house never was *nor* ever will be mine."

How unfair. He'd never thought about it, but her husband *would* own everything if she married. No wonder she wasn't keen on marrying except for love. That would be the only way she could ensure with any amount of certainty that she would be treated well.

Could he draft a contract which would allow her to keep everything in her name should she marry? It depended on how tight the second half of the will was. And if the man she married would agree to sign it and abide by it. Doubtful. What man would marry her for all this and then give it all up?

She smoothed her hands down her skirt. "Now, you must remain out of sight while his lordship is here. He mustn't know you are even in the house."

"I'm not going to leave you alone in a room with him."

"He can't be allowed to see you. I'll be perfectly safe." She walked down the hallway to a second, smaller door in an alcove that led into the parlor. "You can listen from here."

He didn't like this one bit. But he was interested in what she would say to Lord Claremont. "Very well. But if I suspect you are in any sort of trouble, I'm going to break up the meeting."

"I won't be in any trouble."

He followed her downstairs and into the kitchen where several servants congregated, including Mr. Dent.

Victoria faced the butler. "Foster, make sure Lord Claremont feels very welcome."

The butler nodded.

"Mrs. Fuller." Victoria turned to the housekeeper. "Wait a few minutes after Lord Claremont arrives to serve the tea."

"Certainly." The housekeeper set the sugar bowl and creamer on the prepared tray.

Victoria picked up the two cups and inspected them. She opened the china cabinet and returned the cups there, then picked up one cup after another and selected two. "Give this one to his lordship when you pour the tea and this one to me."

Graham noticed that the two cups had chips on the rims. What was the little minx up to?

Muriel scuttled in. "He's coming up the driveway."

Victoria straightened her shoulders and nodded to Mr. Dent, who hurried out of the room. "It's time." She spoke to the room at large. Or was it to herself?

Graham followed her up the servants' stairwell.

She seemed to be in no particular hurry. She waited at the top behind the heavy oak door.

After a moment, the front door latch clacked, and distant voices filtered through the doorframe.

Another moment later, the servants' door opened from the other side, and Mr. Dent moved aside. "He's in the parlor."

"Thank you." She stepped out and took several deep breaths.

Graham stood next to her. "You don't have to do this if you don't want to." He would gladly confront his lordship on her behalf.

"Oh, I *want* to do this. I'm just preparing myself." She fluttered her hand toward him. "To the alcove, and don't come into the parlor for any reason."

He would be the judge if he had *reason* to go into the parlor.

She strolled the length of the hallway to the parlor doorway, pulled a black handkerchief from her sleeve, and slumped her shoulders.

He tiptoed to the door that had been left cracked open a bit. A tall potted palm with a cluster of other plants hid him from view. Perfect. He slipped inside, crouched, and peered through the leaves.

Lord Claremont stood as she entered. "Victoria, thank you for your invitation."

She waved her handkerchief toward him. "I am so grateful you came." She sat on the end of the sofa closest to the crackling fire.

He sat next to her. "I thought after the theater you might be upset with me for taking Mr. Berg's place. Since the plans were all made, I felt I would have been negligent if I left you waiting."

Negligent only because *he* was the reason Mr. Berg didn't show. Graham wished he could see Claremont's face straight on to read him. Women rarely could tell what truly hid behind men's words, and men had no clue what danced around in women's heads.

Victoria gave a halfhearted smile. "That was so kind of you. And your box offered a far better view of the performance than the lower seats would have. Truly thoughtful."

Claremont straightened his shoulders, no doubt pleased with her compliment. "You are welcome in my opera house box *any* time."

Graham bet his lordship would love to have a beautiful lady of Victoria's station on his arm everywhere he went. But she could be ugly for all Claremont cared if he could have her uncle's money.

Mrs. Fuller entered through the door behind Graham. She smiled down at him and continued into the room with the tray. "Tea, miss."

"Thank you."

The housekeeper set it on the table in front of the pair. "Shall I pour, or would you like to?"

Victoria nodded at the tray. "Please do."

The first cup, Mrs. Fuller handed to his lordship, then one for her mistress. "Anything else?"

"No, thank you." Victoria spooned sugar into her cup. . .one. . .two. . .three. . .and stirred with soft clinking sounds.

The housekeeper left the way she'd come in. She winked at Graham as she passed by. Her footsteps stopped just outside the door.

Graham glanced back to see the housekeeper, butler, Muriel, and one other maid standing behind him, straining to hear.

Claremont took a drink of tea, pulled the cup from his lip, and glared at it. He touched the chip on the rim. His eyebrows pulled together.

No doubt he thought the same thing as Graham. Why serve a guest with chipped china?

But the man didn't mention the damaged cup. "Your message sounded as though you had something specific you wished to speak to me about."

Victoria dabbed the corner of her eye with her black handkerchief. "I'm in quite a quandary. I don't know what to do. I need your counsel."

"I will help in any way I can."

Graham bet he would. Help himself to Mr. Helmsworthy's money.

"My uncle had debts."

They weren't much. Nominal at best. She knew that as well as Graham did.

"Go on." Lord Claremont took another sip, glared at his cup again, and set it and the saucer on the table in front of him.

"I had three months from the reading of the will. I'm going to be out of this house in a little over two weeks."

Claremont pulled back. "But your uncle had so much."

"Debts."

"What about all his holdings?"

"Debts."

From his lordship's pinched expression, Graham could tell the man struggled to believe the fortune that he'd thought was within his grasp had slipped away.

Claremont swallowed hard. "Certainly your uncle left you something."

"I will receive a small stipend."

His lordship shifted on the sofa. "How small?"

"Oh, not to worry. If I scrimp, I can rent a modest apartment, hopefully one with a separate bedroom."

Claremont leaned forward as though about to spring off the sofa.

She sucked in a quick breath and continued. "I had hoped to supplement the allowance by working at a local school for girls, but none of them are hiring."

His lordship stood. "I am so sorry to run out on you like this, but I just remembered a prior engagement." He backed toward the door. "Thank you for a nice time."

Graham struggled not to laugh and give away his refuge.

Victoria followed her guest into the foyer. "But whatever shall I do?"

Graham and the servants watching shifted as one to peer down the main hallway.

Lord Claremont snatched his overcoat and hat from Mr. Dent. "Sorry, I am unable to help you. I'll make some inquiries and get back to you. Good day." Claremont swung his coat on and, without bothering to fasten it, hurried outside into the freezing December air.

Graham came out of hiding and strode to the foyer.

Mr. Dent closed the door.

Victoria burst out laughing. "Did you see him? He couldn't get out of here fast enough."

"That was *brilliant*." Graham applauded her. "I dare say that's the last we'll see of him."

And nothing she'd said was a lie. She merely omitted some key information. But if she didn't find a suitable husband soon, it would all be the cold hard truth.

Chapter 9

Graham stared in disbelief as Victoria wrapped a set of plain white plates in table linens and placed them into a crate. "You're packing? Why?"

With one finger held aloft, she glanced up at him, and her blue eyes melted his ire. "I have one week left. I have failed my uncle's test. As he knew I would. So I'm packing necessities and making inquiries into apartments I can afford on my stipend. Don't worry. I won't take anything of value."

He never imagined she would. But then again, he never imagined her living anywhere but here. . .in her home. "I'm sure you'll be given ample time to find a place and move after the rest of the will is read."

"Why put off the inevitable? I would rather be done with it all when the final sentence is rendered." She went back to her task.

"You have a week. You never know what the Lord will do."

She stilled her hands and sighed but didn't look up. "If He was going to make all my dreams come true, He would have by now. Besides, all my marriage prospects—not that any were suitable to begin with—have been scared away."

Not *all*. "There has to be one agreeable man in the greater Boston area."

She turned to face him. "Do you have someone in mind?"

Was that hope in her voice and eyes?

Staring intently, she blinked several times. "Anyone?"

Soon after he had met her, his heart had secretly hoped. But he hadn't let his thoughts go there, because he knew that even faced with a life of near poverty, she would never consider him. He could mention Stanley Browning. She got on well with him, and his sister was her best friend. But what if she took him up on Browning? Then she would be lost to him.

Would he rather have her in poverty and still have a glimmer of hope than have her financially secure? "I'll marry you." He hadn't meant to say that. But he couldn't take it back. Didn't want to.

She gripped the chairback closest to her and appeared not to breathe for a moment. Her voice came out small, almost childlike. "You?"

He swallowed hard and nodded like an errant schoolboy.

One eyebrow rose gracefully. "Why would I want to spend the rest of my life with a man who doesn't even like me and thinks I'm nothing but a spoiled debutante?"

"I don't dislike you." *In fact, quite the opposite.*

"Do you deny that when we met, you wanted nothing to do with me?"

"Well. . .I. . .my cases. . ."

"Do you deny you thought me among the snobbish privileged who couldn't do anything for myself?"

"Well. . .I suppose. . ."

Her eyes glistened, and she blinked several times. She folded her arms. "So *what* about your oh-so-romantic proposal am I supposed to swoon over and say yes to?"

He was mucking this up. He drew in a deep breath to order his thoughts. Just like closing statements to a jury. "My proposal is not meant to be romantic but practical. To keep you from losing everything."

She thinned her lips. "So you want my uncle's money, too. You would be sitting pretty then. You are no different than Lord Claremont and all the others."

Ouch! "That's not true. I'm not after your money. But I don't want you to lose it."

"I'm not losing my uncle's money."

"Yes, you are."

"I can't lose something I never had in the first place. And if I marry, it all becomes my husband's—in this case *you*. So I was never, ever going to have my uncle's money, married or not. I would rather be a pauper and control my own life than be at the whim of a man who cares naught for me."

He rubbed the back of his neck. He was making a flying mess of this whole thing. "What I mean is, I would allow you to have full control over your uncle's money—your money."

"*Allow.* How generous. That's easy to say now. I'm sure Lord Claremont would have said the same thing."

"True. But I will draft a contract we'll both sign before we marry, giving you full control."

She narrowed her eyes. "You could do that?"

"Of course."

"But wouldn't that go against my uncle's will? And therefore not be binding?"

"I think I could word things to take effect the moment all your uncle's assets are transferred to m—the man you marry."

Through squinted eyes, she studied him. "Why didn't you suggest this before? With one of the men my uncle had chosen?"

"I hadn't thought of it until now." And he didn't want her to marry anyone else. "You can't be sure that one of those other men would keep his word and not try to break the contract after the wedding. I give you my solemn promise."

"Why would you do this? What would you gain out of the deal?"

You. "Nothing. You deserve and are entitled to your uncle's holdings. You're his only heir."

Her stoic expression didn't budge.

"Would you at least think about it?"

She gave a curt nod. "I would like to be alone to contemplate my future."

From the start, she had been trying to send him away. Was there anything more he could say to persuade her? "I'll be in the library."

◆ ◆ ◆

Victoria's heart broke as Graham walked away.

He had proposed a business arrangement.

Nothing more.

She had hoped for more.

A lot more.

But what would he gain from his proposal? Certainly not a wife to love and cherish. Social position?

The tears she had held at bay during their discussion broke free. She slapped them away. Why did she think she was special enough to find a man to *love* her when so many women failed? Or settled.

Her uncle must be laughing at her high ideals now. Shaking his head and saying she had fanciful notions.

Stanley had obviously been wrong in his declaration that Graham held affection for her. Maybe Stanley would be willing to marry her if he learned of her uncle's stipulation. He might not agree to her having *full* control but at least a large allowance.

Victoria stayed in the dining room for a good hour, packing the dishes and linens she would take with her. The time gave her a chance to get a handle on her emotions.

Prepared to face Graham again, she strode into the library and studied him busy at work behind the desk. "Write the contract, and I'll read it."

Graham jumped to his feet. "Really?" He strode around the desk. "So you're agreeable to my proposal?"

"I don't know." She clearly wasn't going to find another man to fall in love with in a week. Wouldn't it be better to marry a man she at least loved even if he didn't return her love than having no love at all? "But I'll read it and consider your offer."

He reached back and picked up the papers he'd been writing on. "It's done."

"How? When? You left me only an hour ago." Had he already had the contract written up before he arrived? Had he been planning this all along? Was he manipulating her? She prayed not.

"I wrote it just now while I was waiting for you."

"You did?"

He nodded.

"Is it legal?"

"Of course. Once you've signed." He motioned toward the desk chair. "Sit and read it. Let me know if you have any questions or would like anything changed."

She hadn't expected something so fast. Her legs felt weak as she rounded the desk, grateful for the cushioned seat to catch her. She dropped the contract onto the desk and flipped through the pages. "You've already signed this. Are you that confident?"

"I wanted you to know that I'm making you a serious offer."

"Why are you so insistent?"

He hesitated. "Because you deserve what's rightfully yours."

She sensed he was holding something back. She drew in a slow breath. "I don't know. Maybe with someone like Stanley. He at least doesn't detest me."

Graham seemed to bristle at the mention of Stanley. "I do *not* detest you. Far from it. I admire your spirit and spunk. You've never let the conditions of your uncle's will get you down. You're smart and have a superb sense of humor. I don't know another lady who could have outsmarted Lord Claremont the way you did. Most would have given up, declared him the victor, and married the manipulating clod. But you stood your ground."

He paused then continued. "Please consider me over Mr. Browning."

"I still can't determine what you would gain out of the arrangement."

"Does it matter?"

"Yes." Consenting to let him write the contract had been a bad idea. "I don't understand your motivation. And until I do, I won't agree to anything." She leaned back in the chair and crossed her arms. "I don't want any surprises. I want to know exactly what I'm getting myself into."

He stared at her, unwilling to speak.

She couldn't take his silence, stood, and rounded the desk, prepared to leave.

"Um—I—*you*!"

She turned slowly to face him. *Me?* "What does that mean?"

He took one of her hands in his. "I would get *you*. That's all I want. I love you."

The air froze in her lungs. Could it be true?

He continued, unaware of her swirling emotions. "Yes, when I first met you, I thought you were spoiled, but then I got to know you. You treat the servants like human beings, and they love you. The household staff is more like family to you. You're not willing to sacrifice your principles for the security of money."

She stared at him, afraid to speak, but finally found the courage. "You don't love me. You're just saying what you know I want to hear." *Tell the silly female what she wants to hear, and she'll do anything you ask.* She didn't know which hurt worse, his declaration of love when he didn't mean it, or his not saying it at all.

"I wish there was something I could say to convince you, but I know that no words would be adequate. They would all sound fabricated. Though words are my profession, I have none but this. I do love you."

Victoria ached to believe him.

"Please read it." Graham guided her around the desk and into the chair.

At the very least, she could scan what he'd written. The contract gave everything back to her. House. Money. Business holdings. As she read, an uneasiness coiled around inside her, and a verse echoed in her mind, drowning out the words on the page. *"It is easier for a camel to go through the eye of a needle, than for a rich man to enter the kingdom of God."*

She allowed her mind to ponder that verse and realized she was no different from all the men who would marry her for her uncle's money. Wasn't she considering Graham's offer partly for her uncle's inheritance? Otherwise there would be no rush. She would always wonder if Graham believed the earnestness of her declaration. She wanted him to have no doubts in her. And hadn't God pricked her heart with that verse?

She stood, came around the desk, and handed him the contract.

He turned to the last page. "You haven't signed it."

"And I'm not going to. If I sign that and marry you, I would be as dishonorable as Lord Claremont or the others."

"What are you saying?"

"Thank you for your offer, but I'm not going to marry for the sake of money." Though she desperately wanted to marry him, she knew the right thing to do was to *not* marry him to receive her uncle's vast wealth.

"So you plan to go to the final reading unmarried."

"Yes."

He lowered to one knee. "Will you marry me after the will is all settled?"

Behind her, someone gasped. She turned to see the household staff bunched together at the bottom of the stairs.

Mrs. Fuller, barely able to contain her grin, waved her on and nodded for Victoria to accept Graham's proposal.

She wanted to say yes. If he truly loved her, she would have everything she ever wanted. But if he didn't love her, then this could all be a big manipulation to marry her before the will was read, and he would take everything. "Do you truly love me?"

His smile spread wider. "I do."

Gazing down at him kneeling patiently, she believed him. Or at least, her heart believed him. And that would be enough for her. "Why would you want to marry a pauper?" She realized she didn't truly believe he loved her. Her uncle's money had always stood in the way of love, or the certainty of love.

"Because I love you. Is this some sort of test? To see if I really do love you? Because I do."

"No. No test." She wouldn't do that to him.

"Then you'll marry me."

"I'll have *nothing*." She never truly believed that anyone would fall in love with her, or at least, she wouldn't be able to believe it.

"I don't care if you have money or not. I want to spend the rest of my life with you. I can provide for you." He spread his hands. "Not at this level, but well enough."

"Then you really do love me."

He nodded.

"Yes, I'll marry you, but not to have my uncle's money, but because I love you, too."

He rose, cupped her face in his hands, and gave her a gentle kiss on the lips.

Her insides tingled with joy and love for this man. It would be a fine Christmas after all.

The servants applauded.

Chapter 10

Victoria shifted in the chair in the lawyer's office. The one she'd sat in three months ago. She couldn't believe she had to endure more of her uncle's criticism on Christmas Eve. She glanced over at Graham seated next to her.

From the folder in front of him, Mr. Frye removed two envelopes, one sealed with red wax, the other with deep indigo. "Since you didn't announce happy news the moment you walked in, shall I assume you are not married?"

She squared her shoulders. "Graham—Mr. Welling—I mean, your grandson and I are going to get married." A giddiness bubbled inside when she spoke the words.

Mr. Frye removed his spectacles. "Going to? But you are not now married?"

She shook her head.

Graham leaned forward in his chair. "We are waiting until after Mr. Helmsworthy's will is all settled." He had never once asked her nor pressured her to marry before.

"You realize that means you will only get a small stipend? Why didn't you marry yesterday?"

It had seemed wrong to her. "I didn't want to marry for money." She had gone back and forth on whether or not to marry Graham before the reading but only ever felt a peace when she landed on the side of not marrying in haste to receive the money. A peace that passed all understanding. She was doing the right thing. What God would want her to do. Trusting Him.

Graham slipped his hand around hers.

And how would Graham feel if she insisted on inheriting? He might feel she didn't think him capable of providing for her.

Mr. Frye cleaned the lenses of his glasses with his handkerchief. "So you willingly chose to *not* receive your uncle's money and holdings?"

She nodded.

The elderly solicitor shook his head, replaced his spectacles, squinted at the writing on the outside of each envelope, and set the blue one aside. He held up the other. "'To be read in the event my niece does not marry in the specified time. Signed Joseph Helmsworthy.'" He held it up for Victoria to inspect. "As you can see, the seal has not been broken."

She gave him a nod of acknowledgement.

Mr. Frye slid a letter opener under the flap and broke the seal with a soft tearing sound. He pulled out several sheets of paper and unfolded them. "'My Dearest Victoria—'"

Victoria leaned forward as much as her corset would allow. "Wait a minute. I thought you said this letter was written by my uncle?"

The old barrister gave a knowing smile. "It is. The letter should explain everything. Shall I continue?"

My Dearest Victoria? Her uncle had always referred to her as "the girl" when he spoke of her to others.

Graham touched her arm. "Let's see what he has to say."

She straightened. "Did you know about these letters?"

Graham shook his head.

Mr. Frye adjusted his position in his chair. "I assure you that Mr. Wellington had no knowledge of this. Only your uncle was privy to the contents. *I* do not even know what it holds. Joseph handed both sealed letters to me with instructions to read whichever one applied. Married or not married. If you are prepared, I will continue."

She doubted she would ever be prepared. It made no difference what was in the letter. "Proceed." But with the opening endearment, she would have a hard time believing the letter *was* from her uncle. Maybe Mr. Frye had written it on his behalf. Or her uncle had been coerced.

The old barrister adjusted his spectacles and focused his gaze back to the pages. "'My Dearest Victoria, If you are hearing this letter read, then you have given up your inheritance for love or the chance for love sometime in the future. I cannot tell you how pleased I am that this is the letter being read.'"

Why didn't he just disinherit her from the start if he hadn't wanted her to have his money? Why play this game?

As though reading her mind, Graham spoke up. "Is this really necessary? We all know what's coming."

"Whether good or bad, the execution of the will cannot be complete until after the reading."

Graham turned to her with a questioning expression.

She nodded. "I'll be fine. I want to get this over with." So she could get on with her life with Graham.

Mr. Frye continued. "'I wish I had figured out what was most important and chosen as you and my brother did, but I was an ambitious young man who could not see clearly. I chose money over the lady I loved. I believed I could earn my fortune and then win my love back. But she no longer wanted or loved me, and married a penniless man. I could see she was happy. I have regretted my decision every day of my life. You will not be living with those regrets the rest of your life.'"

How sad. Her uncle had loved but not known the worth of that love. No wonder he was so closed and distant.

"'You are a better person than I. A stronger person.'"

She couldn't believe her uncle was praising her.

"'When you first came to live in my house, I was put out. You were as foreign to me as a mermaid from the deep. I would sit and listen to your lilting voice and laughter ringing through the rooms and down the halls. I would stand at the window and watch you play in the yard and garden, not knowing how to approach you. I was afraid if I got too close, you would disappear.'"

She had never known. What she had thought was cold and aloof behavior was really fear?

"'I hope you find a man who will love you and treat you like a princess.'"

She glanced at Graham. She had.

"'Since you have again not disappointed me, I have something to add to your monthly stipend.'" Mr. Frye quit reading aloud, but his eyes still moved back and forth as though reading.

"What is it?" Victoria asked.

Mr. Frye removed his spectacles and looked up. "He's left you everything."

"What do you mean?"

He replaced his glasses. "'You chose love over money, so you shall have both. I give you the money, now go find love.'"

He turned to the next page. "'Now for the business of business. Though Collin Nelson has been an exemplary manager over all my holdings, he has a low opinion of women's ability to manage business affairs. I have arranged for a generous departing bonus for him, and today he will be given a one-month notice to leave. I have no doubt you will be able to manage things once you learn about my—*your* different businesses. Run them, sell them, do what you like with them. The overseers of my businesses are all good, trustworthy men. I hope you choose to keep them on.'"

Victoria couldn't believe what she was hearing.

"'As I do not wish for you to trouble yourself with the day-to-day business affairs, I have a list of suggested men to step into Mr. Nelson's place as overall manager. One possibility is Mr. Max Hodges, who oversees all of my shipping endeavors, a strong choice to promote to manager over all your holdings. Another could be Mr. Henry Forthright, who looks after my steel and gold mine holdings. He would do a fine job for you as well. Or perhaps, Mr. Graham Wellington—'"

Graham shot to his feet. "Me?"

Victoria gazed up at him.

He stared at her. "I had no knowledge of this. I *am* capable of providing for a wife. For you. I love you."

She knew all of that. Mr. Frye had said neither of them knew the contents of the letter. She took his hand. "I know. Please sit."

He remained standing.

"Mr. Helmsworthy and I spoke at length about you. I had no idea all his inquiries were for this purpose. May I continue?"

"Pardon my outburst." Graham lowered himself back into the chair.

"'Mr. Graham Wellington, Mr. Frye's grandson, is younger than the other two candidates, and you might be more comfortable with someone closer to your age. Mr. Frye vouches for his trustworthiness.'" The old attorney folded the letter and shifted a stack of papers in front of him. "I just need you to sign a few documents."

Victoria sat silent for a long moment while both men stared, waiting for her to say something. She couldn't believe this turn of events. She had been prepared to receive only the small stipend and had been content with that. She didn't know if she wanted all that wealth and responsibility. "What if I don't sign?"

Mr. Frye sputtered before speaking. "Don't sign? Why ever not?"

Shifting in his chair, Graham faced her. "Then the courts will decide who and where your uncle's assets will go. Don't worry. I will provide for you either way, but I don't want you to have to sacrifice."

He didn't seem concerned at all about not having her uncle's money. He respected her and was leaving the decision up to her.

Mr. Frye sputtered again. "You entered my office a pauper. You don't have to leave that way."

Victoria had spent the past three months accepting that she wouldn't receive a penny over the stipend the will had allotted, preparing herself for that inevitability.

True, her uncle had never been openly affectionate toward her, but neither had he been cruel. He had bought her expensive things when she wanted them, like pretty dresses, a string of pearls, and the automobiles. Maybe those gifts had been the only way he knew to express his affection for her.

Her uncle had loved her after all. She wished she had realized as much while he was still alive. Love came in all manner of varieties. Her uncle's was expressed with patience, freedom to make her own choices, and the showering of gifts. She could see where he had been generous with his money.

She picked up the pen and hesitated. But what about God? What did He want her to do? She sensed a nod of approval. She gazed at Graham. He loved her with or without her uncle's money. A sudden glee bubbled up inside her. She was loved by the man she was in love with *and* wealthy. The good she could do with the money was unimaginable. With a confident smile, she signed the required documents. "Shall we go find a minister?"

Graham wore a cautious expression. "I don't have the contract giving you control of all your uncle's—*your* assets."

"It's not necessary." With love on her side, she felt safe. "We'll manage everything together."

Graham wrapped her in his arms and kissed her soundly.

A merry Christmas after all!

Mary Davis is an award-winning author of over a dozen novels in both historical and contemporary themes, four novellas, two compilations, and three short stories, as well as being included in various collections. She is a member of American Christian Fiction Writers and is active in two critique groups.

Mary lives in the Colorado Rocky Mountains with her husband of over thirty years and two cats. She has three adult children and one grandchild. She enjoys playing board and card games, rain, and cats. She would enjoy gardening if she didn't have a black thumb. Her hobbies include quilting, porcelain doll making, sewing, crafts, crocheting, and knitting.

In for a Penny

by Susanne Dietze

Dedication

For my patient, encouraging, hilarious family. I am blessed to love and be loved by you.
With loving thanks to Anita Mae Draper, Debra E. Marvin, and Gina Welborn
for their friendship and gracious help when I wrote this story.

Are not two sparrows sold for a penny? and not one of them shall fall on the ground without your Father. . . . Fear not therefore: ye are of more value than many sparrows.
Matthew 10:29, 31 ASV

In for a penny, in for a pound.
English Proverb

Chapter 1

Philadelphia
September, 1894

"Did you see it, Penny? You're famous." Fair-haired Alma Shore hurried forward, grinning and waving a crisp sheet of newsprint like a fan.

Penelope Beale's steps faltered. She'd asked Alma, her dearest friend, to meet her at the Pennsylvania Museum and School of Industrial Art so she might escape that sheet of newspaper—or rather, what it reported.

Apparently, escape was impossible. "Mother was pleased." An understatement if ever Penny had uttered one.

"Now your mama can keep one, and you can paste this one in a memory book." Alma held out the sheet, so Penny tucked it into her beaded bag.

The thought of pasting the tidbit in a memory book made Penny's jaw clench. Nevertheless, Alma's intentions were kind, and it wasn't Alma's fault Penny was in this mess.

Penny took Alma's arm as raindrops began pattering in slow percussion against their picture hats. "You're thoughtful, dear. Thank you."

Alma squeezed Penny closer as they hurried inside the museum. "I confess to all manner of shock that you wished to leave the house today, what with tonight's huge event."

Huge? Hardly. But Penny understood Alma's meaning. While the guest list was tiny compared to most of Mother's parties, the evening was colossal in terms of its impact on Penny's future.

But she'd rather not think of her duty. Not while she still had a few precious hours of freedom left. "I need distraction today. I spent the morning at the Home for Friendless Girls, but I wanted to spend time with you, too."

Distraction wasn't on Mother's mind, however, when she allowed Penny out of the house today. She'd insisted that it might be of benefit for Penny to be spied around town after this morning's mention in the society pages. That way, it would not appear as if Penny languished at home over a gentleman.

Appearances mattered a great deal in the Beale household. Every objet d'art on every stick of fashionable furniture in their grand house spoke to the Beale family's wealth. So did every stitch of clothing they wore, including Penny's blue-and-cocoa Worth ensemble from Paris.

Perhaps that was the biggest reason Mother wasn't enthusiastic about Penny's work at the Home for Friendless Girls. No one saw fit to describe it in the society pages.

A pity. The home would need a new patroness once Penny moved to England. She could continue to send financial support, but who would step into her place, reading to the girls?

The tightening of her chest started Penny down a road of anxiety she must stop now, before it got too late. She took a deep breath, remembering the kind face of her governess, Miss Foster—a name Penny couldn't pronounce as a small child and had shortened to Frosty.

Frosty used to hold Penny close when she was anxious, cradling Penny's cheeks in her hands and reminding her to breathe. *God is with you.*

If Frosty were here, she'd look Penny in the eye and do the same. Frosty was with God now, but her love and wisdom remained in Penny's heart. Thankful that Frosty had taught her about God's care, Penny breathed and remembered she could trust Him to provide for the girls' home.

And for her own life, too, at this time of change.

Alma sighed, drawing Penny's attention to the present. Her friend scrutinized a sculpture, a quizzical look wrinkling her delicate nose. Everything about Alma was delicate: her tiny build and diminutive stature made her look like a fashionable doll. Alma nudged Penny. "I am poor company in a museum. I pretend to understand art for the sake of appearances."

Appearances again. Penny shook her head. "No need to pretend with a dear friend."

Except, perhaps, when it came to the topic of today's society pages. Penny couldn't dishonor her parents by confiding in Alma—at least, not yet, and not in public.

Besides, the facts listed in the newspaper were true. There was no disputing them:

Lionel Retford, Earl of Hawton, of Nottinghamshire, England, arrived in Philadelphia yesterday, taking rooms at the Bellevue. His lordship dines tonight at the Rittenhouse Square home of Mr. and Mrs. Edwin Beale and their daughter, Miss Penelope Beale, and is expected to attend the family's upcoming ball.

The report was true, but tantalizing in its suggestion. One needn't speculate overlong to suspect the earl did not cross the Atlantic to attend a ball. . . .

Unless it was held to celebrate his betrothal to the Beales' daughter.

Anxiety squeezed Penny's rib cage tighter than her corset. She couldn't get enough air to quell the panicky feeling swirling in her stomach.

You are with me, God. You are with me—

"You'll be a lady, a titled English lady," Alma whispered. "Can you credit such a thing?"

Oh, this wasn't helping at all. "Lord Hawton has not asked yet. My, look at this sculpture—"

"He'll propose," Alma interrupted. "Why wouldn't he? You're kind, well mannered, exquisite to look at, and your hair was the envy of Newport this summer—don't tell me it wasn't." Her gaze raked Penny's chestnut coiffure, pinned under her picture hat.

Ridiculous. It wasn't Penny's pompadour style that Lionel, the well-bred but cash-poor Lord Hawton, wanted.

It was her inheritance. But she couldn't tell Alma that.

Panicky jitters spread to Penny's legs and arms. Thinking of Lord Hawton tended to do that to her. She'd met him a handful of times in London, and while he was pleasant enough, they'd discussed naught but weather, a play they saw, and his enjoyment of grouse hunting in August. There had been no spark of attraction, no meeting of minds, no talk of anything spiritual—all things Penny had wished for in a husband. Yet her parents thought him perfect for her.

Or rather, they thought his title perfect, a fair exchange for a significant dowry that would shore up his crumbling estate.

"Lord Hawton already has a little daughter for you to love, too." Alma's hand landed over her heart. "I cannot wait for a family of my own. But Mama doesn't want to part from me."

What a twist. Penny's parents were shipping her to England while Alma's mother couldn't bear to say goodbye.

Alma released her arm, as if mistaking Penny's quaver for the desire to examine something else.

Breathe. God is here. Look at the art.

Then she saw it, a painting on the opposite wall, beckoning her to step closer. She strolled toward it, her gaze locked on the pastoral scene of a stable's interior, complete with sheep and chickens illumined by shafts of sunlight peeking through the rough wooden planks of the barn. A peaceful image, it reminded her of scenes of Jesus' birth, although no baby lay in the feeding trough. Another museum patron viewed the painting, but there was ample room beside him for her to admire the canvas, too.

Nevertheless, her gaze flickered to the man beside her. Tall and slender, he wore a gray suit and a moss-green ascot tie that complemented his coffee-brown hair. To her surprise, he smiled down at her.

"Serene, isn't it?" His accent betrayed him as an Englishman.

Mother would never approve of her exchanging anything more than a curt nod with a strange man, yet he'd said nothing untoward. And something about him beckoned her to continue a conversation. "That's what I like best about it. I might have commented about the composition, or Verboeckhoven's talent, but you phrased it best. The serenity of the scene."

Dark eyes twinkled at her from a lean, handsome face. "You're familiar with the artist?"

Caught. Heat surged up from her chest to her neck. "Not in the least. His name is labeled on the plaque."

He laughed, and she joined in. My, he was attractive. She'd encountered her share of well-to-do, nice-looking fellows, both at home and on her European trip earlier this year with her parents. But none had captured her attention quite like this one.

Penny compressed her lips. She'd best stop this at once—whatever this was. A flutter of attraction for a complete stranger? She was not at liberty to entertain such a notion. She returned her attention to the painting.

He shifted. "I'm glad you're not familiar with the artist. It frees you to interpret the work on your own, without someone telling you how it's supposed to make you feel or what to think about it."

Not being told how to feel or what to think? The idea of such liberty made Penny's chest ache. "I've never thought of art that way."

Or that her feelings and thoughts mattered, beyond shoving them down so she might better obey her parents. Frosty had listened to her, but that was so long ago now.

"A true tragedy." The gentleman smiled, revealing even teeth and charming dimples in his clean-shaven cheeks. "I hope such perspective helps you view things differently in the future."

By *things* he meant art, of course, but it applied to her life, too. In her twenty-one years, she'd never needed to hear another's words more. Peace settled over her shoulders like a cozy cashmere scarf. "It will."

Thank You for dropping this man on my path today, Lord. No matter what happens this evening, I will remember what this man's words made me realize: that You care about my feelings and thoughts, and You alone can help them become what You wish them to be.

And what God seemed to wish was that she wed Lord Hawton.

"I enjoyed our chat." His accent made the words sound like honey and cream.

A man of thirty or so years in a brown plaid suit blustered into the room, dripping wet from the rain. When he spied the gentleman beside Penny, his shoulders sagged in relief. "Sorry to be late, chap." Another Englishman.

"I scarcely noticed, Whitacre." The gentleman bowed his head at her. "Good day."

"Good day, sir. And thank you."

Alma studied a painting as if trying to memorize it. Penny drew alongside, curving her arm through her friend's. A few more paintings and it would be time to go home and get ready to receive Lionel, Lord Hawton, her future husband.

Perhaps she should ask the Lord to help her be happier about it.

◆ ◆ ◆

"I say." Seymour Whitacre waved his hand before Emmett Retford's nose. "Quit looking at her."

Emmett dragged his gaze from the lady in blue, who sauntered from the room arm in arm with her friend. "Sorry, Whitacre. You were saying?"

"If you find the master of the house trustworthy, then I trust your instincts. Tell him. It's easier to get the information we need when amateurs like you aren't skulking about for it."

"Amateur?" Emmett laughed. "You wound me. My previous task for you went off quite well, thank you very much."

"Don't be smug. All you had to do was verify the authenticity of that Rubens."

"At no small cost. I was stuck at that abysmal house party."

Whitacre scratched behind his ear, mussing his macassar-slick black hair. "Let's hope tonight isn't so dreary for you then, eh? I'll meet you at my hotel tomorrow for a report."

The rest of the afternoon, Emmett couldn't stop smiling. Whitacre was one to lift the spirits, of course, but the young lady in blue he'd encountered in the art museum charmed him to his shoes.

What was her name? It would have been bold and impertinent to ask her outright, but he hoped they'd encounter one another again.

Then he'd learn her name.

If it's Your will, God, anything is possible.

Even achieving his secret task for the Crown, the real reason he came to Philadelphia.

Well, that bit of spy work, and his niece, Viola.

Viola's rap on his wrist dragged him to the present, where they sat on the plush-carpeted floor of their suite at the Bellevue. "Uncle Emmett, you aren't listening."

"Sorry, poppet. Lost in thought." He shifted positions, crossing his legs on the other side of the pretend tea table Viola had built of several stacked books. "What was it Amelie did?"

Amelie, Viola's doll, slumped on the cushions at his side, her porcelain face smeared with scarlet.

"Ate all the strawberry jam." Viola shook her head, making her brown curls bounce. Even at seven years of age, she looked like a dowager when she made that disapproving face. "How rude of her."

"Amelie must be hungry." But where had Viola hidden the jam while Emmett daydreamed about the dark-haired miss from the museum? Some doting uncle he was. He peeked under the floral cobalt fabric skirting the chair beside them. Ah, there was the pot of jam. Better that he found it than the hotel's housekeeping staff. America may lack some of the formalities of home, or so he'd heard, but forgotten jam pots moldering under the furniture were no doubt unpleasant surprises in every country.

He was wiping sticky jam off his fingers when Viola's governess, Miss Partridge, bustled into the parlor. A woman of middle years, she wore a plain gray gown, a starched cap, and a sweet expression. She bobbed a curtsy. "Mr. Retford, sir."

Viola pointed at her doll. "Amelie ate the jam, Miss Partridge."

"We shall clean the both of you up at once, then." Miss Partridge's smile was indulgent. Emmett once again thanked God that Viola was cared for by such a compassionate woman.

It must be time for Viola's bath. And for Emmett to leave for dinner. He rose to his full height and stretched his cramped legs. "Did you finish your pudding, poppet?"

Viola scraped her fork over her plate to capture every crumb of the jam-and-biscuit dessert. "It wasn't pudding, Uncle Emmett. It was a tea party."

"Of course. Thank you for the tea, Lady Viola, Miss Amelie. Until morning?"

She spun to Miss Partridge. "I want to go with Uncle and Papa."

"Not this time." Miss Partridge patted Viola's shoulder.

"Tomorrow." Emmett bent to wipe the smear of jam from Amelie's porcelain face with his linen napkin before the matter was forgotten and Viola clutched the doll to her white pinafore. "Tonight is for the adults."

Her tiny lips curled into a pout, even as her father, Emmett's eldest brother Lionel, entered the parlor from his chamber. His evening finery resembled Emmett's, although it was sharper; no doubt helped by his valet, Lionel looked the heir he was, from the soles of his leather shoes to the silk of his top hat. Emmett managed to knot a reasonable-looking white tie about his neck himself, and his black wool tailcoat didn't sport a speck of lint, but he would never make the sort of impression Lionel did because he lacked that indescribable something in manner that conveyed nobility. And as a fourth son, he never would.

Not that he minded. How could he, when his life was so rich? Uncle to Viola, with work he enjoyed, and now this secret errand for Queen and country?

A thrill of anticipation shot through his limbs. He'd come to Philadelphia for this purpose. Now he had an additional objective for his visit, to return to the museum he visited today, in hopes that the dark-haired lady in blue visited, too.

"Are you whistling?" Lionel's brow scrunched.

Emmett caught his lips midpucker. "I daresay I was."

"Uncle Emmett isn't attending today." Viola stood on tiptoe for Lionel's brief kiss to her crown. "Good night, Papa."

Emmett bent to hug her. "Sleep well, poppet."

Lionel waited in the vestibule, smoothing his neat mustache. "We mustn't be tardy."

With a nod to Miss Partridge, Emmett hastened after Lionel. The cool evening air swirled down his collar and chilled his spine, and the carriage wasn't much warmer. He'd heard Americans overheated their homes, however, and he wondered if it would be so tonight.

"Nervous, Lionel?"

"Not too. It's a solid arrangement, and the lady is a decent sort."

Emmett shook his head. "Sounds like a merger, not a marriage."

"It is both. Look where marrying for love got me the first time. Brief happiness, but now we've had to sell off anything that wasn't entailed. If I don't make a practical alliance this time, it'll devastate us."

Us? Emmett didn't live at Hawton Park anymore. Still, the estate was part of his heritage. "Have faith."

"I don't need faith. I need a million pounds sterling."

"And a mother for Viola?" That would have been Emmett's top priority.

Lionel shrugged. "Miss Partridge does what needs doing, but speaking of mothers... I should like an heir, although the line is secure enough, between you and our brothers—ah, we are here." The carriage pulled to a halt in a neat neighborhood of fine houses built around a grassy park. The dwelling to their right appeared crafted of stone, with a grand entrance flanked by Greek-style columns and marble statuary.

Mr. Beale's banking fortune was enormous to afford such a residence.

Lionel smoothed his mustache again. "Ready to meet my bride?"

Pity for the young lady soured Emmett's stomach. "She hasn't said yes yet, brother."

They stepped out of the carriage, and Lionel's confused features were illumined in the streetlamps. "Why wouldn't she? She'll be a countess."

Her money for Lionel's title. The exquisite town manor before them for the freezing cold, crumbling pile of stone back in England. What an exchange.

At least Emmett wouldn't share such a fate. "Some of us wish to marry for love."

"Some of us can't afford to. All we Retfords have is our breeding and a pile of debt."

"And our dignity."

Emmett also had a modest salary from the university and a faith in God. And when he wed, he'd want a woman who was his friend. Someone with a giving heart. And yes, he wanted love, too. For there to be a flash of attraction, as he'd experienced with the lady in blue today at the museum, a spark that would grow into something lasting and deep.

Lionel rapped the massive front door with his silver-tipped walking stick. Emmett squared his shoulders as the door opened to admit them.

Within a moment they were ensconced in a grand foyer, decorated with marble and gold. A manservant took their coats and led them to an elaborate parlor trimmed in red and dark wood, where a couple with gray tingeing their dark hair waited near the marble hearth. Behind them was a slender woman. Lionel's intended—

Her. The lady in blue from the museum.

Emmett almost forgot to bow and smile when Lionel introduced him to Mr. and Mrs. Beale and their daughter, Penelope.

Her name was Penelope.

He'd daydreamed about visiting the museum tomorrow at the same time on the chance she would be there again, too. But now, she'd be in his life through the decades to come.

As his brother's wife.

Chapter 2

Penny's mouth stuck around the polite words of greeting she'd rehearsed for Lionel and his youngest brother. *So good to see you again, Lord Hawton. Nice to meet you, Mr. Retford.*

But the words weren't appropriate anymore. She'd already met Emmett Retford at the museum.

Everyone peered at her with expectant expressions, except for him. His chocolate-brown eyes reflected her sense of astonishment.

Penny! The voice in her head might as well have been Mother's scold, but it broke her tongue loose. "Welcome, Lord Hawton. Mr. Retford. So good to see you again."

So good to see *Lord Hawton* again, she should have said. Mother's glance was sharp.

Mr. Retford tipped his head toward Mother. "Miss Beale and I shared a few passing comments on a canvas at the museum today. I'd no idea she was Miss Beale, of course."

How kind of him to save her from her slip. Penny smiled her thanks. His return smile melted something in her knees.

"Please." Father bade them to be seated. Then he coughed, a dry, unproductive sound that made Penny's stomach swoop. Father coughed like that when he experienced a heart palpitation, as a way to "get the drum beating again," he would say. The palpitations were harmless, he'd said, but induced by too much work. Would he rest easier soon? She prayed so.

Penny took a spot on the brocade sofa, expecting Lord Hawton—oh, she must think of him as Lionel if she was to become his wife—to sit beside her.

Instead, he settled into a wingback chair near Father. "Emmett cannot stay away from museums and galleries, I fear. You may recall he is an art historian."

Mother tipped her head to the side, allowing the lamplight to land on the diamonds at her throat. "You are a collector, Mr. Retford?"

"A professor." Mr. Retford—Emmett, since he was to be family—sat across from Penny in the lone available seat.

He did not look much like Lionel. There was the same trim build, but Emmett was taller, more solid. If Lionel didn't slick back his hair, it might prove to be the same gold-tinged brown of Emmett's. Lionel's mustache might be fashionable, but Penny preferred Emmett's clean-shaven look—

Mother cleared her throat, drawing Penny to attention. Heat prickled at her cheeks. She should be conversing, not comparing her almost-fiancé to his brother. "You teach, then, Mr. Retford?"

"At Oxford, but I am a consultant, too. I won't bore you with details."

"I am not bored in the least." It was true. Mother must have found the prospect dull, however, because she turned toward Father and Lionel. "Did you enjoy your visit with your friend?"

"Whitacre and I were at university together. Faithful friend. He gave me a ride home from school when Viola was born."

Lionel's daughter. All Penny knew was Viola's mother died in childbirth. "I look forward to meeting her tomorrow."

Emmett's face transformed. "She's amazing, you'll see."

"You're fond of her." Odd how she'd not yet had a full conversation with Lionel about Viola. Nor had Lionel's features brightened at the mention of her the way Emmett's did.

"As if she were my own."

"Does she know how to read?" The moment she asked, she regretted it. Now Emmett would think her as odd as Mother did.

His brows rose. "Simple sentences, yes."

"I teach reading at the Home for Friendless Girls. They were orphaned by a cholera epidemic four years ago. I missed them while I was in Europe and then in Newport for the summer. But please do not judge me as ungrateful for my travels." She knew how blessed she was to see the world.

"On the contrary, Miss Beale. I have formed quite the opposite impression of you."

A kind comment, since he hardly knew her.

But something passed between them at the museum and again here in the parlor, right under the noses of her parents and his brother. Something as bright and unexpected as a bolt of lightning before a storm, lifting the hairs on her arms and capturing her breath.

Perhaps this was what poets described as infatuation. Penny had never experienced it before, but she knew a marriage forged on attraction alone would not fare well without friendship and love.

Unless you were Mother, who thought an English title more important than compatibility.

But a title of nobility didn't mean a man was noble in spirit, did it? One's lineage didn't indicate one's worth, and marriage should be based on more than money.

Perhaps she shouldn't be thinking about marriage while looking at Emmett, whose smile made her toes curl in her silk shoes.

She was to marry Lionel. This attraction to Emmett would pass. She must not give in to it. Indeed, she must introduce a new, nonthreatening subject of conversation until Lionel and her parents included them in their conversation. Art again, or England?

She settled on both. "One of my favorite memories of London was the art."

"Did you have a favorite piece?" He looked like he wanted to know. Then again, he was an art historian.

"Everything. Sculpture. The glass and architecture of the cathedrals. Tapestries. The illuminations in medieval manuscripts."

"The work of skilled craftsmen gifted by God." His broad, approving smile did not help her smother her attraction to him. "Your parents acquired several new pieces on their voyage, did they not?"

Panels and tapestries. Paintings and vases. Mother thought such items lent an air of wealth and history to their homes. "Indeed."

His eyes darkened. "Including a pair of paintings by Gainsborough, perchance? A gentleman poses with books, and a lady with a map?"

"They hang in Father's office. You're familiar with them?"

"They used to hang in Hawton Park, our home in Nottinghamshire. The subjects were our mother's ancestors."

How awkward. To think Mother had asked Emmett if he was a collector, when his family had found it necessary to part with paintings of family members to pay bills. "I am sorry."

"Don't be. The paintings were relegated to the attic some time ago. I'm relieved they are appreciated once again."

"Would you like to see them?"

His feet planted, as if preparing to stand. "Please."

Now? She'd meant after dinner. But he seemed so eager.

Farrow, the English butler her parents had brought back some years ago, entered the parlor. "Dinner is served."

Emmett's fingers fidgeted against his sides. "Another time, perhaps."

She stood. "Soon."

After all, she'd be seeing plenty of Lionel, who must be excited about marrying her, given that he had brought his daughter and brother all the way to America to meet her.

The thought cheered her, until Lionel offered her the most mechanical of smiles before escorting her into dinner.

If he was happy to make her his bride, he hid it well.

◆ ◆ ◆

The next morning, Emmett struggled to hide his good opinion of Penny. Not that he could say aloud that she was the loveliest woman of his acquaintance, so he settled for something else. "Bang-up shot, Miss Beale."

Penny grinned, a vision under a grass-green picture hat that matched her dress and the stripes on her croquet mallet and ball—a becoming coincidence. Her steps were light on the lawn behind the house, as if she didn't mind a whit if her shoes or hem would be stained by dewy grass. "You may call me Penny, if you like, Mr. Retford."

He'd called her that in his thoughts since meeting her last night. "And I am Emmett." He probably should have tacked on *your new brother*.

"Viola and I are in the lead now."

Naturally, the mallet and ball Viola chose were trimmed with yellow, her favorite color. "Do not be sad, Uncle Emmett. One must be a good sport, win or lose."

"True, Viola," he said, exchanging amused glances with Penny.

Viola squatted to view her shot. "You tell me all the time."

Penny's laugh tickled his ears, and it was impossible not to join in.

Viola took her shot. It missed the hoop by several inches, and she frowned. He sauntered to where his red ball awaited him on the grass, patting the top of her miniature picture hat as he passed. "Think of it as a kindness, poppet. You've offered me the opportunity to redeem myself."

"To win, you mean." Viola looked to Penny. "He thinks he is funny."

"He is." Penny grinned. "Although we are not truly competing. I thought Father would join us as he loves a good match, but with three of us, we play for enjoyment, not the contest."

Emmett gave it his best shot, anyway. *Thwack.* The ball rolled through the hoop, knocking Penny's green ball to the left. She'd not mind the hit, since it gave her a better angle for her next shot.

"Thank you for setting me up, sir." Her voice was teasing. "He plays well, Viola, but I think we may best him, after all."

"Oh, I do hope so. Despite what I said earlier, winning is more enjoyable than losing."

"I thought we were not competing," Emmett reminded them.

Giggles overtook Viola, and he and Penny laughed with her. Their subsequent shots all missed their marks, but no one minded the silliness.

At least, Emmett didn't think anyone minded. Lionel and Penny's parents sat on the veranda, chairs facing the expanse of lawn and an excellent view of the game, but it didn't appear that any of them watched. Instead, Mr. and Mrs. Beale's heads turned toward Lionel.

Rather than woo Penny's parents, Lionel might have done better to play croquet and grow better acquainted with Penny—and his daughter, who skipped toward a bed of fading pink roses. She reached to take one in hand.

"Take care, Viola." Penny's tone was gentle. "The thorns on that bush are tiny but sharp. Like puppy teeth."

"I want a puppy, but Papa says no. The hounds are enough." Viola's fingers stroked rosy petals. "But hounds don't live inside, and their mouths foam. And there are so many of them at Hawton Park."

"How many?" Penny paused over her shot, her expression tentative.

"Dozens."

Emmett shook his head at Penny. *Not quite*, he mouthed.

She laughed and struck the ball with the mallet. "If you like, Viola, I will ensure a bouquet of those roses goes back to the Bellevue with you. They are a sorry substitute for a puppy, but I hope you enjoy them nonetheless."

"They smell better than the hounds." Viola danced back.

"I second that." Emmett stepped up to his red ball. *Thwack.* A solid shot. The ladies clapped for him.

They continued the round, with Viola twirling and Penny chatting and Emmett teasing, but something gnawed at his abdomen. Lionel.

How could he miss out on spending time with his daughter and future wife?

Perhaps Lionel still felt the need to solidify things with her parents, but in Emmett's understanding, the arrangement was secure, or else Lionel wouldn't have made the trip across the Atlantic.

Did Penny find the prospect of marrying Lionel suitable, too?

If Penny felt affection for Lionel, it didn't show. And he'd been watching her. Couldn't stop watching her.

So she didn't necessarily love Lionel. Did she want to be Countess of Hawton as badly as her parents seemed to wish it? Or did she do this in obedience to them?

The answer mattered a great deal to him.

A blond servant set a tray of lemonade and petits fours on a white wicker table nearby. Penny bade the young fellow pause. "Clark, I'd like to send a bouquet of roses home with Lady Viola. And if there are enough, I'd like a few more bouquets for tomorrow. This may be the last of the season."

"Yes, miss."

"What's tomorrow?" Viola gave voice to Emmett's question.

"I'll visit the Home for Friendless Girls. I like to take a few bouquets of whatever is in bloom. Every young lady enjoys flowers, don't you think?"

Ah, the orphans she'd mentioned last night. "You mentioned reading to the girls, but clearly you do more."

"Flowers aren't the same as a kettle of porridge or new stockings, but if I can add cheer to their rooms with flowers or rugs, it is not much. I receive more from them than I give. Viola, your turn."

Emmett knew then why she was marrying Lionel. Not out of greed for his title. Not because she wanted to leave Philadelphia, either, because her heart resided with those girls. She was marrying Lionel out of obedience to her parents.

She tapped her green ball to strike the center peg and end the croquet match. And even though he shouldn't, he couldn't help liking everything about her. Even the obedience that led to her engagement to his brother.

"We've won, Miss Beale!"

"Well done, Viola." She embraced his niece and then shook Emmett's hand. "A fine game."

"I thought we were not competing," he teased, still holding her hand.

Lionel sauntered toward them across the lawn. It felt as if the day grew dimmer.

"Now, Viola," Lionel said in that tone of his that stiffened Emmett's shoulders, "Miss Partridge wouldn't like you leaping about like a hoyden."

Viola's shoulders slumped.

"Viola has been most ladylike." Penny's defense of Viola made Emmett's shoulders relax. "We made an excellent team."

Viola's countenance brightened again. "We won, Papa. Ladies over lads. But Uncle Emmett will be a good loser."

"Of course I will." Emmett chucked her chin.

He'd be a good loser in the game, and in the coming years if the burgeoning pull in his chest for Penny didn't die.

I shouldn't be drawn to my brother's intended. Please, God. Kill this attraction, so I can feel for her as a brother would.

He'd never before been jealous of his eldest brother, but the visceral twist of envy coiled in his chest now. Lionel, Penny, and Viola stood conversing on the grass, creating a tableau of familial bliss. And he wanted what his brother had. Not the title or estates, but Penny.

Focus on your task. Emmett turned away, stuffing the jealousy down. He was not in Philadelphia to fall in love with someone he could never have. Or even to lend support for Lionel and Viola as they welcomed Penny into their family.

He was sent here by the Prince of Wales for one reason. The portrait of his ancestor Lady Dunwood, sold by Lionel and purchased by Mr. Beale. Penny said it now hung in her father's study. There hadn't been opportunity for him to view it after dinner last night—not with Lionel dominating the conversation.

Emmett must gain entrance to Mr. Beale's study and do what must be done.

His old college chum, Seymour Whitacre, would be waiting tonight for a report of Emmett's progress. Yet so far, he had naught but a sorry tale of romantic angst to share.

Some spy he made.

Chapter 3

The next morning, Penny straightened the cuffs of her serviceable russet gown and ordered the carriage to be brought around.

"The food and flowers are already packed, miss." Clark's smile revealed twin dimples in his cheeks, as if he enjoyed visiting the girls' home as much as she did.

Penny hastened to the morning room, where Mother enjoyed tea and the society pages. "Good morning, Mother."

Mother eyed Penny's gown with distaste. "Really, Penny? Today?"

"I am the home's patroness."

"I do not take umbrage with your spending time there. 'Tis your timing that grieves me. Lord Hawton and his brother are expected for luncheon, and you invited Alma and her mother, too."

"I shall be home well in advance." Penny's gloves felt damp against her palms. "This isn't a typical visit to the home. I must know the girls are taken care of when I m–marry. They need a new patroness, so I invited Alma to accompany me."

"And you think Alma a suitable replacement?" Mother's eyes widened in surprise. "What a charming idea."

Suddenly it was easier to breathe. "I thought so."

"If Alma appears charitable, maybe she'll land more suitors. She's richer than we are, so it's a wonder she hasn't been pursued. If she'd gone to England, she might be a duchess by now. Pity her mother's kept her on such a tight rein since her father died."

Penny's fingers twisted. The true pity was that Mother thought Alma's most attractive quality was her wealth. "Alma has love to spare, and her father passed in the cholera epidemic, too. Just like their parents."

"Mm." Mother's gaze was back on the newspaper.

She should just go, but something held her back. "I'm not certain Lionel cares for me, Mother."

Mother gaped. "What nonsense is this? You're charming." Mother's favorite word.

"He doesn't speak to me." She'd tried yesterday, but the conversation had been so stilted. Not at all like it was with Emmett—

She *must* stop comparing them. It served no purpose but to make her wish for something she couldn't have.

"Those Englishmen hide their emotions." Mother sighed. "He wouldn't be here if he didn't wish to marry you."

"It's the money he wants."

"It would grieve your father's heart if you brought such concerns to him as you've brought to me." Mother didn't mean it metaphorically, either. Father's palpitations—harmless though Father claimed them to be—were of cause for concern.

Maybe Penny should give it more of a chance. She bent to kiss Mother's rose-scented cheek. "I won't say a word to Father."

"Perhaps Lord Hawton will have a friend for Alma. Then she could move to England, too."

How cheerful Mother was at the prospect of sending her only child across the ocean. Penny cast the thought aside. Mother didn't mean it that way, but sometimes her careless words made Penny feel small. Unnecessary.

That was not the case at the Home for Friendless Girls.

Friendless was a horrid euphemism for the orphans, but Penny determined not a one of them would feel friendless, ever. They stood in a line in the vestibule, fourteen in all, aged six to thirteen, donned in matching navy pinafores. Miss Brice, the tall headmistress with a wide smile, bade them curtsy.

"How pretty you are," Alma pronounced. And it was obvious she meant it. Penny's chest warmed.

Miss Brice exclaimed over the fragrant roses and set the bouquets in the main room, where clean benches and tables offered work, study, and dining space. Penny and Alma spent the next hour reading aloud while Miss Brice unpacked the provisions Clark had brought around to the kitchen.

Wind rattled the shutters against the window, startling Penny. Then she consulted the watch pinned to her shirtwaist. "Alma, we will be late."

They bid the girls and Miss Brice farewell, hastening into the carriage. Alma took Penny's hand. "What a wonderful day. Time with your girls and now luncheon with an honest-to-goodness earl."

But it wasn't the earl Penny most wished to see today. Nevertheless, once the guests arrived, Penny bade Lionel to sit beside her on the settee. Her ribs ached with each breath, but she must get over this anxiety if she ever hoped to breathe comfortably again. Speaking of something—or someone—familiar seemed a good place to start.

"Viola is delightful." She smiled. "How does she enjoy Philadelphia?"

Lionel seemed surprised by the question. "Well, I suppose."

She waited a moment, but he didn't elaborate. If only he'd furthered the conversation, rather than simply answering her query. Penny tipped her head. "How does she spend her time?"

"Lessons with her governess."

"And adventures with Amelie, her doll," Emmett added. "Today they are flying a kite in the park."

Father laughed. "Good day for it, with this wind."

"Did you say doll?" Alma's question drew every eye. Then she flushed a becoming shade of rose. "Pardon me, but I didn't notice a one at the girls' home this morning."

Penny searched her memory. "I've not seen one, either."

"Perhaps we should remedy that." Alma glanced at Lionel.

"A capital idea. I should be happy to fund the endeavor." Lionel smiled, showing far more enthusiasm than Penny had observed before.

"Perhaps your daughter should help pick them out," Alma suggested. "She would know best what other girls like."

Lionel nodded. "I'll speak to her governess."

Emmett's gaze drew Penny's again, sending flutters through her abdomen. He looked so dapper in his dark blue suit.

"I had wondered about something for the girls' home, too," he said. "Art for the girls."

"A course of appreciation?"

"Application. They've had such rough lives, and time with a brush or pastel could offer them a way to express themselves creatively. I'd be happy to donate the supplies. Viola and I could come with you and show your girls how to use them."

Art to express themselves. Dolls to love and tend. God was answering her prayer. The girls were under the Lord's wing, and He would care for them. What a blessing that He'd chosen to provide through Alma, Lionel, and Emmett.

His hand was at work in her life. Even in this marriage she didn't want.

"They would like it very much." She smiled at Emmett.

After luncheon the group fractured into smaller conversations in the parlor. Lionel perched near Alma in the chairs by the windows, explaining grouse hunting. Penny wasn't certain whether to feel slighted or relieved, but Alma, bless her, looked enraptured. Mrs. Shore and Mother shared the settee, and Father and Emmett—

Weren't here. Curious.

But their absence inspired Penny to slip out for a moment, too. She nodded at her mother and quit the parlor.

At once, the air seemed cooler, easier to inhale. Penny caught sight of the windblown elms outside the tall, wide windows that flanked the grand staircase. Their swaying beckoned her to watch for a moment before she decided to sneak into Father's study, which offered a more private view of the elms.

Emmett stood beside Father's desk, one hand on Father's pen-and-ink stand.

"Emmett?" Shivers of unease skittered up her arms. "What are you doing here?"

◆ ◆ ◆

Emmett was not doing well as a spy. He'd managed authenticating a suspected forgery of a Rubens for Whitacre at that house party last spring, but this attempt wasn't going as well. Caught at his first attempt to be alone with the painting? He'd have to improve at skulking and skulduggery if he wanted to continue to serve in this capacity.

Which he did. Badly.

Penny waited, lips parted, eyes wide. If only he'd met her before Lionel had—

God help me. That train of thought wouldn't do.

"I wanted paper." It wasn't a lie. He didn't have his sketchbook.

Her face relaxed. "Take whatever you need—"

"That's not all." Spying might be part of the job, but lying was not in his nature, and he wouldn't start now with Penny. He had permission to inform her family, but he'd hesitated. Now, however, it was best to make a clean breast of it. He hadn't known Penny long, but he'd seen her kindness and compassion. He knew in the marrow of his bones he could trust her. "I'm here because of the Gainsboroughs."

Her gaze flickered to the paintings behind him, and her eyes softened in concern. "Father bought them from a dealer. If he knew Lionel sold them without your blessing, he might return them. They're clearly important to you."

His head shook. "Not to me. To the Crown."

She took a step into the room, disbelief widening her eyes. "Queen Victoria?"

"The Prince of Wales, actually." He took a deep breath. "And only the painting of Lady Dunwood. Or rather, the map at her side."

Penny drew closer. Her floral perfume wafted around him, filling his brain with thoughts he should not have about his brother's intended. *Focus on the painting.*

How did Penny view the image? He gazed at it afresh, taking in the scene as if for the first time. Bewigged and decked in a pale gown, his great-great-grandmother Lady Dunwood seemed the epitome of a well-bred, educated lady of her time, seated before a desk piled with books and, of course, the map. It hung upside down, hanging off the edge of the desk like a prop.

"What is so valuable about this map?" Penny turned her head to the side.

She'd laugh, but it was rather incredible. "It leads to King John's treasure of crown jewels."

She did laugh, a sound of surprise. "The prince wishes to add John's bounty to the royal coffers, then?"

If only. "A group of anarchists wishes to overthrow the Crown. So far they've made attempts to assassinate members of Parliament and destroy government buildings."

Her mouth popped open. "I'd no idea."

Little wonder. Mrs. Beale probably limited the sorts of newspapers Penny read to the society pages. "Thus far the group has been foiled, but government intelligence learned this group seeks to take hold of symbolic objects."

"Such as the treasure of King John? Whatever for?"

"The prince fears they would disrespect the crown or scepter somehow, but I suspect if the anarchists found the treasure, they would sell it to fund their violent pursuits." He peered at the map, praying Gainsborough had been precise with his brush. "In any case, the government hopes to find the treasure before anyone else."

"How did they know about the map?"

"My friend Seymour Whitacre—he was the chap at the museum—works for the prince. He remembered me telling him about the painting and asked for it. I told him our family had parted with it but that Lionel was, er, visiting the family to whom it had been sold, and, well, here I am."

"So that is why you accompanied Lionel and Viola to Philadelphia. To copy the map."

"I'm glad to be here with Viola. And to meet you. But yes."

She turned to him, her face so close he could see the flecks of green in her brown eyes and the tiny mole above her lip—

"Does Lionel know?"

Lionel? Oh. Enough looking at her lips. Emmett turned back to the painting. "I have permission to tell him, but I haven't done so. I'd not want him upset that he sold a painting sought by violent thugs."

She stiffened. "Beg pardon, but these *thugs* know about the painting, too? Are we in danger for owning this thing?" She gripped the gilt frame as if preparing to yank it from the wall.

"Wait, please." He covered her clenched fingers with his hand. "If they know, which

I doubt, they wouldn't cross the Atlantic for it when there are other means to find the treasure."

"None as easy as a map, I imagine." Her voice was high and tight.

"No one will come, but if anyone tried, I'd protect you. I'd die protecting you."

The words hung in the air, soft as breath.

Their hands were still touching. Their gazes held, unblinking, for too long.

Why didn't she jerk her hand away? Why must she stare up at him, wide-eyed and trembling, as if she might care for him, too?

One of them must stop this madness. But he wasn't certain he had strength enough to look away. It was all he could do not to kiss her.

He'd hoped that the attraction he'd felt was a trifle, but her friendship and her heart drew him like nothing he'd known before.

This was more than passing fancy. This was dangerous.

So, praying for strength, he lowered his hand and dragged his gaze back to the portrait, where he stared unseeing for the span of several breaths.

Then she took a deep, ragged breath. "How did poor King John lose his royal crown?"

Her tone was different. Conversational, but forced, as if she pretended the moment between them hadn't happened.

He should follow her lead. "King John was not a popular king, as you may recall from the legend of Robin Hood."

He glanced at her. Good, he'd made her smile.

"It was during the First Barons' War, 1216 to be precise. During a military campaign, John grew ill and parted from his slower-moving baggage wagons. Unfortunately, the route the wagons took crossed the mouth of the Wellstream."

"What is that?"

"A tidal stream. At low tide it was passable, but the wagons were not fast enough, and they were sucked into quicksand, lost in whirlpools, or washed away with the tide—depending upon which account one reads. Regardless, the crown, silver plate, gold, and an Arthurian relic called the Sword of Tristram were lost."

"How does one locate wagons washed away or sunk in quicksand, even with a map?"

"An excellent question. Nevertheless, Lady Dunwood's ancestor, who was with the baggage train, drew one anyway. He either chose not to search for the treasure or never found it, despite his map, because it was buried or swept away. Either way, Lady Dunwood wanted the map captured in this painting. The original map was never seen again, and this is the only clue that remains."

"And what a tantalizing clue it is." Penny's lips turned up in a gentle smile. "You should tell Father. He'll grant you access."

"Access to what?"

Emmett twisted at Mr. Beale's baritone, which held more than a little curiosity in its tone.

"The paintings, Father." Penny swept away from Emmett, leaving a whirl of her floral scent in her wake. "Emmett has a tale to tell about them."

She offered an encouraging smile before exiting, but the room grew colder without her in it.

"How so?" Mr. Beale took Penny's place beside him, so Emmett shared the story. His thoughts diverged between his government task and Penny, however.

He was fulfilling his duty to the Crown. He should feel relieved, happy, but longing panged his abdomen like hunger pains.

Emmett had always believed he didn't need to seek out a wife; if God wanted him wed, He'd see fit to provide. So far, Emmett's head hadn't been turned by anyone, and he'd trusted that was part of God's provision, too.

Until now. Much as he did not wish to admit it, he was falling in love with Penny.

And nothing but heartache would come of it.

Chapter 4

The next afternoon, Penny's thoughts still swirled from her conversation with Emmett. Treasure, villains, maps—the stuff of novels.

But as she wandered a toy store with Alma and Viola, her thoughts had less to do with King John than with Emmett.

She'd been drawn to him the moment she first saw him, although she felt guilty having such feelings because of Lionel. Then she'd learned who Emmett was, and she'd determined to squash her attraction like a bug under her boot heel.

But when they started to become friends, the feelings only increased. How could they not, when he was such a likable fellow? His devotion to Viola, his humor, their shared faith, all made him even more appealing.

She'd hoped—prayed—that her traitorous emotions would subside so she could appreciate Lionel as a fiancé and Emmett as a brother-in-law.

Then in Father's office, Emmett's touch on her hand sent a flame up her arm. And she wasn't so certain she could ever view Emmett as a brother.

Her steps paused. Should she follow through with marrying Lionel when she didn't love him? They weren't engaged yet. He hadn't asked. And when he did, what if she said no—

A porcelain head the size of a small apple was thrust before Penny's eyes, almost smacking her in the nose.

"Look at this one." Viola waved the doll, shaking its blond curls so Penny's vision swam yellow. "She looks like Amelie's sister."

Viola's high-pitched English accent made Penny smile. So did Viola's side-by-side comparison of the new doll in one hand with Amelie in the other. Aside from their clothing and the evidence of Amelie having been well loved, the dolls might indeed be twins.

"I agree."

"So do I." Alma cupped Viola's shoulders in a brief hug. "The girls at the home will love the dolls you've chosen, Viola."

It had been Alma's idea for the three of them to go doll shopping, trailed by Miss Partridge, with Clark to handle the packages. Penny hoped it would be a memorable outing for Lionel's little girl. The toy store held all manner of delights, but Viola hurried straight to the section shelved with dolls. It hadn't taken long to select fourteen for the girls at the home, with a few extras should new residents come along.

Penny fingered the doll's plaid frock. "Do you think the dolls require changes of clothing, Viola?"

Viola tapped her chin in thought before nodding. "Miss Partridge says a coat and spare frock are always wise to pack, so the dolls should have such, too."

At the mention of her name, Miss Partridge stepped forward. Penny smiled at the governess, who then nodded understanding that she wasn't being summoned. Penny warmed at the careful note the governess paid to her young charge. Her obvious care for Viola reminded Penny of her own governess, Frosty.

Frosty was the woman who had truly raised Penny and taught her about God. Much of the year, Mother and Father left Penny in Philadelphia while they spent time in New York, Newport, or abroad—until this year, that is. It seemed as if Viola experienced a similar childhood to Penny's, with a servant as the most constant figure in her life.

The similarity between Penny and Viola, attended by servants rather than parents, pricked at Penny's skin like ant bites. The wounds were small but sharp. Not that Penny or Viola suffered like the girls at the home; on the contrary, they had Miss Partridge and Frosty.

But what would it have been like if Mother had been the one to guide Penny, instead of Frosty? Or if Lionel went against the conventions of his class and took a larger role in raising his daughter?

A moment ago, Penny had entertained the scandalous thought that she could decline Lionel's proposal. Then Viola had thrust the doll in her face, reminding her that a marriage between Penny and Lionel was about more than just the two of them.

Show me what is best for Viola, Lord.

Alma's eyes brightened. "Viola, may I sew a few ensembles for Amelie? I used to sew things for my dolls when I was younger."

"Oh, yes, please." Viola dashed off to Miss Partridge. "Did you hear? Miss Shore will sew clothes for Amelie."

Alma, her gaze fixed on Viola, clutched Penny's arm. Were those tears in Alma's eyes? Penny dug a handkerchief out of her bag. "What troubles you, dear?"

Alma dabbed her eyes with the lacy edges of Penny's hankie. "I would trade places with you in an instant, marrying such a fine man and mothering that little girl."

Lionel was a fine man, Penny supposed. And Viola was a darling, but surely it was the circumstance, not Lionel and Viola themselves, that Alma envied. Although envy implied bitterness, and Alma was surely motivated by loneliness. Penny patted Alma's hand. "Is your mother still hesitant to allow you to be courted?"

Alma blanched. "She is amenable now that it is too late—oh, never mind. In the meantime I have the perfect tiny buttons in my basket at home for a ball gown for Amelie."

"What is too late?" Had Alma met a gentleman she wished to marry? But Alma slipped from Penny's touch and rushed to Viola, babbling about the petite buttons.

It was all Penny could do not to drag Alma aside when they returned to Penny's house, but the moment was never right to question her, especially with Viola in their company. The girl accompanied them to the parlor, where Penny released Miss Partridge for her afternoon tea and then asked Clark to bring the newly purchased dolls into the parlor.

"We must line them up and show them off." Penny tugged off her gloves. Alma was already helping Viola do the same.

Within minutes, they'd removed the lids from the dolls' boxes and propped them against the sofa and hearth. Viola scooted on her knees, introducing Amelie to each one, while Alma studied their clothes. Penny rang the bell for tea just as Lionel poked his head in the door.

"I thought I heard noise. We gentlemen were in the study. My, what a sight," he exclaimed. "Is this the parlor or the nursery?"

"Do you like our purchases?" Penny moved beside him.

"I chose them all, Papa. Aren't they pretty?" Viola made Amelie shake hands with a black-haired doll.

"I should say so." He turned to Penny—at last. It seemed he hadn't initiated a single conversation with her since his arrival in Philadelphia. "Thank you."

Maybe she expected too much, but the date of the ball was approaching—the ball when her parents planned to announce their betrothal, although he hadn't proposed yet. Or talked to her beyond commenting on the weather or food.

Spending time with Lionel strained her breathing, but she must get to know him better. She forced a smile.

"Perhaps we can speak later about Hawton Park." *Or anything. Anything at all.*

"Mmm."

That was as good as a yes from him, she supposed, because he stepped away to peer at the dolls where Alma and Viola curled on the floor.

Penny stood alone, feeling a stranger in her own parlor. Perhaps Lionel thought there was no need to get to know her because it wouldn't change anything. Perhaps he didn't want to be friends and planned to go on with his life apart from her once she'd birthed an heir.

Abandon her, like her parents had done.

Viola checked a doll's ears for aches, and Lionel and Alma made sympathetic noises for the poor sick dolly. Penny, unsure whether to join in or run away, caught the sounds of the tea tray being brought in. Relief. "I shall see if Father or Emmett wishes tea."

"That would be splendid." Lionel looked up from the floor. At least he was paying attention to his daughter.

Father wasn't in his office, however. Emmett alone stood before the painting of Lady Dunwood, studying the map with a brass-handled magnifying glass. He didn't hear her come in but continued on his task, pausing to swipe a lock of unruly hair from his brow.

Penny's heart pounded, and her mouth went dry. *Take this from me, Lord. I want to be faithful, not torn.*

Even though she hadn't made a sound, Emmett turned. His grin warmed her to her toes. "Good afternoon. Success with the dolls?"

She nodded, walking toward him. "They are lined up for Viola's inspection in the parlor. One appears to have an earache."

"I hope she's well enough to be delivered to the home tomorrow. I had hoped I might come with you. Viola, too. It would be good for her to give the dolls to them personally. But I also thought perhaps we could bring the art supplies and show the girls how to use them."

"I will write the headmistress to be certain, but I am sure she will agree." She glanced at the magnifying glass in his hand. "Father gave you permission to copy the map, I see."

"First, I'm ensuring the painting wasn't tampered with at some point. Painted over, that sort of thing—but it looks to be free of alterations. Are you looking for your father?"

"Both of you. Tea's in the parlor."

He set the magnifying glass on Father's desk. "Your mother desired a consultation with him on a matter pertaining to the ball Saturday."

Ah, yes. The ball. Every mention of it made her stomach twist and her chest tighten. Emmett's fingers clenched at his sides, as if he wished to speak, but he didn't.

So she leaned against Father's desk. "Tell me about Hawton Park."

He leaned against the desk beside her so they were side by side, their hands almost touching. "What's Lionel told you?"

"About grouse hunting season. Nothing about the house." Her future home.

Emmett ran a hand through his hair, mussing it to dashing effect. "The estate was built over time. Two of the towers are six hundred years old."

She nodded, understanding his meaning. "I imagine they require extensive repair."

"In medieval days, the earls of Hawton were among the richest men in England, thanks to their prominent roles in wars and intrigues. Nowadays, life is far different, and Lionel is in the same position as other members of the nobility: saddled with estates built for far different purposes in far different times. The costs of running the estate are crippling him."

"How difficult that must be."

"More than a hundred servants are in his employ, from chambermaids to the men who tend the two hundred square miles of grounds. Then there are everyday expenses and repairs. He's sold medieval weaponry from the armory and artwork." He tipped his chin at the painting. "But it isn't enough."

"He needs a wealthy wife." More than wealthy. Someone as affluent as the daughter of a banking magnate. "And my parents wish me to be titled. A fair exchange."

He didn't join in her humorless laugh. "Is there anything in it for you, Penny?"

"Viola." She didn't need to think before answering. "I see myself in her. She's parented more by Miss Partridge than Lionel, as is typical of his class, I know, but I was raised by my nanny, too. I called her Frosty."

"*Frosty?*"

His wide smile lightened the mood, and she was grateful for the reprieve. "Are you laughing at me? In the middle of my tender story?"

"Never." Of course he was.

She forced a mock glare. "I couldn't pronounce Foster. Didn't you have a nickname for your governess?"

"Nanny Macklin was a stickler. I called her Mack once, to my detriment. My knuckles still hurt." He waved his hand.

"What faradiddle."

"Fara—what?" His eyes widened.

"Diddle. You don't say faradiddle in England?"

"Do I look like the sort of person who says faradiddle?"

"One doesn't need to say faradiddle to know what it is."

He snickered. "My old auntie said faradiddle, but I have never once uttered the word."

"Until today."

"Until today." His smile was soft. Sweet.

She had to look away. With a deep breath, she placed Lionel back in his rightful place, between her and Emmett.

"Was Macklin Lionel's nanny, too?"

Even though she didn't look at Emmett, she could tell he shook his head. "Lionel was seven when I was born and already off at school, but Cyril and Vernon were still at home."

"Vernon is the clergyman, and Cyril is the soldier?" She'd worked to keep them straight, although she hadn't met them.

"As is fitting for second and third sons of earls. Fourth sons like me? No one knows quite what to do with us."

"So you are twenty-eight." Seven years younger than Lionel's thirty-five.

"I am."

"A young professor."

"And a map copier." There was that saucy grin again.

It was easy talking to him, sharing jokes. Maybe God had sought to care for her by giving her a friend in Emmett, a companion in her new family. A brother. But she'd ruined it all by developing feelings for him that were not at all those of one sibling for another.

Her heart hammered once, hard against her ribs.

She shouldn't be alone with Emmett anymore. Not until her feelings were under control. So she pushed off from the desk and inclined her head toward the door.

"Come, before the tea is cold and the dolls get packed for tomorrow."

He nodded and joined her. Every hair on her arms stood at attention just because he walked at her side.

Penny crossed her arms. She was wise to avoid being alone with him. The sooner she got over these wretched feelings for him, the better.

◆ ◆ ◆

The following afternoon, Emmett had prayed a hundred times or more for God to remove his feelings for Penny. Now, the only male at the Home for Friendless Girls with Penny, Alma, Viola, a host of dollies, and fourteen girls busy with brushes and watercolors, he prayed it again.

So far, God hadn't answered the way Emmett thought best.

Penny's declaration that she cared for Viola touched his heart in yet another new way. How could he not love her?

Penny, her smile wide, squeezed the shoulders of an orphan girl, Vera, who painted a tree in three shades of green. "My favorite color. So soothing."

Looking up from her own painting, Viola shot him a triumphant smile. "I told you Miss Beale likes green, Uncle. That's why you wore the tie, remember?"

Penny looked at his tie. Did she remember as well as he that he'd been wearing it when first they met at the museum? Suddenly, it felt too tight, and he tugged at it with a forefinger.

She looked away, her cheeks pinking like cherries.

How do I stop falling in love with her, Lord?

It was more than he could accomplish on his own. It was like chasing an already-moving train in an attempt to prevent it from leaving the station. No matter how vigorous his efforts, the train was well on its way to chugging well out of sight.

"Mr. Retford." A little girl Viola's age raised her hand. "Did I do this right?"

He took a deep breath to clear his head, relaxing as the familiar wet-paper smell wafted about him. Young Mary's watercolor revealed a family, all with yellow hair. Her with her lost parents, perhaps? He'd prayed one or more of the girls would find solace or comfort through art, and maybe this was an answer. "You did indeed, Mary. It's beautiful."

Then all the girls sought his opinion, about colors and whether or not their paintings were beautiful, too.

"They all are," he and Penny said at the same time. Their gazes met and then dropped away as if it was a crime to be caught looking at one another.

She'd certainly given that impression since their private talk in her father's study yesterday. Like she was afraid to look at him.

Viola beckoned him to bend down. She cupped her hand around her mouth, as if to impart a secret. "Dolls now, Uncle?"

"When Miss Beale says so." The boxed dolls waited in the parlor until after the art lesson.

"When Miss Brice, the headmistress, says so," Penny countered with a wink. "But I am as eager as you, Viola."

Viola hurried to where Alma exclaimed over a girl's painting of her old house, leaving Emmett and Penny side by side, watching.

She glanced at him, smiled, and flushed. The pause between them grew long, and Emmett struggled for something to say to her. So he smiled. "It seems we're always in front of art, doesn't it?"

What a dull-witted observation. Emmett could have kicked himself.

"But those other times, we studied paintings. Now we watch young artists at work, enjoying themselves and perhaps even healing, thanks to you."

"I'm the inspired one."

Penny made him want to write poetry—whole sonnets about the pink of her cheeks. They would turn out terrible, but she made him want to try, anyway. Inspiration did that to a fellow. Which reminded him—

"I consult for several museums, at home and even the Metropolitan—"

"In New York?" she interrupted.

He nodded. "Have you been?"

"Yes, and the—forgive me, I could talk all day about it, but you were saying?" Her eyes were so wide and lovely it made his breath hitch.

"I could talk art all day, too. And often do."

"Because you're a professor." There, she was looking at him again.

"And map copier," he teased, just as he had yesterday. "But I wonder if there might be ways to introduce art to children who otherwise would not be exposed to it."

Her hand clutched his arm, and her face shone with eagerness. "What a wonderful thought. Remember what you said when we met, when I admitted I didn't know much about the artist of the painting we viewed?"

How could he forget? "I said it allowed you to approach the canvas without prejudgment."

"I think there is benefit in knowing about the artist, sometimes, too. Like today. Their paintings are all the more precious because of who they are and what they've been through." She squeezed his arm, and it was all he could do not to take her hand and squeeze back. "The girls are enjoying this so much, and with your donations, they'll be able to continue to paint and sketch and express themselves—"

"I say, Penny." Alma's voice was sharp.

Neither he nor Penny had noticed the girls leaving the table and queueing up at the door. Alma mouthed, *the dolls.*

"The parlor, Miss Beale?" The headmistress, Miss Brice, tipped her head.

Penny's hand jerked from his arm. "Oh, yes. Girls, our guests have brought something special for you today."

Without a backward glance, she bustled out the door, the girls at her heels. When Alma passed Emmett, she didn't spare him a look, either, and her mouth was set in a disapproving line.

Emmett pinched the bridge of his nose. He'd made his interest in Penny obvious. Again. Alma recognized it. Lionel might next time.

But Penny had forgotten herself, too. As a well-bred lady, she would not have touched his arm had she not been caught up in her excitement. *Assume it was for the project, Emmett. Not you. Keep your mind on art.*

Art was not on anyone's minds when the girls opened their boxes, however. He leaned against the doorjamb and watched the scene. Some girls hugged their dolls, and the two littlest girls immediately changed their dolls' clothes. Viola fluttered among them, Amelie in arms and Alma at her side, while Penny held back, swiping tears from her lashes. Then, one of the tiny girls brought her a doll midchange, and Penny bent to help with the buttons.

You cannot love her.

He told himself that the entire carriage ride back to the house, where Mr. Beale had left the study free for him to work. He told himself again as he measured and scrutinized and sketched the lines of the map, reminding himself he was the worst type of cad for making moon-eyes at his brother's almost-fiancée. He was still telling himself when Lionel sauntered into the room, surrounded in a cloud of his expensive bergamot cologne.

"So this is the famous map."

Emmett had told Lionel about it last night. Whitacre was right; it was easier to copy the painting when he didn't have to creep about. Nevertheless, Lionel hadn't expressed much interest, so it was a surprise to see him here.

"I didn't know you'd arrived."

"Thought I'd fetch you and Viola. The females are at tea, and Mr. Beale had business in the library, so I came in search of you." Lionel squinted. "Looks like a bunch of squiggles and whatnot."

"It is." Emmett set down his pencil. "But it's up to Whitacre to find a landmark in it. My job is to copy the map with precision."

Lionel drifted to sit in one of the wingback chairs by the hearth, where a small fire crackled in the grate. "Pleasant way to execute your duty."

Emmett shouldn't, but he couldn't help himself. "And is your duty pleasant, Lionel?"

Lionel glanced at the open doorway, as if he feared being overheard. "Penny's a kind woman. Good with Viola."

And so much more that Lionel was blind to. Emmett dropped into the wingback chair across from his brother and bent toward him, the better to keep his voice low. "You didn't answer my question. If you have doubts, you don't have to go through with it."

"The contracts are drawn."

"I admire your commitment, Lionel, but—"

"Call me all manner of names for marrying for money. Mercenary, heartless. But I won't dishonor her by backing out. No, we're in in for a penny, in for a pound now."

In Lionel's vehemence, he hadn't noticed his pun, an ironic choice since it used Penny's name. But the idiom was apt, since it meant once one began something, one had to see it through to its completion.

It didn't make it right, though.

"How many pounds, Lionel?" What was Penny worth in this exchange?

"Two million, American currency. Enough to set a good amount right."

Like paying the boot maker for the fashionable *congress gaiters* on Lionel's feet.

"You haven't proposed." Which seemed odd.

"Her mother wants a production of it." Lionel rose. "I'm to propose at the ball. Penny doesn't know. It's to be a surprise."

Emmett stood, his stomach dropping to his soles. "Lionel."

"I'm not keen on humbling myself before a crowd, but it is a moment of mortification for two million dollars."

A *lifetime* for two million dollars, not a moment—Lionel's tender pride was least on Emmett's mind. How could Penny, traded for such a sum, say no to Lionel in front of all those people?

She couldn't, even if she wavered from her obedience to her parents and her determination to care for Viola.

"I'm sorry." For Penny. For this mess.

"Thank you." Lionel shrugged, mistaking Emmett's apology. "Ready to return to the Bellevue with us?"

His head shook. "I've more work to do with the map."

Once Lionel left, Emmett took up the pencil and sketchbook, which was open to a drawing of the map. He'd drawn several versions, in fact: in its entirety and in quadrants, both to scale and enlarged. He wasn't quite finished, and these renderings were the whole reason he'd come to Philadelphia. He must be ready with them before his scheduled return to England after the ball. Or sooner, the way Whitacre pestered him with notes left each night at the Bellevue.

Shame pinched his gut. He should have come to America to support Lionel, but his brother had been an excuse to get a job done.

Lionel hadn't asked for support, though. Their family was fractured—distant and formal since the deaths of their parents several years ago. If it wasn't for Viola, Emmett wouldn't see much of Lionel. He saw little of Vernon and Cyril, too.

The Retford brothers, almost strangers nowadays.

Nothing was beyond repair, however. Emmett sank onto the expanse of Mr. Beale's desk and prayed for healing between him and his brothers.

Of course, his relationship with Lionel wouldn't be helped a whit if Emmett confessed to loving Penny. Penny felt something for him—he knew she did—but was it love? And even if it was, he had nothing to offer her but a modest cottage and a shot at a new career path he didn't have yet. Whitacre hadn't heard back from the prince.

Emmett snatched up the pencil and paper and returned to his sketching. If the Lord didn't free him of his affections for Penny, Emmett prayed God would at least free Penny from whatever she seemed to feel for him, so she could be happy with Lionel.

And that his family—his whole family, including Penny—would grow together again.

Chapter 5

The next two days passed in a whirl for Penny. Fittings for her ball gown, food tastings, and two nights out with Lionel, Alma, and Emmett had left her weary. At luncheon, Mother expressed concern over the bags under Penny's eyes and sent her for a rest, but Penny feared shutting her eyes.

When she did, she saw Emmett's face. Then Lionel's, and Viola's. Her dangerous feelings for Emmett prevented her from resting, so it was far better to do something else. Like read.

But after trying for half an hour to get lost in the pages of a novel, Penny conceded defeat. Curled on the gold lounge in the parlor, she was still on the same page she'd started on, unable to focus for more than a sentence or two before her mind flitted to Emmett. Again. She shut the book and smacked it onto the lounge in a huff.

She'd thought she'd done the right thing, deciding not to be alone with Emmett because she couldn't trust herself. But then at the girls' home two days past, he'd looked down at her with his soft brown eyes, and she'd forgotten anyone else was in the room.

It hadn't mattered that they weren't alone. She couldn't keep being lost in his conversation, drawn to him no matter who else was around.

It did not bode well for her future.

She retrieved the book and carried it upstairs. She should select something suitable to wear, since Lionel would be arriving soon for dinner. He had yet to propose, and the ball to announce their betrothal was tomorrow evening. Even now, servants bustled about the house polishing and sweeping and scrubbing, preparing for something she dreaded.

Unless—

What if, instead of fighting the warring in her chest, she listened to it?

She loved Emmett. Stopping halfway up the staircase, hand pressed against the wild beating of her heart, she admitted it to herself.

She'd tried dismissing her attraction, tried avoiding him, and she'd prayed to view Lionel differently, although God had answered that prayer. She now felt compassion for him, since he bore the heavy weight of a responsibility he couldn't afford. Still, sympathy for Lionel wasn't the same as being in love with him.

Penny gripped the banister. What if she said no to her parents, to Lionel?

"There you are." Mother peered over the landing above. "You've failed to select a gown for tonight, so I've chosen for you."

Penny climbed the rest of the stairs and set the book on her bureau. Mother—and the maid who curtsied and dashed from the room—had been busy. An ecru silk gown trimmed with pink rosettes lay across her bed, alongside white gloves and stockings. Beside the ensemble lay her ball gown for tomorrow. Something bright and glittering rested on the bodice.

"Your pink rubies." Penny's hand went to her mouth. Mother prized this necklace above all others.

"I should say they're worthy of the future Countess of Hawton, wouldn't you?"

She'd wanted Mother's approval for so long. Now she had it, symbolized in a necklace. But she shook her head. "I cannot wear them."

"Don't be a goose, Penny. It's just for the evening. You can't hurt them."

"That's not it." Tears stung Penny's eyes. "I do not wish to marry Lionel."

There. She'd said it. Her breathing eased, as if her corset had loosened, but the matter wasn't over yet. *God, help me.*

Mother blinked. "Your nerves are overset. You're fatigued."

"I'm sorry. I know you worked hard for this—"

"I have, and this is the gratitude you show?" Mother stared at a spot on the wall, as if she couldn't bear to look at Penny. "What brings this on, hmm? You still don't love him?"

"No." Penny's swallow grated her throat. "This is a business deal."

"To your advantage. You're getting a title."

But not love. "I'm in love with Emmett."

For a moment, it looked as if Mother might throw something. Then she took a deep breath and shut her eyes. "You and Emmett have discussed your feelings, then? You think this is romantic, the two of you against the world, breaking his brother's heart?"

"I do not know how he feels about me, but it doesn't matter. It isn't fair to Lionel, marrying him when I love his brother."

"That spark flooding your veins? It isn't love. It's fickle attraction and rebellion."

Penny had thought so, too. But not anymore. "I've tried to ignore it, Mother. Tried to get past it."

"And done a shoddy job."

"I care for Viola, enough that I thought it a good enough reason to marry her father, but Lionel and I do not suit. I've tried to better know him, but he seems as unaffected by me as I am by him. I should free us both before we make a mistake."

Mother's look was pitying. "Rejecting him will not free you, Penny. Your shortsighted decision will shackle you in ways you cannot imagine. Emmett wouldn't marry you even if he wanted to, because of the damage it would cause in his family—as if your father and I would allow it, with him being a teacher or whatever he is."

The hair at Penny's nape stood on end. "He has an honorable profession, Mother—"

"He has no money, which would be well and good if he was *somebody*, but he isn't." Mother rubbed her temples, as if the conversation ached. "And if you do not marry Lionel, you'll bear a reputation in England and America as a finicky female who thinks she's too good for nobility, and who will have you then?"

"I need not marry." Penny had money of her own from her grandmother—enough to get a start. And she could find work as a teacher, perhaps. Serve children the way Miss Brice did at the Home for Friendless Girls.

Mother rolled her eyes. "Make a pariah of yourself? You have the opportunity to do as I did, to marry into a better family. One that will show those sticklers in New York that we're as good as they are. Better, because you're marrying nobility. The Astors will be so envious."

The Astors, members of the "List of 400" elite of New York society, were among those who'd snubbed Mother over the years because her father was a cotton broker. Father might have had money when she married him, inherited banking interests he'd multiplied tenfold, but his money was newer than theirs.

Mother wouldn't be ignored, however. When the New York Academy of Music refused to admit the Beales into its circles, Mother helped form the Metropolitan Opera, alongside Alva Vanderbilt. When one harridan announced Mother would never dine at her New York table, Mother managed to book passage on the same transatlantic voyage and arrange to be seated at the woman's table, all for the irony of it.

Mother refused to take *no* for an answer—then or now. But Penny had to keep trying. "I don't care a whit what the Astors think. But I do care about Lionel and how he might feel, knowing I care for his brother."

Mother's hands flew in the air. "You will never utter a word about Emmett to him. So Lionel hasn't given you the attention you crave, but pish-posh! He thinks enough of you to give you his title. I'd say that's worth two million dollars."

Two million dollars? Penny's jaw dropped. So that was the sum her parents offered to someone to marry her. Lionel accepted two million to put up with her for the rest of his life.

A great sum of money that Mother seemed to believe Penny would be flattered by, but actually made her feel as if she were worth nothing at all.

Her glance landed then on her Bible, lying on her nightstand. No, she wasn't worthless. She was priceless to God.

She had to trust Him. "Marriage shouldn't be about money, Mother—"

"Should it be about feelings? Yours and Emmett's and Lionel's? What about ours, your father's and mine?" Mother's features settled into a tired look that made her look older than her middle years. "All your father ever wanted was your security. Yet you would hurt him? You know he isn't well."

Penny's veins iced. "You mean the heart palpitations?"

"It's far more than palpitations. He didn't want you to know, but there's a problem with an artery to his brain." Mother tapped the side of her neck. "The physician made it clear Edwin is not to engage in any physical activity whatsoever."

"No exercise?" It made sense now, his watching from the veranda while she played croquet.

"Or worry. Anxiety is not good for him, Penny. When he moves too fast or experiences strain, he could faint. . .or worse."

Panic clawed Penny's throat. "Is he dying?"

"We are not certain, but it is imperative he is kept calm."

She sank onto the corner of her bed. So this was it? She had to marry Lionel or risk causing her father anxiety, which could lead to his death?

Emotions warred in her chest. Disbelief, guilt, anger, fear for Father. And her feelings for Emmett, crying out not to be ignored.

But she must, or Father could die.

The answer seemed clear now. Her feelings were a trifle compared to Father's life.

With God's help, she must choose to forget Emmett. She'd just determined to trust Him. This was how she would start that journey. She nodded, but tears slipped down her cheeks.

Mother stepped closer—enough to touch Penny, but her fingers caressed the rubies instead. "You will come to love Lionel. You already care about Viola. A year from now, you may have a baby of your own. You'll forget Emmett."

"He's Lionel's brother. I cannot disremember someone I see every Christmas, regardless of whether or not I am—or was once—in love with him." A bleak prospect indeed.

But she mustn't forget Viola. She'd be the best mother to her she could be.

"I'll send a maid to clean you up. Oh, and I invited Alma and Mrs. Shore to dine with us, as well."

The presence of Alma and her mother would stave off any unpleasant histrionics Penny might consider throwing, as well. Penny's mother had planned well.

"I will be ready, Mother."

Mother smiled from the threshold. "That's a good girl. Your father will be so pleased. Should we try on the rubies before I leave?"

Pretty as they were, they were heavy against Penny's throat, a weighty reminder that she was not free to choose for herself. Except when it came to trusting God.

Right now, that felt very hard to do. But it was her only option, so she took it with both hands.

◆ ◆ ◆

Emmett's supper tasted like chalk, although the platters on the dining room table looked delicious: bright vegetables, a standing rib roast, potatoes whipped and piped the shapes of swans, and ribbons of jellies created a palette of color and artistry. A far cry from the suppers he sat down to at Oxford, or the modest concoctions he managed at his cottage.

Another reminder that Penny deserved much more than he could provide.

That didn't ease the ache in his gullet, however. He loved Penny. So much that he had no choice but to avoid her for the rest of his life, if need be, so he didn't do something foolish and declare himself, jeopardizing her future happiness.

Even if it meant keeping his distance from Viola and Lionel, too.

A quick glance revealed Lionel hadn't eaten much, either. Nor had Alma or Penny, whose gaze met his at long last and then darted away.

So she was avoiding him, too.

After supper, Lionel cleared his throat before anyone could be seated. "Perhaps I might borrow Penny for a moment?"

Emmett's hands fisted. Was Lionel proposing? He was supposed to do it tomorrow, publicly at the ball, but why else would he seek privacy with Penny tonight?

"Certainly." Mr. Beale nodded. "The fire is still lit in the library."

Emmett had no option but to watch his brother escort Penny out.

The Beales and Mrs. Shore sat near the hearth, but Alma wandered to study an oil painting of a horse. Emmett joined her and was about to make a comment on the painting when she sniffed.

Her face mottled and her eyes were suspiciously bright.

Emmett withdrew his linen handkerchief. "Alma?"

With hasty motions, she swiped her tears and crumpled the hankie, as if determined her mother wouldn't notice. "Lio—Lord Hawton is proposing, isn't he? I'm happy for Penny."

And miserable for herself. Understanding dawned. "You love Lionel. I don't know why I didn't see it before."

"You mustn't tell a soul." Alma's blue eyes blazed. "He's not done a thing to encourage me. It's all my foolishness. I fought it, but here I am."

"The heart can be a disobedient thing, can't it?" He should know. "I have struggled in vain against my own heart."

She sighed. "I wondered, but the past two days Penny and Lionel have spent more time together and she hasn't looked at you once, so I thought I'd been wrong."

He bent down toward her, as if they shared a joke. But a sorry one. "Now we know one another's secrets."

"Unrequited love. Lio—Lord Hawton thinks of me as a friend."

Which was a world more than he seemed to think of Penny. *Lord, should Alma and I speak up?*

Where had that prayer come from? Still, it saturated his bones, easing the ache. Honor, duty, contracts all fell beneath the desire to tell the truth.

"What if we told them how we feel? Now, as it says in the wedding service: speak now or forever hold your peace. I'll hold my peace, forever and always, once they're married, but if we talk to them, they'll be informed before they wed. And then they'd understand why we find it too painful to visit them."

"But Lionel is proposing, isn't he?"

"He isn't supposed to until the ball."

She blinked. "So there's time to stop them? Could we?"

"We *could*. Whether or not we *should* is debatable."

Alma looked up at him, her eyes free of tears but full of determination. "Do you think we should?"

He was about to nod when Farrow, the butler, paused inside the door, his gaze on Emmett. "A gentleman to see you, Mr. Retford."

Mrs. Beale's brows rose. It was an extraordinary occurrence, for a guest to be hunted down like this. Unless—

"Did he give his name?"

"Mr. Whitacre, sir. He says it's most urgent."

With a quick nod to his hosts and Alma, Emmett hastened from the parlor. Whitacre paced the foyer, a look of relief smoothing his features when Emmett drew near.

"Apologies, old chap." His smile was tight, and his gaze on Farrow.

Emmett understood his meaning. He nodded at the butler. "Thank you, Farrow."

When the butler retreated and left them alone, Whitacre's shoulders relaxed. "I'm sailing back tonight. Another anarchist attack, and it's definite they want items and property important to the Crown. I need the map."

"I've made several renderings." Emmett tipped his head toward the hall, leading the way to Mr. Beale's office. The sketchbook was where he had left it, on the end table by the paintings of Lord and Lady Dunwood. Emmett flipped it open to one of the enlarged quadrants and pointed to a curve. "I think this is Sutton Bridge."

"I'll make a note of it for the fellows who get this."

Emmett handed over the book. "Godspeed, then."

"You seem in as much a hurry as I am."

"You've no idea." What were Lionel and Penny doing, anyway, if Lionel wasn't proposing?

"Then I'll thank you for your service to the Crown. The prince will be well pleased with your efforts, and I sent a telegram to London tonight inquiring about that position for you." Whitacre nodded.

To Emmett's surprise, Alma waited in the foyer, shredding his handkerchief in her trembling fingers. Once Whitacre let himself out, she took Emmett's hand in her soggy one. "Come on."

The library door was wide open. Their pace quickened.

"Alma, dear." The feminine voice halted their steps. Mrs. Beale followed after them, her mouth turned down. "I never dreamed you'd be so selfish as to interrupt Penny's special moment."

Emmett's molars ground together. Clearly Mrs. Beale had been watching in case he and Alma got any ideas.

"No one interrupted anything." Penny's voice was flat. She and Lionel stood in the doorway, not touching. "We were getting better acquainted, that's all."

She glanced at Emmett, almost a pleading look, but there was more in it. Confusion, perhaps. Lionel hadn't proposed, and she didn't know about the plan to surprise her at the ball. Maybe she wondered what was taking Lionel so long.

But Mrs. Beale grinned, a triumphant look. She took Penny's arm, preventing her from speaking to Emmett or Alma.

"Take heart," Emmett whispered to Alma. "There is still time. The Hawton emerald isn't on Penny's finger yet."

And if God was willing and Lionel agreed, the emerald never would be.

Chapter 6

An hour before the ball, Penny stood before her looking glass. Her Worth ball gown was a confection of pink and snowy silk. Her dark hair swept into a fashionable pompadour held in place with diamond-tipped pins, and Mother's pink rubies twinkled on her throat. If Penny's cheeks were pale or her lips drawn, well, it was to be expected that a lady suffered nerves the night her betrothal would be announced.

God would give her strength.

Penny was waiting in the foyer when Lionel, Emmett, and Viola arrived, dressed in exquisite evening clothes. She hadn't seen any of them since last night, although the gentlemen had called today while Penny was out on one of a half-dozen errands for Mother.

"You look lovely." Lionel kissed her hand and then moved on to greet Mother before she could thank him.

"You really do," Emmett agreed.

"Thank you."

She started to do it again, that state of looking into Emmett's eyes and forgetting who else was in the room.

At least, until Amelie's porcelain hand patted Penny's arm. Viola stared up at her. "Miss Partridge says I am to thank you for inviting me to stay the night and watch the ball."

Penny hugged her. "I enjoyed peeking when my parents hosted parties. Come, let me show you and Miss Partridge the best vantage."

Emmett was smiling at her, making her knees—and her resolve—weak. But she had to be stronger than that.

With Miss Partridge in tow, she and Viola ascended the stairs. They rounded the corner and Penny pointed. "There is your bedchamber, and here, around this corner, the hall has tiny openings. Windows without glass that overlook the ballroom. See?"

Viola was just the right height to rest her elbows on the ledge. "Will they see me?"

"If they look up, yes."

"It is fancy."

It was. Mother had ordered the mirrored walls bedecked with flowers and greenery. Bright green smilax leaves and darker ivy dripped from the chandeliers, and white bouquets filled a dozen gold jardinieres. Behind a gilt screen, musicians tuned their instruments. "You can watch the guests arrive and see some dancing before bedtime."

"Amelie, too." Viola lifted her into Penny's face.

"Viola!" Alma rushed down the hall, a vision in pale blue satin. Clark followed her bearing a small trunk. "Look what I brought for Amelie."

"A wardrobe!" Viola rushed into Alma's arms as Clark opened the trunk for their inspection. Satin ball gowns. A red cloak. A nightdress with matching cap. All perfect and sewn with care.

Clark and Miss Partridge moved the trunk to the designated bedchamber, and Alma and Viola followed, dropping to the floor to change Amelie for the ball.

Something speared Penny's chest. Again, that feeling that she didn't belong—in her own home, with her best friend, or with her soon-to-be stepdaughter. *I'm trying, Lord.* But her rib cage grew tight again. She turned on her heel.

The hall wasn't empty. Emmett, resplendent in his evening finery, leaned against the windows overlooking the ballroom. "Penny?"

She couldn't be alone with him. If she was, she might betray her feelings and ruin everything. Her head shook, shifting the rubies at her throat.

Emmett held out a hand. "Please. It's important."

This moment would be all they had, so with a puff of breath she hadn't known she held, she gave in and joined him at the window.

"I meant what I said." His eyes sparkled in the lamplight. "You look beautiful. But you have always looked beautiful to me, from the moment I saw you."

"Don't say that." It made everything so much harder.

"You must hear this before you allow the betrothal to be announced. I love you, Penny."

Her knees wobbled. "You can't."

"I don't know how you feel, but you don't love Lionel. Any more than he loves you. In fact, I am certain he loves Alma. I had a frank talk with him last night after our return to the hotel, and he all but admitted it after I told him how I feel for you."

Penny's brain spun from so much news. "Then why—does Alma know?"

"Your mother kept you two so busy all day we've not had the opportunities to speak to either of you until this moment. She caught Lionel downstairs, but I managed to sneak away from her."

"Is Lionel withdrawing from the agreement?"

Emmett shook his head. "His word is his bond and all that. He won't dishonor you."

It made sense now. They wanted her to do the breaking. Cowards. "So I should dishonor him? For Alma's sake? Or for his brother?"

"Not for me." His eyes grew sad. "I cannot marry you, Penny. Your parents wouldn't approve, you'd be cut off from them, and I have nothing to offer you. I'm the fourth son. I work for my wage, and I cannot give you this." He gestured at the ballroom.

"I do not want this." She wanted love. Emmett's. And her parents', but it seemed all she'd have was her parents' satisfaction that she'd married an earl.

"I will never be worthy of you, but I wanted you to know, eyes open, before Lionel proposes tonight."

Oh. The proposal was to be a spectacle, then. "My groom is taking two million dollars to marry me. My eyes were open to that, even if I was too disheartened to figure out how the proposal was being accomplished. Or that you cared for me, something I both wished for and dreaded, because I love you, too. But now I know you do not love me enough to marry me."

"You love me?" He smiled, took her hand, but then lowered his head. "I'm poorer than Lionel. Love isn't enough sometimes."

"You sound like my mother." She looked down. "But unless Lionel breaks it off, I will marry him."

"What about Alma's heart? Lionel's?"

"It's my father's heart that I'm thinking of right now." *Lord, help me.* "Mother says any anxiety or exertion could cause him to lose consciousness or even die. If I defy Father, I could hurt him."

Emmett's free hand cupped her cheek. "I'm sorry. For your father's health and that your mother uses such manipulative means to bend you to her will. This could have been prevented, without danger to your father, if we'd had more time."

Her chest felt torn open from the inside. "But we don't, and if Father fell or—something—because of me, I'd never forgive myself."

"Your compassion is but one of the things I love about you, Penny." His gaze raked her features, as if to memorize them.

It required all her strength to smile at him. "We should go down now. Guests will be arriving."

His hand lowered.

When she turned, her gaze passed the window and caught on two people below, looking up at her. From the horrified looks on their faces, they'd seen Emmett touch her face.

Her parents.

◆ ◆ ◆

After Penny dashed away without another word, Emmett made his miserable way downstairs, where the foyer crowded with guests. He greeted a few, but the effort of keeping a brave face was unbearable. Maybe he should leave the ball. Claim a headache and return to the Bellevue. Or leave Philadelphia altogether. He could drop by the Metropolitan Museum in New York and sail home in the next few days.

He'd have to run upstairs and explain to Viola he wouldn't be crossing back to England with her. Before he could get far, Alma emerged from the library, her eyes bright with unshed tears.

He hadn't seen her leave Viola's room. "You found Lionel?"

"Mrs. Beale turned away for a moment and I stole him." Her voice was flat. "I told him how I feel, but he won't back out of things with Penny because he signed the contract. Unless Penny can convince her parents—"

Emmett's head shook. "Her mother's convinced her of grave consequences, should that happen."

"So we are stuck." She lifted her chin, patted his arm, and moved toward her mother, who watched with red-tinged eyes. So Mrs. Shore knew, too.

Emmett hurried to the library, where Lionel stared into the fire. Emmett touched his shoulder.

"What a sorry business." Lionel tried to smile. "If I'd met Alma first. . .she's an heiress, too. All this could have been avoided."

Emmett's fingers fisted. "Is Hawton Park all you care about? Four people are brokenhearted tonight."

"Gentlemen?" Mr. Beale poked into the room, his hand extended. "I'd like to start the ball. What say you, eh?"

"Of course." But Lionel didn't look any happier about it than Emmett.

Emmett couldn't leave now without causing a scene. Already, the eyes of dozens of guests fixed on them as they entered the ballroom. Emmett clenched his jaw and joined Alma and her mother, lurking beside a potted palm.

Lionel offered Penny his arm. Mr. Beale tapped a silver spoon against an empty crystal goblet, creating a melodic *clink* that drew the attention of everyone in the ballroom.

"Ladies and gentlemen, thank you for attending tonight, some of you from great distances." He chuckled, eyeing Lionel. "I should like to begin the dancing, but first, an announcement. Or rather, a very special question."

The proposal.

Lionel's fingers fidgeted, ready to withdraw the Hawton emerald from his pocket, no doubt.

Emmett prayed. Alma's breath hitched as if she fought against sobs. Mrs. Beale grinned, triumphant beside her husband.

But Mr. Beale's gaze was on his daughter. Penny nodded, communicating her compliance.

Mr. Beale nodded back.

Emmett could say something. Speak now or forever hold his peace. He took a step forward.

Mr. Beale held out his hand, reaching out to Penny, but his palm faced Emmett as if staying him. It was enough to make Emmett pause.

"I would like to ask my daughter to share the first dance with me." Mr. Beale smiled. "If she will have me."

Chapter 7

Penny gripped Father's hand as he led her to the center of the floor. "We shouldn't do this, Father."

"Can't I enjoy one song with my beautiful daughter? If I am to dance the first dance with your mother, everyone will forgive the breach in etiquette."

"You're not supposed to dance at all."

"She told you? Pity." He bowed as was customary as the first strains of the waltz began.

Penny hastened to curtsy. "Sit down before you exert yourself."

"I shall, after you tell me what is going on tonight."

"I thought Lionel would be proposing." Penny placed her hand on Father's shoulder and they began to move to the music.

"Your mother planned it as a surprise."

"It slipped out. Regardless, the contract is signed."

"But you've yet to accept him." Father smiled. "One, two, three, oh I'm hopeless."

"Father, please stop the dance. Pass me to Lionel and sit down before you collapse."

"I shan't have the opportunity to speak to you in private again, and even now, every eye watches us until I invite the guests to join us on the floor. So speak. You fancy Emmett?"

If he was angry, he hid it, although his face was purpling. Maybe from concentration on his steps—Father was not the best dancer.

"If I tell you, you'll sit down?"

"Yes."

She puffed out a breath. "Lionel and Alma are in love, and Emmett and I love each other, but we are all too honorable or poor or obedient or stubborn to do a thing about it. And I'm determined Viola will not grow up with naught but paid servants to love her."

She shouldn't have said it. The look of pain in Father's eyes was something she'd never forget, not if she lived to be a hundred. She deserved to rot in one of the moldering towers in Hawton Park for wounding Father's feelings—

And no. His heart. Father's knees gave way and he slipped toward the ground.

◆ ◆ ◆

Emmett dashed forward, catching Mr. Beale's neck and shoulders before his head could smack the hard floor.

"Father!" Penny gripped Mr. Beale's hand.

Mr. Beale's cheeks were cool, but a pulse beat at his neck—a good sign. Loosening the elder man's tie, Emmett looked up. "Is a physician present?"

A gentleman pushed through the gathered crowd. "I am."

Emmett sat back, ready to assist but allowing the doctor space to work. Within moments, Mr. Beale's eyelids fluttered. "Penny?"

"I'm here." She kissed Mr. Beale's hand. "Don't worry. Everything will be the way it's supposed to be."

Mr. Beale started to speak, but Mrs. Beale's sobs drowned out the words. The next twenty minutes passed in a flurry of activity: Mr. Beale was carried to his bedchamber and the guests were sent home, except for Lionel and Emmett, who gathered with Penny and her mother in the parlor to await the doctor's news.

Penny stood by the hearth, staring into the flames. Without caring what her mother thought, Emmett rushed to her side. "This isn't your fault."

"Of course it is. I told him the truth, and he fell."

He squeezed her elbow, just beneath the lacy pouf of her sleeve. "You are not to blame. I pushed things too far. That wasn't love, what I did to you, telling you I loved you and offering nothing but guilt."

Her hand covered his. "You offered me knowledge to make an informed choice. I thought I chose well, but I still managed to ruin it all."

"Mr. Retford." Mrs. Beale's sharp retort made Penny jump. "You forget yourself."

His hand fell away.

"Pardon me." Alma's soft voice carried through the room. Viola clung to her hand, and Mrs. Shore lurked behind. "Mother and I do not wish to intrude, but Viola was watching the ballroom from the window in the hall above. She requires reassurance."

Lionel stepped forward. "Poor duck. Everything's fine."

Viola didn't look convinced. Emmett knelt and chucked Viola's chin. "It was frightening, I'm sure, poppet. But Mr. Beale woke up."

"It's true." Penny stroked Viola's curls then looked up at Alma. "How kind you were to check on her."

Farrow paused at the threshold. "Madam, Mr. Beale asks for you."

"At last." Mrs. Beale rose from her seat on the settee, glaring at Emmett as she passed out the door.

"Back to Miss Partridge you go." Lionel thumped Viola's head in an awkward pat.

"I'd like to stay here." Viola's eyes were wide.

"Why don't you, then?" Penny shot Lionel a beseeching look.

Alma nodded. "I can fetch Amelie and some coloring pages."

Lionel smiled. "Your consideration is touching, Miss Shore."

Miss Shore indeed, as if everyone in the room but Viola didn't know how he felt about Alma.

When Alma returned, she and her mother bid them all good night. If her farewell to Lionel was too long or quiet, no one objected.

Emmett reached for Penny's hand, but she pulled away. "I'm going to check on Father."

"It is not your fault," he whispered so Viola wouldn't overhear.

Penny shook her head as if she didn't believe him.

Viola squatted on the floor before the coffee table and opened her box of pastels. To think, Emmett had prayed to repair his family. Instead, he'd caused further harm—and not just between him and Lionel, but to the Beale family, as well.

Emmett settled into a chair to pray. For Mr. Beale. For forgiveness for pushing too hard.

When he looked up again, Viola had created a stack of colored pages. He sat beside her and examined the top sheet. "A pretty meadow."

"It's the green at Hawton Park, of course."

"Ah, yes." There was the house in the distance. Emmett lifted the next sheet. It looked like a family scene. A rather curious one, at that.

At movement from the door, Emmett looked up. Clark held a salver. "Urgent telegram for you, Mr. Retford."

Emmett stood and thanked Clark. He opened it, read the contents twice, and slipped the telegram into his breast pocket.

"Good news?" Lionel peered at him.

"Indeed." When Viola yawned, he chuckled. "It's bedtime, I believe. Would you like your father to take you up?"

"No." But she yawned again.

Lionel lifted Viola into his arms—something Emmett hadn't seen happen in ages. "Come on, darling."

"Wait." Emmett scooped up Viola's picture. "May I borrow this, sweetheart?"

"What for?"

"I'd like to show it to Mr. Beale, if I may."

"So he will feel better?"

"That is my hope, yes." So they all would feel better.

She nodded against her father's chest.

Emmett bid his niece good night and mounted the stairs. Penny paced the hall before a shut door. Before he could reach her, Mrs. Beale slipped out of the room, leaving the door ajar. When she saw him, her lips pursed.

"Madam?" He bowed. "How fares Mr. Beale?"

"Alive," she snipped.

"And well." Mr. Beale's exasperated tone carried through the doorway. "Come in, Retford."

Mrs. Beale gaped. "I do not think—"

"Send him in, Marjorie."

Penny lifted her hand, as if to touch him, but didn't. "Emmett?"

He took her hand and squeezed it. "I must speak to him, man to man. I'll do my utmost not to upset him, though."

Emmett squared his shoulders. It wasn't every day one had the chance to speak now or forever hold his peace.

Chapter 8

"This is your doing." Mother pointed to the shut door, her nostrils flaring. "Sneaking off with Emmett—"

"We didn't sneak." Penny slumped into the Chippendale chair outside her parents' room that no one ever sat in. "We were saying goodbye."

"—And letting your father dance, after I'd warned you. You hurt your father and ruined Lionel's *surprise* proposal. Oh yes, he was going to propose! Nothing went right tonight."

At least they'd be certain to make the society pages tomorrow. Penny sighed. "I'm marrying Lionel, Mother. Isn't that enough?"

"It's not for me." Emmett had opened the door and paused in the threshold, staring at Penny. It had taken courage for him to face her father.

Mother pretended he wasn't there. "Come, Penny. Let's see your father."

Penny didn't want to leave Emmett this way, but to her surprise, he nodded that she should. And then he followed her into the room.

"You aren't welcome here." Mother glared at Emmett.

"Hush, Marjorie." Father shifted against the headboard of his bed. Praise God, his coloring had returned. "I've something to say to our daughter."

She rushed toward him. "Don't exert yourself, Father. And I've something to say to you. I'm so sorry for saying what I did. And letting you dance."

"I knew well what I was doing, dancing. Someone had to put a stop to the nonsense."

Penny and her mother gasped together. "Father?"

Father took Penny's hand. "I'm the one who seeks forgiveness. I thought you'd want Hawton. A title goes a long way in this world, you know."

"I know." She smiled. "But so does love."

He kissed her fingers. "It does indeed. So I'm freeing you from any obligation you may feel to marry Lionel. I'll give him something for his trouble, but it won't be a dowry. Now do me a favor and go speak to that fellow there while I convince your mother."

Emmett stood at the door wearing a hopeful grin for her.

"Him?" Mother said it like Emmett was a pirate. "Unchaperoned?"

"It's the hallway, Marjorie." Father shooed Penny and Emmett out.

"What is this?" Penny turned on Emmett once they stood in the hallway. It was empty, although her parents' loudly whispered argument couldn't quite be ignored.

He led her back to the Chippendale chair. "I apologized to him for going about everything the wrong way. I should have spoken to him from the start, but I thought you'd be better off without me. Marrying Lionel is better for you, after all."

"You are as bad as he is, if you think I need not be consulted in the matter."

"I should have consulted Viola, too." He held out the paper.

Penny studied the drawing. A dark-haired man and woman stood off to the side. A smaller figure, dressed in yellow, stood in the foreground, flanked by a mustachioed gent and a lady, with whom she held hands. The lady was yellow haired, donned in blue, and held a baby—no, the body was too adult-like. It was a doll.

Viola, with Lionel and Alma, and dolly Amelie. Emmett and Penny were still valued enough to be in the picture but nevertheless on the fringe.

Emmett smiled. "Remember when we met?"

"I'll never forget it."

"Me neither, but do you recall when we studied that painting and you confessed you didn't know the artist? I said it's sometimes of benefit to approach a piece of artwork without prejudice, do you remember?"

"It was a kind comment to cover my ignorance."

"It was nothing of the sort. Although what I said isn't always true. Sometimes knowing the artist can enrich a viewer's experience. Like with this picture."

She studied it and gasped. "Viola wants Alma to be her mother. Not me."

"Alma and Lionel want it, too. Are you sad?"

Penny should feel sad, maybe, but she didn't. Instead, warmth suffused her from her heart to her limbs. Lionel was a different man with Alma. Kinder, and more available to Viola. His friendship had been good for Alma, too—Penny saw that now. Alma was happy, blossoming with love for Lionel and Viola, the family she long had craved.

So Penny shook her head. "I'm not sad in the least. I wanted Viola to be loved. For everyone to be happy."

"Viola loves you, too. She'd enjoy having you as an aunt."

After he'd said he wouldn't marry her, not two hours ago? She hopped to her feet. "I beg your pardon?"

"I thought I was clear." His lips twitched.

So he thought this amusing, did he? "That is the worst proposal I've ever heard."

"You've heard many, then?"

"Not a one, and you know it." She let him take her hands, but she wasn't about to let him get away with such a weak declaration. "A proposal should be sweet, and also explain how a marriage might be achieved without giving my father a heart attack."

"First of all, I showed him Viola's picture."

"That was all it took?"

"For him, yes, but for the sake of your mother's need to see you married to someone more suitable than an earl's youngest brother, I told him about my new position."

"You shouldn't stop being a professor for my sake." She didn't want him to change a thing. She'd argue it if she must, but it was becoming harder to concentrate with him holding her hands to his chest.

"I'll teach here and there." His heart pounded under her fingers. "But tonight I received word from London. The Prince of Wales is so grateful for my efforts with the Dunwood map that he's asked me to serve in a capacity that is somewhat diplomatic, somewhat academic, with a dash of espionage thrown in. I'll assist Britain and America with sensitive cases that include art—and there are more than one would believe. Forgeries, stolen pieces, historical disputes."

"Or maps to lost treasure?"

"Especially maps to lost treasure." He grinned, his lips so close she could stand on tiptoe and kiss them. "I should still have time for my newest passion, sharing art with children in need so they can express their emotions."

Like her girls at the home. "I am so pleased for you." And the children he'd help. And that he'd be in America. Close enough, perhaps, to court until Mother accepted that appearances weren't as important as things like love.

"I can afford a larger house, as well as a flat in Mayfair. And I won't be in shabby lodgings in New York. Or Philadelphia. But it won't be this." He glanced at the rich furnishings. "No title. No grand estate. If you want more, I'll go and not say a word, for I'm still the fourth son. Not the heir to anything."

"Except my heart." There was no one else she'd ever want to give it to.

"I'll spend every day treasuring the masterpiece you are. Precious." His lips grazed her forehead. "Unique." Then her cheek, just under her eye. "Beautiful, without and within."

She swayed, expecting his lips to touch hers. Instead, still holding her hands, he dropped to his knee.

"I'm in for a penny, in for a pound now. I started something and will see it through to its end." His eyes twinkled. "And yes, it's my favorite pun, Penny of mine. Will you marry me?" He gazed up at her with such devotion in his eyes that she tugged him to his feet.

"That is a suitable proposal." When she smiled, their noses touched.

He bent forward, his lips a mere inch from hers. "Is that a yes?"

"Yes, Emmett, I will marry you."

And then he kissed her as properly as he'd proposed.

Sometime later she opened her eyes to see Lionel slip from Viola's room. He didn't seem at all unhappy to spy her kissing his brother, but she still gasped.

Emmett turned and slipped his arm about her shoulder.

Lionel held up his hands in a gesture of peace. "Congratulations."

"You aren't angry?" About her, or the two million?

"Emmett helped me see that God will provide, but in the meantime I shouldn't ignore the gifts He's placed into my hands, like Viola and Alma. I wish you both happiness."

"Thank you, Lionel."

After he descended the stair, Penny curled back into Emmett's arms. "So Lionel turned down two million dollars."

"So did I."

Her head snapped back. "Father offered it to you?"

"Yes, but I suggested it go into a fund for you. And your children."

"*Our* children."

He kissed her again. "Now what do you say we give your parents the good news?"

Mother wouldn't find it good at all. But Penny took Emmett's hand and prayed that in God's good time, Mother would come around.

God hadn't let her down yet.

◆ ◆ ◆

Three weeks later

Penny spun from her looking glass as Alma, a vision in a bridal gown of white satin, entered the bedchamber.

Alma gasped. "You look beautiful, Penny! Your wedding gown is perfect."

"As is yours, Alma." Penny hugged her dearest friend, even as she recalled her mother's order not to embrace anyone, lest she wrinkle her Worth gown.

"We are in the society pages today." Alma hopped on her toes. "Mama sent for extra copies, so I brought one for you."

"I'll paste it in my memory book." Although she already knew the words by heart:

> *Lionel Retford, Earl of Hawton, of Nottinghamshire, England, and his brother the Honourable Mr. Emmett Retford, have chosen Philadelphia brides. Today the church in Rittenhouse Square will be the scene of a double wedding. . . .*

Hand in hand, Penny and Alma made their way downstairs where Mother, Mrs. Shore, and Viola waited.

"I hear church bells." Viola twirled in her buttercup frock.

"That means it's time." Mrs. Shore, who weeks ago had found it so difficult to part from Alma, had quickly taken to the idea of moving to England—and having a step-granddaughter to love.

Mother fluffed a portion of Penny's veil. "Your father wants to dance at the reception. He knows full well he could faint or worse."

Penny patted Mother's shoulder. "I'll allow him a few bars of music but no more."

At least Father was healthy. And as she'd prayed, Mother's opinion of Emmett had changed dramatically. His relationship with the Prince of Wales helped matters immensely, as far as appearances were concerned to Mother. Maybe someday she'd come to faith. Penny wouldn't stop praying.

"Are you packed for New York?" Mother took her arm.

There, Emmett was to examine paintings and, God willing, break a ring of international art forgers in the process. Meanwhile, the search for King John's treasure had begun back in England, and this summer Emmett and Penny would visit the area.

"I'm ready." Penny nodded. "My one regret is leaving the girls' home. They still lack a patroness."

"Didn't I tell you? I volunteered." Mother laughed. "While you had your final dress fitting yesterday, I visited to see what the fuss was about. What charming girls."

Despite the muss it would cause their gowns, Penny embraced her. "You've given me the best wedding present I could have hoped for."

But it wasn't the best one, after all. That came when she entered the church on Father's arm, Alma on his other side, Viola ahead scattering flower petals on the aisle. At the aisle's end, the grooms waited, grinning like children. Emmett was resplendent—there was no other word for it. He was the best wedding present, one for her to keep forever.

When she reached the front of the church, before Emmett could take her hands, Lionel stepped forward and kissed her cheek. For the first time, his nearness didn't make her chest tighten or her stomach clench.

"Welcome to the family, Sister."

Beside her, Emmett offered the same gesture to Alma.

"Now me!" Viola hopped for kisses before sitting with Mrs. Shore.

"Now me," Emmett murmured when he took Penny's hands at last.

"Not yet," Penny whispered. "You have to marry me first."

And so he did, and when they were pronounced husband and wife, he gave her a kiss she'd not soon forget.

Historical Note:

Lady Dunwood, her painting, and the map to King John's lost treasure are pure fiction, but the treasure itself is quite real. King John's crown, scepter, and other valuables were lost between King's Lynn and Lincoln just days before King John's death in 1216. Over the past eight hundred years, despite numerous searches by historians, archaeologists, and amateurs in those fields, the treasure has yet to be found.

Susanne Dietze began writing love stories in high school, casting her friends in the starring roles. Today, she's the award-winning author of a dozen new and upcoming historical romances who's seen her work on the ECPA and Publisher's Weekly Bestseller Lists for Inspirational Fiction. Married to a pastor and the mom of two, Susanne lives in California and enjoys fancy-schmancy tea parties, the beach, and curling up on the couch with a costume drama and a plate of nachos. You can visit her online at www.susannedietze.com and subscribe to her newsletters at http://eepurl.com/bieza5.

Sweet Love Grows

by Anita Mae Draper

Dedication

To Susanne Dietze and Gina Welborn for their laughter, encouragement, and candor, and especially to Gina for inviting me to be a part of this exciting project. And to my Barbour editor, Jessie Fioritto, for raising my novella to a higher level.

I can do all things through Christ which strengtheneth me.
PHILIPPIANS 4:13

Chapter 1

1890
McLeod County, Minnesota

Jeremy placed his well-fingered Bible on the corner of his wide oak desk as a reminder that laws allowed the correct dispensation of property and valuables during times of grief when people acted from their hearts instead of their heads. He believed he could perform any task assigned to him in the course of his duties without allowing emotions to cloud the facts, regardless of who was on the losing end.

Yet as he prepared to meet Robertson's daughter, a bitter taste coated his tongue. Due to past grievances, common sense and generosity were missing in this case, and there was nothing he could do but carry out the law and then leave with his emotions intact.

From his paisley-patterned vest he took out his favorite pen, a graceful, well-balanced instrument made of fine silver with a smooth gold nib. He'd received it upon completing his legal apprenticeship under Winston, along with the implication that he might be offered a partnership in his law firm if he could take care of one troublesome legal matter. A week of isolation in return for a future of security? Jeremy had practically run to the train.

He set his pen down beside the small stack of legal documents made out to Robertson's daughter.

The bitter taste flooded back.

Reaching for the pitcher of water and one of the glasses he'd set out in case she needed refreshment after hearing his news, he poured one for himself.

If only the taste of pure water could wash down the filth of his task.

◆ ◆ ◆

Amelia tightened the black shawl around her shoulders more for the familiar security it provided than from the breeze that rocked the attorney's shingle under the eave.

Hesitantly, she knocked on the door.

Footsteps on the other side advanced in her direction. The door opened to show an impeccably dressed man with trouser creases as straight as those of her butler.

After a quick appraisal he leaned against the doorframe with a wry, appreciative smile. "Another member of the Glencoe welcoming committee? I appreciate all the attention, but I do have work to tend to, Miss. . . ?"

"Miss Robertson."

"Oh?" Straightening, he wiped his hand across his mouth. "You're not what I expected."

He was younger and more attractive than she'd expected as well, yet she wasn't going to admit it. At least not while standing on the street where all of Glencoe could hear.

"Come in." He swept his hand toward a chair facing his desk before turning to close the door. "I'm sorry about your father."

She bit her bottom lip. Perhaps it was distress and strain that made her feel as she did, but he didn't sound a bit sorry that Father had passed away.

"Did you know him?"

"No, not personally." Curt and to the point, he splayed his hands on the documents as if to keep the words from jumping off the pages. "I'm sure you are aware that your father died intestate? That is to say, without having left a will?"

She remembered a long-ago conversation when Father had said that one day she would receive everything he owned, but he had never mentioned a written paper proving it, and someday had come sooner than either of them expected. "It appears that is the case, Mr. Moore. Is that a problem?"

Steepling his fingers, he tapped his fingertips together. "Yes, in your case it is." His voice held a quality she tried to define—not remorse or sorrow. Perhaps resignation.

She fiddled with the black crepe trim of her bodice. "Mr. Moore, my father left me everything he owned—the house, the estate, and the mill. All that is required is for me to sign the official papers so that the bank recognizes me as his heir and I can continue the work he began." She eyed the pen on his desk.

As if following her line of sight, he picked it up and rolled it between his fingers. "Your state of finances wasn't included in your father's financial report, so am I to assume you have your own means of support separate from the estate?"

"What do you mean? Why would I need my own funds?" She stared at him. "I have everything I need at home."

His eyes darkened. "The question of who owns the Robertson estate is what we are discussing here."

"What do you mean, who? I told you, Father left it to me."

"And yet after two days of searching, no one has produced the will that proves it."

"Mr. Moore, I have a mill to run." She rose from the chair, her hands clenched around her handbag to keep her from shaking them at him.

He rose as she did. "Please sit down and I'll attempt to explain further."

Amelia had no wish to stay. Moore was playing games with her, pulling her along like a toy horse on wheels. And yet the bank required completed paperwork to prove ownership. She sat back down.

"This is a delicate situation." He tapped his mouth with the fingertips of his right hand. "Your mother was Angela Cord. Correct?"

"Yes. She was a Cord before she married Father, and then she died on the day I was born. Really, Mr. Moore, what has that to do with Father's will?"

"Everything. Henry Robertson never married Angela Cord."

Although he seemed to be relaying logical information, she couldn't quite grasp the meaning behind his words. And then, as a rushing sound filled her ears, the room blackened, sucking her down into darkness as thick as pitch.

◆ ◆ ◆

"Miss Cord?" Jeremy dipped his fingers into the pitcher of water and then dabbed his fingertips on her face. He had known his news would be a shock, but he hadn't thought she would fall out of her chair. He slid his left arm under her neck and raised her head.

"Miss Cord? Can you hear me?"

Long silky lashes opened over sky-blue eyes. She stared up at him with a puzzled expression. "What happened? Why did you call me Miss Cord?"

No sooner had she spoken than she cried out in alarm and then covered her eyes with her forearm.

He grimaced at the awful taste in his mouth, knowing he could have broken the brutal news with more compassion instead of the harshness that had erupted. But that meant he was responding to her with his heart and not his head, and if he allowed that, he might as well walk away and call himself a failure right now.

A few minutes later she faced him from the chair across his desk. Except for some mussed hair and a hat that was tilted slightly more than when she'd entered his office, she appeared composed. "Mr. Moore, what does my father's state of matrimony have to do with all of this?"

"You can't be his legal heir if he hasn't claimed you as his daughter."

"Hasn't claimed me? Of course he's claimed me. The whole county knows I'm his daughter."

He steepled his fingers. "He didn't claim you legally on paper. These are all the pertinent documents concerning Henry Robertson's estate." He motioned to the papers on his desk. "There is proof that he owned the house and the land it sits on, the estate, and the mill. Your name doesn't appear anywhere."

She stared at the documents as if she could read them upside down and through all the layers of the pile. "How can you be sure my parents never married?"

"Because there is no record of it in the county courthouse records or in any county church."

"They could have gone to another county, or to Minneapolis or Chicago."

"Yes, they could have." She was wrong, but he liked that she was presenting possibilities. It showed an intelligence that she would need in the months to come. He slid the top document across the desk. "This is a copy of your birth record, signed and dated by the midwife who delivered you."

A myriad of expressions crossed her face as she read the words. With a sniffle she opened her handbag to take out a frilly handkerchief. Holding it to her mouth, she read the record again.

Jeremy knew the words would rip her world apart, but it was all legal. The best thing for everyone concerned would be for her to run back home to pack her bags and leave on her own volition thereby saving him the misery of evicting her.

His gaze fell on the Bible as the scripture about taking care of widows and orphans came to mind. He gulped more water. He had been the orphan whom Winston had taken home to look after. Winston had fed, clothed, and educated him. If Winston wanted what was rightfully his, then Jeremy would get it for him—as long as it was legal.

He chanced a glance at Miss Cord, who still clung to her birth record as if reading it again would change the words. If she produced a will or even a statement of intention written by Robertson, Jeremy would sign over everything to her without a qualm. But if she couldn't. . .

He gulped more water to wash the sourness from his mouth.

◆ ◆ ◆

Pain arced across Amelia's chest as if Moore had reached across his desk and squeezed her heart himself. With her hand on her bodice as if to keep her heart in place, she reread her birth record while mentally checking off each fact. Her father was Henry Robertson. Her mother was Angela Cord. She was Amelia Cord. Not Amelia Robertson, but Amelia Cord. And instead of writing a date for her parents' marriage, the blank line was filled in with the word *illegitimate*.

With shimmering eyes, she handed the document back to Moore.

He laid it on the stack and then picked the whole thing up to tap all the papers into place with all edges plumb before laying them on the desk again. "To summarize, you are *not* the legal heir of Henry Robertson's estate and mill, which includes the house and Robertson's Syrup."

She shivered as if the words had stripped her of everything.

"And since you are not the heir, you have no legal right to reside on the premises."

She flinched. "What do you mean?"

Three quick knocks rapped against Moore's office door.

Moore rose from his chair. "That could be my next client." He walked around the desk and offered his hand. "Let me know if I can be of further assistance."

"Assistance? Help me keep my home!"

He led her toward the door. "That's not possible."

"But what will happen to it all? Will there be an auction?" The thought of buying it back caused elation for a moment until she remembered she had no funds.

"I think we'd better let the *legal* heir decide that."

She pulled away from him. "Who's that?"

"I'll be out in a couple of days and we'll talk more. Good day." He pulled open the door and greeted the older man standing on the sidewalk.

With one short meeting, Moore had erased her past as well as her future.

◆ ◆ ◆

Williams waited at the front entrance beside the large black wreath. "I hope you enjoyed your drive, Miss Amelia."

She untied the silk ribbons of her black crepe-bedecked hat. "It was the best part of my afternoon. I noticed things I've never seen before."

"The death of a loved one has a way of opening our eyes, miss." His eyes portrayed his own profound sadness of losing a man he'd admired and worked with every day for two decades or more. "Dinner will be served at six o'clock."

She was about to say she didn't feel like eating tonight, but then Mrs. Fielding would worry about her health, and that wouldn't do at all. "Thank you, Williams."

Up in her chamber, she took off the mourning outfit she'd purchased ready-made due to the time constraint and hung it carefully on a hanger. As she donned her black silk evening gown, she wondered for the first time how much it had cost. Like the rest of the shopkeepers around town, the subject of payment hadn't been mentioned because it was a foregone conclusion that the estate bookkeeper would pay for any purchases on her account. But who was paying them now? Did her bookkeeper know she was no longer the heiress without any right to charge anything to the estate account?

She caressed the black silk as if it was the last time she'd wear it. If Moore demanded payment, how could she pay him? With her jewels?

She picked up her jewelry chest from its place on the bureau and set it beside her on the bed. Her fingers trailed across the inlaid mother-of-pearl leaves draping the sides of the box. She opened it and took out the gold chain locket that held a tiny image of the woman who had borne her and then died. Amelia stared at her mother's image for a long time, trying to see a resemblance between their faces and not seeing anything, although Father said they had the same chin in likeness and temperament. She closed the locket and placed it on the bed.

Next came the pearl starburst brooch, which she set on the bed beside the locket.

Half a dozen other pieces remained in the box, but they held no sentimental value. She scooped them out and put them on her bureau for the legal heir.

With the jewelry box empty, she put the brooch and locket back inside and then hugged it to her chest. Father had said the sewing box and brooch were the only items of note her mother had owned when they met. It was after her death that Father had taken her sewing box, lined it with velvet, and given it to Amelia with strict instructions to keep it with her always.

Regardless of what Moore said belonged to the legal heir, he would have a monumental fight on his hands if he tried to take the only three items she considered rightfully hers.

Chapter 2

Amelia pushed open the conservatory's glass door and inhaled the familiar humid air laced with the scent of sodden soil and damp vegetation. Over the past three days everywhere she looked—everything she touched—emphasized the magnitude of her loss. Here under the tutelage of Woodward, she'd learned how to grow tropical shrubs, luscious ferns, and colorful flowers—triumphs against the frigid Minnesota winter and the searing summer sun.

After filling her watering can with rain water from the outside barrel, she sprinkled the rows of terra-cotta pots holding the sorghum seedlings. Another week and they would be ready to plant out in a special plot reserved for testing different varieties of sorghum to see which had the shorter growing period and which were more resistant to pests, drought, and other adversities.

She'd spent years studying under Woodward, and then when he deemed she was ready, she began her own research of developing and breeding sorghum plants. If she left, what would happen to her research? Her plants?

As she watered, the seedlings blurred before her eyes, and soon her tears were sliding down her cheeks in accompaniment to the gently flowing water from her spout.

Perhaps the new heir would allow Woodward to continue her work after she left. Sniffling, she moved to the next row.

Years of selective plant breeding—which could benefit the whole Minnesota sorghum industry—were on the verge of being lost. Was there nothing she could do? No, that was the wrong attitude. There must be something she could do. But what? Who would be interested?

The crunch of footsteps on the walkway leading to the conservatory drew her attention. Through the condensation coating the window, she made out the form of the man she least wanted to see on this weepy morning. He said he'd be out in a couple of days. When those had passed without his presence, she prayed he'd gone back to Chicago. His visit could only mean more disappointment.

On impulse she hid behind some five-feet-high palm fronds.

He reached the door and entered without knocking, his eyes darting straight to her location as if he'd spotted her black clothing on his way up the walk. "Good morning, Miss Cord. Your butler said I would find you puttering out here."

She bristled. Emerging from her sheltered spot, she reached for her watering can. "Please give me the courtesy of using Miss Robertson, the name my father introduced me as and one I've used my entire life. As for the puttering, I don't consider botanical research puttering, but perhaps to someone who spends his day with books it may seem like that."

"I see." He clasped his hands behind his back and watched her. A few minutes later, he wandered off to explore her favorite place on earth.

She kept a wary eye on him, holding her breath every time he fondled a leaf or bent to get a closer look. He even whiffed two different orchids before completing the circuitous path and returning to her side.

"Do you have an affinity to plants, Mr. Moore?" Knowing his level of botanical experience would tell her how far she could plead her case concerning her eviction date.

"Only when they please one of the lovely recipients of my floral tributes."

His what? She stood her watering can upright so she wouldn't drown something while being distracted and took a really good look at Moore. He'd pushed his hat back so that two inches of wavy dark hair framed his forehead. The sunlight flowing through the glass panes showed soft brown eyes that reminded her of cattails in July.

His eyes widened as he grinned.

She tried to recall his last sentence and failed.

"Ladies, Miss Cord. I give flowers to ladies."

Feeling as if her face was on fire, she turned back to the seedlings, thankful she had something to look at besides him.

"So you're a botanist." He gestured to her potting table with its special shelves for books and drawers for her botany laboratory instruments.

"Not officially, but Woodward, the estate's groundskeeper, studied in England and I've studied under him. These sorghum seedlings, for instance"—she gestured to the seedlings—"they are the result of several years' worth of research, records, and plant breeding."

"It looks like grass."

"Most grains start out looking that way and then they take on the characteristics of their variety as they grow. These stakes"—she pointed to the small pieces of wood at the beginning of each row— "are marked with the name of their parent strains. We plant out the seedlings, tend them, harvest them, and evaluate them. In the spring I'll choose strains with particular superior traits and breed them with other strains. The resulting seedlings will be grown in our test plot next year."

"I see." He dropped his gaze to where his finger tapped the closest wooden stake.

What had she said that changed his features from interest to something indiscernible? Ah. . .there wouldn't be a next year. A heavy feeling pushed against her chest. There probably wouldn't even be a harvest. Would these seedlings even leave the conservatory?

She summoned her courage from a place deep inside. "What are your plans for the conservatory, Mr. Moore?"

In the silence that followed, she held her breath, trying to be ready for whatever action he announced.

◆ ◆ ◆

Instead of answering, Jeremy sauntered over to where he'd seen a tray of funny-looking cactus plants, some with a huge red ball, and others with a yellow ball on top. If it hadn't been for the pricks, he wouldn't have recognized them as cactus. There wasn't a lot he did recognize in the glass-enclosed structure where greenery and flowers hung from the ironworks and filled every bit of floor space that wasn't taken by the walkway or the furniture.

He had seen engravings of tall palm trees, but these ones—like the one she had tried to hide behind—were perfect as a background feature for her wicker chairs and table. If his visit were purely social instead of for business reasons, he thought he would enjoy a moment to sit among the beautiful surroundings without having to think about who owned what.

Abruptly, he headed to the door. What had he been thinking? Wicker and tea among the flowers and trees? How Winston would laugh if he heard such a thing. Jeremy's ears burned at the thought.

He paused at the door. "Tea will be served in the study, Miss Cord. Please join me there."

He closed the door firmly behind him and then followed the walkway to the house. He didn't need to see her face to imagine the shock she must have felt at his implicit request that she join him for tea in her own home. But it wasn't her home any longer and she needed to get used to the idea.

As the twin peaked turrets of the Robertson mansion caught his eye, his chest tightened. As Henry Robertson's daughter, Miss Cord had led a life as sheltered as any royal princess. Without the social status that Robertson's life afforded, she would be just another person on the street looking for work. Would she survive or succumb? When his swallow didn't clear away the taste in his mouth, he increased his pace.

At the house he strode through the foyer as if he'd lived there for years, and yet his first entrance had only been minutes before when he had informed the butler of the change in ownership before being directed to the conservatory.

The butler followed him. "Mr. Moore, Miss Amelia hasn't—"

Jeremy whipped around to face him. "No, she probably didn't. Bring in the tea and I'll see that she does."

The butler puffed out his chest like a grouse trying to scare the competition off.

As Jeremy strode down the corridor, he realized that the home was probably the butler's as well. Back in Chicago, most of the employees in the big houses were day staff who went to their own homes in the evenings. Out here in the backwoods though, where would they go unless they wanted to make the long trip to town each day and night?

Having to room and board the staff would explain the reasoning behind the huge three-story house Henry Robertson had built on his estate. Winston might even let them all stay once Miss Cord was gone.

Yet as he stood in the study before the multipaned glass door that led out to the side veranda, Jeremy suspected that Winston's hatred for Robertson had deepened to such an extent over the years that even the staff would be ordered out because they had served to make his life comfortable.

He crossed his arms at thoughts of Winston. The man had taken him in because he'd wanted his mother, and then treated Jeremy as fair as any son. It used to rankle Jeremy that Winston hadn't married his mother or legally adopted him, but the more Jeremy learned of the law, the more he understood how signatures placed on a poorly written document could be detrimental to a person's financial status. Having lived on the street once, Jeremy wasn't about to try it again and could well understand Winston's reluctance to take that chance with him.

The bitterness returned to his mouth at the sound of a door closing. As footsteps approached, he told himself that putting Amelia Cord out onto the street had to be done for Winston's sake. With her connections though, it wouldn't be the same as what his mother had experienced.

Amelia Cord strode through the open study door with her eyes blazing. "Mr. Moore, you take unwelcome liberties with my staff."

Jeremy tapped his chest pocket to locate his pen. His loyalty lay with Winston. No matter how Amelia affected him, he needed to remember that.

"Tea, Miss Cord?" He held the silver teapot over a dainty porcelain cup as if it were a natural occurrence that he should be pouring tea in her father's study.

She stopped before a pair of leather-tufted wing chairs strategically placed in front of the large walnut desk.

Jeremy poured tea into a cup, aware of her fists hanging down the sides of her dress in his peripheral vision but choosing to ignore her display of emotions. With one cup filled he started on the next.

"Yes, with honey," she huffed. She dropped into one of the chairs and crossed her arms. Within moments, she uncrossed them and placed her hands on the chair arms where her fingers curled over the edge until they stopped on worn spots on the leather—spots perfectly fitted to her fingertips as if she'd performed the same action a hundred times or more.

As Jeremy set the teapot down, the glint of his silver pen bolstered him. She may have sat here and spent time with Robertson, but he was the one in control of the teapot and they both knew it.

With his saucer in hand, he sat beside her in the matching chair. Although he would have felt more authoritative sitting across the desk from her, he wanted her guard down so they could discuss the unpleasant details of the case without emotions—and tears—getting in the way.

"Miss Cord, as I sit in this room and look at all the books, I can't help but wonder if you've flipped through every one in the search for your father's will."

Her cup rattled as she set it on the saucer. "We've been over the entire house twice, shaking and checking behind and under everything movable. Short of tearing up the floor or pulling the walls down, I don't know where else to look."

"I see." He sipped his tea. How was he supposed to evict her when she looked at him with sky-blue eyes filled with concern? Her eyes had been the first thing he thought of when he had woken during the night with the case on his mind, and that wasn't going to work at all.

She looked around Robertson's study as if allowing her memories free rein. "I don't understand why Father didn't leave a will." Her deep chest-heaving sigh jumped the wall he was trying to build around his heart. He wanted to embrace her and reassure her that all would be fine.

Her sky-blue eyes found him. "You mentioned an heir. Please explain how that is possible."

His dreamy state shattered. He rose and set his cup and saucer on the service tray. Deciding that he needed the security of a desk to play the part of an attorney, he sat in Henry Robertson's large wooden chair where brass tacks held down the russet-colored leather and displayed the fine craftsmanship of the piece. Another item to add to his report and one more item for Winston to hate. He had a suspicion that Winston would rather burn everything than sell it, but that would mean a financial loss and Winston didn't like losing money.

Amelia leaned forward in her seat. "Mr. Moore? Who inherits instead of me?"

He tapped his pen against the desk. "Since no will has been found, your father's only legal heir, Mr. Winston Kent of Chicago, inherits everything."

"And who is Mr. Kent?" She raised her chin.

"Your father's heir," he said, merely to test her mettle now that her pluck had returned.

It seemed she didn't wish to be tested. She rose and put her cup and saucer down hard on the service tray so that the cup clinked with abandon as it settled.

He raised his finger. "Careful, that's no longer yours."

He almost ducked from the glare she threw him, thankful she hadn't reached for a dish. Standing, he tugged his vest down. "If you've finished, I would like you to give me a tour."

"Of what?"

"Everything."

"Why?"

"Because it's necessary for my report."

"But we haven't discussed why Mr. Kent is the heir."

"I understand the mill is down the road. Why don't I explain on the way over?"

Chapter 3

The sight of plowed fields and the earthy smell that surrounded them tugged on Amelia's heart. She pointed them out as Moore drove the buggy past them. "This week we're plowing and harrowing. If the weather holds, we'll be planting next week."

He glanced at the field and then at her. "Perhaps."

"Perhaps? What does that mean?"

"It means Winston may not want them planted. Especially in sorghum."

"Not plant sorghum?" The idea was ludicrous. She gestured to the mill. "How can you run a mill without its main product?" She stared at his profile, ready to pounce on whatever ignorant answer came out of his mouth.

A muscle twitched along his jawline as if he'd locked his tongue in place and it wanted to get out. "Very well. Winston Kent is your father's stepson. He was ten years old when Henry Robertson abandoned him."

"My father would never abandon his child."

Moore shrugged. "And yet he did."

Only a foolish man would accuse Henry Robertson of doing such a thing. "You are slandering my father's name, sir. I'll not have it."

"It's not slander when it's the truth, Miss Cord. I can provide evidence if you wish, but wait to hear the whole truth before you start demanding justice."

Despite the outrage that urged her to pummel him with her clenched hands, the conviction behind his words made her pause. The father she knew would never abandon his child, but the Bible portrayed dozens of people who changed over time, or due to a momentous event. What if her father had done the same? Was she being fair if she didn't at least listen to his story?

"Tell me about my father, then. I don't know anything about his life before he met my mother. Was he born in Chicago?"

"According to his marriage record, yes."

She winced. It wasn't what she wanted to hear, yet it could explain why they hadn't found a record for her father marrying her mother.

He glanced at her and then looked away. "Winston's mother married for love when she was very young, but her family didn't approve of her choice and disinherited her. When no riches were forthcoming, her husband decided he loved the bottle and carousing more than her. Winston was barely two when his father died in a drunken brawl."

"The poor woman." He didn't respond, and it struck her that while telling the story, his voice had an edge she hadn't heard before. An idea began to form. "What happened to her?"

"She went back to her family and asked them to take Winston in because he shouldn't pay for her sins. They forgave her and welcomed Winston into the family."

Minutes passed as she waited for him to continue. When he didn't, she voiced her suspicions. "Are you Winston?"

"Whoa!" He pulled back so hard the horse reared. The sun reflected in his eyes as he stared at her. "Am I Winston? Of course I'm not Winston. Do I act like a rich, spoiled dandy?"

"Well, no, but it seems possible. I have no idea if you're rich. Yes, you act spoiled at times. As for being a dandy, you know how to dress well without being extravagant, so no, I wouldn't say you're a dandy." She lifted one shoulder. "I merely wondered."

He slapped the lines against the buggy and they moved forward once more. "When Winston was nine"—he threw her a look that said she should know better—"Winston, not me, when Winston was nine, his mother married Henry Robertson. The way Winston tells it his mother didn't want to remarry, but her parents were worried about her in the event of their death and made arrangements with Robertson to provide his name and protection to her and her son. She went along with it because she wanted her son to have a father. In return, Robertson received funds for a business venture."

Amelia's heart thumped beneath her bodice. She placed her hand over it and tried to take deep even breaths to slow it down. Something important was about to be spilled, and she had an awful feeling it concerned her.

"What was the business venture?"

"A syrup mill in Minnesota."

Her stomach twisted. "Oh." She stared at the mill and waited for the rush of familiar pride that always struck when she looked at the large structure. She couldn't feel anything except pain for Winston's mother who sacrificed so much for her son. "Tell me the rest."

Moore reined in the horse to a slow walk. "Henry Robertson married Winston's mother and formally adopted Winston as his son. I can provide a copy of that as well. Ten months later, Robertson left for Minnesota to get the mill started. He never returned to Chicago."

"Oh." She placed her hand on his and he stopped the horse. "Winston never saw him again?"

"No. When Winston was twelve, his mother died. He never speaks of it, but the servants hint that she drank something and never woke up. His grandparents sent word to Robertson, but the man didn't have the decency to show up for his wife's funeral."

Amelia swallowed the lump in her throat. "When was that?"

He shrugged as if it didn't matter then added a date.

She sat in stunned silence, blinking her tears into submission. "Henry Robertson hadn't returned to Chicago to bury his wife because he'd been tending his newborn daughter while the woman he loved died."

His brown eyes searched hers as if trying to find the root of her lie. He blinked once, then twice, and looked away. "As I said, your father abandoned his legal heir."

God in heaven, how does this happen?

And it all became clear. Winston was the rightful heir who felt the need to revenge his mother's death by hurting someone his stepfather had loved. By virtue of default, Amelia was the target.

And she didn't like it one bit.

◆ ◆ ◆

Three days later, Jeremy rode his livery mount back to Robertson's mill. He'd been up until the early morning hours finishing the report detailing all aspects of the sorghum cane operation yet wanted a final look at the books before sending his findings on to Winston. During the tour, Amelia and her men had showed him a near-perfect operation, but a bit of snooping around on his own might turn up something a new owner would want to know.

It was still early when he arrived at the mill and tied the chestnut to the rail. The last time he'd been here, workers had loaded barrels of syrup onto a wagon hooked to a four-hitch team of draft horses. This time the yard was devoid of anything that moved unless you counted the two-odd dozen empty barrels stacked along one wall.

He tried the door, found it unlocked, and walked into the large, warm interior, stopping for his eyes to grow accustomed to the low light level. The place needed more lights. Definitely an added expense for a buyer but not the huge problem he anticipated.

The mill foreman entered from a door on the right side of the large processing room. He nodded somberly to Jeremy. "Mr. Moore, I didn't expect you today."

Exactly what he wanted to hear. Jeremy offered his hand. "George Hanover, wasn't it?"

As he moved closer, the foreman wiped his right hand with a rag he'd been holding. He stretched his hand out to shake Jeremy's. "Yes, sir. Is there something you needed?"

Jeremy's gesture encompassed the whole mill. "Henry Robertson was a blessed man, George. Sometimes an operation falls into ruin when an owner dies—yet you've managed to keep his high standard as if he never left."

"That's Miss Amelia's doing. She followed her father around, mimicking his movements and absorbing everything like a sponge. We were worried about her when Mr. Robertson passed, but she comes down every afternoon, hiding her pain and carrying on as usual."

This isn't what Jeremy expected—or wanted—to hear. He would have to be square with Hanover if he wanted to get to the truth. "Did Miss Amelia explain why I'm here, George?"

"You're the attorney for Mr. Robertson's estate."

"That's correct. And did she give any indication for the mill's future?"

Hanover leaned back as if affronted by the question. "What do you mean? Miss Amelia would never sell the mill."

Just as he suspected, Amelia hadn't explained the situation to her staff. She wasn't doing her workers any favors by withholding the information, because they could be out looking and lining up jobs instead of waiting until they were dismissed. But he wasn't about to break the news until he had Winston's final word.

He motioned to the office. "Can I see the books, George? I need more information before I can do the final figures on Mr. Robertson's net worth."

The foreman scratched his head above his ear. He looked at the main entrance as if expecting someone to walk in and take charge of the situation. When the door didn't open, he moved aside. "I guess it would be all right. The sooner this is all settled, the sooner Miss Amelia will be happy again."

It was becoming clear that the relationship between Miss Amelia and her employees touched on a level that brought affection as well as respect into the equation. He would have to watch his step when it became known that he was evicting her from the property. The bitter taste returned as it often did when he thought of his mission. He wanted the taste gone for good.

"You're right, Hanover. Let's get this done so everything is settled."

As he followed the foreman into the office, he took out his pen. His loyalty lay with Winston, the true heir who'd had two fathers and lost them both. In Jeremy's eyes, Henry Robertson had done the unpardonable by abandoning the boy he had adopted. If Robertson had landed in Jeremy's court instead of God's, Jeremy would have done everything he could to see he paid for his neglect because that was just and right according to the law.

Yet as he went over the figures, his own words distracted him. If man's law was all that mattered, how would God judge him after he helped a vengeful man throw an innocent woman onto the street?

◆ ◆ ◆

The next morning Jeremy sealed his completed report into an envelope addressed to Winston. His trip to the mill hadn't yielded anything negative about the operation. On the contrary, it proved that Amelia's new sorghum varieties had increased production without cultivating more land. If she were a man, any number of companies would hire her. As a woman, she had a steep uphill climb to be accepted in the same manner. Did she have the fortitude to do it? He believed she did, and that would ease his mind some when she was on her own.

He hadn't quite figured out how and when to get her off the property, but it wouldn't happen until Winston responded to the report.

Unlike Chicago's big and busy post office, Glencoe's was located in the mercantile where the postal worker gave each customer a dose of advice along with the mail. Jeremy didn't mind the slower pace since he didn't have anything to do except sit in his office and wait for Winston's response. He advised potential clients on their rights and then sent them elsewhere for representation because he didn't want to be involved with a court case here after the Robertson case had closed.

Since several people were ahead of him in line, he checked out the store while he waited.

As his roaming gaze settled on a new travel trunk, an idea formed that would aid Amelia's plight while not being disloyal to Winston. After mailing off his report, he explored the trunk. It reeked of quality from its canvas cover to its iron bottom. Double-bound wide iron corners, leather-covered planked sides, and sliding handles with iron caps. Heavy and built to last. He opened the lid with its fine tumbler lock and found a bonnet box, a jewelry box, and an umbrella case. Everything a traveling lady would need.

Chapter 4

Later that afternoon with the new trunk in the back of a rented wagon, Jeremy drove past the empty Robertson fields. Regardless of who owned the estate, it was a crime to let fertile fields stand unseeded for a season. It was also a crime to leave special crops untended, such as Amelia's research seedlings, which is why he had included them along with the conservatory holdings and seed inventory in his report. If Winston included them on a sales list, they might attract someone interested in botany. Or would Winston view the loss as another way to get back at Robertson?

Soon enough he brought his team to a stop at the base of Amelia's veranda steps.

Someone must have seen him driving up because Amelia waited at the top. "Mr. Moore, I didn't expect you today. Especially not at this late hour."

Wisps of damp hair framed her forehead, proving he'd interrupted something strenuous.

"I won't be long, Miss Cord. I brought you something." He jumped from the wagon seat to the ground and circled around to the back where a canvas tarp provided added protection to the trunk's own cover. With a great deal of aplomb, he whipped the tarp and then the cover off the trunk.

"What's this?" Clasping her hands together, she held them waist high as if locking them into position so they wouldn't touch anything.

Jeremy swallowed. What he had thought was a great plan didn't look so good with the recipient and her butler eyeing him with the same sharp look he'd received from policemen as a young boy. Winston had saved him then. Jeremy would return the favor.

He signaled the butler, and together they carried the trunk up the stairs and set it near the hem of Amelia's skirt.

"It's for you." He opened the lid to show her the compartments and cases hidden inside. "Everything you need in one trunk."

Her brows furrowed. She glanced from him to the trunk and back to him. "Since I assume this is your way of telling me I need to pack, I'm finding it hard to thank you for your generosity."

"No need. I quite understand."

"I'm surprised you're letting me take my clothes, Mr. Moore. Does Winston know?"

Her verbal dig caught him between the ribs where it hurt. It made what he had to say easier. "I don't think you understand, Miss Cord. This is the only luggage you will leave here with. You can take anything you wish, your jewels, your gowns, even the crystal decanter and your silver tea service if you prefer. But anything you take must fit in this single trunk."

"You can't be serious." Unclasping her hands, she forced her fists down her sides and gripped her skirt in what he was beginning to realize was an emotional reaction to something unpleasant. "Have you seen a woman's gown, Mr. Moore?"

He raised his brow at the absurd statement. "Oh yes, I've had my fill of many a fine lady in a gown."

A light rose color bloomed on her cheeks. She looked skyward for a moment as if asking for help. "One of my gowns would completely fill that trunk."

"That's your problem, Miss Cord, not mine. I've always believed that modern fashion wastes yards of material that could be used for better purposes elsewhere." He marched down the steps before she decided to grab one of the cases in the trunk and throw it at him. "I'll be back in five days. I expect you and your trunk to be waiting on the steps."

"Five days? What about the seedlings? And the fields?"

"The estate is no longer your concern, Miss Cord. If you're not waiting when I return, I'll assume you've already moved on."

Five days. What was he supposed to do in this backwoods for the next five days?

◆ ◆ ◆

The next morning Amelia saw her father's watch lying on her bedside table. She reached for it, marveling that it felt as warm as if he had taken it out of his pocket only moments before. Holding it close to her cheek, she remembered the teasing he used to receive because of the florals etched on its cover instead of a hunting or fishing scene like so many other men depicted on theirs. But Father loved his plants no matter if they were in the garden, the conservatory, or out in the fields.

Her gaze strayed to the trunk. Without Father's will, she had no recourse but to do as Moore wanted. Williams advised her to challenge the legality of Winston's adoption, but she didn't have the heart for holding up the planting season while the courts decided who owned what.

With Father's watch in her hand, she opened the trunk and then the jewelry box that came with it. There was more than enough room for all her jewels, but she would stick with her plan and leave everything behind except for her mother's jewelry box, brooch, and locket.

A lump formed in her throat as she rubbed her thumb across the floral etching of the watch. Even a vengeful stepson deserved his father's watch.

The hallway shimmered as she moved toward Father's room, determined to do what was right before she changed her mind. At the closed door to his room, she paused to wipe her tears.

Henry Robertson had given her life, been her father and mother, taught her to love and laugh and believe in God. She'd thought he was perfect. He hadn't been and had left her in dire straits.

Using the skills he'd taught and the faith he'd instilled, she would survive whatever trials awaited. She laid his watch among his other personal effects and with a final goodbye, fled the room.

◆ ◆ ◆

Later that morning, Amelia stood in the parlor looking over her assembled staff. Along with the five members of her household, the group included the groundskeeper, groomsman, and stable boy, as well as the estate manager and mill foreman, who would be responsible for relaying the information to their respective employees. Their faces conveyed a mix of concern, sadness, and questions.

"First, I want to thank you for your service to my father." She licked her lips as the words came out weaker than she wished. Williams handed her a glass of water and she drank, trying to quench her parched mouth that felt as dry as the Dakota badlands.

In as calm a state as she could manage, she explained the facts surrounding the missing will. "What it means is that my father's stepson, Mr. Winston Kent of Chicago, is the legal heir to everything Henry Robertson owned at the time of his death."

As they started to protest, she held up her hands. "I don't know how long I can stay, but I will as long as I am able."

The young groomsman stepped forward, twisting his cap as if wringing the moisture out. "Will we be sent packing?"

Her father had hired the youth only the summer before. "I don't know, Jimmy."

She addressed the gathering. "I really don't know much beyond my own plight and that Mr. Moore is now in charge of everything. If he hasn't told you otherwise, continue as if Father were still here."

They waited in expectation.

What else could she tell them? She sipped her water and tried to swallow past the lump forming in her throat. She realized that they needed familiar tasks to take their mind off their troubles.

She singled out the mill foreman. "Mr. Hanover, with the mill on the verge of closing for the season, see that the maintenance and shipping schedules are taken care of, or there'll be havoc for the new owner come harvest."

"Consider it done, miss."

"Mr. Thornby," she said to the estate manager. "Continue preparing the fields including the test plot. Since you have the seed, plant on schedule. Leave the seedlings in the conservatory as their future is yet to be decided."

"Yes, miss."

"Woodward."

The groundskeeper straightened.

"I want the grounds in peak shape in case prospective buyers come to take a look."

"As always, miss."

"Yes, as always. I know you'll all do your best as you have always done. However"—she looked at each briefly in turn—"despite what I've just said, I don't know if you'll have a job next month, or next week even. So if you want to search for another job, let me know and I'll give you time off to look. But please, don't all leave at once."

Her desperate attempt to soften the news didn't even bring a smile.

As if rehearsed, they all looked to Williams, who stepped forward. He cleared his throat. "Might we inquire as to your future?"

She closed her eyes to stop the sudden pool of tears. As the silence lengthened, she opened her eyes and allowed the tears to fall. In the silence, their sniffles and discreet coughs caressed her heart. She raised her chin.

"I believe I'll see if Rosie needs a hand in the mercantile. I always enjoyed my time there with her when Father had things to do."

Twelve-year-old Charlie, the stable boy and the youngest employee, piped up. "You could marry a rich man, miss, and buy it back."

She smiled. "What a grand idea, Charlie. Then no one would ever have to leave. Thank you all."

She had no plans to marry for money, but she loved that they were thinking of ways to keep everything going as before.

◆ ◆ ◆

Penny nudged Amelia's arm as she tied off her lines in front of the mercantile. Amelia responded by scratching the length of Penny's nose. Why hadn't she realized before that all the horses would be included in the estate?

"Are you all right, dear?"

Amelia turned to face Rosie, the mercantile owner, who had taken her mother in when she needed a job and then taught her to be a lady. Father had found her serving customers with a smile he couldn't forget.

With a final pat on Penny's nose, Amelia climbed the mercantile steps. "As long as you're here I am, Rosie." She embraced the older woman as she always had.

"Time for tea, I'd say." Rosie led the way through to the back counter. "Mind the store, there's a dearie."

A few minutes later, the floorboards of Rosie's quarters creaked above Amelia's head.

When Rosie returned, Amelia took her tray. "You should have let me do that. I can tell your arthritis is acting up."

Rosie rubbed her knees. "I'll admit the steps are wearing me down." She glanced around the store. "Did those Smith brothers pick up their tools?"

"Yes, they did." Amelia poured the tea. "And the Moodie girl dropped off her eggs."

"Is it true?" Rosie asked without warning.

Amelia's cup clinked against the saucer. "If you're asking if I've lost everything that I hold close to my heart, then yes, it's true." She patted Rosie's forearm. "Except you. I still have you."

"I didn't believe it." Rosie shook her head. "When the rumor started flying, I told them they were wrong. Even now that I've heard it straight from your mouth I still don't believe it."

Amelia jumped up as a young woman approached the counter. "I'll get it," she said to Rosie. "Rest your knees while you can."

When Amelia returned to her cold tea, Rosie bore red-rimmed eyes. She reached down and held Rosie's hand. "It's all right," she soothed. "It's in God's hands. I'll be fine."

"I wish I could take you in, but with Aaron and the girls coming, every bit of space I have will be taken."

"Hmm. When are they arriving?"

"About two weeks if they follow the timetable they sent me a while back. Could be here sooner or later, too."

Amelia thought of the single trunk waiting for everything she owned. It wouldn't take much to unpack and then repack later.

"Rosie, can I stay with you for a few days until Aaron and the girls arrive? I'll work down here for my room and board and save you the trouble of climbing the stairs." She gripped Rosie's hand. "I only have a few more days at home before Mr. Moore brings the wagon out for me and my trunk."

"What's that you say?" Rosie's hand trembled.

"Mr. Moore is the attorney for Father's estate. He's the one who's evicting me from my home."

Rosie paled. "What trunk?"

"Mr. Moore brought one out for me. It's very strong and high quality."

Rosie shrank into her chair like an old apple that had been sitting in the cellar too long.

Amelia followed Rosie's line of sight to the cash box hiding under the counter. Now why was Rosie glaring at her money box as if she wanted to smash it to bits?

Chapter 5

Jeremy left the telegraph office empty-handed. Five days had passed since he'd mailed off his report to Winston—ample time to read the report and get back to him about the Robertson estate. Even without a firm answer, Jeremy needed to continue the course of action they'd planned before he left Chicago.

Alone in his office, he flipped open his calendar. Sure enough, a large red circle proved it was the day he was supposed to drive out to the Robertson mansion and collect Amelia and the trunk. He would do it, too.

Yet each time he thought of his last visit when her initial shock had been followed by quiet acceptance he wanted to slink down in his chair. He would've felt better if she'd let out a wild tirade, gone on about the unfairness of it all, screamed that her father left it to her, or even threatened him with a countersuit. But no, she had looked at the trunk as if it was a special blessing.

With frustration surging through his veins, he slapped his calendar closed.

◆ ◆ ◆

Amelia must have seen Jeremy coming because she was ready when he arrived, sitting demurely on the trunk, parasol over her shoulder even though she was under the cover of the veranda roof. A tactic to throw him off guard? He took a wide stance, fists on his hips, and said the first thing that came to mind.

"I suppose you have another parasol in the trunk. Trying to get away with two of them?"

Her mouth opened in that cute little circle women make when they express surprise.

"Why no, Mr. Moore. This is the only one." She rose with elegance, bent over, and opened the lid. "See for yourself."

Oh, he'd see all right. He ran up the steps two at a time to peer around her.

With the trunk open, the umbrella case lay nestled on the inside of the lid. Amelia popped the latches and then held it open for him to inspect the empty interior. "Would it matter if I took two parasols when you said I could take anything that would fit in the trunk, including the silver tea service?"

The repetition of his own words directed back at him by Robertson's daughter caused his common sense to flee. "I don't care what you take as long as I know about it."

"In that case..." She retrieved a wooden box and lifted the lid to show him two items nestled in velvet. "The starburst pin is the only thing my mother owned when Father met her. The locket was a birthday gift from Father and holds her image inside."

She closed the jewelry box slowly, eyeing the pieces inside as if it would be her last chance to look at them. Her hand caressed the smooth wood. "And this was Mother's sewing box before Father gave it to me. These are the items I hold most dear, Mr. Moore. I can't bear to leave them behind, but if you feel it would be unfair for me to take them, here." She held her treasures out like an offering, waiting for him to snatch the last bit of familiarity from her hands.

His chest hurt, and he didn't like it. He'd expected tears and whining, or at least a drawn-out shouting match to work his frustrations out. Not her complete surrender to someone who didn't give a whit.

Williams stepped forward. "A word, sir. Years ago when Mr. Robertson first altered his wife's sewing chest into a jewelry box, he tasked me with ensuring it remain in Miss Amelia's possession. I will honor him, Mr. Moore, even in death."

"Put it away." Jeremy scowled for effect, relieved that Williams's admonition had saved him from looking soft by giving in to her sacrificial attitude.

With the jewelry box back in the trunk, she looked at him with an arched brow.

A memory of sitting in the corner of the classroom with a dunce cap on his head while his pretty teacher pointed to him wasn't the image he wanted to remember. Not when Amelia, attractive as she was, regarded him in the same manner. He hadn't been stupid then, and he wasn't now.

With his blood pounding through his veins, he grabbed the sides of the tray that held her jewelry box and personal items and yanked it up. Instead of being chock-full of silk and satin outfits, a stack of neatly folded black cotton clothes met his eyes.

"What game are you playing? Where are your gowns? Or the crystal and silver?"

Guileless eyes as blue as the sky searched his as if looking for something. "It's not a game, Mr. Moore. If I am to leave my sheltered home and make my way among those with less, why would I dress in fancy clothes? Without protection, I will be open to anyone who wants what I have whether I am wearing it or carrying it in my arms. To put it bluntly, once I leave here I am a woman alone. I need practical clothes if I am to survive."

He rammed the tray back in the trunk. "You need money to survive. I've given you the chance to take jewelry, silver, whatever is valuable so that you can exchange it for money." He was spurting out the words so fast he had to stop to catch his breath. Couldn't she see that he was trying to help her?

His head was pounding along with his heart. He moved to the railing and braced himself on it with his head bent. "Once you leave you can't come back for anything." He turned to face her. "Go inside and try again."

She crossed her arms. "You've made it quite clear that none of this is mine. Why would I take what belongs to someone else? That borders on theft and it goes against the law as well as biblical principles, Mr. Moore. You ought to know that."

What could he possibly say in the face of such stubbornness? Nothing at all. Shaking his head, he marched down the steps and across to his wagon. Hearing footsteps echoing his, he turned to find her following him. Behind her, Williams and the groomsman carried her trunk.

"Leave it!"

She balked. "But you said—"

"I changed my mind. I'll come back for you another day."

"I don't understand."

No, she wouldn't. He rambled out the first thing that came to mind. "Change of plans. Until I hear something solid back from Winston, there's no reason for you to leave your home."

She narrowed her eyes. "What game are you playing now?"

"Look, do you want to leave today? Or would you rather stay as long as possible?"

"How can you ask that?"

"How? You're the one arguing with me."

Her lower lip trembled, and he knew she was on the verge of an explosion—wet or dry, but an eruption of emotion that surprisingly, he didn't want to see or hear. Without saying another word, he climbed onto the wagon seat.

She'd asked if he was playing a game and he hadn't answered. If he had, the answer would have been yes. Otherwise, he'd have no reason to travel down the road from town and visit the only person who made him feel alive.

He glanced over his shoulder without thinking. She stood on the veranda, hand shielding her eyes from the sun's glare, looking in his direction.

He flicked the lines. So much for not letting his emotions get involved. She'd been the levelheaded practical one while he'd almost melted at the thought of her out on the street alone and fighting for survival. It was only because he'd been there and knew what it was like. For the first time he wondered if Winston really knew what awaited Amelia on the street.

◆ ◆ ◆

Golden rays warmed Amelia as she lingered in the garden that stretched from the house to the trees along the drive. Precious times had been spent with Father guiding her from one plant to another, his love of botany pouring out with explanations of plant traits and requirements—not as knowledgeable as Woodward, but special nonetheless.

Their forays always ended at the old well, where they sat on the raised wooden platform hidden from view behind the taller perennials.

She sat on the well platform and closed her eyes as the bees buzzed in the garden. A familiar memory returned of her knocking on the boards.

"What's this, Father?" she always asked with laughter in her voice.

"Something to stop my little girl from falling in," he would answer with a twinkle in his eye. She would hug him for caring and look up in expectation, waiting for the tickle that wouldn't end until she screamed for mercy.

Those memories of whispered secrets, dreams, and laughter were things that no one could take from her.

Four days had passed since Moore left her and the trunk behind. Four days of living with nervous staff who worked and lived under the same umbrella of insecurity. Each morning she'd woken worried that it would be her last in her family home.

But no more.

While waiting for breakfast, she'd read the apostle Paul's inspiring verse in Philippians 4:13. It reminded her that she wasn't alone. But more than that it gave her strength. Even when surrounded by the unpleasantness of men like Moore, the Lord was always with her. And with His strength, she'd move forward with the newness of the shiny green leaves unfurling under the warmth of the May sun.

Spotting Woodward near the edge of the garden, she headed his way.

He tugged the front of his cap. "Morning, Miss Amelia. It's good to see you out and exploring the gardens."

"Good morning, Woodward. The peonies are growing well."

"Yes, miss. Your father would be pulling up a chair to watch them grow on a day like this."

She smiled at the thought. "Yes, they were special to him. Now that the ground is fit for growth, perhaps you could dig up his favorite one and plant it by his grave?"

"That would be a grand idea. I'll get to it today. Is there anything else I can do for you, miss?"

Amelia was struck by his gracious manner—not that it was different from any of the other times he'd addressed her, but that it was always the same. For as long as she could remember he had been the caretaker of everything that grew on the house grounds. He'd taught both her and her father about botany, and while Father loved his garden, Woodward had been keen to share the conservatory with her. But most of all, not once had Woodward shown impatience at being pestered by a little girl's questions.

Suddenly, it was very important that he understood how his presence affected her life. "Woodward, I—"

He raised his index finger. "If I may interrupt, miss, I have a surprise waiting for you in the conservatory."

His eagerness persuaded her that any sentiments could wait until later. "That sounds interesting." She strolled toward the glass structure with him by her side. "Your surprises are always a delight."

"I hope this will be as well."

With the outside temperature increasing, the conservatory door stood open, inviting her inside. Were the colors more vibrant today, or was she the one who had changed?

"What's this?" She spied her surprise within seconds of entering the scented surroundings. It sat on the potting counter beside her botany instruments, an empty glass and metal structure about a foot high and long, and half as wide with a peaked roof. "It looks like your terrarium, but it's new and there's nothing inside."

"I ordered it the day you told us of your leaving. I used mine as a model to make a case so you can take it with you." He lifted a wooden box off the ground. It was higher than the terrarium, but flat on top with a carrying handle. Holding it up, he pointed out the open bottom. "Slide it on the top, and lock the latches in place. Like this." He lowered the case until it met the wooden base.

Amelia clasped her hands to her bodice. "It's wonderful, Woodward. Oh. . ." On impulse she reached out and gave him a quick hug then backed off as propriety demanded.

"What shall I put in it?" Every plant in the conservatory was as familiar to her as the pearls on her mother's pin. Yet, only the most compact ones would have the growth characteristics required for the miniature greenhouse. That still left many choices.

A sudden thought sobered her. "And what about Mr. Moore? He might say I'm taking Mr. Kent's property if I fill it with plants from here."

"I thought as much. If you'll tell me which you prefer, I'll bring my own over and keep a cutting or two for myself. Yours will be jiggled about if you're traveling and you need strong plants with good root systems to survive the stress."

Footsteps crunching on the gravel walkway drew their attention outside. Amelia's joy fled as her gaze locked with Moore's sardonic one.

He stepped into the conservatory. "I thought perhaps you'd be out here."

Woodward turned to Amelia. "I'll be waiting for your list, miss." A quick tip of his hat and he strode out the door.

"Woodward doesn't appear to be worried about leaving you alone with me."

"Should he?" She raised her brows for effect. "Then again, killing me off would be one way to dispose of someone who's overstayed her welcome."

He slipped his right hand into the front pocket of his trousers. "You may choose not to believe me, but the thought never entered my mind." His eyes widened, giving him the maniacal expression of an asylum patient. "Until now," he added in a haunting voice.

Her laugh slipped out. "Be warned, Woodward may have left your sight, but you can be sure he's watching from some corner. It is a glass structure, after all."

"Speaking of glass structures." He tapped the terrarium. "Did this shrink?"

She expected a response about stones and people living in glass houses. Instead, he'd tossed out a comment so ludicrous she couldn't stop another laugh from bubbling out. "Oh dear." She pressed her lips together before yet another traitorous action escaped, and then sealed them with her cupped hands.

Moore cocked his head, a strange expression on his face. "You seem different today."

She felt different after her morning's decision to live each day knowing God had blessed her abundantly. And the terrarium proved it. She opened one side of its roof to expose the emptiness within. If Moore told her to leave today, she'd be ready.

From the corner where she kept her potting supplies, she scooped out smooth pebbles gleaned from a fast-flowing riverbed. After spreading them in a thick later at the bottom of the terrarium, she went back for a double handful of coconut fibers as if Moore wasn't standing there watching her with his hands tucked into trouser pockets.

"Was this here all along? I don't remember it from my first visit."

"Woodward brought it over this morning." She spread the coconut fibers over the layer of pebbles. If she told him she would use it to carry precious plants for sentimental reasons, how would he respond? A sideways glance proved that he seemed different today as well—more relaxed if that were possible, especially in his face where lines weren't furrowing his forehead. Quite attractive if she wanted to admit it—which she didn't.

As she continued adding layers of peat and soil, Moore wandered over to the sorghum seedlings. With the slowest of motions, he reached out and flicked a grassy blade making it sway ever so slightly.

"They've grown."

"Yes, they have," she admitted, for it was no use denying it.

She closed the lid on the terrarium and stepped back to admire it. All it needed was plants to enhance its beauty.

Moore hadn't moved from the seedlings.

Amelia wiped her hands on a garden rag. Woodward was the only one who knew the schedule called for them to be planted the next morning. Even Thornby, the estate manager, didn't know the timing although he'd reported that the trial plot was ready.

Instinct told her not to tell Moore. It wasn't a matter of spoiling his pensive mood, but if the seedlings were to have any chance of survival, they needed to be in the ground.

Chapter 6

Jeremy dragged his gaze from the grassy seedlings. They reflected hours—weeks—of work that would be lost unless Winston decided to sell them. But who would buy them? Some scientific research university? A botany company? Or would they be allowed to wither and die because they had belonged to someone named Robertson?

The sound of horses approaching the conservatory caused him to look outside, where the lack of condensation due to the open door gave him a clear view of the groomsman riding one horse and leading another.

Amelia rushed outside. "What is it, Jimmy?"

"They're here, Miss Amelia." He jumped down, grinning. "I spotted them on the northwest quarter on the other side of the hill. Not sure for how long, though." Keeping a grip on his own reins, he handed the ones for the other horse to Amelia.

Jeremy didn't know who they were talking about, but he wasn't about to let Amelia run off and leave him alone. He strode after her. "Who's here?"

Jimmy hoisted Amelia into the sidesaddle and then turned away while she adjusted the skirts covering her raised right leg and lower left one.

"Come with me and see." Her eyes sparkled as she tossed out the challenge.

Jeremy didn't need a second urging. He slipped his left foot in the stirrup of Jimmy's horse, grabbed hold of the horn, and swung up.

With a forlorn expression, Jimmy passed up the reins.

Clearly, Jimmy had expected to be part of the adventure. While Jeremy wasn't about to give up his ride, he didn't want the lad to carry a grudge over it. "Thanks, Jimmy. I appreciate you lending your horse to me. I don't know what this is about, but if you're sorry you're not going, then it must be someone important."

"Oh, it is, Mr. Moore. A sight you'll never forget. Keep your ears and eyes open."

"Let's go." Amelia wheeled her horse on its back hooves and started off at a lope.

They headed northwest through the estate, crossing the prairie and circling the woods. Several times he inquired who they were hoping to meet, but each time she smiled and answered that he'd see.

After a while he heard a croaking sound. Not like a frog, but something strange that reminded him of a dinosaur exhibit that had passed through Chicago the year before. Only a couple of smaller prehistoric creatures had been displayed, one a runner and the other a flier, both with bones missing, but enough in place to give an impression of what may have been. Of course the paleontologist hadn't known what sound they would have made, leaving it up to the attendees' imaginations. But the strange croaking hitting his ears sounded prehistoric.

Amelia slowed at the base of a small hill. She tapped her finger to her mouth and he got her message. With diagrams of flying dinosaurs filling his thoughts he wasn't about to utter a sound and take a chance on scaring off whatever was waiting on the other side.

After tying off his horse, he lifted her out of the sidesaddle. Setting her down, he allowed his hands to stay at her waist while her upturned face caught his attention. Wide blue eyes sparkling and expectant, with a full smile that expressed her excitement.

Her hands were still on his forearms, and she squeezed them gently. "Ready?"

Caught in the moment, he nodded. With her looking at him like that, he would have agreed to anything.

Turning, she grabbed one of his hands and practically pulled him up the grassy hill, lowering her body as they climbed. Near the top she dropped to her knees.

He stopped to watch her crawl forward while tugging her troublesome skirts out of the way. Was she unaware of the soil marks she'd endure? Or that he could see her ankles? Or in this new state she was in, didn't she care?

She looked back, her face more animated than he'd ever seen, and he knew right then that she didn't care for convention when it balanced against something better.

Moving quickly, he crept up beside her before dropping flat. After the frenzy of activity, he was almost afraid to look and instead watched her glee as she looked down on whatever sight was so special that she had held his hand and crawled through grass to get here.

"Look, they're dancing." Shining blue eyes cast a quick glance at him. "Aren't they beautiful?"

He looked down on a swath of large gray birds, bowing and jumping on long legs, and a few bigger white ones with black wingtips. Red patches on their heads flashed with their movement, like beacons beaming out across a stormy sea.

"Over there. Look." She placed her hand on his and pointed to where one of the large white ones twirled in a circle like a ballerina. "The gray ones are sandhill cranes, and we see lots of them. The bigger white ones are the whoopers, but there seems to be less every year."

One sandhill stabbed at the ground. Another one tossed a stick in the air as if playing with it. "What are they doing?"

"Dancing. They bob and pose and give each other the eye like roosters do, so I suppose it's part of their threat stance." She sighed. "But it's also a beautiful courtship dance when two of them perform it together. They say cranes mate for life and teach their offspring how to dance."

"Breathtaking. I've never seen anything so inspiring." As soon as the words were out he regretted them.

Her knowing glance didn't help.

He couldn't allow her to think him soft and tender and mooning over some stupid dancing birds. With his gut clenching at the thought, he jumped to his feet.

A tremendous roar resounded through the air as waves of cranes took flight, their white, black, and gray markings mixing in a flapping frenzy, first against the wooded background and then higher against the blue sky. They flew northwest, filling the air with a raucous croaking that stayed with him long after they'd disappeared from view.

Without a word, Amelia shook out her skirt and led the way back to the horses.

Jeremy didn't feel like talking, either. The beauty of the cranes, their dinosaur-like croaking, the way he'd let his guard down—all emotion-draining events that left him wanting to find a hole and hide from the world. Considering that he was on Winston's land, he could have done it if he wanted.

Amelia waited by her horse, her expression showing how much she hated having to wait for assistance.

◆ ◆ ◆

"Will you stay for tea?"

After a quick and quiet return ride, her question was the last thing he expected. He tried to gauge her mood. She had every right to yell at him for scaring off the cranes, and she hadn't even mentioned it. Probably wouldn't, as social custom dictated such a response would be unnecessary, yet visiting at such a time would allow the topic to be opened and dissected. "No."

She dipped her head in response. Williams opened the door for her entry.

"Amelia."

She glanced back. "Yes?"

"Thank you for showing me. I'm sorry I scared them off."

She shook her skirt as if to rid herself of him. "We all have to leave sometime, don't we?"

Her parting shot grated all the way back to town. She didn't have to tell him that everyone leaves. If no one left, he wouldn't be in this distasteful predicament.

◆ ◆ ◆

Later as he waited in line for his mail, memories of the day teased him. The time he'd spent with Amelia in the conservatory had been his most relaxing minutes since arriving in Minnesota. It probably had to do with all the luscious greenery, which seemed to buffer the outside world even with the glass windows, but he had a feeling it was due to Amelia's presence. And although she hadn't mentioned why, her new attitude intrigued him.

He'd never been a bird watcher, and yet lying in the grass beside Amelia while they watched the dancing cranes had affected him. For a brief time, they had shared something special. Something so unique he doubted he would ever see it again. And never again with Amelia at his side because just one word from Winston and she would be gone.

"Mr. Moore!"

He came out of his musings to find Rosie marching toward him.

"Here." She pushed some bills at him. "I don't want your money."

A glance told him it was the amount he'd paid for the trunk. "What's this for?"

With her hands on her hips, she glared up at him. "I never would have sold you that trunk if I knew it was meant for Amelia. That's dirty money, Mr. Moore. I won't accept it." She started to walk away but turned back for more. "You should be ashamed of yourself for what you're doing to that girl."

Jeremy's ire rose. He didn't need to be whipped in public for reasonable legal actions. And it wasn't like he was making the decisions. Winston was doing that. He was only carrying them out. Any day there'd be instructions on what to do, and there was just as much a chance that Winston would drop the whole thing as there was that he would pursue his plan to devastate the Robertson holdings. Not likely, but possible.

Despite Rosie's verbal lashing, he wanted to hold on to the special moments of the day for a while longer, and he wouldn't be able to do that if he received a letter from Winston. Making a flash decision, he stepped out of the postal line and left the mercantile.

"Mr. Moore."

Instinctively he looked back.

The postmistress waved a white envelope. "Mr. Moore. A letter came for you. From Chicago!"

◆ ◆ ◆

The morning after the crane sighting, Amelia awoke thinking of Moore. The way he'd nudged the sorghum seedling. His rapt attention as the cranes danced. Both were tender moments she wanted to keep close to her heart for the times when Winston's force pressured him to do things against his better judgment.

She didn't know when, but sometime between the conservatory and the cranes she'd begun to understand that although Moore was Winston's puppet, tenderness and affection might be the way to cut his strings and free them both. And it would have to start with her.

Right after breakfast she headed to the conservatory to prepare the seedlings for transplant. Once in the ground they stood a better chance of survival than the ones that depended on human care.

In preparation for the task, Woodward had left several shallow basins of water on the potting table. Taking each terra-cotta pot in her hands, she tapped out its root ball and laid it in a basin with its name stake and the rest of its variety. By the time the last pot was empty, the first basin of root balls had started to dissolve in the water. Gently, she teased the roots apart but left them in the water so they wouldn't dry out.

"Are you ready?" Woodward asked a bit later.

She replaced the final seedlings in their basin. "Yes. Let's go before it gets too hot."

Between the two of them, they carried all the bowls outside and laid them in the back of the wagon, up close to the seats where they would receive the least jostling. As she ran back for her wide-brimmed planting hat, Woodward covered them with a blanket to absorb any spillage while keeping the roots moist.

Although the sun was warm on her shoulders, white puffy clouds hung in the distance. "It's a good day to plant, isn't it, Woodward?"

"I believe you're right. Once those clouds roll in, they'll stop the sun from burning the seedlings. By tomorrow they should be standing as straight as new trees."

"It won't get too cold tonight, will it?"

He lifted his nose to the prairie wind. "I don't believe so, but once they're in the ground, they're in God's hands."

It was the confirmation she needed. She was like the seedling taken from its home and transplanted in a new place. Yes, she was in God's hands, but it was up to her to ease the transition and not allow herself to be torn by the experience. Leaving would be hard, but she would find a new home. His love would strengthen her.

She could withstand anything.

Chapter 7

With the letter in his pocket, Jeremy walked to his hotel lugging his feet as if his socks were filled with Amelia's river-washed stones. Winston had intruded on his special day, and if Jeremy was right about what the letter entailed, there wouldn't be any more of them.

In his room, he tossed the envelope on his bed and turned to watch the traffic go by.

Each time he glanced at his bed, waves of turmoil rolled in his gut. He owed Winston for taking him and his mother off the street and giving them a home. Winston had been the father figure in his life, the man who paid for his education, who taught him everything there was to know about life and the law.

But with Winston's loathing against Henry Robertson and anything to do with Minnesota, Jeremy knew that whatever was in that envelope, it was going to hurt Amelia.

When he couldn't stand the suspense any longer, he slipped his pocketknife under the fold and cut the envelope open. Six words jumped off the paper.

BURN IT ALL AND WALK AWAY.

He dropped the letter as if it seared his hands, and then stomped on it hard with his right foot. Backing away, he covered his mouth with his hands to stop the roar from escaping.

As his wits returned, he picked up the paper and read it again. This wasn't simple loathing. This was a huge financial loss and total destruction of property for no reason.

He stooped to pick up the single sheet of paper as his legal training flooded back. No salutation or date. And no signature. He reached for the envelope, noting the lack of a return address. A postmark indicated it came from the city of Chicago but nothing to prove who sent it.

He tossed it on his washstand and began pacing. Winston was crazy to think Jeremy could do something so destructive. It bordered on the workings of a madman. He stopped in his tracks. Had Winston crossed the line between hatred and insanity?

There was only one way to find out. With Winston's letter safely in his coat pocket, he slapped his hat on his head and rushed out the door.

Minutes later at the telegraph office he tossed a coin onto his newly written telegram. "Send that right away." He added a second coin to the first one. "I'll be at the Grand Hotel tonight and the Robertson place tomorrow. Send someone with the answer." He added a third coin to the pile. "Consider it urgent."

◆ ◆ ◆

Amelia inhaled the sweet scent of the syrup room for the final time. "So that's everything then?"

"That's it, miss." Hanover slipped his handkerchief from his back pocket and wiped his hands with it. He nodded to the rack of turned-over syrup pans. "Everything's sterilized and ready for the harvest."

"And the wood?"

"Delivered and stacked. Both wood sheds are full to the door. Mr. Robertson kept to his schedule to the very last." He tucked his rag away. "Your father was a good man, miss. He'd be heartbroken to see the fix he left you in. You sure Moore's on the level?"

She shrugged as they walked to the front entrance. "It doesn't matter. Without a will, there's nothing I can do."

After placing a huge padlock on the door, he handed her the key. "The boys and I checked every nook and cranny in the mill."

"Thank you, Hanover. I hope you all will be working on the estate this year until harvest starts, but until I know what's going to happen I can't make promises."

He handed her into the buggy. "Don't you worry, miss. We've talked it over and will stay as long as you need us. We owe your father that much."

She drove homeward with warmth surrounding her heart. Her father had been a special man, not only to her, but to his employees. Whoever ended up with the mill would be wise to keep the same loyal men working it.

Halfway home she saw the dust trail of a rider heading her way, but it was minutes before she recognized Moore. Her heart thumped against her rib cage, keeping time with his loping horse. Letting go of the buggy lines with one hand, she placed it on her errant heart. Since when did the sight of Moore receive such a response? Since they'd watched the cranes dance with abandon.

But as the distance closed and she saw his expression, she knew his visit wasn't due to a matter of the heart.

"What is it," she called out, unable to keep silent.

He pulled up beside her, both he and his horse breathing heavily. "We need to find your father's will."

It wasn't what she'd expected to hear. "But we looked everywhere."

He set his horse to a walk beside the buggy. "Is there any place you haven't checked? Somewhere he liked to go alone?"

"What's this about?"

"It's—" Pursing his lips, he shook his head. "It would make everything easier."

He was hiding something. She could tell by the way he wasn't catching her eye. "Have you heard from Winston?"

He looked away. "How's the mill?"

So, he had heard from Winston and the news wasn't good. Should she push him? No, because his lack of an answer meant he was second-guessing Winston and that could only be good for her and her staff.

"The mill's closed for the season. We'll open as soon as the harvest starts." His look made her realize what she'd said. "Or someone will."

He cocked his head as a bemused expression settled on his face.

Now that he was looking at her, she wondered why. Reaching up, she tucked a small batch of hair tendrils behind her ear and then tugged her wide-brimmed hat down over them to keep them in place.

"What are you doing, Mr. Moore?" She asked as her cheeks warmed.

"Looking. It appears you've been out in the sun too long."

So much for preening. "I was out planting this morning."

He threw her a sharp look. "You were?"

"Yes, the seedlings are safely in the ground."

"You think they're safer in the ground?" Something dark crossed his face.

"At least they have a fighting chance with the weather instead of being left to wither away in the conservatory."

"You don't know what you've done."

She turned into the tree-lined drive to the house. "I know exactly what I've done, Mr. Moore. I have responsibilities, and I'm taking care of them before I leave."

His face reddened. He shook his finger at her, his voice rising with each shake. "If you find the will, you won't have to leave."

"Quit shouting, Mr. Moore. Everyone in the county can hear you." What was wrong with him? Didn't he want her to leave? She sent him a furtive glance. Something had riled him to the extent he'd boiled over like an unwatched syrup tray. He thought she hadn't searched everywhere for Father's will when her whole life depended on its existence? Moore was the one who appeared to have been out in the sun too long.

As they approached the house, Jimmy ran out to take the buggy. "Shall I take your horse, Mr. Moore?"

"No, Jimmy, I won't be staying."

"Good-bye, Mr. Moore." Amelia climbed the steps with the aid of the banister as soreness from the morning's activity stiffened her muscles.

"Amelia," Moore called after her.

Williams opened the door and then closed it after she'd entered.

"Amelia!"

She dragged herself to the stairs. "I'm done for the day, Williams. Please have a bath prepared and send someone up with my dinner." Heaven help her, it may be the last ones ever in her childhood home.

◆ ◆ ◆

Amelia!

Fire flicked toward Jeremy as he ran through the burning mansion. "Ame—"

The sound of his voice shattered the nightmare. He lay in bed with his pulse pounding in his ears as awareness of his hotel room returned. After several moments of reassurance that the nightmare had been a manifestation of his worry over Winston's order, he swung his legs over the side of the bed and sat up.

Outside his window, the light gray sky heralded the dawn of a new day. What would it bring? The messenger carrying Winston's response to his final plea to save the Robertson holdings from destruction had shown up as he'd eaten his dinner in the hotel dining room. He hadn't possessed the courage to unfold the telegram at the table, and his appetite had fled with its arrival. Alone in his room, he'd read three little words.

You owe me.

Jeremy hung his head between his knees. It wasn't the house and mill only that would be wasted, but all the plants in the conservatory. As memories of dancing cranes flooded back, he thought of farther-reaching consequences. If fire from the buildings started a wildfire across the grassland, where would the cranes dance? How many animals would lose their lives and habitats? How many human homes would the voracious flames devour?

No, he couldn't do it.

Jeremy reached for his clothes. He had always believed that the law was the ultimate legal authority, and Winston had a right to his revenge as long as it was within that boundary. Yet he'd lagged in his duty to escort Amelia off the Robertson estate because it hadn't been morally right. Winston's destruction order served as the knife that cut Jeremy free of any remaining loyalty.

◆ ◆ ◆

"Fire!" The voice ripped through the house like a lightning bolt.

Amelia paused brushing in midstroke. As the word sunk in, she threw her brush onto her bureau and ran to the door. Clutching her dressing gown closed, she sniffed the air, relieved that smoke wasn't barreling through the house. At the balcony railing, she looked down to see Williams, Woodward, and Thornby in the foyer.

"Where's the fire?"

They all looked up.

Thornby yanked his hat off his head. "We think it's the mill. Hanover's gone over. I've sent Jimmy to warn the neighbors. We're heading over now."

"The mill? But how—"

"We'll see, miss. I'll report when I can."

He rushed out the door with Woodward right behind.

The mill? Her conversation with Hanover about the wood delivery popped into her head. Two woodsheds would throw off a big fire with a lot of heat. And with the dry spring they'd had and a good prairie breeze it wouldn't take much for the fire to spread to the mill. Maybe farther.

She ran back into her room and across to her balcony door. Black smoke billowed against the early morning horizon. Nothing to indicate what was burning, but the mill was the only large structure in that direction for miles. And they'd need every hand to fight it.

Minutes later, wearing her planting outfit, she strode past Williams in the foyer.

"Miss Amelia, where are you going?"

"To help, Williams. Have Mrs. Fielding and the girls prepare soup and sandwiches for a large crowd. Something that will be ready whenever the fire is out." She whipped open the door.

"But, miss—"

She slammed the door behind her, cutting off his voice.

Down the steps she ran toward the stables. With a clear blue sky overhead, she knew it would take a miracle for rain to fall without the clouds.

At the drive shed she yelled out, "Anyone here?" When no one answered, she kept going until she entered the low light level of the stable. The stalls were empty, their doors open as if there hadn't been time to close them. It didn't matter—she'd walk all the way if that's what it took. She turned back to the house.

"Miss Amelia!" Her youngest staff member, the twelve-year-old stable boy, appeared around the corner of the drive shed.

"Oh, Charlie, am I ever glad to see you." She cast a critical eye on the old mule Charlie towed behind him. "I need a ride. Is he all that's left?"

"Yes, miss. Jimmy chased the rest into the pasture, just in case, but Digs wouldn't go."

Thank the Lord for Digs. "We'll take the wagon, then."

While Charlie harnessed Digs, Amelia rounded up as many buckets as she could find and tossed them into the wagon.

Williams hailed them as they passed the house on their way out. Not wanting to hear more objections, she almost told Charlie to keep driving until she noticed the pile of blankets and jars of water stacked on the bottom step.

Soon they were off. Charlie coaxed Digs toward the fire until the mule balked and refused to move when they were still several hundred yards away.

"It's all right, Charlie." Amelia climbed to the ground. "Do your best to keep him quiet and we'll come to you." With her skirts clutched in one hand and carrying two blankets and buckets with her other arm, she headed toward a scene that was worse than she'd imagined.

A wall of dancing heat threatened to smother her as she approached the mill, where flames licked up the walls above broken windows and high ventilators. One man worked the pump above the well. Buckets of water were passed on down the line of eager hands until they were thrown against the mill wall. Amelia couldn't tell if they were having an effect, but she prayed it was so.

As if they'd been the first to go, two piles of burning embers marred an area on one side of the building where the woodsheds had stood. On the other side of the mill, two men furiously pushed empty barrels off their stacks and rolled them into the newly planted field.

Hanover approached with his handkerchief in his hand. "The sheds were on fire when we arrived, so we put our effort into stopping it from spreading. Not sure how, but we didn't notice the fire inside the mill until the glass started busting from the pressure." He wiped the back of his neck. "The door was still padlocked, miss."

Above the snapping of the flames, the timbers groaned under their crushing load.

"Run!" Hanover grabbed her arm and herded her back the way she'd come.

She ran toward Charlie as fast as her skirts would allow but couldn't stop herself from craning her head around to see what was happening.

Barrels littered the area as Hanover's men scrambled into the field.

Chunks of burning debris flew in all directions as the mill caved into itself with a horrendous crash, leaving blackened timbers with burning ends jutting out at strange angles like dropped cigars.

"Amelia?"

Moore's emotion-filled voice was like a steadying hand on her arm—until her sanity returned. Of course he had a legal right to be there.

"Amelia, what happened?" His voice sounded strangled, as if trying to keep his anger under tight control.

Did he think she started the fire to keep Winston from inheriting Father's accomplishment? She crossed her arms. "I don't know what happened. Hanover said the fire was going when he got here and the door was still locked."

"Fire!" A shout from one of the field hands rippled through the workers.

"Look!" Hanover pointed to the northwest.

A plume of gray smoke rose toward the blue sky, close to the area they'd watched the cranes dance.

Moore sucked in a sharp breath. "What's over there?"

"Pasture up to the woods that border the estate." She judged the distance between the two fires. "I don't understand how it got there. It couldn't have been lightning. There wasn't a storm last night." She backed away. "I have to see."

Hanover shouted an order to the workers. Several of them left the bucket brigade and ran toward the wagon, only stopping long enough to pick up shovels. "The mill's gone, miss," Hanover said as he wiped his neck. "Take the men. I'll meet you there as soon as I can."

◆ ◆ ◆

The wildfire skipped from treetop to treetop, dropping burning limbs which started smaller fires in the dry underbrush. What had been a plume of gray smoke when they first spotted it had turned into a billowing mass as the flames spread through the woods, consuming everything in its path. Across the razed land, black poles stood as sentinels on the ash-spewn ground—black and gray, nothing green.

Thornby shook his head. "I'm sorry, miss, there's nothing to be done."

"How long do you think it'll burn?" Her worries turned to the few neighbors who lived near this part of the estate.

"Until it hits the river," Thornby said. "It'll miss the farms unless the wind changes."

"I didn't hear a storm last night." Moore picked up a twig and then bent it. *Snap.* "Don't you need a storm for a lightning strike?"

Amelia eyed him. "Yes, you do. But if someone was bent on revenge, all they would need is a match after the spring we've had."

He looked away.

She wondered if the idea hadn't crossed his mind and then immediately regretted it. She hadn't eaten anything yet, and the lack of nourishment made her crabby. "Thornby, I'm going back to the house. Stay with the fire, and let me know if it changes direction. I'll send someone out with refreshments."

As they left the woods behind and headed across the fields, it took a moment to recognize the black smoke curdling up from the area of the house. "No!"

Startled, Digs reared. His brazen *hee-haw* filled her ears as if he, too, felt the unfolding horror.

She grabbed the lines from Charlie and slapped them down against the board. "Yaw!"

Digs sprang off so fast they lost a bucket or two. She didn't care. She raced homeward with her heart in her throat. *Why, God, why?*

◆ ◆ ◆

"I don't understand." Amelia stared at the charred wreckage of her home. "Who would do this to me? To us?" She gestured to Mrs. Fielding and the members of her small staff who sat on the old well cover as if in a stupor.

"Only a madman, Amelia." Jeremy walked up to her carrying his coat, which he'd shed when they first arrived. Tucking it under his arm, he unrolled his long sleeves.

"Let me take that." She reached for his coat so he could perform the task easier. As he handed it to her, a sheet of paper slipped out. She grabbed for it.

It caught the wind and opened as it fell.

"No, wait." He reached down and picked it up—but not before she read the six incriminating words.

Chapter 8

"You." She jerked away from him. "You started the fires?"

"No, not me. I—" He floundered for words. "It was Winston." How could he explain that he hadn't even considered carrying out Winston's diabolical conflagration?

"You work for Winston!" She pushed her fists straight down her sides as if to keep them under her tight control. "First you set fire to the mill. And while we were working on that, you started the woods on fire."

"No, it wasn't me. He ordered me to do it, but I refused."

"How could you do it? Why you? Or did you have help? Oh." Closing her eyes, she shook her head as if she hadn't heard him.

He opened his mouth to lay more protestations at her feet when he realized there wasn't anything he could say when she'd read the proof of his misdeeds with her own eyes. Or at least the proof of what appeared to be his crime.

"Please leave, Mr. Moore. I need to see to the comfort of my staff."

He raised his hands to stop her from walking toward the smoldering, burned-out shell of her home and then dropped them by his side. She needed to be surrounded by people who cared for her. Although his arms ached to hold her as her staff were doing, he needed to clear his name before he could ever hope to receive any sort of affection in return.

But if he didn't start the fires, who did?

◆ ◆ ◆

Amelia had felt abandoned at being forced to leave her home to a man who didn't deserve it, yet she would have given it willingly if it would have saved her beautiful home from devastation. Everything made of wood had burned away, both inside and out, on the sides and back of the house only. Due to the wind, the garden, the lawn, and the trees lining the drive were untouched, creating an eerie contrast between the past and present.

Scorched brick walls stood as a testament to their strength, while other walls lay in rubble among the charred timbers that had held the flammable roof in place. Here and there wisps of smoke rose from dying embers turning into ash.

At the corner of her eye the conservatory stood with blackened glass. She'd studiously ignored it, unable to face the disaster within, but she had to see for herself. To remember this day and all that she'd lost.

She trudged along the familiar walk, eyes shimmering at the darkness within the glass building. She hoped the moisture in the structure and inside the green wooded plants had saved them, but at the door she gasped. Instead of greenery and brown limbs, drooping black stalks crowded together in misery. Mounds of ash where wicker had stood. Her potting table a pile of rubble with botany instruments poking up proving they were there.

Footsteps crunched up the walk.

She turned from her dreams and walked outside. "It's all gone, Williams."

"Not quite, miss. I have something to show you."

"You should have gone with the rest, Williams."

He turned to face her with the hulking mess she'd called a home forming a background she couldn't miss.

"Sorry, Miss Amelia, but you're stuck with me." To prove his statement, he linked her arms in his and led her toward the old well. She pulled back, unwilling to share her special place with anyone other than Father. But Williams kept his grip on her arm, patting it like Father would have done. "Come, I have something to show you. When I noticed the second fire, I suspected foul play."

"You did? Why?"

"Because there was no connection between them. No natural reason to explain their existence."

"It was Moore." She covered her heart as a piercing pain radiated outward. "Winston told him to do it, and he did. Like a little puppet with no morals of his own."

With the well platform upon them, she sank onto it with her head resting on her arms and knees.

"I smelled kerosene as soon as I approached the kitchen, where the first fire started. I suspect they splashed it about and added a lit match. Not just once, but on the verandas as well. I believe he—or they—would have done the same through the front door but didn't want to risk being discovered. We could have caught the culprit if we hadn't been otherwise occupied."

"I'm so thankful you all got out alive." She shivered at what might have been.

"Which brings me to the reason we are here."

She looked at the shambles of her life. "I know exactly why I'm here, Williams, and it's all because of Moore and his fiendish family."

"Not quite." He held his hand out to her. "If you will."

Oh dear, now Williams was acting strange. But she allowed him to pull her to her feet.

Williams moved to the back of the well and dropped to his haunches.

"What are you doing?"

Instead of answering, he raised half the platform like a cellar door opening and then laid it on top of its mate.

Amelia gasped as she realized it wasn't a well at all but simply a three-foot hole in the same shape as the platform that covered it.

"What's this?" Close to the side where Williams stood sat the new trunk that Moore gave her.

"You'd already packed it, miss. But in the rush I dragged it down the stairs myself, and it's not a light one by any means and it got away from me and tumbled twice before stopping. And then I somehow managed to get it out here."

He drew such a comical picture of what must have been the most harrowing experience of his life. She flicked the latch and opened the trunk lid. Instead of neat and orderly, her things were topsy-turvy and a complete mess, but one sight of her jewelry box and she was in tears. "Williams, I can't imagine I'll ever be able to thank you for this."

He straightened like his old self. "Don't say that until you've seen the damage, miss."

She opened the jewelry box her father had made from her mother's sewing chest. Both the pin and the locket were safe inside, although the locket chain would need some patience straightening out. It wavered before her. "Thank you, Williams. You've given me something precious. Something I thought I'd lost forever."

He turned away and sniffed. "You're very welcome, miss. It's what your father would have wanted me to do."

She wanted to hug him, but propriety demanded she not. Propriety? She didn't give a toot about correct behavior when her home was in ruins and Williams had saved the only things that truly mattered.

"And this." He pulled out Father's gold watch and placed it in her hand. "I managed to grab that, too."

That did it. She threw her arms around his waist and hugged as hard as she could. "Thank you, Williams. Thank you."

His arms surrounded her with the lightness of someone unsure what was expected. "There, there. It's going to be all right. You'll see."

◆ ◆ ◆

Jeremy bent low in the saddle and urged his already galloping horse faster, faster, as if he could outrun the black and empty future dragging in the dust behind him.

But he hadn't even gone a few hundred yards when the high-pitched, raspy breathing of his horse infiltrated the disturbing images he'd witnessed a few hours before.

"Whoa, boy." He dismounted and then slid the reins over the horse's head, annoyed that he'd allowed his frustrations to threaten the well-being of the gentle animal. With the horse walking beside him, he wiped the lather from his long, silky neck. "Easy, boy. We'll walk a spell. It'll do us both a world of good."

As the horse's wheezing diminished, Jeremy's thoughts were overtaken by Amelia's expression as the words of the telegram registered. Her shock that he'd been the instigator had brought out his denials. But her pain at his alleged betrayal had silenced him.

Why did she feel betrayed? They had been on opposite sides since their first meeting. No, before that even, because Winston had raised Jeremy to believe that Robertson had stolen from Winston's family, and his main purpose in life was to enact revenge.

Spotting a rock in his path, Jeremy kicked it with every ounce of frustration that clung to his muscles. It flew down the road a bit and then skittered to the side. He stared at the rock as they walked past it. Amelia was like that rock. He'd kicked her whole world apart by pointing out her illegitimacy, but all she did was roll along, and when she stopped, she stood straighter than before. She's the one he should be admiring, not some madman with no sense of morality.

And he did admire her. More than admire her. She pulled at his heart so that each time he'd had a harder time leaving, and it had only been his loyalty to Winston that had ensured his distance.

While his attachment to her had grown stronger, the one he'd felt for Winston had thinned with brittleness at each hurtful deed to Amelia, until finally it had snapped like Winston's mind.

Jeremy stopped walking. Closing his eyes, he looked heavenward and sniffed the air. Dust, prairie grasses, and newly turned earth mingled together. For the first time in a long time he sent up a prayer asking for wisdom, help, and forgiveness.

Later in town after returning the horse to the livery, he headed for the sheriff's office. No more regrets, he knew exactly what he had to do before he could even think of presenting himself to the woman who'd come to mean more to him than anything or anyone else on earth.

◆ ◆ ◆

In the middle of the night, Amelia awoke disoriented by the strange room and the gently snoring woman beside her. Within moments, events of the previous day rushed in with stark reality. If she hadn't opposed Moore when he told her to leave, would the mill, woods, and house still be standing? The pressure on her chest kept her still while the familiar lump grew in her throat. Had it been her fault?

Moonbeams shone through Rosie's window and fell across Amelia. She had prayed that the overcast weather meant God would send the rain to put the mill fire out, but not a drop fell anywhere in the county on a day they needed it the most.

As good as her word, Rosie had been waiting in front of the mercantile when Williams drove up with everything she owned in the back of the wagon. Funny how she'd packed it with the future in mind without realizing the devastation attached.

Bless Williams for having the wisdom to see the danger and act upon it. With the stumble he'd taken, had he really managed to save her things intact?

She slid off the bed, careful not to wake Rosie, who would get up at first light on her own.

Sitting on the floor, Amelia opened the trunk lid and took out her jewelry chest. The mother-of-pearl leaves picked up the moonlight, presenting a surreal picture, inviting her caress. She opened it and one by one took out the only items she had left that her parents had touched. She held the items against her heart—a pin, locket, and watch. Mere items devoid of anything resembling affection, and yet she felt connected through them to her loved ones.

By the light of the slow-moving moon, her gaze fell on a splash of white in the jewelry box interior. She didn't remember anything else inside, but perhaps Williams had added something and in the turmoil forgot to mention it.

Holding the box up to the light for a closer look, she found that an inch of the velvet interior had torn away from the wooden side, and between the lining and the wood poked the corner of a white paper.

Williams wouldn't have had time to rip the fabric away from the side, add a note, and then reseal the lining save for the one inch that had caught her eye. And even if he did, there was no guarantee she would find it—unless he told her about it. Yet they'd driven the whole way to town yesterday with barely a word between them.

As she replaced her pin, locket, and watch safely back in the box, she couldn't stop looking at the white corner. Father had made the jewelry box for her with her mother's sewing box. In all the years she'd owned it, it hadn't strayed from its spot on her bureau.

So whatever was on the paper had been placed there by Father or the person who added the lining.

Her hands trembled as she ripped the velvet away from the wood, little bits at a time, stopping after each tear to ensure Rosie didn't wake. When the opening was three inches long, she pulled out a folded sheet of notepaper.

At the sight of her mother's iris-emblazoned paper, her tears poured out. She dropped the paper and hid her face in the hem of her nightshirt to muffle the sounds she couldn't hold back.

Many minutes later, she moved her position into the moonbeam once more. With a deep cleansing breath, she unfolded the paper to find Father's masterful script. Disappointment that it wasn't from the mother she never knew was short-lived as she read the letter addressed to her and written so many years ago. Although his words didn't explain her parentage, it acknowledged her as his blood kin and sole heir of all that he owned.

She tucked Father's will back into its hiding spot, closed the lid, and put the box back into the trunk Moore had provided, all the while feeling that she hadn't won anything at all.

Thanks to Williams, they would rebuild. Not elaborate, but a house big enough for her and the staff, who wouldn't have to worry about jobs—unless they wanted to leave. She'd rebuild the mill, maybe with new technology and a coal-fired steam heating system. They could be ready for harvest if they were diligent. With the seedlings safely planted, she'd be able to continue her botany work in a new conservatory as funds permitted.

Planning her future should have made her content.

It didn't.

She stood by the window hugging herself. What good was re-creating the past, when all she really wanted was a future with a man she could never trust?

Chapter 9

A few hours later Williams drove Amelia back to the ruins she had inherited. On the way, she told him about the will and asked him to keep it to himself as she hadn't decided what to do with the information yet. It was his reward for the action he'd taken to ensure her future. Even Rosie wouldn't know that the will was hidden upstairs in her quarters.

During the night the wind had weakened the wall of bricks supporting her princess turret and it had fallen into the rubble of the blackened shell. Amelia grieved for her loss, yet the discovery of the will not only eased a portion of the calamity, it gave her energy to start the rebuilding process. And before that could start, the old and broken had to go.

She didn't expect to see Moore again, so when he didn't show that day, she wasn't surprised. The next day, either. However, over the next few days she found herself looking down the empty drive hoping to see him riding toward her.

"He'll be back, miss, one of these days." Williams tossed a charred board onto the pile they would set on fire later. He hadn't wanted to wear the denim overalls that Rosie had pressed into her hands the first morning of their return, but after hours of wear, he had admitted they saved his suit from dirt and tears and were comfortable while working.

She sent another peek down the drive. "Do you really think so?"

"Yes, I do. And although you haven't asked my opinion, I don't believe he set the fires."

"You don't? Why?"

"He was with you when the fire in the woods started, as well as the house."

"He could have paid someone to do it for him just like Winston did."

Williams nodded. "Yes, miss. Just like Winston did. That doesn't prove it was Moore." He pulled a sodden handkerchief out of his back pocket—the gesture reminding her that she needed to check with Hanover about the mill's progress later.

"I don't believe Mr. Moore would do anything to hurt you intentionally, miss. He had ample opportunities to evict you empty-handed. First, he let you stay even though, by your own words, you had no legal right to be here. Then he allowed you to pack anything you wanted so long as it would fit into the trunk. Yes, he turned it into a game and toyed with you, but I believe it was more pretension than a wish to run you off."

Her pulse raced as he said his piece, but then it slowed as memories of her first meeting in Moore's office flooded back. Williams hadn't seen Moore's face as he'd delivered his brutal news. "I must get you a hat, Williams. I believe the sun has touched your head."

"If that's what you think, miss, but I saw how he looked at you."

She felt as if she stood on the edge of a raging river and needed Williams's answer to ferry her across. "How did he look at me?" She held her breath.

Williams focused on the charred wood he'd thrown on the pile. "Tortured, miss."

◆ ◆ ◆

Several days after Williams's revelation, the sheriff stopped by the estate to say he'd completed his investigation and he'd charged two men with arson for setting all three of the fires on her property.

"Does Mr. Moore know?"

If the sheriff was surprised by her response he didn't show it. "Yep. As the attorney handling all your affairs, I thought he should know."

Moore was Winston's attorney, not hers, but since it didn't matter one way or the other to the case, she didn't feel the need to explain. "Thank you, Sheriff."

So Moore had spoken the truth when he'd claimed innocence. If he refused Winston's order, was he still working for him? Or was all forgiven because he was family?

Amelia brought the water jug and cups around to the men. As they drank, she couldn't stop herself from glancing down the drive.

And then she took a second successive glance because she wasn't sure if the sight of Moore was real or imaginary. Her pulse quickened. Yes, he was riding up her drive.

Aware of her soil-stained outfit and windblown hair, she strode to the tent Williams had erected as shelter from the June sun. At the washstand inside, she poured water out of the pitcher and into the basin so fast that it sloshed over the side. Ignoring her mess, she scrubbed her face and fixed her hair.

If it was going to be their last meeting, then what he saw today would be the memory he took back to Chicago.

She emerged from the tent to find him standing by his horse watching the workers. He looked tired and worn as if he hadn't slept much in the past week. Since a sincere social salutation didn't come to mind, she simply nodded and waited for him to speak.

"Miss Amelia." He tipped his hat with formality. "You're looking well."

"Thank you." Suddenly, she wanted him to leave because it was hurting too much to go on. Perhaps it was the mental and emotional games he had played at her expense, or the physical activity of the past week, or the knowledge of what might have been if he'd come under different circumstances, but a lump was growing in her throat, and she was so very tired of it all. "State your business, Moore."

"I came to say I'm sorry for all the suffering I've caused."

She crossed her arms because she couldn't argue with him, and she wasn't ready to forgive him yet, either.

"You're making good progress here."

She raised her chin. "At the mill, too." She braced herself, ready to counteract his order to stop work and get off the property.

"That's good." He shoved his hands in his pockets. "I've parted ways with Winston."

She stared at him. "How? Isn't he your stepfather or something?"

"Something like that." His wry smile didn't reach his eyes. "But it's all formal with signatures so I can't be held responsible for any of his future actions."

"That was wise."

This time his smile was genuine. "Yes, I think so, too. But the best part is this..." He handed her a stamped envelope with Winston's return address.

She accepted it with trembling fingers and then held it by her side. "If you're not Winston's attorney, does that mean he's sending someone else to evict me?"

"No, you'll never be evicted again, because look—" He reached down and snatched the envelope out of her hand. With an experienced flick, the letter was out of the envelope and open toward her. "Winston gave me the Robertson estate as payment for services rendered. He wanted to be rid of the whole thing."

She saw the flash of pain in his eyes and instinctively knew that his refusal to do Winston's bidding had broken whatever strings had tied them together. But what did that mean for her?

"Are you saying that *you* own my land now?"

"Yes—no! I want to give it back to you, dearest, as a wedding present. Look. . ." He held the paper close to her eyes when she refused to touch it. "Down here I've annotated that I give up all rights to the property known as the Henry Robertson estate and Robertson's Syrup Mill out of McLeod County, Minnesota, and bestow them on one Amelia Cord Robertson of the same location."

He searched her eyes as if desperate for a response.

She couldn't respond—she couldn't even think straight. He had broken all his ties with his family and life in Chicago because of her. And then when he'd been given valuable property, he'd given that to her as well. And somewhere in his speech he'd slipped in something about a wedding.

"Repeat the part about the wedding."

Chuckling, he cupped her chin with his hand. "I'm asking you to marry me, Amelia."

"Sweet words, but why? If you have the land already, you don't need—"

"Because I love you. I've loved you since you fainted in my office and looked up at me with your sky-blue eyes. Because I felt I had to return to Chicago I tried so very hard not to love you, but I can't help it. I do."

She wanted to believe him so very much, and yet doubts lingered. "If I say no, what happens to the property?"

He dropped his hands and stepped back. A muscle twitched along his jawline. She knew how hard he was clenching his teeth, trying not to show what emotion or frustration he was feeling. "If you say no, you can keep the deed and I walk away."

"You would do that?"

"If that's what you want. I haven't put any effort into gaining clients here, so no one will miss me if I hang my shingle somewhere else. I hear they need attorneys out in the Territories, especially with statehood upon them. I'll get by." He shrugged as if it wasn't a big deal, but his dark eyes said otherwise.

Taking one of her hands, he curled her fingers around the letter. "Keep this somewhere safe and you'll never have to worry about some ornery attorney trying to chase you out of your home."

As he walked toward his horse she shivered, already missing the warmth from his hand on her face. If she allowed him to leave, she would miss his warmth for the rest of her life.

"Wait." She hurried to his side. "I don't want you to leave."

He faced her with his emotions hidden behind a somber curtain.

"You're a hard person to love, Jeremy Moore, but somehow against my better judgment I've developed feelings for you as well."

Hope flared in his eyes, yet he kept it in check.

She waved the deed he'd given her. "What if we didn't have this?" She ripped it in half and then threw the pieces into the prairie wind while he watched in stunned silence. "What if we walked away and started fresh somewhere else, just the two of us?"

He swallowed hard and then blinked. A moment later he smiled. "I never knew what freedom was until I met you. For the first time in my life I don't have someone looking over my shoulder or telling me what to do. You, on the other hand, could have gone anywhere you wanted, but you chose to stay here and ensure your staff and your father's legacy were looked after. It doesn't matter to me where we go, what we do, or who you bring as long as we do it together."

Wrapping his arms around her, he glanced over her shoulder. "However, we should let your staff know what's going on because it looks like they're about to pummel me with bricks."

She laid her head on his shoulder. "You know they won't."

"Not if I keep holding you like this, anyway."

Social convention dictated that she pull away from him. She snuggled closer instead. Secure in his arms, she closed her mind to everything else until a persistent nagging took hold of her thoughts.

Leaning back, she gazed up at him. "There's one more thing you ought to know." This close, she realized his eyes were lighter than she thought and flecked with gold that sparkled when he smiled. Why hadn't she noticed that before?

"Mmm-hmm. I'd like to know if you're going to marry me."

"Oh, didn't I say?"

"No, I'm sure I would have remembered that."

"I wouldn't have let you forget it." She'd never been one to exchange banter, and yet the simple teasing confirmed that she was well on her way to happiness.

"Ahem, Miss Amelia," Williams interrupted in a loud voice. "Is there something you would like to tell us?"

She dragged herself away from Jeremy to find the workers and whatever staff were on hand that day waiting with animated expectation.

"Yes, please tell us, Miss Amelia." Jeremy clasped his hands together. "We would *all* like to know."

She licked her lips. She would give them more than they'd asked, and everything they needed. "Mr. Moore has asked me to marry him."

Cheers went up.

"And what did you say?" Charlie called out.

"Yes."

More cheers.

"Then we don't have to leave?"

A hush fell over the group while many of them turned in Charlie's direction.

The scene shimmered before Amelia as she realized the toll the fires and insecurity over the past couple of weeks must have taken on the young boy. She set her hand on the twelve-year-old's shoulder. "No, Charlie, you don't have to leave until you're ready to go."

His tremulous sigh was all she needed to know everything was going to work out.

Jeremy appeared at her side, his hand on her arm. "Amelia."

"As a matter of fact"—she placed her hand over Jeremy's as a token of assurance—"I found my father's will, and in his own words it states that everything he owned passes on down to me. So you see"—she raised her hands to encompass them all—"this is our home and no one can make us leave."

She smiled as her men slapped each other on the back.

Charlie stood alone looking like he would burst. She did the only thing she could. She wrapped him in her arms and hugged him tightly.

"Please tell me you weren't just saying that," Jeremy said later as they drove back to town.

"No, it's true. When he altered my mother's sewing box, he hid his will behind the velvet lining. I never would have found it if Williams hadn't dropped the trunk in his haste to get it out of the burning house."

He nudged his shoulder against her. "I've always liked Williams. He's a good man." A moment later, he chuckled. "So that's why you ripped up Winston's letter without a hint of remorse. My heart almost stopped right there."

"You didn't look worried."

"No, because I was trying to show strength and courage. At least until you said yes."

She linked her arm in his and leaned her head against his shoulder. "Yes."

"You're sure?"

"Yes." She yawned. "Are you?"

"Yes."

"Good, because I've fallen in love with you, and I'm so exhausted I'd rather not go through it again."

His chuckles warmed her heart.

Epilogue

Among the mixed scent of a multitude of flowers Amelia detected the faint odors of wallpaper paste, plaster, paint, and varnish. Not the fragrance she'd expected when she had dreamed of her wedding day, yet it signaled a new beginning.

"There, I think you're ready, dearie." With one final adjustment of the veil, Rosie stepped back.

Amelia looked into her new mirror and wondered what Jeremy would think and feel as he saw her dressed in her lilac finery, the color specifically chosen to honor her father's passing only half a year before. In tribute to her mother she wore the locket beneath her bodice where it nestled against her skin, and her pearl starburst brooch pinned to the lace on the outside for all the world to see.

A knock at her door heralded the arrival of Woodward, who had patiently answered her questions and given his time throughout her growing years and would now escort her into the future. He led her down the stairs and through the foyer, all new and different yet with enough familiar details to remind her of the home she'd loved before.

Outside she paused on the veranda and tried to capture the vivid scene before her. Two dozen white benches were filled with friends in colorful outfits. Their guests turned as she exited her new home. Behind them, the glass panes of the conservatory gleamed in the sunlight, hiding the new growth of resilient plants that had survived the scorching flames.

Soon the cranes would return, dancing for whatever reason cranes dance, in the same valley as before, or others; it didn't matter to Amelia, as long as they returned. Like the plants and shrubs that were returning to the burned-out areas of the woods, bright green testaments to nature's survival.

In contrast, the sorghum was ready for harvest, while the new and updated mill sat ready to receive the canes.

Cycles of life and death, of destruction and new beginnings. Of hope and love and the promise a new day brings. And with that realization she set aside all the disappointments of the past and looked to her future.

As if on cue, Jeremy left the minister's side and walked toward her, his face embodying the same things she'd been feeling as she stood on the veranda appreciating the blessings in her life.

He reached the bottom of the steps and raised his open hand to her. "I love you. You are everything I didn't know I wanted until you showed me the dancing cranes. God instilled in them the instinct to dance, to mate for life, and to always return home. Shall we follow their example and spend the rest of our lives together?"

She would have flown down the steps if her dress had allowed it, but soon enough she was by his side, heading toward the minister who would join them together, under God and before their friends, a testimony of how the sweetest love can grow when it seems that life is hopeless.

Anita Mae Draper historical romances are woven under the western skies of the Saskatchewan prairie where her love of research and genealogy yield fascinating truths that layer her writing with rich historical details. Her Christian faith is reflected in her stories of forgiveness and redemption as her characters struggle to find their way to that place in our heart we call home. Anita loves to correspond with her readers through any of the social media links found on her website at www.anitamaedraper.com.

Readers can enrich their reading experience by checking out Anita's story boards on Pinterest at www.pinterest.com/anitamaedraper.

Hometown Heiress

by Patty Smith Hall

Chapter 1

Atlanta, 1895

It wasn't every day a plum job dropped in Matthew Langley's lap, but today looked to be his day. He studied the impeccably dressed gentleman opposite him and wondered how the man even knew him. Granted, Matt was making a name for himself at the *Atlanta Journal and Constitution*, but this was Senator George Evers. The man was already well respected in the Georgia political landscape. Why, he had almost single-handedly pushed the notion of the Cotton States and International Exposition through the state house, picking up financial backing as well as making a name for himself on the national political stage along the way. In some high-ranking circles, a possible run for the governorship was already being whispered about.

Today, Evers had given Matt the scoop he'd waited his entire career for. The senator would run for governor, and he'd offered Matt the plummy job of press liaison.

"I expected more of a response from my future press liaison than silence." Evers's salt-and-pepper eyebrows knitted together in slight annoyance.

Matt chuckled. "Even wordsmiths are rendered mute at times. Of course, I'm honored." He paused to pick his next words carefully. "I'm just not sure why you picked me for this position. Many others are far more experienced in political journalism than I am. Take my editor, Mr. Taylor. He actually has experience on Capitol Hill."

"Are you trying to talk me out of hiring you, young man?"

"No, I'm..." Matt wasn't certain what point he was trying to make, only that the man needed to know he had other more experienced options. "It just seems a little unusual that you'd want a beat reporter to be in charge of your press office."

Evers sat back and studied him for a long moment. "You did write those exposés concerning the social ills of our state that everyone is talking about, correct?"

Matt didn't know where the senator was going with this. "Yes, sir."

"And you're moving people to respond. I tell you when I read your piece on the continued decline of the working class thirty years after the war and the effects of the recent depression, I thought you provided some extraordinary insight into the mind-set of the working poor."

Not insights but realities. Ones he was very familiar with growing up on the outskirts of Athens. Some nights he hadn't known where his next meal was coming from. "Thank you."

"It made me want to storm the halls of the state capitol and get to work on legislation that would help our people."

Exactly the kind of reaction Matt had hoped to provoke. He smiled slightly. "I'm glad it prompted you to act, sir."

"A person would have to be dead not to feel for those people." The senator hesitated for a moment. "I truly believe it was your article that was the deciding factor in my decision to run for governor."

Matt wasn't sure whether to believe the man—he was, after all, a politician—but he couldn't deny the sense of pride he felt at the senator's comment. "Thank you."

"And it's why I'm offering you the job as my press liaison rather than one of those other journalists you mentioned. You see, I believe my campaign should focus on the issues that plague our society like poverty and inhumane living conditions. Certainly, I can do some of that in the state senate, and I have. But there, I'm just one of many. As governor, I can influence the house and senate to consider these problems and write bills that can make a difference."

The senator sounded earnest, but then most politicians did until they were elected. True, Evers had voted for a recent relief bill, but most of his record favored state industry leaders. "This is a mighty big shift in your public policy, more than a simple article could sway you to make."

"Yes, well, I recently visited a friend. You might know him, Martin Eison."

Who didn't know of Mr. Eison? He owned the largest textile mills in south Georgia. Matt nodded. "I've heard of him."

"Most people have. Anyway, I went to see him at his office and was stunned by what I found." Evers leaned forward, his fingers white from their grip on the chair. "Children, some as young as five or six, on the floor of his mill. Some were running around barefoot, and I couldn't help but wonder when was the last time any of them had eaten."

Five years old! Matt's temper spiked. Working in a mill wasn't any place for a kid. He should know. "Did you confront Mr. Eison with your concerns?"

"Of course I did. Even told him the legal working age in Georgia was twelve. But Martin refused to be swayed. Said the children's paychecks were the only thing keeping food on the family's dinner table."

Probably true, but still. To have a five-year-old running a machine. Even Mr. Perkinson, the owner of the mill where he'd worked as a boy, didn't hire anyone younger than eight.

Matt studied the senator. Was he truly interested in improving the lives of the poor? Or was it just a way to win the governor's mansion? "Well, I don't think you should take on too much. Maybe focus on one hot-button issue like unsafe work conditions or low pay."

"You've got a point there." Evers tapped his finger against his lips as though rummaging through the possibilities, then glanced over at Matt. "After what I saw, I want to focus my attention on abolishing child labor."

A tingle of excitement nestled in the pit of Matt's stomach. It was a topic he himself was passionate about, but every article he'd turned in to his editor had been rejected for the same reason. He was too close to the subject matter to be objective.

Maybe this was his opportunity. His chance to help a young boy or girl not endure the same kind of childhood he'd had. "I think that will work well with the public."

Evers leaned back in his chair. "I think you're right, son, though it most likely won't sit well with Martin."

"He backed your last campaign, didn't he?"

The man nodded, something almost sad in his expression. "Martin was like a brother to me and had been one of my staunchest supporters. We haven't spoken since I confronted him about the children he employs in his mills. I have to admit I didn't worry about the older children working there—Martin had always been good to them—but five-year-olds." He drew in a sharp breath. "Martin claims he stood to lose his fortune if he complied with my request, though I don't see how that's possible. The entire operation is run by children."

Matt sat back. Wasn't this the reason he'd studied journalism in the first place? To help right the wrongs in society, to make a difference in the world? And here was a man willing to fight alongside him at great peril to his political career. "You know I'll have to confirm everything you've told me."

"Of course, and I have someone I think might be able to help you with that." The senator reached down, opened his satchel, and pulled out a file. He handed it to Matt. "Dania Eison is extremely knowledgeable on this subject and could turn out to be a valuable asset."

Matt looked at the file in his hands then back at Evers. "Dan. . . ?"

"It's pronounced Dan-ya. She's heiress to the Eison textile mills. I don't know how much she understands about the business—you know how young women with money are—but I'm sure if you ask her the right questions, she can confirm that there are young children working at the family mill." The senator nodded. "Yes, I'd start with her."

An heiress with no thought to the needs of others as long as her own comforts were met, the heartless creature. Yes, he'd like to meet Miss Eison and put her in her place. But he couldn't just walk up to an heiress and start a conversation. "How can I make her acquaintance?"

"Oh, I've taken care of that." Evers gripped the arms of the chair and pushed to his feet. "Dania is due to arrive tomorrow to attend the exposition and do some shopping in the city. I told her I've made arrangements for an escort while she's here."

"She's traveling by herself?" It seemed odd that an heiress, particularly one as wealthy as Miss Eison, would be traveling alone. Maybe she had other entertainments planned, ones where a chaperone would be an inconvenience.

Evers laughed. "Dania likes to think of herself as a modern woman, but I'm sure she's made arrangements for a maid to attend her while she's here."

Of course she had. It wouldn't do for her to button her own skirt or tie up her boots. She probably had a town house full of servants ready to act on her tiniest whim. "What time does her train arrive?"

"Around noon, though she hasn't made any plans until the next day." He seemed almost embarrassed for her. "You know how young ladies are. Probably wants to rest after the strenuous journey."

A four-hour train trip strenuous? What was the woman made of, crystal? Matt swallowed his disdain. "Do you know what other exhibits Miss Eison is interested in visiting while she's here?"

The senator cocked his head to the side as if to think. "The fine arts building, I presume. Perhaps, the women's building. Dania thinks she's a very progressive thinker, though why she thinks that when she's never been out of Tifton is beyond me."

Matt nodded. It sounded as if Miss Eison thought she was still on the plantation, complete with crinolines and a mammy. Maybe a few days in his company would jolt the woman into the new century that was coming.

And if he enjoyed watching her stumble, so much the better.

Chapter 2

Dania Eison tugged at the edges of her woolen shawl as she stepped down onto the train platform, the cool air a relief compared to the heavy stuffiness of the passenger cabin. She thought to step farther into the rush of people then paused, her heart hammering against her chest. She'd never liked Atlanta, still didn't. Too many people for her taste.

Well, this wasn't a pleasure trip. Mr. Ernest Young, one of the most noteworthy industrial engineers in the country, was speaking at the Cotton States Exposition in two days, and she planned on being there. True, she had almost canceled when the bobbin had broken on her main threader. Why come for a demonstration that may not be feasible for the mill? But what if it was? What if Ernest Young's ideas on automation could be put to use on the floor of her mill? It would cost a pretty penny, but the welfare and safety of her young employees outweighed the cost. If only she could secure a meeting with the man, but all her attempts had been rebuffed.

There was much to do in the next two days. Clasping her valise with both hands, she headed down the platform to the stairs that led to the street. Maybe the carriage Uncle George had promised would be waiting there.

"Miss?"

Dania had barely turned when she felt a strong pull on the valise in her hand. Shock tinged with anger exploded in her chest. "What do you think you're doing?"

"Just let go, missy, and no one will get hurt."

"You just might!" Long hours of setting the thread and carrying cotton had strengthened her arms, and she was too stubborn to give up without a fight. She clutched the leather handle of her case and held on for dear life. "Police!"

The man seemed startled by her response. "Let go!"

The man yanked so hard Dania feared he'd dislocate her arm. But she refused to give up. Clasping the valise as tight as she could, she lifted her leg and kicked him hard just below the knee.

Letting go of her case, the man stumbled back, clutching his knee as if she'd landed a mortal blow. "You didn't have to do that, you little minx."

"The lady was much kinder than I would have been," a masculine voice behind her said. "I would have shot you myself."

Dania turned. If she'd had any doubts about this man's words, the infuriated expression on his face repelled them. "Too bad you weren't here to demonstrate."

He gave her a cockeyed grin that caused her stomach to flutter. Probably shock from facing down a would-be thief. "You seemed to have the situation well under control."

Dania's mouth fell open then snapped shut. Any of the men back in Tifton wouldn't have thought twice at helping her, but then this wasn't home, was it? "I appreciate your concern, but I'm sure you have somewhere you need to be, Mr. . . ."

"No, I'm exactly where I belong. And the name is Langley, Miss Eison." He walked over to her assailant and jerked him upright, causing the man to wince. "There's a police officer just around the corner. I'll be back as soon as I introduce this man to the authorities."

Dania blinked as she watched the two hurry down the platform. How did he know her name? Why did that name sound so familiar? Could he be one of the men she'd hoped to meet with at the exposition? Or. . .

Dropping her valise, she opened her reticule and pulled out a neatly folded sheet of telegraph paper. Uncle George had begged off meeting her at the station, but he'd promised to send an associate in his place. She scanned over the telegram then smirked. A Mr. Matthew Langley.

"Lovely." Dania stuffed the paper back into her purse and clicked it shut. How Uncle George even knew she would be in Atlanta was anyone's guess. After his unsuccessful bid to buy the mill out from under them, Papa had broken all ties with him. A thirty-year friendship destroyed over a business Dania wasn't even sure could survive. But Papa had been adamant: *"Don't trust anything Uncle George might say. The mill will provide financial security to our family and the families of those who work there."*

Papa. The sadness that accompanied any thoughts about her father brought a knot to her chest. Four long months since a heart seizure had claimed Papa's life, yet it still felt so fresh. Mama could make it through the day now without crying, or at least, she hid it well. Katie, her younger sister, had returned to school in Savannah while her sister Gilly had taken the semester off from college to help out at the mill.

"Miss Eison?"

Gracious gravy, but the man was quick! Dania opened her reticule, retrieved a fifty cent piece from her coin purse, and handed it to him. "Thank you for alerting the police, Mr. Langley. I do appreciate it."

He glanced down at her hand as if she held a water moccasin. "Do you always pay people for doing the right thing?"

"No, but—"

"Then don't insult me by offering me money."

She'd insulted him? Dania pulled her hand back as if it had been slapped. "I'm sorry. That wasn't my intention. When I was planning this trip, I wasn't expecting Uncle George to secure me an escort."

Confusion furrowed the man's handsome brow. "The senator is your uncle?"

She gave a humorless chuckle. "No. It's just that my father and Uncle George have been friends since before I was born. Neither had any siblings, so they always considered themselves brothers." That was until Uncle George tried to buy the mill out from under her family.

"Miss Eison, is something wrong?"

Dania lifted her head and met blue-green eyes touched by a hint of concern. Matthew Langley was quite an attractive man, probably the most handsome of her acquaintance. When he stared at her, as if his complete attention was focused on her, her heart skipped a beat. Dania shook her head. "Probably just tired from the train ride. I don't travel very much."

"You don't?"

"Why would you think that I do?"

If he thought her question odd, his expression didn't show it. "Isn't that what most young heiresses do? Travel around the country, shopping and attending teas? Dancing the night away in the arms of any one of a number of matrimonial candidates?"

Dania didn't know whether to be angry or fall down laughing. "I wouldn't know. I've spent the last several years learning the family business."

He blinked at her response. "You work for your father?"

The man seem surprised by her news, but at least he wasn't mortified like most of the men she knew. "I'm the oldest of three sisters, Mr. Langley. With no male heirs, Papa felt it was important that I learn all aspects involved in the daily running of our mill. It is a family business after all."

"Oh." He looked slightly amused, as if the idea of her running the mill was humorous in some way.

What exactly had Uncle George told this man about her? Whatever it was, he hadn't painted an accurate picture of her or her life. Why did that bother her so much? Dania drew in a deep breath. "I appreciate your offer to escort me on Uncle George's behalf, but there's really no need."

Mr. Langley nodded, sitting back on his heels. "If that's what you'd like."

An odd response, so very different from the men back home. For some odd reason, she wanted to know why. "You're not going to remind me of the dangers of traveling alone or the damage that could be done to my reputation."

He studied her for a long moment then shrugged. "You appear to know all the arguments. Why bother repeating them?"

Shaking her head, she gave him a slight smile. "Uncle George might not see it that way. As your employer. . ."

"Oh, I don't work for Senator Evers. At least, not yet."

This was getting confusing. Dania pressed her lips together. "Then why did my uncle ask you to escort me?"

"Well, to be honest"—he gave her another of those lopsided grins and she forgot to breathe—"escorting you around is kind of my job interview."

She stiffened. "Excuse me?"

"The senator said you had some ideas on how to change the textile industry that piqued my interest. Is that true?"

Dania tensed; Uncle George's resistance to changes at her mill was still an embarrassing memory. Why would Uncle George tell this man about the changes she hoped to make? How did he think Mr. Langley could help? "Are you on the state house committee that oversees the textile business?"

"Oh no," he chuckled. "I'm too honest to be a politician. I'm a news reporter for the *Atlanta Journal and Constitution.*"

"Some people might say that's almost as bad."

The rich timbre of his laugh sent a pleasant tingle up Dania's spine. "You're sharp as a tack, aren't you?"

"It comes in quite handy when you're operating a business." She shifted the focus back to Mr. Langley. "Might I have read some of your articles?"

"You read the *Journal*?"

"When I can get it. For the business news, of course," Dania added, feeling herself blush. Truth be told, she devoured every paper she could get her hands on, a habit she'd started when she was barely old enough to read. Mama had always frowned upon it—young ladies needed to be protected against the harsh realities of the world—but it hadn't stopped her papa from sneaking papers to her.

"I just finished a piece on how the recession of 1890 widened the divide between social classes."

"That was your work?" Dania forgot her embarrassment and smiled. "We had quite an interesting conversation about that piece over the dinner table a few nights ago."

"That's all I can hope for when I write on those vital topics."

Dania nodded. It had been more than just a discussion. Mr. Langley's article had made her all the more determined to help those who worked for her and her family. Maybe he was just the man to help her. "I think I may have spoken too soon. If you'd still like to escort me to my appointments, I would be grateful."

His gaze settled on her, studying her as if she were the subject of one of his articles. "You changed your mind mighty fast."

"A lady can change her mind, can't she?" Dania shifted from one foot to the other and decided to be completely honest. "Truth is, I'd like to hear more about the research you did for your article. I'd like to know what I can do to help those people you mentioned in the piece."

"You're interested?"

Why did the man sound so surprised? Did he think she was some kind of monster? "I do care about people, Mr. Langley."

"Of course." He didn't smile, but there was a light in his eyes when he offered her his arm. "And please. Call me Matt."

"Matt." His name came out airy as if she was whispering her nightly prayers. Dania cleared her throat as she took his arm. "I'm Dania."

"Like its male counterpart, Daniel." A warm tingle shot up her arm as he covered her gloved hand with his. "It suits you."

Her heart did a little flutter. It shouldn't matter what Matthew Langley thought of her name or anything else, for that matter. Her first concern would always be her family and the children working in their mill. The only reason she was here in Atlanta was her business. She didn't have time for romantic entanglements, no matter how attractive the man was.

Chapter 3

Dania Eison was up to something. Matt could feel it deep in his bones. Instinct, his editor had once told him. The scent of a story.

There was certainly a story here. Matt glanced around the lobby of the Edgemont Hotel. A comfortable place with its hand-crocheted doilies, well-worn rugs, and comfortable chairs, but not exactly what he'd had in mind for a textile heiress. He'd been more than a little surprised when Miss Eison had given him the address to the clean but reasonably priced hotel; even more so when the owner, a Mr. Cooper, had greeted Dania like an old family friend.

But then Dania Eison hadn't been quite what Matt had expected. There was nothing in her manner to suggest her elevated social status, except for her well-made traveling suit that was the perfect shade of blue to match her luminous eyes. She was lovely, a beauty some might say, yet her manner seemed down-to-earth, as if she were unaware of her striking appearance. And she couldn't have been more straightforward when she'd refused his escort.

So why had she changed her mind?

Footsteps on the stairs drew his attention. Dressed in a snowy white shirt, a dark blue serge skirt, and a no-nonsense straw hat, Dania could have passed for any one of the many young women hurrying around the city streets to their jobs. For some odd reason, the thought made Matt smile. "Miss Eison?"

She turned and gave him a wide smile. "Mr. Langley. I'm sorry if I've kept you waiting."

"No apologies are necessary. It gave me time to make a few notes on my next article." Notes about her, though in all honesty, most were from his meeting with Senator Evers. Today, he would write down his own observations.

Her smile widened, but there was a sense of relief in her eyes. "Good. I hate to think of me wasting your time simply because I couldn't wake up this morning. I must be more tired than I thought."

Matt nodded. "Travel has a way of wearing a person out."

She stopped and gave him a worried look. "Do you find train travel exhausting?"

What an odd question! "No, I find it quite relaxing myself. Why do you ask?"

"Well, I have a full schedule today, and I wonder if it might be too taxing for you."

His brow furrowed in confusion. "Too taxing?"

"Well, you just said travel wears you out, and I wouldn't want you to get all tuckered out chasing me around Atlanta."

"I. . ." He pressed his lips together to keep from laughing. "You certainly speak your mind."

Her cheeks turned a lovely shade of pink. "One of my worst faults. Mama says it's most unladylike."

"I don't know." He thought for a second. "I think it's most refreshing."

Her eyes met his, and his breath caught in his throat. "That's a very modern way of thinking."

Matt forced himself to breathe. "How else are we going to know what the fairer sex is thinking unless you tell us?"

She chuckled softly. "You do have a point."

Matt wasn't quite sure why, but the thought he could make her smile, as if he were the only man in the world who had that particular talent, gave him a sense of satisfaction. "So, Miss Eison, what is on the agenda for today?"

"I'd hoped to do a bit of shopping." Opening the clasp of her reticule, she retrieved a folded piece of paper. "There's a fabric shop near Little Five Points that has large quantities of material for very good prices." She handed him the paper. "I'm not quite sure how to say the last name."

"Mr. Shonkwiler." The man who'd made Matt's first shirt when he'd come to Atlanta. Though his wares were good, they were beneath the quality most fashionable young ladies would consider. "I'm sure there are other merchants who would be more than happy to accommodate you."

"Is something wrong with Mr. Shonkwiler's material? He came highly recommended."

"No, he's very good but. . . ," Matt spurted.

Dania didn't give him an opportunity to finish. "His shop is open this morning, isn't it?"

"Yes, but. . ." He was confused. Why would someone of Dania's social status seek out a second-rate vendor? Was the Eison mill not as profitable as Evers thought? Or was it that Dania wasn't aware where the fashionable ladies shopped? "If you're having a new wardrobe made, you might find the shops along Peachtree more to your taste."

"A new wardrobe?" A smile played along her lips. "No, I wanted to go to him because his establishment is located next to the boot maker."

The woman was talking in riddles. "And you want a new pair of boots?"

"No. I mean, yes." She grimaced. "I'm not making any sense, am I?"

He shook his head. "Not really. Maybe if you tell me what you're hoping to achieve with your visit."

She bit her lip as if she were considering the idea. "I'd hoped it would remain a secret."

Gracious! Withholding a secret from him was like waving a red flag in front of an angry bull! Surely he could get her to share it. Maybe he could rattle it out of her. Matt stepped closer until the folds of her skirts touched his pant legs. "I promise not to tell."

"I have my reasons, Mr. Langley." Her gentle response belied the merriment in her eyes. "If you feel you can't escort me to Mr. Shonkwiler's, then I can find my own way there."

The woman had piqued his interest. There was no walking away from this assignment now. She might not have told him her secret yet, but she would. He bowed slightly at the waist. "I am at your disposal, Miss Eison."

"Thank you." She didn't say anything more, simply tugged on her worn leather gloves and started for the front entrance. Matt followed in her wake, the blue material of her skirts swaying in a lovely rhythm with each step.

Dania didn't speak again until they were settled in a hired carriage. "It's really no big secret, why I need to go to Mr. Shonkwiler's. It's just I don't want it to get back to the folks at home."

Well, that sounded interesting. Maybe Miss Eison was more like the heiresses he knew than he'd first thought. He leaned back into his seat. "Well, if the fabric isn't for you, maybe it's for your younger siblings?"

Dania glanced at him. "Do you promise not to tell anyone?"

"I'm a reporter, Miss Eison. It's my job to tell people's secrets."

"All right then." She turned to look out the window.

Oh, for Pete's sake, her secret couldn't be *that* newsworthy. "Fine, your secret is safe with me. But I do ask one thing in return."

There was a wariness in her eyes when she turned to look at him. "What would that be?"

"Please." He leaned toward her. "Call me Matt."

Her lips trembled into a slight smile that sent his pulse racing. "Okay, Matt. As long as you call me Dania."

"Dania." The name still struck him as unusual, yet he liked the way it came off his lips. "So? What's your secret?"

"Are you always this nosy?"

He shrugged. "It's a vice of the trade."

"A very annoying vice," she huffed, fiddling with the reticule in her lap.

"For those with something to hide." Matt waited for her response. If past experiences were anything to go by, Dania would either clam up or give him a dressing down.

Her laughter surprised him. "You must be terribly good at your job then."

Something about her response made his heart do a little flip in his chest. Matt shifted away from her slightly. "Only if I can get people to talk."

"Which, I'm certain, you have no trouble doing." Color stole into her cheeks making her eyes an even brighter shade of blue. "It's nothing really. I just noticed that most of the children who work in our mill are in need of clothes. So I thought I'd buy some material and offer it to their mothers. Those without anyone at home who sews, I'll make clothing for."

She'd just given him his confirmation. There were children working at the Eisons' mill, the information Evers wanted, yet her explanation was so unexpected. Most mill owners concerned themselves with their profits, not the basic needs of their young employees. Were the Eisons different? Or were they working some kind of angle he hadn't uncovered yet? "You're not doing this out of your company store, are you? Because those families might want food on the dinner table more than clothes."

"I don't understand." Confusion clouded her expression. "What do you mean by a company store?"

He'd have to push a little harder. "Your employees might not be able to manage the bill for both."

Sudden anger flashed in her eyes. "I'm not charging for the fabric. It's a bonus, along with the boots I'm having made for them."

Sweet mercy. Giving away clothes and boots without a thought to her profits. If true,

Dania was full of surprises. "That's a strange philosophy for a business owner."

"Yes, well." He felt her relax slightly. "I feel that mill owners have a moral obligation to make sure their workers are fed and cared for. It's like my papa always used to say—you can't expect a person to understand the goodness of the Lord when they're cold or hungry. I think it works in business, too."

Strange indeed, Matt thought. Had this been her father's idea, or was Dania doing this behind his back? Did it really matter? It was an incredibly kind thing to do. "Why did you want to keep it a secret?"

She gave a small sigh. "People have their pride, even those without very much. I didn't want word to get back home that this is anything other than what it is: a benefit of employment. If folks thought it was something else, they might refuse the garments, and that would be bad for the children."

She'd considered the workers' feelings. No business owners did that, at least, not the ones Matt was acquainted with. But then he'd known Dania was different from the moment he saw her kick her assailant in the shin. She took care of herself and those around her. Maybe that's why she'd drifted into his thoughts at odd moments last night. Despite everything Senator Evers had told him about Dania, she was telling him a different story. Not of a self-absorbed heiress, but of a woman who took her responsibilities seriously.

He hadn't expected to like her, but he did. He liked her very much.

"Matt, are you all right?"

"Just thinking," he answered, trying to put his jangled thoughts back in some order. "What does your father say about all this?"

"My father?" Her lips trembled slightly.

Matt didn't know why, but he felt a sudden need to put his arms around her and offer his shoulder to lean on. Reassure her everything would be okay. Instead, he took her gloved hand in his and gave it a reassuring squeeze. "You want to talk about it?"

"It's just that. . ." She sniffled then glanced up at him, her lashes wet with unshed tears. "My father passed away a few months ago. Since then, I've been running the mill."

"You. . ." The carriage came to a stop before he had a chance to ask the million questions running through his mind. Why had Dania been left in charge? Was there no Eison male relatives to take over the family business? And if she felt such a moral obligation to her workers, why did Dania still employ children?

Chapter 4

The morning flew by. Mr. Shonkwiler was everything Dania had been told to expect, helping her pick out soft yet durable fabrics that even the youngest of her charges would have a tough time ripping. The prices he'd given her left enough money to buy several bolts of white cotton for undergarments and bedsheets.

Waiting at the counter for the bill, Dania glanced over at Matt as he studied fabric samples. Talking about her father's death had been impossible these past few months, yet with Matt, it had felt right, as if he alone understood.

He glanced up at her, and she jerked around, her cheeks suddenly warm. She didn't make it a habit of staring at men, though in all honesty she hadn't noticed that many before Matt. Maybe it was because she'd caught him watching her a time or two. Well, as far as she was concerned, turnabout was fair play.

Dania turned her head to find him watching her again. "What?"

He shook his head. "Excuse me?"

"You've stopped asking me questions, but now you're studying me like I'm some animal in the zoo."

"I'm sorry." He came and stood in front of her. "I just find you. . .interesting."

Her, interesting? "You need to get out among young people more."

He chuckled. "You don't think you're interesting?"

"No," she huffed. "Why would I?"

Matt watched her for a second longer than was comfortable. "Are you asking my opinion?"

"You're the one who thinks I'm interesting, not me." And not anyone who really knew her. To most, she was simply Dania: reliable, practical Dania. They found nothing remotely interesting about that.

"Well," he began. "You're a woman in a man's world, yet you're running your family mill on your own terms. You care about the people who work for you—so much so you're taking some of your profits and putting clothes on their back, which I think is quite admirable." He leaned toward her, close enough to where only she could hear his next words. "You're too lovely for your own good. And I can tell from the color in your cheeks that you don't take compliments easily."

Dania's heart skipped a beat as Matt stepped away. He thought she was lovely? She thought he'd expected someone with a little more polish, more like the debutantes at the Peachtree Driving Club. What would he think if he saw the calluses on her hands? Or the old shirt and linen pants she wore to work on the equipment at the mill? If he saw her then, he wouldn't find her nearly as interesting.

She didn't have time to thank Matt before Mr. Shonkwiler hurried back. The pencil trembled in her hand as she wrote down her address for the delivery.

She thanked the tailor then turned and placed her receipt in her reticule. This was silly, of course, these emotions Matt sparked inside of her. She had a community that depended too much on the jobs she provided to be allowed to have her head turned by the first handsome man to pay her any notice. A brief flirtation, maybe? No, she'd never been one for such nonsense. She was simply too practical for that.

"What are you thinking about so hard?" Matt asked as he took her elbow and steered her toward the door.

A warm tingle ran up her arm, and she had to stop herself from leaning into him. "How did you know I was thinking about anything?"

There was a soft smile in his voice. "I just notice things."

"Like what?"

"People's expressions. A scowl here, a tiny line there. It helps me figure out what question to ask next or whether to take the interview in another direction entirely."

Goodness gracious. She prayed the man couldn't read her mind! "That must come in handy in your profession."

"Very." He slid her a glance. "Like you, for instance. You nibble at your lower lip when you're deep in thought."

She did? She'd never known that. "Anything else?"

"You normally smile a lot, but you're a little out of practice, probably because of your father's passing and the responsibility of running the mill." He gently squeezed her elbow. "That's a lot for one woman to take on."

She stiffened. "You don't think I can manage the family business because I'm a woman?"

"No, that's not what I meant at all." Matt turned to face her, concern written in his expression. "I just think it doesn't give you very much time to mourn your father, whom you clearly adored."

Matt was right. Since Papa's passing, she'd thrown herself into running the mill, implementing changes, trying to convince the parents of her young charges they needed to be in school, not working from dawn to dusk. Only in the quiet of her bedroom, when it was just her and the Lord, did she pour out her sorrow for the one man who believed she could move mountains. "I miss him."

Matt walked her to a nearby bench. As she sat down, he settled in next to her. "Tell me about him."

That was all the invitation she needed. Over the next hour, she shared stories of Papa's dry sense of humor, of his concern for their small community, of his love of the Lord and his family. With each memory she shared, it was as if Papa was with them. Matt had been right. Talking about her father made her feel unmeasurably better.

He must have sensed she was finished because he pulled out his handkerchief and handed it to her. "You okay?"

"Yes. Thank you for listening." She blotted the snowy white square against her lips and inhaled Matt's clean scent. "I don't know about you, but I could do with a cup of coffee and a sandwich."

"Is it lunchtime already?" He pulled out his pocket watch and glanced at it. "One o'clock."

One o'clock! If she didn't hurry, she'd miss Mr. Young's secretary and any chance she had at meeting him. But she hadn't had a real meal since what? Yesterday morning? If she didn't get something in her soon, she might pass out in front of Mr. Young, and that wouldn't do. "Well, maybe a quick bite."

"Good, because I made reservations for us at a nice little café around the corner."

Any other time, the action would have irritated her, but with Matthew, she only smiled and took the arm he offered her. "Pretty confident I'd have lunch with you."

He shook his head. "No, just ruled by my stomach. Besides, you need a break after all the work you've done this morning."

She chuckled. "I don't call buying material and arranging for a boot maker to come to Tifton work, Matt."

"Maybe not, but it should be. You went through more fabric swatches than my mother when she's making a quilt."

Dania felt a smile tug at the corners of her mouth. "Well, if you had suggested jeans for the boys earlier, it wouldn't have taken so long. That was a brilliant idea."

"I'm sure Mr. Shonkwiler would have suggested it eventually." Matt looked down the street then back at her.

Was it her imagination or was the man blushing? She lowered her gaze. "Still, what made you think of giving the boys those?"

"I had a pair when I was growing up." Matt opened the door to the café then stepped aside for her to enter. "Ma must have figured the expense would be better than constantly mending my clothes."

Dania waited as Matt talked to a primly dressed waitress. He'd probably been a rambunctious little boy, always into something, trying to figure out how the world worked. What kinds of activities had he liked? She'd wondered what it would have been like to go fishing or climb trees. Whatever Matt did, it had to be more exciting than the hours she spent learning every aspect of the mill.

"You're thinking again." His low whisper rumbled against her ear.

She waited until they were seated at their table before answering. "I was wondering what things you liked to do when you were a little boy."

"Not much," he said, staring at his menu. "There wasn't time."

Why had he not had time? She lowered her menu to look at him. "But you said your mother spent all her time mending your clothes. I thought you must have torn them climbing trees or something."

Matt glanced up at her. What she saw in his gaze caused a sudden ache in her chest. "I didn't play a lot when I was a kid."

"But—"

He interrupted her. "I worked from the time I was seven."

Matt worked as a boy? "What did you do, sell newspapers after school? Or did the grocer hire you to make deliveries?"

He hesitated. "I was a threader at the Perkinson Mill in Athens."

Dania's heart sank. Her father had refused to do business with Marvin Perkinson. Said he was a tyrant to his family and even worse to the children who worked for him. "How long were you there?"

"Almost ten years."

That didn't make any sense. How could he go to school if he worked long hours at the mill? How did he get into college? "But I read you graduated from the University of Georgia. How could you go to school if you worked twelve hours a day?"

"I studied for two hours every night and Sunday afternoons after church." His smile had turned melancholy. "I didn't want to work in a mill for the rest of my life."

"I don't blame you. And the university?"

He focused his attention back on the menu. "I was offered a full scholarship."

A full scholarship. She'd known the man was intelligent, but it had taken more than smarts to get him into the university. "That took a lot of get-up-and-go."

"Ma called it plain old stubbornness."

"She must be mighty proud of you." She relaxed a bit into her chair. "Is she still in Athens?"

"No, she and my sister, Mary, live here in town. Mary is on scholarship to Agnes Scott."

"So determination runs in the family."

Dania glanced down at her menu. "I keep telling the children education is important. That's why we started a mill school during the middle of the workday. We furnish lunch and provide instruction in math and reading during the hottest part of the day." She glanced up to find him staring at her. "What?"

"You really think about those kids a lot."

"Every waking moment, and sometimes in my sleep." She chuckled.

"You know, most people wouldn't do that."

Dania was all too aware of that fact. Her father, for all his goodness, thought her ideas a bit too progressive for the textile industry. Now that she was in charge, she fully intended to live up to her convictions concerning the mill.

Or at least most of them.

"You're very different than what I expected."

Dania grimaced. What exactly had the man expected? Queen Victoria or something? "You must not be keeping company with the right kind of ladies."

"Miss Eison," he replied, his lips turning up in a crooked smile. "Is that your way of asking if I'm courting someone?"

"Of course not," she stammered, scorching heat flaming her cheeks. Why would she care if the man was in a courtship or even engaged for that matter? "Are you?"

"No. What about you?"

She shook her head, strangely relieved by his response. It was time to change the subject to something less personal. "Why am I not what you expected?"

"Well"—he cleared his throat, his cheeks ruddy as if he was actually ashamed of himself—"I figured you would be more like Mr. Perkinson's daughters."

"I'm nothing like those two." Dania pressed her lips together. "Heddy and Matilda Perkinson are more interested in the number of flounces in their skirts than the poor people who work for them."

"You're right. You are nothing like them. Will you please forgive me for my assumptions?"

Dania bit her lower lip then released it. It was perfectly normal for Matt to think that way. He had worked under Mr. Perkinson's iron rule. Yet she wanted him to judge her for herself, maybe even like her just a little. "Working for their father like you did, I can understand why you might have drawn that conclusion."

"Still, it was wrong." Matt's gaze softened. "I hope you can forgive me."

The man said it with such conviction, almost as if he hated the thought that he'd hurt her in some way. Without thinking, she covered his hand with hers. "There's nothing to forgive."

"Thank you." He lifted her gloved hand to his mouth and placed a gentle kiss against her knuckles, a pleasant warmth traveling up her arm and into her chest.

The more she learned about Matt—from his work ethic to his undeniable pride in his family—the more she liked him. If she ever considered marriage, it would be with someone like him.

As if she would ever marry. Between her family and her workers, a home and family of her own was just a far-fetched dream.

Chapter 5

Their late lunch turned into dinner. Not that Matt was complaining. The more time he spent with Dania, the more convinced he was that Senator Evers was hiding something. Why would the man suggest the Eisons' mill be the focal point of his article on the need for child labor laws if he knew what Dania was doing to help her young employees? And why had Evers led Matt to believe Dania was just another spoiled society girl? What had been the real reason for the division between the senator and his lifelong friend?

What about Dania? There was no denying she cared about her young employees, even went so far as to educate them. Then why didn't she change her employment policies to exclude children up to the state's mandated age of twelve?

"Dinner was lovely, Matt." Dania took the arm he offered and settled in beside him as they stepped out onto the sidewalk. "I usually don't eat dessert, but that peach cobbler was too tempting to pass up."

Matt covered her hand with his and smiled. "Maybe we can eat here again before you return home."

She turned her head and studied a store window display. "I shouldn't be here now, but I'd hoped to discuss the mill with Mr. Young."

"The industrial engineer?"

"Hmmm." She nodded. "He has some theories on employee safety and facility layout that I think could be useful at the mill." She pressed her lips into a slight frown. "Only I can't get an appointment with him."

"That's odd."

"Not really," she replied. "Young is very well respected in his field."

Matt shook his head. "No, I mean, the man's secretary called on me at the paper yesterday morning and arranged an interview. He even gave me my pick of appointment times."

Dania's face fell. "Oh."

"Why would he do that? I can't imagine his appointment book filled up that quickly."

"It didn't." The pain in her eyes when she glanced up at him was almost his undoing. "Mr. Young won't see me because he doesn't believe women should be business owners. Or at least, his secretary believes that."

"That's ridiculous. Many women own their own businesses these days."

"Maybe, but most do things like sewing or cooking or running a boardinghouse." She sucked in a deep breath. "Very few are in manufacturing or textiles."

Matt's temper flared. "That's all the more reason for Young to mentor those who are in the field."

Dania stopped walking and turned to face him, a soft smile on her face. "You know, you're not what I expected, either."

He wasn't sure he wanted to hear this. He was, after all, working in Senator Evers's interest, though the position had not been finalized. But something deep down inside wanted to know what this woman thought about him. "How's that?"

"Well, I thought you'd be like Uncle George. A little stuffy at times." She blushed. "Very set in his ways. Why, Uncle George was completely against Papa leaving me in charge of the mill. He said no man would want a woman in business. Said Papa would be better off leaving it to him, that he would see to our well-being, and that I and my sisters would marry well. But you—" She gave him a shy smile. "You've been a pleasant surprise."

Matt wanted to bask in her compliment, but this might be his only chance to discover what happened between the men. "How did your father react to his suggestion?"

"Papa laughed it off." She hesitated. "But he broke off his friendship with Uncle George soon after that and told me to never trust him. Papa didn't like getting unsolicited advice, even from his best friend, so I didn't take it too seriously."

Mr. Eison broke off the friendship, not the other way around as the senator had claimed. What other suggestions had Evers made to Dania's father? Had Evers even asked Mr. Eison to get rid of his child employees? Is that why the men broke ties? "Why do you think your uncle didn't come to your father's funeral?"

Dania squeezed his arm then turned and started down the street. "Your mother must have gone mad with all the questions you asked as a child."

Matt laughed. "I believe if you don't ask, you'll never know."

"That's very wise of you." The sparkle went out of her expression. "I only wished I had the opportunity to ask."

She was thinking about Mr. Young again. Well, that was easily fixed. "You're coming with me tomorrow."

Startled blue eyes gazed up at him. "What?"

"Young's secretary gave me two hours with him tomorrow morning starting at ten. I've already gotten most of the information I need, so if you'd like to ask him some of your questions..."

"You would do that for me?" Her lips spread into a wide smile, and he forgot to breathe. He had a feeling he would do a great deal more for her if given the chance.

"Of course," Matt said when he finally caught his breath. "I'll pick you up in the morning. Just have a list of your questions ready."

"Then I'd better get back to my room." He could almost feel her tremble with excitement. "I have so many questions. How am I going to figure out which ones to ask?"

"I could help you, you know," Matt offered before he could stop himself. Questions about Senator Evers still lingered in his mind, questions that might be answered by some of his sources around town. But that could wait. Dania needed him, and for the moment at least, that was simply enough.

◆ ◆ ◆

Matt watched Dania pace the lobby of Ernest Young's hotel room the next morning. Her hair secured in a loose chignon at the base of her neck, she looked every bit the young businesswoman, but even dressed in a pale blue waist shirt, black skirt, and sensible boots, she still managed to steal every rational thought out of his head. "You're going to wear a hole in the rug if you keep doing that."

The corners of her mouth lifted into a sweet smile, one that he was growing quite fond of. "I'm afraid I'll forget everything I want to ask."

"You wrote your questions down, didn't you?"

She pulled a notebook similar to his out of her skirt pocket. "It took some time, but I think I got everything."

Matt nodded. It had taken the better part of the evening to hone in on what Dania felt would best help the mill. Some questions had surprised Matt in their simplicity, but each focused on the safety and care of her young employees. It had struck him sometime last night that she truly cared for these people, even at the cost of her own profits. This made him like her all the more.

Like? Who was he kidding? The feelings he had toward Dania Eison had evolved far beyond that simple term. He wasn't ready to put a name to it yet, only that she might possibly be the most interesting woman he'd ever met.

And he was springing her on Mr. Young without a word of warning. Whatever questions Dania had, she needed to make them count. "Did you narrow them down to the most important one or two?"

Dania stopped midstep and glanced at him, her wide blue eyes focused and determined. "I picked the most pressing ones about safety, but depending on his answers, I probably have follow-up questions." She walked back and sat down in the chair beside him. "I only wished I didn't need to ask them at all."

Her statement surprised him. In the short time he'd known her, it was apparent Dania loved her work, but man or woman, it was a huge responsibility to carry. "Why's that?"

She sighed then shook her head. "It's nothing. Forget I even said that."

But Matt couldn't. He'd never liked unanswered questions, not in interviews he conducted or in the stories he researched. It displayed a lack of trust, almost as if she were hiding something, though he couldn't for his life think why.

Unless she didn't trust him.

"Matt?" He turned to find her staring at him. "You're thinking."

He shook his head. "No, I'm not."

"Your brows furrow and you get this terribly serious look on your face." Dania stood in front of him, her hands clasped behind her back. "You're wondering why I didn't explain myself."

How was she able to read him so well? He guessed turnaround was fair play. "It's the reporter in me."

She gave him a soft smile. "That makes you an excellent journalist." Her lips flattened into a straight line. "It's just that if I had my choice, I wouldn't have children on the payroll."

Dania didn't want to use child labor in her mill? Matt asked the question before he could stop himself. "Then why do you?"

She drew in a deep breath. "After Papa died, I worked out a plan to replace all the children in the mill with adults. We would pay a living wage to any man or woman over sixteen we hired. It meant a significant decrease in my family's fortune, but it was the right thing to do." She knotted her hands in her lap. "Only I didn't expect such opposition from the children's parents."

"Why?"

"Tifton is a small farming community, so most of the older boys work the land while their younger siblings make ends meet working at the mill."

"I hadn't thought of that," Matt said more to himself than to her. His family had been too busy just trying to survive to worry about making ends meet.

"If I give jobs to adults, it's as if I'm taking food off those children's plates." She turned worried eyes to stare at him. "They could lose their homes."

Matt knew the feeling all too well. Many a night after his parents thought he was asleep, he'd listened to them worry about how they would pay the rent or put food on the table. More than a few times, he'd stolen sweet potatoes from one of the farms on his way to work, just so he'd have something to eat. Even now, all these years later, the thought of it made him sick.

Yet here Dania was, trying her best to help the children under her care. Everything she'd done in these last few days—buying fabric, hiring a boot maker, speaking to Mr. Young—spoke of her commitment to her young employees.

"Who can find a virtuous woman? for her price is far above rubies." The scripture his mama use to read from her old Bible whispered through him. Those were hard verses for anyone to live up to, yet he could see them being lived out in Dania. She was a rare jewel in their materialistic world—someone who actually cared more for others than herself.

What he would give to have her in his life!

But that wasn't possible, not until he discovered why George Evers wanted to destroy her family. Matt glanced at her. He couldn't ask Dania outright; finding out her uncle was using the Eisons as a springboard to the governor's mansion would hurt her badly. Still, she might be able to give him a lead. He'd just have to be careful how he phrased his questions. "Did you ever talk to your uncle George about this?"

"Once, a long time ago." She gave a feminine snort. "He thought that I would lose everything Papa had worked for and leave our family destitute. It was the reason he suggested I find a husband."

The idea irked Matt. If Evers had succeeded, Dania would be married, and he would have never had the chance to know her, to love her, to make her his wife.

His wife?

Matt cleared his throat, his heart pounding like a piston on one of the machines in the industry pavilion at the exposition. "Did the senator suggest anyone for the position?"

Dania grimaced then whispered, "He said he would take care of me and my family, make sure my sisters married well, and that Mama was cared for. I didn't understand it. I mean, I thought of him as a relative but not a. . ." Her throat worked as she tried to get out the word. "Husband."

No wonder Martin Eison broke off his friendship with Evers. The man wanted to get his hands on Dania's fortune. Was this how he'd hoped to fund his gubernatorial campaign? By using the Eisons' funds? And when Dania and her father didn't fall in line, did the senator plan to exact his revenge by running them out of business? Matt intended to find out.

Chapter 6

I'm afraid that's all the time I have."

Dania scribbled the answer to her last question in her notebook then glanced at the massive grandfather clock in the corner. Two fifteen? That couldn't be right. Matt's appointment was scheduled to end at twelve o'clock, and he'd only needed ten minutes to clarify some points. That would mean. . .

Dania turned to the gentleman across from her, collecting her things as she spoke. "Mr. Young, I'm so sorry. I didn't mean to keep you this long."

The man gave her a reassuring smile. "It was my pleasure, Miss Eison. I only wished I had more time to answer your questions, but if I don't leave now, I'll be late for my introduction at the exposition."

"Mr. Young," Matt said from where he stood in the corner. "Neither one of us expected such generosity of your time. I'm sure I speak for the both of us when I say thank you."

Was it her imagination or was there a hint of irritation in Matt's voice, but why? Was it possible that Matt was jealous? The thought came to Dania out of nowhere. That was impossible. Mr. Young had been nothing short of professional in answering her questions and asking some of his own—nothing to indicate a more personal interest. Besides, the man was too full of himself to take an interest in anyone else.

Maybe Matt was irritated with her. She had taken up most of Mr. Young's time this afternoon, and Matt had an article to get out. Yes, that had to be it, but that didn't stop her from hoping he might be the tiniest bit jealous. Because that would mean Matt cared about her, and she so wanted him to care.

Dania closed her notebook and put it along with her pencil in her reticule, half listening as the men talked about the exposition. Mama had always told her that her heart would know when she met the man God had picked out just for her. But wasn't that something mothers told their spinster daughters so they didn't give up hope? Dania had thought so.

But then she met Matt.

"I thought you weren't scheduled to speak until tomorrow, Mr. Young," Matt said as he came to stand alongside her chair and placed his hand gently on her shoulder, as if declaring himself to the man.

But Mr. Young didn't seem put off by it. "I'm not, but they're introducing some of the more important speakers this afternoon at the state pavilion." He glanced down at Dania and smiled. "Were you planning on attending tomorrow, Miss Eison?"

"Why, yes. I am—"

"We both do," Matt added before she could finish her sentence. Though it was a simple response, there was a warning in Matt's words, as if he were protecting her from Mr. Young's perceived advances.

Dania rolled her eyes. Men!

"Then allow me to reserve you two seats. I've been told to expect a rather large gathering, and I'd hate to think of Miss Eison fighting the crowd to hear my lecture."

A rather pompous statement but probably true. Shaking off Matt's hold, Dania stood and held out her hand to Mr. Young. "How very kind of you."

"Yes," Matt bit out. "Very kind."

Taking her hand, Young bent down and placed a soft kiss against her knuckles that made her go tense. Of all the. . . Dania drew her hand back and grasped her reticule to keep her hands from shaking. "Until tomorrow then."

"I'll walk you to the door."

"That's all right." Matt's fingers cupped around her elbow. "We can see ourselves out."

Dania hurried out of the suite alongside Matt, matching him step for step until they stood in the hallway. She finally drew in a breath when the door to the hotel room mercifully clicked shut.

Strong hands came down gently on her shoulders. "Are you okay?"

Dania rubbed her hands together, desperate to rid herself of the feel of Young's lips on her skin. "I wasn't expecting him to kiss my hand like that. It was. . ."

"What?" Matt asked. "You're not going to say noble, are you?"

Dania's heart tumbled around in her chest. Matt was more than a little bit jealous if his reaction was anything to go by. Well, there was one way to find out. She sucked in a calming breath and lifted her head to look at him. "I was going to say gallant. Like something you might read in one of Jane Austen's books."

"I wouldn't know. I don't read British romance novels." He smirked, then turned, dropping one hand to the small of her back. He gave her a slight push in the direction of the stairs. "If you ask me, the man was rather forward toward you."

Dania ducked her head, biting her lip to keep from smiling. "Forward?"

"Couldn't you see the man was flirting with you?"

If that was flirting, Mr. Young had better stick with his perk diagrams. "Flirting? Mr. Young only answered my questions. He was a perfect gentleman."

"You may not have realized his intentions, but I saw what he was up to." He must have noticed her confusion because his brows furrowed into deep lines. "The man canceled two appointments so he could spend more time with you."

Maybe Matt was right. Maybe Mr. Young had been flirting, not that she would recognize a flirtation if it reached up and bit her on the nose. But Matt had noticed it and had acted to protect her from the man. Did that mean he cared for her, or was he simply being a gentleman?

Why was she even thinking about it? The mill owned her body and spirit for the foreseeable future, and whatever time she had to spare was devoted to her mother and sisters. There wasn't enough hours in the day to explore a relationship with Matt right now or for several years to come.

But she did love to tease Matt. "He's not too old for me."

Matt slammed his hat on his head once they'd reached the lobby. "Old enough to be your father."

Dania chuckled. "I don't think he's that old. Maybe thirty-five."

"Forty, if he's a day." He opened the door then stepped back to allow her to walk through.

She had to bite her lip to keep from laughing out loud. Matt really was quite fun to work into a lather. Dania took his offered arm once they were on the sidewalk. "Mr. Young is quite attractive."

The muscles in his arm tensed beneath her fingertips, and she struggled to breathe. "I didn't notice."

"Really?" Dania stole a glance at him. Poor man might break his jaw if he gritted his teeth together any harder. "I thought a newspaperman like you would notice every little detail."

"I remember the important stuff, not whether the man can button his shirt correctly."

As much fun as this was, it was time to stop this little game. "Well, he can flirt all he likes, just not with me."

If she thought that would set Matt at ease, she was mistaken. "You don't like him in a romantic sort of way?"

"Not that it's any of your business, but no. I do not see myself with someone like Mr. Young."

"Then what kind of man do you see yourself with, Dania?"

She'd hoped to avoid so intimate a question from Matt, but what could she expect? He was a reporter, for heaven's sake, and more inquisitive than any man had the right to be. Best to be truthful. "I've been so busy learning the ropes of the mill, I've not had much time to think about it. I'm not looking to get married, at least, not in the near future."

She felt his eyes on her. "Isn't marriage the goal of every woman?"

"Another one of your assumptions?" She met his gaze. "Or have you researched it for a future article?"

The corners of his mouth lifted. "Touché."

They started down the street once again. The sun warmed her face, and she scolded herself for forgetting her parasol. Her freckles would pop out across her nose, not the creamy complexion her mother assured her attracted a man. But really, what was the point? "Besides, most men wouldn't want a wife who runs a textile mill."

"Why do you say that?"

She must have spoken her thoughts out loud. Unfortunately, Matt had heard her. "It's true, isn't it?"

Matt seemed to give it some thought. "Some men might appreciate a wife with a head for business."

"Oh, really?" Shoppers and visitors to the exposition crowded the sidewalk, so she pressed closer to him. "And where might I find one of these heroes among men?"

Matt didn't answer, only studied the store windows as if his very life depended on it. Well, she didn't need his answer to know the truth. Papa had always been honest with her. That Dania's responsibilities, that her decision to run the mill, would scare off any marriage prospects. She'd come to terms with it, or at least she'd thought she had until she met Matt. Now, she wondered if she'd accepted her father's prognosis too soon.

They reached the street corner before Matt spoke again. "I'd be proud to have a wife who had the knowledge and wherewithal to run a business."

Dania turned around to face him and suddenly found it hard to breathe. From her perch, she was at the perfect height to stare into his earnest blue-green eyes, to take in the tiny scar at the tip of his chin, to note the firmness of his lips.

She leaned back slightly to give herself some room. "You really believe that?"

"If a woman wants to pursue a career, she should have the right to do so."

"Even if she's your wife?"

The crooked smile Matt gave her tugged at her heart. "If that's what she wants, yes."

"That's a very modern attitude."

He shook his head. "Not really. I figure if it was good enough for King Solomon to write about, it's good enough for me."

"Proverbs 31." Dania's smile grew. It wasn't every day an attractive man shared scripture with her. She stepped into the carriage and got settled, pleased when Matt sat beside her. "How do you know about that passage of scripture?"

"My ma thought it was just as important for me to memorize as it was my sister." He leaned closer, brushing his shoulder against hers. "It is advice to the prince on what to look for in a good wife."

Dania hadn't known the history behind the verses. "Your mother sounds like a very wise woman."

He nodded. "She read the Bible to us at the breakfast table every morning before Pa and I went to work."

"Mama was the same way, only she'd read to us once Papa and I got home from the mill." The memory of those times filled Dania with longing. "I'd be so dirty with little pieces of thread clinging to me like dandelion seeds. Mama always put a pitcher of hot water and a cake of soap out on the porch so I could wash off the oil and dirt from the machines before I came inside. Then we'd sit down to supper, and Mama would read. She liked the book of Proverbs and all of the New Testament." She smiled. "Those were such good times."

The world around them went quiet for a long moment. Finally, Dania turned toward Matt, only to find him staring at her, confusion darkening his eyes. "Your father forced you to work in the mill?"

Dear goodness, Matt made it sound as though her father had held a gun to her head. "It wasn't like that. As the oldest, I always knew I would need to learn the workings of the mill. That meant every piece of machinery, all the different materials we use. Everything." She paused for a moment, still remembering the day she'd gone to Papa and told him her plans. "I'm the one who made the decision to work at the mill, Matt, not Papa."

"Most girls of your social status would be more interested in dresses and dances than going to work."

Dania pressed her lips together. "You're doing it again."

"What?"

"Making assumptions about me." She drew in a deep breath to calm herself. "Don't paint me with the same brush just because you had a bad experience with a so-called 'lady.'"

Matt captured her hand in his then gave it a gentle squeeze. "I'm sorry. It's just that. . ." He hesitated. "You're a very unusual woman, Dania Eison. Kind and generous, and so beautiful."

She tried to speak but could only manage a whisper. "You think I'm beautiful?"

Her pulse kicked up a notch at the interest in his eyes. "Surely this isn't the first time you've heard that?"

"No." But the other times had felt wrong—as if it were expected rather than a compliment. Matt wouldn't say something like that unless he truly believed it. A blush warmed her cheeks. "Thank you."

"You're welcome." He gave her hand another squeeze then let it go, much to her dismay. "So what would you like to do now? We could grab a sandwich and head over to Piedmont Park. I might be able to rustle up some day-old bread so we could feed the ducks."

Oh, how she'd love to spend the afternoon strolling around the lake with Matt, learning more about him. A day without the burdens of home weighing her down. But she had taken up a great deal of his time. "You don't have any obligations at the paper?"

He shook his head. "My assignment was turned in last night, so I'm all yours."

I'm all yours. Three short words, yet spoken by this man, they had the ability to tilt her world slightly off-center. How could that be? She'd known him for scarcely two days, yet it felt as if she'd known him a lifetime. Was this what falling in love felt like? Dania didn't know; she'd never been in love before. With Matt, it made perfect sense.

How could such a relationship work? Everything Matt held dear—his mother and sister, his career—was here in Atlanta. Moving to Tifton was out of the question. If she moved, her family as well as the community that depended on her would suffer. Papa had told her she'd have to make hard decisions, but did she have to give up her chance at happiness, too?

Dania's chest squeezed into a painful knot. They only had this afternoon. A few wonderful hours to remember when the responsibilities of her life bore down on her in the years to come. Dania met his gaze and nodded. "A picnic in the park sounds lovely."

Chapter 7

The sun hung low on the horizon by the time Dania and Matt packed up their things for the trip back to her hotel. Matt flagged down a carriage, and once Dania was safely settled, he instructed the driver to take the longest route to her hotel, and if the horse wanted to walk slow, all the better. The man gave Matt a knowing wink, but he didn't care. All he wanted was for the afternoon to last a little longer.

Which wasn't really the truth, Matt told himself as he climbed in and took the seat beside Dania. A few hours would never be enough with this woman. No, he'd need years to discover the depths of Dania's character—the kindness she showed to everyone she met, the grace that glowed within her, her loyalty to her family and workers. It might even take a lifetime, but it would be more than worth it if he could spend every moment with her.

"I had a lovely day, Matt." Dania brushed some stray blades of grass from her skirt. "I even liked that new game those men were playing at the park. What was it called?"

"I believe they called it football." He laughed, remembering her vivid expressions during the course of the game. "I wasn't sure you enjoyed it or not."

"Only when that gentleman got hurt." She turned worried eyes on him. "Do you think he's okay?"

Matt took her hand in his and gave it a reassuring pat. "I heard it was only a minor sprain."

Dania breathed out a relieved sigh. "Well, other than that, I found the whole experience quite exciting."

"Very exciting." He liked hearing her talk, watching the animation in her expression about the new sport or her devotion to her family and friends back home. She made him laugh at times, made him think of others. He felt like Adam to her Eve, a perfect complement to each other as God had designed.

"Oh, I meant to ask you." She turned to face him. "Did you know Uncle George was running for governor?"

Her question hurled him back into reality. "Where did you hear that from?"

"Two gentlemen in front of us were talking about it while you went to get us some lemonade. Why didn't you tell me?"

"He didn't want the news getting out until he was ready to announce his intentions," Matt replied. That much was true, but why hadn't the senator kept him in the loop? Had he learned Matt was snooping around, trying to discover the senator's reasons for targeting the Eisons? Was it simply sour grapes over Mr. Eison's refusal to sell the senator the mill? Or the fact that Dania had rejected his marriage proposal? What had he expected when she clearly thought of him as her uncle?

Matt only hoped the runners he'd sent in search of information last night had found something on the senator, anything that could explain his vendetta against Dania and her family.

"What are you thinking about so hard?"

"What?" He smiled down at her, taking in her clear blue eyes, the slight upturn of her nose, her pink lips. What would it be like to kiss her? Had Evers tried to when he'd proposed to her? The thought made him want to sink his fist in the man's face.

"Now, you're scowling."

Matt shook his head. "No, I'm not."

"All right." She shifted to face forward. "You just look like you will let out a growl at any minute."

She wasn't too far off the mark. He couldn't tell her the truth. George Evers's betrayal would wound both her and her family very deeply. He riffled through some possibilities and chose a safe subject. "I was thinking about an article I'm working on."

"It must be something you're very concerned about, judging by your expression." Her voice held a spark of excitement. "If you'd like to discuss it, I'd be happy to. That is, if you can talk about it."

"It's not that I can't discuss it." In fact, there was nothing he wanted more than to tell her what her good old 'uncle' George was up to, but Matt couldn't, not until he had proof of the senator's betrayal. "It's just..."

"You have to keep your information confidential until you have all your facts," she finished for him. "I understand." She gave him a playful grin. "It's probably something that would put me in danger if I knew."

"I would protect you with my life, Dania." And he would. He'd do anything to keep her safe and happy.

"I believe you," she whispered, her soft gaze meeting his, the tenderness in her expression causing his heart to almost burst out of his chest.

Matt leaned toward her, watching her, waiting for her to push him away, to remind him they'd only known each other for a short time. Instead, she leaned toward him, her lips parted, her eyes fluttering shut. He gently brushed his lips against hers before claiming her mouth in a sweet kiss. He'd kissed a woman or two in his time, but never had he felt this sense of belonging, this feeling of home as he did in Dania's arms.

Too soon, he broke off the kiss and leaned back, close but not holding her. "I know I should probably apologize..."

"Please don't." Her words sounded a little breathless as if she was as affected by the kiss as he was. She lifted her gaze to meet his, and he found himself falling into depths of the deepest blue. "I've been waiting all afternoon for you to kiss me."

His breath caught in his chest. "You have?"

Her hat drooped slightly as she nodded. "Not very ladylike, I know, but the truth nevertheless."

The high color in her cheeks spoke of her honesty. Matt clasped her hand—why had he never noticed the small calluses on the tender flesh of her fingertips before?—then met her gaze. "I could never be sorry for kissing you, not in a million years."

The corners of her mouth tilted up in a shy smile. "Me neither."

Goodness gracious! Did the woman have any idea that when she looked at him like that, he had to fight to keep from kissing her again! He needed some distance, at least until he figured out what was happening to him. He shifted to the bench seat across from her, still holding her hand. "What would you like to do tomorrow? We could visit the art venue in the morning then make our way over to the industry pavilion in time for Mr. Young's speech. Maybe get some lunch at one of the cafés nearby?"

"I'd love to, Matt, but I promised my lead foreman I would telephone him in the morning, just to see how things are going." The note of disappointment in her voice was a balm to his own. "Maybe we could meet for lunch?"

The carriage slowed to a stop. Matt gave her hand one last squeeze then let go. "That gives me the morning to do some research."

"For that secretive article you were thinking about so hard," she teased, her eyes flashing with humor.

"Maybe." He chuckled as he leaned forward, brushed a soft kiss against her lips, then opened the door. He was barely down the steps before he turned and offered her his hand. She slid her fingers over his, the peaks and valleys of their palms a perfect fit, as if God had made Dania especially for him, and he for her.

Matt was still processing that thought when she let go of his hand, rather reluctantly he thought, and put some distance between them. "Thank you for the day, Matt. I can't remember when I've had such a good time."

"I agree." He held out his arm to her. "May I walk you to the front door?"

She shook her head. "I've got work to do, and so do you."

He snorted. "On my elusive article."

"I'm hoping you'll finish it before I go home day after tomorrow." She gave him a soft smile. "I'd like to read it while I'm here."

If his runners dug up the information Matt was looking for, it would be front-page news in the morning. "I'll bring you a copy of the paper so we can read it together."

"I'd enjoy that very much."

No, she wouldn't. When George Evers's intentions were revealed, when Dania realized her uncle's betrayal, she'd be hurt. Matt would do everything in his power to keep her name out of the papers, protect her and her family from public ridicule. Whatever it took, even if it meant the end of his aspirations of writing on the national stage. The crushing disappointment he expected never came, only the peace of knowing he was protecting the woman he loved.

Matt took Dania's hand in his, brought it to his lips, and placed a soft kiss against her knuckles. "Tomorrow then."

The shy smile she gave him melted any lingering doubts he might have. "I'll be waiting."

Long moments went by before she reluctantly let go of his hand and turned toward the hotel entrance. He watched her as she bought a newspaper from the stand nearby, then waited as the doorman opened the door. She turned then, her expression so full of joy, the same bubbled up inside him. Only when she disappeared from view did the bubble burst, leaving him feeling vaguely morose. If he felt like this now, how would it be when Dania went home in a couple of days? He didn't want to think about their parting just yet.

For now, he needed to find out what Senator Evers was hiding and protect Dania as best he could. The short walk to the newspaper gave Matt time to brainstorm possibilities. Money, perhaps? But Evers's war chest was rumored to be double that of any other candidate, though how that was possible with the man's reputation of alienating his colleagues and potential backers, Matt didn't know. One question kept gnawing at Matt. Why would the senator want possession of the Eisons' mill if he planned to abolish child labor? The financial fallout would take years to recover, Dania had said so herself.

Matt slowed as he turned down Constitution Avenue. Something else Dania had said—about Evers thinking her ideas of helping her young employees being too progressive—needled Matt. What was more progressive than labor reform? Unless the man never intended to introduce his reform bill.

But why? Matt shoved open the door of the newspaper office. Maybe his runners had uncovered some answers.

He'd barely made it to his desk when John Randall, the city beat reporter, hurried over. "Great article, Langley. You really gave it to the owners of that textile mill. They would have been run out of town if they lived here."

Matt sat down and shuffled through the messages left on his desk. From the brief glance, it looked as if his sources had uncovered something. "I haven't the faintest clue what you're talking about."

"Your article. On the front page." John grabbed a paper off a desk nearby and held it out, pointing at an article above the fold. "It made quite a stir around here this afternoon."

Matt grabbed it out of John's hands and glared at it, his blood running cold. SENATOR EVERS THROWS HIS HAT INTO THE GUBERNATORIAL RACE. Matt's article, and yet it wasn't. Entire conversations had been taken out of context, exhorting Senator Evers's social conscience, his ideas for reform, while painting Dania and her family with a dark brush. "I didn't write this."

"No sense denying it." The man slapped Matt on the back. "Everyone in the newsroom knows this is right up your alley."

"No." The longer Matt thought about it, the angrier he felt. "I'm telling you, I didn't write this, and I don't have a clue who did."

"But isn't this the story you've been working on the last few days?"

"Yes, but. . ." Matt glanced over it again. Parts of it he'd written, mainly Dania's quotes on why she continued to employ child laborers. But everything else—her distaste for the practice, her determination to help the children have a chance at a better life—had been skillfully edited out or worse, attributed to Evers. There was no balance in the piece, slanting heavily in Senator Evers's favor while making Dania look like a rich society girl without a care for the working poor. If only his readers knew the truth. "Someone used my first draft but left out most of the truth."

"That's a serious accusation, Matt. One I wouldn't make too lightly."

Matt leaned back in his chair and glared at the man. "I wouldn't say it if it weren't true."

John considered that for a moment. "No, I guess you wouldn't. But who would write an article and then give you a front-page byline?"

Somebody on the senator's payroll who controlled what went into the newspaper. Someone who had access to Matt's work. He glanced at the managing editor's closed office door. "Where's Taylor?"

John followed his gaze. "He left early this afternoon. Said something about an important dinner he had to attend."

It had all been a setup. Evers never planned on hiring him as his press agent. Somehow the man had learned about Matt's time working in the mill, knew his reputation concerning social injustice, and decided to use it to his advantage. Well, Matt wouldn't go down without a fight, not where Dania was concerned. He stood up, grabbed his notebook and a sharpened pencil, and stuffed them in his coat pocket. "How would you like to share a front-page byline?"

John stared at him as if he'd lost his mind. "What are you talking about?"

"Taylor is Evers's new press secretary. He took those notes off my desk and wrote that article." Matt grabbed his hat and headed for the door. "So are you coming with me?"

The man scurried to his desk to retrieve his things. "Where are we going?"

Matt held open the door. "First, we've got to stop by Mr. Abernathy's."

"The publisher?"

Matt nodded. "He needs to know what is going on. Then we're going to pay a visit to Mr. Taylor and his guests."

The next few hours went by in a blur. His meeting with Mr. Abernathy. The confrontation with Evers and Taylor. The evidence he'd collected from his runners proving that the senator along with several mill owners intended to run the Eisons out of business. The prolonged meeting that went into the early hours of this morning, trying to decide the best way to proceed. In the end, the newspaper printed a retraction and an apology to Dania and her family. An article highlighting the improvements Dania had made in her young laborers' lives would soon follow.

With the morning paper neatly folded under his arm, Matt jumped out of the carriage the moment it pulled up to the front door of Dania's hotel, paid the driver, and hurried inside. The lobby was empty, almost somber without the usual hustle and bustle from visitors to the exposition. A reflection of his mood.

At least they'd be able to find a quiet corner so he could talk to Dania. He still wasn't sure what he was going to say just yet. An apology, certainly, but then what? He bowed his head and closed his eyes. *Lord, forgive me for the pain I've caused Dania. I made assumptions about her that just weren't true. Give me the words to make this right with her. Help her to forgive me. And thank You for bringing her into my life. I love her, Lord. In Jesus' name, I pray. Amen.*

With that off his chest, Matt approached the registration desk. A man with a handlebar mustache glanced up and smiled. "May I help you, sir?"

"I know it's rather early, but I have a note for Miss Eison in room 326 that I need delivered immediately." Matt retrieved the note from his pocket and held it out to the man. He'd never struggled with the written word before, but constructing a note to Dania ranked among the most difficult assignments of his life.

"I'm sorry, sir, but Miss Eison is no longer a guest here."

Matt blinked. No longer a guest? "Where did she go?"

The man looked at him with pity in his eyes. "Miss Eison took the six-fifteen train to Tifton last night."

Chapter 8

Dania leaned her head against her office window. Usually the hustle and bustle of the mill floor filled her with a sense of excitement, made her think of all the possibilities for the future, both for her workers and herself. But not today. Today, the clattering of the machinery's pistons and the tense expression worn by more of her workers only reminded her of her own dismal outlook these last two weeks since she'd fled Atlanta.

She walked over to her desk, picked up the tattered newspaper, and read Matt's article again. She shouldn't have picked up and left the way she did, scurrying away in the night like she had something to feel guilty about. Hearing Matt out, getting his side of the story, would have been the right thing to do. Uncle George's betrayal had hurt, but what Matt had done had broken her heart.

Or what Dania had thought he'd done. The newspaper with the retraction and apology had only reached her a few days ago. By then, what anger she'd felt toward Matt had dissipated. After all, he was only doing his job. Maybe, if she'd stayed, heard what he had to say, left on friendly terms, maybe even made plans to see each other. . . The what-ifs were killing her.

Dania let out a heavy sigh. Wallowing in this wasn't helping anyone. No, she needed to focus on the changes she was making, changes brought about because of Matt's article. Because he'd been right. No matter how she sugarcoated it, the Eisons had made their fortune on the backs of young children.

Not anymore. Today, the first group of men who'd answered her ad for factory workers would be interviewed. She hoped by the end of the month she'd be able to let the youngest of her workers go, with six months' pay to help the families adjust to the change. Some of the parents had grumbled when she'd announced the change, but as Matt had predicted in his article, most were adjusting to the idea.

Matt. She'd tried to put him out of her thoughts and failed, so tight was his grip on her heart. Sewing the children's new clothes only brought back the memory of their time in Mr. Shonkwiler's shop; a walk along the lake behind her house, a reminder of their picnic in the park. Dreams of their last few moments together when he'd kissed her so tenderly awoke her in the night, her pillow damp with tears. She'd even avoided reading her Bible, fearful she'd open it to Proverbs 31, knowing she lacked those qualities Matt valued in a wife.

A knock at the door startled Dania out of her thoughts. "Yes?"

The door opened, and her sister Gilly poked her head inside. "I'm sorry to interrupt you, but you're needed on the floor."

Dania dropped the newspaper on her desk. "Is it the threader again?"

Gilly nodded. "Peter Ward has been working on it for nearly an hour now but can't get it up and running. I think he could use your help."

"Tell him I'll be right there." Unpinning her braid, she walked over to the closet where she kept a pair of men's pants and an old shirt for such work.

Ten minutes later, she was staring at a tangle of thread deep in the inner workings of her main threader. There was no way to reach the knotted mess from the top or sides. The only way to fix it was to climb into the machinery and cut the thread loose.

"I tried to get in there, Miss Dania, but my hands are too big," Peter said beside her. "I'm afraid I'll bend one of the smaller bobbins if I pull on it too hard."

"You were right to call me." Dania gave him a reassuring pat on his shoulder. They couldn't afford the time or money replacing a bobbin would cost. "Where are the children?"

"I sent them to lunch. Thought I'd kill two birds with one stone. Get them fed and get them out of your way."

The boy had a good head on his shoulders, and at fifteen, he was old enough to keep his job rather than be let go. "Good. Now, let's see what I can do."

"Just be careful, ma'am. It's awfully tight in there," the boy warned.

"I'll be fine. Remember, I've done this before." Dania smiled slightly as she tucked her braid into the back of her shirt.

"I'm still going to pray, ma'am."

She nodded. No doubt, she'd need it. If this machine went down, she'd have to shut down the entire mill until it could be repaired. No, she couldn't allow that, not when families depended on the mill for their evening supper, including her own.

She squeezed herself into a small opening in the undercarriage of the machine then slowly made her way through the maze of wires and piping until she neared the row of bobbins. She inched forward slowly then groaned. Two of the bobbins looked bent from the pressure already placed on them. Hopefully, it was just her angle. She'd have to get a closer look to know for sure. She moved forward.

Her pant leg caught. Probably a loose screw. Dania yanked as hard as she dared, but the machine wouldn't let go. Maybe if she backed up. A piece of metal dug into her calf, and she yelped.

"Are you all right?"

Matt? Dania jerked her head back too quick and scraped her scalp. But it didn't matter. Matt was here, staring down at her with such a look of concern, it made her stomach flip. "What are you doing here?"

"I came to see you." He gave her a nervous smile then glanced around as if measuring the seriousness of her situation. "Why are you in there?"

"The threader got jammed, and as I have slender hands, it only made sense. . ." She trailed off, her mouth suddenly dry as startling blue-green eyes met hers. Dear goodness, how she'd missed the man. Was this what love felt like? As if she'd found the missing part of herself in him?

"You're caught in a wire that broke lose." He leaned toward her, his nimble fingers working on her pant leg until the machine released its hold on her. "There, that should do it."

"Thank you." Dania inched forward.

"What are you doing?"

Had he forgotten she had a threader to fix? "I still have a knot to untangle."

He gave a slight nod. "Right. Maybe I can help you there, too."

Dania stopped for a moment and looked up at him. "How do you plan to do that?"

The crooked smile he gave her made her heart flip. "If you cut the knot from below and I work from above, we should have this fixed in half the time."

It might work. "You're forgetting one thing."

"What's that?"

"Your hands are too big to squeeze into the area where the knot is."

He gave her another toe-curling grin. "Leave that to me, okay?"

Dania opened her mouth to protest then slammed it shut. If Matt wanted to help, she wouldn't stop him. "Thank you."

By the time she got into position, Matt had rolled up his sleeves and was working on the stubborn knot with the help of his pocketknife. "When I imagined seeing you again, this particular circumstance never crossed my mind."

Her hand shook as she plunked at the threads with the small knife her papa had given her. "You wanted to see me again?"

"Of course I did." He sunk the blade in deeper. "I would have been here sooner, but it took me two weeks to work up the nerve."

Matt had been nervous about seeing her? If it was possible, she fell a little bit more in love with him. "I'm glad you're here now."

He gave her a slight smile. "Me, too."

They worked in silence for the next few minutes, tearing apart the knot until only a few scrapes of thread remained. A machinist would have to be called in to replace the bent bobbins. As Matt plucked the remaining threads, Dania slowly made her way out of the machine, her mind racing in every direction. He said he wanted to see her, but why? Was he writing a follow-up article about her mill? Was he there because he cared for her even just a little bit?

She did know one thing. She would tell him of the changes she was making with her employees. He needed to know his article had made a difference, at least in her family's mill.

"Are you coming out, or do I need to come in there and get you?"

Really, the man could be so impatient at times, but while she hated to admit it, that was part of his charm. "I can do it myself."

She couldn't be certain, but she thought she heard him mutter, "I have no doubt of it."

When she finally stepped free of the machine, Matt's strong hand at her elbow steadied her as she stood. Dania lifted her hand to push strands of hair out of her face when Matt gently grasped her wrist. With his free hand, he pulled a clean handkerchief from his pocket and pressed it against her forehead. "You're hurt."

"Oh." She hadn't even felt it. "I must have scratched it on my way out. Thank you."

Gilly came toward them, her fists knotted in the folds of her skirts. "I'm so sorry, Dania. I told Mr. Langley to wait in your office, but he insisted that it was an emergency."

Dania cocked her eyebrow at him. "An emergency, huh?"

"Patience isn't exactly my strong suit."

"Yes, I know." But then, that's what made Matt such a brilliant reporter. Tenacious, her father would say. Persistent. Good qualities in a reporter and a husband.

She couldn't help the giddy feeling that started in her stomach. Yes, Matt would make a perfect husband for her.

But she wasn't even certain the man cared for her that way. Dania drew in a steadying breath then turned to her sister. "It's all right, Gilly. Mr. Langley is a friend from Atlanta."

Matt slid her a look then turned to face her sister. "A good friend."

"Oh, Mr. Langley!" Gilly glanced from one to the other, then giggled as she walked to the door. "It's about time you showed up."

Heat flooded Dania's face. She would throttle Gilly if she wasn't such a dear. "I'm sorry. My sister Gilly has a habit of speaking her mind."

"A family trait, no doubt." He stared past her to the massive machine. "This isn't the first time you've crawled around inside of that beast, I gather."

Dania shook her head. "And I doubt it will be my last."

"Why didn't your lead boy fix it?" He pushed a stray lock of hair behind her ear, pausing for a moment as he tenderly examined the sensitive bump she'd earned. "That's what he's being paid to do."

Words jumbled around in her head until Matt's hand dropped to his side. She stepped back then, her mind needing some distance to think clearly. "Peter would have gotten stuck if he'd tried to crawl inside, the way that boy has grown these last few months." She hesitated. "Besides, I'll have a mechanic working here soon."

"Yes, I read your advertisement in the papers." Matt pulled one rolled-up sleeve down his arm, then the other. "Only men or women fifteen years and older need apply."

Dania pressed her lips into a tight line. She'd hoped to put her decision into action before they met again. Well, so much for that happening. Best to get this over with so that she could get back to work. "Your article made me realize I couldn't ignore my conscience just because folks disagreed with me."

"Dania, I. . . ," he started.

Tears pricked the back of her eyelids, but she refused to cry. "I don't think you were right in saying I was motivated by guilt. I bought that fabric from Mr. Shonkwiler and arranged for a boot maker to come here because I truly wanted to do what was right for the children." Dania bowed her head to keep from seeing the disappointment in Matt's eyes.

The next moment, she was pulled against him, his arms banded around her as if he never intended to let her go. "Sweetheart, I am so sorry. After I met you, I never thought you were anything but kind and compassionate and everything wonderful."

She leaned back to look at him. "But your article. . ."

"Wasn't mine." He stroked her shoulder blades until she relaxed into him. "Well, some of it was. I made some assumptions about you before I'd even met you. Then the managing editor for the paper stole notes off my desk and edited them to fit his story on Senator Evers's campaign."

"Uncle George intentionally did this?"

Matt brushed a kiss against her hair. "Evers needed the textile mill owners to back his candidacy for governor, and the only way to do that was to get Eison mills out of your hands."

"They thought I was too progressive."

He nodded. "The owners feared if their workers found out what you were doing to improve the lives of your employees, they'd riot. The state legislature would have to step in, and the mill owners couldn't run the risk of having child labor outlawed. With Evers in the governor's mansion and you put in your place, a reform bill would never come to a vote."

Dania reluctantly pulled out of his arms. "I guess they got their way then."

Matt tilted his head to one side. "You haven't been reading the newspaper, have you?"

She folded the handkerchief he'd given her and handed it back to him. "I don't enjoy it as much as I used to."

"You would have enjoyed the last couple of weeks." He opened his jacket, pulled out a folded piece of paper, and handed it to her. "This will be in tomorrow's newspaper, but I thought you ought to see it first."

Taking it, Dania slowly unfolded it. The large font caught her attention and she struggled to suck in a breath as she read: SENATOR EVERS RESIGNS AMID TEXTILE SCANDAL.

Questions tumbled around in Dania's head, but when she looked up at Matt, she couldn't find the words. He must have sensed her struggle because he took her hand in his. "I was an idiot, Dania, letting Evers use me to hurt you and your family. It will always be the biggest regret of my life."

She should step away from him, but it felt too wonderful being this close to him. "Why did you have notes about me?"

"Not going to make this easy for me, are you?" He took a shuddered breath. "The senator offered me the same position he gave Taylor. Those notes about you were direct quotes he gave me the afternoon of our interview. Once I met you, I knew you were nothing like the woman the senator described, so I tossed them in the garbage pail. Taylor must have fished them out."

"So much for respectfulness," she sighed, lacing her fingers with his.

"I wanted to get here sooner, but I had to make sure Evers and his cronies couldn't hurt you again." She felt him relax. "I didn't know an investigative committee could convene that fast."

She lifted her head to look at him. "You testified."

"You bet I did. It was the only way to assure Evers wouldn't hold a public office in the state of Georgia again." He laughed. "The funny thing is this situation got the other senators and representatives talking about child labor laws. I wouldn't be surprised if a reform bill isn't introduced in the next session."

Dania smiled up at him. "The power of the press at work."

"Maybe." The torment in his eyes made her heart ache. "But it doesn't mean anything if you don't forgive me. I let my past experiences cloud my judgement and hurt you in the process."

"Oh, Matt." She took a step toward him then stopped. "I forgave you before I ever got off that train."

He cut the distance between them, drawing her hand to his chest. "You did?"

Dania could hardly breathe when he stood this close. "Of course I did. I had to." There was something else she needed to tell him, but what if he didn't share her feelings? Still, he needed to know. "I guess that's what you do when you love someone."

Before she could blink, Matt pulled her into his arms, his gaze searching then holding hers. Dania's mouth went dry at the play of emotions on his face. "I love you, too."

"You do?"

He gathered her closer. "I think I've loved you since you stood up to the thief at the train station."

"Love at first sight, hmm?" she teased, confident in his feelings for her. "I wouldn't have thought that of a hard-nosed reporter like yourself."

"Me neither." He kissed the tip of her nose. "But then I'd never met you before."

"You've only known me for a short while," Dania reminded him, wishing her practical side would be quiet for once.

"A situation I intend to correct starting now." Dania almost groaned when he let go of her and stepped back to put some distance between them. "I paid a visit to your mother this morning."

That surprised her. "You did?"

Matt nodded, his lips turned up in a rather rakish smile. "You might be progressive in your business practices, but I thought you might still like me to ask your mother's permission to court you."

Dania's heart threatened to flutter out of control. "What did she say?"

"She had some concerns, one being I live and work in Atlanta and you're here in Tifton."

Dania had thought about that, too. Matt's life was in Atlanta, his job was there, and he was far too talented to give it up to move here. But she had responsibilities, a community that depended on her for its livelihood. "That would be a problem."

"Anyway, I told her about my recent promotion, and that seemed to satisfy her question."

"You got a promotion?"

He gave her a wicked grin. "Meet the new editor in chief of the *Tifton Gazette*."

She took a step toward him. "You're moving here? But what about Mr. Hornsby? He's been the editor of the paper since before I was born."

"Always worried about everyone in your community, aren't you? Another thing I love about you." He stared at her for a long moment before he continued. "No need to worry. Hornsby is the new managing editor of the *Constitution* now that Taylor has been sacked."

"And you're moving here." A sudden giddiness overwhelmed her. Matt was staying. In Tifton. And he wanted to court her!

"I did tell your mother it would be a very short courtship as I have every intention of marrying you." He hesitated for a moment. "If you'll have me, Dania."

There was a note of vulnerability in his voice, as if he'd laid out his heart and the wrong word from her would crush it. It only made her love him more. Dania smiled up at him, the thought of spending her life with him, of raising a family, making a home, was almost too much happiness to bear.

Dania lifted her arms and linked them around his neck. His eyes shone, clear and brighter than a summer ocean, as she met his gaze. "Yes, Matt, I'd like nothing more than to be your wife."

Then she kissed him.

Epilogue

Almost a year later

As weddings go, it was fairly simple. Dania had insisted that all the mill employees, past and present, be invited if for no other reason than to ensure they had at least one meal that day. But Matt would do anything for his lovely bride-to-be, even share her with every citizen in the county. For a few hours, at least.

But as Matt stood at the makeshift altar, looking out at the multitude of faces here to wish them well, he realized how much Dania had changed the lives of these people. She'd taken her small corner of the world and made it a better place to live. A woman of noble character if ever there was one.

And in a few minutes, she would join her life with his.

Movement on the front porch caused people to turn, and for one moment, Matt had to fight the urge to stand up on tiptoe just to get a brief glimpse of his bride. First Katie, Dania's younger sister; then his own sister, Mary; and finally Gilly came down the aisle.

Then Matt saw her. She was beautiful in her simple white gown made of silk and lace, her veil floating around her shoulders, the wildflowers she carried a reflection of the independent spirit that he loved. Her mother walked beside her, there at Dania's request. If her father couldn't give her away, she told him, it only seemed right to offer that honor to her mother.

Matt knew the minute she saw him. Her smile blossomed, and if he wasn't mistaken, she walked a bit faster as if she couldn't wait to reach him. His heart burst at the thought.

Finally, Dania stood beside him. Her mother lifted her veil, gave her a kiss on the cheek, then took Dania's flowers and walked to her seat nearby. Dania turned to him, and for just a moment, the world faded from view.

Matt leaned toward her. "Hi."

"Hi."

"You look so beautiful that I almost met you halfway down the aisle. I didn't want to wait another minute."

She gave him a shy smile. "Didn't you see me almost pick up my skirts and run to you once I got a glimpse of you waiting for me?"

"Ready, my love?" He held out his arm to her then covered her hand as they moved forward to stand before the preacher.

"Yes, Matt." Dania covered his hand with hers. "I'm more than ready to start our lives together."

Patty Smith Hall is a multi-published author with Love Inspired Historical and Barbour Publishing. She calls North Georgia her home which she shares with her husband of 33+ years, Danny; two daughters, a son-in-love and a grandson who will make his debut in January, 2017.

Savannah's Trial

by Cynthia Hickey

Blessed is the man that endureth temptation: for when he is tried,
he shall receive the crown of life, which the Lord hath promised to them that love him.
James 1:12

Chapter 1

1866, Ozark Mountains

Savannah Worthington!"

Her mother's voice rang across the yard to the barn where Savannah brushed her horse's coat. She sighed, brushing faster. Mama most likely had another lecture in store about the perils of riding at breakneck speeds. She sighed again, kissed Bullet on the muzzle, and strolled toward the sprawling ranch house.

Mama greeted her on the veranda, hands on her hips, a scowl on her still-pretty face. "Are you trying to put me in the grave next to your father?"

"That's an unkind thing to say." Savannah removed her gloves, slapped them against her split skirt, and marched into the house. How could Mama bring up Pa's death like this? He'd been gone less than a year, and the agony was as raw as the day his body was discovered in the cotton fields. His heart, the doctor said.

"Bills are due." Mama followed her into the kitchen. "I've let the cook go and one of the maids."

Savannah whirled. "Not Mrs. Wilson." They'd had the same cook for years, and Mama burned water if she tried to cook.

"I had to do something in order to pay for the man I hired. If we don't get help, we'll be tossed out on our skirts before winter."

Normally, Mama cried doom at the slightest provocation, but this time. . . Savannah groaned. "I hope the hired hand is worth his keep."

"I will be."

She turned at the sound of a deep voice rumbling through the open doorway. Broad shoulders filled the space. When the stranger stepped into the light, Savannah was mesmerized by eyes the color of bluebonnets and hair the color of fresh straw. She held out her hand. "Savannah Worthington."

His large hand engulfed hers, pleasing in the fact he sported calluses. Not afraid of hard work, then. "Wyatt Jamison."

"You're a lifesaver, Mr. Jamison," Mama said. "Genteel women such as my daughter and I are not accustomed to physical labor. I fear my daughter is losing her roots working like a field hand."

Savannah's face heated. "I'm not fragile, Mama."

To the man's credit, he chose to ignore Mama's outlandish idea of what was proper. The ranch was in danger of failing despite Savannah's efforts, and if roughening her hands got the work done, then she'd proudly sport calluses as big as the Ozark Mountains.

A knock sounded on the front door. Savannah excused herself to greet their visitor. The banker, Mr. Morrillton, stood there in a suit no speck of dust would dare settle on.

The man would have no good news.

She stepped onto the veranda rather than invite him inside. "Good morning."

"I wish I could say the same in return." He removed his hat. "There's no gentle way to say this, so I'll come right out and say it. The taxes are overdue on this ranch."

"I'm aware of that. We're struggling to dig ourselves out after my father's death."

"And I have empathy for your loss, but financial matters don't wait."

"Give us six months." The door banged open behind her as Mr. Jamison joined them. "I'm the new foreman. We'll have you your money."

"Six months and not a day more." Mr. Morrillton plopped his hat back on his head and headed for his buggy.

Savannah turned. "You take a lot upon yourself, Mr. Jamison."

He grinned, revealing a dimple in his right cheek that made her stomach do flips. "If I can't pay those taxes, then you fire me on the very day the bank forecloses."

Really, the man was incorrigible and seemed to be a terrible flirt! "Of course you'd be out of a job, sir, just as we'll be out of a home."

"Perhaps, rather than argue over whether I've overstepped my boundaries, you show me around? Then you and I can come up with a plan to turn this ranch into making a profit."

At least he didn't plan on completely pushing her aside for his own ideas. She led him to the barn, where Bullet stuck his head over the stall door and nickered. She paused long enough to give him a rub. "This is my pride and joy."

"Do you mind if I take a look?" He reached for the handle before she agreed. "Have you thought of using him for stud? I'm sure you could get a good price."

"We've used him several times. The funds from his last service is what keeps food on the table." She leaned on the stable wall. "We have several mares of good bloodlines, too."

"Are they pregnant?" He ran his hands up and down Bullet's legs. "Since the war, the army is looking for good horse stock. Are these all of the horses you have?"

"We're a horse ranch, mostly, but we do have a few heads of cattle. Of course we have more horses." She led him out of the barn and to the pasture where twenty-five horses grazed. "These horses, while of good stock, don't meet the same criteria as the ones in the barn."

"But quite worthy of the army." He propped one foot on the fence and cut her a sideways glance. "You seem like a smart woman. Why haven't you considered selling them?"

"I've been too busy with the cotton." Which was failing miserably.

"Forget the cotton. Plant sorghum and sell the painted stallion and two mares. One stallion is enough for a herd of this size. Keep the next colt born. With half the proceeds, buy a few beef cows. Grow what your father started. Buy a bull. You'll be out of the hole in no time."

She sighed. She'd have to admit the real reason she hadn't sold to the army. "I've avoided selling horses to the army at all costs. My brother, Luke, left home to serve in the Union and never returned. He's presumed dead, although his body was never found. I've been reluctant to help other men ride to their deaths."

"The war is over, Miss Worthington. It's time for you to make money from what is left of that crisis."

◆ ◆ ◆

Wyatt continued following his employer around the ranch, dismayed at the amount of work involved. No wonder the women were struggling. How one little gal could do what she had managed to accomplish was nothing short of a miracle. Somehow, they needed to hire a couple more hands to work the fields. At least get the small crop of cotton in and plant the sorghum.

He spotted the vegetable garden, where Mrs. Worthington roamed the rows looking as out of place in her fashionable gown as a pig in church. He glanced to a couple of shacks on the edge of the property. "Are those slave cabins?"

Miss Worthington stiffened. "We never owned slaves. Pa built those for migrant workers."

"We need help, ma'am. I'd like to hire two men with the understanding they get paid when the cotton is in. If we provide food and lodging, I'm sure I can hire a couple of freed men. Would you have any objection to my doing so?"

She twisted her mouth in thought. "No, that sounds like a fine plan. I wish I would have thought of it."

"I'll head to town when we've finished the tour to hire some men and send a telegram to my cousin in the army. We'll get your taxes paid, Miss Worthington, but it will be a lot of hard work."

Eyes the color of a summer meadow flashed. "I'm not afraid of hard work, nor do I relish selling any of my horses. But, I see your point, as painful as it may be."

"I can see that you aren't." Her spirit and determination would make this ranch a success if anything. If not, then that same grit would help her and her mother survive whatever might come.

After a quick lunch of leftover biscuits and ham, Wyatt rode into the town of Pineville. After sending a telegram to his cousin, he headed to the shantytown a few miles away. Not wanting to get shot, he kept his hands in plain sight as he rode up to a group of men gathered in front of the general store.

"What do you want?" A tall man with coffee-colored skin stepped forward. Behind him stood ten more, all with serious expressions.

"I'm looking for two men to work for food and board. Once the crops are in, they'll be paid a fair wage from the proceeds."

"When do you want them?"

"Now." Wyatt grinned. "How about you and one other of your choosing?"

The man frowned. "Why me?"

"You seem to be the take-charge type. That's the kind of man I want to hire. Name's Wyatt Jamison."

"Did you fight in the war?"

"Yes sir, on the Confederate side." He held up his hands as cries of outrage echoed. "I fought with my father, not because I shared his beliefs, but because family sticks together. He didn't come home from the war."

The man stepped forward, hand extended. "Name's Lincoln Jones."

Wyatt leaned forward and accepted his offer of a handshake. "Pleased to meet you. The ranch is the Rocking W. Can you be there in the morning?"

Lincoln nodded. "My wife's a fair cook. Would there be work for her?"

"You bet." If the hard biscuits were any indication of the type of food he'd be eating from the hands of Mrs. Worthington, he'd pay a good cook out of his own funds if need be. "There's work in the house garden, too."

"We'll see you before the sun sets tonight." Lincoln turned and ambled away.

Summarily dismissed, Wyatt steered his horse toward his new home. Things were already looking positive for the ranch. He had high hopes the taxes would be paid on time with a bit of money to spare.

Instead of returning to the main house, he chose instead to ride the perimeter he and his boss lady hadn't covered during their walking tour. Three hundred and fifty acres of rich farm land. They could sell fifty acres and still be sitting pretty.

He gazed upon a creek barely providing enough water for the horses. Dismounting, he knelt in the damp soil next to the water. There'd been no lack of rain to dry up the creek. He stood and wiped his hands on his britches before strolling along the bank.

Just as he'd feared. The creek was dammed by a fallen tree and some boulders. At first glance, a person might think it had happened by accident. Maybe the tree falling, but not the rocks that took a man to move. Someone wanted the Rocking W's water.

He returned to his horse then rode to the ranch. As he led his horse to the barn, he glanced across the fields to see Miss Worthington riding as if the hounds of hell were on her heels. He jumped back into the saddle and galloped after her. When he got within shouting distance, he gave a shrill whistle.

She reined to a stop and turned. "What's wrong?"

"I was going to ask you the same thing?"

"I'm only out for a ride. Please don't tell me that you share my mother's views on how fast a proper lady should ride."

He chuckled. "Not at all. Seeing you tearing past the ranch had me fearing the worst. Have you thought about racing that horse of yours?"

"As a matter of fact, I have. But this backwards town doesn't believe in a woman racing. Not to mention I've bucked enough of Mama's convictions to scandalize her by racing. I'm not sure her heart could take more. Mama believes a woman should be genteel and quiet." She eyed him up and down until he squirmed in the saddle. "Maybe you could race for me."

"I'm too heavy." He fixed a serious look on her. "Besides, you have bigger worries than that, Miss Worthington. It seems someone is stealing your water."

Chapter 2

But the creek is running." Savannah frowned. "How does someone steal water?"

"By building a dam. You aren't out of water at this point, but it's only a matter of time." He folded his arms on his saddle horn. "Who owns the land west of here?"

She sighed. "Mr. Morrillton." It all made sense. If he couldn't get her land by foreclosure, he'd run her off with a lack of water. "What do we do?"

"I have workers arriving this afternoon. I'll set them to work destroying the dam before they start in the fields. If the matter escalates, you may want to think of hiring men to guard the creek."

One more thing to worry about. One more thing to need funds for. When would it end? Lately, the only time Savannah felt free of trials was on Bullet's back, galloping across the land. "We'll do what we must do."

"One of the men's wives will help cook and tend the garden."

She glared at him. "Is my money so easily spent that it trickles through your fingers like sand?"

"Whoa." He held up his hands. "It's included in the original plan. Your mother hired me to take charge of the ranch and see whether I can make it profitable. That's what I intend to do."

She moved Bullet closer to his horse. "It's my ranch, Mr. Jamison. Mine. I make the decisions. My mother hired you without discussing the matter with me. Any decisions, no matter how trivial they may seem to you, are to be run through me from now on. Is that understood?" She jabbed him in the chest with her forefinger.

"Perfectly clear, *boss*. See you at the house." He turned and trotted away from her.

She closed her eyes and exhaled deeply, feeling like a worm. The man was only doing what her mother had hired him to do. From his suggestions it was obvious he had a good head on his shoulders and might actually succeed in pulling the ranch away from the edge of an abyss. Still, the ranch was her inheritance. The only piece of her father she had left. She didn't want to relinquish all of the control to a stranger.

A cloud of dust rose on the road leading to the ranch. As the owner, it was her job to welcome the new hired hands and appease her mother, who would not be pleased to have strangers in the house. Much less ex-slaves, whom she suspected were all thieves. Prayer was the only thing Savannah could do to change her mother's narrow-minded ways. Sometimes she feared her prayers didn't pass the ceiling of the ranch house.

Sure enough, Mama stood on the veranda, arms crossed, eyes wide, and stared at the two families pulling up in rickety buckboards full of furniture and children. "What is this, Mr. Jamison?"

"Workers, ma'am." He strode forward and shook the hand of the man in the first wagon. "They're going to help me make this ranch profitable again."

"You, sir, are responsible for them." With a twitch of her skirt, she stomped into the house.

"I apologize for my mother's rudeness." Savannah dismounted and pulled off her gloves, offering her hand to the same man her foreman had shook hands with. "I'm Savannah Worthington, owner of the Rocking W. Welcome. I look forward to working with you."

The man stared at her for a moment before accepting her hand. "Lincoln Jones, missus. This is my wife, Irma. That fellow back there is Lee Brown and his missus, Rose. My wife will help in the kitchen and house while Rose tends garden, iff'n that be all right with you."

"That sounds marvelous." She grinned, actually looking forward to the explosion that would be Mama when she found out not one but two strangers would be traipsing through the house. "Let me show you to your new homes."

"I'll do that, Miss Worthington," Mr. Jamison said. "You might want to soothe your mother's ruffled feathers."

"Right." With a nod and a grin to those in the back wagon, Savannah headed into the house. "Mama?"

"Did you know about this?" Her mother whirled from where she stood in front of the parlor fireplace. "We have so little left. Are you willing to have it stolen from us in the middle of the night while we're murdered in our beds?"

"Mr. Jamison has vouched for these people, Mama. We can't turn the ranch around without help."

"Then hire men from town."

"These are people from town." Savannah rubbed her temples. "You might as well resign yourself to the fact that one of the women will be working in the kitchen and the other will help in the garden. You've complained often enough about not having the help a woman of your caliber should have. Now, you have what you've asked for."

"I'll keep my eyes peeled, young lady. You can count on that for a fact." Mama sat in her rocker and set it moving fast enough it actually scooted a couple of inches across the floor.

Savannah groaned and moved out the back door. The wagons had pulled in front of the nearest vacant cabins. The families didn't have much, and what they did possess looked barely usable. Not one of the children wore shoes, and while the adults' clothing was clean, every article sported more patches than original fabric.

She turned and climbed the stairs to her room. Surely she had a housedress or two the women could use. The men could make good use of Pa's clothes still hanging in the bureau. There wasn't anything she could do right away for the children, but she'd figure out something to make sure they were better clothed.

Opening the bureau in her parents' room, she began laying her father's things on the bed, keeping aside her favorite shirt of his. A blue chambray he'd worn to church. That, she couldn't part with. Perhaps, once she had the items collected, she could explain to

Mama the need and she would—

"What are you doing?" Mama rushed into the room.

"Giving Pa's things to the workers. He would love to know they were being put to good use."

Mama plopped on the bed and fingered the shirt. "Are you sure?" Her voice broke. "Is it really time?"

Savannah wrapped her arms around her. She'd expected more opposition. "Yes, Mama. It's time."

◆ ◆ ◆

"I hope these cabins will suit your needs." Wyatt pushed open the door.

"This is better than where we were living," Lincoln said. "I'm much obliged."

The cabin was one large room with a fireplace designed for cooking and heating. The front wall was broken up by the door and two small windows. The roof seemed in good repair and the wood plank floor, while covered with a film of dust, didn't seem to have too many splinters.

"Let me know what you need and I'll see whether we can get ahold of it for you." Wyatt was pleased. The cabins were of sturdy quality, much like the bunkhouse he had the privilege of living in. "Once you're settled, I need the dam above the creek cleared." He explained his suspicions. "Can you shoot?"

"We'd be hung if we point a gun at a white man." Lincoln's face remained stoic.

"You have my permission to protect yourself." Wyatt held out his pistol. "I can trust you." He wasn't sure whether he meant the statement as that or as a question.

"Yes sir." Lincoln took the gun. "I can shoot, but if men come after me with a rope, I 'spect you to get me free from here."

"You have my word." Wyatt prayed it wouldn't come to that, but if he was right about someone trying to keep the water, things could get ugly. "It's only until I can hire someone to guard the creek. I'll be working right along with you. I'll meet you on the porch in half an hour." He stepped outside and headed for the main house in order to give the newcomers privacy and a bit of time to settle in.

"Mr. Jamison." Miss Worthington waved to him from the front porch.

"Please, call me Wyatt. It's too much to say my surname."

"Very well. You may call me Savannah." She folded her hands in front of her serviceable navy split skirt. "I have finally brought myself to clean out my father's things." Her voice shuddered. When she regained control, she continued. "I'd like you to escort me to the cabins so I may offer the clothes to our workers. I don't want them to think of my offering as charity. Getting his things out of my mother's room will help her heal. I also have a couple of housedresses that, with the right skill, could be taken in or let out, depending on the need."

Wyatt rubbed his chin. "I'm not rightly sure how our new friends will take to being offered the clothing, but I'll go with you."

"Thank you." She scooped up a pile of folded clothing and joined him. "I really hope they aren't offended."

"We can pray they won't be."

She cut him a sideways glance. "You're a religious man?"

"Couldn't get through this life without God. I know for a fact I wouldn't have survived the war without Him."

"My brother was a believer. It didn't bring him home." She took a deep breath and squared her shoulders. "Our ways are not His." She marched toward the cabins, a smile plastered on her face.

"Missus, sir." Lincoln and his family greeted them. "We're ready for work."

Savannah held out her offering. "My father died last year. I am finally able to offer his clothing to someone who may appreciate them. Please, take these as early payment for your services. There are also some things I hope the women and children can use."

The two families stared at Savannah as if she were a two-headed critter. Then Irma stepped forward. "Thank you. We appreciate the offer."

"You're doing me and my mother a favor. My father would have wanted someone to use his things rather than have them hanging unused." Savannah grinned then turned to Wyatt. "What are we working on today?"

"Undamming the creek." He glanced at her hands. "You need gloves if you're going to help."

She pulled a pair from her pocket. "I'm ready. Mrs. Jones, Mrs. Brown, my mother is expecting you. Please ignore any rude behavior from her. She's a bit. . .biased since my brother didn't return from the war. She'll come around in time."

The women nodded and, after setting the clothes inside the cabin, headed for the main house. The children trotted after the adults who walked to the creek.

With four adults and nine children ranging in ages from three to twelve, judging by their sizes, they'd have the creek cleared in no time. Wyatt almost felt like whistling except for the unlawful act of Savannah's neighboring rancher.

"I don't approve of small children doing heavy labor," he said once they reached the creek. "Let the little ones play in that shallow pool."

Lincoln and Lee glanced at each other then sent the children off to play, keeping the oldest close to help. By the supper hour, the creek was flowing swiftly and had risen by a foot. Hot, muddy, and feeling better than he had in a long time, Wyatt used the supplies he'd brought along and posted a sign warning against damming the creek anywhere along its path, and led his group of tired workers home.

Irma and Rose greeted them at a makeshift table set up behind the main house. "Sit. Food is ready," Irma said. "Mrs. Worthington has retired with a bowl of soup to her room." The look on the woman's face spoke volumes about the reason Mrs. Worthington had retired. "We thought it easiest to all eat together out here. Mr. Jamison, Miss Worthington, your supper is on the stove."

"We'll eat out here with you, if you don't mind." Savannah grinned and took her seat.

Wyatt couldn't be more proud of the boss lady than he was at that moment. She'd worked just as hard as the rest and wasn't above breaking bread with them. Yep, he was going to enjoy working at the Rocking W.

Chapter 3

Savannah shuffled into the kitchen the next morning more sore than she could remember having been in her entire life. Every muscle screamed. She poured herself a cup of coffee and groaned as she sat at the table.

"That's what happens when a genteel woman works like a field hand." Mama glared at her over the top of her cup.

Savannah shot an embarrassed glance at Irma. When she was small, they'd had several servants flittering around the house like ghosts who wanted their presence known, invisible but not. She'd been taught not to speak about private matters in front of them. Now here she was being scolded in front of others like that child from long ago.

"I'm a little sore, but otherwise. . .I feel better than I can remember. Hard work is nothing to be ashamed of."

"Now that we have help, there's no need for you to work so hard."

Savannah frowned. "What would you have me do? Would you prefer I sit and do needlepoint? While away the hours, steeping in boredom? No thank you. As owner of this ranch, I intend to be involved in all aspects of running the place."

"You could spend time learning to run a household, organize charitable events, and find a husband." Mama set her cup down with a thud. "A man is better suited for running a ranch."

"There isn't a man around, Mama."

"Excuse me?" Wyatt stood in the doorway, an amused smile on his face. "What am I? A lily flower?"

Heat started in Savannah's stomach and traveled to her face until she was certain her skin was as red as the flame on the stove. "May I help you?"

"Well, I know a man who has a steer you might be interested in purchasing. Not to mention that young stallion we want to keep for stud doesn't seem to know what he's supposed to do." His grin grew wider. "I was going to handle these things myself, but after our conversation about me running all decisions through you, I thought it best to pay you a visit and ask if you want to see how the steer works with your cattle."

Mama gasped at the word *stud*, and Savannah's face grew hotter. "I'd, uh, like to take a look at the steer."

"There's also twenty-five head of cattle he's willing to take in trade for two strong horses that can pull a wagon. The family is moving west. I await your permission to proceed, my lady." He waved his hat and bowed.

"At least someone around here knows how to act properly." Mama stood and left the room.

For goodness' sake. Savannah shook her head and stood, carrying both coffee cups to the washboard. "Twenty-five head of cattle is a lot for two horses, Wyatt." She wasn't happy about the idea of her precious horses pulling a wagon, either.

"He's taking an extra axle and wheel I found in the barn, too. He doesn't want to raise cattle when he gets to his new home. Wants to farm."

She nodded. "Do you want a cup before we head out?"

"Thanks to Miss Irma, I've already had two. Best coffee I ever drank."

"Oh, go on with you now, Mr. Jamison." Irma waved away his comment. "You ain't nothin' but a sweet-talkin' man."

"Lincoln needs to be careful or I might just steal you away." Wyatt winked.

"It was delicious, Irma. Thank you." Savannah tugged on her gloves, uncomfortable with the flirtation, harmless though it may be. "I'm ready."

With a sweep of his arm, Wyatt waved her in front of him. "After you."

"You may stop with the theatrics." She marched past, nose in the air, and headed for the patch of grassland closest to the house.

A man in a buckboard jumped down when he spotted them approaching. "I've picked out the two horses I want." He pointed to two large mares. "They ought to be able to pull this wagon, don't you think?"

"I would think you would need mules or oxen." Savannah frowned. "These are quarterhorses, made for riding, not pulling a wagon. I can't bear to think my horses will be mistreated."

"Do you happen to have the mules you're talking about?"

"No." Savannah exhaled sharply, afraid of losing the trade, but she couldn't in good conscience let the man believe he would make it to California with these horses. "I do know of a man who might take the horses in trade for what you need. If you're willing to take that chance, then we have a deal." She thrust her hand forward.

"I'll take that chance and thank you." The man returned her handshake. "These horses are for riding, miss. I'll make arrangements to pull the wagon."

"I'll tie the horses to the back of the wagon for you." Wyatt stepped into the corral.

Wyatt moved with a long-legged grace reminiscent of a mountain lion Savannah had seen once. Why wasn't such a man married? With women outnumbering men since the war, there should be a line of eager ladies knocking on his door. If her life wasn't so consumed with preserving her inheritance, she might set her cap for him herself. As it was, a husband and a family were not in her future.

A few weeks ago, the thought would have been nothing more than a flicker in her mind. Now, she experienced regret that what she should have could not be. Feeling as if the weight of the world was on her shoulders, she watched while Wyatt tied two of the horses Pa had raised to the back of a stranger's wagon.

She blinked back tears and squared her shoulders. It needed to be done if they were to keep the land. She turned and headed back to the house before Wyatt could see her emotion.

◆ ◆ ◆

Wyatt didn't miss the sheen of tears in Savannah's eyes. If he had the funds, he'd pay her taxes. As it was, he was lucky to have a roof over his head and food in his belly. What was left of his army money had gone toward purchasing the horse he still hadn't named.

Once the son of a wealthy plantation owner, he didn't have a dollar to his name now. His childhood home burned to the ground, Pa dead of heart failure, and Ma. . .well, she'd died soon after of a broken heart. Carpetbaggers had scooped in after that and taken what was left. It was all gone by the time he'd returned home. Saving the Rocking W was Wyatt's attempt at regaining purpose in his life. He wouldn't allow himself to fail. Seeing Savannah's tears only reinforced that fact.

Once the new owner of two fine mares drove off, Wyatt whistled for Lincoln and Lee. "Can you men ride a horse?"

The men nodded.

"Let me ask the boss where we can graze these cattle." He strode toward the house, finally locating Savannah helping in the kitchen despite Irma's protests.

"Where can we put these cattle, Boss Lady?" He grinned as she heaved a sigh. "If you know of a small canyon, it would prevent us constantly chasing after the critters."

"I know of a place." She left the dough she'd been kneading on the counter. "I'll meet you in the barn."

"I'll saddle your horse." He tipped his hat at the women and headed for the barn. If he had her horse ready for her, they could leave as soon as she joined them. Hopefully, finishing one task quickly meant the cotton could be picked over the next day or two. Once sold, it would provide payment to the hired hands and put a bit in the ranch's coffers to tide them over until he heard back from his army buddy.

He mentally concocted a to-do list in his head, praying Lincoln and Lee would stay on after the fields were picked and replanted. With horses, now cattle, the fields, and keeping the creek free of dams, it was more work than one man could handle.

"I'm ready." Savannah entered the barn, tugging gloves onto her hands. "The canyon is a little less than an hour's ride from here."

So far? He'd hoped for somewhere closer. A place easier to keep an eye on. "Is there a patch of rich grass closer?"

She twisted her lips in thought. "The creek meets up with another smaller one not too far away. If you put the cattle there, they probably won't wander too far. The greatest threat would be bears and cougars."

"We need to hire another hand. Someone who won't mind sleeping with the herd."

"I hear money trickling again." She checked the cinch on the saddle then put her foot in the stirrup and swung onto the horse's back.

"Maybe I can find someone willing to work for food until we get back on our feet." He grabbed the reins to his horse and two others. "I'm doing the best I can not to spend money you don't have. But, as amazing as I am, I can't do it all myself."

"I can help."

"You do help. But it'll take more than us two, even with Lincoln and Lee." He cut her a sideways glance. "Lack of workers is one of the reasons this ranch is failing."

Her face darkened. "That couldn't be helped! Our workers left to fight and never returned. You saw how Mama acts toward the freed men and their wives."

"Use the backbone God gave you and don't let her rule the roost. You're the boss here."

She reined to a stop. "Excuse me? Who do you think has kept the roof over our heads for the last year?" She slapped her chest. "Me."

He grinned. "There's the spunk I want to see. Harvest that. Work as if you are successful, Savannah, and I promise you, this ranch will be something to envy someday."

"I'm not one to give up. There's no need to light a fire under me." She urged her horse closer to the waiting workers. "They sure don't look like cowboys."

Wyatt laughed, his horse's ears twitching at the sound. "As long as they can ride and follow directions, they'll do." He froze in his tracks, his smile fading. "Don't look now, but trouble in a tailored suit is coming."

Mr. Morrillton marched toward them. "So, it's true. You've hired shanty people."

"What is your objection, Mr. Morrillton?" Savannah squared her shoulders. "I told you we would have the taxes paid, and so we shall. Or did you think damming the creek would set us too far back?"

"I have no idea what you're talking about." He adjusted his tie.

"We've posted a warning, sir," Wyatt said, "and we'll be hiring a guard. If such behavior persists, we'll have to get the law involved."

The man's gaze clashed with Wyatt's. "I'll get this ranch lawfully, Mr. Jamison. Mark my words. Hiring. . .those people won't save this place from being purchased right out from under Miss Worthington's pretty little feet. By me, I might add." He spun on a polished boot and stomped back to his buggy.

"What a vile man. Where is he going?" Savannah asked.

Wyatt shrugged.

The banker switched directions at the last moment and approached the house. Mrs. Worthington stood from her rocker and smiled. The man took her hand and kissed the back of it.

Wyatt's blood ran cold. The worm wouldn't consider courting and marrying Savannah's mother in order to obtain the ranch, would he? If so, nothing Wyatt did would make a difference. All his plans for success would be wasted.

From the look on Savannah's pale face, she feared the same thing. "I'm afraid you'll have to take the cattle without me." She slid from her saddle. "There are. . .some papers I need to find."

"Papers?"

She lifted her chin. "Pa wrote up a new will where he left me the ranch, not Mama. But the will has been. . .misplaced. Without it, people will naturally think he left the ranch to Mama. I have to find it before she does something foolish. . .like marry that snake in a dark suit."

Chapter 4

Savannah sat back, staring at the trunk in front of her. A week had passed since she'd begun her search for Pa's will. Nothing. Where could Mama have put it? The worst part. . .Mr. Morrillton made a point of visiting the ranch every day to prey on Mama's affections.

"Are you still looking?" Mama entered Pa's office. "Your father handed me a stack of papers tied with twine and told me to put them in a safe place. I wish I could remember where that place is. I'm sorry, dear, but you needn't worry. Leaving the ranch in my hands is the same as leaving it in yours."

Savannah stood, dusting her hands on her brown skirt. "Not as long as that man is courting you."

"Oh, pshaw, he's only being friendly."

Savannah had suspected for a while that her mother's mind might have been affected by the loss of her only son and husband within months of each other. Her blindness regarding Mr. Morrillton confirmed the notion. "Please think again where you might have put them. Think back to last year when Pa handed the papers to you."

Mama tapped a finger against her lips. "I'm trying. He would have handed them to me in the house. I'm sure of it."

"Could you have stuck them in your skirt pocket? Maybe carried them to the barn?" *Please, God, don't let Mama have thrown them in the fire thinking they were garbage.*

"You know I don't go to the barn." Mama narrowed her eyes. "They're in the house somewhere."

"Hidden panels, false drawers?"

"I have a headache from all this thinking. I'm going to lie down."

Savannah fell into Pa's office chair. If there were hidden places in the house, surely he would have told her. There'd been no secrets between the two of them since her brother's presumed death. He'd openly stated that she would inherit the ranch.

Tears pricked her eyes remembering the day she'd found him facedown in the cotton. With the workers having left to fight in the war, he'd not bothered to hire help, instead doing it all himself. Savannah had managed to get neighbors to help get that crop in and replanted, but by then they were already so far in the hole financially, she'd feared they couldn't return to a life of prosperity. With Wyatt, she'd again had hope, until now. If Mama remarried, the ranch might succeed, but Savannah would lose her inheritance for sure.

Where would she go? What would she do? Pa had bought the land when she was five. It was all she knew.

"Tea, Miss Worthington?" Irma carried a silver tray into the office.

"Thank you." Savannah took a cup and set it on the desk. "If you lived here and needed to hide important documents, where would you put them?"

"You're asking me?" The woman's brows rose.

"Yes. You're a smart woman, and I'm at my wit's end." Savannah waved a hand toward the only other place in the room for a body to sit. A cane-seated, straight-back chair. "Please. Sit and help me think this through."

Irma was obviously not used to such an invitation, but with a slight shrug of her thin shoulders, she set the tray on the desk and sat down. "I've cleaned every inch of this house; let me ponder a moment."

Wyatt stood in the doorway. "Cotton is ready to go to town. Will you be coming?"

Torn between wanting to continue her search and wanting to make sure the cotton got the best price, staying won out. If anyone could keep the buyer from cheating them, it would be Wyatt. "I'll stay. But, I would like to be the one to pay our friends." She smiled at Irma. "I hope your family will stay on. There is plenty of work to be done. I'm sure we can find ways to pay you."

Irma nodded. "I'll talk to my husband. As it is, the lodging you've provided is better than anywhere we've lived so far. Will my Lincoln be going with you, sir?"

"No, he's elected to stay behind. He said I'd be treated with more fairness if I went alone." Wyatt shook his head, started to say something, then clamped his lips shut. "I'll look for you, Savannah, when I return."

When he'd left, Savannah reached over and put her hand on top of Irma's. "Don't despair. Small-minded ideas won't last forever."

"I reckon." Irma straightened. "Let's go back to thinking on our current problem."

"What did you do. . .before?"

"Before the war freed me? I was a house slave."

"I thought so. You speak with education. Can you read?"

"Yes ma'am."

"Good. You'll know what you find when you find it. Now"—Savannah rubbed her hands together—"where should we look next?"

"Does the desk have a hidden compartment anywhere?"

Savannah shook her head. "I've gone over the entire piece of furniture. Besides, if it did, Mama wouldn't have known. She's horrible about keeping secrets. Pa would not have told her about one of his hiding places. We need to think like her."

"Jewelry box?"

"I've looked." They were getting nowhere.

"Attic?"

"A cursory search. Are you willing to get dusty?" Savannah grinned.

"I live for it." Irma returned her smile and removed the spotless apron she wore. "I have some time before I need to get lunch. There's no time like the present."

Savannah stood and lifted the tray. "I'll put this away and meet you at the stairs."

"That's my job, missus." Irma moved to take the tray from her.

"You're helping me with mine, I can help you with yours." Savannah gave her new friend a look she hoped would not allow room for argument and headed for the kitchen.

◆ ◆ ◆

Wyatt returned at lunchtime, sorghum seed in the back of the wagon and his pockets full of money. He'd gotten more than a fair price for the cotton, promising to help the buyer when the time came for the man to purchase a horse.

He turned the wagon and team over to Lee and went in search of Savannah. He was surprised not to find either her or Irma in the kitchen. Instead, Mrs. Worthington stood at the stove, staring at it as if she'd never seen one before. "Ma'am?"

"I'm wanting a cup of tea. Mr. Morrillton will be arriving soon and will want refreshments. Where is my daughter?"

A thud overhead gave him a clue. "I'll find her." He took the woman by the elbow. "Why don't you wait in the parlor for your guest?"

He'd barely got her seated when a cry from above sent him flying to the attic. "What's wrong?"

Savannah, tears in her eyes, hugged Irma. "We found it. We found Pa's will hidden in one of Mama's old petticoats. Irma is a gift from God."

Irma chuckled. "I've never been called that before."

"Well, gift from God," Wyatt said with a grin, "there's a woman downstairs distraught because she can't boil water and is having a guest arrive soon."

"Mercy me." Irma dusted her hands. "I'll see to her right away." She hurried down the stairs.

"I need to put on my best dress if we have company coming." Savannah's smile lit up the room. "I'm sure Mr. Morrillton will be pleased."

Wyatt laughed. "I've a gift for you." He handed her the money. "The man will be wanting a horse in a month or two and I promised him a fair deal."

"The way you're selling off the horses, I hope the mares produce soon." She slipped her arm through his. "I can't thank you enough, Wyatt."

"Three of the mares are expecting soon. I reckon a few more will be in the coming months." He led her to her room. "I'll be out by the barn when you're ready to pay the workers."

"Give me half an hour." She entered her room and closed the door. Before he'd turned to walk away, she thrust the money back at him. "Go ahead and pay Lincoln and Lee. See if they're willing to stay on. I'll tackle Mr. Morrillton instead. Then we'll have a feast, all of us, to celebrate."

Her joy was infectious. His steps light, Wyatt headed to the worker cabins.

Lincoln and Lee whittled on their porches but stood when he arrived. "Did you get a fair price?" Lincoln asked.

"I did." Wyatt counted off their share. "I want to ask whether you're willing to stay on as hired help. I can't guarantee regular pay until funds come in, but you will get paid."

The men looked at each other then back at Wyatt. "Yes sir, we's happy here," Lincoln said. "It's a safe place for our young'uns and we're treated fairly." He glanced over Wyatt's shoulder. "Company's coming."

Wyatt sighed and headed back to the house. He didn't want Savannah to be alone when she told the man his motives were going to be unrewarded.

"You can turn right around and leave, Mr. Morrillton," Savannah said when Wyatt approached. "I've located the papers leaving the ranch to me. Courting my mother will not get you my land."

"Savannah Marilyn Worthington!" Her mother stepped through the front door. "That is not why Mr. Morrillton is spending time with me." She glanced at the banker. "Is it?"

He didn't glance her way. "There are other ways of getting what I want, Miss Worthington."

"Is that a threat?" Wyatt stepped to Savannah's side. "I suggest you take your leave immediately."

"Mark my words. This ranch will be mine." He got back in his buggy and drove away.

"Well!" Mrs. Worthington plopped into a rocker. "He was only after the land. It's all right. No one can compare to your father in my heart anyway." She set the rocker into motion. "Thank you for your assistance, Mr. Jamison."

"Walk with me, Wyatt." Savannah stepped off the veranda and headed around the corner of the house. "How close are we to paying off the taxes?"

"Two-thirds of the way."

"If you hire a couple of armed men, will we make the deadline?"

"It will be close."

She glanced at the barn. "I've been offered good money for Bullet. Would it be enough?"

"I won't allow you to sell your horse. We'll get the taxes paid another way."

Lincoln came up behind them. "Mr. Jamison, Miss Worthington." He held out his wages. "Irma and I are willing to hold off a bit on getting paid. We've kept some, but the majority is here. You put this toward keeping the ranch."

Tears shimmered in Savannah's eyes. "That's kind of you, Lincoln, but what if we lose the ranch? You'd never get your money."

"You's been good to us. We's willing to take that chance. You've given us clothing, food, and a right fine place to live. Please. Let us help."

Savannah glanced up at Wyatt. "How close does that get us?"

"If we sell off two more horses, you'll have the money necessary to pay your taxes." He scratched his chin. "But you'll be very low on funds. You'll need to be frugal for a few months."

"What if we sell off twenty acres? I know it isn't a lot, but the neighbor to our east may be willing to purchase the land to increase his wheat fields. That would tide us over for a good while."

"You could sell ten acres and we'd be fine. No need to get rid of so much of your land. Not yet." Not ever, he hoped, and she wouldn't miss ten acres. That way, the livestock could stay to help build for their future.

He reached for her then pulled back, realizing he'd almost overstepped his boundaries. He wanted to hold her, caress her face, and rejoice in the fact they had a solution. As it was, he was her hired help, and it would do him well to remember that.

Chapter 5

Savannah stepped onto the veranda, coffee in hand, and stretched. Having found Pa's will filled her with more hope than she'd had in a long time. She grinned and mouthed a "thank you" heavenward. While her heart ached for Mama, knowing the wealthy banker had only wanted her for the ranch, Savannah couldn't help but feel relieved.

She glanced toward the corral where Wyatt, Lincoln, and Lee all stood as rigid as soldiers. The empty corral. She set her coffee cup on the top step and dashed to their side. "Where are the cattle? The horses?" The missing section of railing answered before they could.

"They're gone." Tears poured down her cheeks. "We're ruined." She covered her face with her hands and sobbed.

Wyatt pulled her hands down then drew her into his arms. "You aren't. We'll find them."

"They're stolen," she mumbled against his chest. A very solid chest, she might add. She peered up at him. "What will we do?"

"We go after them." With his thumbs, he wiped away her tears. "They can't have gone far. Lincoln said they were here when he went to bed last night."

"That's right, missus. I came out to use the necessary and the animals were here. That was five hours ago."

She nodded and stepped back, embarrassed at her emotional outburst. "What would I do without you, Wyatt? Without your ideas and support for making this ranch prosper in the future, I'd have no hope and would have given up." No truer words had ever left her lips. Their foreman wasn't only a hired hand, he was the one to save them. She knew without a doubt that he'd do everything humanly possible to keep her from losing her ranch. She still had the land to sell. Now that the shock was gone, she knew they would be fine.

"We could plant more crops, but this isn't a farm. It's a ranch. It's always been intended to be a ranch. We need those animals. Please saddle my horse." She turned and marched to the house.

Inside, she made a beeline for the mantel and took down Pa's rifle. While she kept it cleaned and ready for use, she hadn't shot it since before he'd passed. She wasn't going after rustlers unarmed. She took down his holster and pistol from a nearby peg, hooked it around her waist, and joined the men in the barn, thinking it best not to tell Mama where she was going.

Wyatt handed her the reins to Bullet. "I know it's useless to ask you to stay behind." He eyed her guns.

"Yes, it is." She slid the rifle into a sling and swung into the saddle. "I trust the rest of you are also armed."

"All but Lee."

"Then leave Lee behind to watch the women and children. He can bang the supper bell if trouble comes. We'll hear it." She kicked her horse into motion. Tears were over. It was time for action. Once she had her property back, she'd pay a visit to the sheriff and demand justice be done.

Wyatt pulled alongside her. "Don't go running off on your own."

She shrugged. "I'm sorry for my weak behavior earlier. Please pretend it never happened."

"I'd rather cherish the moment. You felt good in my arms, Boss Lady." He gave her a smug grin.

Her face heated. "This is not the time for flirtation, Mr. Jamison."

He flicked the reins and moved ahead of her as they traveled through a narrow pass. "Do you know where we're going?"

"Follow the trail. It leads to the canyon I mentioned the other day. If the cattle aren't there, then we check Morrillton's ranch." She wasn't sure what she would do if the animals were found on the Lazy M, but it wouldn't be good.

Wyatt held up a hand for them to stop then slid to the ground. "I hear cows. Stay here while I scout it out. If you hear gunfire, ride back to the ranch."

"I will not. If shots are fired, we're coming to help. Right, Lincoln?" She glanced over her shoulder.

He swallowed audibly. "Yes ma'am. But I'm not accustomed to shooting."

"Just aim and pull the trigger." She switched her attention back to Wyatt. "We're waiting and ready."

He shook his head and stepped into the bushes.

"You scared, Miss Worthington?" Lincoln's shaky whisper told her he was terrified.

"More angry than anything. Have you ever had something taken from you? Something that would alter your future?"

"Yes ma'am. My firstborn son was sold out of my arms."

"Oh." Shame flooded through her. Her trials were mild in comparison. "Do you know where he is?"

"He'd be fifteen now. I've put out the word I'm looking for him. His name is Abraham."

She glanced back again. "I give you my word, Lincoln, that I will help you find your son."

Tears sprang to his eyes. "You'd do that for me?"

"In a heartbeat. Let's save my ranch, and then we'll find your boy no matter how long it takes." She choked back tears. "We'll pray, Lincoln. Without ceasing."

"Thank you, ma'am." He ducked his head, but not before she saw his tears fall.

She had just started to get off her horse to approach his and offer more consolation when Wyatt returned. "Are they there?" she asked him.

"Yes, along with two armed guards."

"Can we take them?"

He narrowed his eyes. "No, *we* cannot."

"They wouldn't dare shoot a woman." She slid from her horse. "If I can just go talk to them—"

"You're plumb loco." Wyatt took her by the shoulders and shook her. "What if they will shoot a woman, or worse? Who will care for your mother? We'll head into town and get the sheriff."

"No." She yanked free of his grasp, grabbed her rifle, and darted into the bushes. She would have gone to the sheriff if they'd found the cattle on the Lazy M, but they were right here, within arm's reach. Before going to the sheriff, she needed to know who was responsible for the rustling.

◆ ◆ ◆

Wyatt groaned, told Lincoln to secure the horses before following, and then headed after Savannah. He was going to wring her pretty little neck. He watched in horror as she stepped in sight of the rustlers, her rifle nestled in her arms.

"Good afternoon, gentlemen." Her voice would have melted butter. "I want to thank you."

"For what?" The two men stood, hands on their holsters, while the dark-bearded one spoke.

"Finding my lost cattle and horses. I'm Savannah Worthington of the Rocking W. My fate lies with these animals. I am forever in your debt."

The two men exchanged glances then started to laugh. As they hooted at her, their rifles loosened in their grips and pointed at the ground.

"You alone, little lady?" Dark Beard asked.

"My hired hands are waiting for me. Is that coffee on the fire? I sure could use a cup."

Wyatt had to admire her spunk, even if he disapproved of what he considered foolishness. He put a finger to his lips as Lincoln joined him. "I think she's trying to distract them," he whispered. "We'll wait for an opportunity then jump out."

"I ain't never done nothing like this before, Mr. Jamison."

"I just need you for moral support, Lincoln." He hoped. If things erupted into a gunfight, he wasn't sure he could count on the man to actually pull the trigger.

"Yeah, it's coffee," Dark Beard said. "But it's old and bitter. We got some hard tack, if you've got something to trade." The way he glanced up and down Savannah's body made Wyatt want to start shooting.

"That's all right. I'll take my animals and head on home." She took a couple of steps backward.

"Hold on, little lady." Dark Beard took a step forward. "Me and my brother think you should visit awhile longer. Now, he don't talk much, but he knows how to treat a woman."

Savannah shouldered her rifle and aimed it at his head. "Who paid you to steal my animals?" Gone was the soft, Southern lady. In her place was an irate woman ready to fight.

Wyatt grabbed Lincoln's arm and pulled him out of the bushes. They stood on either side of Savannah, their own weapons aimed at the rustlers.

"I suggest you keep your hands away from your guns," Wyatt said. "You'll be dead before you get them out of the holsters. Now, answer the lady's question."

"Some man in a suit." Dark Beard shrugged. "Looked like a rich man. Said if we took these animals and held them here until he sent someone for them, we'd be paid real good. Doesn't look like that's going to happen."

"No, it does not. Toss your guns over here real nice like and my friend will collect them. Then, you two skedaddle and tell your rich friend he isn't going to run the Rocking W into the ground. Got it?" Wyatt lifted his gun just a tad to help get his point across.

"You're letting us go?"

"Hurry, before I change my mind."

The men dropped their guns, jumped on their horses, and rode off.

Wyatt turned to Savannah. "Don't ever do anything like that again."

"It worked, didn't it?" She smiled. "Lincoln, would you fetch the horses so we can herd these animals home? Wyatt, I think you need to hire guards when we visit the sheriff."

He agreed, even though he had no idea how they were going to pay them. Plus, he needed to find honest, hardworking men that would work well with Lincoln and Lee. Not an easy task in this part of the country.

The ride back to the ranch was a busy one, with the three riders circling the animals. Wyatt didn't mind. It kept him from dwelling on what could have happened to Savannah with those rustlers. Boss or not, his feelings for her were growing. He didn't know whether to rejoice or run away in fear.

What if he failed her? What if she shared his feelings, then something happened to separate them? There were so many variables that could pull a man and a woman apart. He admired her spirit, but could he live with a woman who would charge recklessly into danger? He wasn't sure his heart could survive the loss of another person he loved. He needed to spend a lot of time in prayer before deciding whether he wanted the life of a bachelor or of a family man.

Lee had the corral fixed by the time they returned to the ranch and a makeshift one next to the barn. "I figured it might be more work for the rustlers if we split the animals up," he said. "Horses in the smaller corral, cattle in the larger one."

Wyatt agreed. Once the danger from Morrillton was past, the cattle would range free. But until then, the future of the ranch needed to stay close to home.

Savannah handed the reins of her horse to Lee and marched to the main house, where Mrs. Worthington stood, arms crossed. Wyatt couldn't see clearly that far, but he figured a scowl marred the woman's face. After all, her daughter had left for hours and taken the guns from the house.

He chuckled. She was a pistol for sure. Maybe a life with Savannah would be worth the trials and possible heartbreak. He'd speak to God before bed and see if he couldn't find an answer in his father's worn Bible.

Chapter 6

On the way to town the next morning, Savannah tilted her head and cast a coy glance Wyatt's way. "Still mad at me?"

"I was never mad at you. I was scared for you. There's a big difference." He continued looking straight ahead.

Which told her he was lying. No matter. His not looking at her gave her a clear view of his strong, and very handsome, profile. "What are your dreams, Wyatt? Everyone has one. Lincoln's is finding his son. I promised to help him." She told him of the sad conversation from the day before.

"How do you propose to keep that promise?" Now he looked at her, his brilliant eyes narrowed. "I doubt you'll find paperwork telling us who the boy was sold to. But I'll put some posters up in nearby towns."

"That would be wonderful. Thank you. We'll ask around, spread the word. I have faith we'll find him, Wyatt. Your dream?"

He shrugged. "I want to live a good life, leave a legacy so my days on this earth will be remembered when I'm gone. It's a simple dream, but every morning when I set my feet on the floor I ask myself, what can I do today to further that along?"

She knew that if he were to leave, she would never forget him. Without Mama's hiring of this wonderful man, Savannah would still be mired in worry about the safety of the ranch. "You've definitely made your mark here. You've helped the ranch, given the hope of a better life to Lincoln's and Lee's families. . . ." And stolen her heart, if she were honest with herself. "Do you want to marry someday?"

"Is that a proposal?" He flashed the crooked grin that set her heart racing.

"No." She turned her face so he couldn't see the heightened color in her cheeks. "Just a question to pass the time."

"I've thought about it, but I don't have a lot to offer a woman. I came from a successful family. We had one of the largest plantations in Georgia. But the war changed all that. Now I'm little more than a drifter."

"Oh, you are far more than that, Wyatt."

Their conversation halted as they crossed the town line and tied their horses to the hitching post in front of the sheriff's office. Savannah had never had reason to meet the sheriff before, but she'd heard stories that the man was on the take and lazy. To him, the least amount of work for a dollar was the best policy. Her heart thudded. Surely the stories were false. A man of the law should be fair and unbiased. She took a deep breath and pushed open the door, grateful for Wyatt's presence at her side.

A man as tall as Wyatt's six feet, but outweighing him by at least forty pounds, sat behind a scarred desk, scuffed boots propped on the desktop. "Sheriff Webster?"

"This is the sheriff's office." The man blew a puff of smoke from the cigar in his mouth and lowered his feet. "What can I do for you folks?"

Savannah waved her hand in front of her face. "I need to file a complaint."

"You don't say. Who against?"

"Mr. Morrillton. He has dammed my creek and hired men to steal my property." She lifted her chin.

"That's a serious statement about a prominent citizen of this town." He stubbed out his cigar on the bottom of his boot. "You got any proof?"

"Just a threat from the man's own lips." She crossed her arms. Why wasn't Wyatt saying anything?

"That's not enough for me to arrest a man, but I can have a talk with him."

"Talk is cheap, Sheriff. While you're *talking*, you might want to mention to the scoundrel that me and mine have taken to wearing our weapons. We won't be threatened again."

"Now, it sounds like you're threatening an officer of the law. But then, a pretty little thing like you wouldn't do that, would she? What about your silent bodyguard here? He got anything to say?"

Savannah glanced at Wyatt. A muscle ticked in his jaw. His eyes shone with a steely glint.

"Only that I'll do what it takes to keep this little lady safe. Thank you for your time." He took Savannah's arm and practically dragged her to the sidewalk. "That was a waste of time."

She glared at him. "You stood there like a tree."

"I was assessing the situation. He's a crooked sheriff."

"What do we do now?"

"We have a slice of pie." He led her toward the diner.

"How is that supposed to help us?"

"It has a big window with a perfect view of the street." He opened the diner door for her and informed the waitress they wanted a table by the window. "Two slices of apple pie, please."

She wasn't sure of his point, but breakfast was a while ago. She wouldn't turn down pie if someone else was buying. Settling onto a chair, she glanced out the window. "Oh, I see."

Sheriff Webster wasted no time marching down the sidewalk and into the bank.

"Wyatt, you're brilliant. But what are we going to do about it?"

"How flirtatious can you be?" He winked.

"Not very." She gave him a stern look. "What crazy plan are you cooking up? Because if it involves me being all soft and sweet to either one of those porcupines, you can forget it."

"All right, let's try the soft and helpless approach. I'll pretend to have quit employment at the Rocking W. We can get by for a few days with Lincoln and Lee caring for things. I'll be close by, but once Morrillton hears I'm gone, I bet my hat he'll come calling. Not on your mother this time, but on you. You can be all upset and flustered, batting your eyelashes and whatever it is that women do when they want a man to follow their whim.

You can get him to confess in no time."

"We'll need a reputable witness for the sheriff to believe us."

"I've got that covered, too. Another army buddy of mine is a marshal. I'll get him to come here, you'll ask all the right questions in this very diner, and he'll hear everything."

She took her bottom lip in her teeth. The idea might be crazy enough to work. "You promise you aren't really leaving me?"

"I promise. I'll never leave."

◆ ◆ ◆

They'd just finished their pie when Webster exited the bank. "Time to act." Wyatt took Savannah's hand. "Remember. You'll be hurt and outraged by what I say, but I'm pretending. Don't take any of it personally." He dragged her outside.

"I cannot work for such a scatterbrained female that doesn't know her horse from a cow's behind!"

Savannah's eyes widened. Her mouth opened silently. Then, realizing they were the center of attention and that the banker and the sheriff were watching, she said, "Then don't! I didn't hire you in the first place. I didn't want you here." She stomped her foot. "Pack your things and be gone by nightfall." She marched to her horse, swung into the saddle, and galloped away.

Wyatt stood there for a second then realized she was riding off alone. He leaped onto his horse and took off after her. Their plan was now in action. He prayed it wouldn't backfire somehow.

Savannah waited for him a mile down the road. "How exhilarating! I should be on the stage." She grinned. "Did you see the smug looks on their faces?"

He laughed. "I did. Morrillton will probably be at the ranch within an hour."

"If he does, you hide in Pa's study. If you leave the window open, you can hear everything that is said on the veranda. If he acts unseemly, you'll be there to save me. Although, I will have the pistol in my pocket." With a click of her tongue, she set her horse into motion.

He should have known she'd step into the role with everything in her. Hopefully, she could keep a civil tongue with Morrillton until he believed her helpless act. "I need to go back and send a telegram to my friend. Please, go straight home."

"Wyatt, I managed perfectly well going back and forth to town on my own before you arrived. I'll see you when you return." She trotted off, leaving him feeling like a fool.

Once she was out of sight, he headed to the telegraph office. After sending his message, he waited for a reply. One came within half an hour. His friend would arrive in the morning. Good. They needed to end this threat to the ranch and focus on building the Rocking W into the ranch it held promise it could be.

"We got problems, Mr. Jamison." Lincoln caught up with Wyatt in the barn. "We got a mare foaling and a cow broke through. We suspect she's gone off to have a calf on her own."

"They do that." Wyatt didn't see a lot of reason for concern. "She'll come back at feeding time."

"We saw signs of a cougar, sir, just this morning."

That changed things. "Let's go find us a cow. Is the mare having trouble?"

"She's in the beginning stages. Lee is with her."

Why did trouble come on top of trouble? Wyatt pulled his rifle from the scabbard and headed for the woods. He really wanted to be back before Morrillton showed his face. As they searched for the cow, he explained the latest plan to Lincoln, who promised to let Lee in on the news.

They found the cow and newborn calf bedded down in a pile of decaying leaves a few yards into the woods. Wyatt checked over mother and baby. Everything looked fine. He slipped a rope around the cow's head. Baby would follow without a problem.

Something screamed. Wyatt whirled. Lincoln shouted.

Wyatt found himself slammed to the ground by an animal weighing almost as much as he did with sharp teeth and claws. "Shoot it! Ahh!" The cougar bit down on his shoulder. "Lincoln, shoot it!"

"I'll hit you!"

Wyatt wrapped his hands around the animal's throat and pushed. His muscles strained as he fought to keep the teeth away from his neck. "Do something!" Another bite and Wyatt feared he'd lose the fight. Pain racked his body.

The cow hurtled down the path, baby following.

The cougar grunted as Lincoln slammed a thick branch across its back. It turned.

Wyatt grabbed his pistol and fired. The animal fell. Wyatt's eyes closed and the world went black. The last thing he thought of was that if he died, Savannah would be alone to fight against Morrillton.

◆ ◆ ◆

When he came to, his good arm was slung over Lincoln's shoulder and the man was doing his best to drag Wyatt down the path. He glanced back at the dead cat that had attacked. Close call. He might be bleeding and half-conscious, but he was alive. For now.

Lincoln had torn the sleeve from his own shirt and bound Wyatt's wounds. "You need a doctor, Boss."

"I reckon I do." He shook his head to clear it. "I counted two bites. Anything else?"

"You've a deep scratch in your side and a graze on your head. You put up a good fight, but the cat was stronger."

"Until I shot it. I want its hide, Lincoln."

"I'll come back for it. You hush now." Lincoln shook his head. "You're going to scare the dickens out of Miss Worthington."

"It's best you take me through the back way, then. Irma will patch me up. Better yet, go straight for the bunkhouse."

"No sir, the first idea was better. My Irma is good with a needle and nursing. We'll patch you up."

Wyatt stared at the man's solemn face. "First thing when I'm on my feet is teaching you how to shoot."

"I can shoot, just not very good."

"You'll be good when I finish with you." They stopped at the edge of the property.

Morrillton's wagon was parked in front of the house.

Chapter 7

Savannah was prepared to do battle by acting helpless. She pasted on a smile as Mr. Morrillton climbed from his buggy. That is, until she spotted a weary Lincoln helping a blood-covered Wyatt toward the house.

"Wyatt!" She leaped from the veranda and sprinted toward them. "What happened?"

"We were searching for a cow and her newborn calf when a cougar jumped Mr. Jamison. We need to get him into the house."

"Of course." Unmindful of the blood, she propped her shoulder under Wyatt's other arm. "Irma! Spread a blanket on the sofa. Hot water." What was she forgetting? If Wyatt died. . .well, she wouldn't think about that. With her heart in her throat, they passed a very confounded-looking banker.

"What's going on here?" He propped fists on his suited hips. "I thought this man was gone."

"Chew on your hat, Mr. Morrillton, and go back to town." Savannah stepped onto the first step. "We've got you, Wyatt. We're almost there."

"I don't play games, Miss Worthington. You'll regret this little charade." He turned and climbed back into his buggy. "Mark my words."

She'd like to mark him with a riding crop. "Good day, sir."

They entered the house with Mama and Irma both scurrying to get the needed medical items.

"Not the sofa!" Mama pointed to the kitchen. "The table, please."

They half carried, half dragged Wyatt to the kitchen and, with the four of them working together, got him on the table. The pallor of his skin made Savannah's knees weak, and she sagged into a chair.

"Go change, honey. You're covered in blood." Mama patted her shoulder on her way past. "Irma and I will patch up Wyatt. We're going to be removing. . .some articles of clothing. As an unmarried woman, you don't need to see."

Gracious. She'd change, but she'd return pronto. Modesty had no place when the man she loved could be dying. Loved. She never expected that emotion to have a place in her life.

With one last glance at Wyatt's face, she headed upstairs, hoping, praying, it wasn't her last look at a living Wyatt. Shedding her stained clothing, she kicked them into a corner of her room and grabbed her plainest housedress. Whether Mama liked it or not, Savannah had every intention of helping nurse Wyatt back to health.

Using what water was left in the basin on her bureau, she cleaned up the best she could, got dressed, and hurried back to the kitchen. The moment she arrived, Mama tossed a towel across certain parts of Wyatt's anatomy.

"Avert your eyes!"

"Mama, please. I'm no shrinking violet." Although the heat rushing to her face at the sight of Wyatt's strong limbs and chest might just kill her. For her sake, and her mother's, she draped a small blanket over the patient. "There. We're all safe."

Irma giggled. "You white people are the strangest things. The trick is not to look at Mr. Jamison as a handsome man right now. He's a body, something that needs caring for."

Maybe she could look at him that way, but Savannah sure couldn't. She wouldn't see him as anything other than the handsome, viral man he was.

"You. . .think. . .I'm handsome. . .Irma?" Wyatt asked, not opening his eyes.

"I may have jumped the broom with Lincoln, but I'm not blind. Hush, now. We got to stitch you up and it's going to hurt. Miss Savannah, fetch me the medicinal whiskey, then help hold him down."

Heavens to Betsy, she was going to have to touch him. Her gaze met Mama's startled one. Then, Savannah grinned. Mama couldn't say no when Irma needed her help. Oh, how scandalous, how glorious, how utterly naughty. She knew she would be consumed with embarrassment once Wyatt was on his feet, but that was another day.

During all this, Lincoln had remained quiet. His stoic expression belied nothing other than weariness.

"Lincoln, would you fetch the whiskey from the top shelf?" Savannah asked. "I'll put on a pot of coffee. You look as if you desperately need a cup. Then, you sit in that chair over there. We'll fuss over you in a bit."

"I ain't never sat down in a white person's kitchen before."

"Don't be silly. We're all family here." She patted his arm as he passed. "You very well may have saved Wyatt's life."

"If you're finished making my man uncomfortable, Miss Savannah, I need your help. Sit on his legs. Lincoln, you can't rest yet. Hand me the whiskey and hold down his shoulders. Mrs. Worthington, you hand me what I need when I need it." Irma barked orders like an army sergeant.

Mama's eyes widened, but she stepped closer to the black woman. There were a lot of firsts happening in the Worthington household that morning.

"First we pray." Irma led them in a simple prayer for God to guide her hands and heal Wyatt. Then she held out her hand for the whiskey. "Open your mouth, Mr. Jamison."

"You've seen me without clothes, Irma. Call me Wyatt. I don't drink." He opened one eye.

"Open. Your. Mouth."

Savannah giggled as he obeyed. Maybe Irma should be the ranch foreman with the way she handed out orders. If Wyatt could argue with her, then he was going to be just fine. She caught sight of the needle in Irma's hand and grew dizzy. She could not faint! She busied herself with the coffee.

"Child, get back over her." Irma's voice cut through her busyness. "Ain't nobody got time for that. Coffee can wait. Mr. Jamison is losing blood all over the kitchen floor."

Mercy. Savannah leaned on the counter and focused on her breathing.

"Now, Miss Savannah."

She nodded and took a deep breath. She climbed onto the table, got a glimpse of the whiskey being poured over Wyatt's open wounds, and collapsed across his legs. The last thing she heard was Lincoln laughing and saying, "I guess that'll work for holding his legs."

◆ ◆ ◆

Wyatt almost screamed as the whiskey poured over him. He thought he preferred the cat's bites to the fire burning through him. "Stop, please."

"Can't." Irma continued to pour. "Not going to allow any infection, Mr. Jamison."

"I can't move my legs."

"That's because Miss Savannah fainted over them."

"What?" He opened his eyes.

"She'll be fine. Let's get you sewed up. Here." She shoved a leather strap in his mouth. "Should have used this from the beginning."

The woman was going to kill him. He bit down on the strap and groaned as the needle punctured his skin.

Warmth coursed through him at the thought of Savannah caring so much she would faint to see him in pain. Or maybe it was the whiskey. Either way, he hadn't taken her for the fainting kind. Maybe he was going to die. He hated Irma to work so hard on saving him if he was going to die anyway.

Irma hadn't finished stitching the first bite when Wyatt passed out. He woke to find himself on a bed in a room he didn't recognize. A cool sheet covered his body. A body that still didn't have on a stitch of clothing. Why in tarnation had they stripped him? The cougar bit his shoulder and arm, right? He turned his head to see Irma asleep in a chair.

He cleared his throat. "Irma."

Her eyes flew open. "Yes sir. You feverish?"

"I'm a bit hot, but not too bad. I, uh. . .why am I naked?"

"That cat got you in the shoulder, the arm, across the rib cage, and scratched up your thigh real good. It took a while to get you cleaned up."

"Can I have my clothes now? I'd like to speak to Savannah." Lord have mercy, she'd been in the kitchen while they'd worked on him. How was he ever going to face her again? "Never mind. I can't."

"Pshaw. I'll get you some tea and company." She sauntered from the room, muttering about crazy white people.

He must have fallen asleep. The next time he opened his eyes, night had fallen. The only light in the room was a low-burning lamp lighting Savannah's sleeping face.

He lay there, content to watch her, even though his throat burned with thirst. He'd ruined the plan to get a confession out of Morrillton. What had happened with him, anyway? He vaguely remembered a thinly veiled threat. Well, Wyatt wouldn't be lying in bed for long. He'd be back out there protecting the people he cared about, especially the woman who had stolen his heart.

Sighing, he stared at the ceiling. Why was he bothering to contemplate a relationship? He had nothing to offer. Just some half-bright ideas to keep the ranch running. What she really needed was money. He lay there like a trussed-up turkey, unable to do a thing. The realization of what couldn't be weighed on his heart. He would help her get the taxes paid then look for his replacement. Savannah needed a husband. One as good at running a ranch as he was, but one who could offer her financial freedom. He turned his head away from her and went back to sleep.

The next time he woke, Mrs. Worthington sat in the chair. "It's about time," she said. "Soup is growing cold." She shoved a couple of pillows behind his back. "While I feed you, we need to talk."

"All right." He grimaced against the pulling of his stitches as he struggled to sit upright. "I can feed myself. It isn't my right arm that's in a sling."

"Very well." She handed him the tray with a cup of tea and a bowl of soup. "I tasted the tea. It's vile, but Irma swears it will help you, so drink up or she'll have my head. She's a very bossy woman." She pulled the chair closer to the bed.

"This is a delicate subject." She twisted a handkerchief in her hands. "But, since my daughter has seen you without apparel, I feel it necessary to save her reputation by the two of you getting married."

He spit soup down the front of him. "Excuse me? There were no other people there, Mrs. Worthington. Only us and the workers. Who was there to form any opinions?"

"Word gets around. I won't have my daughter sullied." She lifted her chin. "Are you adverse to marrying Savannah, or only to marriage in particular?"

A proposition of this sort was the last thing Wyatt expected to hear upon waking. "This is a lot to throw at a man lying in bed, Mrs. Worthington."

"You are still without apparel, Mr. Jamison. Savannah spent the night in your room!"

"Watching over me as I slept!" Of all the ridiculous—

"Others do not know that." She crossed her arms. "I have tried to do right by my daughter. I will not stand down now."

He shoved the tray to the side, spilling some of the soup. "I've lost my appetite."

"The idea of marrying my Savannah curdles your stomach?"

"No ma'am. She would make any man very lucky to have her as his wife. My reluctance has nothing to do with her personally." He met her steely gaze with one of his own. "I have nothing to offer your daughter."

"Except your name. That alone will keep her reputation intact."

He exhaled heavily. The woman would not listen to reason. "Mrs. Worthington. Please. I plan on leaving the Rocking W as soon as the taxes are paid. I'm not the type of man to stay in one place. I've always compared myself to a tumbleweed, going where the wind blows."

"Balderdash. I had someone look into your background before I hired you. You may have lost everything in the war, but you come from good lineage."

Savannah stepped through the door, face pale, eyes brimming with tears. "You're leaving me?"

Chapter 8

She couldn't believe the words coming out of his mouth. He'd said he would never leave. What kind of man goes back on his word? With a sob, she whirled and fled his room. She wouldn't marry him now if he were the last man on earth.

"Savannah!" His cry followed her down the hall.

She barged through the kitchen and out the back door, letting it slam behind her. Running in the house and slamming doors was something a lady never did, according to Mama. Well, Savannah didn't care. She needed to get away.

"I don't think you should ride in your state of mind." Lincoln stepped around the stall next to where Bullet was stabled.

"I didn't ask for your opinion." She grabbed a bridle.

"Miss Savannah." He gave her a sad look. "That man is hurting. He don't mean nothing by what he said."

"You heard?" How did he beat her here?

"Irma told me. That woman's ears can catch a mouse scurrying across the floor. She hears a lot listening through the back window while she tends the herbs. Mr. Jamison will marry you without hesitation."

"Marry me?" She stared at him. "What do you mean?"

"Ah. You didn't hear the entire conversation." He scuffed the toe of his worn boot in the dirt. "Your Mama is insisting he marry you to save your reputation. Because, well, uh. . ."

"Because he was covered with only a blanket?" Of all the outlandish. . . "I need to speak with her right now before she continues this absurd idea." She marched back to the house, blood boiling. Mama's outdated notions needed to stop before something was done that couldn't be undone.

Ignoring Wyatt, who still sat up in bed rather than lying down as an invalid should, she approached Mama and planted her fists on her hips. "What crazy thing are you trying to do now?"

"I have no idea what you mean." Mama stood and picked up Wyatt's tray. "Now that you are here, the two of you need to talk, and I've work to do."

"I will no longer play nursemaid to this. . .this. . .man!"

"At least now you acknowledge that I'm a man," Wyatt said.

"Hush." She huffed and plopped into the seat Mama had vacated. "I suppose we do have some things to talk over. I won't hold you to your promise to stay and help me. That was said under the emotion of the moment." She stared at a loose thread on her cuff. "I will also not marry you because Mama thinks I saw something. . .improper."

"I have nothing, Savannah." His whispered words brought her head up. "I've lost everything. I can't bring you down to my level."

"If not for you, I'd be in the same situation." Not able to voice the words, she tried to tell him she loved him with her eyes, to implore him to stay. "When will you leave?"

"As soon as your taxes are paid." He looked away, ripping her heart into pieces.

As she sat there, sorrow gave way to anger. How dare he get so close to her only to take it all away? She wanted to thrash him with one of the pillows behind his back. Instead, she clenched her fists and sat while he fell asleep. Once he had, she rested her gaze on his face, clouded with stubble, and dreamed of what might have been.

"Tea?" Irma handed her a cup. "Two sugars, just as you like it."

"Thank you." If only tea could mend a broken heart.

"This is in God's hands, sweetie. Wyatt will survive, and your heart will mend." She leaned closer. "Men are not the sharpest tacks in the box. If he does leave, he'll come running back the moment he realizes what he's up and left behind. Which will be about a mile down the road."

"Will you watch him? I'd like to take a walk. I know Lincoln and Lee are more than capable of running the ranch, but I'd like to make sure the corral is secure and the calves all right."

"I have something better." She pulled a small bell from her pocket and set it on the nightstand. "Your Mama found this in your Pa's study."

They left the room, Irma heading for the kitchen and Savannah for the corrals. Savannah waved at Rose, who stirred a pot of laundry. Since the arrival of the two women, she had less work to do. A good thing, since Wyatt wanted to leave. The full running of the ranch, harvest, selling of goods, would all fall on her shoulders.

She propped a booted foot on the corral and watched the calves frolic beside their mothers. Maybe she could get Wyatt to help move them to a better place before he left. Then, when the time came and the birthing season started again, she'd hire someone new to bring the animals home. Of course, now that they had cattle, they needed to be branded. A task she was not equipped to do. Maybe she could get him to do that, too. After all, taxes weren't due for another three months. They had time.

First off, she needed to arrange the sale of ten acres to their neighbor. She headed to the barn to saddle Bullet. Not long after, she rode east, armed with a rifle and pistol, and hope that Mr. Johansson still wanted the land for hay.

The sun shone through the trees, dappling the trail in front of her. Birds serenaded from oak and pine trees. If not for her heavy heart, the day would be perfect. Pa had always said to rejoice in each day. But what could she find, other than the beauty around her, to rejoice in? Mama wanted to marry her off to a man who only desired to leave at the first opportunity. She glanced heavenward. Irma was right, though. God had everything in control. Savannah would do her best to remember that.

◆ ◆ ◆

Wyatt opened his eyes to an empty room. A cold cup of tea rested on the nightstand next to a bell. He groaned, stretching as far as his stitches would allow, and swung his legs over the side of the bed. No more using the chamber pot or having others wait on him. Other than a mild throbbing in his right thigh, his legs worked fine. He might not be able to work the fields or rope a cow, but he could still supervise while others worked.

Dizziness overcame him. Maybe he wasn't as ready as he thought. One day was obviously not enough to recover from the blood he'd lost. He lay back against the pillows and stared at the ceiling.

God help him, he didn't want to leave the Rocking W. He wanted to stay, marry Savannah, and have a passel of young'uns. If only his father were alive to advise him. He'd most likely box Wyatt's ears, tell him to stop acting like a fool, and go after his girl. He just might, if he could stand up without his head swimming.

What was the worst thing that could happen if he married Savannah? They worked together to keep the ranch afloat? What if she couldn't manage without him? She was a strong, intelligent woman, but a partnership was always better. He had knowledge and experience to offer her. That, and his heart. Would it be enough?

"You're awake." Mrs. Worthington carried a tray into the room. "Beef stew?"

"I am hungry. Thank you."

She set the tray on the nightstand. "I'll set out some clothes so you can at least drape a shirt around you. Irma took a pair of your long underwear and cut off one leg. We'll have you as respectable as possible. Let's get you on your feet."

Heat rose to his neck. "I'll eat, then you send Lincoln or Lee in. They can help me dress." The woman was loco for sure.

"I'm a widowed woman, Mr. Jamison. I've seen all there is to see."

"If it's all the same to you, I'd prefer one of the men." He fixed a stern glance on her. "I appreciate all you've done, but other than bringing me my tray, one of them can now help me."

"Very well." She folded her hands in front of her. "Have you thought more on my proposition?"

"Still thinking."

"Well, don't take too long. She isn't getting any younger." She turned and left him staring after her.

Did he love Savannah enough to put up with her mother? He grinned. Yes, he supposed he did.

By the time he'd finished the stew and coffee, setting all the dirty dishes back on the tray, Lincoln arrived in his room. The man grinned, his teeth startlingly white against his dark skin. "Modest, Mr. Jamison?"

"Shut up and help me get respectable, as Mrs. Worthington says." He reached an arm out to the man who was quickly becoming a dear friend.

Through pain and breathlessness, they managed to get his underwear on and a shirt fastened around his shoulders. "Tell me what's going on. Has Morrillton been back? Any more calves? What about the mares?"

"Slow down, boss." Lincoln glanced at the chair.

"Sit, please."

He did. "Two more calves birthed just fine. Three mares due any day now. No, the banker hasn't been back. That seems suspicious to me."

"I agree." Wyatt rested his head back against the pillows. "How do you feel about going into town and listening around?"

"We aren't welcome there."

Wyatt sighed. "Sorry. Sometimes, I tend to forget such ridiculousness." He gnawed the inside of his cheek. "I guess there's nothing to do but keep an eye out and hope the man gave up."

"Men like him don't give up."

That's what he was afraid of. Anything could happen, and he was as weak as one of those newborn animals outside. "I need to get out of this bed."

"Irma said if I did more than help you get dressed, she'd thrash me. I believe her." Lincoln flashed another grin. "I don't make her mad, not if I'm using my head."

"Wise man." Wyatt shook his head, looking forward to the day a woman bossed him around. A woman other than Mrs. Worthington. "Could you find Savannah and send her to me?"

"Sure thing. I saw her out by the corral a while ago." He hurried from the room, taking the tray with him.

Wyatt smiled. Maybe lying in bed, stitched up and hurting, wasn't the way most men proposed to a woman, but he didn't want to wait until he was back on his feet. He needed to reassure her, right now, that he'd decided he was going to keep his earlier promise and not go anywhere she wasn't.

Lincoln returned within minutes. "Her horse is gone. Tracks show she headed east."

"To sell ten acres." He'd speak with her when she returned. Closing his eyes, he slept.

When he opened his eyes again, night had fallen. He reached for the bell beside his bed and rang for someone to come.

Irma, her arm full of folded linens, stopped in his doorway. "You hungry? Want Lincoln to take you to the privy?"

"No, I'd like to speak to Savannah, please." Time was wasting. He'd waited long enough to tell her how he felt.

"She ain't here."

"What do you mean? She left hours ago."

"Yes sir, and her mama is worried. Lee went looking for her."

Wyatt's blood ran cold. Any number of things could have prevented Savannah from returning home. Her horse could have thrown her or a shoe. She could have met up with a bear or cougar. He shuddered, knowing her chances of coming out of such an encounter alive. "Get me Lincoln." He swung his legs over the side of the bed.

"I's here. A deaf man could hear you hollering from the barn."

"Get me up and on my horse."

With Lincoln's help, he shuffled toward the barn, turning at the sound of galloping hoofbeats. The marshal had arrived. From the other direction came Savannah's riderless horse.

Chapter 9

Savannah glared at Mr. Morrillton's back and pulled against the restraints keeping her in the back of the wagon. If she could get free, she'd bound out and race for home. It was a good thing for the snake that her hands were tied. If she were free, she'd throttle him!

"Settle down back there. You're upsetting my horse."

"Your horse? What about my Bullet?"

"He's heading for home as we speak with a nice little message tacked to his saddle." His shoulders shook as he chuckled. "I told you that one way or the other I was getting that ranch."

"Why mine?"

"You know as well as I do, Miss Worthington, that it's easier to take something from a woman than it is three brothers. The Mason boys would just as soon shoot me as look at me. I need your land to expand."

"Here's an idea." Was that a loosening of her knots? "Sell out and move somewhere else and buy a larger parcel."

"This is my home. I was born and raised here." He glanced over his shoulder. "Why don't you sell to me and follow your own advice? I'll pay just under the ranch's value."

"Go chew on your hat." She slammed back against the backboard, regretting her childish action immediately.

A bruise would form from where she'd banged against a sharp piece of wood not sitting flush. Wait. Not wood. She smiled and began the arduous work of rubbing the rope against the protruding nail. She winced as the nail scraped her wrist.

The wagon stopped in a clearing in the center of thick pine trees. Mr. Morrillton set the brake on the wagon and jumped to the ground. "Now, we wait for the ransom."

She stopped sawing the rope. "The deed to my ranch, I presume. I'm the only one capable of giving you that."

He grinned, the expression sending shivers down her back that had nothing to do with the setting sun. "I have that all planned. Don't worry your pretty little head about it." He grabbed her ankles and yanked her toward him.

Once her feet were on the ground, he all but dragged her to a tree. As he tied her to it, he made a clicking sound with his teeth. "I see you were trying to free yourself. Silly girl. All you've done is cause your wrist to bleed."

She kicked out at him, feeling great satisfaction as he grunted when she connected with his shin.

"There goes your biscuit." He turned and set to work building a fire. Once he had a flame going, he laid a pistol next to him and sat staring into the flames.

"May I at least have a drink of water?" Her stomach rumbled at the thought of the biscuit. "You don't want a dead hostage, do you?"

"You won't die with one day of no water." He didn't turn to look at her.

Savannah sighed. Who would come for her? Lincoln, perhaps. Wyatt was bedridden and wouldn't have the strength. Otherwise, if he loved her, as she had hoped he was beginning to, she doubted anything on earth would keep him away. Now, she'd have to rely on a couple of hired hands afraid to pull the trigger on a white man.

She rested her head against the rough bark of the tree. Her situation seemed bleak. Well, Savannah Worthington wasn't one to lie down without a fight. Working the binding around her wrists against the tree, she ignored the pain in her shoulders. Eventually, she'd free herself. Persistence was the key. Then she'd head into town and demand the sheriff do something. Kidnapping was not something to be ignored. She glared at her captor's back.

She thought more about what could have been with Wyatt. Foolish man. She didn't care whether he had money or a bloodline that went back to the Mayflower. What mattered was that he loved God, loved the ranch, and loved her. She blinked away tears, realizing he didn't love the third on her list of requirements.

But as long as there was breath in her body, there was hope. She would declare her love for him as soon as she saw his face. What happened then was up to Wyatt and God.

"You'll go blind staring at the fire like that." Not that she cared one way or the other, but the silence was deafening.

"I'm thinking."

Hmm. She wouldn't have thought him capable of it. If he was, he wouldn't have chosen to take the path of kidnapping. "What about?"

"How this is all going to turn out and how rich I'll be. You should have followed through with letting that cowboy leave. Then we could have wed and I'd have what I wanted."

Savannah shuddered. Being locked into a marriage with such a despicable man was the worst fate imaginable. "If you untie me, we can discuss this in a more civilized manner. I had no control over Mr. Jamison being attacked by a cougar and having to return to the ranch. We can go to town, get married, and tell everyone we eloped and that the ransom note was nothing more than a joke." Plus, it would provide her with the opportunity to escape.

"It's too late for that, Miss Worthington." He narrowed his eyes over his shoulder. "You told me to chew on my hat. I can't marry someone so unladylike. Not to mention the way you ride that horse of yours. Scandalous. I'm a very important man in town."

Maybe to himself. If she were to take a poll, she doubted very much that others shared the same view. She returned to working on her bindings. They seemed to be loosening, sending hope surging through her tired arms. She was so thirsty. So hungry. How could the man be so cruel to a woman? Oh, when she freed herself. . . .

◆ ◆ ◆

If that man hurt Savannah, he'd feel the fullness of Wyatt's wrath. *Please, God, don't let Savannah open her mouth and make the man angry.* He smiled, knowing she had a special talent for speaking her thoughts.

"This man sure isn't trying to hide his tracks." Larry West, Wyatt's marshal friend, pointed to a set of wagon tracks. "Is he really dumb enough to think you'd ride up with the deed in hand and give it to him without a fight?"

"No. That's a cover-up for something else." Wyatt rotated his shoulder, careful not to pull too hard on his stitches. He could only pray he'd have the strength to save Savannah once they found her. The energy spurred by fear and anger was quickly ebbing away to be replaced by exhaustion. "I think he's going to use me to get Savannah to turn over the deed."

"Would she?"

Wyatt shook his head, sliding a pistol into his sling. "She's the type to die for her friends." If his suspicions were correct, and the pained look in her eyes when she heard he was leaving was one of spurned love, it increased the risk she would take to keep him safe. If she didn't give him a boot in the rear. No, Morrillton would use Wyatt as an incentive for Savannah to hand over the deed without violence. Then. . . Wyatt had no idea what the man intended.

"We need to sneak up on the man and take him down before he has the opportunity to act."

Things were going to get messy. Wyatt closed his eyes and prayed for safety, wisdom, and a favorable outcome.

Larry held up his hand then pointed to the trees ahead of them. This was it. The moment of truth.

Wyatt slid from his horse, grunting as the impact jarred his wounds. He grabbed his rifle from the scabbard and checked the pistol in his sling. They were as ready as they could be.

They made their way slowly through the trees, stopping at a thick clump of prickly evergreen bushes. Through the branches, Wyatt spotted Savannah tied to a tree and Morrillton outlined by the fire's glow. Wyatt squatted. A twig snapped under his boot.

Morrillton jumped to Savannah's side and aimed a pistol at her head. "Come on out, Mr. Jamison. I'd hate to ruin this pretty gal's face."

Wyatt closed his eyes at his carelessness then stood and stepped into the clearing. "Don't harm her."

"Leave, Wyatt. I have this under control," Savannah said.

"It doesn't look like it from here, dearest." In fact, she looked as if she was in pain, and dirt covered her clothes.

"Did you bring the deed, Mr. Jamison?" Morrillton cocked his head.

"I did."

Morrillton took a knife from a sheath on his belt and cut the ropes binding Savannah then hauled her to her feet. "Hand it to the little lady, real careful like, after you set your gun on the ground where you stand."

Wyatt laid down his rifle and pulled a folded sheet of yellowed paper from his pocket. It wasn't the deed. There'd been no time to search for the real thing. Moving slowly, he handed the paper to Savannah, narrowing his eyes at the sight of blood on her wrists.

She glanced at the paper, not batting an eye. "Let him go now. There's no need to kill him."

Kill him? Wyatt narrowed his eyes. So it was intended to be a trap.

"I can't do that," Morrillton said. "Not until you sign the paper over to me. If you don't, I shoot him where he stands. You sign, and we all walk away from here."

The obstinate look on her face told Wyatt she had no intention of carrying the charade of compliance much further. She glanced over his shoulder toward the trees. Smart girl. She knew he wouldn't have come alone.

"I'll tell everyone that I signed under duress," she said. "It will never hold up in court."

"Shall I shoot him in the leg first?" Morrillton rapped the barrel of the gun on her shoulder.

Wyatt stepped forward at her cry, halting when the gun swung his way. He put his good hand up.

"I don't see why you care for this woman, Mr. Jamison. She is a trial, for sure."

"I happen to love her," Wyatt replied.

"I love you, too." Tears streamed down Savannah's face. "I wanted to tell you the moment I saw you."

"How touching." Morrillton fired at Wyatt's feet. "That's a warning. There's a pen and ink in my saddlebags. Be a good girl and fetch them for me." He gave Savannah a shove.

Her eyes glittered with hate in the firelight, but she did as he instructed. She returned, clutching the pen in one hand, the bottle of ink in another. "Where shall I sign?"

"Use that rock over there." He motioned with his head.

She turned as if to obey then whirled back and plunged the pen into his hand.

Morrillton howled. His gun went off, the bullet whizzing past Wyatt's head.

Wyatt pulled the pistol he'd shoved into his sling free and fired, taking the man in the leg as Larry bolted from the bushes. The marshal tackled the banker to the ground and snapped a pair of handcuffs over his wrists.

"Let's see the sheriff help you now," Larry said, yanking the man up. "I heard every threat you made to these people. You, sir, are going to jail for a very long time." He pushed Morrillton toward his horse. The man stumbled, almost falling to his knees.

Wyatt turned and grinned at Savannah. "Did you mean it? When you said you loved me?"

She ran to him and threw her arms around his neck. "I'll tell you every morning and every night until the day I die."

"Then I reckon we need to let your mother know there will be a wedding after all."

"When?"

"As soon as I'm able to put both arms around you."

She pouted. "So long."

He laughed. "Come on, Miss Impatient. Let's go home." How sweet those words. He had a home, a family, a woman who loved him. How stupid he had been to contemplate leaving. No force on heaven or earth could get him to leave now.

"You might have to hold me on my horse," he said. "I'm that tired."

"I'll hold you forever, Mr. Jamison."

Chapter 10

Savannah stared at the cream-colored gown her mother held up. "That will never fit me." Mama was more buxom, wider in the hips. While Savannah wasn't rail thin, she didn't possess her mother's curves.

"We'll alter it, add a bit of new lace. It will be the perfect wedding dress." Mama gave a smug smile. "Who knew that my proposition to save your reputation would end with the two of you falling in love. Divine providence!"

Savannah grinned. If Mama wanted to believe she had a hand in her and Wyatt falling in love, then so be it. She wasn't too far off. If she hadn't hired Wyatt, Savannah would be selling the ranch and the two of them would be making a new start somewhere else. As it was, the taxes were paid, to a new—and honest—banker. She had no doubts that, with Wyatt beside her, the taxes would be paid every year.

It had been a trial for sure, but God worked it for good. She fingered the yellowed lace on the sleeve of the gown. "It will be perfect, Mama. I want to get married here, at the ranch, so Irma and the others can attend."

"People will talk."

"I don't care."

Mama gave a nod, then another. "You know. . .I don't care either. Our new friends have been a godsend. It's wonderful to live as we were meant to and to have someone to converse with when you're out doing unladylike activities."

Savannah had witnessed another miracle. The softening of her mother's heart and the opening of her mind. A bright future loomed before them all.

"Of course," Mama added, making Savannah rethink her new views on Mama's thoughts, "once you're married, Wyatt can take over the outside chores completely, leaving you to do as a lady should."

"I fully intend this marriage to be a partnership in all aspects, Mama. I cannot sit and sew all day or sip tea. I'd be committed to an asylum within six months." She retrieved a pair of scissors from Mama's sewing basket. "Shall I start snipping?"

"Not on your life." Mama clutched the dress to her chest. "You'll ruin it. Leave the sewing to me." Her look clearly said that if Savannah spent more time at the sewing machine, she could be trusted with such important matters.

"I'm going to check on the new foal." Savannah left and headed to the barn where Bullet was now a daddy. The little red baby with black feet looked just like his papa.

"I hope to be a mama someday," she said, kneeling next to the wobbly legged foal. "A little boy who looks just like his pa, as you do."

"I'm hoping for a girl that looks like her mama." Wyatt peered over the top of the stall, his folded arms resting on the edge.

"Your sling is gone." Savannah grinned. "We can get married."

"This instant, if you want." He winked.

She couldn't believe she was contemplating it. "No, Mama is looking forward to inviting the entire church. She has agreed to let us hold the ceremony here."

"That's a big step for her. How do folks spread the word around these parts?"

She laughed, pushing to her feet. "Tell one person and it will spread like wildfire. I need a few things from the mercantile. I'll tell a couple of loose-lipped people. We'll have quite the crowd."

"I'll ride with you and visit the preacher." He stepped around the wall and drew her into his arms. "I can't wait for Saturday."

"So, it's Saturday?" Her heart leaped.

"And not a day longer. I want to attend church on Sunday as husband and wife."

"Let's take the wagon. I know Mama will have a list. It's been awhile since we've been able to stock the pantry, and with guests coming—" The ladies of the church would be more than happy to provide the food, but Mama insisted on making a cake.

Hand in hand, they strolled back to the house. Savannah couldn't imagine life being any better. She glanced at the cabins where Lincoln's and Lee's little ones played. Someday, her children would play right alongside them.

"I'm glad I didn't fight Mama and race Bullet."

"Why?" Wyatt glanced down at her. "You would have won."

She shrugged. "What if I had fallen? I could have been killed." She nestled against him. "Then I wouldn't be marrying you."

"I didn't think you were prone to worrying."

"I'm not, but I am good at looking backward and seeing what might have happened." She laughed.

After she retrieved the list of items Mama needed, Wyatt helped Savannah into the wagon. With the flick of the reins, he sent them toward town.

She glanced at his serious expression. "What's wrong?"

"You aren't the only one thinking backward today. When I think of what could have happened with Morrillton—" He cleared his throat.

She put her hand on his arm. "You rescued me. Even injured, you came."

A slow smile spread across his face. "I think you would have managed."

"Oh, definitely, but it's always nice to know someone will come for you even when they're severely injured."

He grasped her hand. "Always. Just please try to stay out of trouble. I'd like us to grow old together, sitting on those rockers on the porch."

"No guarantees, but I'll do my best." She gave his hand a squeeze. Growing old with him sounded wonderful.

He dropped her off at the mercantile with the promise to return in half an hour. Smiling, warmed with love, Savannah pushed open the door. "Good afternoon, Mrs. Warren."

"Savannah!" The portly woman bustled around the counter. "How are you after your ordeal?"

"Just fine. I'm marrying Mr. Jamison on Saturday. Will you spread the word? The ceremony will be at the ranch."

"You bet I will." She wiggled her fingers. "Let me have your list while you go browse the ready-mades and see what you want for a gift."

Savannah made a beeline for the children's shoes. "I need nine pairs of these, and I'm willing to pay for them."

"For your workers?"

She turned at the woman's bitter tone. "No, for their children." She fixed a stern look on the woman. "They can't help the color of their skin, no more than we can. If it bothers you, I can order through the mail."

"No, I'm sorry. You know I lost my son and husband in that war."

"And I lost a brother."

"You're a good girl, Savannah. The rest of us can learn from you. Take the shoes. They're on the house, my first step toward forgiveness."

"Oh, Mrs. Warren." Savannah rushed over and pulled the woman into a hug. "So much death, so much hatred. But, together, we can help change people's minds, don't you think?"

The older woman sniffed. "Yes. Now let me fill this order so you can get married."

Married. What a wonderful word.

◆ ◆ ◆

Saturday dawned bright and sunny. Warm for the beginning of fall, but the day wouldn't be unbearable under the oak trees where Lincoln and Lee set up benches for the guests to sit.

"Get away from the window," Mama scolded. "Wyatt will see you."

"I'm not in my wedding gown yet."

"Even worse. You're in your underclothes."

Savannah sighed and let the drapes fall into place. "The dress is beautiful, Mama." Cream-colored lace cascaded from the sleeves and high collar. A brooch winked from the neckline. "I'll look like royalty."

"I'm pleased to see you wearing the same dress I married your pa in. It's as if he is here with us."

"He isn't the only one here with you."

Savannah gasped and turned. "Luke!" She threw her arms around her brother, who looked every bit the stranger in clothes that fell from his too thin frame, and a face thick with a dark beard. "Oh, Luke." Tears poured down her cheeks.

"I came just in time to give you away." His arms wrapped around her.

"Where were you?" Mama asked, a hand clutched to her chest. "We feared you dead."

"A prisoner for a while. Then I wandered a bit, letting go of ghosts." He glanced around the room. "It's good to be back."

"Irma!" Mama yelled. "My boy is home. He needs a shave."

"I didn't come alone. Hold on." Luke ducked out of the room and returned with a young black man. "I spotted a poster looking for this boy. I ran across him in my travels. Mama, Savannah, this is—"

"Abraham?" Irma dropped the porcelain bowl of water. It shattered on the floor seconds before she crumbled.

Savannah hefted the hem of her dress and raced from the house and into the bunkhouse. Wyatt turned from the washstand. "What is it?"

"You found him." She smiled through her tears. "You found Lincoln and Irma's son."

"Well, Luke did, actually." He grinned through his shaving cream. "You look beautiful, by the way."

"My brother is home, too. Oh, Wyatt, this day is perfect."

"I'll meet them after we're wed. Go on back to the house before your mother has a conniption."

Savannah nodded and, careful to keep her dress from trailing in the dirt, stepped into the yard. She glanced toward heaven. "Thank You, God. I know You can't send Pa back to us, but I hope he is watching from his heavenly home and that he is proud of me."

She returned to the parlor where Irma and Lincoln cried over their son and Mama carefully shaved the beard from Luke's face. Savannah hovered in the door, taking in God's goodness in fulfilling His promises. From outside came the sound of buggies arriving and the chatter of voices ready to celebrate.

"You let Wyatt see you, didn't you?" Mama frowned.

"I had to thank him for reuniting a family. Besides, no bad luck can come from such a perfect day."

Once Luke looked himself, albeit a lot skinnier and dressed in the only suit of Pa's still hanging in the closet, he crooked his arm. "Ready, little sister?"

"I am, big brother." She slipped her arm in his. "I can't wait for you to meet Wyatt. You'll love him."

"Since you do, I already do. It takes a special man to win your heart and keep this ranch afloat. Mama told me what he's done with the cattle and horses. He sounds like a good man."

"He is." She beamed up at him. "With the three of us running this place, we can't fail."

They stepped onto the porch. It seemed as if the entire town was seated on the benches provided. Lincoln and the others grinned from the shade of a tree. On the feet of the workers' children were new, shiny shoes.

Everyone Savannah cared about, everyone that helped make this moment possible, was here. She knew without a doubt that Pa smiled down from heaven.

From the front of the crowd, Wyatt, resplendent in a gray suit, grinned in her direction. Savannah's joy overflowed. With one more glance at her brother, she took her first step toward her groom.

Luke placed her hand in Wyatt's. "Take care of her, sir."

"With my life." Wyatt's eyes shimmered. "She's the most precious thing I have."

Together, they turned to face the preacher. "Dearly Beloved. . ."

Savannah barely heard the rest of the preacher's words, so engrossed was she on her groom. She responded when prompted, laughed when one of the men cheered, and cried tears of joy when they were pronounced man and wife.

"You may kiss your bride," the preacher said.

Wyatt dipped her over his arm and laid a heated kiss on her lips. More cheers arose. When Savannah straightened, she knew her face had to be as red as an apple.

"I introduce to you, Mr. and Mrs. Wyatt Jamison."

They'd come through so much. One trial after another strove to keep Savannah and Wyatt apart, not to mention the loss of the ranch. But, together, with God's grace, they'd come out the other side stronger than before.

Savannah slipped her hand into her husband's and smiled. She couldn't wait to see what the future held.

Cynthia Hickey grew up in a family of storytellers and moved around the country a lot as an army brat. Her desire is to write about real but flawed characters in a wholesome way that her seven children and five grandchildren can all be proud of. She and her husband live in Arizona where Cynthia is a full-time writer.

A Family Inheritance

by Lisa Karon Richardson

Chapter 1

San Francisco, California
May, 1883

Anne Shepherd nibbled on the tip of one silk-gloved finger as she craned to see the length of the railroad track.

"You're going to chew clean through that glove." Lottie, her maid, stood next to her on the platform.

"Then I'll buy a dozen more."

"But none of those gloves will be here to help you make a good impression on your aunt."

"Mm." This indisputable logic swayed Anne where anything flimsier would have failed. She resorted to twisting her fingers together instead. "What is taking so long? The train should have been here ages ago."

"It's exactly two minutes late."

"I guess you have a point." Anne's fingers drifted to her mouth again and she jerked them away. "I was hoping it would be early."

"Which is why we've been waiting for near on an hour." Lottie looked past Anne's shoulder. "Wait. Is that steam from the engine?"

Anne held her hands up in surrender. "I understand. I'm being ridiculous. Wishing for the train won't make it come any faster."

"No, really." Lottie turned her around. "I think that plume of smoke is from the train."

Anne gasped. "I think you're right." She glanced in both directions to make sure no potentially disapproving officials were nearby then hopped off the platform and put a hand to the track. The metal vibrated beneath her fingers. "It's coming." She held up her hand and with Lottie's help scrambled back up on the platform. "Oh, feathers. I didn't think that through. Did I get anything on my dress?" She fluffed her skirts, trying to inspect the beautifully rich damask of claret red for spots. It would be just like her...

"Spin."

Anne obediently made a slow turn.

"No. Looks just fine." Lottie gave a critical squint at Anne's hair and tucked back one of the flyaway auburn strands. She frowned and gave Anne's jaunty little hat a tug.

Anne yelped. "For heaven's sake, it's pinned in place."

"I wanted to make sure."

Anne smoothed down her skirt and found to her astonishment that her hands were trembling. Other than shivering with cold, which didn't count, she didn't think she'd ever trembled before. "I do look all right?"

"That's your nicest dress. And you in it is the prettiest thing I've ever seen."

"Thanks, Lottie." Anne squeezed her hand.

The rumble of the train was audible now, and its low tidal swell was pierced by a scream from the steam whistle. Intermittent squeals came from the brakes as the train began to slow for its entrance to the station. Steam billowed around its wheels. At last the great metal bully shouldered its way alongside the platform.

Anne took a few running steps alongside it. Then, clasping her hands, she waited more decorously for it to come to a full stop. The porter slid a step alongside the door and passengers began to disembark. A pair of prim Mormon ladies in plain cotton dresses were followed by a cross-looking old man with impressive muttonchop whiskers. Behind them an exceptionally tall fellow with dark, slightly curly hair and moderate sideburns emerged. One leg was wrapped in a mass of bandages, and he looked weary enough to drop. Immediately after he hobbled his way off the train he reached back to help the passenger who had been waiting somewhat less than patiently for him to descend the stairs. This was an older lady with streaks of steel gray in her tightly reined hair. She was dressed head to toe in black that seemed not so much to absorb light, as repel it. On second glance this lady was younger than she first appeared, and Anne chalked them up to a mother and son.

She watched eagerly as the passengers continued to spill from the train. But the flood soon became a trickle, and at last a uniformed conductor stepped off the train, patting his belly in search of his watch chain. Fumbling, he pulled out the fob and tapped it.

Anne approached him. "Isn't there anyone else on board?"

"Nope. Everyone's off."

"That can't be. My aunt was supposed to be on this train. It was all confirmed."

"Don't know what to tell you. There ain't any old ladies hiding back there. Something must have stopped her making the train."

Brow furrowed, Anne turned away. "I sure hope nothing awful has happened."

Lottie touched her arm and then jerked her chin toward the mother and son, who were the only passengers remaining on the platform. They were looking about them as if waiting for someone, though studiously ignoring Anne and Lottie. "Maybe that's her."

Turning, Anne gave her skirt's short train a kick out of the way and marched over to them. "Excuse me, folks. I'm looking for Irene Carver. Is that you, ma'am? Or maybe did you meet her on the train?"

The woman looked horrified and raised a lorgnette to her eyes. She peered at Anne through the little slivers of glass like she was examining something repulsive under a magnifying lens. "Who might you be, young woman?"

"I'm Anne Shepherd. I'm her niece."

"That's impossible." The woman's lips were twisted as if she smelled something rotten.

Anne straightened her spine. "Why would I make it up? Are you Mrs. Carver?"

There was a flicker in the woman's eye.

"You are, aren't you?" Anne pressed. "I know I don't favor my father much." She moved in to embrace her aunt. The woman wasn't very friendly, but this must all be very strange for her. Moving all the way across the country could make anyone cranky. Anne was determined to make allowances.

The woman stood stiffly, responding to the hug with a bare raising of her arms.

"And that must make you my cousin." Anne moved to embrace the young man who had accompanied her aunt. He smelled nice. A little bit of the coal smoke from the train, but also cloves and a touch of hair tonic and clean linen. He felt nice, too. Warm and solid, and he was less shy than her aunt about returning the embrace.

"Move away from him at once. That is not your cousin."

"Oh." Anne pulled away, cheeks stinging. She looked again at the older woman. "You are. . . ?"

"Yes." The woman sighed. "I'm Irene Carver, and this is Perseus Jackson Wilberforce the Second. He is the son of family friends and graciously accompanied me."

Despite his cane, Mr. Wilberforce swept off his hat and managed a creditable bow. His movements were lithe, and Anne surmised that when he wasn't injured he was probably fairly athletic.

"I prefer Jack." His voice was an undertone. Anne was pretty sure only she could hear him.

Anne extended her hand. "Nice to meet you. I'm sure sorry I grabbed hold of you."

"Don't give it a second thought, Miss Shepherd. I've never been more pleasantly attacked." His warm smile as he spoke took any possible sting from the words.

Anne chortled. "You're a good sport about it anyway."

"Miss Shepherd." Mrs. Carver's imperious tone froze the humor of the situation. "Am I correct in believing that you are wearing a ball gown?"

"Yes. Isn't it pretty? I wanted to wear my nicest dress to welcome you to town. I figured if there's anything worth celebrating, it's finding family when you thought you were alone."

Her aunt started to speak, but Mr. Wilberforce cut across whatever it was she might have said. "That is a lovely sentiment and very kind of you." He glanced at his companion, who was turning a vivid shade of pink. "I'm afraid Mrs. Carver is exhausted from her travels. Can we get her someplace she might lie down and refresh herself?"

"Of course." Anne was instantly remorseful for keeping them both standing and waiting so long. "I've got the carriage waiting."

◆ ◆ ◆

Jack peered at the modern city sprawling around them as they left the railroad depot on Market Street. Miss Shepherd's carriage was luxuriously appointed, and the city around them was nothing like the shantytown he'd expected. It looked as prosperous and permanent as any of the cities out east. More so than some. He grimaced at the well-tended shop windows and bustling businessmen. There was nothing remotely wild about this west.

It looked like he'd have to head up into Alaska territory to find real, untouched wilderness. Just as soon as his foot was healed he would figure out the best way to get there. One thing was for certain, there was no way he was returning to hidebound Boston. This was his chance, and he was grabbing hold of it.

The streets of San Francisco seemed to be made of nothing but hills, and the carriage was once more climbing at a grade that made Jack's calves ache just looking at it. The homes were growing larger and larger until they came to a neighborhood of great sprawling palaces that shouted their wealth to passersby.

This most certainly was a departure from Boston, where wealth hid itself behind a pretense of genteel shabbiness. This flamboyance had an air about it, and he began to suspect that Miss Shepherd's scarlet-and-gold ball gown was more fitting to this place and these people than Mrs. Carver's black. He glanced at his family's formidable neighbor and knew without a doubt that she was having no such reflections. The set expression on her face made it clear that she would make every effort to bring this city, and most especially Miss Shepherd, to heel.

In the meantime, Miss Shepherd was chattily pointing out features of the city and trying to make herself agreeable. She was appealing, with auburn hair that seemed determined to caress her face, pale blue-gray eyes, and a smattering of freckles over apple cheeks. It was difficult to imagine that after her father's death, this slip of a girl had single-handedly worked his claim and uncovered one of the biggest lodes in California. Not only that, but she had been managing her own affairs since then. Beneath the sunny smile, she must have a spine of steel.

The carriage paused in front of an enormous turreted palace. He was still trying to absorb the ostentation when the carriage turned into the drive. He counted at least five stories if one included the tallest central tower. A glass-domed greenhouse was affixed to one side of the house. Great windows and slender columns proliferated. Of course this would be Miss Shepherd's house—blindingly new and obvious, yet charming in its eccentricity, with an open, welcoming air. It was perfect.

The driver pulled up smartly and the front door of the house was immediately flung open. A neat row of uniformed maids paraded out followed by a uniformed footman and finally an Asian man dressed in a frock coat. The staff lined up on the steps, hands clasped behind their backs. The coachman opened the carriage door and handed down Mrs. Carver then Miss Shepherd.

Miss Shepherd waited politely for Jack to extract himself from the vehicle. Then she linked her arm through her aunt's. Jack could see the older woman stiffen, but Miss Shepherd seemed not to notice. She walked her aunt along the line of waiting staff members, introducing each one. Mrs. Carver seemed to be making an effort to be gracious. She indulged each person with a regal nod.

Having run the gauntlet, Miss Shepherd conducted them inside. Used as he was to the restraint of Boston, Jack nearly choked as they entered. The front door opened on a central atrium that soared all the way to the roof. This central area was lined by balconies with doors leading off to various rooms. Dark, polished wood was carved into banisters and posts and columns. The floor beneath their feet was of gleaming marble, dotted by gorgeous Turkish carpets in vivid reds, golds, and blues.

"Refreshments in the parlor first, then I believe Mrs. Carver would like to rest." Miss Shepherd spoke to the Asian man, who Jack had to assume was her butler. She turned inquisitively to Mrs. Carver. "Perhaps you'd like to have a bath drawn as well?"

"No." The ring of finality in the woman's tone made it sound as if she never intended to bathe again.

Miss Shepherd turned her gaze to Jack. "And you, Mr. Wilberforce? Would you care to have a bath?"

Practically salivating at the thought of being free from grit and the smell of smoke, Jack was grateful for her consideration. "You have no idea how welcome that would be, Miss Shepherd."

She offered a winsome smile as she ushered them into an opulent parlor fitted out with every modern convenience. "Oh, believe me, Mr. Wilberforce, I've come in off a long trail quite a few times. There's nothing like a warm bath to make a body feel human again."

Mrs. Carver cleared her throat loudly.

Miss Shepherd put a hand on the older woman's back and ushered her to a chair. "Goodness, you sound dreadful. Let me go check on rushing that tea along for you."

She swept from the room, and Mrs. Carver lay back in her chair and pulled a handkerchief from her sleeve, waving it before her face as if she felt faint.

Jack had seen a number of these spells on the long train journey, but he tried to remain kind. "Are you well, Mrs. Carver? I'm sure we can call in a doctor if need be."

"It's this girl. This dreadful, vulgar girl. She doesn't have the first notion of proper behavior." She lowered her voice and leaned forward. "When I saw her on the platform wearing that—that getup, I thought she must be a woman of. . ." She couldn't seem to bring herself to say it. "I thought she was not as she should be."

Jack refrained from saying what came to mind.

Mrs. Carver continued to fan herself weakly. "I've never seen such an ostentatious display as this house. It's grotesque. And did you see? I think her butler is Chinese."

"Oh, he is." Miss Shepherd's voice was a silvery rush. "Bao Chang is wonderful. He takes care of simply everything around the house. I swear I don't lift a finger. His wife, Mei Lin, is my cook." She settled herself on a settee across from her aunt. "That woman knows her way around noodles. She has opened my eyes to a whole new way of eating."

"You have a Chinese cook?" Mrs. Carver sounded as if she hoped she had heard incorrectly.

"Sure enough do. You are in for a treat."

Bao Chang entered at that moment with a tray laden with tea things.

"Bao Chang, I've been talking you up to my aunt."

"Miss is too kind." His voice was quiet, the accent very slight. He placed the tray at Miss Shepherd's right hand and gave a bow before slipping out of the room again.

Miss Shepherd poured and offered a selection of cakes and savories that looked good to Jack, Chinese cook or no. He piled his plate high and ate his fill, though Mrs. Carver refused everything but the tea itself.

Jack felt it incumbent upon himself to keep the conversation going. It wasn't as difficult as it might have been. Miss Shepherd was quite willing to be pleased and interested, unlike her aunt, who seemed determined to find fault with everything.

Poor Miss Shepherd, she had no idea what her generous impulse to bring her widowed aunt to live with her would cost.

Chapter 2

Silently, Anne sat and scraped butter on her toast. She reached for the little bowl of strawberry jelly then decided against it. Three days with Mrs. Carver had left her quivering like that poor jelly. Nothing she did was quite right: her manner was too frivolous, her dresses were too showy, her home too gaudy, and her cook too Chinese.

Anne had done everything she could think of to welcome the older woman to San Francisco, but she was out of ideas and almost out of patience. Having invited Mrs. Carver to come live with her, however, she could hardly pitch her into the street after less than a week.

As if Anne's musings had summoned her, Mrs. Carver sailed into the room. As usual, she was kitted out in stiff black bombazine. She passed a critical eye over Anne's far livelier dress of persimmon-colored silk done up with bows of sea-foam green. Anne immediately corrected her posture and removed her left hand from the table to lie primly in her lap.

"Good morning, Mrs. Carver. I hope you slept well." Always Mrs. Carver, never Aunt or Aunt Carver. The older woman had made it very clear that one ought to be invited before using such titles.

Mrs. Carver surveyed the selection of food on the buffet. "How anyone can get a solid night's sleep with the sound of those dreadful foghorns blaring away at all hours, I'll never know."

"I've always liked the foghorns. They sound so melancholy and sort of romantic to me." Mrs. Carver's back stiffened and Anne hastened to amend her comment. "Lord willing, you'll grow used to the sound and maybe even grow fond of it one day, too."

"Yes, well. We'll see about that." Mrs. Carver claimed a seat at the table and set down a plate graced by a single slice of toast and one slice of bacon.

"If you'll tell me what sort of food you prefer, I'll be pleased as Punch to provide it for you."

"You needn't concern yourself. I wouldn't want to put anyone out on my account."

Mr. Wilberforce tromped in with his cane, sparing Anne the necessity of a reply. She greeted him enthusiastically, and he gamely joined in with sunny morning chatter. It seemed to Anne that he made an effort to be pleasant in direct proportion to her aunt's grumpiness. By the time he took his seat, his plate was piled high with pancakes, sausages, bacon, and a mound of fluffy scrambled eggs.

Anne passed him a jug of warmed maple syrup.

Mrs. Carver cleared her throat. "Do you know anyone in this city?"

"I know a lot of people."

"People worth knowing, I mean." Mrs. Carver pinched her lips together in a way that made it clear she was wondering why she bothered. "It is customary that a relative would take a newcomer visiting when she arrives and make the appropriate introductions."

"Oh." Anne's breakfast felt like ashes in her throat. "I don't—"

Her aunt sighed. She looked at the toast she held poised delicately between two fingers, put it back down, then pushed away from the table. "I will be resting in my room for a while."

Mr. Wilberforce scrambled to stand as she left.

Anne let her own piece of toast drop back on her plate. She stared at the eggs congealing on her plate for a long moment. Things could not go on like this. "Mr. Wilberforce?"

He laid aside the newspaper he had reached for. "Yes, Miss Shepherd?"

"My aunt thinks I'm vulgar and cheap and. . .and ignorant."

"Miss Shepherd, I don't think—"

She raised a hand. "I'd just as soon call a spade a spade. I grew up in mining and logging camps. I can climb trees, catch my own food, even make my own shelter in the woods if I need to, but I don't know much about the world you and she come from. While you're here, would you teach me how to be a more proper lady? The etiquette and stuff that she sets so much store by."

Mr. Wilberforce cocked his head at her request as if it had taken him completely by surprise. "You are a very unusual young lady, Miss Shepherd."

"I know. Like I said, I never learned—"

He smiled gently. "It's a compliment. Perhaps you'd be willing to work a trade?"

She raised her eyebrows. "What do you have in mind?"

He glanced in both directions as if afraid that someone was listening in on their conversation. "I don't intend to go back to Boston. I've come west to make my own way in the world. I want to test my mettle."

"You sound like my father."

He nodded. "I always looked up to him. He seemed like some larger-than-life figure."

"What's all this got to do with a deal?"

"I'll teach you about social niceties, if you agree to teach me wilderness lore in return. You're clear-eyed about your situation, and I'd be a fool if I didn't take the same attitude. I've read plenty of books, but I've never actually spent a night in the woods."

Before that moment Anne believed that jaws only dropped open in books. "Not ever?"

"Not ever. Do you think you can teach me a thing or two?"

"Or three." She grinned and offered her hand. "It's a deal."

They shook on it.

She tilted her head. "How should we get started?"

"Your need seems more immediate than mine, Miss Shepherd. Where would you like to begin?"

"You can call me Anne, you know. I've never been Miss Shepherded so much in my life."

He shook his head. "That's a fine honor, but we don't know one another well enough for such liberties yet." His correction was tactful.

"How well do you have to know someone to call them by their given name?"

"With someone of the opposite sex, you'd need to be blood relations or very close family friends since childhood. Or. . ."

"Or what?"

"Or be engaged."

"Seems awful stuffy to me."

Mr. Wilberforce gave a short bark of laughter. "Just you wait."

Anne's cheeks grew unaccountably warm. "But really, so long as I've given permission and everyone's respectful, what's the harm?"

"It's not about harm. It's about appearances." He leaned closer. "How about this. I'll call you Anne, and you call me Jack, but only when we're alone. That way we stay on your aunt's good side."

"I'm not sure she has one." Once more feeling as if she could face her food, Anne took a bite of crunchy toast.

"If she does, we'll find it." Apparently, Mr. Wilberforce was an optimist.

"Why do you want to be called Jack when your name is Perseus?"

He sighed. "I prefer Jack."

"Why's that?"

She was surprised to see his ears turn pink. "No one would voluntarily be saddled with a name like Perseus."

She shrugged. "I don't know. He was a hero of mythology, a doer of mighty deeds. It seems like a noble name. Certainly it has more character than Jack."

"You know about mythology?"

She gave him a look over her toast. "I'm not uneducated or stupid, Jack. I've simply never had the opportunity to learn the particular skills my aunt sets so much store by."

He was quick to respond. "Of course." Though he still looked chagrined as if she had caught him out.

She relented and changed the subject. "Perhaps you can tell me why Mrs. Carver doesn't like my dresses, especially the dress I wore to meet her?"

Once again color bloomed in his features, bleeding into his cheeks. His gaze darted around the room like he had been cornered.

"Have I said something wrong?"

"It's um—it's—I wouldn't generally presume to comment on a lady's appearance or costume."

"But if I don't ask, and you never tell me, how am I going to know?"

Gazing haplessly at the newspaper still lying neatly folded on the table, he spoke. "I don't think it was the dress itself, although it is rather bright for an unmarried young lady. It was the fact that it wasn't the right kind of dress for the time and place. It's a ball gown, and you weren't at a ball."

"She thought it was too fancy?"

"Yes. And too revealing for a train platform."

"What does that matter? If I'd reveal that much of myself at a ball, why not at a train platform?"

"It's just not done that way."

"It's all pretty arbitrary, isn't it?"

"In a way."

"No wonder I can't make head nor tails of what she wants." She sighed. "So what should I have worn?"

"Again, I'm no expert on ladies' costumes, but an afternoon dress of good-quality fabric. Three-quarter-length sleeves are acceptable in summer if it's hot. The neckline shouldn't reach below the base of the throat."

"That doesn't sound very festive." She shrugged. "Do you think the counter girls at City of Paris will know what I'm after?"

Undisguised relief crossed his features. "Better than I would."

"All right. I'll take Lottie with me. We'll both get an education. I can see I have a lot to learn." She could tell he had been worried that he would offend her, and she tried to reassure him. "I'm glad to have you for a teacher."

"Keep referring to me like that and I'll have to figure out how to be professorial."

"I think my aunt believes I've slighted her, by not driving her around and introducing her to folks, but I don't know many people she'd think 'worth knowing.' How can I make it up to her?"

He considered, pursing his lips together. "You could host a small dinner party."

"A dinner party." She bounced to her feet. "Perfect."

◆ ◆ ◆

Anne nudged the end of one gleaming silver fork then stood back and raised her book. She glanced from it to the table and back again. "I think I've done it just as the book says."

Jack nodded. He would never have guessed that coming west would see him spending more time on the minutiae of etiquette and dinner parties. But he had to admit, Anne had been an enthusiastic student. In fact, teaching her had been somewhat humbling. She was quick enough that he was sometimes left scrambling.

Now they surveyed the long dinner table together and he had to admit, she had made amazing progress in just a couple of weeks. The silver gleamed and was laid properly. The china glowed as if it were made of pearls. Crystal stemware sparkled. Fresh flowers dotted the table, not so high that they would impede conversation, but enough that they added interest and freshness to the table.

"And this dress is all right?"

The dress in question was a confection of soft blue with a froth of gold lace in a standing collar and at the edge of three-quarter-length sleeves. The skirt was narrow but blossomed into an elaborate bustle at the back. "It's just right."

She rubbed her hands together in glee. "It's been a day and a half since Mrs. Carver has said anything to me about being too loud or boisterous. She still sniffs at the house, but she's even softened on that subject since she's ordered curtains she likes better." She stepped closer to him in a conspiratorial move. "I think the hot water taps and radiant heat may have softened her up, too. I know they sold me on buying this house when I first saw it."

"I never had any doubt you would win her over."

She breathed out a little exhalation of pent-up breath. "Growing up, I always imagined what it would be like to be cultured and refined. That's why I moved to San Francisco. I don't know that I ever would have found my way if it wasn't for you, Jack." She reached out and gave his hand a little squeeze.

Her fingers were warm inside silk gloves, and Jack squeezed back before she pulled away. "I think I hear guests arriving." Her voice was higher pitched than normal. She darted toward the door, then, as if someone had yanked her back, stopped at the doorway, straightened her spine, and glided, sedately, into the hall.

Jack followed more slowly. He had never met a woman so candid. There was simply no pretense about Anne. You always knew where you stood with her, and he found that very. . .likable. As likable as her blue-gray eyes that could flash with humor or spark with anger, and that flyaway auburn hair that seemed to cry out to be caressed.

Most of the invitations Anne had peppered the neighborhood with had been declined. Something she told him she'd expected since she'd never met most of the recipients. Being a single, rather eccentric, young lady living alone, he could just imagine what they thought and how they had responded to her presence in their midst. In spite of all that she had managed to entice six couples to the dinner party. Cynically, Jack was fairly certain that they had accepted more out of curiosity than anything else, but at least they had accepted. He only hoped that Mrs. Carver appreciated all the effort to which her niece had gone.

◆ ◆ ◆

Most of Anne's nervousness had faded. Everyone seemed to be enjoying themselves, but particularly, Mrs. Carver was animated and engaged in discussion. Anne had never heard her speak at such length or so genially. It was like she had finally found a place in which she could be comfortable.

Bao Chang came in carrying an enormous almond charlotte piled high with whipped cream and berries. There were gasps of delight and oohs from the guests. He was followed by a couple of footmen to do the actual serving while he supervised, just as had been done with every course and as was customarily the job of a butler.

Mrs. Miller, a wiry woman with a fringe of dishwater-colored hair hanging limply against her forehead, spoke from the middle of the table. "I don't know how your white servants bear it."

The smile shriveled on Anne's lips. "Excuse me?"

The other conversations around the table trailed away.

Mrs. Miller waved a hand at Bao Chang, who was carefully slicing the dessert and placing it on plates for service. "I can't imagine putting a Chinese in charge of anything. We have a few as houseboys of course, but most of them are stupid and lazy."

"Madam, Mr. Chang is in the room." Anne was rather proud of how even her voice was. She glanced at Bao Chang's back, but he made no change in his posture. He simply kept apportioning the dessert.

"It's all right." Mrs. Miller waved a hand. "He's only Chinese."

Her husband intervened. "Now, dear, it's not polite to criticize the running of a host's household."

"I wouldn't say a word normally, but Miss Shepherd is so young, and new to the city. I feel it's my duty to help her understand how things are done in San Francisco. It will save her a lot of heartache in the end."

Anne stood hastily, her napkin balled up in her fist. "Bao Chang has been a second father to me from the time I was a young girl. He is classically educated and speaks four languages. Aside from that, he is kind and wise and the farthest thing from lazy that could be imagined. By rights, he should be my business partner, but while he owns shares in my mine, he refused to accept an equal share because he didn't think it was appropriate. In fact, I invited him to this dinner this evening so that my aunt could understand his merits, and he declined in order to wait on you all."

One of the other women, Mrs. Hopkins, spoke in a stage whisper. "At least someone has a sense of the proper order of things."

There were titters among the guests. Anne looked from face to face. Her aunt's face was red and she was staring fixedly ahead, wearing a sickly smile.

"That's it." Anne's cheeks burned. She flung down her napkin.

Jack stood hastily. "Miss Shepherd, you don't look well. Perhaps you'd like to rest?"

"Yes, and I'm afraid I'm going to have to ask everyone to leave."

The faces around the table reflected stunned indignation.

Bao Chang's demeanor when he turned around was impassive. "I will fetch your wraps and hats." It was only because she knew him so well that Anne was able to spot the smile playing at the corner of his mouth.

Seething, Anne swept from the room, head high, and left them to sort themselves out. If these were the people with whom her aunt wished to consort, she was welcome to them.

◆ ◆ ◆

Jack half expected that Anne would call off the day's tutorial after the dinner party debacle. But she was waiting for him the next morning, looking grimly determined. He swept right into the lesson, without trying to rehash the previous evening's events.

"No, don't bend forward. You should keep your back straight." He demonstrated a curtsy again. He ought to have felt like a prize chump as he did so, but with Anne he never felt that way, even though by now he was having to think hard to dredge up every memory he could in order to determine what was proper in the random scenarios she regularly flung his way. They had covered everything from table etiquette to conduct in the street and letter writing. All the rigid rules he had wanted to escape when he jumped at the chance to escort Mrs. Carver to San Francisco.

Despite all that, he'd come to find himself enjoying their lesson time. It was what had caused him to linger in the city far longer than he had planned.

"Is this better?"

"Very good."

Her grin was infectious, and Jack couldn't help but join in. He took her hand and bowed, raising it to his lips for a brief kiss. "One final lesson. Now that my leg is finally healed, you need to know how to dance."

She waved a hand. "Oh, I know how to dance. I can do a jig with the best of them." She caught his eye and sighed. "You're talking about some fancy dance, aren't you?" It wasn't a question so much as a statement of wonder that society could even rein in and restrain something as fundamentally free and natural as dancing.

He smiled. "I'm going to teach you a waltz. They are played at every ball, and it's a hard dance to fake. We stand like this." He took her hand and positioned it on his shoulder, then took her other hand in his while placing his own lightly at her waist.

She pulled away, one eyebrow raised. "This is a dance? A proper dance?"

"Promise."

"I had to check. I've known too many fellas who'll use any excuse to try to steal a kiss." She allowed him to reposition her, and he tried to concentrate on explaining the steps and rhythm of the dance, but it was apparent that she wasn't wearing a stiff, whale-boned corset beneath her dress. Instead, he could feel the soft warmth of her waist. His throat felt dry as the desert he had traveled through when crossing the country, and he swallowed hard.

He began to hum "The Blue Danube" and swept her into the steps of the waltz, trying not to focus on the supple movement of her body as she allowed him to lead her through the swirling steps. She laughed, and they both grew a little breathless as they spun round and round the room together.

He came to a stop but couldn't seem to tear his eyes away from hers for a long moment. The spark of laughter in her eyes grew into something softer and yet more intense.

From the hall came the uncompromising staccato clack of swift heels on the marble tile.

Jack stepped back and cleared his throat. "Um, if you were in a ball gown, you would have a loop sewn in the skirt that you could hook over your wrist to hold it out of the way."

"That's good to know."

"Yes." He'd never before grown breathless after he'd *stopped* dancing.

"Yes." It was almost a whisper.

The parlor door was thrust open and Mrs. Carver barreled in. Even having heard her steps in the hall, Jack started at the sudden intrusion.

"Good afternoon, Mrs. Carver." Anne executed a perfect curtsy.

Her aunt stopped and pulled her head back a little as if trying to get a better view of this phenomenon. "Mm."

The sound, at least, was disapproving.

"I went to make amends with your—our neighbors this afternoon." Mrs. Carver settled herself in the most comfortable chair and reached for the bell cord. "They are the first persons of refinement I've met in this. . .outpost. We are lucky that they were gracious and understanding when I explained the shortcomings of your upbringing. The Hopkins are going to hold a ball and have promised an invitation. Between now and then, Anne, you and I will have a great deal of work to do. We need to make you presentable to society."

Jack knew Anne well enough by now that he could see the telltale sign of her biting the inside of her lip to keep from saying something as Mrs. Carver outlined a rigorous course of study for her niece in social niceties. The older woman patted Anne's arm. "With the exception of last night's deplorable display, I think my presence is already having a beneficial effect, my dear. I've noticed an improvement in your deportment in the last few days."

Bao Chang appeared with a tray of refreshments, and Mrs. Carver snapped her mouth shut then managed the usual sickly smile she exhibited whenever she saw the butler. "Oh, good. I'm parched."

Chang elected to set the tray down on the table nearest Anne before he left the room again. As he did so, Jack thought he caught the faintest whiff of a smile on the Chinese man's face as he glanced at her. And she responded with a demure smile of her own. Jack glanced between the two of them again, and his eyebrows shot up. Anne hadn't been exaggerating. They were more than employer and servant. They were friends.

Chapter 3

"As I was saying," Mrs. Carver continued.

Anne picked up the teapot and, keeping all that Jack had taught her firmly in mind, she poured a cup of tea for Mrs. Carver as she knew she liked it.

Her aunt kept talking though Anne had only half an ear trained on what she was saying, too intent on making sure she poured well. "Mrs. Hopkins was very clear that no one of any standing would hire a Chinese butler. It's just not done. They are fine for the railroads or even as a houseboy. But it isn't appropriate to put a Chinese in charge of whites. And don't even get me started on cooks. Only a European cook truly understands fine cuisine."

At last the tenor of Mrs. Carver's monologue invaded Anne's consciousness. She looked up, frowning.

"Again, I'm sure a Chinese would be fine as an assist—"

"I'm not getting rid of Bao Chang and Mei Lin." Anne stared hard at her aunt.

"My dear, I'm sure they've done their best, but—watch!"

Anne's hand jerked at the outburst. The cup overflowed and tipped over, drenching the tray and her skirt with steaming, hot tea. She jumped to her feet and began dabbing at the mess, wishing she still carried a real handkerchief, rather than the miniscule lace scrap she had been assured was more ladylike.

"Oh dear, and you were doing so well until then." Mrs. Carver sighed. "Now, I think the issue is that you simply haven't been exposed to the quality of service you could expect from a better class of servant. You don't know what you've been missing."

"Mrs. Carver." Anne's voice was even sharper than she had intended. Bao Chang appeared again with an expression of polite inquiry on his face, and she realized that Jack must have pulled the cord for him. At the sight of her, the butler instantly produced a towel seemingly from nowhere. He whisked the sopping tray away without spilling a single drop.

Anne dabbed at her dress, too agitated to sit again even though she knew that Jack was forced to stand because she was on her feet. She made an effort to control her voice. "Mrs. Carver, I will not send Bao Chang and Mei Lin away."

"My dear, you don't understand. It's simply not done." This was said with the air of a pronouncement from on high.

"It is done. By. Me."

"You will never advance your social position if you cannot—"

Anne flung her hands wide. "I don't want to advance my social position if it means firing my friends. Bao Chang worked the mine with me. He helped keep me safe in the bad days. And it is by his wise advice that I have the fortune I have today."

Mrs. Carver's eyes were wide in astonishment.

"Because of the ridiculous nature of the current laws, we were able to bring Mei Lin to him only with the greatest difficulty. She is the gentlest, kindest creature you've ever met. You would have me bring her from China with the promise of a life in the United States and then kick her out on the street because I now deem her inconvenient?"

"A reference—"

Anne leaned over the older woman. "But as you said, no one will give a Chinese a decent place." She stepped back and carefully resumed her seat, scrubbing futilely at the tea stains on her skirt.

"Well." Her aunt's lips were tightly pursed. "I can see you feel strongly about them, so I'll say no more on the subject."

"Thank you."

"But I do feel it incumbent upon me to bring another situation to your attention."

Anne stilled.

"Your maid, Lois—"

"Lottie."

"Lottie. I'm afraid that her reputation is far from spotless. There are rumors that she was something known as a 'pretty waitress girl.'" She said the words as if they were curdling on her tongue. "She worked at a dance hall down in some terrible district called the Barbary Coast. I am assured that the women who work at these places are of the lowest imaginable character."

Anne's cheeks prickled with heat and her hands were trembling. "Are you quite finished?"

Mrs. Carver gave a single jerk of her chin.

"I am well aware of where Lottie came from. Thank you."

"My girl, you don't understand. You cannot have her in a position so close to you. Her presence will tarnish your own reputation."

"No. You are the one who does not understand. Lottie has been my friend for years. She fed me when I was starving and half-drowned from the rains. And she took care of me when I was sick. The people who work for me are not just employees. They are my friends." Anne stood again. "I have tried to change everything about myself to suit you." She waved a hand at the sober navy day dress she wore. "And I've let you have free rein to change my house to better suit your tastes. But you will leave my friends alone. They have been family to me far longer than I have known of your existence."

Once more Bao Chang appeared in the doorway with a tray. With quiet dignity he brought it in and set it before Anne. Then he produced a thin, yellow telegram and handed it to her. "This has arrived for you, Miss Anne."

"Thank you, Bao Chang." She gave a nod that bordered on a bow.

He withdrew with his usual dignified air.

Her hands were still trembling as she took the flimsy sheet, but they stilled as she read.

"Is something wrong, Miss Shepherd?" Jack's voice intruded on thoughts that had grown suddenly jumbled. He stood at her elbow as if she might faint and he would need to catch her.

She did feel dreadfully cold. "I—um, yes. There is trouble at the mine. Someone has tried to take it over."

◆ ◆ ◆

Jack watched Anne closely. All the blood had drained from her face, and where a moment ago she had been full of magnificent fire as she squared off against her aunt, now she looked suddenly fragile. She let the telegram slip from her fingers and flutter to rest on the tray.

"Excuse me, I need to go."

Politeness would have required an acknowledgment and a gracious farewell, but she had spoken with too much finality. "Go? Where are you going?"

She raised her eyebrows as if the answer was obvious. "To the mine. I have to go take care of this."

"The mine? But isn't that some distance from here?"

"About a hundred and eighty miles."

Her aunt sat up at that, spluttering. "You want to travel so far, alone in the wilderness?"

"I'll take the train as far as Stockton." Anne smiled.

"But that still leaves some one hundred miles to your destination, doesn't it?" Jack asked.

"You needn't worry. I've made the trip many times."

Jack had been waiting for just this opportunity to head out into the wilderness. He cocked his head, trying to signal to her that this was the opportunity for her to follow through on her part of their deal. His chance to test his mettle against the wilderness. "But the territory is hardly tamed."

"That's true. Many of the mining towns between here and there have dried up." Anne looked at his facial contortions as if she feared for his sanity. Then her expression cleared. "Of course, having a gentleman along to keep me safe would be most welcome."

Mrs. Carver slammed her cup into its saucer. "You absolutely cannot go into the wilds alone with a young man. It would be suicide for your reputation."

Jack's rising hopes spiraled to the earth, but Anne merely smiled. "Then you're welcome to join us."

Flustered, Mrs. Carver waved her hands. "I couldn't possibly. The idea—there's too much. The—" She seemed to latch on to a thought. "Perseus can't go into the wilderness either. His foot is still healing, and he ought to stay home and take care of it. You can send someone. Surely you have someone you trust—"

"I have a number of people I trust, but this is personal. That mine is my father's legacy, and I worked it with blood, sweat, and tears. I'm not going to let someone come in and try to take it away."

"And I've got a clean bill of health on my foot. I can't in good conscience allow a delicate young lady to face the rigors of the wilderness alone." Jack knew he was laying it on a bit thick, and he thought he saw Anne hide a grin behind her cup, but she was so quick he couldn't be sure.

The lacy handkerchief in Mrs. Carver's hand looked like a white flag of surrender. "When must we leave?"

"Immediately." Anne had a curious look on her face, as if she were regretting the rash decision to invite her aunt now that it looked as if it might be accepted. "There's no time to be lost. But it will be rigorous. We will need to ride hard."

"Don't you worry about me. I am an accomplished horsewoman."

The lines of Anne's face hardened once more. "We leave in one hour."

Mrs. Carver's mouth hung open and her hands dropped to her lap. "Such a thing simply isn't possible."

"It certainly is. I would give you longer, but we need to catch the afternoon train for Stockton. I'll send Lottie to help you. Take only the essentials."

Without a backward glance, Anne marched from the room, and Jack could hear her issuing orders. Within a few minutes the sounds of scurrying feet could be heard throughout the house.

Mrs. Carver remained seated, staring forward. She had an almost windblown look about her, as if she had been caught in a tornado.

"Well, ma'am." Jack offered his arm. "It appears we both have packing to do in a very short amount of time."

"Hm? Yes." She allowed him to help her up and escort her from the room. "She's a rather forceful young woman, isn't she? Not at all docile."

Jack nodded gravely. "I think that's fair to say." Personally, his unease about how Anne would be able to manage her opinionated relative had been put to rest, and in the process he had a bubbling, fizzing sort of sensation in his chest. Like he was standing on the edge of a precipice and looking forward to the leap.

Chapter 4

Anne had been hard-pressed not to pace the length of the train car during their journey the previous day. They had arrived in Stockton too late to make any headway before they lost the sun. So she had led their small party to the Occidental Hotel, which was located not far from the station.

Though she had slept fitfully, she was ready to go, dressed in a divided skirt and cambric shirtwaist, as soon as dawn broke. She pinned her hair into a neat chignon at the nape of her neck then drew on her battered old Stetson. She caught a glimpse of herself in the tarnished surface of a mirror, and a spark of recognition flew through her. For the first time in months she looked like herself. It was nice. She slipped on her heavy trail gloves and slung her saddlebag over her shoulder. Maybe it was time to stop pretending that she could ever be a lady of refinement and get back to the business of running the mine and her investments. If she had been out at the mine and paying attention, there might never have been any trouble.

In the lobby she spoke to the clerk, who summoned a boy. The boy took her saddlebag and sped off through the hotel. When she turned back to the lobby, she found her aunt descending the stairs stiffly, Jack at her side, though she was waving away the assistance he offered.

Anne met them at the base of the stairs. "Are you all right? Perhaps you ought to rest here, while we head out to the mine."

"I'll be fine." Mrs. Carver brushed away all attempts to assist her, standing on her dignity as she had since Anne had insisted that she could bring no more than a single bag.

"I could also get you a ticket back to San Francisco."

Her aunt might have replied, but her attention was diverted by something behind Anne. Anne turned to find the clerk to whom she had spoken.

"They're ready, miss." He led the way outside. Standing in the street was the boy he'd sent running earlier, along with four horses.

"We're riding? Are these your horses, or did you hire them?" Jack sounded intrigued.

Anne signed the paperwork the clerk handed her. "These beauties are mine. They came with us on the train yesterday. You didn't think I was going to make you walk a hundred miles on foot, did you?"

"I, for one, had no idea as to your intent." Her aunt sniffed. "You've been very high-handed."

Anne gave the clerk and boy each a handsome tip and took the reins of the animals. Jack immediately stepped forward to assist her.

"I apologize if my manner has offended, Mrs. Carver. It's too slow to go around by the cart roads. I've brought horses so that we can take more of a straight shot. The terrain is rough. It will take three or four days to get out to the mine." She thought about offering to send the woman back to San Francisco again but decided that it might seem too pushy.

The packhorse had already been loaded down with essential supplies, and the other animals had been groomed and saddled. Anne made a quick circuit, inspecting each animal to make sure they didn't have any injuries. Then she clapped her hands together. "I think we're ready to hit the trail." The thought of getting up into the mountains made her tingle. She was going home.

A thought suddenly occurred to her as her guests made no immediate move forward. "My goodness, are you able to ride?"

"I assure you, I can ride perfectly well. I just don't know which of these brutes is supposed to be mine." Her aunt's words were tart, but Anne was relieved.

"Mrs. Carver, I think you might find June Bug an agreeable mount. She's. . .tractable."

"I suppose it's too much to hope there is a sidesaddle available."

Anne opened her mouth, but her aunt forestalled her apology with a raised hand. "I'll manage."

Anne glanced at Jack, who gave a miniscule shrug. It was clear that her aunt was uninterested in any solicitousness from Anne, so she nodded and they mounted up.

The eastern horizon was still a watercolor painting washed with the gray tinge of night, the sun still lazing behind the mountains as they rode out of Stockton. Anne set a swift pace. They needed to make time as quickly as they could while the terrain was still good.

Anne glanced back a number of times to make sure Mrs. Carver was able to keep up. Somewhat to her surprise, her aunt had outfitted herself with a split skirt. She sat a horse with the ease of long habit.

The town puttered out around them, fading into the occasional farmer's homestead. They wended around cherry and walnut orchards and fields of waving grains. Jack alternated, sometimes riding next to Anne, other times falling back to ride beside her aunt. He was nothing if not a gentleman. Anne wondered, not for the first time, if there was anything more to his leaving Boston and coming west. He seemed so accomplished, she couldn't imagine what would cause him to abandon the life he'd always known. Or—she looked out at the unspoiled country and breathed in deeply of the fresh air—perhaps there wasn't anything strange about it at all.

Anne called a halt for lunch beside a rippling little stream. Dismounting, she felt the ache of muscles she had not been putting to good use for a while. She welcomed the pain. It meant she was doing something to correct the deficiency, but she wasn't so naive as to think that everyone would feel the same way she did. Jack was walking slightly bandy-legged, and her aunt moved slowly, though neither of them voiced any complaints.

They were tougher than she might have given them credit for, but as soon as they had eaten, she mounted up again. She led them relentlessly on through pasturelands. Through marshes. Always bearing toward the mountains and the mine. She felt like the proverbial homing pigeon.

By late afternoon they reached the Sierra Nevada foothills, a scrubby-looking stretch, windswept and home to only the most tenacious species. She finally saw what she had been aiming for, a ramshackle fence made of scrub brush bound together with everything from bits of rusty barbed wire to twine.

"What is this place?" Jack asked.

"This is a Yokut Rancheria." Anne swung herself down from her horse and opened a gate that no one would suspect existed if one didn't know it was there.

There was a moment of silence, and Anne glanced up to see Jack and her aunt exchanging a look.

Her aunt spoke after a moment. "You mean Indians."

"Yes, it's their village. They've been granted this land back from the federal government rather than having to go to a reservation."

"Indians aren't safe."

Anne couldn't hold in her laugh. "We were in far more danger of being robbed and beaten in Stockton than we are here." She held the gate open for them and they rode through.

Jack gazed about appraisingly. "How big is this place?"

"Mm, I'd say maybe twenty acres. It's meant to support almost four dozen Yokut."

"How does that work?" Surprisingly, this question was from her aunt.

"Not very well sometimes." Anne shrugged. "But they prefer this to the reservation. This is their homeland."

◆ ◆ ◆

Now this was more like it. He'd finally found his way to the real west if he was going to see an Indian village.

A little girl of perhaps seven darted from around an evergreen.

Anne inclined her head. "*Hil-Lé.*"

"*Hileu ma tannin.*" The little girl looked up at them from under breathtakingly long lashes.

"Where's your mama?"

The little girl took to her heels, scampering through the trees. Anne snorted a laugh. "We'll have a welcoming party soon enough."

"Just so long as it's not the kind of welcoming party that is interested in scalping their guests." Jack lowered himself gingerly from his mount and walked with her, trying not to show how sore he was. He had discovered why cowboys had the reputation of being bowlegged.

"Not a chance. Your mangy scalp wouldn't interest anybody."

He put on a show of mock outrage. "I resent that. I don't have fleas."

"Well now, there's a recommendation."

They walked side by side, leading their mounts, following the path the little girl had taken, albeit at a slower pace. Mrs. Carver remained firmly in her saddle, as if she might need to gallop for safety. Jack glanced back to check on her a time or two, and each time Mrs. Carver's eyes were examining the trees and shrubbery suspiciously, as if she expected Indian warriors to spring from the underbrush with war whoops and tomahawks flying.

What they found instead was what appeared at first glance to be a handful of large, round haystacks. Closer inspection revealed that these were actually carefully constructed dwellings covered in thatch. In the center of the small gathering, a number of women were working around a large central fire pit. They straightened at the approach of visitors.

Anne raised her arm and called a greeting.

The women responded in kind and a couple moved forward. The travelers were quickly overtaken then surrounded by a herd of stampeding children led by the little girl. The children were like a tide encircling Anne. Even knowing that it was idiotic, Jack felt fear tickle the back of his throat. Resolving not to read any more dime-store novels, he stood tall, trying to see the horde as children rather than the savages of legend.

Anne, meanwhile, did not flinch. She remained perfectly composed, even happy. She laughed as she was all but nearly overrun by some two dozen small bodies with outstretched hands. She held up a brown paper bag. The children let out a cheer. Anne gave the bag to the tallest of the boys, and just as quickly as they had appeared they dispersed, following the boy with the bag as if he was the pied piper.

"What was that?"

Anne gave him a smile over her shoulder. "Candy."

The first Indian woman reached her. "You spoil them."

"They deserve a treat. As do you." From somewhere she produced another bag and pulled a handful of brightly colored silk ribbons from inside.

The other women had come alongside them now, and they gasped at the brilliant rainbow in Anne's fingers. Their eyes lit up, and one of them reached forward as if to stroke the soft fabric. Anne pressed the ribbons into her hands.

"We can't..."

"Don't be silly. You have shown me such kindness, I must repay my debt."

"You will eat?"

"If you will have us. I would love another of your wonderful meals." Anne turned to bring her aunt and Jack into the conversation. "May I present Mrs. Irene Carver and Mr. Perseus Wilberforce." With the hand holding the reins she gestured at the women beside her. "This is Huyana, Papi, and Mary."

The women smiled at their visitors shyly, looking up through their lashes. Anne linked her arm through Huyana's. "Now, tell me how Captain Frank is doing. The last I heard, he had big plans to get the rancheria expanded."

Jack let them move ahead of him and hung back to walk alongside Mrs. Carver's horse. "Are you all right, ma'am? You look pale."

The lady swallowed hard but then gave him a little grimace that might have been meant for a smile. "My friends in Boston will never believe it when I write to them of this."

"I wouldn't be so sure." He gave her smile back with interest. "I'm sure they are aware of your intrepid nature."

"Pish. They may think I'm bossy, but I doubt they consider me intrepid." She grimaced again. "Perseus, might I ask a favor."

"Of course, ma'am."

"I'm afraid I am in need of assistance to dismount."

"Of course!" He stopped instantly, letting his own horse's reins fall to the ground.

Mrs. Carver all but fell off the horse into his arms. He staggered backward and his healing ankle gave a howl, but he managed to keep them both upright and steady the lady while she gathered her composure. She did not stand up straight immediately, however.

"Have you perhaps injured your back?"

"Go ahead with the others." She sounded cross. "I'm fine."

"I would prefer to make sure you are all right."

"I told you, young man, I am fine." She put her hands to her back and straightened with agonizing slowness. She modified her tone. "It's been a while since I've spent all day in a saddle."

Jack leaned toward her. "I thought she was never going to stop. Your niece is quite the slave driver."

Mrs. Carver's response was muffled, but he could have sworn she said that she thought it ran in the family. It was the first hint he'd ever had that she might have a sense of humor.

The three of them were made to sit on stools while the Indian women bustled about them. A few moments later a small party of Indian men appeared. They seemed to be joking among themselves, carrying something in large sacks over their shoulders. The jollity halted when they caught sight of their visitors.

A man of average height with gray streaking his dark hair stepped forward and greeted them. "Hil-Lé. Hil-Lé."

Anne rose and greeted him in return.

Jack rose as well, feeling awkward and wishing he knew the protocol. It hadn't occurred to him that he ought to have Anne teach him lessons on manners as part of his wilderness training. He stepped to her side and extended a hand to the man.

Anne facilitated the introductions. "Captain Frank, this is Perseus Wilberforce."

"Jack, please."

"Jack, this is the headman, Captain Frank."

"You are welcome, Jack." The cadence was slow and formal, the expression solemn.

"Thank you, sir."

Mrs. Carver remained seated but nodded graciously as she was introduced. Formalities complete, the women presented them with plates of corn mush, freshwater mussels, some sort of berries, and some sort of bread. He'd never encountered the like.

He glanced at Anne, and she gave his plate a significant look before meeting his gaze again. With deliberate movements she scooped up a bit of mush in her fingers and popped it in her mouth. Her eyes went from him to her aunt and she repeated the action. Definitely should have gotten a few lessons.

Anne's were not the only eyes on him, and he followed suit tentatively. Eating with his fingers was novel but not so terrible as his mother and a parade of nannies from his childhood would have had him believe. The mush wasn't bad—a bit tasteless, but not bad. He scooped up another couple of fingers' worth. The Indian woman who had served his meal gave a relieved smile and bobbed her head.

The headman turned to speak to a young man who arrived. Anne switched from whatever tongue she had been using, to speak to Jack and Mrs. Carver in a low tone. "They value hospitality here. Thank you for showing them respect by receiving it gratefully."

The headman finished greeting the newcomers and returned his attention back to his guests. He spoke in careful English. "What brings you to our valley, Mr. Jack?"

Somehow confessing that he had simply wanted to escape the strictures and expectations of his wealthy family seemed the wrong thing to say to this man who held the burden of responsibility for an entire village and for whom his ideas of adventure would probably seem childish. "Mrs. Carver needed an escort, and I was lucky enough that she chose me to accompany her on her journey."

Captain Frank listened politely, but Jack got the sense that he wasn't buying his story, and he wondered how many times Anne might have traveled through this place all alone. He swallowed and fought down the desire to explain further. It would just make him look wishy-washy.

"You are a man who says the right thing always." The words contained no particular inflection, but still they did not seem to be a compliment.

Jack's shoulders tensed, but he measured his words carefully. "I try always to be polite."

"Jack trained as a lawyer. I think it's a requirement that they speak well." Anne spoke brightly. She seemed unaware of any possible undercurrents to the conversation.

"Ah, an important man. You keep the law."

"Not so much keep—"

"The headman is the law among the Yokuts."

"You have great responsibility."

"Yes." The headman seemed to be done with him. The conversation veered from there with Captain Frank showing Mrs. Carver attention, which was accepted with more good grace than Jack might have expected. In fact, now that she was past her first shock, she was remarkably engaged. Speaking to the women near her and watching the activity around them with keen interest.

At last, as the meal was wrapping up, Captain Frank returned his attention to Anne. "You will stay with us tonight?"

"That's kind of you, but we need to be going. I'd like to make a few more miles before the sun goes down."

Jack could have sworn he heard her aunt groan at this, but when he looked, her face was utterly unreadable.

"It would be wise to stay here for the night. There are rumors of bandits in the forest."

"There are always rumors of bandits."

Captain Frank shrugged. "True, but there have been more lately. These rumors may be more than talk."

"I will watch for the signs and be careful to avoid them. Besides"—she flashed a grin—"we have Jack to protect us."

Jack searched her face for sarcasm but saw no malice there.

Within a few moments they had mounted up again, and as the children ran alongside them, Anne led them from the rancheria.

"Why didn't you wish to stay in the village? Surely it would be safer than sleeping in the wilderness." Mrs. Carver sounded aggravated, but her tone had changed. She did not sound patronizing.

Anne held her shoulders very still, but when she spoke, her words sounded cheery enough. "The Yokut are a proud people. They would have felt the need to offer us the best hospitality they can. But with their lives and livelihoods restricted to the rancheria, they have very little. I couldn't bear to take any more from them than necessary. Also, I would like to make a few more miles today. We've got a long way to go before we reach the mine." She glanced back at them. "If you're worried about the talk of bandits, you don't need to be."

"It's not that," Mrs. Carver said and shifted in her saddle.

"I promise to help make our campsite as comfortable as possible. I know exactly where we are going."

Her aunt seemed to accept this reassurance, though Jack got the sense that this had more to do with her reluctance to discuss why she would prefer to stay at the rancheria than with any confidence she felt in Anne's plan.

The mountains looked close enough to touch now even as they remained stubbornly elusive. The scrub and rock gave way to groves of spreading oak trees and verdant evergreens and pines. He even spotted his first giant sequoia. The green canopy overhead protected them from the sun's heat but was so high that it didn't feel claustrophobic. The clop of their horses' hooves was muffled by innumerable leaves. Occasionally their passage startled a bird or sent a squirrel scampering for cover, but otherwise it was as if they were the last creatures in existence. He inhaled deeply and let the breath out on a sigh. Here the rush and bustle of the city was as irrelevant as a bathing costume to an Eskimo.

His legs and hindquarters ached from riding, but he had to admit that this was a better way to get to know the country than the railroad. There was nothing like the rich, loamy smell of the forest. And there was no way to get a real feel for the scale of the great sequoia trees as one barreled by in a train. But, passing beneath its mighty boughs, he had a whole new appreciation for his own finiteness.

"Hold." Anne held her hand up.

Jack reined in hard.

Anne pointed to a hole that a casual observer might simply have thought was deep shadow at the edge of a mass of brush. "There are mining pits like that all over the place. Miners turned over just about every bit of ground in the state. A lot of it they didn't put back."

"That is very dangerous." Mrs. Carver had a hand to her chest as if she had almost fallen into the pit.

"It's important to stay alert." A smiled softened Anne's briskness. "We'll stop before it gets dark."

"I suppose that's some comfort."

It was another hour before she finally called a halt. Jack had begun wondering if she was simply growing contrary. But as he drew up beside her, he saw the reason she had made them come so far. A tiny cabin nestled at the edge of a clearing. On the far side a brook burbled merrily.

"Is this a friend's house?"

"It's mine."

"We're near the mine then?"

"We're days away from the mine still. This is a way station." She clicked to her horse, and they started down the slight grade to the cabin. "It's not much, but by the time we come back this way, it will feel downright luxurious."

Considering his aching bones, that sounded ominous.

To enter, Anne produced no key, merely pushed the door open.

"Aren't you worried about thieves?" her aunt asked.

"There's nothing here worth stealing." Anne turned to her aunt and ushered her inside. "Besides, it can't be stolen if it's a gift."

"Don't speak in riddles, girl. I am far too tired for foolishness."

"Out here, cabins like this are left unlocked in case of an emergency, especially in winter. This place might save someone's life if a blizzard blows up unexpectedly. Anyone in need is welcome to help themselves to its stores of wood or supplies, therefore they cannot be said to have stolen anything."

"That's very. . .practical." Jack didn't know what else to call it.

He followed the ladies inside to find the cabin was larger than it looked from outside but still very simply furnished. A wooden bed frame with a mattress and a pile of quilts folded at the foot. A single cane-back chair sat in front of a wide fireplace with a stack of wood piled neatly beside it and a rag rug before it. And, pressed up against one wall, a workbench with a few pots and pans, utensils and tins. A thick layer of dust overlay everything.

"Home sweet home." Anne opened her arms wide. "At least for the night."

Mrs. Carver sneezed.

Anne grimaced. "I suppose it does need a good airing out." She planted her hands on her hips.

Sensing that he was about to get an assignment, Jack placed his saddlebags against the wall and straightened. As suspected, he was set to bringing in additional firewood and getting a blaze started while the ladies took the quilts out to hang on some bushes.

He then led the grazing horses to a small paddock and brushed and watered them. More manual labor than he had performed in the past year. But it felt good to be moving and working out the kinks in his muscles, so he couldn't complain too much.

After a few moments he found himself humming. It was quiet here. Some might say lonely, but his only concern was the grumbling of his belly. He was getting hungry. As he headed back to the cabin, Mrs. Carver was enthusiastically whacking the blankets. A cloud of dust billowed out of the door followed by Anne, broom in hand. To his left, Jack heard something between a grunt, a growl, and a question mark.

He turned to find a pair of small eyes examining him from a great shaggy head.

Some sound must have escaped his throat because Anne looked up and stiffened. "Don't run and don't look him in the eye. He might take it as a challenge."

Jack focused furiously on the animal's nose, which twitched and sniffled in a sinister way.

"It's a black bear. They're not usually aggressive." Anne's voice was low and calm.

"What should I do?" It wasn't much more than a whisper, but she heard him.

"Back away from him slowly. Don't make any sudden movements."

The bear was glaring at him now, and Jack caught a whiff of its heavy, brackish odor. With his heart hammering to be let out of his chest, he took a careful step backward.

The bear cocked its great head at him as if wondering why he was walking in such a strange manner. It took a step forward, its great paws making no sounds, but the great claws at the end of them scoring the ground. Jack took another step and another. The bear matched him. It wasn't particularly tall, about chest height, but it had great, broad shoulders. Jack figured it weighed a good three hundred pounds.

"Are you carrying any food?"

"I have some licorice in my pocket."

"Pull it out slowly and drop it to the ground, then back away from it."

Jack did as he was told. The overly sweet scent of the licorice wafting up to him made him want to vomit as he pulled it out. He dropped it on the ground. The bear's ever-twitching nose seemed to grow more dramatic in its gyrations, and he lumbered forward. Jack hastily backed away.

"Slowly. Calmly."

He made sure not to make any sudden jerky movements but continued to move toward the cabin while the bear's attention was occupied.

The bear reached the place Jack had been and snuffled around in the dirt, pawing at the bits of candy. A long, sinuous tongue escaped its jaws and claimed one piece of licorice after the other. He looked up at Jack and let out another growl that ended in a question mark, for all the world as if he were wondering where Jack was going when they had been having such a good time.

Jack nearly jumped out of his skin as small hands grabbed the back of his jacket.

"I'm right here." Anne's voice remained steady. "Go ahead and get in the cabin."

Jack glanced inside and saw Mrs. Carver had already managed to obtain relative safety. She peered at him, her white face seeming extra pale as it looked out from the shadows.

"What are you doing?" Jack asked.

"I think someone has been feeding this bear. If I'm right, he won't want to take no for an answer, and I may need to take more desperate measures."

"I'm not cowering inside and leaving you to deal with a bear alone." An image of the long rifle she'd carried strapped to her saddlebags came to his mind.

"I've dealt with worse than a black bear."

"Not while I was around. If he stopped because of the licorice in my pockets, then this is my fault. I'm not leaving you to handle the consequences." He looked at the bear, who had run out of licorice and was moving toward them again. "Just tell me what to do."

"You're sure?"

Jack wanted to shake her. Couldn't she see the bear coming? "Yes."

"Raise your hands above your head to make yourself as big as possible, and yell at it. Move forward, but not too quickly."

Jack raised his hands above his head and shook them wildly. Why this addition to the program seemed appropriate he didn't know, it just did. He moved toward the bear, who seemed more surprised at his change in demeanor than anything else. Jack followed this up with the biggest, deepest bellow he could manage. The bear jerked away, one paw held high in the air, and Jack would have sworn that the expression on its face was the same Mrs. Carver had worn when they had been accosted by a beggar at one of the innumerable train stops on their journey out west.

Jack roared again, and the bear turned and began to lumber away. It gave a single glance over its shoulder as it went. Jack gave another menacing shake of his hands. Within a few moments the bear was swallowed by the shadows of the woods.

"Nicely done." Anne came up beside him.

"If I'd been alone, I'd have taken off running for sure."

"Well, now you know what to do." She shrugged, sounding nonchalant, as she stared into the woods after the big animal, but he noticed that her knuckles around the broom still showed white. "It's better to avoid confrontation if you can, but if you can't, then you have to look as big and scary as possible and make them decide *they* don't want the confrontation."

As he looked down at her profile, Jack's throat felt unaccountably dry again. "I'll keep that in mind." His voice sounded husky.

She looked up at him then, and the moment seemed to stretch out between them as rich and melting as honey. Her lips curved in an enigmatic, almost searching way. "You sure you're all right?"

"Never better." He managed a smile.

"Good." Her more habitual flash of a smile burst across her face, and she handed him the broom. "Then you can finish sweeping. I need to start supper."

His fingers covered hers as he accepted the broom. His throat constricted. He should have left Boston years ago. The west was invigorating like nothing back east.

Chapter 5

Before they started out the next morning, Anne tried to give Mrs. Carver a liniment to rub into sore muscles, but the older woman pushed it away.

"I'm fine, thank you."

Anne could tell by the way the older woman sat and held herself with utmost care that she wasn't fine. "If you change your mind, just say the word."

Anne took care throughout the day to slow their pace as they climbed higher and to take more breaks than they had taken the day before. Perversely, she was reluctant to call a halt to the ride for the day. She wanted to find the best possible campsite. There would be no cabin tonight, and as they climbed higher, it was growing cooler.

At last she found the spot. A small clearing, well sheltered by trees and within feet of a brook. There was a scant hour until they would be engulfed by darkness, so they didn't have much time.

She swung herself down from her horse, which gladly bent to drink its fill. "All right." She reached for her saddlebag. "We'll need to rig a couple of lean-tos, find firewood, build a fire, and gather moss and pine needles to make comfortable and warmer places to lay. We'll also need to care for the horses. There is plenty of grass for them to graze upon, but they should be brushed down and staked for the night." Irritated, she looked around. "What is that buzzing noise?" Then she found the source. Suspended at the edge of the clearing, not far from where she stood, was a beehive. She smiled. "I just found a nice addition to our supper."

"I can take care of the horses," Jack said.

"Thank you, Mr. Wilberforce. Mrs. Carver, I have some tarpaulins and rope in this pack here. We can work on rigging the lean-tos. We need to get all this done before we lose the light."

Say what one would about Mrs. Carver, the woman was not stupid. And despite the achy slowness of her movements, she readily grasped the basics of lean-to construction. Anne left her to finish while she went to gather moss and pine needles. It was arduous work after a day in the saddle, all bending and standing, squatting and lifting.

How much would it cost to run a branch line of the railroad up to the mine? She began working through the calculations in her head. At Bao Chang's advice, she had taken a substantial share of her earnings from the gold mine and invested in the railroads, among other things. By train this journey would have ended the day before, or possibly even the day before that if they hadn't stopped in Sacramento. Once she got home she'd have to look into the possibilities.

Huh. She was thinking of San Francisco as home. Back in the city, she'd always thought of the mine as home.

When she returned with her umpteenth and final basket of bedding materials, she found that Jack had made a creditable place for a fire, neatly circled by stones, and had laid kindling and wood within. Her tenderfoot was coming along nicely.

"Do you want to do the honors?" he asked as she approached.

"I wouldn't dream of stealing your thunder."

With an air of suppressed excitement he struck a match, and Anne wondered if this might not be the first time he'd ever laid and lit his own fire. The thought was so preposterous she rejected it, but then, he had grown up in a city with a number of household servants. Would he have ever had cause to light a fire for himself?

A piercing howl pulled her from her reveries as she piled moss in the first lean-to.

"What was that?" For the first time Anne thought she detected a quiver in Mrs. Carver's voice. "Was it wolves?"

An impulse shivered through Anne. She could repay Mrs. Carver's haughty meanness with a dose of terror. But, no. "Sounds more like coyotes to me."

"You're sure?" Mrs. Carver's gaze roamed wildly over the thick trees that surrounded them.

Anne placed a gentle hand on her arm and waited until the woman's eyes rested on hers. "I'm sure."

Mrs. Carver pressed her lips together and nodded.

Time for a distraction. "We've got the biscuits I made at the cabin to eat tonight, but you know what would go really well with some biscuits?"

The response was wary. "What?"

"Honey." Anne grinned wickedly and pointed toward the beehive hanging pendulously from the nearby tree.

"You can't be serious."

"I certainly am."

Jack drew nearer. "What do you have in mind?"

"We're going to use your fire."

"Surely fire would make the bees angry."

"To be strictly accurate, we don't want the fire, we want the smoke. It makes the bees sleepy. Then we can borrow some honey without any protests."

"Won't it simply irritate them?" Mrs. Carver wasn't buying her explanation.

"Don't worry. My father taught me how to get honey when I was real little." She held her arms out in a circle in front of her. "I need a good-size bundle of green branches with the leaves still on them. They need to be green so they'll burn very slowly and produce a lot of smoke."

Jack nodded. "I'll be right back."

Meanwhile, Anne retrieved a bucket and a rope from among their supplies and checked the edge of the knife she carried in a scabbard on her hip. It was gratifyingly sharp. She tied a large handkerchief around her nose and mouth as Jack returned with an armful of branches.

"Don't tell me, you're really the bandit the Indians were warning us about."

"The bees might feel that way." She tied the rope around the bucket handle and then approached the tree.

Jack walked with her. "We could do without honey. You don't have to go through all this."

"I've got a taste for it now." She smiled at him, though he probably couldn't tell because of the bandanna around her face. "Don't worry." She plucked a burning twig from the fire and wrapped it in the branches, which she quickly tied tight in a bundle.

With the rope looped over her shoulder, the branches in the bucket, and the bucket handle looped over her arm, she shinnied up the tree. By the time she reached the high limb, the bundle of branches was smoking. She pulled it from the bucket and pushed it in front of her as she found a seat on the limb and scooted along to the hive. The bundled branches were producing a good amount of smoke now. It billowed in a white cloud as she leaned forward, passing the bundle below the hive and letting the smoke saturate it.

The aggressive buzzing gradually became a low drone. She glanced down to see her audience of two watching with rapt expressions.

Anne rested the smoldering branches on the tree limb in front of her, slid her knife out of its sheath, and sliced away a large chunk of beeswax, which she dropped into the bucket.

This she lowered to the ground with the rope. As soon as Jack had retrieved it, she let go of the end of the rope. "I'm going to toss down the branches next. Douse them in the stream."

She did so, and Jack snatched up the smoldering bundle and dashed toward the stream. Anne was already scooting her way back toward the tree's trunk. The bees would rouse quickly now that the smoke was gone.

At the base she found Jack returning from the stream. He was grinning from ear to ear and clapping. "That was quite the performance."

She bowed. "Why, thank you. Thank you."

"My brother taught you how to do that?" Mrs. Carver's voice was curious, without a single note of criticism.

Anne straightened. "Oh yes. He loved the forest. Growing up, I think I lived half my life in a tent, but I don't recall ever wanting for much. The forest had a way of providing for our needs when he was around." A deep nostalgic longing for her father made her eyes fill with tears, and she blinked them away. In her desire to become refined, she had moved to the city and had lost her sense of freedom and her connection to him. Maybe she shouldn't try to be something she wasn't. She busied herself with retrieving the rest of the makings for supper in order to have an excuse to turn away.

Silently, Jack came to assist her. He was a true gentleman. It seemed to come naturally, effortlessly to him. For him, etiquette wasn't a list of rules; it was about trying to be respectful and put people at ease. He wasn't just well mannered, he was gracious. And kind. His manner reminded Anne of her father. She'd say it was in the blood, but if that was the case, why didn't she have it? Maybe it came with their upbringing. The to-the-manor-born confidence made Jack very attractive.

Not that she cared. She swallowed. Who did she think she was fooling?

"You're quiet all of a sudden," he said at last. Not pushing for a response.

She summoned the brightest smile she could manage. "No choice. My mouth keeps watering when I think about that honey."

"Of course, you've listened to my instruction well. Active drooling is frowned upon in polite society." He took the pack of foodstuffs and large pot and carried it to the fire for her.

"I am glad you taught me that. It would have been embarrassing to be the only drooler at my next dinner party." She used tongs to mound hot embers around the base of the large pot and smiled ruefully. "Although to be fair, I don't think anyone back in San Francisco is likely to invite me to any dinner parties any time soon."

Jack put a hand on her arm, forcing her gaze up to his. "That's their loss, Anne. You're worth any ten of them."

She froze, unsure of what to do or say, waiting for the punch line, the joke.

"I just thought you should know." He removed his hand but left behind turmoil. Was it possible that he cared for her as she had come to care for him? She wasn't one of the fancy ladies he grew up around. She never would be. How could she ever please someone as polished and educated as he was? Should she try?

She didn't know what or who she was anymore.

Mrs. Carver returned from a discreet trip into the woods, and Jack withdrew, heading toward the stream. Anne jabbed at the embers with a stick as her aunt approached and began pulling foodstuffs and tin plates from their bags.

"Mrs. Carver, you know good and well I've made this trip on my own plenty of times. Why did you really insist on coming?"

Her aunt swallowed and was silent for so long that Anne was certain she wasn't going to answer. Finally she pulled out the carefully wrapped packet of biscuits and looked up. "You may not believe it, but when I was a young woman, I had many beaux, and not just because of the family's wealth. But not a one of them captured my fancy."

She paused, but Anne didn't try to fill in the silence. This was the most her aunt had revealed of herself since her arrival in California.

After a moment Mrs. Carver continued. "Not until I met my mountain man. He'd come back east to fight for the North in the war, and I was a nurse."

Anne stilled her restless hands at this revelation, fearful of drawing her aunt's ire and halting the flow of confidence.

"Of course, my parents didn't approve. I ended up listening to their counsel, but a part of me has always wondered."

Anne cocked her head, trying to understand the emotions behind the words.

"Wondered how I would have managed. What my life would have been like if I'd run away with him. I suppose I thought that this trip might answer some of my questions."

Impulsively, Anne laid a hand on her shoulder. "I have no doubt that you could have done it, but if your parents were able to talk you out of it, then he wasn't the man for you. You're a woman who acts on her convictions."

Mrs. Carver didn't pull away, but there was a sudden sheen of moisture in her eyes and she blinked rapidly. "Yes, well, while we're on the subject of my stubbornness, I think I could do with some of that liniment, if you still have it."

Anne swallowed a smile and hurried to fetch the medicine. Maybe there was more to her aunt than her abrasive exterior would suggest.

◆ ◆ ◆

Jack stared out at the vista spreading before him. This was truly God's country. He'd never seen a more beautiful spot. Even knowing how rugged and demanding the landscape could be after climbing up into the mountains for three and a half days straight, he couldn't quite get past the beauty of this wilderness. "I have never seen anything so stunning," he whispered. He glanced up to catch a glimpse of Anne's profile as she, too, gazed out over the forest, and he realized that he might have to qualify his statement. With love for this place shining in her eyes, she was easily a match for the scenery.

She glanced his way and gave him a reassuring smile. "It's not much farther." She raised her hand and pointed about halfway down the mountain, opposite to a bit of a plateau. With her guidance he spied a thin stream of smoke and a clearing with a handful of shingle-sided buildings.

"That's it?" It was hard to believe that the fabled mine was within sight. Or, more accurately, it was hard to believe that that sight was the fabled mine.

"Yes." She beamed at him, and he decided to reserve judgment. Some things were most impressive only after you came close to them.

Chapter 6

Anne had managed to keep anxiety at bay in the last few days by focusing on the goal of getting herself and the others safely to the mine. Now that it was in sight she could feel worry expanding like a noxious bubble within her chest. The closer they drew, the more immediate her concern became. It was more than the natural concern that would have been prompted by the maddeningly nonspecific telegram.

She watched the site carefully as they approached. It wasn't until they were about to break from the cover of the forest that she finally realized what had her on edge. There was no movement in the yard and not a sound from any of the outbuildings. She pulled up hard on her horse's reins.

She heard her aunt's grunt and the jingle of her horse's bridle as she reacted to Anne's move, drawing to the side to avoid a collision.

Anne turned back to them both. "I know you're as anxious to get there as I am, but would you indulge me and wait here?"

Her aunt frowned. "What kind of trouble are you expecting?"

"I'd like to look around first and, um, make sure they know I've brought guests before you arrive."

Jack shook his head. "Anne—"

Mrs. Carver gave him a sharp look.

He cleared his throat. "Miss Shepherd, I know you well enough by now to know that you're not riding ahead to make sure your men have the place tidied up for our arrival. How about you tell us what's going on."

"I don't know what's wrong. It's just that it's. . .it's too *quiet*."

"Then you're not going in there alone."

"It's my mine and my horse. I can ride where I like."

"No doubt, but I'm riding with you."

"As am I," her aunt added stoutly.

It took some doing, but at last Anne was able to convince her aunt to remain where she was so she could go for help if necessary. Considering that the woman had no idea where they were or how to find the nearest settlement, it seemed unlikely that any help she might bring to bear was going to be of material use, but Anne very carefully did not point this out. Jack proved more stubborn. At last her anxiousness to find out what was going on outweighed her objections to his presence.

Together they rode from the woods. Nothing stirred in the little mining settlement.

The whole place hadn't caved in or burned down. Whatever had happened could be fixed. At least that's what she meant to keep telling herself.

She reined up in front of the office, hitched her horse to the post, and headed inside. To her surprise, there was a man sitting behind the desk with his feet propped up. He was a stocky fellow with bushy black eyebrows and a bristly beard. He wore a grimy, sweat-rimmed hat on his head, and there was a hole in the sole of one of his boots. He was reading a dime-store novel and wiping tobacco juice from his mouth with a large handkerchief. At their entrance he lowered the book and peered at them over the top.

His eyebrows rose and the chair legs thumped to the floor. "Who are you?"

"Who are you?"

Their questions rang out simultaneously.

Anne could practically hear her blood begin to simmer. "I'm the owner of this mine. Now tell me who you are and what you're doing here before I forget that I'm a lady."

"I'd suppose you'd say this mine has come under new management."

"Don't be ridiculous. Where is An Wei?"

The door opened behind them, letting light stream in like a river through the office. It was bisected by a dark shadow. Anne turned to see who had arrived. This man was broad in the chest and wore a Stetson like he was some sort of cowboy. Spurs jingled as he stepped inside the office.

"Mornin', folks, how can I help you?"

Holey Shoes jumped in. "This lady claims to own the mine."

"Own the mine?" The newcomer's brow grew rutted, as if he was perplexed. "Why, you must be Anne Shepherd. I'm Sam Holt." He planted a hand on her shoulder. "I'm afraid I've got some bad news for you, honey. Your pa was a claim jumper. This is my mine." He hustled her to a chair. "I'm sure this comes as a surprise."

The whooshing in her ears almost drowned him out. "This is not your mine, and my father was no claim jumper."

"I'm sure it's a bitter pill to swallow. I can understand that, sure enough." He claimed a seat next to her and leaned forward earnestly and much too closely. "I've been wondering how to handle this matter, but I can see you're a nice young lady. I don't want to make things hard on you. And neither of us wants a legal wrangle." He offered a grin that revealed a row of oddly even, white teeth. "You're my witness, Clint. I'm pledging here and now that I'm not going to pursue this young lady for the gold that's been stolen from my mine already."

"How dare you!" Anne was back on her feet in an instant. "I don't know what you're trying to pull, but you're about to get me riled."

Jack placed a hand at the small of her back. The slight pressure at once a warning and an encouragement to resume her seat. She quieted, but she was too wound up to sit again.

"Gentlemen, I assume you have some proof of what you're saying?"

"I wouldn't make such claims willy-nilly." The fellow flapped a hand in the air. "Clint, where's the file?"

Clint prodded the only papers on the desk. "Is this what you're looking for, boss?"

"I do believe that's it." The fellow stood and accepted the documents from his underling. He glanced through them, nodding. "I believe everything is here." He pulled back just as Jack reached to take the documents. "And who might you be?"

"I'm Perseus Wilberforce the Second, Miss Shepherd's lawyer."

"A lawyer. We are in distinguished company." He handed Jack the papers.

There was a long pause as Jack paged through each document. At last he shuffled them back into order. "I'm afraid I have some bad news, Anne."

She could not believe what she was hearing. There was no way this man could have a legitimate claim to her mine. Was there?

A wide, froggy smile crossed Mr. Holt's face.

Jack set the documents neatly on the corner of the desk. "It seems that you are going to be forced to deal with a forger and a would-be claim jumper."

For a heartbeat there was silence as everyone in the room absorbed what he'd said, then the grin faded from Holt's face. "I think you're getting some bad legal advice."

A sneer curled Jack's lips. "The patents are terrible forgeries. You boys should clear on out now before the law arrives. We won't try to stop you."

A whisper of leather and then Anne heard the unmistakable sound of a gun being cocked.

"'Fraid that's not how this is going to go, lawyer." Holt looked almost rueful as he stood up, gun in hand, and trained it right between Anne's eyes. "I hate to do this. I sure enough do. I tried to get you all to just move along, but you forced my hand. I call it unfortunate." He gave a little flick of the gun tip. "Clint, I'm gonna need you to tie these folks up."

"You can't possibly think you're going to get away with this." Anne shook her head. "Even if you kill me, my heirs will own the mine, and they'll come to check it out. You can't steal a mine without someone noticing."

While Holt kept the gun trained on Anne, Clint grabbed hold of Jack's hands and began binding them behind his back with a piece of rope. Undeterred, Jack spoke. "Anyone looking at those will know they're forgeries. You didn't even spell California correctly."

"We're not trying to steal the mine."

Anne had no idea what he was getting at but refused to give him the satisfaction of asking.

He gave her a look that was the equivalent of a pat on the head. "We're stealing the gold, sweetheart."

"What?" Jack's question had an incredulous little laugh at its tail.

"We are stealing the gold," Holt enunciated carefully. He looked back to Anne. "Your men are very kindly helping us out."

"You're using them as slave labor." The heat in Anne's blood began to climb again. Clint reached for her arm and she jerked away in revulsion, bringing her other hand around and boxing him soundly on the ear.

"Ow." His grunt of pain was loud but almost drowned out by Holt's bark of laughter.

"You're going to have to keep an eye on this one. She put up more of a fight than all them other boys put together." He tipped his hat to her. "I suppose that's why you're the boss, ma'am."

Clint approached her more warily this time, and she backed away from him one step and then another. Unfortunately, this put her too close to Holt. Lightning fast, he stepped forward and grabbed her by the throat. The pressure of his fingers digging into her windpipe held her in place.

Hands tied behind him, Jack dove toward him headfirst. "Let her go."

Holt clouted him on the head with the butt of the gun and bright red blood immediately welled up from a gash on Jack's forehead. He slumped to the ground with a groan.

Dark spots swam in Anne's vision. Her feet had only the most tenuous purchase on the ground. She couldn't get leverage. Couldn't get a breath. She wanted to claw the hand away from her throat, but Clint had jerked her arms behind her as he bound her wrists. The cord bit deep into her skin, and her last panicked thought was a plea for air.

◆ ◆ ◆

Dazed, Jack lay on the floor. Something dripped into his eyes, burning, and blurring his vision even more. He blinked furiously. A groan escaped him, and he tried to stand.

"Hurry up, you idiot."

"I'm working on it, boss."

"Now you've gone and done it. She's passed out. I told you to hurry up."

Jack struggled to right himself. It was difficult with the world spinning around him and without his hands.

"Sorry, Holt."

"What did you do to her?" Jack demanded.

"She'll be all right." Holt was dismissive as he let Anne's limp form slump to a chair. Her head lolled and she sat at an unnatural angle, with her arms behind her.

"Why are you doing this?"

Holt looked mildly confused. "Gold."

"Why not rob a bank?"

Holt laughed. "We've done that, too, but there's no percentage in it." He holstered his gun and sat on the edge of the desk. Seemingly happy to explain the depths of his brilliance. "Banks are in towns where they got police, and folks get together posses. It gets messy. We could try the trains, but they ain't as easy to hit as you'd think. They're moving targets for one thing, and for another, every would-be crook in the west is trying to make his name robbing trains. We practically have to stand in line to take our turn. But I got to thinking, we needed a quiet place to lay low for a while, and we needed some big money. So I thought to myself, why not kill a bunch of birds with one rock. This mine had a few guards, of course, but it was easy picking them off, and then it was just a matter of rounding up the other guns and putting everybody to work. When we leave, we'll be loaded down with all the gold them miners is digging up for us right now, and no one to say it ain't ours fair and square."

Jack was impressed in spite of himself. "That's pretty smart."

Holt nodded smugly.

"But where are you going to get it smelted?"

"You don't need to worry about that none. Suffice it to say I got it all worked out."

"What are you going to do with us?"

"I'll give you options. Either you can join your pals in the mine and dig us up gold faster, or I'll have Clint here throw you off the cliffs."

"Not much of a choice."

Holt shrugged. Jack longed to punch the smirk off the man's face.

Anne stirred and then straightened up with a tiny moan. "I'm not going to work my mine for you." Her voice sounded hoarse.

"Your choice." The smirk grew darker. "We might be able to find another way to make you useful."

Jack seethed, his wrists straining against the ropes. He should never have allowed himself to be tied up so easily. His struggles struck Holt as funny. The fellow began chortling and he pulled a face, evidently in imitation of Jack's expression.

"Just wait until I get loose."

"Ooh." Holt waved his hands nervously. "I guess I gotta make sure you don't get loose then." His contempt hung in the air. "Clint, take the girl into the back room. I think I've got something she can do for me."

Clint moved to do Holt's bidding, but the instant he came within range, Anne lashed out with a kick that caught him square in the stomach. He doubled over, retching. Holt moved toward her, hand drawn back as if he was going to strike her. Jack lunged at the fellow, catching him just behind the knees with his shoulders. They both crashed to the ground in a tangle. The breath was driven from Jack's lungs in a great whoosh. He gasped for air.

At that moment the door opened. Jack's heart sank. It must be one of the gang, and any remote chance of escape they'd won by taking the captors by surprise was lost.

"Everyone hold still."

That cut-crystal voice could only belong to one person. Jack raised his head. Mrs. Carver stood in the doorway with a rifle in her hands and a pistol tucked in her waistband.

Clint went rigid in his bent-over posture. Holt flopped onto his belly and stared at the newcomer with an expression of mingled surprise, annoyance, and amusement.

Anne bounced to her feet. "Aunt, you were not supposed to follow us."

"Seems lucky that I did." The hands holding the rifle were absolutely steady, her words precise. "Keep your hands where I can see them."

Laboriously, Jack gained his knees and then his feet.

"Jack, if you would be so good as to kick that man's gun away."

Jack glanced back at her. It was the first time she had ever used his preferred name. "Yes ma'am."

He toed the gun away from Holt and kicked it into the corner.

"And then if you would be so kind as to step on his hands and keep them in place while I release you both."

"It would be a pleasure."

He must have sounded too gung ho. She frowned. "There is no need to be cruel. Simply apply enough pressure to keep him from moving his hands. I don't want him to get the drop on us while I'm working to untie you two."

"It's going to be fun when my men come and catch you. I'm going to take my time," Holt snarled.

"What? Telling them how you were bested by a woman?" Anne was smiling now as her aunt tugged at the ropes binding her wrists. It took but a moment to release her. "You're good with those ropes."

"Yachting was very fashionable when I was young. I became quite the sailor."

Anne rubbed her wrists. "I imagine you have become everything you ever set your mind to."

Her aunt returned her smile fully for the first time in their acquaintance. "Let's just say that there are very few who have ever been able to deny me something I wanted."

Mrs. Carver set to work on Jack's bonds while Anne collected Holt's gun and their own weapons from around the room.

By the time Jack's wrists were loose, Anne was pressing a peacemaker into his hands. He took it eagerly. "I say we return the favor to these two fellows."

"By all means, they need to be tied up," Anne agreed.

Mrs. Carver's lip had a supercilious curl to it. "We'll make a better job of it than they managed."

She and Jack set to work. Hauling Holt to his feet first then pushing him down into the nearest chair, Jack made absolutely certain that the man's hands were securely tied behind him, weaving the ropes through the chair slats, then took the extra measure of tying his legs to the chair legs.

Anne had busied herself making sure Clint was secured.

She stepped back to admire their handiwork, hands on her hips. "Now we just need to rescue my workers."

A smile curled its way across Holt's lips and he exchanged a look with Clint.

"What's so funny?" Jack demanded.

"Nothing."

Anne's sneer at the man was full of loathing. "He thinks we're stupid and that we haven't figured out that he must have several men down in the mine keeping watch over my crew."

Holt's shoulders slumped ever so slightly. "If you're stupid enough to go after them fellers, you're stupid enough for anything."

Jack had had more than enough of Holt. Snatching up Clint's handkerchief from the desk where it had been discarded, he shoved it into Holt's mouth. Using his own bandanna, he tied the gag into place.

"Thank you, Jack. We should have done that ten minutes ago." Anne made a similar gag for Clint to prevent him from calling for help. Their problem was that they had no idea how many gang members there might be. While most might be in the mine, there was no guarantee there weren't some on the surface, working in a kitchen or tending animals or something.

"We need to spread out and make sure all the buildings are empty." Anne's voice came from the back room. She returned a moment later with two more pistols and a box of bullets. "Let's meet at the mine entrance in ten minutes."

Jack and Mrs. Carver each took their share of spare bullets, and then they fanned out through the small settlement. Jack headed toward the building Anne had identified as the bunkhouse, gazing this way and that as he did so, watching for the slightest movement that would hint at the presence of one of the gang.

He eased open the bunkhouse door and stepped inside. No one. The musky stench of stale sweat and dirty clothes filled the air, but there was little enough inside, a half-dozen bunk beds and a couple of chairs was the extent of the furniture. He crouched, and the single move was enough to see under the whole row of beds.

He exited the bunkhouse and headed for the stables. The stench here was different but no less noxious. He eased the door open a couple of inches and glanced inside. A man was humming to himself and listlessly shoveling fresh hay at the far end of the barn. Why did he have to be so far away?

Pulling his hat low so that it shadowed most of his face, Jack stepped inside. He grabbed a shovel propped by the door and raised a hand. "Holt sent me to come give you a hand."

"Huh?" The fellow looked up.

"I'm supposed to help you muck out this place."

"Who are y—" He got no further before the broad blade of the shovel caught him on the head and he sagged to the ground. Jack rolled him to his side and got his hands and feet tied in record time. Maybe once all this was sorted he'd become a cowboy. He seemed to have a knack for roping.

His captive jerked awake as he tied the last knot. "You're making a mistake, pal. You have no idea who you're dealing with."

Jack had run out of patience with these brigands, but he'd also run out of materials for a gag. He pulled free the fellow's own bandanna and used that, but the makeshift gag was a fragile barrier to further trouble. "If you know what's good for you, you'll stay quiet, and I won't send the others from my posse in here to string you up." Let the fellow think that making a ruckus would only cause him more trouble.

Jack pushed himself up and headed out the door. His ten minutes were up. It was time to see what the mines held.

Chapter 7

Anne kept her back to the wall of the mountain as she edged toward the mine's open maw. She'd seen no one in the kitchen or storehouse. That had to be a good thing. It meant they couldn't have too many men to spare. Or at least, that's what she hoped it meant.

The skitter of a pebble made her freeze in place. She scanned the area and spotted her aunt crouching low behind a bush. Rifle at the ready, Mrs. Carver gave her a jaunty salute with her free hand. The woman was full of surprises today. Anne nodded acknowledgment and looked for Jack.

The minutes trickled by, but they couldn't launch their assault without him. They were already outnumbered and, even though they were armed, the bandits would be just as heavily armed, and they would have no compunction about the miners getting caught in the cross fire. Anne adjusted the heavy rope slung over her shoulder, away from her neck, and looked to make sure her aunt was managing okay with the rope looped around her as well. Mrs. Carver didn't even seem to notice the additional burden.

At last Jack appeared behind the corner of the paddock. The three of them crept from hiding, and together they abandoned the sun for the gloom of the mine.

The mine had started life as a cave, and Anne had explored it all at one time or another, but the mining had changed it in subtle ways since she had last been there. She took one of the lanterns from the hooks by the entrance and lit it. It might alert a guard to their presence, but she had to trust that the gang's focus was on their prisoners and that they wouldn't be expecting trouble from their flank. Once she and her companions got a few hundred feet from the cave entrance they wouldn't be able to see a thing unless they had a lamp.

"There are four branches in the mine. I don't know which one they will be working." Her whisper seemed to ricochet off the walls and echo through the long passage.

"Should we split up again?" Her aunt sounded reluctant.

"I think we'd be wiser to stay together. They will have more than one man guarding the miners."

"How many workers?"

"If everyone is here, there should be thirty-one." She grimaced as they all tried to move forward quietly but seemed to make an enormous racket.

"If we can get the guards isolated, it will be a whole lot easier to manage them." Jack patted a large coil of rope he'd brought along, draped over one shoulder.

Anne nodded then realized he probably couldn't see the gesture. "But what if they're not isolated?"

"Then we make the dark work for us and play like Gideon."

"Make them *think* we outnumber them?" Anne was impressed. It was a good strategy, probably the only one with any chance of success.

"Keep them off-kilter," he confirmed.

The darkness edged closer, hemming them in as they moved deeper into the mine. Anne's senses strained to determine which direction might hold the workers. They explored the first branch of the mine, but it seemed to absorb every sound as they moved through it, giving nothing back. She was convinced that the miners weren't in this branch, but they explored it to the end. Her pulse was hammering against her throat, and she endeavored to hold the lamp steady, quelling the shaking in her hands. They turned around and returned to where they'd branched away from the main shaft.

Just before they reached the second branch Anne glimpsed the blush of another light against the wall around a bend.

"Someone's coming," she hissed. She blew out their lamp and pressed herself against the wall.

The rustle of fabric and scrape of boots told her the others were doing the same. The light moved steadily forward. Anne held her breath. The fellow was humming some barroom song in a painfully off-tune monotone. By the time his lazy stroll brought him near, Anne had decided he deserved to be trussed up just for the torture he had done to her ears.

He swung his lantern in a lazy arc. It illuminated his face in its flickering glow and then plunged him back into darkness. He appeared far younger than Anne would have guessed, perhaps sixteen or seventeen, with a narrow-jawed face still pocked by acne.

As the lamp arced away from them, Jack moved. Anne heard a thud, and the bandit slumped to the ground. Somehow Jack managed to catch the lamp before it smashed to the ground and started an oil fire. Anne heard his hiss of pain, and he moved his fingers to his mouth.

"Did you burn yourself?"

"I'm just singed. I'll be fine."

Mrs. Carver tied up the lad while Anne took Jack's hand in hers and examined his fingers. Angry red welts seared across the first three digits.

"These are going to blister." She pulled her last clean handkerchief from her pocket and wound it around the fingers.

"I need to be able to move my fingers."

"You need to not die of infection. Use your thumb to pull the trigger if you must. I'm hoping it doesn't come to that."

"Me, too." His voice was full of anxiety and rueful humor, and something else she couldn't define.

She glanced at his face, but it was too deeply shadowed to read. "Have you shot much?"

"Not at people."

"Me neither." Anne relit their lamp.

"I thought about trying to get information from him, but there was the chance he'd yell and bring reinforcements running, so knocking him out was the safest option."

Anne put a hand on his arm. "You were wonderful. I'm glad you're here."

Leaving their newest captive and his lamp in the main shaft, they continued on down the side branch. It was shallower than the first branch, and they'd gone only a couple dozen steps before they rounded a curve and could see the glow of lantern light on the wall. Anne set the lamp against the mine wall. She wanted her hands free to handle her gun. If they retreated this way, they could retrieve it then, either at speed or at leisure.

Faint voices reached her. Men talking louder than strictly necessary, as if trying to show the mountain how big and tough they were, how they weren't afraid of its vast reaches and immeasurable weight towering above them, as if they were, in fact, terrified. In short, not the voices of miners.

Good. The bandits were on edge. They wouldn't be thinking clearly. With the Lord's help, they'd be easy to confuse.

Jack led the way, and Mrs. Carver brought up the rear as they moved to enact their plan. Light from numerous lamps washed back toward them down the passage as glaring as if they were stepping into a spotlight, but there was no avoiding it. The best they could do was to edge their way along the wall.

There was a shout and some angry scuffling. A thud and a yelp of pain. Anne's fingers tightened on her gun. Her heartbeat thrummed loudly in her ears. They came to the final bend and Jack peered around the corner. Anne couldn't wait. She crouched and leaned around him until she, too, could see what was going on.

A mere ten feet away the cavern widened into a sort of room. It looked like all of her workers were there together. There was none of the gossipy chitchat in the singsong cadence of Mandarin that she was used to hearing. They were dead silent.

One man lay on the ground. A skinny fellow wearing an ill-fitting shirt stood over him. "Unless you want me to cut that pigtail of yours off, then you'll get back to work and not give us any more trouble."

There was a collective gasp at the threat. A man's queue was a sign of his loyalty to the emperor. To lose it would be a deep humiliation. "Now get up."

Jack inched back from the opening, forcing Anne to withdraw as well. For some reason, the three of them crouched low. They put their heads close together.

Jack spoke in a whisper. "There are five bandits."

Anne was glad he had kept his wits about him. She had been too distracted by the drama playing out before them to count.

"Are you both ready?"

She nodded. Mrs. Carver held aloft a length of rope.

Jack stood and stepped into the light. "Jig's up. Throw down your guns." His words, loud and authoritative, echoed and bounced around the rock chamber like billiard balls on a break.

Holt's men looked around them, trying to figure out where the threat was coming from though there was only one entrance. It took several seconds before they had all turned toward Jack.

"Don't move. We've got you covered."

Anne's palms were slick with sweat, and she held her gun tight but kept it level, the barrel protruding into the light far enough so that the bandits would have no doubt that Jack had backup, but not far enough that they would realize how limited that backup was.

"Drop your guns and put your hands in the air."

The bandits looked at one another, a question telegraphing between them as plain as words. Fight or surrender?

They had to act. Anne barked a command in Mandarin.

Instantly the miners overwhelmed their captors, swarming over them and striking the guns from their hands. Anne waved to her comrades. “C’mon.”

By the time they reached the melee, the battle was over. Mrs. Carver passed over her rope, and the bandits were very efficiently trussed up.

Chapter 8

It was only as he approached the men now tied up on the floor that Jack realized his knees were a little shaky. Anne, of course, moved with her usual confidence. She strode into the middle of the crowd of men, who all seemed to be speaking loudly and gesticulating wildly.

Jack kept pace, not about to let her go anywhere near the bandits without protection. Mrs. Carver was right behind them as well. The men quieted as Anne slipped among them.

She stopped before an older Chinese man with glasses whose queue had gone gray. She put her palms together and bowed her head. He responded in kind, and she spoke to him in Chinese for a moment. Jack stood behind her feeling redundant until she turned to him.

"May I introduce An Wei. He is the mine foreman."

She made all the introductions just as Jack had taught her a lifetime ago. No one could fault her memory.

Polite bows and smiles were exchanged all around, and the men bowed especially deeply to Mrs. Carver.

"Can he confirm that there were just nine bandits? We didn't miss any, did we?" Jack asked. He didn't want to celebrate prematurely.

"No. Only nine bandits." An Wei's English was accented but understandable.

"Ah, you speak English."

An Wei smiled and nodded another bow.

With a few words from him, the bandits were gathered up, cursing and bucking and carried out of the mine.

Jack and Anne followed more slowly. "What did you say to them at the end that made them go after the bandits?"

"I told them this was their chance, to attack. I thought those fellows were leaning towards fighting, and people were going to be hurt if they went down that road."

"I think you were right. All I can say is that God was looking out for us."

"True enough."

The next few hours were a whirlwind as they secured their captives and summoned the nearest law enforcement. It was two days before a sheriff and two deputies appeared. It turned out the Holt gang had a whole list of crimes to answer for, and the sheriff was more than happy to lock them up with promises to throw away the key.

A week after that found them disembarking wearily at the train station in San Francisco. Bao Chang awaited them with the carriage, and Jack thought he'd never looked forward to anything so much as a hot bath and a good night's sleep in a soft bed. He rubbed at the stubble on his chin. He understood now why men resorted to wearing beards. When a shave required all the effort of fetching water, warming it, and preparing a razor, it just didn't happen that often.

At Anne's house he dragged himself up the front stairs, using the last of his remaining energy. They were met by Anne's maid. She embraced her mistress in a wholly inappropriate display of affection from a servant, but rather than remonstrating, Mrs. Carver smiled.

Jack blinked. Come to think of it, the older woman had been quiet and pleasant on the entire journey back. Including the stop at the Indian village. Not a single word of complaint or criticism. Perhaps the wilderness agreed with her.

"Oh, Mr. Wilberforce." The maid pulled away and smoothed her apron. "Your mother arrived about twenty minutes ago. I told her your train was expected, so she decided to wait." She misinterpreted his stricken response. "Don't worry, I took her refreshments."

A weight settled on his shoulders, nothing like the honest exhaustion he'd felt before. This was different—bone deep and enough to make him sick to his stomach. He nodded numbly to the maid and headed across the marble hallway to the parlor.

He opened the door to find his mother sitting enthroned inside. Her nose wrinkled at his appearance, and she set aside the teacup she held.

"Hello, Mother."

"My dear, what have you been doing?" She tilted her cheek up for a kiss and he crossed the room to comply.

"It's a long story. But this is a surprise. What brings you to San Francisco?"

"You. I've been hearing rumors."

"About me. . . ? In Boston?"

"The world is a much smaller place than it used to be what with the Transcontinental Railroad and the telegraph." She broke off as Anne and her aunt entered. "Irene Carver, you look a sight. I'm not sure the West agrees with you."

"Martha." Mrs. Carver nodded. "You've come a long way."

His mother's smile was thin. "I thought I'd take the opportunity to return to Boston with Perseus. He's more than fulfilled his duty of delivering you to your niece."

"He has done impeccably." The smile Mrs. Carver turned on him was markedly warmer.

He smiled back, her praise unexpectedly endearing.

"And who do we have here?"

At this, Anne stepped from her position behind her aunt. Jack made the introductions.

"It's a pleasure to meet you, ma'am. You've raised a fine son. A credit to his name."

"Mm-hmm." Now his mother's smile was no more than a stretching of her lips. Her eyes were full of sharp appraisal as she took in Anne's travel-stained garments.

"Mother, you will never convince me that you simply decided on a jaunt across the country without Father. What have you come to say?"

His mother looked from him to Mrs. Carver to Anne and back again. "As I said, just silly rumors. I merely wanted to make sure there was nothing to them. My telegrams went unanswered."

"We haven't been here," Anne said.

"I see."

"What rumors, Mother?" His jaw was tight from the effort of holding back his temper. Anne was never like this. There was no one truer or more straightforward. He adored that about her.

A flush splotched along his mother's jawline and up into her cheeks. "It's—that is. . .I heard a rumor that you might be interested in. . .in Miss Shepherd here, in a romantic way. I simply want to know if it is true or not."

◆ ◆ ◆

Anne's mouth gaped open. "I can assure you there's no truth—"

There was a hiss of drawn-in breath from Mrs. Carver. "You came to warn him off and drag him home, didn't you?"

"His father does want him to come back to Boston."

"Martha Wilberforce, are you implying that my niece isn't good enough for this washed-up lawyer son of yours?"

"Well, no, Irene; of course, your family is of good stock. The best. But we don't know this girl. Don't have any way to know she's who she says she is. From what I've heard, she certainly doesn't act like a Shepherd. She could be after money."

Jack snorted. "Mother, she could buy and sell us three or four times over." He moved to stand directly in front of her. "I spoke to Father before I left. I'm not coming back."

"You're throwing away your future."

"No, Mother. California is my future." He turned from her and reached for Anne's hand. She had been uncharacteristically quiet throughout this whole exchange. "And Anne is my future. It would be my highest achievement to marry her, if she'll have me."

His mother began sputtering, but he had eyes and ears only for Anne.

She looked at him, wondering. "You're asking me to marry you?"

He nodded.

"But you know I'm not cultured, and I made a hash of that dinner party. I'm not a hostess. I'd end up embarrassing you."

"I don't want to marry a society hostess. I want to marry a woman who is loyal and kind, courageous and daring, and wise and so very beautiful." He raised his hand to cup her cheek, and she leaned into his palm ever so slightly. "Believe me, I'd be getting the better part of the bargain."

She searched his gaze, and it dawned upon her that perhaps she had been posing a false choice. Might it be possible to have both refinement and freedom? She could bring culture to the wilderness or independence to the city; the capacity for both lay within her.

She still had a choice to make, but it was the easiest decision she'd ever confronted. "Yes, oh yes." She flung her arms around Jack, and he whooped and lifted her up above his head before returning her to the ground and sealing the engagement with a kiss. At first it was exuberant, but as his lips lingered it grew more heated. His fingers cupped the back of her neck and she shivered. Dimly she heard her aunt speaking.

"Don't bother to fight it, Martha," Aunt Carver advised. "Give her some time and she'll grow on you."

Lisa Karon Richardson is an award-winning author and a member of American Christian Fiction Writers. Influenced by books like *The Little Princess*, Lisa's early books were heavy on creepy boarding schools. Though she's mostly all grown-up now, she still loves a healthy dash of adventure in any story she creates, even her real-life story. She's been a missionary to the Seychelles and Gabon, and now that she and her husband are back in America, they are tackling new adventures—starting a daughter-work church and raising two precocious kids.

Maggie's Newport Caper

by Lynette Sowell

Chapter 1

New York City, 1895

I always knew that James Blankenship would come to no good. He ought to be fired." Mother tossed the newspaper onto the tea table, making Maggie Livingston jump and nearly drop her book—or books, rather.

Maggie glanced up from the latest installment of *The Perils of Phoebe*, tucked discreetly inside a volume of *Great American Poets*. Mother's favorite activity on a rainy afternoon in New York was to read poetry aloud; therefore, such an activity must be Maggie's favorite, too. Mother would typically fall asleep after approximately twenty to thirty minutes, but today's slumber hadn't lasted for long after she began reading the newspaper.

Maggie tried not to squirm on the cushioned settee, lest she receive another admonishment on the value of proper posture.

"Why is that, Mother?" Maggie clutched the books against her bodice.

"Your father likes to tell me that I shouldn't read the newspaper, and I do wish that I had listened to him." She shook her head, snapping up the paper in one hand as she did so.

Maggie risked her book's discovery by standing then setting the books on the settee's cushion. Palms sweating, she crossed the parlor and stood before her mother.

"Here." Mother held up the newspaper. "You're bound to hear of it, anyway."

Maggie took the newspaper and read the headline. "'Livingston prospects fading, bank denies loan.'"

She swallowed hard. "Mother, things aren't that bad, are they?"

"No, of course not." Mother pulled the paper from Maggie's hand. "Your father's business is quite solvent, as he puts it. He merely sought a loan to build a new ship, and the bank refused him. He's inquiring into other possible avenues to secure funding. But this—this James Blankenship makes it sound as if we are headed to the poorhouse."

"But we're not heading to the 'poorhouse'?" Maggie tried not to smile at her mother's dramatic flair.

"No. You needn't worry of anything like that. You only need worry about what you shall wear to your debut next week. The seamstress—Clothilde Dubois—is meeting us Thursday morning at the cottage, where she shall bring an assortment of gowns for you to try."

More gowns.

"But I already have a gown to wear."

"Dear, that was last year's gown. It simply won't do. Everyone will know."

"I suppose you're right." But she'd loved the shade of jade-green silk and how the color made her brown hair seem a touch redder in the proper light.

Maggie bit her lip. Mother had tried to redirect her attention from Father's affairs to that of her upcoming official introduction to society.

She scanned their parlor, with its French furniture, carpet from China, and an Italian fresco on one wall. She had breakfasted this morning, and while a noonday dinner in the city with two of her friends had been canceled due to the rain, she had partaken of a more-than-adequate luncheon here at her family's city residence. She had comforts many only dreamed of. The thought of losing it made her heart beat a bit faster. Yet others not in her station could live comfortable and contented lives despite their lack of ornate surroundings.

She stepped over to the front windows overlooking Central Park. Despite the rain, her heart sang because tomorrow morning they were set to travel to Newport for the summer, to Tidewaters, their cottage—all thirty-five rooms of it.

The front door opened, making them both glance toward the entry.

"Father—you're home early." The fine lines around her father's eyes seemed a bit deeper this afternoon.

"Yes, I'm home early for a good supper before I see the two of you to Newport in the morning."

Mother rose, laying the newspaper on the tea table beside her as she did so. "You didn't tell me you would be coming as well."

Father nodded, removing his hat. "I shall stay the weekend then depart for the city on Sunday afternoon."

He paused in the parlor's doorway and glanced between both of them. "I can see the concern in your expressions. Is it that newspaper article by Mr. Blankenship?"

"Of course it is." Mother frowned. "You ought to sue him for libel, or slander, especially if what he says isn't true."

Father waved her words away. "Nonsense. It's simply a misleading headline, nothing more. His father and I have had discussions over James's writing before. There is something else, though, you must know."

He glanced over his shoulder before continuing. "It might make the news tomorrow, or may not. But I heard from Benjamin Morris that his residence was broken into and all of his wife's jewelry is missing."

"Stolen?" Mother gasped.

Maggie touched the brooch pinned to her shirtwaist. "Does he know who might have done it?"

"No," Father said.

Webster approached, smiling as he did so. "Mr. Livingston."

Father handed Webster his hat. "Thank you, Mr. Webster."

The houseman hurried away, giving Maggie a grandfatherly smile. She'd never known either of her grandfathers, and the courtly older man displayed his warm side for her and few others.

"We must secure our things." Mother nodded. "I certainly hope they don't come here. All the lovely pieces you've bought for me over the years."

"I find it highly unlikely they will. I've already instructed Mr. Webster to keep a close eye on our household." His eyes narrowed as he looked at her, then twinkled mischievously. "And I'm sure you will bring all your baubles to the cottage with you and not leave them here."

Mother grinned at him, her glance sliding sideways toward Maggie, who took her seat on the settee and snatched up her books with care.

"Mr. Livingston, you know me too well."

Maggie shifted on the cushioned seat and tried to find her place in the book she'd put aside moments earlier.

Instead, her mind swirled with news of the break-in and robbery. Would anyone come after their valuables as well? Who would do such a thing?

Upon arriving in Newport, her first order of business would be to speak with one of her best friends, Elizabeth Morris. She hadn't seen Elizabeth since Easter time and missed her. What had it been like to know that someone, possibly a stranger, had been in their home going through their belongings?

Or perhaps it was one of the Morrises' household staff. Yet the Morrises paid their staff well. Maggie's mother had hired one of the Morrises' former cooks, and Maggie had overhead two of the cooks discussing what the new woman had been paid at the other house.

However, being well paid wouldn't overcome some failures of human nature, like greed. The words on the page in front of her blurred as she thought over the break-in.

She hoped and prayed no one else would fall prey to the thief and that if the thief was someone in need, their need would be discovered and met.

◆ ◆ ◆

James Blankenship settled into the chair across the desk from his editor at the *New York Empire News*. He already knew what was coming next. He also wasn't sure his editor's idea would work.

"So, Blankenship, you ready to rub shoulders again with the upper-crust set from whence you came?" William Burrows steepled his fingers under his chin.

"What exactly do you need me to do?"

"Look into the recent burglary and theft at the Benjamin Morris residence. They're not going public with it, but I hear it's happened more than once this year among the gilded bunch. I'd like you to head to Newport and follow the summer social season, see what turns up."

James nodded slowly, trying to school his features at the idea of returning to Newport, even temporarily. "My family won't exactly be happy to see me." Perhaps Mother would; but her tears would cut him to the core and remind him of where he'd fallen short in her estimation.

"You're not there to make them happy; you're there to find the story." Burrows picked up a cigar on a nearby ashtray, tapped it, then put out the smoldering tip. "Tell 'em whatever you want, that you're the prodigal son come home, whatever comes to mind. But find the story."

"I'll find the story. It's. . .it's about time I visit them, anyhow. I've been too busy to consider it."

"Until now." Burrows handed him an envelope. "There's enough in here for a train ticket and money for essentials. Your family will let you stay with them?"

"I imagine they will." And they'll be after me, once again, to return to that fishbowl of a life. As he picked up the envelope and tucked it into his jacket pocket, the echoes of the last argument he'd had with his father echoed in his mind.

"Stay until the story is over." Burrows waved him away. "Pay a visit to the Morrises and see what they'll tell you. Sit on the story, but not too long. We don't want the *Times* to scoop us. Something tells me this could be a big one."

James stood, tugging the hem of his jacket. "I understand. I'll keep you informed."

"Call me on Fridays, let me know what's going on, and we'll go from there."

"I'll call you a week from tomorrow unless I find something significant."

"I'll be waiting for that call."

He left Burrows's office, closing the door behind him as he did so. The newsroom buzzed with the familiar click-clack of typewriter keys and the murmured and sometimes shouted conversations on telephones.

This was his place he'd grown to know, doing the work he loved. Making discoveries, breaking the news, following history in the making.

Father never understood his fascination with the printed word, especially news, James mused as he headed into the sunny afternoon. The leftover puddles from today's rain at lunchtime made the air thick and heavy. Some time at the Rhode Island coast would be the thing, to breathe in some fresh, salty air.

After a streetcar ride to his walk-up apartment, James paused at his mailbox. A letter waited for him. He pulled out the envelope and immediately recognized his mother's elegant penmanship. While standing at the mailbox, he opened the envelope, pulled out a single page, and read:

My dear James,

I hope and pray this finds you well. Christmas seems like a long time ago—nearly six months! A far too long time to go without seeing my youngest son.

Your father's health is adequate at the moment, yet I believe he is not feeling quite as well as he puts out to others. He is grooming Frank for the business. I am quite certain, however, he would welcome another Blankenship son back to the fold.

I do understand your compulsion to follow the news and the written word, but I must be honest that your father still does not understand, nor is he pleased. But I believe he would not be at all unhappy to see you should you come to a visit.

Happy news! No one else knows at this time, but your brother is soon to be engaged to the young Miss Margaret Livingston, of Livingston Shipping and Manufacturing. She makes her debut in Newport very soon, during which the announcement shall be made. How glad I will be to have a daughter!

Please write to me as you are able. A visit from my James would be even better.

Your devoted, loving
Mother

James stood holding the letter in the apartment entryway. Margaret—Maggie—Livingston. Now that was a name he hadn't heard in a long time. Last time he'd seen her, she'd been ten or eleven years old with an impish grin at a supper party that the Livingstons and Blankenships had attended here in Manhattan. He'd been full of himself, thinking that night mostly of the college days that lay ahead of him, all while a pesky little girl with big brown eyes peppered him with questions about the book he'd been reading in a corner because he was bored.

"I like books," he recalled her saying. "Adventure books are the best of all."

He'd been reading *Robinson Crusoe* and was surprised at the time to hear she'd read it, too.

Her precocious nature surprised him. Then the entire party laughed when she promptly announced to everyone that one day she was going to go on a safari, or perhaps to India, all by herself.

She'd fought off tears then, he could see, but her slim, young jaw had been stiff.

He remembered thinking then he liked her pluck, how she didn't want to bend to what "they" expected of her.

He wondered if her nature had tempered over the years. Otherwise, he imagined his older brother, Frank, might soon be tied to a handful.

Chapter 2

Maggie inhaled the salty air as she and Elizabeth Morris walked arm in arm along Newport's beach walk. They'd stolen an hour or so from the demands that came with a summer by the sea, forgoing an afternoon of boating with other friends.

Of course, Maggie brought up the break-in, and Elizabeth immediately expressed her doubts as to whether it was a break-in after all.

"You're certain it wasn't a break-in?" Maggie squinted out at the waves pounding a gentle rhythm on the shore.

"Yes. Father seemed to think it appeared as though someone had tried to pick the lock to the front door on that Wednesday afternoon. But I was home that day and I can clearly see the entry from the street. I was. . .I was waiting for someone." At her last words, Elizabeth's cheeks colored.

Maggie stood stock-still on the walkway, causing Elizabeth to skid to a stop as well. "What? Who? You look as flush as if you've been out all day without your hat."

"Someone." Elizabeth glanced back toward the edge of the walkway. "You will not tell?"

"I promise."

Her friend swallowed hard. "Henry Blankenship, a cousin of the New York Blankenships. He's entirely unsuitable to my parents, but he asked if he could call, and so I said it would be. . .nice."

"Oh, Elizabeth. But you haven't had your debut yet."

Elizabeth squared her shoulders. "I am eighteen, and I am prepared to speak to my parents about an arrangement between Henry and me. He is not as well-off as his cousins, Frank and James, but that doesn't matter to me. He has good prospects. All we did was have conversations on the porch. If things do not go well, I have another plan in mind."

They continued walking, further out of earshot of the maids who accompanied them for propriety's sake. All the better. Maggie's own cheeks burned.

"Good prospects—perhaps. But will your family approve?"

"I can only pray they will. Otherwise I have no idea who they might choose for me. I simply cannot abide the idea of anyone else but Henry."

Maggie nodded slowly and said no more.

Elizabeth nudged her. "But what about you? Your debut is coming. Have your parents hinted at a match?"

"Not at all." The idea of being attached to someone as if she were an extra appendage made her stomach roil. Her parents loved each other, but their love had come before the family's wealth, before she was born. Add on the fact she had money now, well, she questioned the motivation of any who might come calling—no matter how precarious their situation may or may not be.

"Has anyone in particular caught your attention?" Elizabeth gave her a pointed look.

"No." Maggie hadn't really looked or paid attention to any eligible men. "Some of the eligible men are old as Methuselah. Anyway, I can't picture being married anytime soon."

"Well, I'd prepare myself for it, if I were you. We're not quite Vanderbilts, so we need to be grateful for what comes our way."

Maggie wasn't so sure about that. She cleared her throat. "So, about the robbery. If you don't believe someone broke in, who do you think might have done it?"

"I would hate to venture a guess." Elizabeth's forehead wrinkled. "I've known most of our staff since I was a young girl. The new ones, well, they came highly recommended, and as best I know, all have impeccable employment records, without a hint of anything improper."

"And all of your mother's jewelry was taken?"

"Yes. Mine as well. Except for one piece."

"That is a curious detail. Why would a thief take everything but one item? What was it?"

"It was a carved ivory brooch that was my grandmother's that my mother gave to me on my sixteenth birthday."

"Curious," Maggie repeated to herself. "It must be worth something. Not as much as diamonds or gemstones."

Elizabeth shrugged, causing her parasol to bobble as she did so. "No, but it is a distinctive piece, and they might not have been able to sell it without gathering questions."

"Perhaps not. What about the other items that were stolen?"

Shouts came from the head of the walkway.

"Miss Maggie, come quickly!" Her maid, Gertrude, waved a handkerchief. "It is most urgent."

Maggie gave Elizabeth a glance. "I must go."

"I'll come with you."

They hurried along, catching up their skirt hems—it wouldn't do to end up on one's face along the beach walk—and soon met the maids at the edge of the way.

"I apologize for shouting so." Gertrude's cheeks flamed redder than usual in her ruddy face. "You are needed right away at the tennis club. Mrs. Livingston presumed you were there with Miss Morris." She bowed her head toward Elizabeth, who nodded in return.

Oh dear. If Mother had sent for her, who knew what had happened?

"Did she say I must go home straightaway?"

"She did not, only that she sent someone to inquire of you at the club."

A short three-minute walk and Maggie, perspiring profusely, entered the tennis club. What a good thing a cold glass of lemonade would be at the moment. She lacked a fan, and she could sense the heat radiating from her head beneath her summer hat.

Mr. Webster stood at the reception area. He looked cool and unruffled as ever, but his face wore a concerned expression.

"Miss Livingston. I apologize for the interruption, but your presence is required at the house."

"Of course." Her heart fluttered inside her chest. "What has happened?"

"I'm afraid there has been a break-in."

◆ ◆ ◆

At the word *break-in*, James flipped his newspaper down so he could stare across the lounge at the tennis club.

Stared at the young woman whom he'd once encountered when she was but a precocious little sprite. Maggie Livingston—she had to be at least eighteen now, or older—had grown into an elegant young woman, it seemed, although she perspired like she'd been walking about town for hours.

She glanced in his direction.

Was that a flicker of recognition in her eyes? Whatever it was, it vanished almost as quickly as he'd glimpsed it.

He folded the paper, set it on a nearby table, and crossed the lounge.

"Good afternoon, Miss Livingston and Miss. . . ?" He glanced at the blond with round blue eyes who stood next to Maggie.

"Morris." She nodded to him. "Miss Elizabeth Morris."

"James Blankenship." He extended his hand to the older man. "Mr., ah, your face is familiar but your name escapes me."

"Webster. I am the houseman for the Livingston family. You have business with the Livingstons?"

"No. I am merely an old family friend of Miss Livingston and her family, here for the summer, or at least the week. Is there something I can do to help?"

"Help?" Maggie asked, darting a look at Mr. Webster. "You seem familiar to me, but as I can't place your name either, I think we will not require your assistance. Unless, of course, you are with the local authorities."

"No." He shook his head. He was a fool for speaking with her under such circumstances. He'd been thinking of the story, not thinking of how his question would appear.

"I remember you." Webster's voice held a warm tone. "You're the younger Blankenship son, gone off to see the world and chase his own fortune. Always full of questions, you were."

James nodded. "I'm a newspaper reporter in New York. My job is to notice things and ask questions."

"Well, as you are a newsman, I am not so sure the family would want you on the property at the moment, son of a family friend or no," Webster said.

"It's quite all right, Mr. Webster." Maggie, her face full of recognition and a hint of a smile on her lips, touched James's arm with one of her gloved hands. She pulled it back swiftly. "Please, come with us. If you are as observant as I think you must be, you might be of some help."

She remembers me.

James didn't know whether that was a good idea at the moment, but he reminded himself he was following his boss's orders. This was a big development, and he needed to be there.

"I will, gladly."

"I've brought the carriage." Webster's eyes narrowed ever so slightly as he gazed at James. "Mr. Blankenship can ride outside with the driver."

They left the tennis club, where a carriage waited for them. Maggie bade her friend farewell, then Webster held the carriage door open for both her and a young maid. He nudged James toward the front seat.

As they headed along to the row of magnificent homes along the waterfront, James could scarcely hide the wonder he felt at seeing them in person. There was Marble House—or its gates, rather. He could glimpse the "cottage" behind the fences and only guess at the opulence inside. Green, green lawns stretched toward the ocean water that lay beyond the yards.

There was Tranquility, the residence of the Wallingford family, if he remembered correctly. His own family's mansion came next, almost modest looking compared to the others but still a stately residence in its own right.

"You have been gone a long time, Mr. Blankenship," Mr. Webster observed.

"Yes, sir, that I have."

"Not in the family business, either, are you?"

"No, sir, I am not. Unless my father were to purchase the newspaper, which I don't believe is something he would do." As he said the words aloud, he wondered if his father would actually make such a business decision.

"You're not interested in the family business, then?"

"No. I preferred to make my own way, which I have done since ending my education."

"I see." They rumbled along, with the women seated behind them making a low conversation.

The "I see" held faint tones of disapproval, much as his father's welcome had when James had arrived at Fairwinds doorstep the other evening, satchel in hand.

"I'm sure it was a disappointment to your family."

"I'm sure of that, too."

Mr. Webster had plenty of nerve, speaking to the son of a Blankenship in such a way. But it didn't really bother James, although his younger self might have considered it mildly rude. The older man was a fixture in the Livingston house. He was older, grayer than James recalled when last seeing him, but his eyes were bright and perceptive.

James truly hoped Webster didn't see right through him. Besides working on his story, James had the inclination to get to see what kind of woman young Maggie Livingston had become.

Not that it mattered. Not if she was going to become his sister-in-law, he reminded himself.

Chapter 3

As she lived and breathed! James Blankenship stood in the entry of Maggie's family home. Stood in the full force of her parents' gaze. No, he definitely wasn't who they expected to have come calling on them—especially not by hitching a ride back from town with her and Gertrude.

In the midst of the discovery of the break-in, no one seemed to mind that Mr. Blankenship had come calling, unannounced.

"What happened?" both Maggie and James asked at once. She didn't miss the slight twitch at the corners of his mouth as they did so.

"It's gone—my jewelry, all of it." Mother held up her hands then wrung them together, rubbing her bare wrists as if someone had pulled bracelets from them.

"When did you notice things were missing?" Margaret asked. "And what about my things?" She didn't want to sound selfish. She was glad no one was hurt.

"After tea." Mother sighed. "I went to lie down because I had the beginnings of a headache, and I noticed the lid to my jewelry case was partly lifted. I knew I had not done that, because I didn't put any jewelry on this morning. I pulled the lid off, and it's—it's all gone."

"Are the authorities on the way?" James asked.

"We've not summoned them," her father said.

"I told him not to," her mother hurriedly followed up Father's words before Maggie could ask. "We don't need the attention. It's embarrassing."

The same as the Morrises. Maggie bit her lip.

"I apologize for inserting myself into your current situation, but I spoke with Mr. Webster at the tennis club and offered my assistance," James said.

"Assistance? How?" Father folded his arms across his chest and regarded James skeptically.

"My specialty in my work is information. I notice things. I listen to people. I would like to help you find whoever has done this." James's voice held a confident air, yet not forceful or rude. Maggie found it entirely convincing.

"I don't know, Mr. Livingston." Mother frowned. "The idea of finding and, I hope, recovering our belongings is appealing to me. Perhaps Mr. Blankenship can help without much public fuss."

"Yet you work as a newspaperman." Now Father wore a frown that matched Mother's. "How will I know you won't use this information somehow to your advantage? After our recent discussion regarding my business outlook, that is."

James hesitated briefly, glancing at Maggie as he did so. "I have to admit, my boss has asked me to spend time in Newport due to what happened at the Benjamin Morris residence. He wonders if this is a pattern, and I'm afraid to say I must agree with him. I would like to help you get to the bottom of this. I promise I will not reveal anything in writing before I consult with you."

"Very well. Come with me, and I will show you what I can." Father gestured to James, who followed him up the stairs to where the bedrooms were located.

Mother's cheeks were flushed. She pulled out a fan, waving it in front of her face. "The weather this summer, and now all this. I'm simply too flustered and warm."

"Mother, is all of your jewelry missing?" Maggie thought back to her earlier conversation with Elizabeth.

"I'm afraid so." Her shoulders drooped, but then she squared them again. "It's simply evil, just evil, that someone would do something like this to us."

Maggie glanced at their staff who waited nearby. "Mother, may we speak privately, in the parlor?"

"Yes. I need to sit down, anyway. Perhaps the breeze will help."

Maggie led her into the parlor with its marble fireplace, only used on damp, wet days in the summer. She slid the pocket doors closed then joined her mother on the chaise.

Mother opened one of the windows facing the ocean, after which a breeze swirled into the room. "And I thought such things would only happen in the city."

"I must ask you some questions, Mother, while others cannot hear us."

With a whirl and widened eyes, Maggie's mother turned from the window to face her. "Margaret Livingston, I'm not sure I approve of your forceful tone."

Maggie paused before continuing. "Mother, I mean no disrespect, but like Mr. Blankenship, I, too, would like to find out what has happened to our jewelry. I was speaking with Elizabeth Morris before Mr. Webster came to fetch me home, and I would like to see if there are any similarities in the robbery."

Mother appeared to ponder that idea for a moment. She inclined her head slightly. "Very well. What would you like to ask?"

"First, why did you agree to allow J—Mr. Blankenship to help us, when but days ago you were calling for him to be fired from his position?"

"It's simple, my dear. I want him nearby where I can hear firsthand what he is saying and doing about our plight." She sighed again. "This is simply unacceptable. People just do not go around stealing things in broad daylight, not here, anyway."

"Do you think. . .do you think it is one of the staff? I don't want to think about any of them taking something then trying to sell it elsewhere. We have known them for many years." Maggie stood, and strode to the open window and inhaled deeply of the air drifting in from outside. So much cleaner, purer, than the air in New York.

"I don't know. Like you, I don't want to think one of the staff might have done it, either. Mr. Webster is going to conduct a search of all their belongings to see if anything turns up."

Maggie nodded. "Well, I am certain Gertrude had nothing to do with this. She has been with me all day in town, except for when she went to the market."

"We will not rush to judgment, either way."

"She was gone less than thirty minutes."

"Your tone, Margaret." Mother's look could freeze the water that crashed on the shore but four hundred yards away were she staring out the window.

"I'm sorry, Mother." Maggie bit her lip.

"Don't worry your lip, dear." Mother patted her on the arm. "I have had more experience with house staff than you. You have known Gertrude for years, as I have. But some employees are good at hiding their true natures, which is why we must always be on guard before—"

"Before something like this happens?" Maggie finished.

"Exactly."

The pocket doors slid open. Father and Mr. Blankenship stood side by side in the doorway.

"Mrs. Livingston," Father said, inclining his head slightly. "We shall look again at your rooms. Mr. Webster is nearly finished assessing the staff quarters."

◆ ◆ ◆

James had rather hoped Maggie—Margaret—would join them, and he was not disappointed when she fell into step behind her parents.

She slid a glance sideways at him. "You are a brave man, Mr. Blankenship."

"Brave? How so?"

"My mother was not pleased with your newspaper article last week."

"Ah, I see."

Mother looked over her shoulder. "Not so much the article itself, but the headline was misleading, and I believe it would lead people to think our situation is not what it seems."

James didn't want to explain himself. Knowing about the arrangement between his family and the Livingstons, he thought it best to remain silent.

He inclined his head slightly. "I understand."

They climbed the grand main staircase, its steps of polished marble, and stopped at a marble landing covered with a woven runner in shades of red and gold. The cost of the runner was likely as much as a year's worth of rent for his tiny one-room apartment in New York.

Mrs. Livingston paused at a closed door. "I'm not certain I'd like a man to see my sleeping arrangements."

"Come, Mrs. Livingston. He will not touch anything. He is merely here to observe." Mr. Livingston studied James's face. "And he has shown his skills of observation, which I welcome."

He opened the door, and James let the three of them pass ahead of him into the room. It was decorated in blue and white, a soft blue that reminded him of a robin's egg.

Nothing seemed amiss, not at first glance. But an empty box with layers of cushioned sections claimed their attention.

"Empty. Just as a I said." Mrs. Livingston shook her head.

What was Maggie doing? He glanced around to see her behind them, at the bedroom door. She studied the lock and the doorknob mechanism, her hands resting on her knees as she bent at the waist.

"Do you see anything?" he asked, joining her near the door.

"No." She squinted, her vivid brown eyes assessing the doorjamb. "I see nothing that looks like someone tried to force the door open."

"Ah, my dear," her father said, turning to face her. "It is very likely someone used a key or picked the lock. Nothing as dramatic as what happens in those penny novels you read."

Maggie stood upright, her cheeks coloring. "Father!"

"Don't deny it. I've seen you slip a book under the table at suppertime."

"Margaret Livingston," her mother said, a hint of outrage tinging her voice. "Surely you can pursue another more profitable form of reading."

"Surely, you can," James echoed. He found her discomfort a bit humorous—was it due to him being there?

"Maybe I could." Maggie gave him a withering expression. "It has been simply ages since I've read *Robinson Crusoe*."

"So you remember, then?"

She nodded. "I do remember. It was a long time ago, but it was one of the best and earliest grown-up-feeling conversations of my childhood."

"Oh, Margaret, whatever are you talking about?" Mother asked.

"We. . .we were at a dinner party long ago with the Blankenships and the Morrises. I'm not sure who else was there. But Mr. Blankenship and I had a very nice conversation about books. He was preparing to go away to the university."

"Well, I think it's a fine thing that you two get along so well," Mother said. "After all, we are practically family."

"Practically family?" Maggie asked, glancing from her mother to her father.

She doesn't know. . .she doesn't know about Frank.

James couldn't believe she had no idea about her upcoming engagement to his brother. How could they do that to her?

Mr. Livingston shook his head as if in warning to James. Aloud, he said, "Your mother and I have been friends with the Blankenship family for many years, Margaret."

"Yes, that you have." But Maggie still wore a confused frown. "Well, this makes it all the better that you're going to help us, J—Mr. Blankenship."

Of course, he wanted to help them. He'd just had a vivid reminder, though, that he could harbor no thoughts of getting to know Miss Margaret Livingston, other than as a sister.

At the moment, though, he wanted nothing more than to ask her to walk with him along the shore, to talk more about books and the big, wide world she had once wanted to see.

His brother remained in the city, not due back until the weekend and the grand ball which would announce his engagement to Maggie.

"I'm afraid I must take my leave of you now," James said aloud, "and I must call on the Morrises to find out their story firsthand. I will see if there are any similarities to this break-in today."

Mr. Livingston crossed the space of the grand bedroom and opened the window. He glanced down. "I see no footprints outside, nor anything on the window ledge that would lead me to believe anyone came in through the window, either."

Mrs. Livingston joined him, murmuring something about a maid—or maids.

"When—when will I get to see you again?" Maggie asked him, her voice low. "I mean, I welcome the chance to talk with you, Mr. Blankenship. Perhaps we can compare notes on the robberies. I would like to help you."

His gut tightened at his next words. He wanted to speak with her—very much, in fact. But nothing good could come of it. "I will see. I'm not sure that I will require your help, but thank you all the same."

Chapter 4

Maggie's cheeks flamed. He'd all but dismissed her. Well, she would investigate on her own. She stood staring at him while her parents left the window.

"We will remove the valuables from our safe immediately and deposit them in the bank," Father announced. "Particularly the jewelry for your debut."

"Yes, especially your jewelry." Mother frowned. "If something happened to that, it would be an absolute catastrophe."

"But my jewelry—why wasn't that taken?" Maggie had to ask. "If it was someone we knew or welcomed to our home, which seems to be a strong possibility, why wouldn't they have taken that, too? Especially since the household knows we have the jewelry."

"Perhaps it would take too long for them to find the combination to the safe, and they do not possess the skills to open it themselves," Father said.

That was true enough. Mother's baubles were valuable. Yet something didn't feel quite right about the whole thing.

James took his leave of them, seeing himself to the front door. Maggie found herself a bit sorry when he departed. The youngest Blankenship son leaving the family to work as a journalist years ago had been a bit of a scandal, as she recalled. It was no secret the patriarch of the family wished his son had chosen differently. She had always wondered what had become of him and how he'd fared.

Today she'd received an answer. The years in the "outside world" had been kind to him, giving him a relaxed demeanor she envied.

"My dear," Father's voice pulled her away from her musings, "you needn't look worried. I believe that this thief, whoever he is, will not visit us again. Now that we have discovered our loss, he knows we will be on the watch all the more. As a matter of fact, I believe I will hire the young Mr. Blankenship to stay nearby, as the time for your debut draws nearer. He has a quick eye and a sure head about him."

"Yes, please see about it," Mother said. "With our connection to the Blankenship family, I feel at ease having him in our home, despite his chosen profession. Once word gets around about the robbery—and I am certain it will—he will be the one to write the story. Also, despite my misgivings about his journalistic qualities, we will have firsthand knowledge of what he will print."

Maggie staved off her fidgets. She knew better than to ask about calling on Elizabeth, who for all she knew might have remained at the tennis club. Perhaps later, after supper, while the twilight was long. Or perhaps she should sit down and make a list of any similarities between the two crimes.

They descended the stairs together, with Father and Mother discussing the upcoming weekend and the debut. Her debut.

"A few more days." Mother beamed as they paused at the bottom of the stairs.

"A few more days," Maggie echoed. The abominable dress had already been fitted by Madame Clothilde, the orchestra booked, the menu planned. Her parents had hinted at a few "surprises" for her debut. She didn't know whether to be excited or frightened.

As if Mother knew what was on her mind, she spoke about the debut. "I hope you enjoy the surprises we have planned for you. One is your gift, of course, from us."

"The only thing I dread is all those people looking at me." She tried not to shudder, nor seem ungrateful. "Perhaps, Mother, I could receive my gifts when it is but you and I, and Father, by ourselves?" She hated the pleading tone in her voice.

"Nonsense. I won't allow that. I want everyone to see what we give you, along with your reaction. That will be a gift to me." Mother squeezed her hand.

Maggie did hope it would be a trip, if not to somewhere exotic, at least to Europe. She had said so earlier in the spring, when her parents asked what she would like for her debut gift. She had mentioned university studies at the time, but Mother had pish-poshed that idea.

"All right, Mother. It is what I'd prefer, but you and Father are so kind, giving me this party."

"It will be the grandest event in Newport, I am sure." Mother had beamed.

Maggie tried not to squirm. No, it likely wouldn't. That would be Consuelo Vanderbilt's or Francesca Wallingford's upcoming events. She didn't say this aloud, though.

Ah, Mother. . .such pomp was but an illusion, and Maggie knew it quite well the time when she saw another debutante, Therese Howe, sobbing in a back hallway during her own debut. The young woman had everything in the world except the freedom to choose whom she would marry. She was summarily married off to a British count and lived in Britain with her title and estate, or so Maggie last heard.

"Ladies, here is where I leave you. I must make a few phone calls before supper." Father nodded to both of them and departed to his study.

As he left, Mr. Webster joined them in the foyer. Gertrude followed, looking white as a sheet, her eyes reddened.

He stopped in front of Mother then turned over his hand to show them an earring on his palm. "After an inspection of the staff's belongings. I have found something. This. Among Gertrude's belongings."

An earring, made of gold, and Maggie recognized it right away. "I thought I lost that one. I still have the other."

"If I can explain, please, Miss Maggie—" Gertrude's voice, full of anguish, echoed off the marble.

"You most certainly may not!" Mother's voice rang out with an anger to match Gertrude's tone. "You are dismissed from our employ, and that straightway. Remove your things from our home. At once."

"Mother, I lost that earring months ago." Maggie took it from Mr. Webster. "The clasp is broken."

"I was going to get it fixed—I promise I was—in time for your big party." Gertrude's shoulders drooped. "I tried them on one day and I broke the clasp. So I was embarrassed and kept it."

"I care not of your intentions." Mother's face looked like a thundercloud. "The fact you would hide something like this from us? I would not be surprised if you were an accomplice to this thief, whoever he might be."

Maggie watched as a sobbing Gertrude left the foyer, with Mr. Webster following, his face sterner than Maggie ever remembered seeing.

"I believe you are making a mistake, Mother."

"Someday soon, when you are mistress of your own household, you will understand." Mother's expression softened.

"What do you mean, someday soon?"

"You will be someone's wife before you know it. My duty has been to prepare you for that."

Maggie nearly said she was tired of duty but stopped herself. "Please excuse me. I must take care of a few things before supper."

She scurried away, feeling like a small child with a lump in her throat. Now, more than ever, she needed to help find whoever did this—especially if suspicions were cast on Gertrude.

◆ ◆ ◆

James left the Morrises' grand estate and headed down the curved driveway toward the street.

A bit flummoxed was one way to describe how he felt at the moment. He'd called on the Morrises unannounced, and the lady of the house, Mrs. Benjamin Morris, did not wish to discuss the matter with him—a person of the press—no matter his family background or good intentions. Or so it had gone. He should have expected such a reception.

He checked his pocket watch. Nearly five o'clock and time for supper. His father was still in the city, as was Frank, so both Mother and he would be the only ones dining together this evening. In a way, he preferred it at the moment, as both Frank's and Father's demeanor toward him could be characterized as aloof at best during his first few days in Newport.

He scaled the front steps of Fairwinds. The place wasn't home to him, but the warm touches his mother had lent to the space made it feel welcoming. Flowers in vases, tapestries of flowers, soft pillows on the elegant yet stiff furniture.

He had grown accustomed to seeing to his own hat and waistcoat and at first would not let the staff put them up in preparation for his next trip out of the house. But this time, he handed his hat and coat to Withers, the old gentleman who saw to the family's household affairs.

"Will you be dining at home today?" the man asked.

"Yes, sir, I will."

"Good. Your mother will be glad to know that."

"Thank you, Mr. Withers." James gave him a nod before following the sounds of a harp that came from the direction of the parlor.

He slid open the pocket doors to find his mother occupied with her latest attraction. She looked up at him and smiled as she let the strings go.

"You're home." She rose from her stool. "I was almost afraid I would dine alone tonight."

"No fear of that, Mother." He glanced at the instrument, nearly six feet tall. "You are quite accomplished. I am impressed."

"I've had plenty of time to amuse myself in the afternoons."

She's lonely.

He'd never realized it until now. Father and Frank, running the business. Him, off pursuing his own path away from them all.

"When will Father and Frank be here?"

"I've been assured they will both be here in time for the weekend and the Livingstons' ball for Miss Margaret." At the mention of Maggie's name, her eyes glowed. "I've invited Margaret and her mother to luncheon with me next week, after the big announcement at her debut. We will likely have much to do as soon as there will be a date to publish for the wedding."

He sank onto the nearest sofa, pushing a pillow aside as he did so. "I've just come from their house. From what I understand, Mag—Margaret doesn't know of this engagement."

"It will be simply wonderful to add a daughter to the family." Mother gazed up at the fireplace, where a family portrait of the four of them hung. "I will have someone with whom to coordinate events."

"What does Frank think of this arrangement?"

"I suppose he's glad enough. She's a smart one, she is. And Frank needs someone smart beside him. Smart and beautiful. I imagine they'll have handsome children."

"Really, Mother?" He nearly chuckled at her reference to children.

Her face flushed. "With marriage comes babies."

James felt the urge to squirm at this conversation, even with him having lived among a bit less genteel—no, a lot less genteel—folk in the city.

A bell rang signifying supper was ready and ending that line of discussion, thankfully. He rose, allowing Mother to pass through the doorway ahead of him.

Frank had been a kind enough young man, but as an adult, James saw a calculating coldness replace that attribute. It concerned him, even more so now that Miss Maggie Livingston was soon to be engaged to his brother.

It concerned him so much he almost began thinking of a way to stop the engagement. Another ulterior motive ate at him, he realized as he entered the ornate dining room in shades of green—green like envy. He wanted the chance to court Maggie or at least explore the idea of it. Right now, he saw no way to make that happen.

Chapter 5

Supper had ended and Maggie had barely touched her plate. They sat on the rear veranda of Tidewaters, the sky beyond them with the first tint of pink before the sun prepared to slide down in the west.

Maggie had no appetite after Gertrude's sudden departure. She'd run after the young woman, whispering promises to help her and that if all went well she would see her back in the Livingstons' employ. Gertrude barely spoke but continued away, tears streaming down her cheeks.

Instead of sheer curiosity which drove her to wonder about the robberies, she now had a larger purpose: clear Gertrude's name. While the authorities weren't involved—yet—she hated to think of what might happen to Gertrude if they were.

She glanced toward her mother. No use in trying to sway her opinion. In Mother's eyes, Gertrude had taken something that didn't belong to her and therefore needed to be dismissed, regardless if she had anything to do with the robbery or not.

The carriage house held bicycles available to use, and Maggie knew how to ride one, her own bicycle still in New York. She would ride over to Fairwinds and tell James straightaway what had happened. Perhaps he had learned something from the Morrises, as well. If she left now, she could be back before dark. She would not let this wait until tomorrow.

"I believe I shall take a turn around the block on the bicycle," she announced, placing her napkin on her plate.

"By yourself? It is a bit unseemly to do so, even in our neighborhood." Mother sounded as if she'd proposed racing around the block in her nightgown and robe.

"Oh, Mrs. Livingston, let her go. There are still others walking about after supper. She will not be alone. And possibly she will meet up with some other young women like herself." Father wiped his mouth with his napkin, dabbing at his mustache as he did so.

"Thank you, Father. I promise I shall not be long." She scooted away from the table to fetch her hat. Thankfully, she still wore her walking skirt from earlier that day, a garment of which her mother did not completely approve but was still perfectly modest.

She was soon pedaling along the lane to the street. She stopped only long enough to open a narrow side gate, meant for leaving the grounds on foot—or in her case, on bicycle. As her father supposed, a few people were out taking a walk after supper. Maggie didn't recognize them—but oh—there was Francesca Wallingford!

"Good evening, Francesca!" She waved at the young debutante, soon to be launched into society like herself. Francesca had joked once that the idea of "launching" the young women into society sounded much like a ship being christened in the harbor.

"I certainly hope no one cracks a bottle at our sterns," the young woman had said, at which they had both laughed.

The flicker of memory of that conversation made Maggie smile as she continued along toward Fairwinds. She was calling on a man unannounced. Perhaps it would be better to inquire of Mrs. Blankenship first and then ask about James.

Her heart beat a bit faster at the thought of asking for him. What if her voice betrayed her with a squeak? She dared not think of that happening. Instead, she cleared her throat a few times as the blocks passed by.

Ahead of her lay Fairwinds, the next home on the right. The massive cottage wasn't surrounded by large fences of iron bars but a stone wall that would not be too difficult for a nimble person to hop over or climb over with the assistance of a mounting block.

The home boasted six fireplaces with grand dormers and no fewer than four porches and one immense terrace on the second floor that faced the sea. Fairwinds wasn't as grand as Marble House or Tranquility, but it spoke of old money and of a family's wealth that had stood longer than her family's own.

Maggie plucked up her courage anew as she rode up the driveway to the porte cochere and glided to a stop. Where to place her bicycle? She dismounted—carefully, not to disrupt her split skirt—and balanced the bicycle.

She leaned her bicycle against one of two stone lions guarding the double doors to the home and made use of the large, cast-iron knocker. Her heart knocked in her throat.

To her surprise, the lady of the house, Mrs. Blankenship herself, answered the front door.

"Ah, Miss Margaret Livingston, what a pleasant surprise." The woman smiled sweetly, her warmth genuine. "What brings you calling after supper on this fine day?"

"I, ah, would like to speak with you, ah, and your son, if you have some time this evening." She inclined her head with a slight bow. "Please excuse my forwardness in calling in this manner. But to me, it is rather urgent."

"My dear, Frank is in the city, with his father. They won't be back until the day of your debut."

"I see. Well, I welcome the chance to visit with you and James, as well."

Mrs. Blankenship glanced over her shoulder toward the street. "Please, come in. We don't have to stand here on the doorstep when we can enjoy the breeze on the rear veranda. I'll call for some lemonade as well. Unless you'd prefer tea?"

A rivulet of perspiration snaked down her back. "Lemonade sounds like just the thing, Mrs. Blankenship."

The older woman stepped back into the grand house. "You may call me Violet, Margaret."

"All right." Maggie smiled as she entered the house's foyer with its dark wooden staircase that curved up the wall. "Violet, lemonade sounds lovely."

Violet Blankenship gestured to the rear of the staircase, where a set of floor-to-ceiling paned doors had been flung open, revealing a seascape behind them. "Join James on the veranda, and I shall be there shortly. You are acquainted with James, are you not?"

"Yes, I am." Again, her heart gave a skipping beat. "Thank you."

Her summer boots sounded too loud on the polished wooden floors as she crossed under the staircase, passed a set of fireplaces that faced each other, and stepped through the open doorways and onto the veranda.

James, not wearing a dinner jacket, leapt up from one of the chairs. "Maggie."

"Hello." She smiled at him but felt it leave her face as she recalled the main reason for her visit.

"What's wrong?"

She shook her head, letting out a pent-up breath. "It's Gertrude. My mother fired her, thinking she is in cahoots with whoever robbed the jewelry. We simply must get to the bottom of whomever did this."

◆ ◆ ◆

Maggie made a pretty picture as she stood on the veranda, her cheeks flushed and a few beads of perspiration on her forehead.

"Please, sit down," James said. "What happened that caused your mother to dismiss Gertrude?"

Maggie settled onto a nearby wooden folding chair and explained about the broken earring as well as Gertrude's explanation for having it.

"So you see, I'd missed the earring long ago. I figured it had come off when I was walking in the garden in New York." She stared out toward the ocean, where twilight reflected on the water. "I didn't remember I'd lost it until Mr. Webster showed it to us."

"I agree with you." He scratched his chin. "I think it is unlikely that Gertrude had anything to do with the robbery."

"I'm glad you think so. Mother wouldn't listen, and Father, well, he leaves the running of the household to her. Mother's word is law where our home is concerned." She leaned on the arm of her chair and looked in his direction. "Did the Morrises speak with you today?"

"No." He paused, not wanting to explain what had transpired. "But you're friends with Miss Elizabeth Morris, aren't you?"

"Yes. In fact, this afternoon we were discussing the robbery at her house when we were interrupted about the one at mine."

"Don't you two look thick as thieves, already?" Mrs. Blankenship strode out onto the veranda. "The lemonade is coming right out. I know night is falling shortly, but there is enough time to sip one glass before you are on your way, Margaret."

A woman clad in a gray dress with a white apron emerged from the house. She carried a tray with three glasses filled with lemony yellow liquid and ice. Without saying a word, she set the tray on a small table nestled between their chairs and slipped back into the house.

Mrs. Blankenship took a seat on the other empty chair and picked up a glass of lemonade, with James picking up the other two glasses. He gave one to Maggie.

The coolness of the glass chilled his fingers and kept them from losing their grip.

"This is very good lemonade, Mrs. Blankenship," Maggie said after taking her first sip. "Thank you."

"You are very welcome."

"Would you care to walk along our ocean-view courtyard?" James heard himself saying.

"That would be very lovely." Maggie took another sip. "Would you like to come with us, Mrs. Blankenship?"

"No, the courtyard is in view of the veranda." She beamed at them. "So glad that you are both getting along so well. Like family."

James desperately wanted to tell Maggie about Frank, but it wasn't his place. He shouldn't have asked her for a walk, but he didn't trust the fidgets he felt the longer he was in Maggie's presence.

They crossed the expanse of green lawn and soon reached the smooth, paved courtyard of stones. It had served the family well as a sort of large checkerboard when he and his brother were much younger.

"I remember this courtyard." Maggie stopped at the edge of a darker stone square. "It seems smaller than I recall."

He laughed at this. "It seemed to grow smaller, gradually, every year we came here when I was younger. I can't recall the last time I took a walk out here." Perhaps it was that last party, before he went to the university.

"Why did you leave your family?"

The question surprised him. "I didn't leave them, not really. Father and I. . .had a disagreement. I wanted to write, and he wanted me to stay in the family business. I told him I would rather write. He told me I wouldn't see another penny if I did. So I did."

"That was very brave of you. Or foolhardy."

He had to smile at her words. "Probably both. I have both regretted and not regretted my decision."

"Have you had the opportunity to travel much as a news writer?"

"No. I went abroad to spend summers in Europe during my university days, which only fueled my desire to write, but I've stayed in Manhattan and the boroughs of the city." He stopped walking, realizing he'd been pacing back and forth on the courtyard. Maggie stood staring at him, a half smile on her face.

"I have always wanted to travel. I believe my parents are giving me a trip to Europe for a present. It's supposed to be a surprise, but Mother has paid extra attention to my wardrobe for the fall and suggested we purchase a few more travel trunks."

"I would have liked to show you the sights in Paris, London, even Rome, perhaps." He still remembered his first trip abroad, and it would be something else to go again and see it anew through someone else's eyes.

She said nothing in response, simply smiled and nodded her head. Yet a pink glow lit her face. Or was it simply the slant of the dwindling sun before it slipped behind the treetops to the west?

Maggie looked back toward the house. "It must be hard for you to be here this summer with them."

"I haven't seen Father much. Frank is due to arrive tomorrow."

He wanted to tell her about Frank but realized it wasn't his news to tell. Even thinking the words, *"By the way, your parents are marrying you off to my older brother,"* left a bitter taste.

"I should go. The light is fading faster than I realized it would."

"You're very right." He led her back toward the veranda where Mother sat, sipping her lemonade. "I enjoyed our conversation. I'm sorry I don't have more helpful information about the Morrises."

"That's quite all right. I, too, enjoyed our conversation."

Mother rose from her chair as they drew closer. "Did you enjoy your walk?"

"Yes, Mrs. Blankenship, I did, thank you." Maggie smiled. "However, I must go now."

"Come again soon, if not before your debut. My husband and sons and I look forward to attending and to our big announcement."

"Oh, a big announcement?"

"Yes, I'm presenting you with a very special gift." Mother clasped her hands together in glee. "I wore it for my wedding, and your mother thought it would be fitting to wear for yours."

"Wedding." The word came from Maggie's lips in a pitiful squeak. Her pretty brown eyes grew round. She glanced at him, a flicker of—something—inside them that went out when he shook his head.

"To our son Frank. We are delighted to have your parents announce your engagement with all of us present at your debut. We shall gain a daughter, and James a sister, come next spring."

Chapter 6

Somehow Maggie made it back to Tidewaters. She didn't recall what she did with the bicycle upon her arrival. She didn't remember whom she saw when she entered the house and climbed the stairs. If anyone had questioned her return in the dusky twilight, she didn't recall.

She could only feel her pulse thudding in her ears as she lay on her bed and stared at the ornate ceiling. The center of the room where the gas chandelier hung had a fresco which reminded her of a bright blue summer sky with fanciful clouds and a scattering of winged birds. She had chosen the design herself because of the birds. Now, she wished she had wings so she could fly away like one of them.

Her? To be engaged? To Frank Blankenship?

She didn't know the man, couldn't recall his hair color, his demeanor, or anything else about him.

James had blue eyes, the color of the sea and lit with an enthusiasm she could feel when he looked at her. She wanted to ask him more about his travels, more about everything he did. Perhaps it was because he'd bucked his family's expectations.

It had been a mistake to visit Fairwinds, and her folly was costing her now, such a silly errand. She should have gone to visit Elizabeth. Calling on her friend wouldn't have been as awkward as it had been calling on the Blankenships. Yet it had pleased her more than anything else at that moment to be sitting with James.

Had he known about the planned engagement? For a split second, when she heard the word *wedding*, she had thought perhaps Mrs. Blankenship had encouraged her and James's conversation because of that. Yet the brother-and-sister reference shouldn't have been lost on her. And the slight furrow to James's brow told her he'd known. She squashed the flicker of hope that her parents' choice was him.

Yes, James had known all along, as well.

Oh, Lord, please deliver me from this.

She was having feelings, feelings of curiosity mostly, toward James. A curiosity she hadn't had with anyone else. Even with her conversation with Elizabeth about marriage earlier that afternoon. . .

Her thoughts trailed off. Mother had mentioned something about Maggie having her own household to run sooner than she imagined.

They'd all known about this, all of them but her.

She felt more foolish and silly than ever.

A soft knock sounded at her door. "Margaret?"

"Yes, Mother?"

"I thought I heard you return." She opened the door and entered her bedroom. "Oh, you're rumpling your skirt."

"It does not matter to me."

"Whatever is wrong, dear? I am a bit concerned that you arrived home when it was a bit too dark for you to be out."

"How long ago did you decide that Frank Blankenship and I should be engaged?" She sat up and swung her legs over the side of the bed in a decidedly unladylike manner which made her feel oddly rebellious.

Her mother gave a long, squeaky sigh. "It has been since the winter. You were not supposed to know this until your debut."

"Well, I know now."

"Who told you?"

"Mrs. Violet Blankenship herself. She appeared to burst with the news this evening when we had lemonade."

Mother pursed her lips. "I would have preferred to call on the Blankenships with you. I cannot believe you had the audacity to call on them by yourself. Why ever did you do such a thing?"

"It doesn't matter now, and I intended no ill manners." Maggie expelled her own sigh. Her eyes hurt from crying. Tears wanted to come again, but she would not crumble in front of Mother. A lady controlled her emotions at all costs.

"I am sure you did not. But don't let something like this happen again. I'm not sure it was the best decision to allow you to ride your bicycle alone, especially so close to nighttime. We don't want anyone getting wrong ideas."

"I promise it will not happen again, Mother." The words meant nothing to her ears.

Married. I'm going to be getting married.

"Very well. I am not trying to be hard on you, my dear. You are our only child, our only hope for the future. The Blankenships are a good, upstanding family, and no matter what happens to our position, yours will be secured, and I pray, because of that, so will ours."

A niggle of worry did battle with her dismay. Father had reassured them their position was secure, but from what Mother had just said, it sounded as though the marriage might be part of a business agreement between the two families.

The Blankenships were considered "old money," and Maggie knew for a fact that Elizabeth hoping to marry a Blankenship cousin would help her as well.

"Well, as you have said nothing, I assume you don't share my hope?" Mother asked.

"I am pondering all of this, Mother, but yes, I pray our position will be secured as well," Maggie managed to say.

"We will not begin to search for a new maid for you until after the ball. There is simply not adequate time to inquire about one now, and I don't want questions about why we are replacing Gertrude."

"I understand." Maggie studied her hands, folded on her lap. She'd neglected to wear gloves while riding the bicycle. If Mother had known, she would have insisted Maggie apply lotion immediately. Tonight, she didn't care.

Mother left after reminding Maggie she needed to arrange her wardrobe of gowns for the weekend so the laundress could press them for her.

She let the tears come, again, but no sobs, else she would have to bury her face in a pillow to allow herself a good wail, which would do no good and might send the staff running to her door.

Maggie prayed for a solution, but she could see none. The robberies paled in comparison to her own situation. The preacher always exhorted them not to fret over the morrow, because the birds of the air were supplied by their heavenly Father. Yet she had more than enough of everything, and her worry was more of the future. What would happen to her, to all of them?

Soft footfalls then a quiet swish near the door caught her attention.

A small piece of paper lay on the floor where someone had slid it underneath the door. She hopped from the bed and hurried to snap up the folded note. She yanked the door open and stared up and down the hallway, lit only by gas lanterns. No one.

She closed the door firmly then opened the note: *The Morris robbery and the Livingston robbery are not the same.*

◆ ◆ ◆

James hadn't had a bad night's sleep like this one since his first night living in a rented apartment all by himself in the city. The tenant next door drank and was prone to argue with his wife, who also drank. The arguments would last into the middle of the night until they both presumably fell asleep, upon which time the tenant on the other side's young child would wake up, crying for milk in the predawn hours.

By midmorning, the fog inside his brain had lifted somewhat, enough for him to pick up the family's telephone to call his editor with an update. This one, he would definitely appreciate. Not one, but now two, robberies. Would he want him to go forward with a story? Perhaps a phone call to Mr. Livingston was in order first. Or a visit to the home to follow up on the events of yesterday.

He donned his morning coat and called for a horse to ride. No need to take out the carriage or buggy. If it wasn't so warm, he might have walked.

James arrived at the gates to Tidewaters and rode through, upon which a horseman met him to take his horse to the stables.

A tiny maid answered his knock. She scurried off to announce him, shortly after which Mr. Livingston entered the foyer.

"Good morning, Mr. Blankenship. I gather you are here to discuss the robbery yet again?"

"Yes and no. Since this is the second robbery in a matter of weeks among the families, I feel I must tell my editor this is story worthy now," he said, removing his hat. "This could be a disturbing trend. Either way, it will be good for people to know they should be on the watch. I gave you my word I would share this with you, and I am due to give a report to my editor this morning."

"Quite right." Mr. Livingston nodded. "If this is a trend among our set, we must discover who it is, or at least hopefully, the attention will make them stop."

"I do have another idea as well. With Mag—Margaret's debut coming tomorrow night, it might be helpful to set a trap for this individual or individuals. This will not go to press before the debut, so we will have the opportunity to continue investigating, and I can keep my editor happy."

"Sounds wise. What do you have in mind?"

James glanced throughout the foyer and at the closed doors. "Is there somewhere we can talk privately? Your study?"

"Of course. Please, follow me." Mr. Livingston led him along the hallway to another closed door then opened it to reveal a room with a massive desk, a bookcase, and a fireplace before which two leather chairs faced each other. The place smelled faintly of pipe tobacco.

James did not speak until the door was firmly closed behind them. "My mother is planning to let Margaret wear her treasured diamond necklace at the debut. In fact, she plans to present it to her in front of everyone. What if—and this is a big *what if*, sir—we spread the news around that the diamond necklace will possibly be presented at the debut?"

"The thief, if they believe they have a chance at a larger prize, might act."

James nodded. "My thought exactly. And if we can somehow arrange for the lights to go out or get Margaret alone on the porch in the dark—"

"I'm not sure I like that idea, but perhaps the lights out in the ballroom might work."

"May we share this plan with Margaret, sir?"

"Yes. She is a smart young woman and will be most agreeable to help us."

Of that, James had no doubt.

Chapter 7

From her bedroom window, Maggie saw James arrive at Tidewaters and depart not thirty minutes later. She needed to tell him about the note she'd received last evening, and she'd just let that chance slip away. But part of her couldn't bear to see him after last night's heartbreaking revelation. Of course she hadn't masked her disappointment and shock last evening at learning the big secret to be revealed at her debut.

The source of her disappointment went a bit deeper, and of that he could not know. Of the two Blankenship brothers, she very much preferred James to Frank. To reveal that to anyone could do her no good, especially not with the plans their families had made.

Did this mysterious Frank Blankenship know anything of her? What did he think? She couldn't pull together a memory of him at all. The idea frightened her, along with another recollection of the sobbing debutante she'd thought of while walking with Elizabeth on the beach yesterday.

Rattling around her room like a wayward pea would do her no good and only serve to magnify her sour mood. Could she plead her case to her father, if not her mother? She preferred the wrong brother, to be sure, but if she made her wishes known, would it even change things?

No, especially since James was the proverbial rogue of the family. He was worse than no choice at all, likely, in everyone else's eyes.

She moved from the window and went to fetch her favorite day dress then changed her mind. Perhaps she would play some tennis after all, to gain some enjoyment from striking a ball instead of throwing a childish tantrum and breaking things in her room—something she wasn't given to doing, but surely seemed tempting, the more she considered it.

A soft knock sounded at her door. "Miss Margaret? Miss Morris is calling to see if you would like to play tennis today, then luncheon at her home?"

It was her mother's maid, Agnes. She missed Gertrude's familiar voice with its accent.

"Please tell her yes, Agnes. I shall be down straightway."

She met Elizabeth in the foyer. Her friend was dressed much like her, with a long white skirt and a white shirtwaist, with a large white hat to fend off the sun.

"I am so looking forward to our match." Elizabeth linked arms with her.

"As am I. Although I can't promise I will show much skill. I'm out of practice." Maggie waited until they were outside at Elizabeth's carriage before continuing. "I do plan to hit that tennis ball as much as possible."

On the way to the tennis club, Maggie explained about her coming engagement, with Elizabeth's expression becoming more crestfallen as she did so.

"Oh, Margaret. It's simply dreadful." Elizabeth shook her head, her curls bouncing. "This is why I and someone would like to take matters into our own hands, before something like that happens. So what do you know about this Frank?"

"Not much. Not much at all."

"His brother, James, is far more appealing, in some ways, I suppose."

"I suppose." Maggie tried not to let her smile betray her, but too late.

"You fancy him, do you?"

"Yes. No. I'm not sure. I dare not think about a possibility with him, not when everyone else has other plans."

"Have you told them your wishes?"

"No. My mother would find him unsuitable, especially given his profession."

Maggie refused to discuss the matter further, all throughout their tennis game, which was cut short by a sudden rain shower.

"Ah, bah," Elizabeth said. "Shall we go home early for lunch? Better than sitting here, waiting for the sun to come out."

"I don't mind having lunch now."

They soon arrived at the Morrises' cottage, where lunch was not yet ready. The two situated themselves in the library, in what Elizabeth called her favorite reading nook. The window seat looked out on the soggy garden.

"I'm going to see how much longer it will be for lunch." Elizabeth left Maggie on the seat, poring over a book she'd selected from the shelf.

While scanning the opening pages, to see if she wanted to ask to borrow the volume, the book slipped from her fingers and bounced onto the floor. She climbed from the window seat's cushion and bent to pick up the book. A small board at the lower edge of the seat appeared loose. She pushed it into place, but to her surprise, it sprang away from the seat, revealing a small cache. Inside the cache glittered a ruby necklace, a sapphire ring, and a pair of diamond earrings.

Maggie sat there staring at it. A movement to the side caught her eye. Elizabeth had returned.

Upon seeing Maggie, Elizabeth colored. "Oh, Maggie. You won't tell, will you?"

"You need to tell."

"I can't. I'm afraid to." A tear slid down from Elizabeth's right eye. "It was mine anyway, mostly mine. I was going to use it for Henry and me. . . ." She sank onto the bench.

Maggie shook her head. "There's an investigation and everything. You need to tell them."

"I don't know if I can. There are other things missing, but I didn't take those."

"You should, you must. Maybe if you tell them about Henry, they will understand."

"I'm not so sure."

Maggie hugged her friend. She understood that feeling.

"Talk to them before they decide something because they don't know your wishes. And maybe you can help them narrow down who the thief is."

Maggie had to find James, and soon, to tell him about this discovery and what it meant for their own investigation.

◆ ◆ ◆

Father had asked James to lunch at the club, to which James had agreed. He might as well spend time with his father and meet that challenge head-on. He wasn't sure who had been avoiding the other, but with Maggie's debut coming up, he was sure Father would share the plans for the family with him. Although, he ought to be surprised at this.

"Good day to you, son." They took their seats at the table. James had ceased receiving curious glances, for which he was grateful. A few had reintroduced themselves to the "wayward" young man, as some had murmured about him.

"Good day to you, Father."

They ordered then sat in silence. James sipped his lemonade, while Father drank coffee. That was one of the things he always remembered about the man. Coffee, with every meal, no matter the time of year and no matter the weather.

"So, how is your assignment going here in Newport?"

"It's going well, although not quite as I expected."

Father nodded. "Mr. Livingston has filled me in. You have a rather unorthodox idea, but it just might work. I like it."

"Thank you. I am trying to help find a resolution for this. I received a message that I need to call my boss at the office. They may have more information on the first robbery."

"Very good. We don't want bad publicity, but I would prefer the full story to come out."

"That is what I am hoping for, as well."

"So. Have you thought about returning to work for me?"

James tried not to sigh. "Yes, and no. I'm happy and content where I am." Although that wasn't entirely true. He missed the old days, such as they were. He didn't miss the tension and posturing like roosters, the cutthroat nature of business sometimes. He wasn't sure where he fit with that, unsure that he wanted to fit with that.

"I. . .I would be willing to find—something—for you to do. A modest living. You wouldn't need to live with us." Father took another sip of coffee. "I'm getting older, James. I don't know how much time I have. A man gets to looking back on his life, and what is the point of having a legacy without anyone to leave it to? I've done this for you and Frank. Both my sons."

"Thank you, Father. I, ah, I miss the old days. But I don't want things to be like they were." James nodded. "But I'll think about it."

Chapter 8

The sight of the glittering diamonds on the necklace Mrs. Blankenship held up made Maggie catch her breath. Why, the bit of jewelry had to be worth as much as their entire cottage, now decked out with lights and lanterns ablaze. The wiring for electricity had not been installed just yet, although Father promised it would be before summer's end.

"Here." Mrs. Blankenship extended the necklace toward Maggie. "I wore these at my debut, and as I never had a daughter, I am glad for you to wear them. Although I still think it would have been more magnificent for me to put the necklace on you with the whole ballroom watching."

"Perhaps," Father interjected, with Mother standing close by. "But we can announce the same when we make the announcement of the engagement before the dancing begins."

Father and James had informed her of their plan yesterday evening. It was known only to the three of them.

"I dare not risk the other ladies knowing of it," Father had said. "I know you can keep a secret. Also, it helps that we let you know of our plan to catch this person in the act, if possible."

She certainly hoped so, she reflected as she turned to let Mrs. Blankenship fasten the necklace behind her. As soon as it was secure, she couldn't resist turning toward the looking glass to see the necklace in all its splendor lying at her throat.

"Consider this necklace my engagement gift to you." Mrs. Blankenship's hands were warm on her shoulders.

"Oh, Violet," gasped Mother. "That's too generous of you. It's simply exquisite."

"It is not, not when family is concerned." Mrs. Blankenship beamed as she stared at the glass with Maggie.

"We should go downstairs," Father said. "Frank is waiting for us, as is your husband, Mrs. Blankenship."

"Has James arrived?" she heard herself say aloud. Or had she merely thought it?

"He is delayed. He received a phone call from his employer in the city." Mrs. Blankenship shook her head. "So sweet, you inquire about your future brother-in-law."

Father shot her a quizzical look that also held a knowing expression. She felt her cheeks color, and she glanced down in the direction of her silken summer boots that matched her dress's shade of lilac.

Mrs. Blankenship appeared disappointed that their big announcement would be lost, with the six of them being announced at the same time. Mother kept staring at the necklace, as if mesmerized by it. Maggie practically felt the facets sparkling in the light of the gas lamps as she descended the stairs.

There was Frank Blankenship, waiting for her along with his father. What should she say? Should she say anything?

"Miss Margaret." Frank extended his arm as she managed the bottom step. She didn't stumble or trip with the last stair, although her heart skittered uncomfortably.

It shouldn't be like this.

"Good evening, Mr. Blankenship." She offered him the best smile she could manage at the moment. The necklace might as well be a neck shackle. She wanted to wrest it from her neck herself and save any thief the trouble.

With a flourish of music from the twelve-piece orchestra, Mr. Webster flung open the doors to the ballroom so they could pass through, with Maggie's parents entering first, followed by the Blankenships, then she and Frank last of all.

She could scarcely hear the applause, their announcements, followed by *the* announcement of the engagement. All eyes were on her, the necklace, the dress. Maggie kept her hand clamped around Frank's arm to still it from shaking.

No one seated themselves until Maggie and her family had found their seats and taken them. As Maggie did so, she scanned the long table. No James. A few empty seats at the end of the table. Maybe he had arranged to arrive after supper. She hadn't asked, because James had said he would be here.

Frank said nothing to her during the meal. Surely a man would speak to a woman to whom he would soon be engaged. As he wasn't inclined to conversation, despite her remarks about the meal and the current state of the weather, she chose to mentally assess those she knew at the table.

No fewer than twenty for this early supper, but when the dancing began later, the numbers would swell to more than one hundred. How could they know who might act? Maybe the thief wasn't among them tonight. Maybe they were wrong and the thief was long gone.

The pheasant was cooked to perfection, as was the rest of the meal, but Maggie could barely swallow. The idea of her engagement, soon to be officially announced, had her numb and her palate dry.

Toward the end of the meal, James stepped into the dining room and took the last empty seat at the table. As he'd already sent word he would be delayed, his arrival wasn't quite a faux pas. A few of the older ladies present frowned, but what else could one expect from the man who had deserted his family and spurned his legacy?

He gave Maggie a nod, and she swiftly ate the last bite of her supper. She tried not to touch the necklace, but she couldn't help but think of it again, and the fact that James sat at the table.

At last, supper was cleared away and the group of them trickled into the ballroom. Maggie knew the plan. During the third song, not long after the announcement, the lights would be shut off in the ballroom—long enough for the thief, if present, to act.

If Mother knew of this plot, she would surely be against it, especially due to the fact it would mar what she had hoped to be an elegant evening.

"May we speak, in the hallway, before the dance and the big announcement?"

The male voice jolted her from her musing. Frank Blankenship had found his voice, at last.

"Oh, yes, of course." He held open the door and they slipped into the hallway, vacant except for a few of the kitchen staff hired for the evening who were still clearing away the supper table.

She clasped her gloved hands together and regarded him. He wore a finely tailored suit and his brow glowed with sweat. Not perspiration, but sweat. Frank mopped the river that streamed down his forehead.

"I suppose this is the most awkward position in which I've found myself in my entire life." He blotted his neck with the handkerchief next.

"I can assure you this was a complete shock to me."

He raised the hand holding the handkerchief. "We shall get through this as best we can, for the sake of our families."

"Perhaps we could call off the engagement, at another time, before we go much farther?" she had to ask.

He looked at her in horror. "This is part of the deal, the merging of my company with your father's company. That you are married to me as well. Canceling our engagement violates the terms of the deal and will rend the entire thing void."

"I don't love you." Maggie choked out the words.

"This marriage will not be based on love. I assure you I will not approach you to obtain any of the duties of marriage. We shall have separate rooms and separate lives. You will not be allowed to travel alone, however, but must be accompanied at all times. I've been told of your desire to travel. I do hope you will keep yourself occupied during our marriage as I will be too busy for anything but my work."

Maggie nodded slowly. A marriage, void of love, years of loneliness. And all the money in the world. She wanted nothing more than to pull the necklace off, run from the house, and disappear somewhere, anywhere.

◆ ◆ ◆

James glanced about the ballroom, which glowed in Italianesque splendor with vivid reds and golds. Brightly colored ball gowns provided a contrast throughout the room. He didn't see one in the shade of lilac that Maggie wore. Where had she—and his brother—gone?

Frank was self-absorbed and so focused on business he likely didn't know what to do with a woman to run his future household. Poor Maggie. He tried not to have selfish thoughts as he strode into the hallway.

There they were, standing outside the other set of doors to the ballroom. They were engaged in conversation, Frank looking intent and Maggie looking perplexed. She fidgeted with the strand of glittering diamonds at her neck.

Mother's necklace became her, but even without it, Maggie sparkled. And Frank had no clue. Why, if he were the one in Frank's position, he would be telling Maggie of everything he hoped for their future home. That he would not insist on his rights as a husband, but they would take their time, getting to know one another better. He would ask her where she wanted to travel first, and they would make plans to visit Paris and as many other sights as she would want to see.

Stop. James schooled his features and approached the two of them.

"May I offer you my congratulations, brother?" He extended his hand to Frank, who shook it in response.

"Thank you." Frank assessed him with disinterest. "So why are you here this evening? Father said you have been on a special assignment from your editor?"

"Yes, I am."

"Yet you came to this supper. May I inquire as to why?"

He looked at Frank narrowly. "I am here for our family."

"You have never concerned yourself with business affairs before."

"I am also here for Miss Margaret." He inclined his head to her, at which she glanced between him and Frank.

James wanted to tell her what he'd just learned from his editor. There had been an arrest made in connection with the robbery at the Morris residence in New York. An employee who had been caught trying to sell the jewelry he'd stolen. This confirmed the truth behind the anonymous note Maggie had received that the robberies were unrelated to each other. The remainder of the jewelry had turned up in the family's Newport home unexpectedly.

He'd already drafted the story of the robbery and promised to deliver it to the newspaper first thing in the morning when the press opened.

This meant, though, that the second robber was still unaccounted for, something he hoped would be remedied this evening.

The strains of the first song began, and with that, Frank pulled Maggie into the ballroom without another look at James. He heard the sounds of a stringed fanfare, of sorts, then the deep timbre of Mr. Livingston's voice making the big announcement.

James ignored the pang of regret. What if he had stayed with his family all this time? Would he be the one standing beside Maggie as the announcement was made? He wouldn't head down that path of thought. It would do no good.

He entered the ballroom to see smiling faces looking at the newly engaged couple. His mother was telling everyone—yet again—of the fact that Maggie would become the daughter she never had, and that Maggie had accepted her gift of diamonds as a welcome to the family.

Nods and smiles. Maggie's smile was thin. She didn't look his way, and it confirmed what he had both hoped and dreaded—she felt something for him. He didn't mistake that, especially not in the hallway moments ago.

Enough musing, he told himself. If they found the real thief, then Maggie might at least be able to hire her Gertrude back once again.

Chapter 9

The minutes dragged on as they waltzed across the dance floor. At least Frank was a good partner in this matter, equally as fumbling as she was. No, a bit more so. Maggie was not fond of the waltz but knew the questions would fly if they did not take a few turns around the floor.

Was it the third song? Or only the second?

Maggie couldn't recall if she'd missed a song, or not.

"You might smile a bit more, Margaret," Frank chided. "You should be happy that your family is attached to ours. From what I understand, your father's interests are slipping and this was saving him from inevitable ruin."

"You may end up with me as your wife due to a business agreement, but I am not, nor will I ever be, your employee, and you may not command me as such."

He laughed, a loud boisterous sound that caused some to stare their way. "I was warned about you, with good reason I see. You will obey me."

She bit her lip when he squeezed her hand a bit harder than necessary. *Dear God, please, help me.* She saw no way out of this.

The strains of the waltz ended and drifted away. The wall of floor-to-ceiling windows was open on the ocean side of the ballroom, letting in the cooler night air. How Maggie longed for the beach walk at the moment. Instead, she was stuck here in the stuffy ballroom.

She pulled—gently—away from Frank and headed to the ocean-side doors. "I need a breath of air."

"I, for one, am ready to wait out the next song, myself." Frank glanced toward the ballroom doors. "I see your father has not retreated to his study as of yet."

"No, he will not. Not for a while, anyway. Father will likely retire there as soon as it is polite to do so." That, and see if anything came of her displaying the necklace.

"Don't be but a minute."

"I shan't be long." Maggie recalled her instructions and paused at the doorway. Would anyone else follow her, particularly if Frank were nearby? She stepped out onto the veranda and inhaled. Another song began inside. She closed her eyes, wanting nothing more than to remain here for the rest of the evening and let Frank do what he might. It sounded as though he planned to do that after the wedding, so she might as well train herself to be accustomed to that.

"There you are. I've been trying to speak with you since supper." Mother stood in the doorway, framed by the golden light behind her. "I'm afraid we've had some bad news regarding your friend Elizabeth."

Maggie nodded. "She admitted to me that she'd taken the jewelry so she and Henry Blankenship could run away together. And she's very sorry."

"Well, I for one am glad of this discovery. Associating with her would only be bad for your reputation, at this point."

"Oh, Mother." Maggie turned her attention to the dark surf beyond the house. Her heart hurt for Elizabeth, that she'd chosen to do what she'd done. It remained to be seen what would happen to her friend, but the scandal alone was bringing embarrassment to her family.

I almost don't blame her.

She faced the ballroom once again. Mother was speaking to another of her friends, Mrs. Agatha Something—Maggie couldn't recall. She slipped past her and headed across the dance floor. In a few moments, the third dance would begin. Yes, she would sit this one out.

Where should she stand?

Another well-wisher gave her their congratulations, which she accepted with thanks and a smile. It felt like lying, and she did not like it a bit.

"You nearly ready?" a familiar voice said at her elbow.

"Nearly." She couldn't help her wide smile at James. Here came Mother again, still chatting with her friend. "Elizabeth admitted to the theft."

"Yes, but there is also another thief. They were caught trying to sell what they'd stolen, while, as you told me, Elizabeth had hidden her part of the jewels away. When the robbery was discovered, she kept silent, believing she would not be discovered. Except, for you."

"I hope she and Henry will still get to be together."

"I'm not sure." His downcast tone made her glance at him again. "We don't always get the ending we hope for."

"Oh, James—"

"Could you please fetch me a cup of punch, and one for yourself?" Frank asked, stopping at her other side.

"I'll get you both some punch," James offered, and then he was gone.

The third waltz began for real this time, and Maggie stayed frozen where she was. There went Mother and Father, taking their turn on the floor. The music played on, and couples swept by them as she and Frank stood by the wall. No one else was close to her where she stood about two paces from the ballroom door to the hallway.

The ballroom was plunged into darkness. Although she'd been half expecting the darkness, she still found her pulse racing. Murmurs filled the room as the players fell silent. A few nervous chuckles sounded. Some moved about the room, calling for a light.

Seconds dragged on, and swift movements and rustling fabric in the dark grabbed Maggie's attention. She could scarcely make out shadows backlit by the sliver of moonlight outside.

A hand grabbed at her neck—a woman's hand. Maggie reached for the hand, and another pushed her back to the wall while the first hand snatched at the necklace.

Pain shot through the back of her neck, and she tried not to scream.

"I say, what is going on?" a voice called out nearby.

More fumbles as the murmurs and call for a light grew louder.

Maggie's neck ached, but she followed the person—whoever they were—and stumbled into the hallway herself. She snatched at air in the darkness.

The lights came on in time for Maggie to see her mother skitter and fall onto the marble floor, the necklace sliding away from her.

"Mother!"

◆ ◆ ◆

James wasn't quite sure who they would discover, if anyone. He certainly hadn't thought of Mrs. Livingston lying prone on the floor, stammering something about trying to keep the necklace safe.

She had no explanation for why she fought Maggie and ripped the necklace from her neck in the darkness. At Mr. Livingston's direction, the orchestra continued to play while Maggie, her parents, and he discussed things in the hallway.

Mrs. Livingston's shoulders sagged. "I admit it. Things are bad, far worse than my husband lets on to everyone. We needed the money and soon. I was starting with the jewelry. I was afraid if I said nothing about the jewelry missing, I'd be questioned about it before long."

His father frowned. "This is simply unbecoming behavior. If this is how you conduct yourselves, I am a bit skeptical about entering into an agreement with the lot of you."

Maggie cleared her throat. "Mr. Blankenship, sir, my father is a good man. He has worked very hard to achieve everything that he has. Please, if you have an agreement, it is with him and not with my mother."

James admired her all the more just then, defending the agreement his father had with hers, despite what it meant for her personally. Frank entered the hallway.

"Ah, there you are." He glanced at each of them. "Have I missed something?"

Father studied James's face then Frank's. "I will fill you in later, much later. Please, dance with your fiancée, and I will go find your mother." He strode into the ballroom.

Frank took in the sight as Maggie picked up the diamond necklace from the floor. She rubbed the back of her neck, and her mother's shoulders drooped lower, if that were possible.

"Mother. You used to tell me that God would take care of us, that He always takes care of us, no matter what."

"I did. But now, I'm not so sure, the way business is going for your father. I feel as if God has forgotten us."

"Mother, it will be all right. If God is God, and He is taking care of us, then whatever state we find ourselves in, we are in His care." She said the words aloud, almost as if she were convincing herself that it was true. Was this something she had forgotten herself lately?

"Come, Margaret." Frank nudged her arm. "We must make at least one more turn on the dance floor."

"Very well," Maggie said. She flung an almost pleading look at James, who knew he could do nothing for either of them at the moment.

When they were gone, Mrs. Livingston headed away from the party, leaving James and Mr. Livingston alone.

"So, what are you going to print about this, young man?" Mr. Livingston regarded him with a stern gaze.

"It is good that this theft was prevented. And you have your answer for the missing jewelry." He wasn't 100 percent certain his boss would let him off the hook for not inserting this into the follow-up about the arrest made for the Morris robbery, but this incident occurred in Newport, not the city. By the time he spoke to him again, the next big thing would be coming along.

"Thank you." Mr. Livingston let out a sigh. "Ah, that woman I married. She is dear to me, far more dear than any riches or jewels. I'm afraid she mistook my business concerns as an impending disaster. She tends to be a bit histrionic. But I assure you nothing like this will happen again. I plan to further assure your father and brother of the same thing."

Chapter 10

Maggie's feet ached for days after the ball, and so did her heart. She didn't see James again after that evening, and she found herself looking for him when she and her mother visited Violet Blankenship at Fairwinds the following Monday morning.

"The men are in the city, all of them." Violet waved her hands. "But no matter. We don't need them to begin wedding planning and household planning. You will, of course, live on the third floor of our building. Mr. Blankenship is already having the apartments prepared so they will be ready for you and my Frank to move into next summer."

If Maggie had thought the ball was a flurry of activity, the morning that followed turned into a blizzard.

She wore a ring on her finger, placed there unceremoniously by Frank in front of everyone, including James. Now she tried to push thoughts of anything other than a warm brotherly friendship with James from her head.

Her parents had indeed revealed their gift to her, the much-desired trip to Paris this coming fall, but she imagined at this point it would be spent with shopping trips and dress designs, not visiting museums and basking in the history of the place.

"Margaret, tea?" Mother asked again.

"Yes, Mother." She smiled at Mrs. Blankenship. "I apologize. My mind seems to be going in all sorts of directions today."

"Well, that is quite all right. I do declare, your debut was one of the best I've attended in the past two seasons." Mrs. Blankenship lifted the porcelain teapot and poured a cup for Maggie. "There. Sugar?"

"Please."

After Mother's grab at the necklace, Maggie sent it to the bank with Father. She didn't want the thing in her jewelry box, and neither did Father, probably for different reasons. Mother didn't mention the incident again, and neither did Maggie or Father.

She wondered again about James. Before Father left for the city this morning, she nearly asked him if the engagement could be called off, but she didn't. Such arrangements were common in their set, and she shouldn't have been surprised that her parents had entered into one for her.

She inhaled deeply and looked across the expanse of Fairwinds lawn. If she could live somewhere like this all the time, being married to Frank would not be so bad. She prayed that God would help her with the loneliness she knew would come and that any ideas she had of James would die forever.

◆ ◆ ◆

James sat at his desk at the *New York Empire News* trying to work on his next assignment. The robbery story was already on its way to print and would soon be part of news history. His present assignment was on the growing suffragette movement among the New York elite.

"You know how to talk to these people," Burrows had told him upon his return to the office that morning. "I've heard you on the telephone. Your voice changes, your manner of speaking. You know how to get them to talk to you."

He would be making the rounds among the upper crust of society again. He wasn't sure how he would like it. Maybe this was a way of rebuilding the bridge with his father, a bridge he'd torn apart years ago. During his brief time in Newport last week, it seemed a few building blocks for a new bridge were set in place. Not that he would be returning to the family business anytime soon.

"Hey! Blankenship. Someone's here to see you," someone called out from their desk near the door.

James squinted across the room. Father? And Frank? What had he done to warrant this visit? They both looked serious as the grave. Well, Frank looked like that nearly all the time. He'd always been a serious one, which served him well in business.

Burrows, his boss, wore a look of surprise that James imagined matched his own.

His father and Frank wound their way through the rows of desks and stopped when they reached his. James stood, wishing he'd worn his nicer coat today. But it didn't matter. They shook hands with him.

"We have a proposal for you," Father said.

"A proposal?" Were they asking him to come back? He realized how he'd missed seeing his mother, but he had no inclination to leap back into that fishbowl of a life again.

"I, ah, I don't want to marry Margaret Livingston," his brother blurted out. "I can't keep up this ruse. I was able to for that debut, but no more. A wife is too much to take care of. I don't want to deal with the responsibility of having to think about a wife."

"I see." He wasn't sure what that had to do with him.

"Yet we have an agreement with the Livingstons," his father continued. "Their interests need protection, and a marriage would only strengthen our companies."

James figured there had to be some other financial benefit for the family, but he didn't ask about that. "So how am I involved with this?"

"We are prepared to offer another agreement to them, but this time naming you as the husband. In our agreement, there must be a Blankenship-Livingston wedding, but no particular son is named."

The hubbub of the office surrounded them, his coworkers wrapped up in their own stories after giving them a few curious looks.

"May we talk somewhere privately?" James asked his boss.

"Use my office." Burrows jabbed his thumb toward his windowed office with a door. "But make it quick. I have an appointment in twenty minutes."

James led them into Burrows's domain and closed the door behind them. "All right, now we may talk without so many listening ears. Father, what do you want me to do?" He almost added, *"Come back to work for you?"*

He wasn't sure he could do that. But a writer's life was hard, odd hours for meager wages. He wasn't at the bottom of the pile, and he'd worked his way to where he was now—as indicated by the fact that Burrows finally called him Blankenship instead of Blandford, for one thing.

"We must have an engagement, followed by a marriage within one year," his father explained. "Whether it is Frank or you matters not."

"One year." He thought it over. He didn't want to be roped into something like this. But then, it was Maggie. . .and she deserved better than being the subject of an arranged marriage.

And there was Frank's blasé attitude toward the nuptials to be considered. His brother probably gave Maggie instructions as if she were a secretary or stenographer. James tried not to roll his eyes at the idea.

"Well, what say you?"

James stared out across the newsroom. "I say I must speak to Margaret Livingston as soon as possible. Then we will let you know our decision—together."

◆ ◆ ◆

Maggie walked along the shore, or as close as she could get to the encroaching tide without getting the hem of her skirt wet. The day had worn her down. After the tea and endless wedding plans that had ensued, she'd faced another supper, this time with the Morrises. No mention had been made of Elizabeth's fate until Maggie managed a whispered conversation with her friend in the foyer before the family departed.

No resolution for Elizabeth and Henry. Perhaps one day, Elizabeth had said. Her mother wanted to let the scandal die down—she was certain the Livingston family understood that position.

Tonight, Maggie wanted to just breathe in the fresh air and wonder what would transpire between now and the wedding in one year. Maybe she and Frank would develop a civil friendship, a mutual respect. Or so she could hope.

Maggie glanced back at the house. A figure approached—a man in a suit. James?

But he was back in the city at his job, their paths now uncrossed as they should be.

"Good evening," he said as he reached her on the edge of the sand.

"Hello." Her mind floundered for a reason why he might be here. "What. . .what are you doing here?"

"I'm here to see you."

"Me?"

He nodded, offering her a slow smile. "There's been a new development with the agreement between our families. I asked that I be the one to tell you about it and see if you agree."

"A development?"

"Well, it seems that my brother doesn't want to be saddled with a wife. He doesn't want to be bothered with the upkeep or something like that."

She almost collapsed with relief. "So there's to be no wedding?"

"Ah, well, there's the rub. There must still be a wedding next year."

"What?"

"Yes. But this is why I asked to be the one to speak with you, and we will tell the family of our decision. You must agree to it. I asked the family for that, as well."

"You mean?"

She could marry James. . .instead?

"This is all so. . .fast." Maggie swallowed hard. "James, I'm not sure what to think. What are your inclinations to having a wife?"

He cleared his throat. "I would find a different job, possibly with my father. Nothing high level. I shy away from that. I'm content and blessed doing what I do. But Father will find something more. . .agreeable to me, in time. I realized I need to ask his forgiveness for leaving like I did. It hurt him very much. I think this. . .this between us. . .will go a long way to doing that."

"You look at me as a way to please your father?" She started to laugh.

"No, that's not it." He practically sputtered. "I mean, Margaret Livingston, I would like to court you. I've spoken to your father about it, and he is agreeable. Would you be agreeable to that? One step at a time."

Being courted by James Blankenship? Was he really smiling at her? Her heart skipped a beat as he took her hand, raised it to his lips, then kissed it.

"Yes, yes. I am most agreeable to that."

"Come with me?" He offered her his arm, which she gladly took. "Let us tell your parents and then mine."

"Oh, James," she said, leaning on his arm as they climbed the low dune, "I look forward to the next year, very much."

"As do I." He stopped long enough to give her a quick kiss.

Epilogue

One year later

New York City had seen more lavish weddings, to be sure, but that mattered not to Margaret Livingston Blankenship. The past year being courted by James had flown by as they walked together, talked together, and discussed the books they read.

No more robberies or anything else like that occurred, but Margaret wondered about the possibility of another caper in her future. James was wont to notice little things that would get their imaginations wondering. But for now, they had more important matters to tend to.

They had plans for a wedding trip to Paris, which, he promised, would have no dress fittings or shopping unless she really wanted it to. She did not.

For tonight, however, they were heading to Fairwinds to spend time at the cottage as husband and wife before heading out on their trip.

Gertrude had returned to their employ and would accompany Margaret to their new apartment at the Blankenships' building in the city after returning from Europe.

"Happy, my wife?" James asked as he helped her from the carriage.

"Very happy, my husband. And thankful."

"What lies ahead of us, I do not know. But I look forward to having you by my side as we go forward together."

"As do I, my love." She smiled up at him, her heart skipping a beat. *Thank You, God, for this ending, and this new beginning.*

He swept her into his arms and carried her into the house.

Lynette Sowell is an award-winning author with New England roots, but she makes her home in Central Texas with her husband and a herd of five cats. When she's not writing, she edits medical reports and chases down stories for the local newspaper.

All That Glitters

by Kimberley Woodhouse

Dedication

To my big sister Mary Margaret.

Wife, mom, sister, daughter, friend. You've worn many hats and done it beautifully.

And you've always been there for me.

I'm so thankful God gave me you.

Thanks for putting up with your kid sister. . .

Which reminds me—I'm sorry for hiding under your bed while you were reading so that we could try to scare you.

Ray made me do it.

Chapter 1

Juneau, Alaska, 1895

I don't know why yer makin' such a fuss." Johnny Jones tugged his jacket a little tighter and stood taller. "It ain't *that* cold." Maybe if he said it enough times, he could convince himself.

"Speak for yerself, Johnny. I don't know why we had to take this job anyway. I'm gonna freeze to death up here, and besides that, I never killed no one." Clive hopped from one foot to the other and smacked his gloved hands together.

"It's good money. More than we've ever seen in our lives, and we won't have to go digging around for it, so quit yer whinin'. Who's gonna catch us up here anyways? Nobody knows us, and we won't be staying." He nodded toward the building. "Just shut up and watch. They should be comin' out any minute."

As soon as the words left his mouth, the door across the street opened. A lady in a blue dress with sleeves almost as wide as the door stepped out followed by two gray-haired men in their fancy suits. That was them.

The Abbots and their lawyer friend.

The trio walked down the street toward their hotel, talking and nodding.

Johnny waved to Clive. The time had come. A job worthy of his skills. "Follow me. If we play our cards right, we can get the job done and catch a boat back to someplace warm by the end of the week."

"Warm sounds awful good. I'd just about kill for it." Clive smiled enough to show his gray teeth.

"Good. No more foolin' around. We have a father and daughter to get rid of."

◆ ◆ ◆

Mary Margaret Abbot listened to Father tell Uncle Dillard about the plans for the new mines. Gold had been struck and was plentiful—especially to those who had the funds to spend on good equipment. With the new Abbot investments here in Juneau, their mines would prosper for generations to come. A little thrill ran through her. While it wasn't her first choice to be unmarried at her age, she did enjoy that it meant Father allowed her to see the business side of things. The world changed at a rapid pace, and she loved watching it happen.

Since Mother died when she was a child, Mary Margaret had grown up knowing that she would become the lady of the house and need to help direct her sisters. But as she'd grown, her interest in business grew along with her, and Father brought her on trips and to business meetings. Three years ago—on her twenty-fifth birthday—Father dubbed her his business partner. As the heiress to the Abbot fortune, she didn't mind one bit, although some of the men she encountered didn't quite know what to do with a woman involved in business discussions.

"Arnold, it's a grand plan. And already a successful one." Dillard tapped his cane on the boardwalk. "As your lawyer and adviser, you have my full support to pursue more ventures such as these. As your brother-in-law, I can congratulate you—the Abbot coffers will grow in abundance."

"High praise indeed, and I don't mind if I do pursue them. Thank you for that." Father smiled. "I'm also thinking of investing in a few of the failing claims that are close to the same underground creek. That places them in proximity of what we hope to be the 'mother lode'—that's how the men put it? Without money and equipment, they wouldn't be able to reach the central vein for years."

"But you can change that. Ah yes, good plan." Uncle made notes in the little leather notebook Mary Margaret had never seen him without. "And you'll keep on the hired hands? The prospectors?"

"I think so. Give them a stake in the claim for their work. I provide the funds and the means, they provide the hard labor. What do you think?"

"Another excellent idea. Build loyalty from the workers and put a good name behind it. You won't just be another gold digger. It'll be respectable and grow." Their family lawyer rubbed his hands together. "Even in this chilly weather, the idea warms my insides."

"I'm glad you approve, let's put them into motion. I'd like it all taken care of before we leave end of the month." Father turned to face her. "What are your thoughts, Mary Margaret?"

"I agree with Uncle Dillard that it is a grand plan, and I look forward to learning more about the gold mines." His last words stayed with her. End of the month? They would return home, of course. But Mary Margaret found that she didn't want to leave Alaska. After months on end in this great northern territory, she fancied staying on a bit longer. It was a beautiful place. And far from Colorado. At twenty-eight years old, she was the eldest of three daughters in the Abbot clan. And the only one who would inherit anything of the Abbot fortune since her sisters chose to marry money-obsessed men and throw away their dowries to worthless husbands. The thought of going home to Colorado and listening to her sisters' constant whining and complaining was enough to tempt her to stay in a shack in Alaska forever. If Mother had lived to see her younger children grow into the women they'd become, she'd join Mary Margaret in solitude. Of that Mary Margaret was most certain.

"That's my girl." Arnold Abbot laid a hand on her shoulder. "You make me proud, daughter." With a nod, he began walking toward the hotel again.

"Thank you, Father." She pasted on a smile. Dare she voice her thoughts? "Must we *really* leave at the end of the month?" He would know the true motivation behind her question—they were so connected. She'd seen firsthand the toll her sisters' poor choices took on Father.

Father stopped and turned. Uncle Dillard followed suit.

"We've spent the better portion of a year up here, and if we can get all our assets in order, I think it's time to head home." Father sighed and offered his arm to her and looked toward the mountains. "Although, I will be sad to leave this beautiful land. But there is business at home to attend to."

She nodded. "You're right. But I've certainly enjoyed Alaska and its quiet." Even though Uncle Dillard knew the reality of the Abbot family dynamics all too well, Father was correct to steer the conversation to neutral ground.

The Abbot businesses always interested her, but something about the gold mines excited her on a new level. Maybe it was the risk so many had taken—giving up anything and everything to come to this unknown land and stake a claim. Or maybe it was that overnight a man of no means—young or old—could turn into a rich man. So different from anything she had known in Denver. And since she was a woman, she could never go off on such an adventure—and didn't need to—but it was still interesting and exciting.

Back at home, in Colorado, the wealthy class had nothing to do with the lower classes. Old money and new money never mixed. It just wasn't done. But here in Alaska? It didn't seem to matter. Not one bit. And with the Abbots investing in mines all over, they'd be helping others attain their dreams as well. If only it were appropriate for a single, young woman of means to stay on and supervise her father's ventures. Then she could stay. And not go home to the torturous attitudes of her sisters. But then, Father would have to deal with them on his own.

She wouldn't inflict that punishment on her worst enemy.

Father pulled her along. "Let's get something to eat. I find I'm quite ravenous."

"I agree." Uncle Dillard pointed his cane toward the hotel. "We can wrap up the final details. I'll plan to stay a few weeks to assure the equipment arrives in good order, and then I can always hire a supervisor for you. Someone who can be on-site each day."

"Good, good." Father nodded and walked up the stairs to the porch of the simple establishment. "I already have a man in mind. We've met a few times, and I've had him thoroughly checked out. Let's go meet him together and we'll offer him the job."

Uncle raised his eyebrows. Mary Margaret was just as shocked to hear Father already had a candidate, but Arnold Abbot never left anything to chance. His businesses had grown because he was always one step ahead.

"Well, then. We have a plan." Uncle Dillard gave her a smile. "The firm will send up a suitable representative to run the office here. Once he's in place, I will make sure he's in good order before I head back to Denver."

Mary Margaret released her grip on her father's elbow and allowed the men to get a few steps in front of her. As she turned, she took in the view of the Coast Mountains and sighed. Sometimes it was harder than others to be the only sensible daughter in the family.

If only she'd been born a boy. Then she could stay in Alaska for as long as she wanted. And if she'd been born a boy, Father wouldn't be dealing with the nastiness from Martha's and Mabel's husbands.

But alas, here she was. A girl. And she loved being a girl—except for maybe corsets. If she could be a fine lady like her mother had been, she'd be happy. But what if she never married?

A shiny glint caught her attention from down the street. Something behind the bank?

The *crack!* of a pistol made her jump off the stairs to the ground.

Pinging sounded from above her head.

"Stay down, Mary Margaret!" Father's voice bellowed from the porch.

Covering her head with her hands, she wondered if she'd be leaving Alaska after all.

Chapter 2

Charles Delaney removed his thick leather gloves and used them to wipe at the dust on his trousers. Today of all days, the new owner of the mine was coming to visit. And while Charles had great news to share with Mr. Abbot, the mine had draped him in at least a half inch of dirt and grime. Not the best way to greet him.

Checking his timepiece, he exited the mine and realized there wasn't any time to worry about his appearance. Abbot and his lawyer would arrive at any moment.

Jasper—his right-hand man—waved at him and ran up from the tunnel. "Exciting news, ain't it, Charles?"

Horses brought a wagon up the road to the mine.

With one last slap at his clothes, Charles smiled. "Indeed, Jasper. Especially with the new owner." He clasped his friend's shoulder. "New equipment will help us get to that vein in no time."

He ventured out into the bright sunlight to meet the party and couldn't keep his smile from widening. All his hard work would pay off. Big-time. This wasn't his last resort to "find his fortune." No. He'd done the research. Knew these mountains. Took on the challenge. Patience and old-fashioned manual labor won the day.

A well-dressed man descended from the wagon.

Charles reached out a hand in greeting. But the other man lifted his hand up to the wagon, and all Charles could see was a blur of white. His eyes hadn't adjusted to the brightness of the day yet, and whatever or whoever held the guest's attention blinded him. He closed his eyes for a moment and wiped at them with the back of his hand.

It didn't help. Hazel eyes looked at him from under an enormous hat and parasol.

He blinked.

"Mr. Delaney, I presume?" The man's voice made him abruptly shift his gaze.

Charles nodded.

"May I introduce you to Miss Mary Margaret Abbot." The older gentleman reached out a hand. "I'm Mr. Dillard, one of the Abbot family lawyers."

Charles nodded and shook the man's hand. Why was there a lady here? He cleared his throat. "Thank you for coming, Mr. Dillard, Miss Abbot. I apologize for my appearance, but it has been a prosperous day."

"I'm glad to hear it." But Mr. Dillard didn't smile. "Miss Abbot's father is the new owner and investor in this mine and several others in the vicinity. But I'm afraid he's taken a bit ill, so we are here to speak with you on his behalf."

"I'm sorry to hear Mr. Abbot is under the weather." The blinding white glow beside him was a bit too distracting. "Why don't we head over to the shade. We have a makeshift office set up."

As they walked, Charles wondered what would possess a woman to wear white when she was headed to a mine. Didn't she have any sense?

Mr. Dillard spoke up before they even sat down. "I'm afraid we don't have a lot of time today, Charles. Let me be frank."

"Please do."

"Mr. Abbot believes that you and your friend Jasper are the best. Honorable men, hardworking, and honest. We've done a lot of digging around in your past and find you to be a suitable candidate. All of that to say, Mr. Abbot would like to hire you as the manager of his mines up here in Alaska, and then Jasper can be the foreman under you or whatever position you think would be best. It's a large task. Multiple mines—twenty at least. But we are willing to offer you large percentages of the profits for a job well done." He pushed a folded piece of paper to him. "We'd like this taken care of today."

Charles opened it and studied the numbers. "This is quite the offer, Mr. Dillard." More than he'd imagined, and it was a bit of a shock. Was this some sort of trick? Or a test? He continued to look down at the paper. "I'm impressed, but I must ask. . .why the rush?"

A huff sounded to his right. He'd quite forgotten about the white-ensconced guest.

"It's quite simple, Mr. Delaney." Miss Mary Margaret Abbot's smooth voice startled him. "My father chose you after much deliberation. Now an offer has been made to you. One that will not be repeated." She stood up—looking quite perturbed even in her angelic, puffed-sleeved getup. "Do you accept the job, or not?"

◆ ◆ ◆

The gall of such a man. Here, he'd been offered a small fortune to work for her father, and he wanted to know the rush? Why, if she weren't a lady, she'd bop him on the nose with her parasol this very moment. Mary Margaret winced at her angry thoughts. What was it about fatigue and stress that made her so unreasonable?

Uncle Dillard heaved a great sigh. "Mr. De—"

"I accept." Steely gray eyes bore into her own. "I apologize for my question, Miss Abbot, and I accept the generous offer." Something in his stare made her soften a touch.

Well, maybe she had judged him too harshly, but she didn't have time for this. Not when her father lay in the hospital. She straightened her shoulders and held his gaze. "Thank you, Mr. Delaney. Mr. Dillard will handle the contract." His scrutiny unnerved her. Not ugly. Not spiteful. Not angry. But solid. Sure. Steadfast. Even sitting down, the man was so tall he was almost eye level to her full height of three inches above five feet.

With a whirl and a nod, she headed back to the wagon. The sooner she was back at Father's side, the better. She could tell him to rest assured that all would be taken care of—by honorable men.

The driver helped her climb back up into the freight wagon, and she looked down at her gown. Brown and black dust covered the hem. Why did she insist on wearing such frippery? Tears burned at the corners of her eyes. Because this was Father's favorite gown on her—he said it made her look like an angel. And he desperately needed an angel right now. And a miracle.

The past two days had been a nightmare. After the shots at the hotel missed them all by mere inches, Father was convinced that someone had tried to kill them. And he didn't have to think too hard to figure out who it was. Mary Margaret's sisters both married unsavory men against their father's advice. All along, they'd been after Father's money and the Abbot empire. Over the years, they'd revealed the depths of their greed to Mary Margaret as they maneuvered and weaseled every way possible to inherit a portion. And their subtlety wore off ages ago. Bolder than ever, her brothers-in-law would stop at nothing. Even murder?

The thought sent a chill up her spine. But didn't they know Father's will was ironclad and they had no place in it? She shook her head. All this time, she'd prayed for the men to give up. She thought Father would outlive them all. Even though they'd escaped the bullets, the attack sent Father into a frenzy, which resulted in a heart episode. The doctors weren't sure when or if he would regain his strength.

A tear escaped and slipped down her cheek. What would she do if something happened to Father? What if he *didn't* recover?

Uncle Dillard returned to the wagon, and she turned her head. The man had seen too many of her tears already. Now she had to be strong. Not only for Father, but for the Abbot assets. Uncle explained at the hospital that her father's directions were explicit. If anything happened to him—sickness or death—she needed to take the reins until he recovered or for the rest of her life. The responsibility weighed heavy upon her, but she could do it. Besides, she wasn't married—nor was she likely to be anytime soon. After watching the disastrous marriages of her sisters, she'd become wary of men. And with good reason.

"It's all settled." Uncle Dillard patted her hand. "Delaney is a good man. Honorable and decent. We can trust him."

"I'm glad. I'm sure that will relieve some of Father's stress." She turned to face him. "I apologize for being so short. Do you think Mr. Delaney was offended by my behavior?"

He chuckled. "Don't you worry about that. If anything, I think you impressed the man by not being a simpleminded, entitled female. He understood you were all about the business. And I explained to him the stressors that have caused the family grief recently."

"Good." Mary Margaret leaned toward the driver. "Please take us back to the hospital." She looked back to Dillard. "We just need to get Father well enough to endure the trip home, and then I will deal with my sisters and their husbands like they should have been dealt with long ago. Family or no, they will no longer be allowed anywhere near Father or the Abbot holdings. This was the last straw."

◆ ◆ ◆

Mary Margaret held Father's limp hand. In the few hours since she'd left his side to attend to business, he'd worsened. His cheeks were gray. "Father, please. Hold on. We just need to help you get your strength back."

The slightest shake of his head appeared to wear him out. "No. . . It's my time."

"Father, don't say that."

"I love you. . .Mary Margaret."

"I love you, too." There was no way to hold back the tears.

"God has been. . .good to me. And I get to see your mother. . . ." A smile lifted his lips in a small curve.

"Oh, Father. What will I do without you?" The pair had been a team for so long now, she couldn't bear to think of life going on without him. Pain ripped through her chest.

"Trust in the Lord, Mary Margaret. He will guide you." Father's voice gained a touch of strength. His eyes focused on the wall behind her. "I'm ready."

Uncle Dillard moved to the other side of the bed and nodded. "Go in peace, Arnold."

Father's smile grew as her tears intensified. His focus no longer resided on this world. This couldn't be the end. Could it?

A gentle squeeze on her hand and then a long last breath.

He was gone.

Her father, mentor, and best friend. Dead.

Mary Margaret collapsed over the body of the man she'd loved more than any other human being and sobbed.

Chapter 3

On his lunch break, Charles studied the papers Mr. Dillard gave him during their meeting. Under the canopy of trees outside the mine, he'd set up a small tent and left the front flaps open. He didn't mind the mist and rain that most people around the Juneau area thought of as dreary. Feeling the wind and rain on his face with the scent of spruce in the air was far better than the closed-up, musty environment of the deep mine shafts.

Jotting down a couple of notes, Charles felt confident. The job was huge, but he was up for the challenge. For two days, he'd planned and figured and discussed all the ideas with Jasper. It would be a lot of hard work, but they were ready. His thoughts turned to lovely Miss Abbot. When she'd arrived in that beautiful dress, he thought she was like all the other rich women he'd met—all fluff and nonsense. But she'd been direct and to the point. Yes, even a bit sharp-tongued. But after Dillard explained, it all made sense. Sounded like she would be running things while her father was ill, and Charles looked forward to seeing her again. She was definitely not what he expected and unlike any other women he'd met.

Horse's hooves sounded along the cavern walls. Seemed at a fast clip, too. Charles put the papers down and went to greet whomever their guest might be.

The sight of Mr. Dillard surprised him.

The man dismounted and nodded. "We need to talk."

"Of course." Charles walked toward his office and fought off the ominous thoughts crowding into his mind.

"Do you have anywhere more private than that tent?"

"I'm afraid not. But I doubt anyone will bother us here. They're all deep in the mine."

Mr. Dillard looked around the small mining camp and nodded.

"I have a bit of coffee I could offer you, but I'm afraid it's probably cold."

The lawyer sat on a rickety stool and sighed. "I'm fine, but thank you for the offer." He took off his hat and wiped his brow. "I'm afraid the news I have to share is grave."

"I guessed that."

"Before I tell you, I need your word that you will not, under any circumstances, discuss these details with anyone else. Not even Jasper."

"You can trust me, Mr. Dillard." His heart raced. Was it all for naught?

"I believe I can, Mr. Delaney. That's why I'm here."

"Please, call me Charles." He sat on the stump he'd been using for a stool and placed his elbows on his knees. "Best to just spit it out. I can handle it." Could he?

"Mr. Abbot is dead. His heart failed him two days ago. We will bury him tomorrow."

He raised his eyebrows. Not at all the news he expected to hear. "I'm very sorry to hear that."

Mr. Dillard turned his hat in his hands. "Miss Mary Margaret Abbot—who you met the other day—will inherit everything. I helped draft the will, so I know it will stand. She's a smart one and quite capable of running the companies. But her two younger sisters have husbands that have been trying to get their hands on the Abbot empire ever since they married into the family. Arnold knew all along and held them at bay, but I fear they have resorted to the worst of treachery." He mopped his brow with his handkerchief. "One attempt was made to kill them both at the hotel where they were staying. It was actually the shooting that caused Mr. Abbot to lose his temper over the whole debacle and sent him into the heart episode."

"Will all this affect the mines, sir?" It had to. That was the only reason the lawyer would be there. Charles's hopes sank to his feet.

"Heavens, no. The mines will be just fine." Mr. Dillard stood. "I'm afraid I'm not being clear. It's not the company or your position that I'm here about. It's about the safety of Miss Abbot."

"Miss Abbot?" The thought of her in danger kindled his anger. Who tried to kill her? "But I don't understand. What does that have to do with me if it's not anything about the mines?"

"Let me start again. I believe Miss Abbot's two brothers-in-law hired someone to kill her father. Now that he's gone, I believe her life is in danger as well. If she dies before her thirtieth birthday, then the other sisters have a chance to inherit everything. But it's even more complicated than that. Mr. Abbot isn't even buried, and somehow the family back in Colorado is contesting the will. My office in Denver tells me that a judge has already read the will, and the sisters are saying since they haven't heard from Mary Margaret in many months and she is out of the country that they can't be sure she is even alive to inherit.

"Now only a foolish judge would rule so quickly, but apparently, he has. Perhaps he's even been paid off. . .it wouldn't be the first time. My testimony to Mary Margaret's well-being via telegram is unacceptable to him—so he's demanded that Mary Margaret appear before him. And the deadline he has set is thirty days. If she doesn't appear by then, he will consider allowing the family to contest the will. And it sounds like he's already made up his mind. If Miss Abbot doesn't get back to Denver as soon as possible, Arnold Abbot's legacy could be destroyed."

"So what's the trouble? Why don't you just take her back to Denver?"

"Therein lies the problem. I must finish all the legalities up here. The Abbots were prepared to leave while I handled everything else. Only the three lawyers tasked with Abbot business are allowed to transact and sign—and as you well know—I'm the only one here. The mines are not all transferred yet, and Alaska is a territory—out of the country to the banks back in Denver. It will take at least two weeks for me to finish all the financial and legal obligations. We don't have that much time." Dillard shook his head. "It seemed simple to me—postpone the business dealings even though we might lose many of the mines, take Mary Margaret back to Colorado, and then return up here—but Miss Abbot refused. She said we would be letting her father down, so she's got this cockamamie plan to go by herself—to which *I* put my foot down and refused."

Charles nodded but didn't understand why the lawyer would need to tell him all this.

Mr. Dillard paced. "I'm afraid that whoever is out to get rid of Miss Abbot is expecting this very thing. They're hoping that I won't accompany her—not that I could offer all that much protection. And she will fall into their hands." He pulled out two pieces of paper. "Look. I've had a private investigator working in Denver for two years—watching the sisters' husbands. He intercepted and copied these two telegrams."

Charles took the papers and scanned them.

NO RETURN FOR THE PAIR TO COLORADO *stop*

YOUR PRICE IS ACCEPTABLE *stop*

With the background Mr. Dillard gave him, Charles could imagine how the telegrams were interpreted as threatening. "This is grave indeed. But I still don't understand what this has to do with me? Do you need my help in some way?"

"I apologize. Let me get to that. I need to stay and handle things, but I will ask my office to send someone to replace me immediately. But it's unacceptable for Miss Abbot to go alone until I can reach her. That's where you come in. You are the only man that I know up here that is trustworthy. Mr. Abbot held a deep respect for you. So, I'm going to offer you a deal. We are willing to sign over this mine completely to you—with the equipment we've already purchased—if you will accompany Miss Abbot back to Denver and act as her bodyguard."

◆ ◆ ◆

Johnny bent over the table and studied the layout of the harbor. He'd paid a pretty penny for the information, but it would be worth it.

Clive bit into his fried chicken and pointed with a greasy finger. "What's yer plan *this* time?"

"I ain't the one who missed outside the hotel. So don't mouth off to me." He swept his arm and knocked Clive's plate off the table. Was it even worth it to have this idiot involved?

"Hey! I paid good money for that."

"Yeah, money I gave ya. Learn some manners, why don'tcha?" Johnny straightened himself and fixed his cuffs. After watching the fancy men for days, he wanted to behave like them. He'd be rich soon, and he'd have to show them all who was boss. "The *plan* is to disable the engine. Delay them so they have to stay another night. I got a maid at the hotel willing to help us." He walked across to the window. "Then we just figure out some way to kill the rich lady in her sleep."

Chapter 4

Hands on her hips, Mary Margaret paced the floor of the hotel room in front of Uncle Dillard. "I don't see why I can't just hire a maid to go with me." Yes, she was angry—furious actually—and taking it out on the poor man. But her uncle had sought out someone to escort her home without even asking her opinion.

Underneath the anger though, there was more. . .she hurt. Ached. Grieved the loss of Father. And no matter what predicament they were in, she didn't believe it warranted her needing to deal with a man she barely knew while she mourned.

It was all too much.

"That's unacceptable and you know it." The man looked as if he'd aged ten years in the past few days. "Whether you admit it or not, you're in more danger than you realize. Even if I were escorting you home, I'd hire someone to help protect us."

She plopped into a wingback chair. Very unladylike, but she didn't care. "But why Mr. Delaney? I've only met him the one time, and I don't believe I made the best first impression, which would make for a very uncomfortable trip."

"Uncomfortable or not doesn't matter. Your father trusted the man. We know everything there is to know about him, and he will be able to protect you. That's all that matters."

"I still don't like it." Tears slipped down her cheeks. She hated sounding like a whiny child, but she'd buried her father just that morning. All she really wanted to do was curl up in a ball on her bed and cry. Her life would never be the same. "Why can't I just wait for you to finish?"

He walked over to her and took her hand. "Because you might miss the deadline, and your father's holdings would be lost." A knock at the door tore his attention away.

Even though he was right, she didn't want to admit it. Whether she liked it or not, it appeared she would be traveling with Mr. Delaney to Colorado.

If the trip didn't upset her enough, the thought of facing her sisters and their husbands made her want to run away to Canada and never return. Martha and Mabel were sure to make life miserable the instant Mary Margaret set foot in Denver. The two were thick as thieves and just as conniving.

Then there was the fact that Father wouldn't be with her. She'd never faced them without him. And what about their wretched husbands? How would she keep them at bay?

"I have an idea." Dillard stood before her. "This telegram just arrived. It appears the firm is working on several matters on their end, and a replacement is already on the way up here." He tapped the paper to his chin. "What if I initiated a rumor in town about how difficult this is for you and that you won't leave without me? We might draw out the killer. I could appeal to the local law enforcement and see if they can apprehend the man. Meanwhile, you and Delaney head out on the steamship for Prince Rupert in Canada. You can rest and hide there a few days to see if I can catch up. We could all travel together from there. But if I'm not there by say, the fifteenth, you all go on without me."

It wasn't her first choice, but it was better than going the entire trip without him. "I guess. . .if we must."

He placed his hands behind his back and walked to the door. "Good. I'll get a maid to help you finish packing and arrange for transportation down to the dock. Mr. Delaney should be here soon." Uncle Dillard turned and looked back to her. "It'll be all right. I'll feel much safer once you are on your way."

When the door clicked shut behind him, Mary Margaret collapsed back into the chair. Everything from the past few days washed over her. While she understood the gravity of the situation, her heart refused to believe it.

Numb. That's how she felt. Father was gone and he wouldn't be coming back. What good was it for her to inherit everything if she couldn't share it with her best friend? She had no one else. Not a single friend or even family member that she could trust with the depths of her heart.

Another knock at the door preceded a maid's entrance. "Miss, I'm here to help you pack."

Mary Margaret took a shaky breath. "Thank you. Please go ahead and finish this trunk. I'll fetch my valise out of the other room."

When she was once again alone, she allowed the tears to flow.

◆ ◆ ◆

The docks teemed with noise and unwashed bodies. Mr. Delaney towered above her on one side, while Uncle Dillard stood on the other. The day was a horrible blur. Beginning with the burial of her father and ending with a good-bye to the only other person she knew up here.

Dillard moved forward. "I'll go find out if they are ready for you to board."

Fiddlesticks. Now she was alone with the big bodyguard. Hopefully, he wouldn't want to talk—

"I'm sorry about your father."

Even though his voice was soothing, his kind words did nothing to help the rough places around her heart. To be frank, she'd prefer not to hear anyone else be sorry for her loss. But she should at least show him manners. "Thank you."

"I know he was the best of men."

"Yes, he was." Now could the big man please be quiet?

"I'm honored that he chose me to manage his mines."

Apparently not. "Uh-huh." She turned her face away from him.

He leaned over into her peripheral vision. "Are you all right?"

Exasperating man. Why couldn't he just leave her be? Despite her every effort, more tears formed at the corners of her eyes. She'd cried enough today for a lifetime and didn't need the man beside her to think any less of her. With a swallow and a deep breath, she found her voice. "I'm fine."

Abrupt. To the point. If she could keep him from talking to her for the next few weeks, they'd do *just* fine.

"Well, if you need someone to talk to, I'm here."

No, she did not. Would not. Ever. She sighed. How did she get into this mess?

Mr. Dillard stomped toward them, a storm brewing on his brow. "It would seem there's damage to the steam engine. And we cannot afford the delay. There isn't another ship for two days."

Was it terrible that she thought of that as good news?

Mr. Talkative crossed his arms. "What do you think we should do?"

"Well, since it's too late in the day to do much, I think we should go back to the hotel and formulate a new plan."

"All right then." Mr. Delaney offered her his elbow.

At least she could go to bed. Maybe sleep would claim her and she wouldn't have to face the coming weeks.

◆ ◆ ◆

A scraping sound brought Charles awake. Not that he slept all that well on a divan that was three feet too short for his frame. But all seemed quiet. He'd been dreaming about the decision he'd made that day and felt a little guilty. Was it wrong for him to choose the path with the largest profit? Dillard agreed that Jasper could know he needed to take a business trip and that he would be the mine's owner when he returned. Jasper had understood and rejoiced with him, but Charles still wished he could be there to see the boys hit the big payout. They were so close—he could feel it. But it wasn't likely he could get back for at least five weeks.

Thump!

Where had that noise come from? He sat up and wiped a hand down his face.

Two more thumps.

From Mary Margaret's bedroom. He jerked his head toward her door. The living area where he slept sat in the middle with Mr. Dillard sleeping in the room her father had occupied on the other side.

In his stocking feet, he headed for the room. Maybe she was having a nightmare?

Three rapid thumps. He ran—she could yell at him later for the unseemliness, but his gut told him something wasn't right.

Storming through the door, Charles was shocked to see a shadowy figure hovering over Miss Abbot's bed. A breeze blew in from the open window. The figure threw something down, ran to the window, and jumped out.

Charles pursued but tripped over a pillow in the dark room—the killer's choice of weapon?—and fell hard. By the time he reached the window, the figure was gone.

All the air had gone out of him. Mr. Dillard hadn't been overly cautious. He'd been right.

He turned toward the bed and heard footsteps from behind. "Are you all right?"

Mr. Dillard turned on the lights, and Charles got a good look at her face.

White as a sheet, Mary Margaret sat on her bed. Eyes wide and hair disheveled. "I. . .I don't know. It all occurred so fast." Gone was the grieving woman from the docks who'd been trying to hold it together. Gone was the businesslike lady from the mine. And in her place sat a small and terrified, young-looking girl.

Dillard went to her side. "What happened?"

She shook her head. "I woke up with a pillow being pressed over my face." Her voice wobbled. "I couldn't breathe. I tried to get free and make noise. . .but. . ." She sucked in a big breath and looked straight into Charles's eyes. "If. . .if Mr. Delaney hadn't heard, I. . .I. . ."

The older man patted her hand. "It's all right. You're all right now." But his expression to Charles told a different story. Fear etched a few more lines into the man's brow. "Thank you, Charles."

"Yes, thank you. . . you. . .you saved my life." Miss Abbot took in a deep breath.

Dillard stood up straight. "Let's give you a minute to compose yourself. Mr. Delaney and I will wait for you in the living area."

Miss Abbot nodded.

The feeling that settled into Charles's chest wasn't describable. He didn't want to leave her alone, she looked shaken to her core—who could blame her? The giant bed swallowed her and she seemed. . .so very fragile. He had the urge to wrap her up and protect her for the rest of her life.

Chapter 5

"You want me to do *what*?" Wrapped in a blanket on the divan, Mary Margaret was certain she hadn't heard correctly. Her whole body shook. While it had been easy to ignore the reality before, now. . .well, it was a different story. But she wasn't up for this. Not at all.

Uncle Dillard stood in front of her, his hands behind his back. He looked over at Mr. Delaney, but the other man just shrugged and nodded. "Charles and I both think that it would be best to disguise you."

"By dressing like a boy?" She couldn't keep the incredulity from her voice. Granted she'd thought just the other day about how life would have been easier on her father if she'd been born a boy—but heavens—she didn't mean it. Especially not now. Not with Father gone. She was very much his little girl. And she missed him so much.

Uncle Dillard cleared his throat. "Mary Margaret, this is very difficult. I know you've been through a lot. We're not trying to upset—"

"I'm sorry to interrupt. Miss Abbot—Mary Margaret, may I call you that?" Tall Mr. Delaney crouched down in front of her. Invading her space.

She blinked. Then nodded and leaned as far back into the settee as she could.

"Mary Margaret." Something in his eyes calmed her. That same look she'd seen before. Steadfast and strong. "I'm sorry, but we don't have time for discussion on this. Your life is in danger, and we need to leave before sunrise. As uncomfortable as it is, I think you are small enough of stature to pass as my younger brother. We could cover you in clothes that are too big and hide your hair under a hat. It would be appropriate for us to travel together, and you wouldn't have to handle anything. I'll take care of it so you don't have to talk to anyone. Even me." His eyes held a twinkle. Had he known her thoughts earlier?

"All right." How did Mr. Talkative convince her so quickly? "But I thought there wasn't another boat for two days?"

Charles stayed crouched in front of her. And she had to admit, she liked his presence. "There isn't. But Mr. Dillard has found a man with a skiff that is heading to Hobart Bay. He will pick us—me and my little brother—up there in two days and take us to Prince Rupert."

She shook her head. "Wait a minute. . .why isn't he just taking us from here?"

"He can't. His skiff is full." Charles inched forward, his voice low and calm like she was a skittish animal about to flee. "Besides, we are afraid there are people watching the docks for you. It'll be safer for us to head out on foot."

"On *foot*? Are you mad?" Maybe fleeing wasn't such a bad idea. "First you want me to dress like a boy, and then you want me to 'head out on foot'? What about my trunks?"

Charles sighed and looked down at the floor. "Mr. Dillard will have to take them with him."

She'd almost forgotten her uncle was in the room. As she shifted her gaze to him, she saw the apologetic look on his face. Full of sorrow. And weariness. Why hadn't she noticed the toll this had taken on the man? Glancing from one man to the other, her heart sank. They were trying to protect her. The least she could do was buck up and carry on. What did it matter that she didn't have her hats, gloves, gowns, parasols, and other things? What did any of it matter if she couldn't make it home alive?

Uncle Dillard came forward and laid his hand on her shoulder. "Your father would be so proud of you, Mary Margaret. This isn't easy. But you're an heiress. To quite a substantial fortune. And you are so brave to endure all this to save your father's legacy. You knew his wishes as well as I—he wouldn't want them to win. . .and he would want you alive."

Charles stood and placed a hand on her other shoulder. "We're going to make sure you get to Denver before the deadline. I'll do everything in my power to protect you."

She nodded. A rush of emotion overwhelmed her—with Father gone—the thought of going home sounded horrible. And lonesome.

One look at Charles and she knew he meant every word.

But who would protect her once she got home?

◆ ◆ ◆

In the early morning hours, Charles realized his plan to leave in the middle of the night wasn't going to happen. Mary Margaret had other ideas. Like making sure they had food and necessities packed. Which was wise since they would be off the beaten path, but that hadn't been his first concerns. Then she closed herself up in her room to try on different clothes. She'd been in there an hour already. He checked his timepiece again.

Dillard paced the room with his hands clasped behind his back. Charles hadn't known the man long but had picked up on his quirks. One was pacing. Same expression. Same hands behind his back. And when he did that, it meant he was worried.

The door to Miss Abbot's room opened.

Dillard gasped. "Oh my."

Charles raised his eyebrows and stood.

Brown boots were covered by rolled-up denims that dragged the floor. A long leather coat draped to her knees. Everything was too big. Loose. Swallowing her up. A wide-brimmed Stetson covered her head and her hair. All he could see was a nose and her lips. Even then, she'd marked up her face with what looked like soot from the fireplace.

Charles applauded. "Miss Abbot, it's perfect."

Dillard went to her and nodded his head. "Amazing disguise. No one will be the wiser."

She frowned. "I need to work on my walk though. But with the way the pants and boots fit"—she kicked a leg out to the side—"I'll be stumbling along anyway." Removing her hat, she shook her head. A mass of hair tumbled down around her shoulders. "I can hardly see with it on, but it will have to do. Mr. Delaney—"

"Charles." He held up his hand. "I must insist you call me Charles or you'll give us away."

"Precisely the direction my thoughts had taken. . .Charles. . ." She twisted the hat. "I think you should call me Martin. I've been toying around with names, and I think I could remember to answer to that one."

Smart, pretty, and good at disguises. His respect grew by the second. "Sounds like a good plan." He stood. "Are you ready? I think we'd better get moving."

With a nod, she leaned toward Mr. Dillard. The older man wrapped her in his arms.

"You'll be fine. Charles will take excellent care of you, and prayerfully, I will meet up with you in Prince Rupert."

Charles watched as she crumpled a bit in the older man's arms. A single tear trailed down her cheek. He'd been so focused on the task at hand that he'd forgotten her father hadn't even been gone a week. Maybe he could find a way to help her on their journey. But how?

Mary Margaret stepped back and straightened her shoulders. "I need to grab my bag." As she walked to her room, she twisted her hair up into a knot on top of her head and plunked the hat back into place.

Within a minute, she was back. "I'm ready."

She looked small and fragile, and for the first time in many years, he wanted to put aside all his thoughts of mines, gold, and business and simply take care of someone else.

Dillard broke through his thoughts and stuck out his hand.

Charles grasped it and shook.

"Thank you, son. More than you will ever know."

With a nod, he picked up his own bag. "Thank you for your trust, sir."

The older man offered him an envelope. "There's plenty of money in here to get you to Denver. Remember, if I'm not in Prince Rupert by the fifteenth. Continue on. I've tucked a list into there that contains all the telegram stops where I will leave you correspondence—the telegrams will be addressed to you so no one is suspicious of Mary Margaret Abbot being there."

"Appreciate that, Mr. Dillard." Charles tucked the envelope into his boot.

"Go on then. I'll be in touch." The man appeared a little teary, but he blinked them away.

"Good-bye." Mary Margaret's soft voice quivered.

Charles led the way out the door, wanting to give her a moment alone with her uncle. But they needed to get out of town while it was still dark if their plan was to be successful.

Crisp air greeted them outside the hotel as the sun began its ascent. The streets were quiet except for a few vendors and miners, but that wouldn't last long. They'd better hurry.

He picked up the pace, and out of the corner of his eye he saw Mary Margaret trip. Reaching his hand out to her, he wanted to keep her from falling, but she smacked it away.

"Leave me alone. I'm fine and I'm not a baby." Her voice was low and scratchy. Then she hiked up her pants and went on without him.

For a second, Charles wanted to laugh out loud. He'd almost blown their cover, but Miss Abbot had the sense to stay in character.

He was impressed. With her hat pulled low and a canvas bag slung over her shoulder, she could *almost* pass for a boy in his book.

Only problem was, he knew she wasn't.

And it had almost gotten him into trouble.

How could he convince himself to picture her as a boy? Thoughts tumbled around in his brain, but no answers came to mind.

As he caught up with her, he nudged her with his elbow and smiled. "I didn't know you were such an actress." He kept his voice low.

She shook her head at him and grinned back. "*One* of us has to keep our wits about us."

After the first hour of trudging along, they finally made it through town and into the woods outside of Juneau. The Sitka spruce, yellow cedar, and mountain ash trees were thick in this area. The going would be much slower. Charles reached out to take the bag from Mary Margaret's shoulder to lighten her load.

Once again he received a smack to his hand. "If I'm going to pass as a boy, I have to look like, talk like, and act like one. Only a child would allow their bag to be carried."

Shaking his head, he realized he'd underestimated the heiress Miss Abbot. "Of course. Again, you are correct."

"And I will *always* be correct, Mr. Delaney." Her grin surprised him. For the first time since her father died, there was a bit of a sparkle in her eyes. "So just remember that."

Ah. So she was teasing him. "Yes ma'am."

"Good. We are in agreement." She gave him a slight nod and marched on ahead. "So what exactly is the plan, and why are you allowing me to lead when I have no idea where I'm going?"

Chapter 6

Because you were doing an excellent job of showing me you were a boy." Charles laughed, and the sound made Mary Margaret want to join in. Father used to make her laugh. A lot.

"I might as well take my task seriously, now shouldn't I?" Placing her hands on her hips, she hoped his laugh would return. "Even if these clothes stink to high heaven. I thought I could take it, but whew!"

"Mary Margaret, you never cease to surprise me."

"Good. And remember, it's Martin."

"All right, *Martin.*" He crossed his arms on his chest. "If I were to be completely honest? You were good at trampling down the brush for me. Made it easier to walk." His laugh returned.

Laughter bubbled up out of her. She picked up a stick and threw it at him. But then she shouldn't be surprised. How many times had she gone off in a direction all her own just because she was stubborn? And the poor man had just followed along. Probably didn't want to be smacked again. She held out an arm in front of her. "Lead the way, Charles."

He smiled and it did something funny to her midsection. Holding her gaze, he reached into his pocket and pulled out a compass. He glimpsed at it and then squinted back up at her. "Not bad for not knowing where you were going. But I think we should go"—he pointed to the right of where she'd been heading, whichever direction that was—"*this* way if we want to make it to Hobart Bay." With a wink, he started down the new path.

The smile that started in her toes made her happy. How Charles wielded that power, she had no idea. Used to be, only Father had the ability to do that.

Used to be.

No. She couldn't go there. Not now. Not when she was running for her life. Sheer determination and willpower needed to be her mainstays right now. Father hadn't built this company with integrity and hard work for her to let those greedy men squander it away.

She would make it to Denver. On time.

But first, she had to survive this horrid trek in the woods.

And if she really thought about it, it wasn't all that horrid. Charles had turned out to be a decent companion. Smart, decent, witty. To think yesterday that she had doubts about him and was embarrassed by the thought of being escorted by him—because her own manners had been lacking. And she was uncomfortable with a man invading her tightly enclosed, heavily guarded. . .space.

Looking down, she giggled at herself. Here she was dressed like a boy, covered in dirt and brush in the middle of. . .some forest in Alaska. Who would've guessed? Definitely not her.

Yet, Charles treated her the same as he had before. With respect.

Charles stopped and turned, apparently waiting for her. "A penny for your thoughts."

"They're not worth that much." She waved her hand at him.

"I beg to differ." He started walking again, a little slower this time. "Do you need to take a rest?"

"I appreciate your consideration, but I am fine. I just let my thoughts wander. . .the past few days. . ." Where could she go with this? To talk about Father would make her cry. Talk about the threat against her and she would get angry. Talk about her new insight into her thoughts about Charles? She shook her head.

"I understand. I don't mean to intrude, truly. But maybe we could talk about something else—to keep us occupied as we walk." He shrugged his shoulders and looked at her with compassion. "Tell me about your childhood. Your likes, dislikes, friends. . .whatever you'd like."

Mr. Talkative was back. And it wasn't so bad. In fact, Mary Margaret kind of liked him. "It's a good idea. But why don't we go ahead and pick up the pace again, or we may never get to Hobart Bay in time."

"Will do. You just let me know if I am pushing too hard. I know my long legs give me an advantage, and your legs are much shorter. . .um. . .not that I've noticed. . .what I meant to say. . ." Red crept up his neck and into his face. "I apologize, I shouldn't have mentioned—"

"Charles. Not another word. Don't apologize, I know my legs are short. Pretty much everything about me is short." She tried to cover their embarrassment with a laugh. It's not like anything improper was going on. They were just talking about legs. Right? Gracious, how did she maneuver out of this one? "And I actually think that was rather considerate because you know that you can go faster and cover more territory than I can. So thank you."

Charles laughed. "As you can tell, I've been around miners a long time. My manners need some polishing."

"So why don't you tell me about *your* background? Family, friends, all of it. I know my father and Uncle Dillard knew everything about you, but I just relied on their knowledge and trust." She smiled. "Now that I know you, I'd like to know more." Switching the conversation to him was safer. And much easier.

"Let's see. My family is all gone. Two brothers died of measles when they were children. My mother and father died ten years ago."

"I'm so sorry. What happened?"

"Shipwreck. Bad storm hit just a hundred miles off the coast of San Francisco. No survivors."

"Is that where you are from?"

"San Francisco? Yes." He looked down and checked the compass again. "My parents were wonderful people. I loved them very much and miss them more than I can say, but I know they are with the Lord now, and that makes all the difference in the world. I know

I'll see them again. Anyway, they ran a dry goods store there—in San Francisco."

She gasped. "Delaney's? Really? That was your parents'?"

He chuckled. "You know it?"

"Gracious, yes. My favorite in San Francisco. We traveled there often."

"That is wonderful to hear. I loved that store. Dreamed of running it one day. But once Mom and Dad were gone and they left everything to me. . .well. . .it was harder than I imagined." Looking back over his shoulder at her, he gave her a sad smile. "Not the work or the running of the business—but seeing them around every corner. In every item on the shelves. In all the catalogs. It's almost as if I couldn't heal there. Couldn't let them go. Couldn't go on for myself. The hardest thing I've ever done is leave the store."

"Ah. So did you sell it?"

"No. I still own it. But I pay the new managers really well and they receive high commission checks on top of their wages if they increase profits. So far the incentive has worked well."

Here she thought he was just another gold miner, looking for his fortune. Sounded like she had misjudged Mr. Delaney on more than one account. "Why did you decide to come to Alaska? Or did you go somewhere else first?"

"I hired the managers—a husband and wife, good people—and then stuck around for two months to make sure they would run things properly. Dad had built a reputation for the store that I didn't want destroyed. I think that would have hurt more than leaving the store." He took at least a dozen steps before he spoke again. "Anyway, I kept hearing about Alaska and I like to research, so I spent my time poring over books, newspapers, journals, magazines, anything I could get my hands on. It kept my mind engaged and my thoughts off the loss of my parents."

So he understood her grief even better than she did. The Lord certainly did work in mysterious ways—giving her the bodyguard she needed. "What made you pursue mining?"

"I'd always been fascinated with the history of the gold rush in San Francisco. So when I read a newspaper article about gold mining in Juneau. I switched from research on Alaska to research on mining. I went and talked to successful miners and studied the mines there."

"So when did you come up here?"

"About eight years ago."

"And you've been successful?"

He looked back and smiled. "I think so. I've certainly learned a lot."

"You don't miss your family's store?"

"Not too much. But I stay in contact with the Bannisters back home."

The terrain was uphill now and Mary Margaret struggled to keep up. But she was determined. "Those are the managers?"

"Yes." He stopped and gazed up the hill and in all directions. "Sorry, Mary Marg—I mean *Martin*."

She laughed. "See? It's good practice for when we are around people."

"I know. But I think the only way forward is to continue over this hill." Charles turned back to her. "And I do believe it will be quite a climb."

"I'm ready if you are." Was she? If she were honest, probably not. But she'd give it a go. What else did she have to lose? At least up here, no one was trying to kill her. Yet.

Two hours passed with little conversation and the most intense work her body had ever done. Good thing she was wearing pants, because otherwise it would have been a disaster. And not just the first time when she fell backward and rolled with her legs going over her head. But every time she had to get into an unladylike posture to hoist one or the other leg up to a decent foothold. Charles was gracious enough to go first and tell her where to step and where to hold on—and since he was ahead, he couldn't see her increasingly shabby efforts. But she wanted to hear a choir of angels singing when she reached the top because this was almost as bad as the forms of medieval torture she'd read about. At least it had to be in her mind.

"Good job. Just one more. . .yes, right there. Pull and step. . ."

Apparently, he was at the top. And watching her. She huffed and threw her words up at him. "Couldn't you just haul me up the rest of the way?"

"I thought you didn't want any help, *Martin*."

"Fiddlesticks. I'm impressed I didn't keel over halfway up. I'm not ashamed to ask for help. . .besides, no one is watching." She held on and waited.

Charles chuckled. "I would love to be of assistance." He knelt and reached down with both hands.

Mary Margaret grabbed on to his arms and pushed up with her feet. Before she knew it, she was colliding with Charles's head. They fell in a heap on the ground.

"Ow." Charles put a hand on his head. "I didn't realize you were so light. I might've pulled too hard."

She held a hand to her own brow. "Might've? I think our heads can attest that that's an understatement." Rubbing the knot, she sat up. "Well, that was my first mountain climbing experience, and quite possibly my last." She picked up her hat that must've flown off in the collision. "How much farther?"

Charles stood and offered a hand.

She grasped it and got to her feet.

"We have quite a ways to go, I'm afraid." Dusting himself off with his hat, he dragged in a deep breath. "Maybe we should eat a light meal and keep going."

"I have to admit I'm starved." Finally, she'd get a moment to rest. "Now what would you like? I put several things in my bag and in yours." She started digging around in the canvas sack.

"Um. . ."

"Speak up, silly, or I might just eat yours." Where did she put that jerky?

"Mary Margaret." His voice was hushed.

"Martin." She huffed and continued digging. "Call me Martin." *Aha!* She found her canteen. Now if she could just find the jerky. It had to be in there, she remembered—

"*Martin!*"

The half whisper, half yell brought her attention up. "What?"

He slung his own bag over his shoulder and grabbed her arm. "Put your canteen back in the bag. We're going to back up very quietly and very, very slowly." Tugging at her, he took a step.

"Why? What's going on?" But she did as she was told.

"Because we have company." He pointed.

Looking in the direction he gestured, she gasped. Two brown bear cubs were headed straight for them. Behind the babies walked the impressive and enormous mama bear—and she'd just spotted Charles and Mary Margaret.

Chapter 7

Something shook him.

"Johnny. . .Johnny, wake up."

Clive's voice broke through the nice dream he was having. He yanked his hat off his face. Why did he saddle himself with this green fool? An experienced killer like himself didn't need the headache. "What do you want?"

"I overheard Mr. Dillard talking outside that office he has. He made it sound like Miss Abbot is already gone."

That news brought him fully awake. He sat up. "But how? There hasn't been another boat."

"I dunno. But that's definitely what he said."

Johnny jumped up. Not the news he wanted to hear. His failed attempt at smothering the heiress must've pushed them to do something drastic. But what? He kicked the wall with his boot. "If you hadn't fallen asleep watching the hotel this morning, I bet we'd know where she went. She'd be dead by now."

"Hey, it ain't my fault that you didn't kill her in her room." Clive crossed his arms. "I stayed up all night. I can't help it that I fell asleep."

Wait a minute. Maybe she hadn't left after all. What if that lawyer was scheming? Trying to make them think that she was gone so they would take off after her? He started laughing. "Oh, now that would be too easy."

"Huh?"

"But we're not idiots, are we, Clive?" Well, *he* wasn't.

"What? No. Of course not."

"That lawyer is playing us for fools. Well, that ain't gonna happen."

Clive looked confused. Stupid man. But at least Johnny had someone to take the fall.

"You get yourself down to the docks and ask around." Johnny dug in his pocket and pulled out a bunch of coins. He dumped them on the table in front of Clive. "Pay them nicely to spill the beans—see if anyone knows anything."

"You got it, Johnny."

He settled his hat back on his head. "I'm gonna pay a visit to that maid and see what she knows. Meet me back here in an hour."

"What if nobody knows nothin'?"

Johnny patted the man on the shoulder. "Well, then we will just have to pay the lawyer a visit, now won't we?"

"What kinda visit?"

"The kind where he talks, or he dies."

◆ ◆ ◆

Charles tugged Mary Margaret's arm and shoved her behind him. It really was a good thing she didn't weigh much, because when he needed to, he could use his strength to protect her. Not that he would ever want to overpower her or hurt her, but she could be stubborn. In her own, cute way. He shook his head. Now was not the time.

He backed them up several steps. There had to be at least fifty yards between them and the bears. But the mama was definitely watching them. Then she started clacking her teeth.

"Oh, that's not a good sign. We need to let her know we are human and not after her cubs." He tried to keep his voice low as he continued to back them up.

Mary Margaret's hands gripped the back of his shirt. She whispered close to his shoulder. "If you keep backing us up, you're going to back us right back down the hill we climbed."

"Good point. I'll steer us to the left, and you keep an eye out behind us, okay?"

"Okay."

"Stay close."

"That is not a problem." She paused and then tapped him on the shoulder. "But I am wondering why we don't just run. Aren't we far enough away?"

He shook his head. "Nuh-uh. With brown bears, we need them to see that we are not a threat and that we are retreating out of respect. If they see us run, their first instinct is to give chase in defense of their cubs or their food, their mate, whatever they are protecting."

"Understood. Let's not run, then."

He chuckled. "Good idea." He felt what must be her forehead press into his back between her hands.

"Are you watching them?" Her whispered words ended in a squeak.

"Yes, ma'am. And they haven't moved."

"Whew." She patted his shoulder blade. "And that's *Martin* to you, remember?"

Her attempt at levity strengthened his admiration of her. This was no simpering female he was protecting. "So does that mean you want me to say, 'yes, sir'?"

The pressure between his shoulder blades increased again as she giggled. "Stop making me laugh, that's not fair. And no, I'm supposed to be your younger brother, so get it right." Another pause. "Mar-tin." She drew out the syllables.

"Mar–tin it is." They were almost out of sight of the bears. "Which reminds me, *Martin*." He couldn't help but be a little sarcastic every time he used it. She was definitely too feminine to be "Martin" in his book. But he would do his best to appease her. "You haven't told me about *you*. You've heard all about me, now it's your turn."

"Ugh. I was hoping you would forget." She smacked him in the back this time. "Did I just say that out loud?"

"Why yes. Yes, you did." He looked over his shoulder. "And I'm pretty sure you grunted. . .and you hit me, too. . . Ow."

More giggles. "Stop it."

Using his right arm, he gently took her right arm and pulled her out from behind him. "I think we're safe."

"Are you sure?" She crouched down a little and looked off into the distance.

"Pretty sure." He grabbed her left hand and led her away. "It's going to take us a little longer to go around them, but now that we know they are there, we should be safe."

Her stomach rumbled loud enough for him to hear. "Sorry. I haven't eaten much lately, so my stomach is protesting." She sighed. "It's very unladylike for me to even say, but I don't care anymore. Maybe more people should spend time in the wild to see what real life is all about, and then maybe we could throw some of these ridiculous rules out the window."

"Why don't we walk for a little while longer to put more distance between us and our furry brown friends, then we can eat." She hadn't taken her hand away, and Charles found he enjoyed it, so he held on to it as they walked side by side through the waist-high brush. He needed to protect her, right?

"Sounds wonderful. I should be able to survive without swooning for a good while yet."

Her sharp wit was amazing. And very unexpected. Especially after all she'd been through. But he understood she was doing what she could to shove her grief aside. "So which rules would you get rid of first?"

"It'll never happen. . .but after today? I'm thinking dresses and skirts. Why must women always wear them? With all the petticoats and such underneath—which is another completely inappropriate topic to discuss with a man, but I'm dressed as a boy, so it shouldn't matter. Good heavens, I wouldn't have made it up that *hill*, as you called it, with all that on." She grimaced.

"But. . ." Maybe he shouldn't mention it.

"But what?"

"Well. . .it's just that. . .women are beautiful in dresses." Especially the one beside him. In that white dress she wore the day he met her.

She yanked her hand away and stopped. "And women dressed up as boys in pants covered in dirt are not?" She planted her hands on her hips.

He chuckled and kept walking. "I don't need to answer that." He cut a glance over his shoulder. "But I will say this. Women in pants are. . .distracting." As he turned back, he winked and caught sight of her mouth forming an O— Good. Enough said.

Chapter 8

Why did she have to yank her hand away? Just because she wanted to make a point? Mary Margaret shook her head and swatted at a mosquito. The grass was so high, with tons of brush, rocks, and tree roots to maneuver around—she could've used his stability. Oh, who was she fooling? She missed the warmth and feel of her hand enveloped in his.

No one other than Father had ever held her hand.

Thoughts tumbled around in her brain. Trying to corral them proved difficult. But one fact remained. She couldn't give in to the grief. Even when she was tired. And sweaty.

Yuck. Another thing ladies were not to discuss. But it was true and a fact of life.

"You still with me, *Martin*?" Charles threw over his shoulder.

"Yes." Her stomach rumbled again. "But I might faint if we don't eat soon."

He laughed. "Please don't tell me you're one of those women that's an expert at fainting?"

"No. In fact, I've never fainted in my life. But I *am* a hearty eater. So please, don't make me wait much longer, or I might get grumpy."

Shaking his head, he stopped walking and laughed even harder. "You do beat all." As he turned, he pointed a finger at her. "I'll make you a deal."

She crossed her arms. This sounded fun. Squinting her eyes, she tapped her foot. "I'm listening. But wait. First, I'd like to say that I think it's unfair to hold my food ransom."

He held his palms up as in surrender. "Who said anything about a ransom? And don't you have half the food in your bag?"

She widened her eyes. Of course! She began to rummage around again. "So what's this deal?"

"We take a short break and eat, but you have to agree to tell me about *you* now."

But that would mean thinking about Father. All the beautiful memories. . .and now he was gone. All of a sudden, she wasn't very hungry anymore.

Charles sat on the ground under a tall mountain ash tree and leaned against the trunk. Chewing a piece of jerky, he stared at her. "Why did you stop digging in your bag?"

"I'm not hungry."

He raised his eyebrows. "That doesn't seem possible. I'm a witness to your stomach's protests. Remember?"

She shook her head as tears burned her eyes. Not now. There would be time to grieve later. Didn't the Bible say that in Ecclesiastes? She hated feeling hot one moment and cold the next. Happy, able to laugh and enjoy life. And then overwhelming sadness.

She didn't know how to control all the emotion rushing through her. Poor Charles. He probably hadn't bargained for escorting an emotional female through the woods.

"I'm sorry. I didn't mean to push, honest. I'll just sit here and be quiet." He leaned back against the tree and closed his eyes.

It was gracious and considerate of him to give her a moment to compose herself. But it made her feel that much worse.

Mary Margaret allowed a few of the tears to burn trails down her cheeks. Who cared what she looked like? She was covered in dirt and grime anyway. She could allow herself a moment or two of grief, and then she could buck up and move on again.

"You know"—so much for giving her a moment, Mr. Talkative was back—"when my parents died, I was crushed. But I still wanted to be happy. Knew they would *want* for me to be happy. And I wanted people to talk about them. Remember them. But instead, they ignored the fact that I'd lost them. They tried to pretend like it didn't happen. Maybe to spare my feelings? To keep from causing me pain? I'm not sure. But what I am sure of is that it hurt *worse*, not to talk about them."

Maybe he was right. Charles was safe. She could talk to him about Father. Besides, he'd asked. Several moments passed as she thought it through. Should she shove her feelings down or open up?

He went back to eating his jerky then drank from his canteen.

She wiped her face and drew in a deep breath. "My mother died when I was only five. Martha and Mabel—my younger sisters—were barely two and three years old." Her stomach growled, and she bit into her own jerky. Not the high-class food she was used to in Denver, but it was sustenance. "Martha and Mabel don't remember our mother, but she was a beautiful and kind lady."

Charles leaned forward as if there were nothing he'd like more in the world than to listen.

"My memories are few of Mother, but I'm grateful for them. When she passed, Father doted on all of us but had his hands full with the business, so he hired a governess. She was prideful and had a huge influence on my sisters. But I was the oldest and didn't want anyone else in my life, so I pushed her away from the very beginning.

"As we got older, I excelled in math and loved to talk about Father's plans and business ideas. Poor man. I didn't understand a lot, but I asked tons of questions. I think he just needed someone to care about what he did. While Mabel and Martha were concerned with dolls and hair ribbons, I wanted nothing more than to follow Father around all the time. Our governess convinced him that if my sisters were to be true ladies that they should be sent to a prestigious finishing school. And so he sent them." She ate a few more bites.

"What about you? Why didn't the governess think you needed it as well?"

"She said I would never succeed as a lady, that I was too stubborn, strong-willed, and fascinated with things that were best left to men." She shrugged her shoulders. "I didn't mind. Father knew I wanted to follow in his footsteps, and he was all right with that. Besides, I think he'd been seeing the true colors of Martha and Mabel—they hurt him so many times." Talking had a way of making her hunger return, so she finished the jerky and started on a biscuit.

"What do you think the problem was?"

She chewed for a minute longer. "Personally. . .it's hard to say, but I think it's because neither one of them have ever had any place for God in their life. They're self-centered and greedy—even though Father provided everything they could have ever wanted. Anyway, off they went to finishing school to become even more selfish, and I stayed at home with Father. Over time, he told me he was proud of me and that I reminded him of Mother. It's the best compliment he could ever give." The memory made her smile.

"When did they marry the ne'er-do-wells?"

"You've been talking to Mr. Dillard, I see." Her uncle was the only one who called her brothers-in-law by that name. "They were both nineteen when they married. Two lavish weddings within a year. Father didn't approve of either one, because—if you haven't noticed—he investigates and thoroughly researches anyone who has anything to do with our family or business. He learned that the hard way a long time ago. And it became a lonely life for him as so many people wanted to befriend the great Arnold Abbot—for his money. From the very beginning he knew that both grooms-to-be were only after the Abbot fortune, but the girls wouldn't listen."

"Your father was a very wise man. I'm sorry I couldn't have known him better."

She smiled at the thought. Father had invested a lot in Charles. Had trusted him. For some reason, that made her very happy. "Me, too."

"What happened after the weddings?"

"I turned twenty-one and everyone then found out that I was the sole heiress to the Abbot money and businesses. Father still gave them rich dowries when the girls married, but he had written them out when they decided to marry against his wishes. I understood and knew that he did it because he loved them, but they thought he was just being mean. I don't think he really thought they would go through with marrying the weasels—and who knows why they did? I don't even know if Martha and Mabel are capable of true love. But they married those horrible men anyway.

"So while I learned everything at my father's side, they connived with their spouses and each other to try and gain access to Father's legacy. Of course, Father has always had the best lawyers—thanks to Uncle—so they've never gained any ground. But if they are truly behind the threats—I think I've sorely underestimated them and how far they are willing to go."

Charles raised his eyebrows. "It sounds like maybe they need to hear a good sermon or two on hellfire and brimstone to straighten them out."

"I don't know. I don't even know how to pray for them anymore. It's sad."

"So what did your friends think about your family and the way your sisters treated you?"

The question was sure to have been innocent, but it stabbed her heart. "I didn't have any friends. Not since I was a small girl." She sniffed and tried to keep the tears at bay. "Father was my best friend."

◆ ◆ ◆

No friends. Of course, it made sense. Especially when you were worth as much as the Abbots financially. She'd already mentioned that her father had been guarded, but how hard was that for Mary Margaret to grow up. . .so alone? Charles hated to think about it.

She shrugged and looked away. "Please don't look at me that way. I don't need your pity, Charles."

"Good. Because I'm not giving you any."

Her head snapped back toward him. "Good."

"But that doesn't mean I can't care about you and what has happened."

She shook her head. "You don't care about me. You're just invested in the business. If you get me to Denver, you will then own the mine you love." She shoved things into her bag.

"That's not fair, Mary Margaret."

"Martin. Call me Martin." She huffed.

"I care about *you*—a human being—and your safety far more than I care about the mine. Is that why you think I came along?"

She shrugged. But he couldn't help but notice the tears shimmering at the corners of her eyes.

"Yes, you and your uncle made me a wonderful offer to help you out. I appreciate it." He reached out and covered her hand with his. "But that is not why I am telling you that I care."

She pulled away and stood. "Maybe we should get moving again." Wiping her hands on her pants, she let out a jagged breath then slung her bag onto her back.

Charles watched her for a moment. She wouldn't look him in the eye. Pain radiated from her small frame. "All right." He would let it go for now, but he'd have to find a way to convince her that people could care about her for *her*.

He packed his bag and started walking. She fell in step just behind him. He could sense her nearness. Silence reigned in the woods as they trekked on, and Charles felt the weight of her loneliness and grief on his shoulders.

When darkness fell, they hadn't spoken for hours. He stopped and looked back at her. Had the quiet caused more damage than good? "I think we need to rest for a few hours and then continue on before the sun rises."

She nodded and took off her bag. Laying it down, she plopped down beside it and then rested her head on it and closed her eyes. Without looking at him, she spoke. "I will make sure that Uncle takes care of everything before you journey home."

Her protective wall was back up. Charles understood a little more clearly. Taught well, she could snap back into business mode without a thought. It must be the way she guarded herself. And it made even more sense that she had responded to his question when they first met with, *"Do you accept the job or not?"*

Mary Margaret Abbot had many layers. He'd seen her quick wit, her fear, a little of her grief, and the stubborn spitfire that must have made her father proud. As he watched her now, she looked exhausted and sad.

He'd just have to do better at encouraging her and showing her that he truly cared. She would do well at the helm of the Abbot empire, of that he was certain. But he had to get her there safely.

So far so good.

Chapter 9

Johnny tightened the ropes around the lawyer's wrists. "Now I'm gonna ask you one more time. Where is the girl?"

The man shrugged. "Like I said before, I don't know. She could be halfway to Denver by now."

He laughed. The man still thought they were idiots. "We're not stupid, Mr. Lawyer."

Clive laughed, too. "Yeah, we're not stupid. There weren't no boat to take her anywhere."

"Who said they went by boat?" The man had the arrogance to sit there and not look worried.

Didn't he know who he was dealing with? They'd been hired to kill. *Kill.* And they would. Why did he think they'd brought him to this shack? Wait a minute. "What did you just say?"

The man sighed. "I simply said, 'Who said they went by boat?'"

Clive huffed. "But there ain't no other way outta here. Yer lyin'."

Johnny smacked the wall with his hand. "Yeah there is. There just aren't any roads." He went back over to the pompous man and wrapped his hands around his throat. "Tell me which way they went." He squeezed.

The lawyer shook his head and choked out his words. "I don't know."

Johnny squinted at him and released his hold. Placing a gag over the man's mouth, he lowered his voice. "We're gonna do some more asking around town, and if we find out yer lyin' to us, I'm going to kill you." He grabbed Clive's arm and then walked out the door, slamming it behind him.

◆ ◆ ◆

Mary Margaret awoke to a nudge on her shoulder.

"Wake up, Martin. We need to go."

She sat up and nodded. As she rubbed her eyes, her body reminded her that she'd slept on the forest floor. Ouch. And the thought of having to find privacy without an outhouse didn't make things better. Then she remembered why she was here to begin with. Father was dead. And she was on the run.

She stood and stretched. Maybe it would be better to just disappear. It would definitely be easier. But Father would encourage her to continue on the hard path, even if it hurt along the way. And he would be right.

For a while yesterday, she'd found comfort in the companionship of Charles. She'd laughed and smiled. Even bantered. If only she could find that again today. Her melancholy thoughts were dangerous.

Lord, please help. I don't know what to ask for. But You know what's going on. You know how I ache. Give me the strength to do what needs to be done.

A breeze blew over her, and she felt a wash of peace. It wasn't any grand miracle, but it was a start. Might as well get the day started, too.

After a quick jaunt into the woods for her necessity, they were on their way. Eating jerky, and Mr. Talkative pointing out flowers and birds. How did he continue on the way he did?

She shook her head. Maybe it was because, of all people, he understood better than most. He'd lost both parents and had inherited the family business. Their situations weren't identical, but it comforted her to know that he did understand. Even when she didn't give him credit for it.

Good heavens. Had she really accused him of only caring about the mine? The memories of yesterday washed over her. She should probably apologize. When she felt like talking again. Right now, she was perfectly content to let him continue on—filling the silence with simple words about the scenery around them.

On any normal day, she would have loved the learning. The softness of the loamy forest floor. The heavily scented trees and wildflowers that only grew in the beautiful Alaskan wilderness. But it was all a blur. Colorless. And it didn't make her feel anything. The numbness was again her companion.

No. She had to fight the gloom that hovered all around her. But how?

Charles moved a little farther up and picked a few flowers. "Here—aren't these beautiful?"

Another nod.

"They're called chocolate lilies." He gave her the little bouquet and then moved on.

Chocolate lilies. Delicate. Small. And the color of satiny chocolate with yellow centers. They were a beautiful and simple flower. "Thank you."

"Ah, she speaks."

"Someone has to, or you'll just keep talking and talking and talking." It felt good to let her voice out again. Good to share a conversation.

Charles's laugh filled the woods.

"I'm sorry about what I said yesterday. That you were just after the mine. I know it's not true."

"Apology accepted. You've got a lot of spunk, *Mar–tin*."

And maybe, just maybe, she needed to be reminded of it.

◆ ◆ ◆

Hours of swatting at mosquitoes gave a new definition to torture. They were as big as birds up here. Well, maybe not quite that big, but Charles was tired of battling the huge insects. "How are you doing back there?"

"I'm covered in red welts, that's how I'm doing." She smacked his back. "Got it!"

"Ow!"

"Just imagine. I probably saved your life."

Their easy banter was back, and Charles smiled. "But you hit me."

"Saved your life."

"Well, all right. Thank you for saving me from that bloodsucking killer."

"Eww, that's too much for a lady's ears."

"But you're not a lady, remember? You're Mar–tin."

She laughed. "I'm glad it's so dry in Colorado. I'd never survive a summer with these monstrosities."

He almost said that he'd gotten used to them, but it wasn't true. Every year, he fought them and complained about them.

Reaching the edge of the woods, Charles walked a little ahead and saw yet another river for them to cross. He'd lost count of how many they had traversed. Most were just the smaller tributaries that he could wade through. But with Mary Margaret's short stature, he normally had to carry her.

This one before them was different. The current seemed fast and the water deep. Looking east, he wondered if they had time to hike around to a shallower spot.

Mary Margaret came and stood beside him, her hands on her hips. "Well. That looks like fun. What do we do?"

"I'm not sure yet." He squatted down to stretch his muscles. The past two days had been a lot different than digging in the mine. "I don't think we can cross here, and it looks to be quite the hike before it thins out."

Mary Margaret walked to a bluff west of them. She pointed in the distance and looked back to him. "Look! There are a couple skiffs out there. Maybe we can ask them to take us across."

Charles nodded. "Good thinking, let's get down there and see if we can flag them down."

They raced down the hill, and Charles used his long legs to carry him across the shore toward the skiffs. Maybe they were just fishing, but it sure would help if he could hire someone to ferry them across.

After running and waving his arms frantically, he finally got the attention of the man in the skiff closest to them. As the man rowed closer to shore, Charles realized that it was just a boy.

"Do you need help?" The young man waved, grabbed the rope attached to the front of the boat, and hopped out.

"We need to get to Hobart Bay. Can we hire you to take us there—or at least across the river?" Charles looked behind him; Mary Margaret was still catching up.

The boy shrugged his shoulders. "Will you help row? That's a long ways. It will take the rest of the day and I will miss my fishing."

Ah. Yes, the lad was wondering how much he would be compensated. "I'll give you ten dollars to take us, and yes, I will help row."

The boy nodded.

Charles stuck out his hand. "So we have a deal?"

"Yes." The young man shook on it. "I'm Eagle Eye. What's your name?"

"I'm Charles." He gestured to Mary Margaret, who'd reached his side. "And this is my brother Martin."

She nodded.

They all waded into the river and climbed into the skiff. Charles took one oar and Eagle Eye took the other. Once they got into a steady rhythm, Charles asked the boy about his life.

For twenty minutes, the young man went on about fishing and hunting. But how he loved being on the water the most. "I was tempted this morning not to go fishing though."

"Oh really? Why's that?"

"Because a man came into the village in a boat and told us he was looking for a lady. Said he'd pay us a hundred dollars if we helped him find her."

Charles worked to keep from reacting. "Did they find her?"

"I don't know. I decided to go fishing anyway." Eagle Eye shrugged.

More than anything, Charles wanted to look back to Mary Margaret and see her face, but he hadn't heard a sound. She was probably listening though. How could he find out more? "Did they say what her name was or why they were looking for her?"

"Are you thinking of looking and trying to get the money?"

"Hey, we might. My brother and I are pretty good trackers."

The boy shrugged again. "I think they were looking for her because she ran away and they were worried about her. I wasn't really listening. But her last name was Abbot."

Chapter 10

The door to the shack slammed behind Johnny. "Good fer nothin'. . ." Now what were they gonna do?

Clive kicked the lawyer, but the man just sat there. "This wasn't supposed to happen this way, Johnny. We were the only ones that were supposed to get that money."

"Well, it looks like we were the fools, because they've hired someone else. Probably several someone elses." He slapped the lawyer. "This is all your fault. If you woulda just told us where she was, we'd been sittin' pretty right now."

The man narrowed his eyes.

"That's right. Your little heiress isn't out of trouble yet. At least we would've killed her noble-like. Who knows what those others will do to her?"

Crash! The shack door splintered into pieces behind him.

"Hands up, Johnny Jones! You're under arrest."

What? Johnny shoved Clive at the officers blocking the door and rounded the table. But there was no escape.

◆ ◆ ◆

"Thank you." Mary Margaret looked at Eagle Eye and used her lowest voice as she stepped out of the skiff. Finally. They were in Hobart Bay.

Everything in her body ached, and she'd had to work hard for hours to keep her fear in check.

Charles led the way, and when they were out of earshot and visibility of Eagle Eye's skiff, he squeezed her elbow and leaned over. "It's okay. I know it's disconcerting, but it just shows that they don't know where you are."

She nodded. "I know. I just hate the thought that they value money more than me. It's horrible to realize my life doesn't matter to them."

He led her to the telegraph office. There wasn't anything he could say to dispute it, and she knew that. But she wished he could.

When he exited empty-handed, she sighed. "I guess we just stick to the plan."

"Yep." He started back to the docks. "Let's find the skiff your uncle hired and get to Prince Rupert. Hopefully, there will be news there."

It didn't take long before they found the correct boat. Larger than Eagle Eye's fishing skiff, this boat had a steam engine and places to sleep. Charles nodded to her and talked to their host—he would keep the man occupied so she could have some privacy. Mary Margaret went straight to a bunk, laid down, and sobbed herself to sleep.

◆ ◆ ◆

Something nudged her.

"Martin, wake up. We're here." Was that Charles's voice?

She pulled her coat closer around her. "Hmmm?"

"Wake up, you lazy bum. We're in Prince Rupert." His voice held an edge.

Lazy bum? She opened her eyes. Thankfully, she was facing the wall. Another man's voice joined Charles's. Oh no. Their host must be down there. Had she said anything? Pull it together; she was a boy. Charles's younger brother. If she ever needed her acting skills it was now.

"I'm awake, I'm awake." She climbed out of the bunk and pushed Charles. A little brother would do that, right? Even though in reality, he'd probably been standing there to guard her.

"It's about time." Charles sounded gruff. "You slept for fourteen hours."

"So what? I was tired." She tried gruff right back at him.

The skiff owner raised an eyebrow. "Well, I need to be on my way, so if you two could get your things." Then he climbed the stairs up to the deck.

"That was a close one." Charles exhaled.

She frowned at him. "What do you mean?"

"Let's just say you don't sleep like a boy and leave it at that." Charles grabbed his bag.

He led her to the telegraph office. This time he exited with a paper in his hand.

"Looks like your uncle can't meet us yet. Let's go. We've got half an hour to be on the boat to San Francisco."

◆ ◆ ◆

For six days they'd been at sea, and for six days, Mary Margaret had been seasick. It was bad enough that she refused a stateroom on the ship, but now he was having to take care of her around a lot of people. Granted, a lot of them were sick as well and weren't paying attention, but it would be a lot easier if they had privacy. How she ever thought she'd keep her femininity a secret aboard ship he couldn't guess, but he was doing his best to keep their cover in place.

Since Eagle Eye told him there were people looking for Mary Margaret Abbot, Charles had bought the tickets under false names. He could only hope there was additional word from Dillard in San Francisco. He hadn't told Mary Margaret the entirety of the telegram—of Dillard's kidnapping and the multiple thugs hired to finish off Mary Margaret Abbot. What if something happened to her uncle before they reached Denver?

Charles shook his head. One step at a time. First, he had to get Mary Margaret back on her feet.

At least he hadn't heard anyone on the ship looking for Mary Margaret. But most of the people kept to themselves. It wasn't a pleasure cruise, that's for sure.

As the days wore on, Charles began to wonder if it was more than just seasickness. She'd spiked a high fever and now slept around the clock. When she couldn't walk herself to the toilet anymore and started talking in her sleep, Charles went to the captain and asked if there was a stateroom available. Who cared about impropriety at this stage? They were traveling as brothers—and everyone on the ship knew that. Mary Margaret wouldn't know until she was better, and he'd risk her wrath at that point. For now, he had to take care of her properly and not give away their secret. The longer she slept, the more she moaned and called out for her father.

The captain *allowed* him to pay a handsome fee for the stateroom, and Charles moved them into the two-bunk room. As he carried Mary Margaret, he noticed that she seemed even smaller. Someone her size probably didn't have a lot to spare, and if she'd lost as much weight as he assumed, she could be in danger of much more than the sickness. She might never be able to recover.

One of the families traveling had a teen girl among them. By the look of her tattered clothes and skinny frame, Charles surmised her father's attempt at finding gold had failed. Desperate to help Mary Margaret but not wishing to cross the lines of decency, he offered the young girl fifty dollars to help him with Mary Margaret's female needs and to keep their secret that she was traveling as a boy.

The days passed in a horrid, long blur. He spooned broth and water down her throat, praying that she would recover. He couldn't have brought her this far—against such odds—to have her die of illness. No. He'd made a promise. And he cared for her more than he was willing to even admit to himself.

The day before they were to dock in San Francisco, Charles was on his bunk thinking through his options.

"Charles?" Her voice cracked.

He bolted up and went to her side. "I'm here." He wiped her brow with a damp cloth. "How are you feeling?"

"May I have. . .some water?"

A tin cup was all they had in the room, so he filled it and brought it to her. Lifting her head with his left hand, he held the cup in his right and tilted it for her to sip.

She lifted her hand and nodded. "Thank you." Looking around the room, she frowned. "Where are we?"

He held up both hands. "Don't get mad."

The slightest of smiles touched her lips, and it was a beautiful sight. "Never."

"I had to purchase a stateroom. You talk in your sleep."

With a nod, she smiled even bigger. "I know. I should have warned you." She reached for his hand. "Thank you. For everything."

He squeezed her fingers.

She held on.

And the connection between them was powerful. Charles could feel it all the way to his toes. Those hazel eyes of hers were stunning. He wished he could spend the rest of his life staring into them. If only she knew how valuable and special she really was. If only he could break through all the barriers separating them. If only. . .

"What smells so bad?" She crinkled her nose.

He leaned back and crossed his arms as he winked at her. "You do."

Chapter 11

Standing on the deck of the steamship took all her strength. But it was worth it for the fresh air. Even if it was just to get the breeze to blow away her own stench. What she wouldn't give for a bath and clean clothes. Hopefully soon.

As she stared ahead at San Francisco, Mary Margaret pondered what the next few days would hold. While she hadn't known Charles very long, she felt a bond to him. And the more she thought about him leaving after they reached Denver, the more she hated the idea.

In and out of consciousness while she'd been ill, Mary Margaret had dreamed some beautiful dreams. Father was there. Happy and smiling down from heaven. Urging her to go on with life. To be happy. To allow herself to love and trust. When she awoke yesterday and realized how sick she'd been, it was time to change things. Turn over a new leaf. Oh, she would grieve her father for some time—probably the rest of her life. But she also wanted to savor every moment. No matter how many of them she had left. But hopefully, she still had a *lot* left.

She wouldn't let her family members win. If they wanted a fight, they would get one. She would protect the Abbot legacy for her father and pass it down to her children one day. But she would love them and show them God's love and mercy.

Movement out of the corner of her eye caught her attention. Charles strode toward her from the bow of the boat, his hands in his pockets and a slight smile on his face. "I can't tell you how good it is to see you up and about. You had me pretty worried."

"Well, you know me. Always trying to keep you on your toes."

He looked around them. "At least no one else is around right now, so I can be honest."

She held her breath. When he got that look in his steel-gray eyes, she wanted to hug him for all she was worth. She felt. . .adored. "Well, go ahead. What is it?"

"I think I need a clothespin for my nose."

A couple of other passengers emerged from below deck. Probably to watch their arrival at the dock. Mary Margaret gave Charles a brotherly shove and tried not to giggle like a schoolgirl.

"Martin. Behave yourself." He looked stern, but she caught the twinkle in his eye.

"I'm just following your good example, big brother."

◆ ◆ ◆

Two hours later, Charles led Mary Margaret through the crowds at the docks. Something didn't seem right, and it made the hair on the back of his neck stand on end. But as much as he wanted to take her hand and protect her, he couldn't.

Not until they were safe.

He already had a plan. Get her situated in a reputable hotel where he could be in the next room. Then he would check the telegraph office, purchase their train tickets in false names to Denver, and get a new dress for Mary Margaret. It would only take three days to get to Colorado, and they could go straight to the courthouse and clear up this mess.

And then? Well, he didn't want to think about leaving her and returning to Juneau alone. He knew he wasn't good enough for her, but if he'd learned anything over the past few days—it was that he loved Miss Abbot. But could he tell her?

"Charles?"

He looked back.

"I can't quite keep up—I'm sorry—could you slow down just a little?"

How foolish of him. She'd barely been able to stand, and here he was making a mad dash through the streets of the city. He stopped and gave her a minute to catch her breath. But when he turned, he saw a face he'd seen before. But then the man spun and went the other direction. What was going on? If he didn't know any better, he'd say the man had been watching him—or rather, *following* them.

When they reached the hotel, Charles paid for adjoining rooms and ordered a bath for Mary Margaret. After he got her settled, he promised to be back in an hour and told her not—under any circumstance—to leave the room or open the door for anyone.

She smiled. "I'll probably take a nap. I'm so tired, I don't think I can stand up another minute."

"Do me a favor?"

"Sure." She yawned. "What is it?"

"Burn those clothes."

Her laughter carried him down the stairs, and he practically ran to the telegraph office. But to his surprise and worry, there was nothing. What could have happened to Mr. Dillard? Especially after his ominous last note.

He wanted to make a stop in his store, but if he went in the front door, there was bound to be a commotion. Sneaking into the back, he found Mr. Bannister in the storeroom and tapped him on the shoulder.

"How can I help. . . Charles! My word. What are you doing here?"

Charles pulled the man aside. "I need you to be very quiet. Don't let anyone know that I've been here."

"Of course, of course. Whatever you need. Are you in danger?"

Charles peeked through the storeroom curtain. "I'm not really sure. But I am protecting someone right now, and I have to ensure they get to their destination. In a few days, hopefully I'll be able to send you news and explain everything."

The man nodded. "What can I do to help?"

Charles made a list and handed it to the manager.

"I'll get to it right now."

◆ ◆ ◆

The bath was glorious. Most likely the best one she'd ever had—and not just because she'd never gone this long without one—well, maybe that *was* the reason. But she'd dumped enough lavender oil into the water that there could be no question when she got out of the tub that she was Mary Margaret again.

The only other clothes she had with her were a simple man's white shirt and a pair of denims that were so big, she could barely tie the rope tight enough at her waist to hold them up. Prayerfully, Charles would return with decent clothes for her to travel in.

She laid down on the soft bed. Maybe she could just lie here and rest for a few minutes.

◆ ◆ ◆

A knock jolted her awake. And it came from the door that led to Charles's room. She padded her way over to the door and yawned as she opened it. "This had better be good. I was taking a lovely nap and you interrupted."

His chuckle emerged from a tower of boxes.

"What is all this?"

"Clothes. For you. The trunk is arriving in a few minutes. But you can't exactly travel like a lady without luggage."

Before she knew what she was doing, she stood on tiptoe and kissed his cheek. "Thank you. I can't believe you thought of all this."

"Mmmm, you smell nice." He grinned and brought the packages in.

Rummaging through the stack of boxes, she found a large, flat one. When she lifted the lid, she gasped. It was a beautiful white dress trimmed with green ribbons. She held it up. "Charles, it's beautiful. I can't wait to wear it." And she was shocked it wasn't too long. How did he guess so accurately?

"Do you remember the day we met?"

"You mean the day I snapped at you about the job?"

"Yes, that's the one."

She bit her lip. Father died later that day.

"I know it doesn't hold the best of memories, but I was hoping we could make some new ones. You were wearing a beautiful white dress that day, and I'd just come out of the mine, so my eyes were still adjusted to the dark." He moved closer to her. "The sunlight made your dress glow. You looked like an angel."

Tears burned her eyes again. Must she always cry in front of this sweet man? She shook her head. "How did you get the right length?"

"I just told the manager at the store that you only came up to here"—he held a hand up to his chest—"and they did the rest."

A knock sounded—but it came from the door in Charles's room.

"I'll be right back." He pulled the door between their rooms closed.

In a couple of minutes, he returned. But a frown etched his face.

"What is it?"

He motioned to her. "They delivered the trunk, and the bellboy was looking around with a little too much curiosity. Then I looked out the window. Come see, but stay back."

Mary Margaret followed him into his room and over to the window.

"See that man?"

"Which one?"

"The one across the street. Studying his notebook."

"Ah, yes."

Charles sighed. "I wasn't sure of it before, but I am quite positive now."

"Of what?"

"That same man was on the ship. And then he was on the docks following us. Now, he's looking for us in the hotels. The bellboy all but gave him away."

She placed a hand over her heart. Could she take much more of this? "What do we do now?"

He walked into Mary Margaret's room. "Sadly, we pack all this up into the trunk and I go find you some more suitable clothes, *Martin*."

As much as she hated the thought of dressing like a boy for longer, she hated the thought of dying more.

"Oh no."

"What?"

"The tickets are for a man and a woman traveling together."

"Well, I guess you'll have to change them, or does it matter?"

"I'll think of something." Charles shook his head.

"Please. . .be careful."

"You, too."

Chapter 12

The three days were up.

Three days of conversations. Three days of her falling asleep on his shoulder. Three days of holding sweet Mary Margaret's hand whenever he could.

And now their journey was almost to an end. *Could* he let it end?

Charles rubbed her knuckles as she slept on his shoulder one last time. They'd be pulling up to Denver soon, and he'd have to take her straight to the courthouse.

If he thought they'd built a friendship before, it had grown into so much more as they'd traveled for miles on the train. But he couldn't be selfish and think of that now.

When he'd gone to the station in San Francisco, he'd been hit with a genius idea. So he'd traded in his tickets for a later train and then stayed to watch their mystery guest board the train they were first going to take.

Now he just needed to get Mary Margaret off the train and to the courthouse without mishap. And that was easier said than done.

He'd purchased a private compartment to keep her as concealed as possible—and selfishly so he could be with her and hold her hand—but there were sure to be people at the station watching and waiting for them.

The train slowed, and she lifted her head and stretched. The travel had at least been restful for her. "Are we there?"

"Just about."

Quiet engulfed them as he retreated to his own thoughts. But as the train came to a stop, he knew his time was up. "Mary Margaret."

"Yes?" She squeezed his hand and didn't reprimand him for not calling her Martin.

"There's something I really need to tell you—some—"

The door to their compartment burst open. "It'll have to wait." The man who'd been following them pointed a gun at Mary Margaret. "All right, let's get a few things straight. You're going to get your bags, keep your heads down, and get off the train like nothing is out of the ordinary. If you don't, I'll put a bullet in little Miss Heiress here. Got it?"

He nodded. Didn't want to give the guy any thought that Charles would try something—which of course he would. Just needed the right moment.

As they exited the train, Charles looked for a distraction.

A police whistle sounded behind them.

Something poked into his back. "Move!" The kidnapper's voice snapped with anger.

"*Oomph.*"

The pressure on his back disappeared. Charles turned around and so did Mary Margaret.

"Uncle!" She hugged the man.

Sure enough, Dillard stood there with a policeman's club in his hand. And their kidnapper lay in a heap on the ground.

"Thank you." Mary Margaret hugged her uncle again. "I know Charles was trying to find a way to get me away from the man. How'd you do it?"

"The policeman gave me this. And so I just bopped him on the head." Dillard shrugged.

"But how did you find us?" Charles shook the man's hand. "I hadn't heard anything more from you."

Dillard laughed. "Let's just say that I had a man watching this man who was watching you." He took Mary Margaret by the arm. "I don't want to waste a minute. Let's get to the courthouse. Everyone is already there." He gestured to another man beside them. "Oh by the way, Charles Delaney, this is Judge Graham. He will be assisting today."

Charles shook the other man's hand, and then all four climbed into a buggy.

◆ ◆ ◆

The courthouse teemed with people. What was going on?

Dillard leaned toward Charles. "There's also a murder trial going on."

"Oh, gotcha."

"I was hoping it would help us sneak her in."

"Sounds like a plan."

Judge Graham had Mary Margaret on his arm. They must be old friends, because she talked to the older man as if she'd known him all her life.

When the judge opened the door to courtroom B, a cacophony of voices filled the air. Yelling from every direction.

The judge on the bench banged his gavel.

"Exactly why have we been summoned here today?" The nasally voice came from a short woman on the right side. "It's apparent that our sister's not returning. Why do we have to wait?"

"It's our money, too!" A lower female voice.

Those must be the sisters. Martha and Mabel.

Charles stepped forward, but Mary Margaret's hand shot out and stopped him. She removed her hat, letting her hair tumble down, and walked forward. "Sorry to disappoint you. But I'm very much alive."

The women and the men beside them all gasped. And then started yelling again.

Charles covered his ears. How could these women be even remotely related to Mary Margaret and Arnold Abbot?

The judge's gavel banged five more times. "Order! I demand order." He pointed to Mary Margaret. "Now come forward. How do we know you are in fact the Miss Mary Margaret Abbot? You could be an imposter."

The sisters agreed from their corner.

Charles just rolled his eyes.

Dillard and Judge Graham walked forward and approached the bench. Judge Graham sent a serious frown to the presiding judge and then whispered for a minute or two.

The judge on the bench went ashen.

Police filled the courtroom.

Charles watched in awe as the sisters, their husbands, and the judge were all arrested.

Dillard smiled and patted Charles on the back. "I've been waiting for this day for a long time."

Mary Margaret walked to him in her boyish getup and took his hand.

Judge Graham joined them. "Judge Scoggins has been suspected of taking bribes for some time. We are grateful for your assistance in helping us put this case to rest once and for all."

"What about Martha and Mabel?" Her sweet voice shared her concern for her sisters, even though they'd been horrid.

"They—along with their husbands—have been arrested for conspiracy to commit murder and a few other small charges, like falsifying papers, forging documents, stealing, and bribing a US court judge."

"Will I be allowed to visit them?"

"Of course. But do you really want to?" The judge furrowed his brow and shook his head.

Mary Margaret looked to Charles. "Yes, I think I do. Will you go with me, Charles?"

"When the time is right. Yes, I will gladly accompany you." If he could just keep his temper in check. He'd have to pray a lot about that one.

Dillard walked back toward them and kissed his niece on the cheek. "I'm so glad you are okay." He chuckled. "But how you ever passed as a boy when you smell so much like lavender is beyond me."

Charles and Mary Margaret shared a look. He winked at her. "You should have smelled her last week."

◆ ◆ ◆

Two crazy days passed with legal paperwork and visits to the local jail. Mary Margaret slept a lot, too. But Uncle Dillard said that he'd kept Charles occupied with business talk whenever she wasn't around.

As she waited for Charles now, she anticipated talking with him alone. There was so much she wanted to say. So much that filled her heart and her mind.

"Have you ever heard the phrase 'All that glitters is not gold'?" Charles's voice from behind her on the veranda made her smile. She turned to him and took in those beautiful gray eyes.

He lifted her hand and kissed her palm.

Heat flared up her arm. "Yes, I have. *Merchant of Venice*... Shakespeare." She smiled. It was unexpected, but oh, so glorious. She loved this man. Yes, she did. And she couldn't wait to tell him. "So...?"

"Well in gold mining, in the panning process, we find a lot of fool's gold—pyrite."

"Go on." Her heart beat a little faster. She knew him so well, she had already figured out where he was going. But she longed to hear him say it. So she forced herself to remain patient and bit her lip.

"Pyrite is much more reflective of light than real gold. So a lot of people would get excited to see glittering, golden specks—only to find out what they'd discovered and worked for was actually worthless." He took both of her hands in his. "But the real gold—the truly precious metal—appeared to be dull in its raw form to most people. Because they didn't realize what they were looking at. They didn't appreciate it and got distracted by the glitter." He paused.

She peered up at him and hoped he saw the admiration she felt for him.

"Too many are looking for the glitter. But I'm looking for the real thing." Charles went down on one knee. "You are the real thing, Mary Margaret Abbot. And I love you with all my heart. You shine and reflect the True Light, you glitter with beauty, wit, and charm, and underneath it all—you are pure gold. Will you marry me?"

She only had to lean down a few inches to kiss him. And she did it with gusto. When she pulled back, she couldn't keep a grin from her face. "On one condition?"

"Oh boy. What is it?"

"That we hire someone to work with Uncle Dillard to run the companies here when we are not in Colorado."

His brow crinkled. "I don't understand. You don't want to stay?"

She shook her head. "At least not right now. I'd like to go back to Alaska and have a real funeral for Father. But I want it to be more of a celebration of his life, and a celebration of our new life together. And then we can run the mines up there for a while. I can watch you work. Learn all about it. That kind of thing." With a wink, she tugged him toward the door. "It could be an extended honeymoon, an adventure."

"Haven't we been on enough adventures already? Where you almost died?"

Laughter bubbled up out of her, and she waved his comment away. "It'll be fun. Besides, we'll be together, and that's all that matters."

He stopped and pulled her back into his arms. Kissed her nose. "I love you, Mary Margaret."

"I love you, too. But how many times do I have to tell you. . .just call me Martin."

Kimberley Woodhouse is a bestselling, multipublished author of fiction and nonfiction. A popular speaker and teacher, she's shared her theme of "Joy Through Trials" with over half a million people across the country and has appeared on National Television to more than 100 million viewers over the past decade. Kim is a pastor's wife and is passionate about music and Bible study. She lives and writes in Colorado with her husband of twenty-plus years and their two amazing kids. Visit her website: www.kimberleywoodhouse.com.

If You Liked This Book, You'll Also Like…

The Rails to Love Romance Collection
Nine historical stories celebrate a spirit of adventure along the Transcontinental Railroad where nine unlikely couples meet. From sightseeing excursions to transports toward new lives, from orphan trains to circus trains, can romances develop into blazing love in a world of cold, hard steel?

Paperback / 978-1-63409-864-9 / $14.99

The Blue Ribbon Brides Collection
Nine inspiring romances heat up at old time state and county fairs. The competition is fierce when nine women between 1889 and 1930 go for the blue ribbon to prove they have something valuable to contribute to society. But who will win the best honor of all—a devoted heart?

Paperback / 978-1-63409-861-8 / $14.99

Seven Brides for Seven Texans Romance Collection
G. W. Hart is tired of waiting for his seven grown sons to marry, and now he may not live long enough to see grandchildren born. So he sets an ultimatum for each son to marry before the end of 1874 or be written out of his will. But can love form on a deadline?

Paperback / 978-1-63409-965-3 / $14.99